MW01343854

FantasyCraft™

WRITING
Alex Flagg, Scott Gearin, Patrick Kapera

ADDITIONAL MATERIAL
Jon Andersen, Mark Newman

ART DIRECTORS
Steve Hough, Patrick Kapera

COVER ART AND PAGE FRAMES
Ben McSweeney

INTERIOR ART
Ben McSweeney, Joseph Caesar Domingo, Kevin Sanborn, Christophe Swal, Dave Wong

EDITING
Alex Flagg, Patrick Kapera

GRAPHIC DESIGN AND LAYOUT
Brendon Goodyear, Steve Hough

PLAY TESTERS
Walter Christensen, Loren Dean, Nathan Devonshyre, Charles Etheridge-Nunn, Amy Gillespie, Brandon Gillespie, Robert Harris, Lisa Murray, Jason Olsan, Andrew M. Popowich, Unit 13 (Alex Flagg, Travis Herron, Evan McLeod, Kevin Ripka, Jimmy Taylor, and Tyler Johnson), Bill Whitmore

Fantasy Craft Second Printing

CONTENTS

INTRODUCTION

You hold in your hands the gateway to unlimited adventure. In *Fantasy Craft*, you can become a mighty warrior, a cunning thief, or a crafty mage, bending primal forces to your will. You can visit impossible places and do things beyond your wildest dreams: explore the long lost tombs of fallen gods, face down armies of the undead and their sorcerous lich lords, and yes, even save the world. Not our world, not this one, but *your* world. *Fantasy Craft* lets you create and visit places in your mind's eye. The only limit is your imagination.

ROLEPLAYING

A **roleplaying game (or RPG)** is part creative workshop and part improvised theater. There is no board or play pieces (though sometimes you might use a play mat to illustrate complex areas in the game world, and you can even use miniature figures to show where various characters are located). Most of the time, the action takes place in your mind, which is why an RPG is so special. You aren't limited to the spaces on a board — you can go anywhere and do anything you can think up.

Each player uses the rules to create a **player character (or PC)**, his alter ego in the game world. A PC doesn't have to be anything like the player (in fact, he doesn't even have to be human). Some PCs can fly, cast spells, speak languages we can't even pronounce, and more. A PC has his or her own philosophy and opinions, which may or may not line up with the player's own, and that's a lot of an RPG's fun: becoming someone entirely different.

The player controls every action his PC takes and every word he says, and guides him through adventures alongside the other players' characters. These adventures, and most of the game world, are also created — by the **Game Master (or GM)**, who also creates and controls all the people the PCs meet in their adventures. Some of these **non-player characters (or NPCs)** are the PCs' friends and foes, while others are just people they meet in their journeys (merchants, bar keeps, town guards, nobles, beggars, prophets, and others).

An RPG is played across one or more **sessions**, each usually four to five hours long (though yours might be longer or shorter). Before the first session, the GM creates the world and prepares an adventure, which is like an open-ended novel with a beginning but no end. The players create their characters and the GM (usually) incorporates some specific ways for the PCs to get involved into the adventure.

The game starts with the GM describing where the characters are and what's going on around them. From that point the game is completely freeform. The players describe their PCs' actions and the GM describes everything they see, hear, and feel, speaking for NPCs when they appear.

YOUR PLAY GROUP

Fantasy Craft collectively refers to all players, including the GM, as a **play group**, or just "group." Conversely, the PCs are collectively referred to as the **party**. There are many kinds of play groups and many kinds of parties, and sometimes the same play group will create lots of different kinds of parties over the course of its time together. In general, there are three choices every group makes about the game, sometimes subconsciously.

SOCIAL PLAY VS. TACTICAL PLAY

Some groups prefer a jovial game where everyone's laughing and goofing off all the time. Others like a serious game where everyone's focused on their characters and the adventure. Social play is more casual and some claim it's easier to get into and maintain over time, but tactical players swear by their approach, claiming that nothing competes with really losing yourself in the RPG experience.

STORYTELLING VS. COMBAT

Similarly, some groups prefer their adventures focus on ideas, plots, and character growth. A few even look for ways to invest emotionally in their characters, fully embracing their alter-ego as a method actor would a new role. Others crave action: the thrill of combat, and the desperate danger of perilous situations. Again, there's no right option, though the parts of the rules used and the types of adventures played are very different.

SAFE PLAY VS. RISKY PLAY

Finally, there's the division between cautious groups seeking as much information as they can find, carefully weighing every decision, and those that rush headlong into each situation, more concerned with keeping the game moving than making the "right" calls. Player characters can get hurt and even die in an RPG, and as in real life you can very rarely if ever change the past, all of which supports safe play, but detractors argue that it's a game and part of the fun is letting go.

FINDING THE BALANCE

Every group and party must decide its own approach. Often, especially when players like different types of fiction, there will be debate. This is healthy, but whenever possible you should leave it for the periods between game sessions. When you're in the moment, run with what seems to entertain the most players at any time, and be sure to give the rest a little of what they want when you can. Like any group activity, an RPG is about people coming together, which requires acceptance and compromise.

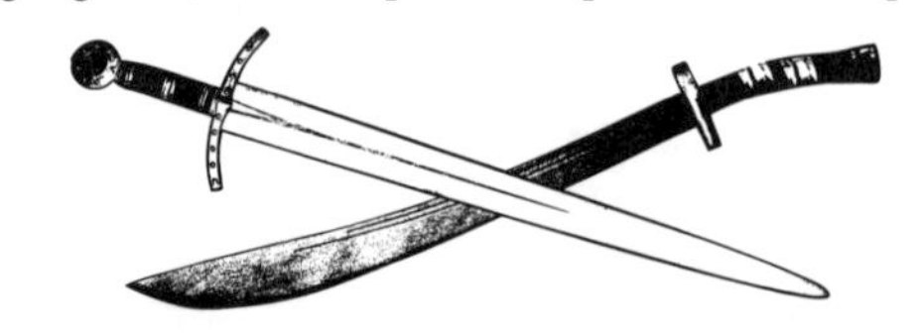

MASTERCRAFT

Fantasy Craft is powered by one of the most robust RPG rule sets available: Mastercraft is the culmination of almost a decade of experience honing a single game system, which is itself based on the oldest, most respected RPG on the market.

Mastercraft's greatest strengths are its incredible versatility and customization. GMs and players have absolute authority to create the characters, worlds, adventures, and NPCs they want without complex, hard-to-find or -use mechanics.

Better still, Mastercraft assumes no genre or time period, making it the ideal vehicle for games of any kind. Crafty Games will be expanding the system with new game lines in many genres and time periods, but it all begins here, with...

FANTASY CRAFT

This Mastercraft game focuses on high adventure fantasy like *The Lord of the Rings*, the Narnia series, *A Song of Ice and Fire*, and the saga of Conan the Cimmerian. Player characters are heroes, villains, or mercenaries in another world where magic and miracles may very well be real. They might adventure for glory, wealth, or to help those less fortunate. In some worlds, they might fight amazing, often hostile creatures that can breathe fire, teleport, and even swallow enemies whole.

Enemies are myriad, ranging from greedy brigands to power-hungry sorcerers to conniving politicians to, perhaps, the gods themselves. Often the strongest of them command legions of inhuman servants — orcs, trolls, imps, devils, abominable monkey men forged of sorrow, and more — that the heroes wade through in their quest for triumph.

Fantasy Craft includes everything you need to tell any fantasy story you can imagine. The players can go from simple stable hands to knights of the realm, break free of slave shackles to rise against an oppressive empire, seek the hallowed knowledge of forbidden kingdoms lost to time, and more.

GETTING STARTED

Expect to spend a little time with this book before your first session — a few hours if you're a player and perhaps a weekend if you're the GM. Initially, you should each read the bits important for your roles at the gaming table *(see next)*, but after that the best way to learn is by doing. Schedule a trial session and try a few skill checks and a mock combat using characters made in your first read-through. See if any questions crop up and if so, spend the time to find the answers as you go.

Fantasy Craft uses a variety of dice (d4, d6, d8, d10, d12, and d20), which you can pick up at any hobby store. Be sure to have at least two sets for the group, as well as plenty of blank character sheets, pencils, and enough munchies to go around.

GENDER AND PRONOUNS

After this introduction, *Fantasy Craft* uses male pronouns. This is merely to keep the text simple and easy to read. There's no expectation that all players or characters will be male. Indeed, your games may well feature both (or either).

Also, this book frequently speaks directly to the reader — sometimes to the player and other times to the character. Again, this is a matter of simplicity. In the event that this gets confusing, consider the context and the intent should become clear.

PLAYERS

Each player's first destination is Chapter 1, which describes the basic process of creating a hero. Parts of this process point to Chapters 2–4, which cover action dice, skills, and feats; magic and spells; and gear, respectively. At least at first, it's probably best to concentrate on the core concepts, choose some options that look fun and easy to use, and read the rules supporting those. Don't try to learn what every option does and above all don't feel the need to make an informed decision about which options are "best" (for you or in general). *Fantasy Craft* can create millions of unique characters and it will take a while to absorb even a fraction of the available combinations.

THE GAME MASTER

The GM's view of the game must necessarily be a bit broader, but fortunately everything he needs to run the game, at least at first, is confined to Chapters 2 (Action Dice and Skills), 5 (Combat), 6 (Bestiary), and 7 (Worlds). Start with the first two, keeping your reading in Chapter 2 to just the basics of action die and skill use. This will give you a firm understanding of the game basics. After that, skim Chapter 7 and come up with a basic adventure (you can build your own world later). Read through Running Fantasy Craft and the rules that follow, choose a few adversaries from Chapter 6, and you're ready to go!

EXPANDING YOUR GAME

When you're ready for more, Crafty Games is there for you! We offer a wide range of expansion products through our website and online store — including pre-made adventures so you don't have to build your own — and one of the most vibrant, supportive online communities in gaming. If you've got rules questions or need advice as a player or GM, stop by **www.crafty-games.com** to take your game to the next level.

CHAPTER 1: HERO

INTRODUCTION

The heroes of any great adventure epic are frequently not the most powerful figures, but they're always the most pivotal and the most involved. It's no surprise then that they're also the most detailed. *Fantasy Craft* offers all the tools you need to create thousands of unique protagonists whose stories are yours to tell. That story might be an epic of moral challenges and great deeds, a bawdy tale of comedy to pass the time, or a simple war story. No approach is superior — it's purely a matter of taste.

This chapter presents all the steps you take to create your character *mechanically* — that is, according to the rules. It shows you the roles you can take and how the experience you gain from adventuring advances your statistics, or "stats" (the terms and numbers used to determine what you can do and whether you succeed when you try something risky). The Game Master uses your stats to develop challenges for your party and it's in these numbers that the game is fun and challenging on a tactical level.

As discussed earlier *(see page 4)*, the social end of the game runs differently for every group. Most of the options in this chapter — especially Interests — lend to the social game, offering seeds for roleplaying and ways to expand the story and setting. These are just the beginning of each character's personal journey and you should always watch for new ways to define your character and make him something truly special. The GM can help and many tools are provided in Chapter 7 to do so.

CREATING A CHARACTER

Creating a *Fantasy Craft* character is a simple process that begins with a blank character sheet. You can download one from **www.crafty-games.com** or photocopy *pages 396–399* of this book. Then just follow these steps. Experienced players may find it easier to skip around in the process but first-timers should follow the steps in order until they're comfortable with them. Detailed instructions are provided for each step beginning on the pages listed in parentheses.

Step 0: Concept ***(below):*** At the core of every hero is a powerful concept. You might become a dashing rogue, a grizzled military veteran, a wandering knight, a cunning spy, or an adventurer of your own creation.

Step 1: Attributes ***(page 8):*** Your basic abilities are set by scores in each of six attributes: Strength, Dexterity, Constitution, Intelligence, Wisdom, and Charisma.

Step 2: Origin ***(page 9):*** Some of your most distinctive traits have been forged 'before the story begins.' Your Origin takes care of this, painting your past in broad strokes with a Species choice and a Specialty that suggests your early history.

Step 3: Career Level ***(page 27):*** Your overall power is determined by your Career Level, which provides several benefits to all heroes, regardless of their other character options.

Step 4: Class ***(page 28):*** Your class shapes your role in the party, offering a themed benefit package that grows as you adventure. Each class offers a unique collection of bonuses, skills, and abilities that customize your strengths and weaknesses.

Step 5: Skills ***(page 63):*** Your class also grants you skill points that you spend to become better at various tasks.

Step 6: Feats ***(page 84):*** Feats let you augment your abilities with unusual actions and spectacular stunts.

Step 7: Interests ***(page 61):*** Craving more depth than your average dungeoneer? Interests include moral and ethical stances, languages, and personal indulgences you pursue between heroic deeds. Beyond rounding out your character, they offer an edge in situations related to your passion.

Step 8: Character Sheet ***(page 61:*** Here you fill in all the boxes on your sheet that are still empty. A few minutes of simple calculation and you're nearly done!

Step 9: Starting Gear ***(page 152):*** Finally, distribute your Lifestyle points to determine how well your character lives and saves, then hit the outfitters to gear up for your first adventure!

STEP 0: CONCEPT

Developing a strong concept greatly increases the chance of an enjoyable play experience, so it's a good idea to make a few key decisions before choosing character options. Generally, the longer you expect to play a character the more time you should invest in crafting the concept, though even a little effort can go a long way.

Always speak with your GM before settling on a concept — he might have some preferences or want to apply some restrictions. Chatting with the other players is often a good idea also, as you can compliment each other's strengths and work the party's history into your own. Every successful concept has three essentials: description, methods, and motivation.

DESCRIPTION

The words and numbers on your character sheet speak to what you can *do*, but they say nothing for who you *are*. What's your gender? What's your name? Where do you come from? Your GM can probably provide a list of common names and cultures to choose from and in a well-defined setting your birthplace might also speak to your appearance and other facets of your concept. In a 'generic' or loose fantasy world just go with a name that sounds cool — maybe one derived from a favorite fantasy novel or movie — and add a few interesting background details that seem easy to fit into lots of adventures.

Next question: What do you look like? A good physical description pays off immediately, rooting you in the action and helping the GM and other players visualize you in the world.

Finally, consider your personality and the things that shaped it. What's your outlook? What are a few of the things you crave and shun? What's your family like and where are they now? Do you have siblings or children? This is often the most complex part of your character's description; fortunately, you can save any of it you're not ready to answer until later, developing and learning about it as the game unfolds.

METHODS

Knowing how you approach problems is especially helpful as it informs your decisions throughout play. As with personality, it's not important to have it all worked out before you dive into your first adventure, though. You might start out with a general theme in mind, such as relying upon brute force, keen wisdom, broad knowledge, fierce skill, or a gift of the tongue. Alternately you could skim the classes and feats to see if something catches your eye. In either case aim for methods that excite you and mesh well with the rest of your concept and the other characters in your party.

MOTIVATION

Heroes tend to launch themselves headlong into deadly situations, hopefully emerging victorious and stronger for the experience. When thinking about why you're more than ordinary, it's crucial to choose goals and motivations powerful enough to justify setting aside the comforts of home for life-threatening adventure. Your motivations also offer the GM hooks so he can sweep you into the action without twisting your arm. Most important of all, a well-crafted motivation gives you a solid reason to work with the other player characters.

WAYS YOU'RE DIFFERENT, WAYS YOU'RE THE SAME

When thinking about your concept, it's a good idea to consider how you stand out from the crowd. What makes you one-of-a-kind in a fantastic world? In centuries to come which of your traits will bards and historians recount first? Be careful — this is one place you can easily stumble. Try too hard to be different and you'll wind up so strange no one can relate. One or two distinguishing characteristics are plenty. They can be physical (unusual eye color, a tattoo or scar, a crest or standout clothing), psychological (distinct mannerism, a notable character flaw, an uncommon fear), a quirk (amusing transposition of words when speaking, fascination with a rare food, peculiar luck), or anything else you can dream up. Be sure to clear your distinguishing characteristics with your GM before working them too deeply into your concept.

STEP 1: ATTRIBUTES

Your most basic strengths and weaknesses are defined by six "attributes" — three physical (Strength, Dexterity, Constitution) and three mental (Intelligence, Wisdom, and Charisma).

Strength (Str): Physical power and musculature
Dexterity (Dex): Physical grace
Constitution (Con): Health and toughness
Intelligence (Int): Ability to learn and reason
Wisdom (Wis): Common sense, intuition, and perception
Charisma (Cha): Attractiveness, personality, persuasiveness, and guile

Each attribute begins with a score of 8 to 18 and generates a modifier. Scores of 10 and 11 are average for most characters and grant a modifier of +0. For every 2 points above or below this range, the modifier increases or decreases by 1, as shown on Table 1.1: Attribute Scores *(see right)*. These modifiers are applied to many things, as shown in the Skills section of Chapter 2 and Table 1.2: Attribute Modifiers *(see below)*.

STARTING ATTRIBUTE SCORES

You have 36 points to spend on attributes. Costs are shown on Table 1.1. Assign the highest scores to represent your strengths and the lowest scores to represent your weaknesses. Keep in mind that many classes benefit from certain attributes and that your Origin often adjusts your starting attributes as well *(see Table 1.3: Origins, page 10)*.

Example: Kevin uses his 36 points to purchase a Strength of 13 (6 points), a Dexterity of 15 (11 points), a Constitution of 11 (3 points), an Intelligence of 12 (4 points), a Wisdom of 12 (4 points), and a Charisma of 14 (8 points).

Table 1.1: Attribute Scores

Score	Cost	Modifier
1	—*	–5
2-3	—*	–4
4-5	—*	–3
6-7	—*	–2
8	0	–1
9	1	–1
10	2	+0
11	3	+0
12	4	+1
13	6	+1
14	8	+2
15	11	+2
16	14	+3
17	18	+3
18	22	+4
19	—*	+4
20-21	—*	+5
22-23	—*	+6
24-25	—*	+7
Etc.	—*	Etc.

*** This score may not be purchased at character creation.**

Table 1.2: Attribute Modifers

Attribute	Applications (Excluding Skill Checks)
Strength	Attacks (Melee, Unarmed), Damage (Melee, Unarmed, Hurled)
Dexterity	Attacks (Hurled, Ranged), Initiative, Defense, Reflex saves
Constitution	Vitality, Wounds, Fortitude saves
Intelligence	Knowledge checks, Skill points
Wisdom	Will saves, Known Spells
Charisma	Lifestyle, Spell Save DC

IMPAIRMENT

Your attribute scores may change over time, sometimes temporarily, sometimes permanently. When a change is permanent, all of your affected scores change accordingly. The same is true of temporary changes, except for vitality, wounds, skill points, known spells, and Lifestyle, which are only affected by permanent attribute changes.

When an attribute is temporarily impaired, it heals at 1 point per day, so long as you get at least 8 hours' sleep in that time.

Example: Kevin temporarily loses 4 points of Dexterity, dropping his score from 15 to 11 and his modifier from +2 to +0. This reduces his ranged attack bonus, Initiative bonus, Defense, Reflex save bonus, and Dexterity-based skill check bonuses by 2 each. After 24 hours of further adventure, he recovers 1 point and his modifier rises to +1. Another 24 hours after that, assuming he's been getting enough shut-eye, he heals another point, but his modifier won't rise again until the end of Day 3. Unless Kevin suffers further Dexterity impairment, he fully recovers the attribute after Day 4.

An attribute may not drop below 0. When one or more of your attributes drop to 0, you fall unconscious until each of your attributes is at least 1. In the meantime, you must make a Fortitude save once per day and each time you suffer additional attribute impairment, against a DC of 10 + 1 per previous save. With failure, your wounds immediately drop to –10, resulting in death.

STEP 2: ORIGIN

All heroes start somewhere. Some are humble commoners before the seeds of adventure take root while others are destined for greatness from their first breath. One of the ways you paint these details into your background is with your **Origin,** which combines a **Species** describing your race with a **Specialty** that suggests your history or profession before joining the ranks of the valiant and virtuous.

Choose 1 Species and 1 Specialty; together they offer a package of benefits supporting a simple name (e.g. "Pech Fencer" or "Orc Tribesman"). If your Species choice is Human, choose a Talent as well. A summary of Origin benefits is found on Table 1.3: Origins *(see page 10)*.

ORIGIN SKILLS

Once you choose your Origin, skip forward to Chapter 2 and choose two skills you feel someone with your background should inherently grasp. These become your "Origin skills," meaning that you can always spend skill points to buy ranks in them, even when they're not currently class skills for you *(see page 63)*.

Some character choices grant Origin skills, which are gained in addition to these two.

SPECIES

Fantasy Craft features 12 playable species, each with its own strengths and weaknesses. Splinter races, like "hill dwarves" and "dark elves," are available through Species feats *(see page 99)*.

Every species is defined by its Type.

TYPE

Your Type sets your Size, means of locomotion, wounds, and various character options and rules that apply to all members of your species. Most fantasy species are 'folk,' a Type that conveys no special rules; other Types are defined in Chapter 6: Foes *(see page 226)*.

DRAKE

You're a drake, proud kin to dragons. Physically, you fit the classic depiction; you possess scaly skin, a serpentine body, wicked talons, destructive breath, and massive wings. Your hide may be red or brown and your scales might be black, blue, green, or gold, depending on your birthplace and ancestry.

Your early life was in all likelihood a solitary existence, spent carving out territory and mastering anything that caught your fleeting interest. You might bear a name granted for notable deeds or traits, or command a title of appropriate stature — for you are due respect and awe. Yours is a cunning and sometimes cruel species, with little patience for those who fail to recognize your greatness, or worse, interfere with your many plans. You regard precious few as allies and still fewer as friends, but for them you harbor deep, enduring affection. They are to be afforded the same rights and privileges as you, for they stand beside legend.

Common Personality Traits: Aloof, greedy, proud, self-centered, wise

Common Physical Traits: Hissing voice, shimmering scales, darting eyes, dagger-like teeth

Example Names: Icebite, Wrathbane, Deathwing, Sunscale, Nighteye

Splinter Race Feats: Elemental Heritage (fire drake, ice drake, wind drake, or other elemental drake), Truescale (cloud drake, mountain drake, swamp drake, or other terrain drake). Unless you choose one of these, you're a 'lesser drake.'

Type: Large (2×3) quadruped beast with a Reach of 2 *(see page 226)*. Your maximum wounds equal your Constitution score × 1.5 (rounded down).

- *Attributes:* +2 to Strength or Intelligence, –2 to Dexterity
- *Base Speed:* 30 ft.
- *Breath Weapon:* Once per round as a full action you may breathe fire in a 20-ft. line, inflicting 2d6 + your Con modifier in fire damage. Make a single ranged attack against all characters and objects in the path; each character hit may make a Reflex Save (DC 10 + the number of Species feats you have + your Con modifier) to suffer only 1/2 damage (rounded down).

Table 1.3: Origins

Species	Attributes	Benefits
Drake	+2 Str or Int, –2 Dex	Large beast (Reach 2, wounds Con × 1.5, Speed 30 ft.), breath weapon (fire), cold-blooded, inquisitive mind, natural attack (Bite I, Claw I), reviled, winged flight 40 ft.
Dwarf	+4 Con, –2 Dex	Medium folk (Reach 1, wounds Con, Speed 20 ft.), darkvision I, enlightened Crafting, improved stability, iron gut, restricted actions (Kick actions, Jump, Swim), thick hide 2
Elf	+4 Wis, –2 Con	Medium fey (Reach 1, wounds Con, Speed 40 ft.), aloof, burden of ages, keen sight, natural elegance, sharp hearing
Giant	—	Large folk (Reach 2, wounds Con × 1.5, Speed 50 ft.), hurled proficiency, improved stability, natural attack (Trample I), sterner stuff
Goblin	+2 Str, –2 Cha	Small folk (Reach 1, wounds Con × 2/3, Speed 20 ft.), agile defense +1, ambush basics, darkvision I, light-sensitive, tenacious spirit
Human	Per Talent	Medium folk (Reach 1, wounds Con, Speed 30 ft.)
Ogre	+2 Str, +4 Con, –2 Int, –2 Cha	Large folk (Reach 1, wounds Con × 1.5, Speed 30 ft.), enlightened athletics, no pain, reviled, restricted actions (Influence, Outmaneuver, Tumble), unbreakable
Orc	+3 Str, +3 Con, –3 Int	Medium folk (Reach 1, wounds Con, Speed 30 ft.), always ready, enlightened intimidate, grueling combatant, light-sensitive. restricted actions (Calm, Decipher, Influence)
Pech	+3 Dex	Small folk (Reach 1, wounds Con × 2/3, Speed 30 ft.), enlightened resolve, hearty appetite, hurled proficiency
Rootwalker	—	Large plant (Reach 1, wounds Con × 1.5, Speed 30 ft.), Achilles heel (fire), bleeding immunity, lean season, lumbering, natural camouflage, thick hide 2
Saurian	+2 Dex, +2 to any, –2 to any	Medium folk (Reach 1, wounds Con, Speed 30 ft.), agile defense +1, cold-blooded, darkvision I, natural attack (Bite I, Tail Slap I)
Unborn	+2 to any, –4 Cha	Medium construct (Reach 1, wounds Con, Speed 20 ft.), achilles heel (electricity), enlightened skill, limited proficiencies, lumbering

Talent	Attributes	Benefits
Adaptable	—	Grace under pressure, inquisitive mind, mix-up, origin skills (any 2)
Agile	+2 Dex	Double boost (Dex), natural elegance, parry
Charismatic	+2 Cha	Charming, double boost (Cha), encouragement
Crusading	+2 to any, –2 to any	Crunch!, iron will, higher calling, sterner stuff
Cunning	+2 Dex, –2 Cha	Charming, cheap shot, sharp mind, tenacious spirit
Educated	+2 Int, –2 Dex	Broad learning, if I recall…, linguist, slow and steady
Gifted	+2 to any, –2 to any	Basic skill mastery, limited proficiencies, origin skill (choose), sharp mind
Grizzled	+2 Con, –2 Dex	Agile defense +1, last chance, rock solid
Hardy	+2 Con	Double boost (Con), iron gut, thick hide 2
Industrious	+1 Con	Charming, encouragement, enlightened crafting, yeoman's work
Intelligent	+2 Int	Double boost (Int), split decision
Methodical	+1 Wis	Enlightened haggle, enlightened investigate, free hint, origin skill (any 1), slow and steady
Nimble	+2 Dex, –2 Str	Speed 40 ft., called shot, cat fall, enlightened acrobatics, last chance
Ruthless	+1 to any, –1 to any	Always ready, cheap shot, menacing threat
Savage	+2 Str, –2 Int	Speed 40 ft., enlightened survival, great fortitude, lean season
Savvy	+2 Wis, –2 Str	Free hint, grace under pressure, if I recall...
Single-minded	+2 Con, –2 Int	Crunch!, relentless attack, enlightened resolve, war of attrition
Stern	+2 Str, –2 Con	Grueling combatant, light sleeper, no pain, relentless attack, unbreakable
Striking	+2 Cha, –2 Con	Celebrated, engaging diversion, natural elegance
Strong	+2 Str	Double boost (Str), improved stability, shove
Svelte	+2 Cha, –2 Wis	Charming, enlightened athletics, rock solid, shove
Unpredictable	+1 Int	Lightning reflexes, mix-up, split decision

Talent	Attributes	Benefits (Cont.)
Vigilant	+2 Wis, –2 Int	Always ready, enlightened notice, lightning reflexes
Wily	+2 Int, –2 Cha	Agile defense +1, engaging diversion, enlightened tactics, mix-up
Wise	+2 Wis	Double boost (Wis), free hint, inquisitive mind

Specialty	Feat	Benefits
Acrobat	Basic Skill Mastery (Robber)	Agile defense +1, attribute training (Str/Dex), fast, practiced athletics
Adept	Any 1 Spellcasting feat	Free hint, heroism, practiced search, turning
Adventurer	Adventurer's Luck	Glory-bound, more than luck, origin skill
Archer	Bow Basics	Animal turning, bow hunter, bow proficiency, camouflage
Aristocrat	Basic Skill Mastery (Actor)	Charming, flashy, noble blood, origin skill
Artisan	Crafting Basics	Celebrated, crafting focus, natural elegance, practiced crafting
Barbarian	Rage Basics	Fast, tenacious spirit, trap sense
Bard	Well-Rounded	Beguiling, encouragement, free hint, practiced impress
Cavalier	Favored Gear (mount)	Crunch!, glory-bound, practiced Ride, triumphant swing
Cleric	Any 1 Chance feat	Charming, field medicine, paired skills (Resolve and Medicine), turning
Corsair	Basic Skill Mastery (Officer)	Agile defense +1, flashy, terrifying look, water vehicle focus
Criminal	Basic Skill Mastery (Pickpocket)	Attribute training (Dex/Int), cheap shot, fast, practiced intimidate
Dragoon	Quick Draw	Black powder proficiency, commissioned, edged proficiency, paired skills (Ride and Tactics)
Druid	Animal Partner	Attribute training (Con/Wis), practiced medicine, practiced survival, trackless step
Fencer	Fencing Basics	Decisive, edged proficiency, fast, parry
Fighter	Armor Basics	Attribute training (Str/Con), extra proficiency (any 4), melee combat expert
Fist	Two-Hit Combo	Attribute training (Str/Wis), fast, practiced acrobatics, unarmed proficiency
Gladiator	Combat Instincts	Crunch!, extra proficiency (any 1), harsh beating, paired skills (Athletics and Impress)
Guardian	Elusive	Practiced notice, step in, tenacious spirit
Lord	Followers	Noble blood, practiced tactics, stand together
Merchant	Basic Skill Mastery (Trader)	Attribute training (Int/Cha), linguist, paired skills (Haggle and Search), thrifty
Miner	Pathfinder Basics (caverns/mountains)	Blunt proficiency, paired skills (Athletics and Crafting), stonecutting focus, unbreakable, warding strike
Musketeer	Bullseye	Attribute training (Dex/Wis), black powder proficiency, called shot, commissioned, heroism
Mystic	The Gift	Attribute training (Con/Cha), inquisitive mind, paired skills (Investigate and Medicine), sharp mind
Nomad	Basic Skill Mastery (Horseman)	Animal empathy, attribute training (Dex/Con), linguist, practiced haggle, trackless step
Physician	Basic Skill Mastery (Healer)	Chemistry focus, contagion sense, edged proficiency, paired skills (Medicine and Crafting)
Ranger	Battlefield Trickery	Animal empathy, camouflage, favored foes
Rogue	Ambush Basics	Practiced sneak, sharp mind, trap sense
Shaman	Blessed	Attribute training (Wis/Cha), contagion sense, origin skill, practiced sense motive
Shield Bearer	Shield Basics	Agile defense +1, blunt proficiency, melee combat expert, practiced resolve, shield block
Sorcerer	Any 1 Species feat	Charming, paired skills (Spellcasting and Intimidate), terrifying look
Swindler	Basic Skill Mastery (Spy)	Attribute training (Dex/Cha), beguiling, charming, practiced bluff
Tribesman	Basic Skill Mastery (Athlete)	Extra proficiency (any 1), game hunter, paired skills (Resolve and Survival), riding mounts focus
Vanguard	Misdirection Basics	Basic combat expert, charming, paired skills (Resolve and Impress), stand together
Warden	Pathfinder Basics (any 1)	Attribute training (Int/Wis), decisive, practiced investigate, unbreakable
Wizard	Spell Library	Broad learning, encouragement, practiced spellcasting, thrifty

- *Cold-Blooded:* You require only 1 common meal per day but suffer 1 additional damage per die from cold and are *sickened* for a number of rounds equal to 1/2 any cold damage taken (rounded down). If you suffer continuous cold damage — such as from the environment — you are *sickened* until you escape the source of the damage.
- *Inquisitive Mind:* You gain 2 additional Interests.
- *Natural Attack:* You gain the Bite I and Claw I natural attacks *(see page 235)*. If you gain a natural attack from multiple sources, the attack's grade becomes equal to the highest single grade + 1 per additional benefit granting the same attack, to a maximum of V (e.g. Bite IV, Bite III, and Bite I become Bite V).
- *Reviled:* The Dispositions of non-drakes decrease by 10.
- *Winged Flight:* You may fly with a Speed of 40 ft.

DWARF

You're a dwarf, a stout and reliable clansman somewhat shorter than a human with similar appearance. Your people are famous for their tenacity and physical toughness, and often develop great skill as craftsmen due to their willingness to set aside frivolity for the simple pleasure of a job well done. Despite frequent accusations that dwarves are curmudgeons, you have a deep appreciation for all things beautiful and are quick to adopt new technologies and innovations.

You most likely came up in a clan — the core of dwarven society — and wear your clan name as a badge of great pride. Your deep familial ties ensure you're quick to honor debts and avenge slights against your ancestors. Through the heat of battle and the chill of conflict, you've also forged strong bonds with your companions, and remain a stout and true-hearted friend to the bitter end.

Common Personality Traits: Brave, gruff, persistent, reliable, stubborn

Common Physical Traits: Beard, barrel chest, sturdy build, heavy brow, incredible endurance

Example First Names: Hrothgar, Durik, Snori, Baldar, Mordn, Gulid

Example Clan Names: Fireheart, Stonehand, Silvermine

Splinter Race Feats: Hill-Born (hill dwarf), Lava-Born (magma dwarf). Unless you choose one of these, you're 'stone born' (a mountain dwarf).

Type: Medium biped folk with a Reach of 1. Your maximum wounds equal your Constitution score.

- *Attributes:* +4 Constitution, –2 Dexterity
- *Base Speed:* 20 ft.
- *Darkvision I:* You ignore the effects of dim and faint light.

- *Enlightened Crafting:* Your maximum Crafting rank increases to your Career Level + 5. Only the highest bonus from any single enlightened ability may apply to each skill.
- *Improved Stability:* You're considered 1 Size category larger for carrying capacity, Trample attacks, and resisting Bull Rush and Trip attempts so long as you are standing firmly on the ground and not climbing, flying, or riding.
- *Iron Gut:* You gain a +2 insight bonus with saves against disease and poisons.
- *Restricted Actions:* Kick attacks, as well as Jump and Swim checks you make are considered untrained *(see page 63)*.
- *Thick Hide 2:* You're considered to be wearing partial armor that provides Damage Reduction 2. This DR does *not* stack with other armor (only the best protection applies). If you gain thick hide from multiple sources, your hide offers the highest single DR value + 1 per additional hide benefit (e.g. thick hide 4, thick hide 3, and thick hide 1 offer DR 6).

ELF

You're an elf, among the few elder races still lingering in the world. Though similar to a human, your form is slim and graceful with fine features and pointed ears. You're gifted with a tremendous lifespan and use it to explore all the world's wonders. You're also deeply attuned to the primal and arcane powers of creation, which is a blessing and a curse as the eras inch forward around you.

Your long life has instilled in you a strong responsibility to preserve and pass on the old ways, though others sometimes view your wisdom and centuries of experience as haughtiness and condescension. You rise above these petty biases and resolve to sway them by example. You're grateful for the few who've embraced your vision — your companions in adventure — and find in their friendship a hope for the future long dwindled among your kind.

Common Personality Traits: Beautiful, determined, graceful, measured, mysterious

Common Physical Traits: Delicate hands, fine clothing, intense gaze, radiant appearance, nimble

Example Names: Aenir, Eldrin, Ilrael, Tevin, Nuada

Splinter Race Feats: Hart Nation (wood elf), Owl Nation (gray elf), Spider Nation (dark elf). Unless you choose one of these, you're a 'high elf.'

Type: Medium biped fey with a Reach of 1 *(see page 227)*. Your maximum wounds equal your Constitution score.

- *Attributes:* +4 Wisdom, –2 Constitution
- *Base Speed:* 40 ft.
- *Aloof:* Your error range increases by 2 when making Impress and Sense Motive checks targeting characters of other species.
- *Burden of Ages:* Your will to live has been worn down by long ages of struggle and you find it difficult to express the fire of the younger species. Any effect that cures or restores your vitality has only 1/2 the normal effect (rounded up).
- *Keen Sight:* Your visual range increments are equal to your Wisdom score × 50 ft. You also ignore range penalties from the 2nd and 4th range increments while you're Aiming.
- *Natural Elegance:* Your Appearance bonus increases by +1.
- *Sharp Hearing:* Your hearing range increments are equal to your Wisdom score × 10 ft. Further, you may always act during a surprise round unless *deafened*.

GIANT

You're a giant, a 10–15 ft. tall humanoid whose heritage dates back to the earliest days of the world. Some call your forefathers "titans" and believe they embodied the most fundamental aspects of creation; you and your modern-day kin still bear this elemental birthright and revel in the mystic awe bestowed to you by "small folk."

Like many elder beings, you have likely withdrawn from the growing race of men, perhaps out of fear or simply for solitude in a shrinking world. You remain intrigued by the exploits of other species, however, and are quick to befriend those that show you kindness and understanding. You're intensely protective of these companions and go to great lengths to protect them from harm. Your enemies, on the other hand, view you as a force of nature, leaving nothing but destruction in your wake.

Common Personality Traits: Jovial, paternal, quick-tempered, straightforward, watchful

Common Physical Traits: Booming voice, towering physique, muscular body, rugged appearance

Example Names: Hruthgar Windwalker, Drath Firebrand, Fafnir Starcrusher

Splinter Race Feats: Elemental Heritage (fire giant, frost giant, stone giant, or other elemental giant). Unless you choose one of these, you're a 'hill giant.'

Type: Large (2×2) biped folk with a Reach of 2. Your maximum wounds equal your Constitution score × 1.5 (rounded down).

- *Attributes:* No modifiers
- *Base Speed:* 50 ft.
- *Hurled Proficiency:* You gain the Hurled proficiency.
- *Improved Stability:* You're considered 1 Size category larger for carrying capacity, Trample attacks, and resisting Bull Rush and Trip attempts so long as you are standing firmly on the ground and not climbing, flying, or riding.
- *Natural Attack:* You gain the Trample I natural attack *(see page 235)*. If you gain a natural attack from multiple sources, the attack's grade becomes equal to the highest single grade + 1 per additional benefit granting the same attack, to a maximum of V (e.g. Bite IV, Bite III, and Bite I become Bite V).
- *Sterner Stuff:* The *keen* quality of each attack made against you decreases by 4.

GOBLIN

You're a goblin, a crude, rambunctious creature notorious for curiosity and mischief. Yours is a small subterranean people with earth-toned skin, pointed ears, course black hair, beady eyes, long noses, and big mouths (literally and figuratively). Though your people share many traits with orcs, you don't take yourself nearly as seriously. Low cunning and humor are time-honored traditions in your culture, making you a natural prankster, rogue, and rapscallion. Despite your ilk's stubby stature and ill-deserved reputation for cowardice, you're a rough-and-tumble little bugger who can be incredibly tenacious when you set your mind to something.

Most goblins are born in pairs or threes and you probably grew up in a subterranean warren with around a dozen others, fighting for limited food and attention. This makes you intensely competitive and self-aggrandizing — the more you can show others up, the better. It sometimes makes life with an adventuring party... *interesting,* but your boisterous nature and loyalty keep things on an even keel.

Common Personality Traits: Exuberant, coarse, grand-standing, nosy, quick-witted, shifty

Common Physical Traits: Dirty skin and clothes, scrawny build, light-fingered touch, hyperactive motion, surprisingly tough and resilient

Example Names: Snorrig, Noblar, Grazbaag, Rord

Splinter Race Feats: Eastern Horde (skull tribe), Great Horde (blood tribe), Northern Horde (bone tribe), Southern Horde (fang tribe), Western Horde (iron tribe). Unless you choose one of these, you're a 'cave goblin.'

Type: Small biped folk with a Reach of 1. Your maximum wounds equal your Constitution score × 2/3 (rounded up).

- *Attributes:* +2 Strength, –2 Charisma
- *Base Speed*: 20 ft.
- *Agile Defense:* Your base Defense increases by 1.
- *Ambush Basics:* You gain the Ambush Basics feat *(see page 95)*.
- *Darkvision I:* You ignore the effects of dim and faint light.
- *Light-Sensitive:* Each time you enter a more brightly lit area, you suffer 20 points of flash damage *(see page 210)*.
- *Tenacious Spirit:* You gain 1 additional vitality point at each Career Level.

HUMAN

You're a human, standing 5 ft. to 6 ft. tall and weighing between 100 to 250 lbs. Your hair, eyes, skin tone, and other physical features vary as much as your culture, which spreads quickly and borrows heavily from all others. You're extremely inquisitive, trading ideas like most trade supplies, and adopting customs and terms from friends and foes alike. You're also wildly ambitious, your culture making in-roads everywhere, sometimes through diplomacy, often through conquest. For all these reasons your appearance, demeanor, society, laws, religion, accumulated knowledge, and even language may be completely different from those of other humans, even your neighbors. Unlike other races, it is this very difference that defines you as a species.

As a relatively short-lived breed, you view life as an adventure, an undiscovered country to explore and command. You blaze new trails every day, sampling and savoring every experience as a great treasure, and with every step you shape your own unique destiny. You haven't the time or the patience for your brother's means and aims, though sometimes you accept those of your father; you're his legacy, after all, and how else will he be remembered? You make your own friends and enemies and cherish both as part of what makes you special.

Talent: Humans are the most diverse of the mortal races and gain 1 Talent to represent their individual heritage, personality, or outlook *(see page 18)*.

Splinter Race Feats: Angelic Heritage (heavenly blood), Devilish Heritage (hellish blood), Draconic Heritage (drake blood), Elemental Heritage (ancient blood), Faerie Heritage (fey blood). Unless you choose one of these, you're a 'true blood.'

Type: Medium biped folk with a Reach of 1. Your maximum wounds equal your Constitution score.

- *Attributes:* No Species modifiers
- *Base Speed:* 30 ft.

OGRE

You're an ogre, a brutish, lumbering humanoid who inspires equal measures of terror and revulsion. Like most of your kind, you have small and darting eyes, a broad muscular frame, a thick-featured face, small tusks or horns, and skin ranging in color from dull yellow, red, or brown to subdued green, blue, or black. Your species is almost universally outcast by other cultures, caring little for the niceties and nuances of society. You tend to be blunt and overbearing in both demeanor and odor.

You've spent most of your life in nomadic tribes, moving constantly to avoid the prejudice of "civilized" folk. Despite your best efforts, many see you as a monster, a man-eater or worse, and overzealous champions and greedy bounty hunters regularly harass and hunt you. If you're lucky, you find work in remote ranks of armies or the company of friends who can see past your foul features. You're grateful for such fortune and treat those who accept you as tribe-mates, wreaking bloody carnage against all who threaten them.

Common Personality Traits: Brusque, guarded, ill-tempered, resolute, uncivilized

Common Physical Traits: Hulking stature, broad body, clumsy gait, bucket jaw, musky smell

Example Names: Gorefang, Zetrix, Bonegnasher, Necksnapper

Splinter Race Feats: Fire Brave (oni), Sea Brave (merrow), Stone Brave (troll). Unless you choose one of these, you're an 'earth brave.'

Type: Large (2×2) biped folk with a Reach of 1. Your maximum wounds equal your Constitution score × 1.5 (rounded down).

- *Attributes:* +2 Strength, +4 Constitution, –2 Intelligence, –2 Charisma
- *Base Speed:* 30 ft.
- *Enlightened Athletics:* Your maximum Athletics rank increases to your Career Level + 5. Only the highest bonus from any single enlightened ability may apply to each skill.
- *No Pain:* You may ignore the first *fatigued* or *shaken* condition you gain each scene.
- *Reviled:* The Disposition of non-ogres decrease by 10.
- *Restricted Actions:* Influence, Outmaneuver, and Tumble checks you make are considered untrained *(see page 63)*.
- *Unbreakable:* Each time you suffer attribute impairment, it decreases by 1 (minimum 0).

ORC

You're an orc, a creature bred in a failed attempt by dark forces to forge elves for war and conquest. Your people vary widely in look and character, particularly between the hordes making up your culture, though all are savage. Your species' tragic history often overshadows your most virtuous deeds and gestures, making the struggle for respect and acceptance yet another war in a long story of endless conflict.

You were expected to mature quickly under the watchful eye (and hobnailed boot) of horde elders, and learned the hard way that each must carve his own path, often in blood. You have little patience for the art of elves or crafts of dwarves, for your legacy must be in the glory of the moment, the fire of battle, and the screams of vanquished foes. Outside the horde, you bind yourself to warriors whose valor and skill you deem worthy, for they can help build your legend.

Common Personality Traits: Argumentative, brave, bloodthirsty, impatient, individualistic

Common Physical Traits: Many scars, pointed teeth, mottled skin, lean ropy physique, blood-curdling roar

Example Names: Nazdreg, Gazghul, Krarug, Vashnak, Erudush

Splinter Race Feats: Eastern Horde (skull tribe), Great Horde (blood tribe), Northern Horde (bone tribe), Southern Horde (fang tribe), Western Horde (iron tribe). Unless you choose one of these, you're a 'black blade.'

Type: Medium biped folk with a Reach of 1. Your maximum wounds equal your Constitution score.

- *Attributes:* +3 Strength, +3 Constitution, –3 Intelligence
- *Base Speed:* 30 ft.
- *Always Ready:* You may always act during surprise rounds.

- *Enlightened Intimidate:* Your maximum Intimidate rank increases to your Career Level + 5. Only the highest bonus from any single enlightened ability may apply to each skill.
- *Grueling Combatant:* Each time an adjacent opponent attacks you and misses, he suffers 2 points of subdual damage.
- *Light-Sensitive:* Each time you enter a more brightly lit area, you suffer 20 points of flash damage *(see page 210)*.
- *Restricted Actions:* Calm, Decipher, and Influence checks you make are considered untrained *(see page 63)*.

PECH

You're a pech, small of stature but quick of mind and limb, a salt-of-the-earth kinsman whose people are known for inattention and cloistered ignorance of the outside world. You were likely brought up in a peaceful, agrarian society, raised on fireside tales of heroes and dragons and big folk doing big things. You, on the other hand, are one of the few bold souls in each generation with an itch to explore, to *live* the stories your people tell with such animated passion.

Before ambition took hold, you lived as most pech do — relishing fine food and company, taking joy in the simple pleasures of the day, and sharing cozy afternoons in stray conversation, letting your mind wander far beyond the confines of your remote community. Perhaps this drifting imagination is what drew you out into the boundless world and urged you to seek new companions. It's certainly what keeps you fierce of heart in the face of adversity, for you know that beyond every misfortune there's a new tale to spin. Someday you'll return to your comfortable home and regale your family and friends about all the amazing things you've seen, the wonderful friends you made, and the fearsome enemies you helped defeat.

Common Personality Traits: Creative, charming, easygoing, persistent, spirited

Common Physical Traits: Hairy feet, fast hands, childlike appearance, expressive features, surprisingly quick

Example Names: Andol, April, Autumn, Banin, Bradoc, Jasmine, Jordo, Malin, May, Rose, Silvertea, Tondol

Splinter Race Feats: Farstride Folk (hairfoot), Quick-Finger Folk (gnome). Unless you choose one of these, you're a 'lightfoot.'

Type: Small biped folk with a Reach of 1. Your maximum wounds equal your Constitution score × 2/3 (rounded up).

- *Attributes:* +3 Dexterity
- *Base Speed:* 30 ft.
- *Enlightened Resolve:* Your maximum Resolve rank increases to your Career Level + 5. Only the highest bonus from any single enlightened ability may apply to each skill.
- *Hearty Appetite:* You benefit from the first 2 food and 2 drink you consume in each day.
- *Hurled Proficiency:* You gain the Hurled proficiency.

ROOTWALKER

You're a rootwalker, a massive living tree with 4 or more twisted branch-limbs, tough bark for skin, and thick foliage that changes with the seasons. As part of an ancient race born of nature, you're eternally dedicated to preserving the balance of life. Your wards are the trees and animals of the deep forest, which you and your kind vow to protect from hunters, woodcutters, and other pillagers.

Your people are solitary, often growing for decades without sentient contact. This cultivates great patience and an exceptionally long view of time, which confounds younger races. They sometimes think you slow-witted or ponderous, but you know the best decisions are those considered carefully — even if that consideration takes weeks! You're often baffled by the rash and impulsive behavior of the younger races. Their "civilization," with all its conflicts and endless racket, is a mystery, but it is also part of the grand design, and as worthy of protection as your precious wilderness.

Common Personality Traits: Calm, indignant, methodical, contemplative, respectful

Common Physical Traits: Colorful foliage, gnarled limbs, inexpressive eyes, whispering voice, gnarled skin bearing the wear of ages

Example Names: Skinbark, Strongbranch, Beechbone, Leaflock, Wandlimb

Splinter Race Feats: New Leaf (evergreen, ironwood, and others). Unless you choose this, you're a 'deeproot.'

Type: Large (2×2) biped plant with a Reach of 1 *(see page 227)*. Your maximum wounds equal your Constitution score × 1.5 (rounded down).

- *Attributes:* No modifiers
- *Base Speed:* 30 ft.
- *Achilles Heel (Fire):* When you suffer fire damage, you also suffer an equal amount of lethal damage.
- *Bleeding Immunity:* You're immune to bleeding *(see page 212)*.
- *Lean Season:* You require only 1 common meal per day.
- *Lumbering:* You suffer a –2 penalty with all Reflex saves and become *flanked* any time two opponents are adjacent to you.
- *Natural Camouflage:* Choose forest/jungle or swamp. You gain a +5 gear bonus with Blend checks while in that terrain.
- *Thick Hide 2:* You're considered to be wearing partial armor that provides Damage Reduction 2. This DR does *not* stack with other armor (only the best protection applies). If you gain thick hide from multiple sources, your hide offers the highest single DR value + 1 per additional hide benefit (e.g. thick hide 4, thick hide 3, and thick hide 1 offer DR 6).

SAURIAN

You're a saurian, a cold-blooded reptilian humanoid hailing from the warmest or wettest parts of your world. Your people are generally covered in fine scales, possess long tails, and have broad lizard-like heads with wide-set eyes and mouths, but your appearance can vary widely. Poisonous saurians are often decorated with brightly contrasting bands of color, while others have rainbow-colored scales, bony crests, rotating eyes, long sticky tongues, or even membranous wings!

Saurians are born in clutches of eggs and hatch alone, their sires having moved on well before. This hard beginning bred in you a deep independence and a knack for innovation. You believe adaptation is the best path to survival and so you're quick to pick up new skills, technologies and other ways to overcome the odds. Though your clutch-mates are your only "family," you get along well with members of all species. Accepting longtime companions as extensions of your clutch is the highest honor you bestow.

Common Personality Traits: Clever, independent, misunderstood, pragmatic, self-reliant

Common Physical Traits: Sleek body, hissing lisp, large protruding eyes, cool skin, clawed hands

Example Names: Ssathryn, Tlaxec, Naryss, Xysstos, Morthyss

Splinter Race Feats: Draconic Heritage (draconian), Jungle Clutch (chameleon), Swamp Clutch (frogman). Unless you choose one of these, you're 'lizard-folk.'

Type: Medium biped folk with a Reach of 1. Your maximum wounds equal your Constitution score.

- *Attributes:* +2 Dexterity, +2 to any 1 attribute, –2 to any 1 attribute
- *Base Speed:* 30 ft.
- *Agile Defense:* Your base Defense increases by 1.
- *Cold-Blooded:* You require only 1 common meal per day but suffer 1 additional damage per die from cold and are *sickened* for a number of rounds equal to 1/2 any cold damage taken (rounded down). If you suffer continuous cold damage — such as from the environment — you are *sickened* until you escape the source of the damage.
- *Darkvision I:* You ignore the effects of dim and faint light.
- *Natural Attack:* You gain the Bite I and Tail Slap I natural attacks *(see page 235)*. If you gain a natural attack from multiple sources, the attack's grade becomes equal to the highest single grade + 1 per additional benefit granting the same attack, to a maximum of V (e.g. Bite IV, Bite III, and Bite I become Bite V).

UNBORN

You're unborn, a being constructed from inanimate materials and given the spark of life by magic or technology. You might be a clay golem, an animated brass statue, a creature of living crystal, or even a clockwork device powered by steam. Regardless of your makeup, you're unique and bizarre enough to forever dwell outside "polite" society.

You were probably built for a single purpose — war, or perhaps labor or companionship — and your master was likely both highly-skilled and wildly eccentric. Some event, maybe your master's death, obsolescence, or the development of free will, now lets you to write your own story and explore a greater world you've never known. You tend to be curious and somewhat naïve about emotions and relationships, meeting new experiences with the wonder and indulgence of a child. Your adventuring companions might be the only friends you've ever had, and their continued acceptance and support is reason enough for you to protect them to your last spark of life.

Common Personality Traits: Curious, impressionable, lonely, loyal, pensive

Common Physical Traits: Glowing eyes, awkward expressions, hollow or tinny voice

Example Names: Whizgig, Tinker, Gadget, The Monster

Splinter Race Feats: Special Construction (clay, clockwork, crystal, and others). Unless you choose this, you're a 'steel golem.'

Type: Medium biped construct with a Reach of 1 *(see page 226)*. Your maximum wounds equal your Constitution score.

- *Attributes:* +2 to any 1 attribute, –4 Charisma
- *Base Speed:* 20 ft.
- *Achilles Heel (Electricity):* When you suffer electrical damage, you also suffer an equal amount of lethal damage.
- *Enlightened Skill:* Choose one skill. Your maximum rank in that skill increases to your Career Level + 5. Only the highest bonus from any single enlightened ability may apply to each skill.
- *Limited Proficiencies:* You begin play with 2 fewer proficiencies (minimum 0).
- *Lumbering:* You suffer a –2 penalty with all Reflex saves and become *flanked* any time two opponents are adjacent to you.

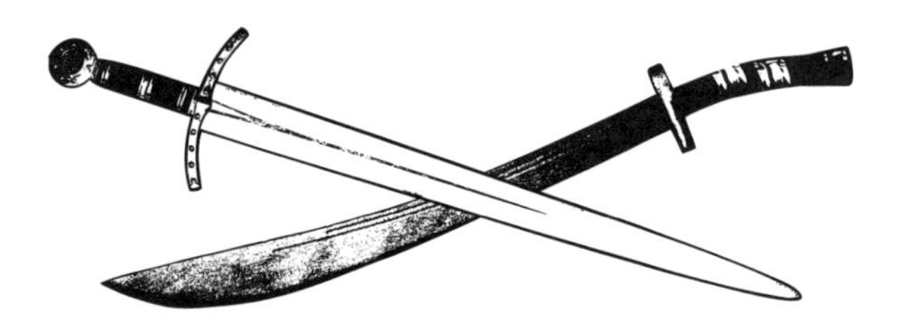

HUMAN TALENTS

Some Talents require you possess an Alignment *(see page 61)*.

ADAPTABLE

You can find a solution to almost any problem and it's often wholly unexpected.

- *Attributes:* No modifiers
- *Base Speed:* 30 ft.
- *Grace under Pressure:* You gain a +2 bonus with any roll you boost with an action die.
- *Inquisitive Mind:* You gain 2 additional Interests.
- *Mix-Up:* You gain the Mix-Up trick *(see page 221)*.
- *Origin Skills:* Choose 2 additional Origin skills.

AGILE

Your body is quicker than most eyes!

- *Attributes:* +2 Dexterity
- *Base Speed:* 30 ft.
- *Double Boost:* You may spend and roll 2 action dice to boost Dexterity-based skill checks.
- *Natural Elegance:* Your Appearance bonus increases by +1.
- *Parry:* You gain the Parry trick *(see page 222)*.

CHARISMATIC

Your natural presence is almost overwhelming.

- *Attributes:* +2 Charisma
- *Base Speed:* 30 ft.
- *Charming:* Once per session, you may improve the Disposition of any 1 non-adversary NPC by 5.
- *Double Boost:* You may spend and roll 2 action dice to boost Charisma-based skill checks.
- *Encouragement:* Once per scene, you may speak to 1 of your teammates for 1 minute to grant them a +1 morale bonus with saving throws until the end of the current scene.

CRUSADING

You focus is... intense.

Requirements: Alignment

- *Attributes:* +2 to any 1 attribute, –2 to any 1 attribute
- *Base Speed:* 30 ft.
- *Crunch!:* Your Strength-based damage rolls inflict 1 additional damage.
- *Iron Will:* You gain the Iron Will feat *(see page 86)*.
- *Higher Calling:* Characters with opposing Alignments suffer a –1 penalty with skill checks targeting or opposed by you.
- *Sterner Stuff:* The *keen* quality of each attack made against you decreases by 4.

CUNNING

You're a survivor who considers every angle and how to exploit it.

- *Attributes:* +2 Dexterity, –2 Charisma
- *Base Speed:* 30 ft.
- *Charming:* Once per session, you may improve the Disposition of any 1 non-adversary NPC by 5.
- *Cheap Shot:* You gain the Cheap Shot trick *(see page 221).*
- *Sharp Mind:* You gain 1 additional skill point per level.
- *Tenacious Spirit:* You gain 1 additional vitality per level.

EDUCATED

You enjoy all the advantages of a higher education.

- *Attributes:* +2 Intelligence, –2 Dexterity
- *Base Speed:* 30 ft.
- *Broad Learning:* You gain 2 additional Studies *(see page 61).*
- *If I Recall...:* You gain a +5 bonus with Knowledge checks *(see page 66).*
- *Linguist:* You gain 2 additional Languages *(see page 61).*
- *Slow and Steady:* The cost to activate your Downtime errors and those of your teammates increases by 2 action dice.

GIFTED

You've found your calling... and mastered it.

- *Attributes:* +2 to any 1 attribute, –2 to any 1 attribute
- *Base Speed:* 30 ft.
- *Basic Skill Mastery:* You gain the Basic Skill Mastery feat *(see page 99).*
- *Limited Proficiencies:* You begin with play with 2 fewer proficiencies (minimum 0).
- *Origin Skill:* Choose 1 additional Origin skill.
- *Sharp Mind:* You gain 1 additional skill point per level.

GRIZZLED

You've survived things other folk can barely imagine.

- *Attributes:* +2 Constitution, –2 Dexterity
- *Base Speed:* 30 ft.
- *Agile Defense:* Your base Defense increases by 1.
- *Last Chance:* You may spend and roll 2 action dice to boost any save.
- *Rock Solid:* You gain 1 additional wound per level.

HARDY

You feel the blows but they don't really bother you much.

- *Attributes:* +2 Constitution
- *Base Speed:* 30 ft.
- *Double Boost:* You may spend and roll 2 action dice to boost Constitution-based skill checks.
- *Iron Gut:* You gain a +2 insight bonus with saves against disease and poisons.
- *Thick Hide 2:* You're considered to be wearing partial armor that provides Damage Reduction 2. This DR does *not* stack with other armor (only the best protection applies). If you gain thick hide from multiple sources, your hide offers the highest single DR value + 1 per additional hide benefit (e.g. thick hide 4, thick hide 3, and thick hide 1 offer DR 6).

INDUSTRIOUS

You always put your time to good use.

- *Attributes:* +1 Constitution
- *Base Speed:* 30 ft.
- *Charming:* Once per session, you may improve the Disposition of any 1 non-adversary NPC by 5.
- *Encouragement:* Once per scene, you may speak to 1 of your teammates for 1 minute to grant them a +1 morale bonus with saving throws until the end of the current scene.
- *Enlightened Crafting:* Your maximum Crafting rank increases to your Career Level + 5. Only the highest bonus from any single enlightened ability may apply to each skill.
- *Yeoman's Work:* You gain the Yeoman's Work feat *(see page 99).*

INTELLIGENT

You've always been the sharpest knife in the drawer.

- *Attributes:* +2 Intelligence
- *Base Speed:* 30 ft.
- *Double Boost:* You may spend and roll 2 action dice to boost Intelligence-based skill checks.
- *Split Decision:* As a full action, you may simultaneously take 2 Ready actions, each with separate triggers and reactions. After the first trigger occurs, the other Ready action is lost.

METHODICAL

Your thinking may sometimes seem slow and ponderous to others, but you tend to uncover the truth of things with few missteps.

- *Attributes:* +1 Wisdom
- *Base Speed:* 30 ft.
- *Enlightened Haggle:* Your maximum Haggle rank increases to your Career Level + 5. Only the highest bonus from any single enlightened ability may apply to each skill.
- *Enlightened Investigate:* Your maximum Investigate rank increases to your Career Level + 5. Only the highest bonus from any single enlightened ability may apply to each skill.
- *Free Hint:* Once per session, you may request a hint from the GM. If he refuses, you gain 1 bonus action die.
- *Origin Skill:* Choose 1 additional Origin skill.
- *Slow and Steady:* The cost to activate your Downtime errors and those of your teammates increases by 2 action dice.

NIMBLE

You're light on your feet and quick to avoid harm.

- *Attributes:* +2 Dexterity, –2 Strength
- *Base Speed:* 40 ft.
- *Called Shot:* You gain the Called Shot trick *(see page 221).*
- *Cat Fall:* You suffer 1 less die of damage from falling.
- *Enlightened Acrobatics:* Your maximum Acrobatics rank increases to your Career Level + 5. Only the highest bonus from any single enlightened ability may apply to each skill.
- *Last Chance:* You may spend and roll 2 action dice to boost any save.

RUTHLESS

Whatever it takes, you're always up for the challenge.

- *Attributes:* +1 to any 1 attribute, –1 to any 1 attribute
- *Base Speed:* 30 ft.
- *Always Ready:* You may always act during surprise rounds.
- *Cheap Shot:* You gain the Cheap Shot trick *(see page 221).*
- *Menacing Threat:* You may Threaten up to 3 opponents at once. You roll only once for the action, while each opponent rolls to resist separately.

SAVAGE

You're untamed, born and bred far outside civilization.

- *Attributes:* +2 Strength, –2 Intelligence
- *Base Speed:* 40 ft.
- *Enlightened Survival:* Your maximum Survival rank increases to your Career Level + 5. Only the highest bonus from any single enlightened ability may apply to each skill.
- *Great Fortitude:* You gain the Great Fortitude feat.
- *Lean Season:* You require only 1 common meal per day.

SAVVY

You always have a plan... or at least *look* like you do.

- *Attributes:* +2 Wisdom, –2 Strength
- *Base Speed:* 30 ft.
- *Free Hint:* Once per session, you may request a hint from the GM. If he refuses, you gain 1 bonus action die.
- *Grace Under Pressure:* You gain a +2 bonus with any roll you boost with an action die.
- *If I Recall...:* You gain a +5 bonus with Knowledge checks *(see page 66).*

SINGLE-MINDED

Your focus and determination cannot be swayed.

- *Attributes:* +2 Constitution, –2 Intelligence
- *Base Speed:* 30 ft.
- *Crunch!:* Your Strength-based damage rolls inflict 1 additional damage.
- *Enlightened Resolve:* Your maximum Resolve rank increases to your Career Level + 5. Only the highest bonus from any single enlightened ability may apply to each skill.
- *Relentless Attack:* You gain the Relentless Attack trick *(see page 222).*
- *War of Attrition:* You may Tire up to 3 opponents at once. You roll only once for the action, while each opponent rolls to resist separately.

STERN

When worn and haggard from your trials, you reveal a core a tough as iron.

- *Attributes:* +2 Strength, –2 Constitution
- *Base Speed:* 30 ft.
- *Grueling Combatant:* Each time an adjacent opponent attacks you and misses, he suffers 2 points of subdual damage.
- *Light Sleeper:* Sleeping is never a Terminal Situation for you.
- *No Pain:* You ignore the first *fatigued* or *shaken* condition you gain in each scene.
- *Relentless Attack:* You gain the Relentless Attack trick *(see page 222).*
- *Unbreakable:* Each time you suffer attribute impairment, it decreases by 1 (minimum 0).

STRIKING

Your good looks set hearts aflutter and keep the poets in business.

- *Attributes:* +2 Charisma, –2 Constitution
- *Base Speed:* 30 ft.
- *Celebrated:* Your Legend increases by 2.
- *Engaging Diversion:* You may Distract up to 3 opponents at once. You roll only once for the action, while each opponent rolls to resist separately.
- *Natural Elegance:* Your Appearance bonus increases by +1.

STRONG

If oxen could arm-wrestle you'd still win every time.

- *Attributes:* +2 Strength
- *Base Speed:* 30 ft.
- *Double Boost:* You may spend and roll 2 action dice to boost Strength-based skill checks.
- *Improved Stability:* You're considered 1 Size category larger for carrying capacity, Trample attacks, and resisting Bull Rush and Trip attempts so long as you are standing firmly on the ground and not climbing, flying, or riding.
- *Shove:* You gain the Shove trick *(see page 222).*

SVELTE

You have a predator's build and natural magnetism.

- *Attributes:* +2 Charisma, –2 Wisdom
- *Base Speed:* 30 ft.
- *Charming:* Once per session, you may improve the Disposition of any 1 non-adversary NPC by 5.

- *Enlightened Athletics:* Your maximum Athletics rank increases to your Career Level + 5. Only the highest bonus from any single enlightened ability may apply to each skill.
- *Rock Solid:* You gain 1 additional wound per level.
- *Shove:* You gain the Shove trick *(see page 222).*

UNPREDICTABLE

Your quicksilver thoughts leave most people reeling.

- *Attributes:* +1 Intelligence
- *Base Speed:* 30 ft.
- *Lightning Reflexes:* You gain the Lightning Reflexes feat *(see page 86).*
- *Mix-Up:* You gain the Mix-Up trick *(see page 221).*
- *Split Decision:* As a full action, you may simultaneously take 2 Ready actions, each with separate triggers and reactions. After the first trigger occurs, the other Ready action is lost.

VIGILANT

You're always on your guard.

- *Attributes:* +2 Wisdom, –2 Intelligence
- *Base Speed:* 30 ft.
- *Always Ready:* You may always act during surprise rounds.
- *Enlightened Notice:* Your maximum Notice rank increases to your Career Level + 5. Only the highest bonus from any single enlightened ability may apply to each skill.
- *Lightning Reflexes:* You gain the Lightning Reflexes feat *(see page 86).*

WILY

People would like you more if you didn't say 'I told you so' quite so often.

- *Attributes:* +2 Intelligence, –2 Charisma
- *Base Speed:* 30 ft.
- *Agile Defense:* Your base Defense increases by 1.
- *Engaging Diversion:* You may Distract up to 3 opponents at once. You roll only once for the action, while each opponent rolls to resist separately.
- *Enlightened Tactics:* Your maximum Tactics rank increases to your Career Level + 5. Only the highest bonus from any single enlightened ability may apply to each skill.
- *Mix-Up:* You gain the Mix-Up trick *(see page 221).*

WISE

When you speak, everyone falls silent to hear it.

- *Attributes:* +2 Wisdom
- *Base Speed:* 30 ft.
- *Double Boost:* You may spend and roll 2 action dice to boost Wisdom-based skill checks.
- *Free Hint:* Once per session, you may request a free hint from the GM. If he refuses, you gain 1 bonus action die.
- *Inquisitive Mind:* You gain 2 additional Interests.

SPECIALTY

Your Specialty grants you a bonus feat. When only one is listed you ignore its prerequisites. When two or more are offered you may choose only one, for which you must meet all prerequisites.

ACROBAT

Your grace and flexibility amaze.

- *Bonus Feat:* Basic Skill Mastery (Robber)
- *Agile Defense:* Your base Defense increases by 1.
- *Attribute Training:* The lower of your Strength or Dexterity scores increases by 1 (your choice if a tie). Apply this bonus after any modifiers from your Species or Talent.
- *Fast:* Your Ground Speed increases by 10 ft.
- *Practiced Athletics:* If you spend an action die to boost an Athletics check and it still fails, you gain the die back after the action is resolved. Against multiple targets you only regain the die if the check fails against all of them.

ADEPT

You collect lost knowledge from all over the world.

- *Bonus Feat:* Any 1 Spellcasting feat
- *Free Hint:* Once per session, you may request a free hint from the GM. If he refuses, you gain 1 bonus action die.
- *Heroism:* You gain a +1 bonus with all attack and skill checks you make during Dramatic scenes.
- *Practiced Search:* If you spend an action die to boost a Search check and it still fails, you gain the die back after the action is resolved. Against multiple targets you only regain the die if the check fails against all of them.
- *Turning:* Choose a Type from the following list: animal, beast, construct, elemental, fey, horror, ooze, outsider, plant, spirit, or undead. Once per combat you may Turn characters of this Type *(see page 223).*

ADVENTURER

You chart your own course, exploring tombs one day and rescuing damsels the next.

- *Bonus Feat:* Adventurer's Luck
- *Glory-Bound:* You may purchase Heroic Renown for 20 Reputation per rank *(see page 187).*
- *More than Luck:* You gain 1 additional starting action die.
- *Origin Skill:* Choose 1 additional Origin skill.

ARCHER

You've made a living by the bow, as a hunter or perhaps a warrior.

- *Bonus Feat:* Bow Basics
- *Animal Turning:* Once per combat you may Turn animals *(see page 223).*
- *Bow Hunter:* You inflict 2 additional damage on standard characters with a bow.

- *Bow Proficiency:* You gain the Bow proficiency.
- *Camouflage:* Choose a terrain: aquatic, arctic, caverns/mountains, desert, forest/jungle, indoors/settled, plains, or swamp. You gain a +5 gear bonus with Blend checks while in that terrain.

ARISTOCRAT

You're a child of nobility or wealthy parents, accustomed to living a life of privilege.

- *Bonus Feat:* Basic Skill Mastery (Actor)
- *Charming:* Once per session, you may improve the Disposition of any 1 non-adversary NPC by 5.
- *Flashy:* Your Panache rises by 2.
- *Noble Blood:* You may purchase Noble Renown for 20 Reputation per rank *(see page 187).*
- *Origin Skill:* Choose 1 additional Origin skill.

ARTISAN

Your mastery of the arts makes you a welcome guest in any land.

- *Bonus Feat:* Crafting Basics
- *Celebrated:* Your Legend increases by 2.
- *Crafting Focus:* You gain 1 Crafting skill focus.
- *Natural Elegance:* Your Appearance bonus increases by +1.
- *Practiced Crafting:* If you spend an action die to boost a Crafting check and it still fails, you gain the die back after the action is resolved. Against multiple targets you only regain the die if the check fails against all of them.

BARBARIAN

You're a savage warrior, driven by sheer fury.

- *Bonus Feat:* Rage Basics
- *Fast:* Your Ground Speed increases by 10 ft.
- *Tenacious Spirit:* You gain 1 additional vitality per level.
- *Trap Sense:* You may roll twice when making Reflex saves prompted by security devices and traps, keeping the result you prefer.

BARD

You hold the night at bay with practical wisdom and good cheer, commonly using stories and song.

- *Bonus Feat:* Well-Rounded
- *Beguiling:* When you successfully Taunt a character, you may decline the standard result to have your target become *fixated* on you for 1d6 rounds. Special characters and villains may spend 1 action die to cancel this effect and become immune to this ability for the rest of the scene. If you gain this benefit from multiple sources, you may also damage the target once without interrupting his fixation (you may do this only once, no matter how many times you gain the benefit).
- *Encouragement:* Once per scene, you may speak to 1 of your teammates for 1 minute to grant them a +1 morale bonus with saving throws until the end of the current scene.
- *Free Hint:* Once per session, you may request a free hint from the GM. If he refuses, you gain 1 bonus action die.
- *Practiced Impress:* If you spend an action die to boost an Impress check and it still fails, you gain the die back after the action is resolved. Against multiple targets you only regain the die if the check fails against all of them.

CAVALIER

You've been trained to fight from the saddle.

- *Bonus Feat:* Favored Gear (mount)
- *Crunch!:* Your Strength-based damage rolls inflict 1 additional damage.
- *Glory-Bound:* You may purchase Heroic Renown for 20 Reputation per rank *(see page 187).*
- *Practiced Ride:* If you spend an action die to boost a Ride check and it still fails, you gain the die back after the action is resolved. Against multiple targets you only regain the die if the check fails against all of them.
- *Triumphant Swing:* You gain the Triumphant Swing trick *(see page 222).*

CLERIC

A servant of faith, you're both herald of their will and shepherd of their followers.

Requirements: Alignment *(see page 61)*

- *Bonus Feat:* Any 1 Chance feat
- *Charming:* Once per session, you may improve the Disposition of any 1 non-adversary NPC by 5.
- *Field Medicine:* You are always considered to have a doctor's bag *(see page 159).*
- *Paired Skills:* Each time you gain ranks in the Resolve skill, you gain equal ranks in the Medicine skill. This may not increase your Medicine skill beyond its maximum rank.
- *Turning:* Choose a Type from the following list: animal, beast, construct, elemental, fey, horror, ooze, outsider, plant, spirit, or undead. Once per combat you may Turn characters of this Type *(see page 223).*

CORSAIR

Yarrrr!

- *Bonus Feat:* Basic Skill Mastery (Officer)
- *Agile Defense:* Your base Defense increases by 1.
- *Flashy:* Your Panache increases by 2.
- *Terrifying Look:* The Will save DCs of stress damage you inflict increase by 4.
- *Water Vehicle Focus:* You gain the Ride skill's Water Vehicles focus.

CRIMINAL

What's mine is mine and what's yours is *about* to be mine.

- *Bonus Feat:* Basic Skill Mastery (Pickpocket)
- *Attribute Training:* The lower of your Dexterity or Intelligence scores increases by 1 (your choice if a tie). Apply this bonus after any modifiers from your Species or Talent.
- *Cheap Shot:* You gain the Cheap Shot trick *(see page 221).*
- *Fast:* Your Ground Speed increases by 10 ft.
- *Practiced Intimidate:* If you spend an action die to boost an Intimidate check and it still fails, you gain the die back after the action is resolved. Against multiple targets you only regain the die if the check fails against all of them.

DRAGOON

You're trained as mounted light infantry, fighting from horseback and on foot with carbine and blade.

Requirements: Reason Era or later *(see page 305)*

- *Bonus Feat:* Quick Draw
- *Black Powder Proficiency:* You gain the Black Powder proficiency.
- *Commissioned:* You may purchase Military Renown for 20 Reputation per rank *(see page 187).*
- *Edged Proficiency:* You gain the Edged proficiency.
- *Paired Skills:* Each time you gain 1 or more ranks in the Ride skill, you gain equal ranks in the Tactics skill. This may not increase your Tactics skill beyond its maximum rank.

DRUID

You're a servant of nature, at home in the world of men and in the wild.

- *Bonus Feat:* Animal Partner
- *Attribute Training:* The lower of your Constitution or Wisdom scores increases by 1 (your choice if a tie). Apply this bonus after any modifiers from your Species or Talent.
- *Practiced Medicine:* If you spend an action die to boost a Medicine check and it still fails, you gain the die back after the action is resolved. Against multiple targets you only regain the die if the check fails against all of them.
- *Practiced Survival:* If you spend an action die to boost a Survival check and it still fails, you gain the die back after the action is resolved. Against multiple targets you only regain the die if the check fails against all of them.
- *Trackless Step:* The DCs of Tracking checks to follow your trail increase by 10.

FENCER

You've made a name for yourself with footwork and swordplay.

- *Bonus Feat:* Fencing Basics
- *Decisive:* You gain a +5 bonus with Initiative.
- *Edged Proficiency:* You gain the Edged proficiency.
- *Fast:* Your Ground Speed increases by 10 ft.
- *Parry:* You gain the Parry trick *(see page 222).*

FIGHTER

You're no stranger to the battlefield; you've already survived some tough fights and have the scars to prove it!

- *Bonus Feat:* Armor Basics
- *Attribute Training:* The lower of your Strength or Constitution scores increases by 1 (your choice if a tie). Apply this bonus after any modifiers from your Species or Talent.
- *Extra Proficiency:* You gain 4 additional proficiencies or tricks.
- *Melee Combat Expert:* You're considered to have 2 additional Melee Combat feats for any ability based on the number of Melee Combat feats you have.

FIST

Your rigorous discipline has toughened your mind and body, turning you into a living weapon of the highest caliber.

- *Bonus Feat:* Two-Hit Combo
- *Attribute Training:* The lower of your Strength or Wisdom scores increases by 1 (your choice if a tie). Apply this bonus after any modifiers from your Species or Talent.
- *Fast:* Your Ground Speed increases by 10 ft.
- *Practiced Acrobatics:* If you spend an action die to boost an Acrobatics check and it still fails, you gain the die back after the action is resolved. Against multiple targets you only regain the die if the check fails against all of them.
- *Unarmed Proficiency:* You gain the Unarmed proficiency.

GLADIATOR

You were raised in the brutal world of death sports, carving out a reputation in blood and steel.

- *Bonus Feat:* Combat Instincts
- *Crunch!:* Your Strength-based damage rolls inflict 1 additional damage.
- *Extra Proficiency:* You gain 1 additional proficiency or trick.
- *Harsh Beating:* The Fortitude save DCs of subdual damage you inflict increase by 4.
- *Paired Skills:* Each time you gain 1 or more ranks in the Athletics skill, you gain equal ranks in the Impress skill. This may not increase your Impress skill beyond its maximum rank.

GUARDIAN

You're a professional bodyguard, trained to be alert and to sacrifice yourself if necessary to save your charge.

- *Bonus Feat:* Elusive
- *Practiced Notice:* If you spend an action die to boost a Notice check and it still fails, you gain the die back after the action is resolved. Against multiple targets you only regain the die if the check fails against all of them.
- *Step In:* Once per combat, you may choose to receive all of 1 attack's damage on an adjacent character. Your Damage Reduction and Damage Resistance apply normally.
- *Tenacious Spirit:* You gain 1 additional vitality per level.

LORD

You're a paragon of your people, a genuine champion who leads from the front in times of strife.

- *Bonus Feat:* Followers
- *Noble Blood:* You may purchase Noble Renown for 20 Reputation per rank *(see page 187).*
- *Practiced Tactics:* If you spend an action die to boost a Tactics check and it still fails, you gain the die back after the action is resolved. Against multiple targets you only regain the die if the check fails against all of them.
- *Stand Together:* You gain a +2 morale bonus to Defense and all saves when at least 2 adjacent characters share your Species.

MERCHANT

The wheels of commerce don't turn *themselves.*

- *Bonus Feat:* Basic Skill Mastery (Trader)
- *Attribute Training:* The lower of your Intelligence or Charisma scores increases by 1 (your choice if a tie). Apply this bonus after any modifiers from your Species or Talent.
- *Linguist:* You gain 2 additional Languages *(see page 61).*
- *Paired Skills:* Each time you gain 1 or more ranks in the Haggle skill, you gain equal ranks in the Search skill. This may not increase your Search skill beyond its maximum rank.
- *Thrifty:* Your Prudence increases by 2.

MINER

You've bent your back digging riches from the earth's bosom — experience that's surprisingly useful in your adventuring career!

- *Bonus Feat:* Pathfinder Basics (caverns/mountains)
- *Blunt Proficiency:* You gain the Blunt proficiency.
- *Paired Skills:* Each time you gain 1 or more ranks in the Athletics skill, you gain equal ranks in the Crafting skill. This may not increase your Crafting skill beyond its maximum rank.
- *Stonecutting Focus:* You gain the Crafting skill's Stonecutting focus.

- *Unbreakable:* Each time you suffer attribute impairment, it decreases by 1 (minimum 0).
- *Warding Strike:* You gain the Warding Strike trick *(see page 222).*

MUSKETEER

You're a member of an elite corps trained to use early blackpowder weapons.

Requirements: Reason Era or later *(see page 305)*

- *Bonus Feat:* Bullseye
- *Attribute Training:* The lower of your Dexterity or Wisdom scores increases by 1 (your choice if a tie). Apply this bonus after any modifiers from your Species or Talent.
- *Black Powder Proficiency:* You gain the Black Powder proficiency.
- *Called Shot:* You gain the Called Shot trick *(see page 221).*
- *Commissioned:* You may purchase Military Renown for 20 Reputation per rank *(see page 187).*
- *Heroism:* You gain a +1 bonus with all attack and skill checks you make during Dramatic scenes.

MYSTIC

You're a folk healer using hidden lore and a hint of magic to assist your community.

- *Bonus Feat:* The Gift
- *Attribute Training:* The lower of your Constitution or Charisma scores increases by 1 (your choice if a tie). Apply this bonus after any modifiers from your Species or Talent.
- *Inquisitive Mind:* You gain 2 additional Interests.
- *Paired Skills:* Each time you gain 1 or more ranks in the Investigate skill, you gain equal ranks in the Medicine skill. This may not increase your Medicine skill beyond its maximum rank.
- *Sharp Mind:* You gain 1 additional skill point per level.

NOMAD

Your travels have led you far and wide and introduced you to many tribes.

- *Bonus Feat:* Basic Skill Mastery (Horseman).
- *Animal Empathy:* The Dispositions of non-adversary animals increase by 5.
- *Attribute Training:* The lower of your Dexterity or Constitution scores increases by 1 (your choice if a tie). Apply this bonus after any modifiers from your Species or Talent.
- *Linguist:* You gain 2 additional Languages *(see page 61).*
- *Practiced Haggle:* If you spend an action die to boost a Haggle check and it still fails, you gain the die back after the action is resolved. Against multiple targets you only regain the die if the check fails against all of them.
- *Trackless Step:* The DCs of Tracking checks to follow your trail increase by 10.

PHYSICIAN

With poultice and scalpel, medicine and bandages, you can hold death itself at bay... for a time.

Requirements: Ancient Era or later *(see page 305)*

- *Bonus Feat:* Basic Skill Mastery (Healer)
- *Chemistry Focus:* You gain the Crafting skill's Chemistry focus.
- *Contagion Sense:* You may roll twice when making Fortitude saves prompted by disease and poison, keeping the result you prefer.
- *Edged Proficiency:* You gain the Edged proficiency.
- *Paired Skills:* Each time you gain 1 or more ranks in the Medicine skill, you gain equal ranks in the Crafting skill. This may not increase your Crafting skill beyond its maximum rank.

RANGER

You're an experienced woodsman specializing in the careful study and decimation of certain enemies.

- *Bonus Feat:* Battlefield Trickery
- *Animal Empathy:* The Dispositions of non-adversary animals increase by 5.
- *Camouflage:* Choose a terrain: aquatic, arctic, caverns/mountains, desert, forest/jungle, indoors/settled, plains, or swamp. You gain a +5 gear bonus with Blend checks while in that terrain.
- *Favored Foes:* Choose 2 Types: animal, beast, construct, elemental, fey, folk, horror, ooze, outsider, plant, spirit, or undead. Your threat range increases by 2 when attacking and making Notice, Sense Motive, and Survival checks targeting standard characters of the chosen Types. You may choose an additional Type at Career Levels 6, 11, and 16.

ROGUE

Your methods are sometimes shifty but also quite effective.

- *Bonus Feat:* Ambush Basics
- *Practiced Sneak:* If you spend an action die to boost a Sneak check and it still fails, you gain the die back after the action is resolved. Against multiple targets you only regain the die if the check fails against all of them.
- *Sharp Mind:* You gain 1 additional skill point per level.
- *Trap Sense:* You may roll twice when making Reflex saves prompted by security devices and traps, keeping the result you prefer.

SHAMAN

You're a holy man, communing with the ancients to pass down their wisdom.

- *Bonus Feat:* Blessed
- *Attribute Training:* The lower of your Wisdom or Charisma scores increases by 1 (your choice if a tie). Apply this bonus after any modifiers from your Species or Talent.

- *Contagion Sense:* You may roll twice when making Fortitude saves prompted by disease and poison, keeping the result you prefer.
- *Origin Skill:* Choose 1 additional Origin skill.
- *Practiced Sense Motive:* If you spend an action die to boost a Sense Motive check and it still fails, you gain the die back after the action is resolved. Against multiple targets you only regain the die if the check fails against all of them.

SHIELD BEARER

As a hoplite, legionnaire, or huscarl, you're trained in the particulars of shoulder-to-shoulder warfare with a shield.

- *Bonus Feat:* Shield Basics
- *Agile Defense:* Your base Defense increases by 1.
- *Blunt Proficiency:* You gain the Blunt proficiency.
- *Melee Combat Expert:* You're considered to have 2 additional Melee Combat feats for any ability based on the number of Melee Combat feats you have.
- *Practiced Resolve:* If you spend an action die to boost a Resolve check and it still fails, you gain the die back after the action is resolved. Against multiple targets you only regain the die if the check fails against all of them.
- *Shield Block:* You gain the Shield Block trick *(see page 222).*

SORCERER

Your cold, calculating demeanor suggests something not quite natural in your ancestry.

- *Bonus Feat:* Any 1 Species feat
- *Charming:* Once per session, you may improve the Disposition of any 1 non-adversary NPC by 5.
- *Paired Skills:* Each time you gain 1 or more ranks in the Spellcasting skill, you gain equal ranks in the Intimidate skill. This may not increase your Intimidate skill beyond its maximum rank.
- *Terrifying Look:* The Will save DCs of stress damage you inflict increase by 4.

SWINDLER

You've learned a lot by keeping your eyes open and your mouth shut.

- *Bonus Feat:* Basic Skill Mastery (Spy)
- *Attribute Training:* The lower of your Dexterity or Charisma scores increases by 1 (your choice if a tie). Apply this bonus after any modifiers from your Species or Talent.
- *Beguiling:* When you successfully Taunt a character, you may decline the standard result to have your target become *fixated* on you for 1d6 rounds. Special characters and villains may spend 1 action die to cancel this effect and become immune to this ability for the rest of the scene. If you gain this benefit from multiple sources, you may also damage the target once without interrupting his fixation (you may do this only once, no matter how many times you gain the benefit).
- *Charming:* Once per session, you may improve the Disposition of any 1 non-adversary NPC by 5.
- *Practiced Bluff:* If you spend an action die to boost a Bluff check and it still fails, you gain the die back after the action is resolved. Against multiple targets you only regain the die if the check fails against all of them.

TRIBESMAN

You hail from a simple society that lives off the land.

- *Bonus Feat:* Basic Skill Mastery (Athlete)
- *Extra Proficiency:* You gain 1 additional proficiency or trick.
- *Game Hunter:* You inflict 2 additional damage on standard animals and beasts.
- *Paired Skills:* Each time you gain ranks in the Resolve skill, you gain equal ranks in the Survival skill. This may not increase your Survival skill beyond its maximum rank.
- *Riding Mounts Focus* You gain the Ride skill's Riding Mounts focus.

VANGUARD

You're an elite guardian of your people, determined to protect them from all threats.

- *Bonus Feat:* Misdirection Basics
- *Basic Combat Expert:* You're considered to have 2 additional Basic Combat feats for any ability based on the number of Basic Combat feats you have.
- *Charming:* Once per session, you may improve the Disposition of any 1 non-adversary NPC by 5.
- *Paired Skills:* Each time you gain 1 or more ranks in the Resolve skill, you gain equal ranks in the Impress skill. This may not increase your Impress skill beyond its maximum rank.
- *Stand Together:* You gain a +2 morale bonus to Defense and all saves when at least 2 adjacent characters share your Species.

WARDEN

You patrol the fringes of civilization to ensure nothing comes upon your community unexpectedly.

- *Bonus Feat:* Pathfinder Basics (any 1)
- *Attribute Training:* The lower of your Intelligence or Wisdom scores increases by 1 (your choice if a tie). Apply this bonus after any modifiers from your Species or Talent.
- *Decisive:* You gain a +5 bonus with Initiative.
- *Practiced Investigate:* If you spend an action die to boost an Investigate check and it still fails, you gain the die back after the action is resolved. Against multiple targets you only regain the die if the check fails against all of them.
- *Unbreakable:* Each time you suffer attribute impairment, it decreases by 1 (minimum 0).

WIZARD

Your mastery of arcane lore ensures you're in high demand as counsel in delicate matters.

- *Bonus Feat:* Spell Library
- *Broad Learning:* You gain 2 additional Studies *(see page 61).*
- *Encouragement:* Once per scene, you may speak to 1 of your teammates for 1 minute to grant them a +1 morale bonus with saving throws until the end of the current scene.
- *Practiced Spellcasting:* If you spend an action die to boost a Spellcasting check and it still fails, you gain the die back after the action is resolved. Against multiple targets you only regain the die if the check fails against all of them.
- *Thrifty:* Your Prudence increases by 2.

STEP 3: CAREER LEVEL

Your Career Level measures your overall power on a scale of 1 to 20 and helps the GM determine appropriate challenges for you and your party. Most campaigns begin at Career Level 1 with each Player Character possessing 0 **Experience Points (XP).** Some games may start at a higher level, in which case each character should start with the same amount of XP (determined by the GM).

As you complete adventures your total XP rises. Each time your total XP reaches the amount needed for the next Career Level it goes up by 1 and you gain all of the benefits shown on Table 1.4: Career Level *(see below).* At this time you may also increase your level with one of your current classes or gain the first level of a new class *(see Step 4: Class, page 28).* Many character options improve as your Career Level increases, so be sure to also review your Origin and feats each time you "level."

Leveling requires a brief period to reflect and train. You may generally only do so between adventures and during Downtime *(see page 68).*

TABLE 1.4: CAREER LEVEL NOTES

Starting Action Dice: The number and size of action dice you gain at the start of each session. Action dice let you tip the odds in your favor *(see page 62).*

Maximum Skill Rank: Your maximum rank in any skill *(see page 63).*

Attribute Bonus: You may apply this bonus to any 1 attribute of your choice.

Table 1.4: Career Level

Career Level	Total XP	Starting Action Dice	Maximum Skill Rank	Attribute Bonus	Extra Proficiency	Extra Interest	Extra Feat
1	0	3 (d4)	4	—	—	—	+1
2	1,000	3 (d4)	5	—	—	+1	—
3	2,500	3 (d4)	6	—	+1	—	+1
4	5,000	3 (d4)	7	+1	—	—	—
5 *	10,000	3 (d4)	8	—	+1	—	—
6	15,000	4 (d6)	9	—	—	+1	+1
7	25,000	4 (d6)	10	—	+1	—	—
8	40,000	4 (d6)	11	+1	—	—	—
9	60,000	4 (d6)	12	—	+1	—	+1
10 **	80,000	4 (d6)	13	—	—	+1	—
11	100,000	5 (d8)	14	—	+1	—	—
12	125,000	5 (d8)	15	+1	—	—	+1
13	150,000	5 (d8)	16	—	+1	—	—
14	200,000	5 (d8)	17	—	—	+1	—
15	250,000	5 (d8)	18	—	+1	—	+1
16	300,000	6 (d10)	19	+1	—	—	—
17	375,000	6 (d10)	20	—	+1	—	—
18	450,000	6 (d10)	21	—	—	+1	+1
19	525,000	6 (d10)	22	—	+1	—	—
20	600,000	6 (d10)	23	+1	—	—	—

* A character may apply his 5th and later levels to expert classes *(see page 28).*

** A character may apply his 10th and later levels to a master class *(see page 28).*

Extra Proficiency: You may choose this number of new proficiencies or tricks *(see below and page 221, respectively).*

Extra Interest: You may choose this number of additional Interests *(see page 61).*

Extra Feat: You may choose this number of additional feats, chosen from any feat tree *(see page 84).*

STEP 4: CLASS

Your class choices provide handy shorthand when describing your character. You begin play with one class but can access others as you gain levels. Your classes are the backbone of your career, showcasing the path you've chosen and what you have to offer your party.

There are three types of classes, each progressively more specialized. **Base Classes** are available at Career Level 1 and have the broadest focus, **Expert Classes** become available at Career Level 5 and offer a little more expertise in a narrower field, and **Master Classes** — available at Level 10 — are the pinnacle of concentrated expertise.

Fantasy Craft features 12 Base Classes designed to portray larger-than-life adventure heroes in a wide range of settings and stories *(see pages 30–52).*

EXPERT CLASSES

Some heroes never deviate from their Base Class, pursuing it to the highest levels of play. Others may diversify or hone themselves for a particular concept or goal. This is where Expert Classes come into play, tailoring your skills and abilities in concentrated ways. Some Expert Classes obviously complement certain Base Classes (e.g. the Beastmaster blends well with the Lancer), but you're free to mix and match class choices so long as you meet all entry requirements.

Fantasy Craft features 6 expert classes common in high adventure campaigns *(see pages 52–61).*

MASTER CLASSES

At the apex of the class progression, Master Classes offer highly specialized training and deep secrets. They're usually linked to specific settings and only available when characters prove themselves to NPCs and groups who can provide the training. Unlike Base and Expert Classes, a character may only take levels in a single Master Class.

Master Classes will be featured in upcoming *Fantasy Craft* products.

MULTI-CLASSING

Taking levels in new classes broadens your range of abilities at the expense of progress in previous classes. This is often helpful to round out a concept or give you more options in play. For example, you might start your career as a Keeper but eventually take levels in Soldier to reveal your growing warrior spirit (and make sure you have more to do in a fight).

When you have levels in multiple classes, you gain their sum vitality, skill points, and table bonuses, as well as all abilities granted by your level in each class.

CLASS DESCRIPTIONS

Classes are laid out in five main sections, allowing you to quickly identify their style, strengths, and benefits.

SUMMARY

Each class begins with a general summary of its theme and capabilities. Several examples demonstrate how you can use this class in a variety of ways. These are intentionally broad — feel free to ignore the obvious stereotypes and pursue your own destiny.

Party Role: This suggests ways you can contribute to the success of your party. Classes can and often do fill more than one role. The five main party roles in *Fantasy Craft* are **Backer** (improves the entire party's performance), **Combatant** (good at fighting), **Specialist** (master of one or more skills), **Solver** (excels at plot advancement and information gathering), and **Talker** (great with NPCs and social situations). A few classes are described as **Wildcards** — they have enough going on that they can fill in for two or more of the other roles depending on how their abilities develop.

CLASS FEATURES

Requirements: Some classes have requirements that you must meet before you can gaining levels in them.

Favored Attributes: These are the most commonly helpful attributes for this class, in order from most to somewhat desirable. These don't have to be your highest attributes (they can even be your lowest!), but beginners may want to focus on them until they become familiar with the game.

Caster: Some classes grant "Casting Levels," which influence spells you cast.

Class Skills: You may only spend your skill points to buy ranks in these skills.

Skill Points: These are used to buy skill ranks *(see page 63).* You get 4 times the usual number at Career Level 1 only.

Vitality: This is a measure of your character's ability to avoid injury *(see page 206).*

Proficiencies: These represent weapon training. You may spend 1 proficiency to become "trained" with each weapon category: Bow, Blunt, Edged, Hurled, Siege, and Unarmed. Some settings also feature Black Powder weapons. Spending an additional proficiency on a category grants you a "forte" with it, which translates to a +1 bonus with attacks made using those weapons. Certain weapons are tricky to use and require a forte to wield *(see footnotes on tables throughout the weapons section, starting on page 176).* You may also spend proficiencies to learn tricks *(see page 221).*

You start with the proficiencies listed in your first base class and do not gain the proficiencies listed in any other class. After Career Level 1, proficiencies are only gained as shown on Table 1.4: Career Level *(see page 27).* Whenever you gain a proficiency you already have, you may choose a different one.

CORE ABILITY

Each class bestows a single "core ability" that serves as its cornerstone. It can be something the class does often, well, or to support later abilities. You only ever gain the core ability of the first Base Class you enter — *the core abilities of all other Base Classes are unavailable to you.* Likewise, you may only ever gain the core ability of the first Expert Class you enter. Master Classes do not offer core abilities.

CLASS ABILITIES

At the heart of every class are abilities gained as your Class Level rises. These are special things you can do, bonuses applied to various skills and actions, and other benefits of training.

Several special rules relate to class abilities.

Allies and Teammates: Abilities that affect "allies" can target any standard or special character on your side, while abilities that affect "teammates" may only target special characters on your side.

Bonus Action Dice: Some abilities grant "bonus action dice." When an ability doesn't specify die type these dice are the same type you gain at the start of each session *(see Table 1.4: Career Level, page 27).*

Doubled Action Dice: Some abilities allow you to roll 2 dice when you spend 1 action die. When two or more of these abilities apply to the same roll, you still only roll 2 dice for each action die spent.

Legacy Abilities: Some abilities are shared by more than one class and grow in stages as the character gains experience. A Roman numeral follows each legacy ability's name (e.g. "*uncanny dodge I*," "*gifts & favors III*," and so on). When you gain a legacy ability from two or more classes, the Roman numeral numbers are added together to determine the ability's overall effectiveness (to a maximum of the highest numbered ability offered by any of your classes).

Location-Specific Abilities: Some abilities may only be used when you're in a specific area, as noted in parentheses following the ability's name (e.g. *"gifts and favors (city)"*). In the case of a city, you must be located in an area with a population of 1,000 or more to use the ability.

Restricted and Temporary Feats: These are explained in the Feats section *(see page 84).*

Starting Action Dice: Many abilities have a number of uses or grant a bonus based on your starting action dice *(see Table 1.4: Career Level, page 27).* Character options that increase or decrease starting action dice affect these abilities normally.

Time-Reducing Abilities: No more than one character option or game effect may reduce an activity's required time.

CLASS TABLE

Your class table sets or improves several of your statistics.

BAB: Your base attack bonus, to which your Strength modifier is added (for unarmed and melee attacks), or your Dexterity modifier is added (for ranged attacks).

Fort: Your base Fortitude save bonus, to which your Constitution modifier is added.

Ref: Your base Reflex save bonus, to which your Dexterity modifier is added.

Will: Your base Will save bonus, to which your Wisdom modifier is added.

Def Bon: Your base Defense bonus, which is added with your Dexterity modifier to a base score of 10 (e.g. with a base Defense bonus of +2 and a Dexterity modifier of +1, your Defense is 13). Unless your Size is Medium, it applies a modifier as well *(see page 217).*

Init: Your base Initiative bonus, to which your Dexterity modifier is added.

Lifestyle: Your base Lifestyle, to which your Charisma modifier is added *(see page 153).*

Legend: The additional Reputation you earn after each adventure *(see page 342).*

SP: You may use these points to cast spells *(see page 110).*

Abilities: Your class abilities.

ASSASSIN

The Assassin is an agent of violent change, a hidden warrior removing key figures for flag or fortune. He's a natural social chameleon, skilled at avoiding notice and gaining entry to so-called secure areas. He does this not by slipping from shadow to shadow but by moving with the flow of people, exploiting the anonymity of crowds. Once in place, he strikes with absolute precision; he can't afford to harm bystanders or leave behind evidence, as it's sloppy and won't earn him any new contracts.

Depending on your campaign, an Assassin could be...

- A black-hearted killer only interested in his employer's coin
- A ruthless spy serving a lord through 'diplomacy of the knife'
- A gentleman-bandit harassing a corrupt monarchy from the shadows
- A holy warrior silently slaying the enemies of his faith — in their own homes
- A servant of Magisters, eliminating wild mages before they can grow to full power

Party Role: Talker/Combatant. You're a master at deception and subterfuge, fooling and confusing enemies long enough to deliver a fatal blow. You also recognize the importance of a clean escape and cultivate the fighting skills needed to cut your way to an exit when events undermine your subtle plans.

CLASS FEATURES

Favored Attributes: Charisma, Strength, Wisdom

Class Skills: Blend, Bluff, Crafting, Disguise, Intimidate, Notice, Prestidigitation, Resolve, Sense Motive, Tactics

Skill Points: 6 + Int modifier per level (×4 at Career Level 1)

Vitality: 9 + Con modifier per level

Starting Proficiencies: 4

CORE ABILITY

Heartseeker: Your base attack bonus is considered equal to your Career Level when you attack a special character. Also, your attacks against special characters gain the *armor-piercing 2* weapon quality *(see page 176)*.

CLASS ABILITIES

Hand of Death: At Level 1, each time you fail a Blend or Resolve check and don't suffer an error, you still succeed as long as the check DC (or your opponent's check result) is equal to or less than your Class Level + 20. If several grades of success are possible, you achieve only the lowest possible positive result.

If you gain this ability for either skill from two or more classes, add together your levels in all classes granting the ability when determining its effect.

Cold Read: You easily pick up people's social cues and details about their private lives. At Level 2, once per session as a free action, you may ask the GM a number of personal questions equal to your starting action dice about a character you can see and hear. Sample questions include "What does he do for a living?" and "What is her favorite author?" The target may conceal an answer by spending 1 action die per question ignored. You may target each character with this ability only once per session.

At Levels 11 and 19, you may use this ability 1 additional time per session.

Quick on Your Feet: You often have to think fast in your line of work. At Level 3, you make trained Disguise checks even when you lack a kit. Also, once per session, you may make a Mask or Ambush check as a free action.

At Levels 7, 11, 15, and 19, you may use this ability 1 additional time per session.

Unspoken Name: People speak of your growing legend, though more often with fear than admiration. At Levels 4, 8, 12, 16, and 20, you gain 1 rank of Heroic renown and a +1 bonus with Intimidate checks targeting any character who knows about at least one of your previous kills.

Blade Practice: You're familiar with many violent tools. At Level 5, once per adventure, you may spend 1 hour practicing to gain 1 temporary Melee Combat feat of your choice until the end of the current adventure.

At Levels 9, 13, and 17, you may use this ability 1 additional time per adventure.

Masks: You hide your motives and even your identity under many layers of misdirection. At Levels 6, 9, 12, 15, and 18, you may choose 1 of the following abilities. Each of these abilities may be chosen only once.

- *Always Ready:* You may always act during surprise rounds.
- *Black Vial:* You gain a +5 bonus with saves against poison. Also, the DC to save against poison you use increases by 5.
- *Convincing:* Once per session, you may force an opponent to re-roll a successful skill check that would penetrate your disguise. You may not force an opponent to re-roll a critical success.
- *Expertise:* Choose one: Blend, Bluff, Crafting, Disguise, Intimidate, Notice, Prestidigitation, Resolve, Sense Motive, or Tactics. Taking 10 with this skill doesn't take twice as long and taking 20 takes only 10 times as long.
- *Fake It:* You may credibly pretend to possess a skill you don't actually have, gaining a +20 bonus with Bluff checks made to feign its use until the end of the scene. This does *not* actually allow you to use the skill — it merely allows you to *act* like you can. Thus, you could stand next to a physician working on the injured and pretend to know what's going on but you couldn't perform a surgery yourself. You may use this ability a number of times per session equal to your starting action dice.
- *Follow My Lead:* Through a mixture of fast-talk and convincing performance you can shield others from scrutiny. Whenever you're present with a hero who's in disguise, they gain a Disguise check bonus equal to your Charisma modifier (minimum +1).
- *Offer They Can't Refuse:* When Coercing, your incentive modifiers are always at least extreme *(see Table 2.12: Persuasion and Coercion, page 75)*.
- *Sneak Attack:* You gain an additional die of sneak attack damage.

Bald-Faced Lie: At Level 10, once per session when you lie to any character, they believe it as truth for a number of minutes equal to your Class Level. Thereafter the target may begin to question the lie, depending on the circumstances. This ability may not support any statement the target absolutely knows to be a lie (e.g. "the sky is green" when it's a clear day and you're both outdoors).

Table 1.5: The Assassin

Level	BAB	Fort	Ref	Will	Def	Init	Lifestyle	Legend	Special
1	+0	+1	+1	+1	+1	+2	+1	+0	Hand of death, *heartseeker*
2	+1	+2	+2	+2	+1	+3	+2	+1	Cold read 1/session
3	+2	+2	+2	+2	+2	+4	+2	+1	Quick on your feet 1/session
4	+3	+2	+2	+2	+2	+5	+2	+1	Unspoken name +1
5	+3	+3	+3	+3	+3	+5	+3	+1	Blade practice
6	+4	+3	+3	+3	+4	+6	+3	+2	Masks
7	+5	+4	+4	+4	+4	+7	+4	+2	Quick on your feet 2/session
8	+6	+4	+4	+4	+5	+8	+4	+2	Unspoken name +2
9	+6	+4	+4	+4	+5	+9	+4	+2	Blade practice, masks
10	+7	+5	+5	+5	+6	+10	+5	+3	Bald-faced lie 1/session
11	+8	+5	+5	+5	+7	+10	+5	+3	Cold read 2/session, quick on your feet 3/session
12	+9	+6	+6	+6	+7	+11	+6	+3	Masks, unspoken name +3
13	+9	+6	+6	+6	+8	+12	+6	+3	Blade practice
14	+10	+6	+6	+6	+8	+13	+6	+4	Finish him!
15	+11	+7	+7	+7	+9	+14	+7	+4	Masks, quick on your feet 4/session
16	+12	+7	+7	+7	+10	+15	+7	+4	Unspoken name +4
17	+12	+8	+8	+8	+10	+15	+8	+4	Blade practice
18	+13	+8	+8	+8	+11	+16	+8	+5	Masks
19	+14	+8	+8	+8	+11	+17	+8	+5	Cold read 3/session, quick on your feet 5/session
20	+15	+9	+9	+9	+12	+18	+9	+5	Bald-faced lie 2/session, unspoken name +5

If you use this ability on a special character, they may make a Will save (DC 10 + your Class Level) to see through the deception.

At Level 20, you may use this ability up to twice per session.

Finish Him!: You've elevated the murder of influential and dangerous foes to an art form. At Level 14, your threat range with attacks and skill checks targeting special characters increases by 4. Also, when one of your attacks or actions would kill a special character, they cannot Cheat Death *(see page 384).*

BURGLAR

In a world of killing things and taking their stuff, thievery is a time-honored profession. The Burglar cuts out the middle man, using guile, stealth, and good old fashioned dirty tricks to pull off daring raids and heists — often without drawing his weapon. He brings a powerful blend of abilities to an adventuring party, helping them overcome dangerous traps and barriers, circumvent guards, and cut through the defenses of particularly dangerous enemies.

Depending on your campaign, a Burglar could be...

- A danger junkie stealing the most highly guarded prizes for the thrill alone
- A pit fighting champion relying on speed and wits to stay on top
- A ninja penetrating fortresses and manor houses to steal secrets and lives
- A criminal mastermind leading a band of cutthroats to glory and riches
- A traveling merchant fending off bandits and other peril on the road

Party Role: Specialist/Combatant. You are the pre-eminent master of stealth, casually slipping past all but the most impressive security and outwitting all but the savviest guards. You specialize in snatch and grab more than fisticuffs but you're not afraid of a scrap when the need arises.

CLASS FEATURES

Favored Attributes: Dexterity, Wisdom

Class Skills: Acrobatics, Athletics, Bluff, Crafting, Haggle, Investigate, Notice, Prestidigitation, Ride, Search, Sneak, Tactics

Skill Points: 8 + Int modifier per level (×4 at Career Level 1)

Vitality: 6 + Con modifier per level

Starting Proficiencies: 3

CORE ABILITY

Dexterous: You excel at tasks requiring nimble fingers and precise eye-hand coordination. Each time you spend 1 action die to boost a Dexterity-based skill check, you roll and add the results of 2 dice (e.g. at Career Level 1, 1d4 becomes 2d4).

CLASS ABILITIES

Very, Very Sneaky: At Level 1, each time you fail an Acrobatics or Sneak check and don't suffer an error, you still succeed as long as the check DC (or your opponent's check result) is equal to or less than your Class Level + 20. If several grades of success are possible, you achieve only the lowest possible positive result.

If you gain this ability for either skill from two or more classes, add together your levels in all classes granting the ability when determining its effect.

Evasion I: At Level 2, whenever you aren't *flat-footed* and make a successful Reflex save to reduce damage, you suffer no damage at all.

Evasion II: At Level 11, whenever you aren't *flat-footed* and fail a Reflex save to reduce damage, you suffer only 1/2 damage (rounded down).

Evasion III: At Level 19, you may forego rolling when making a Reflex save, instead setting your result to your Reflex save bonus + 10.

Bonus Feat: You're focused and cunning, engaging in larceny and assault with equal ease. At Levels 3, 5, 7, 9, 11, 13, 15, 17, and 19, you gain 1 additional Melee Combat or Covert feat.

Uncanny Dodge I: Your senses are supremely sharp, letting you react quickly to danger. At Level 4, you retain your Dexterity bonus to Defense (if any) even when *flat-footed.*

Uncanny Dodge II: At Level 8, you never become flanked.

Uncanny Dodge III: At Level 12, you gain a +4 bonus with Reflex saves made to avoid traps, as well as a +4 bonus to Defense against attacks made by traps.

Uncanny Dodge IV: At Level 16, the first time in each scene when an attack reduces you to 0 or fewer wounds, the attack instead misses you.

Table 1.6: The Burglar

Level	BAB	Fort	Ref	Will	Def	Init	Lifestyle	Legend	Special
1	+0	+0	+2	+0	+2	+2	+0	+1	*Dexterous*, very, very sneaky
2	+1	+0	+3	+0	+3	+3	+0	+1	Evasion I
3	+2	+1	+3	+1	+3	+4	+1	+2	Bonus feat
4	+3	+1	+4	+1	+4	+5	+1	+2	Uncanny dodge I
5	+3	+1	+4	+1	+5	+5	+1	+3	Bonus feat
6	+4	+2	+5	+2	+6	+6	+2	+3	Bag of tricks
7	+5	+2	+5	+2	+6	+7	+2	+4	Bonus feat
8	+6	+2	+6	+2	+7	+8	+2	+4	Uncanny dodge II
9	+6	+3	+6	+3	+8	+9	+3	+5	Bag of tricks, bonus feat
10	+7	+3	+7	+3	+9	+10	+3	+5	I'll cut you! I
11	+8	+3	+7	+3	+9	+10	+3	+6	Bonus feat, evasion II
12	+9	+4	+8	+4	+10	+11	+4	+6	Bag of tricks, uncanny dodge III
13	+9	+4	+8	+4	+11	+12	+4	+7	Bonus feat
14	+10	+4	+9	+4	+12	+13	+4	+7	Prince of thieves
15	+11	+5	+9	+5	+12	+14	+5	+8	Bag of tricks, bonus feat
16	+12	+5	+10	+5	+13	+15	+5	+8	Uncanny dodge IV
17	+12	+5	+10	+5	+14	+15	+5	+9	Bonus feat
18	+13	+6	+11	+6	+15	+16	+6	+9	Bag of tricks
19	+14	+6	+11	+6	+15	+17	+6	+10	Bonus feat, evasion III
20	+15	+6	+12	+6	+16	+18	+6	+10	I'll cut you! II, uncanny dodge V

Uncanny Dodge V: At Level 20, you never become *flat-footed* and may not be targeted with Coup de Grace actions unless you're *held, paralyzed,* or *unconscious.*

Bag of Tricks: You know a hundred ways to use the shadows to your advantage. At Levels 6, 9, 12, 15, and 18, you may choose 1 of the following abilities. Each of these abilities may be chosen only once.

- *Bloody Mess:* You inflict particularly heinous wounds. At the start of each round when an opponent is *bleeding* from one of your attacks, he suffers additional damage equal to your Wisdom modifier (minimum 1).
- *Expertise:* Choose one: Acrobatics, Athletics, Bluff, Crafting, Haggle, Investigate, Notice, Prestidigitation, Ride, Search, Sneak, or Tactics. Taking 10 with this skill doesn't take twice as long and taking 20 takes only 10 times as long.
- *He Did It!:* When you successfully Taunt an opponent you may force him to attack any character adjacent to you (other than himself). You may use this ability a number of times per scene equal to your starting action dice.
- *Look Out!:* Each ally and teammate within 10 ft. who can see and hear you gains the benefits of *uncanny dodge I.* This does *not* stack with *uncanny dodge* abilities they already have.
- *Slippery:* You often trip opponents up with their own attacks. Once per round when an adjacent opponent's attack misses you by 5 or more, you may immediately attempt to Tire the opponent as a free action. You may substitute Acrobatics in place of Resolve for this action.
- *Sneak Attack:* You gain an additional die of sneak attack damage.
- *Stick Close and Don't Make a Sound:* When you make a Sneak check, a single adjacent ally or teammate may share your result. The character must remain within 10 ft. of you to retain this benefit.
- *Stash it:* As a free action, you may make a Stash check to hide 1 object weighing up to 1 lb. Inspection fails to find the object unless a threat or critical success is scored.

I'll Cut You! I: At Level 10, each time you successfully Anticipate, Disarm, Distract, Feint, Taunt, or Tire an adjacent opponent, he must also make a Reflex save (DC 10 + the number of Covert feats you possess + your Dex modifier) or begin *bleeding.*

I'll Cut You! II: At Level 20, if the opponent fails the save and is already *bleeding,* he is *stunned* for 1 round.

Prince of Thieves: You've carved out a tidy little empire for yourself. At Level 14, your maximum Prizes increase by 4 and you gain 400 Reputation that must immediately be spent on contacts, holdings, or magic items.

CAPTAIN

An accomplished strategist and commander, the Captain guides allies through the fiercest tides of war with ease. His leadership and confidence are only matched by his incredible versatility — from precision planning to troop motivation to piercing the mind of the enemy, the Captain is an inspiration on and off the battlefield.

Depending on your campaign, a Captain could be...

- The leader of a mercenary band famed for its ruthless efficiency
- The helmsman of a great ship, loved and feared by a crew he's seen through countless epic battles
- A lordly knight inspiring the people with selfless and heroic deeds
- A barbarian chieftain in the twilight of his life, seeking a glorious end in battle
- An academy instructor passing along decades of experience to the virgins of war

Party Role: Backer/Combatant. You're a powerful 'force multiplier,' providing party-wide benefits tailored to the situation at hand. While not a focused combatant, you have no trouble leading the charge and engaging the enemy directly.

CLASS FEATURES

Favored Attributes: Charisma, Strength, Wisdom

Class Skills: Athletics, Impress, Intimidate, Medicine, Notice, Resolve, Ride, Sense Motive, Survival, Tactics

Skill Points: 6 + Int modifier per level (×4 at Career Level 1)

Vitality: 9 + Con modifier per level

Starting Proficiencies: 4

CORE ABILITY

Cadre: Your leadership inspires your team to excellence. Once per scene as a free action, you may temporarily grant your teammates 1 of your Basic Combat feats until the end of the scene.

CLASS ABILITIES

Right-Hand Man: At Level 1, you gain the Personal Lieutenant feat *(see page 108).* Your Basic Combat feats count as Style feats when determining your lieutenant's XP value.

Master and Commander I: You've proven your worth on the front line and in the seat of command. At Level 2, you gain 1 additional Terrain feat and your maximum Tactics rank increases to your Career Level + 6.

Master and Commander II: At Level 11, you gain 1 additional Terrain feat and your maximum Tactics rank increases to your Career Level + 7.

Master and Commander III: At Level 19, you gain 1 additional Terrain feat and your maximum Tactics rank increases to your Career Level + 8.

Battle Planning I: At Level 3, you gain 2 of the following battle plans. You may begin each combat with 1 battle plan already in effect and may enact a new one as a full action. Each plan's benefits last until the end of the current combat or until you enact a different battle plan. A battle plan grants you and each teammate who can see or hear you a +2 morale bonus with the following rolls and values.

- *Crush Them!:* Melee and unarmed attack checks
- *Fire at Will!:* Ranged attack checks
- *Guard Yourselves!:* Defense
- *I Want Them Alive!:* Subdual damage rolls
- *No Prisoners!:* Lethal damage rolls
- *Press On!:* Base Speed (morale bonus × 5 ft.)
- *Stand Fast!:* Vitality (morale bonus × target's Career Level)
- *Steady Now!:* Saves

Battle Planning II: At Level 7, you gain 2 additional battle plans (total 4).

Battle Planning III: At Level 11, your battle plan morale bonus increases to +3.

Battle Planning IV: At Level 15, you gain 2 additional battle plans (total 6).

Battle Planning V: At Level 19, your battle plan morale bonus increases to +4.

Take Command: At Level 4, you may choose 1 specific mount or vehicle at the start of each adventure. It gains a +1 bonus to Defense and Damage saves and you gain the same bonus with Ride checks to control it, as well as Crafting or Medicine checks to repair or heal it. You may choose a new mount or vehicle during an adventure by spending 1 day practicing with a new one.

At Levels 8, 12, 16, and 20, this bonus increases by +1.

Allure: A great leader must also command respect and trust. At Levels 5, 9, 13, and 17, your Charisma score rises by 1.

Art of War: At Level 6, you gain 1 temporary Basic Combat feat at the start of each adventure until the adventure's end.

At Levels 12 and 18, you may use this ability 1 additional time per adventure.

Virtues of Command I: You bring out the best in your friends. At Level 9, at the start of each adventure you may choose 1 other hero and 1 of that hero's classes. He gains the abilities of the next 2 levels in the class until the end of the current adventure. The hero's Class Level is also considered 2 higher when determining the effects of the chosen class' abilities. This does *not* grant other class benefits, such as class features or table modifiers. Each hero may benefit from only 1 *virtues of command* ability at a time and this ability cannot grant the *virtues of command* class ability.

Virtues of Command II: At Level 15, you may use this ability at the beginning of each scene and its benefits last until the end of the current scene.

Take Measure: Sometimes critical details can be gleaned from an enemy's style on the battlefield. At Level 10, once per session when you make a successful Outmaneuver check, you also gain 1 clue about the target *(see page 335)*.

At Level 20, you may use this ability twice per session.

Number One: Your trusted lieutenant continues to prove himself time and again. At Level 14, your Personal Lieutenant's Threat Level increases to your Career Level minus 1. Also, you may enact up to 2 battle plans at the same time when your Personal Lieutenant can see and hear you.

Table 1.7: The Captain

Level	BAB	Fort	Ref	Will	Def	Init	Lifestyle	Legend	Special
1	+0	+1	+0	+2	+0	+1	+1	+1	*Cadre*, right-hand man
2	+1	+2	+0	+3	+1	+1	+2	+2	Master and commander I
3	+2	+2	+1	+3	+1	+2	+2	+3	Battle planning I
4	+3	+2	+1	+4	+2	+2	+2	+3	Take command +1
5	+3	+3	+1	+4	+2	+3	+3	+4	Allure +1
6	+4	+3	+2	+5	+2	+4	+3	+5	Art of war (1 feat)
7	+5	+4	+2	+5	+3	+4	+4	+6	Battle planning II
8	+6	+4	+2	+6	+3	+5	+4	+6	Take command +2
9	+6	+4	+3	+6	+4	+5	+4	+7	Allure +2, virtues of command I
10	+7	+5	+3	+7	+4	+6	+5	+8	Take measure 1/session
11	+8	+5	+3	+7	+4	+7	+5	+9	Battle planning III, master and commander II
12	+9	+6	+4	+8	+5	+7	+6	+9	Art of war (2 feats), take command +3
13	+9	+6	+4	+8	+5	+8	+6	+10	Allure +3
14	+10	+6	+4	+9	+6	+8	+6	+11	Number one
15	+11	+7	+5	+9	+6	+9	+7	+12	Battle planning IV, virtues of command II
16	+12	+7	+5	+10	+6	+10	+7	+12	Take command +4
17	+12	+8	+5	+10	+7	+10	+8	+13	Allure +4
18	+13	+8	+6	+11	+7	+11	+8	+14	Art of war (3 feats)
19	+14	+8	+6	+11	+8	+11	+8	+15	Battle planning V, master and commander III
20	+15	+9	+6	+12	+8	+12	+9	+15	Take command +5, take measure 2/session

COURTIER

Not all adventurers live and die by the sword; some, like the Courtier, prefer to exploit words. This silken-tongued schemer is part nobleman and part swindler, manipulating the dreams and desires of friend and foe alike. His plots shape kingdoms, make fortunes, incite riots, destroy reputations, and shatter worlds.

Depending on your campaign, a Courtier could be...

- An eloquent aristocrat whose family has navigated the royal court for generations
- A cunning criminal mastermind amassing a horde of ill-gotten gold
- A fiery revolutionary leading the people against an evil tyrant
- A well-spoken elder commanding the respect of many tribes
- A warrior-prince selling his devious services to the highest bidder

Party Role: Talker/Backer. Your golden tongue gives your party a decisive edge whenever a changed mind or a new perspective might save the day (or your skins). You can influence anyone, anywhere — even the heat of battle — and the incredible diversity of your abilities ensures your party is never without options.

CLASS FEATURES

Favored Attributes: Charisma, Wisdom, Dexterity

Class Skills: Bluff, Haggle, Impress, Intimidate, Investigate, Notice, Prestidigitation, Resolve, Ride, Sense Motive

Skill Points: 6 + Int modifier per level (×4 at Career Level 1)

Vitality: 9 + Con modifier per level

Starting Proficiencies: 3

CORE ABILITY

Only the Finest: You reputation relies on impressions — of you and your teammates. Your Appearance bonus and that of each teammate increases by 2.

CLASS ABILITIES

With a Word: Shaping the thoughts and feelings of others is second nature to you. At Level 1, each time you fail a Haggle or Impress check and don't suffer an error, you still succeed as long as the check DC (or your opponent's check result) is equal to or less than your Class Level + 20. If several grades of success are possible, you achieve only the lowest possible positive result.

If you gain this ability for either skill from two or more classes, add together your levels in all classes granting the ability when determining its effect.

Gifts and Favors I (city): At Level 2, you gain an additional pool of money equal to your Lifestyle × your Class Level × 5 silver at the beginning of each adventure that may only be spent on Supplies and bribes. This represents the wide array of tools at your disposal, from desired trinkets to making and calling in favors to leveraging your position and influence.

Gifts and Favors II (city): At Level 11, you may also spend this money on Services.

Gifts and Favors III (city): At Level 19, you've become a great patron and may also spend this money on Crafting checks.

Obligations: You've developed a spanning web of debts and exchanges and can pull strings all over. At Levels 3, 7, 11, 15, and 19, you gain 30 Reputation that must be spent to purchase or improve contacts.

Eloquence: At Levels 4, 12, and 20, the lower of your Intelligence or Charisma scores rises by 1.

Rise to Power: At Levels 5, 9, 13, and 17, you gain 1 Lifestyle or your Noble Renown increases by 1.

Table 1.8: The Courtier

Level	BAB	Fort	Ref	Will	Def	Init	Lifestyle	Legend	Special
1	+0	+1	+0	+2	+0	+2	+2	+1	*Only the finest,* with a word
2	+1	+2	+0	+3	+1	+3	+3	+1	Gifts and favors I
3	+1	+2	+1	+3	+1	+4	+3	+2	Obligations
4	+2	+2	+1	+4	+2	+5	+4	+2	Eloquence
5	+2	+3	+1	+4	+2	+5	+4	+3	Rise to power
6	+3	+3	+2	+5	+2	+6	+5	+3	Power play
7	+3	+4	+2	+5	+3	+7	+5	+4	Obligations
8	+4	+4	+2	+6	+3	+8	+6	+4	Master Plan I
9	+4	+4	+3	+6	+4	+9	+6	+5	Power play, rise to power
10	+5	+5	+3	+7	+4	+10	+7	+5	Master of graces I
11	+5	+5	+3	+7	+4	+10	+7	+6	Gifts and favors II, obligations
12	+6	+6	+4	+8	+5	+11	+8	+6	Eloquence, power play
13	+6	+6	+4	+8	+5	+12	+8	+7	Rise to power
14	+7	+6	+4	+9	+6	+13	+9	+7	Never outdone 1/scene
15	+7	+7	+5	+9	+6	+14	+9	+8	Obligations, power play
16	+8	+7	+5	+10	+6	+15	+10	+8	Master plan II
17	+8	+8	+5	+10	+7	+15	+10	+9	Rise to power
18	+9	+8	+6	+11	+7	+16	+11	+9	Power play
19	+9	+8	+6	+11	+8	+17	+11	+10	Gifts and favors III, obligations
20	+10	+9	+6	+12	+8	+18	+12	+10	Eloquence, master of graces II

Power Play: If politics is war by other means then you're a mighty general indeed. At Levels 6, 9, 12, 15, and 18, you may choose 1 of the following abilities. Each of these abilities may be chosen only once.

- *Beguiling:* When you successfully Taunt a character, you may decline the standard result to have your target become *fixated* on you for 1d6 rounds. Special characters and villains may spend 1 action die to cancel this effect and become immune to this ability for the rest of the scene. If you gain this benefit from multiple sources, you may also damage the target once without interrupting his fixation (you may do this only once, no matter how many times you gain the benefit).
- *Entourage:* You gain the Followers feat *(see page 98),* the NPC group consisting of Attendants *(see page 244).* You may gain the Followers feat a second time later, as your character options allow.
- *Expertise:* Choose one: Bluff, Haggle, Impress, Intimidate, Investigate, Notice, Prestidigitation, Resolve, Ride, or Sense Motive. Taking 10 with this skill doesn't take twice as long and taking 20 takes only 10 times as long.
- *Hoard:* Your maximum Prizes increase by 2.
- *Land and Title:* You receive a 20% discount when purchasing holdings. Also, NPCs automatically know your name and title.
- *Man of the Court:* Once per adventure as a free action, you may gain a free Invitation Favor with a cost equal to your Class Level + 5. Unless used, this Favor is lost at the end of the scene.
- *Slanderous:* The threat ranges of your Influence and Browbeat checks to reduce Disposition increase by your Intelligence modifier (minimum +1).
- *Sterling Reputation:* When you or your allies lose Reputation, the loss decreases by 2 (minimum 0).

Master Plan I: At Level 8, once per adventure as a free action, you gain a number of bonus d4 action dice equal to your Intelligence modifier (minimum 2). These dice are lost if not spent by the end of the current scene.

Master Plan II: At Level 16, these bonus action dice increase to d6s and you may distribute some or all of them to allies able to see or hear you.

Master of Graces I: At Level 10, once per adventure as a free action, you may gain 2 temporary Style feats that last until the end of the adventure.

Master of Graces II: At Level 20, you may use this ability once per scene and its benefits last until the end of the scene.

Never Outdone: You really, *really* hate to lose. At Level 14, once per scene after making an opposed skill check but before the check is resolved, you may set your result to 1 higher than that of your opponent. This cannot result in an error or threat. If both characters use abilities that set their result based on the other character's result, both abilities are expended without effect (canceling each other out).

EXPLORER

At the remote edges of civilization, the Explorer lives a thrilling life of rough-and-tumble adventure, exploring long-buried dungeons, unearthing lost civilizations, and piecing together secrets unknown for millennia. He's most at home in the uncharted expanses most would call "wild" but his unique talents are just as helpful in the tight confines of city streets and along the winding roads between them.

Depending on your campaign, an Explorer could be...

- A mercenary looting treasures of the past for his own wealth and glory
- A dashing and reckless adventurer surviving on luck and innate toughness
- An academic forsaking the scholastic life to see the world's wonders
- A seeker of lost tribes struggling to save them against foreign invaders
- A ruin-delver looking to unlock the secrets of forsaken history

Party Role: Solver. You excel at overcoming a broad selection of obstacles, from traps to riddles and other life-threatening dangers. You're the one your party comes to for just the right answer to save the day. Your spirit is never diminished — you keep hope alive even against the grimmest odds.

CLASS FEATURES

Favored Attributes: Intelligence, Dexterity, Constitution

Class Skills: Athletics, Blend, Haggle, Investigate, Notice, Prestidigitation, Resolve, Ride, Search, Survival

Skill Points: 6 + Int modifier per level (×4 at Career Level 1)

Vitality: 9 + Con modifier per level

Starting Proficiencies: 4

CORE ABILITY

Friends All Over: You gain the Extra Contact feat. You may gain the Extra Contact feat a second time later, as your character options allow. Also, once per adventure you may spend 1d6 hours and 1 action die to summon one of your contacts, even if you're nowhere near their residence, so long as there are at least 40 people within a 25-mile radius (e.g. a small swamp-side dock, a nomad camp in a vast desert, etc.).

CLASS ABILITIES

Tomb Raider: You're familiar with all manner of dangerous locations — how to get in, and how to get out alive. At Level 1, each time you fail an Athletics or Search check and don't suffer an error, you still succeed as long as the check DC (or your opponent's check result) is equal to or less than your Class Level + 20. If several grades of success are possible, you achieve only the lowest possible positive result.

If you gain this ability for either skill from two or more classes, add together your levels in all classes granting the ability when determining its effect.

Bookworm I: You can 'walk up to the right part of a library' or 'flip open a book to the right page' with eerie accuracy. At Level 2, you make Research checks in 1/2 the usual time (rounded up).

Bookworm II: At Level 11, you may make Research checks in 1/4 the usual time (rounded up).

Bookworm III: At Level 19, you may make Research checks in 1/10 the usual time (rounded up).

Bonus Feat: At Levels 3, 5, 7, 9, 11, 13, 15, 17, and 19, you gain 1 additional Basic Combat or Chance feat.

Table 1.9: The Explorer

Level	BAB	Fort	Ref	Will	Def	Init	Lifestyle	Legend	Special
1	+0	+2	+1	+0	+1	+1	+1	+1	*Friends all over,* tomb raider
2	+1	+3	+2	+0	+1	+1	+2	+1	Bookworm I (1/2 time)
3	+2	+3	+2	+1	+2	+2	+2	+2	Bonus feat
4	+3	+4	+2	+1	+2	+2	+2	+2	Uncanny dodge I
5	+3	+4	+3	+1	+3	+3	+3	+3	Bonus feat
6	+4	+5	+3	+2	+4	+4	+3	+3	Rugged +1
7	+5	+5	+4	+2	+4	+4	+4	+4	Bonus feat
8	+6	+6	+4	+2	+5	+5	+4	+4	Uncanny dodge II
9	+6	+6	+4	+3	+5	+5	+4	+5	Bonus feat, rugged +2
10	+7	+7	+5	+3	+6	+6	+5	+5	Notebook 1/session
11	+8	+7	+5	+3	+7	+7	+5	+6	Bonus feat, bookworm II (1/4 time)
12	+9	+8	+6	+4	+7	+7	+6	+6	Rugged +3, uncanny dodge III
13	+9	+8	+6	+4	+8	+8	+6	+7	Bonus feat
14	+10	+9	+6	+4	+8	+8	+6	+7	Lifeline
15	+11	+9	+7	+5	+9	+9	+7	+8	Bonus feat, rugged +4
16	+12	+10	+7	+5	+10	+10	+7	+8	Uncanny dodge IV
17	+12	+10	+8	+5	+10	+10	+8	+9	Bonus feat
18	+13	+11	+8	+6	+11	+11	+8	+9	Rugged +5
19	+14	+11	+8	+6	+11	+11	+8	+10	Bonus feat, bookworm III (1/10 time)
20	+15	+12	+9	+6	+12	+12	+9	+10	Notebook 2/session, Uncanny dodge V

Uncanny Dodge I: Your senses are supremely sharp, letting you react quickly to danger. At Level 4, you retain your Dexterity bonus to Defense (if any) even when *flat-footed.*

Uncanny Dodge II: At Level 8, you never become *flanked.*

Uncanny Dodge III: At Level 12, you gain a +4 bonus with Reflex saves made to avoid traps, as well as a +4 bonus to Defense against attacks made by traps.

Uncanny Dodge IV: At Level 16, the first time in each scene when an attack reduces you to 0 or fewer wounds, the attack instead misses you.

Uncanny Dodge V: At Level 20, you never become flat-footed and may not be targeted with Coup de Grace actions unless you're *held, paralyzed,* or unconscious.

Rugged: At Levels 6, 9, 12, 15, and 18, your Constitution score rises by 1.

Notebook: You keep a record of every interesting fact and detail you encounter, often referring to this notebook — or collection of scrolls, or other small reference tool — to help solve difficult puzzles or suggest unseen courses of action. At Level 10, once per session when you make a successful Research check, you also gain 1 clue about the target.

At Level 20, you may use this ability twice per session.

Lifeline: You and your teammates often slip out of even the most shocking circumstances (largely) unscathed. At Level 14, the first time in each scene your vitality or that of an adjacent teammate drops below 0, it instead drops to 0 and they become *flat-footed.*

KEEPER

In every culture the most learned thinkers and builders set standards for trade, invention, healing, and other roots of culture. When these scholars scramble for an answer they look to the Keeper, a fiendishly clever academic icon whose knowledge is only eclipsed by his desire for more. With a greater view of the world than most ever envision, the Keeper turns facts into weapons, secrets into victory, and questions into adventure.

Depending on your campaign, a Keeper could be...

- A master artisan beloved and respected throughout the land
- A shrewd guild-master conducting trade in all the fair cities of the kingdom
- An astute general whose strategies seem unbeatable
- An astrologer guiding the tribe's chieftain with clever plans and keen observations
- An honored riddle-master preserving the traditions of a lost world

Party Role: Specialist. You're at your best focusing on a few skills and using them to run roughshod over the opposition. In most cases you're also your party's most skilled craftsman and healer, making you important just before and right after combat, though you know a few ways to help during as well.

CLASS FEATURES

Favored Attributes: Intelligence

Class Skills: Bluff, Crafting, Haggle, Impress, Investigate, Medicine, Notice, Resolve, Search, Sense Motive, Survival, Tactics

Skill Points: 8 + Int modifier per level (×4 at Career Level 1)

Vitality: 6 + Con modifier per level

Starting Proficiencies: 2

CORE ABILITY

Teacher: You're a skilled teacher, passing along practical lessons gleaned from your incredible store of knowledge. Once per scene as a free action, you may temporarily grant your teammates 1 of your Basic Skill Mastery feats until the end of the scene.

CLASS ABILITIES

Man of Reason: You're well-versed in the most advanced techniques of your time. At Level 1, each time you fail a Crafting or Medicine check and don't suffer an error, you still succeed as long as the check DC (or your opponent's check result) is equal to or less than your Class Level + 20. If several grades of success are possible, you achieve only the lowest possible positive result.

If you gain this ability for either skill from two or more classes, add together your levels in all classes granting the ability when determining its effect.

Trade Secrets: At Levels 2, 11, and 19, choose one: Bluff, Crafting, Haggle, Impress, Investigate, Medicine, Notice, Resolve, Search, Sense Motive, Survival, or Tactics. Your maximum rank in the chosen skill increases to your Career Level + 8. Only the highest bonus to maximum rank, including any enlightened skill bonuses from Origin or elsewhere, may apply to each skill.

Bright Idea: At Level 3, once per session when making an Intelligence-, Wisdom-, or Charisma-based skill check, you may roll twice, keeping the result you prefer.

At Levels 7, 11, 15, and 19, you may use this ability 1 additional time per session.

Bonus Feat: You work constantly to hone your crafts and the rewards are substantial. At Levels 4, 8, 12, 16, and 20, you gain 1 additional Gear or Skill feat.

The Right Tools: You have precise and comprehensive knowledge about the tools of your craft. At Levels 5, 9, 13, and 17, you may choose 1 of the following abilities. Each of these abilities may be chosen only once.

- *Adaptable Toolbox:* Choose 1 kit *(see page 159).* Your threat range when making skill checks with this kit increases by 1.
- *Apprentices:* You gain the Followers feat *(see page 98),* the NPC group consisting of Apprentices *(see page 244).* You may gain the Followers feat a second time later, as your character options allow.
- *Crafting Recognition:* Your advances have earned the respect of your peers. The Disposition of any NPC with a Crafting focus matching one of yours improves by 5.
- *Elbow Grease:* You gain a +4 gear bonus with Repair checks.
- *Expertise:* Choose one: Bluff, Crafting, Haggle, Impress, Investigate, Medicine, Notice, Resolve, Search, Sense Motive, Survival, or Tactics. Taking 10 with this skill doesn't take twice as long and taking 20 takes only 10 times as long.
- *Improvised Toolbox:* Choose 1 kit *(see page 159).* You're always considered to have this kit when making an associated skill check.
- *Miser:* You gain +2 Prudence.

Table 1.10: The Keeper

Level	BAB	Fort	Ref	Will	Def	Init	Lifestyle	Legend	Special
1	+0	+0	+0	+2	+2	+0	+2	+1	Man of reason, *teacher*
2	+1	+0	+0	+3	+3	+0	+3	+2	Trade secrets (1 skill)
3	+1	+1	+1	+3	+3	+1	+3	+3	Bright idea 1/session
4	+2	+1	+1	+4	+4	+1	+4	+3	Bonus feat
5	+2	+1	+1	+4	+5	+1	+4	+4	The right tools
6	+3	+2	+2	+5	+6	+2	+5	+5	Brilliant +1
7	+3	+2	+2	+5	+6	+2	+5	+6	Bright idea 2/session
8	+4	+2	+2	+6	+7	+2	+6	+6	Bonus feat
9	+4	+3	+3	+6	+8	+3	+6	+7	Brilliant +2, the right tools
10	+5	+3	+3	+7	+9	+3	+7	+8	Know it all I
11	+5	+3	+3	+7	+9	+3	+7	+9	Bright idea 3/session, trade secrets (2 skills)
12	+6	+4	+4	+8	+10	+4	+8	+9	Bonus feat, brilliant +3
13	+6	+4	+4	+8	+11	+4	+8	+10	The right tools
14	+7	+4	+4	+9	+12	+4	+9	+11	Instant solution 1/session
15	+7	+5	+5	+9	+12	+5	+9	+12	Bright idea 4/session, brilliant +4
16	+8	+5	+5	+10	+13	+5	+10	+12	Bonus feat
17	+8	+5	+5	+10	+14	+5	+10	+13	The right tools
18	+9	+6	+6	+11	+15	+6	+11	+14	Brilliant +1
19	+9	+6	+6	+11	+15	+6	+11	+15	Bright idea 5/session, trade secrets (3 skills)
20	+10	+6	+6	+12	+16	+6	+12	+15	Bonus feat, know it all II

- *Stash it:* As a free action, you may make a Stash check to hide 1 object weighing up to 1 lb. Inspection fails to find the object unless a threat or critical success is scored.

Brilliant: At Levels 6, 9, 12, 15, and 18, your Intelligence score rises by 1.

Know It All I: At Level 10, once per adventure as a free action, you may gain any 2 temporary Skill feats that last until the end of the adventure.

Know It All II: At Level 20, you may use this ability once per scene and its benefits last until the end of the scene.

Instant Solution: People rely on you for last-moment solutions… that *work.* At Level 14, once per session, you may make 1 Intelligence-based skill check, automatically scoring a natural 20. This roll is a threat and may be activated as a critical success. You may not be forced to re-roll this natural 20. Also, if the check normally takes 5 minutes or less, you accomplish it as a free action. Otherwise, the time required is reduced to 1/2 normal (rounded up).

LANCER

Since man first rode, cavalry has decided the course of history. The Lancer exemplifies this, lording over the open battlefield and brutally trampling opponents. At the reins he's an unbridled terror, able to push his mount to incredible, some might say "impossible" acts, but even on his feet he manages to give enemies pause. None are fiercer, more disciplined, or more ready to face death.

Depending on your campaign, a Lancer could be...

- A prosperous nomad scouting dangerous territory for his people, leading them from oasis to oasis
- A chivalrous knight errant for whom right makes might, and vice-versa
- A samurai warrior as comfortable on the battlefield as in the imperial court
- A bold tribesman taming mighty mammoths and unleashing their herds upon his enemies
- A wyrm-rider delivering news from village to village in a land overrun by evil

Party Role: Combatant/Talker. Your focus is mounted combat, blending your steed's strengths with personal training in the art of war. Yet your skills aren't limited to the battlefield — your martial techniques translate well to social confrontations, especially when you need to get someone to see things your way.

CLASS FEATURES

Favored Attributes: Strength, Charisma, Constitution

Class Skills: Athletics, Impress, Intimidate, Notice, Resolve, Ride, Survival, Tactics

Skill Points: 4 + Int modifier per level (×4 at Career Level 1)

Vitality: 12 + Con modifier per level

Starting Proficiencies: 6

CORE ABILITY

Lifetime Companion: You gain a mount per the Animal Partner feat *(see page 108)*. You may gain the Animal Partner feat a second time later, as your character options allow. Your mount is replaced at no cost if lost or killed. Also, you receive a 20% discount with mounts and mount-related gear.

CLASS ABILITIES

Born in the Saddle: It takes tremendous ego to command nature, especially when it's prone to bucking and crushing the meek; fortunately, these traits help with two-legged beasts as well. At Level 1, each time you fail an Intimidate or Ride check and don't suffer an error, you still succeed as long as the check DC (or your opponent's check result) is equal to or less than your Class Level + 20. If several grades of success are possible, you achieve only the lowest possible positive result.

If you gain this ability for either skill from two or more classes, add together your levels in all classes granting the ability when determining its effect.

Mettle I: At Level 2, you gain the Armor Basics feat and your maximum Resolve rank increases to your Career Level + 6.

Mettle II: At Level 11, you gain the Armor Mastery feat and your maximum Resolve rank increases to your Career Level + 7.

Mettle III: At Level 19, you gain the Armor Supremacy feat and your maximum Resolve rank increases to your Career Level + 8.

Bonus Feat: The art of war extends well beyond the battlefield. At Levels 3, 5, 7, 9, 11, 13, 15, 17, and 19, you gain 1 additional Melee Combat or Style feat.

Bred for War: At Level 4, you gain a +2 bonus with Refresh rolls. When mounted, this bonus increases to +4 and your mount also benefits from the action.

At Levels 8, 12, 16, and 20, this bonus increases by an additional +2.

Promotion: At Levels 6, 12, and 18, you gain 1 Renown rank of your choice.

Excellence: At Levels 9 and 15, your highest attribute rises by 1.

Master Rider: Together, you and your steed can accomplish the impossible! At Levels 10 and 20, once per session when riding a mount, you automatically succeed with 1 Ride check (DC up to 50).

Last Stand: At Level 14, once per adventure as a full action, you may declare a last stand. For a number of rounds equal to your Class Level, you and each hero within 10 ft. suffer only 1/2 damage after Damage Reduction and Damage Resistance are applied (rounded down).

Also, you — but *not* affected heroes — may continue to act normally even if your wounds drop below 0. At the end of the last stand you become *fatigued*. You still die if you have less than –9 wounds.

Table 1.11: The Lancer

Level	BAB	Fort	Ref	Will	Def	Init	Lifestyle	Legend	Special
1	+1	+1	+0	+1	+0	+2	+2	+0	Born in the saddle, *lifetime companion*
2	+2	+2	+0	+2	+1	+3	+3	+1	Mettle I
3	+3	+2	+1	+2	+1	+4	+3	+1	Bonus feat
4	+4	+2	+1	+2	+2	+5	+4	+1	Bred for war
5	+5	+3	+1	+3	+2	+5	+4	+1	Bonus feat
6	+6	+3	+2	+3	+2	+6	+5	+2	Promotion
7	+7	+4	+2	+4	+3	+7	+5	+2	Bonus feat
8	+8	+4	+2	+4	+3	+8	+6	+2	Bred for war
9	+9	+4	+3	+4	+4	+9	+6	+2	Bonus feat, excellence
10	+10	+5	+3	+5	+4	+10	+7	+3	Master rider 1/misson
11	+11	+5	+3	+5	+4	+10	+7	+3	Bonus feat, mettle II
12	+12	+6	+4	+6	+5	+11	+8	+3	Bred for war, promotion
13	+13	+6	+4	+6	+5	+12	+8	+3	Bonus feat
14	+14	+6	+4	+6	+6	+13	+9	+4	Last stand 1/session
15	+15	+7	+5	+7	+6	+14	+9	+4	Bonus feat, excellence
16	+16	+7	+5	+7	+6	+15	+10	+4	Bred for war
17	+17	+8	+5	+8	+7	+15	+10	+4	Bonus feat
18	+18	+8	+6	+8	+7	+16	+11	+5	Promotion
19	+19	+8	+6	+8	+8	+17	+11	+5	Bonus feat, mettle III
20	+20	+9	+6	+9	+8	+18	+12	+5	Bred for war, master rider 2/misson

MAGE

The mysterious figure in robes decorated with symbols of power, the studious scholar of lost secrets, the master of magical forces great and small, the Mage is all these things and more. His comprehension and control of the arcane grant him dominion of all creation but they also set him apart and compel him to research fearsome truths that shake the very pillars of heaven. Even fellow spellcasters cannot see his path for each Mage is unique, viewing the world through alien eyes.

Depending on your campaign, a Mage could be...

- A hardened war-mage casting destruction across enemy lines
- A wizened necromancer trading the souls of his victims for unholy might
- A traditional robe-and-staff wizard
- A primitive mystic, struggling to harness the power of creation
- A Magister policing the next generation of up and coming spellcasters

Party Role: Wildcard. Your role is determined by your choice of spells and how you use them.

CLASS FEATURES

Requirements: *Sorcery* campaign quality

Favored Attributes: Intelligence, Wisdom, Charisma

Caster: Each level in this class increases your Casting Level by 1.

Class Skills: Bluff, Crafting, Impress, Intimidate, Investigate, Medicine, Notice, Prestidigitation, Resolve, Ride, Search, Sense Motive

Skill Points: 8 + Int modifier per level (×4 at Career Level 1)

Vitality: 6 + Con modifier per level

Starting Proficiencies: 2

CORE ABILITY

Arcane Adept: You learn 4 additional Level 0 spells from any School. Also, once per scene as a free action, you may spend and roll up to 3 action dice to gain a number of spell points equal to the result. These action dice cannot explode.

CLASS ABILITIES

Subtle and Quick to Anger: At Level 1, you may purchase ranks in the Spellcasting skill, learn spells from any School, and cast Level 0 spells you know.

If you already have this ability, you gain an additional Spellcasting feat instead.

Arcane Might: At Levels 2, 11, and 19, the highest of your Intelligence, Wisdom, or Charisma scores rises by 1. Also, you may choose up to 3 spells you know, gaining a +2 bonus with Spellcasting checks to cast them.

Circle of Power I: At Level 3, you may cast Level 1 and lower spells you know.

Circle of Power II: At Level 5, you may cast Level 2 and lower spells you know.

Circle of Power III: At Level 7, you may cast Level 3 and lower spells you know.

Circle of Power IV: At Level 9, you may cast Level 4 and lower spells you know.

Circle of Power V: At Level 11, you may cast Level 5 and lower spells you know.

Circle of Power VI: At Level 13, you may cast Level 6 and lower spells you know.

Circle of Power VII: At Level 15, you may cast Level 7 and lower spells you know.

Circle of Power VIII: At Level 17, you may cast Level 8 and lower spells you know.

Circle of Power IX: At Level 19, you may cast Level 9 and lower spells you know.

Bonus Feat: At Levels 4, 8, 12, 16, and 20, you gain 1 additional Skill or Spellcasting feat.

Spell Secret: At Levels 6, 9, 12, 15, and 18, you may choose 1 spell you know. Its spell level is considered to be 1 lower than normal for you. You may not apply this ability to the same spell more than once.

Arcane Wellspring I: Your magical reserves run deep. At Level 10, when you have no spell points remaining, you may cast Level 1 spells without spending spell points. However, you may not apply spellcasting tricks to these spells.

Arcane Wellspring II: At Level 20, you may cast Level 2 spells without spell points as well.

Master of Magic: While the mightiest of spells still require your full attention, lesser spells are now trivial for you. At Level 14, you may always take 10 with Spellcasting checks and the time required is not doubled when you do. You may use this ability a number of times per scene equal to your starting action dice.

PRIEST

The Priest is a shaman, druid, cleric, acolyte, or other purveyor of the faith who anchors communities and conveys the will of the universe. His power derives from his close connection to the divine; the strength of his faith grants access to special skills, strange and sometimes magical powers, and even miracles. The particulars of these abilities depend on the Priest's faith — if he's devoted to nature he might be a healer, for example, but if he follows an evil trickster god his offerings could include perversions of the mind and body.

Depending on your campaign, a Priest could be...

- A humble parishioner tending the faith of a small community at the edge of an expanding empire of unbelievers
- A fledgling warrior-monk seeking enlightenment and grace in a savage world
- An armored cleric, healing the pious and converting or eliminating unbelievers across the land
- A beleaguered chaplain treating the bodies and souls of soldiers during a bitter war
- The most renowned healer in a major city, trading the gifts of his faith for a life of luxury

Party Role: Wildcard/Backer. Your class abilities often provide direct or indirect support to your teammates, though your specific role largely depends on the Paths you walk. Common choices include War and Strength, which are helpful to holy warriors, and Protection and Life, which fit the classic "cleric" role.

CLASS FEATURES

Requirements: *Miracles* campaign quality, Alignment *(see page 61)*

Favored Attributes: Wisdom, Charisma

Caster: Each level in this class increases your Casting Level by 1.

Class Skills: Impress, Intimidate, Medicine, Notice, Resolve, Sense Motive, Alignment skills

Skill Points: 6 + Int modifier per level (×4 at Career Level 1)

Vitality: 9 + Con modifier per level

Starting Proficiencies: 4

CORE ABILITY

Devout: You've been appointed by a higher power to represent divine will in the world of mortals. This divine will is sometimes felt in the form of miracles. When you fail an attack check with your ritual weapon or a skill check with a Priest class skill and don't suffer an error, you may spend an action die to re-roll the check. You may use this ability only once per check.

CLASS ABILITIES

Acolyte: At Level 1, you take the first Step along any 1 of your Alignment's Paths and gain your Alignment's ritual weapon

Table 1.12: The Mage

Level	BAB	Fort	Ref	Will	Def	Init	Lifestyle	Legend	SP	Abilities
1	+0	+0	+0	+2	+0	+1	+1	+1	2	*Arcane adept,* subtle and quick to anger
2	+1	+0	+0	+3	+1	+1	+2	+2	4	Arcane might
3	+1	+1	+1	+3	+1	+2	+2	+3	6	Circle of power I
4	+2	+1	+1	+4	+2	+2	+2	+3	8	Bonus feat
5	+2	+1	+1	+4	+2	+3	+3	+4	10	Circle of power II
6	+3	+2	+2	+5	+2	+4	+3	+5	12	Spell secret
7	+3	+2	+2	+5	+3	+4	+4	+6	14	Circle of power III
8	+4	+2	+2	+6	+3	+5	+4	+6	16	Bonus feat
9	+4	+3	+3	+6	+4	+5	+4	+7	18	Circle of power IV, spell secret
10	+5	+3	+3	+7	+4	+6	+5	+8	20	Arcane wellspring I
11	+5	+3	+3	+7	+4	+7	+5	+9	22	Arcane might, circle of power V
12	+6	+4	+4	+8	+5	+7	+6	+9	24	Bonus feat, spell secret
13	+6	+4	+4	+8	+5	+8	+6	+10	26	Circle of power VI
14	+7	+4	+4	+9	+6	+8	+6	+11	28	Master of magic
15	+7	+5	+5	+9	+6	+9	+7	+12	30	Circle of power VII, spell secret
16	+8	+5	+5	+10	+6	+10	+7	+12	32	Bonus feat
17	+8	+5	+5	+10	+7	+10	+8	+13	34	Circle of power VIII
18	+9	+6	+6	+11	+7	+11	+8	+14	36	Spell secret
19	+9	+6	+6	+11	+8	+11	+8	+15	38	Arcane might, circle of power IX
20	+10	+6	+6	+12	+8	+12	+9	+15	40	Arcane wellspring II, bonus feat

at no cost. This weapon may not be sold and when it's lost or destroyed it's replaced at no cost at the end of the next Downtime lasting 1 day or more.

Signs & Portents I: You may contact higher powers for guidance in times of need. At Level 2, as a 1-minute action, you may request a hint from the GM. If he refuses, you gain 1 bonus action die. You may use this ability a number of times per adventure equal to your starting action dice.

Signs & Portents II: At Level 11, if the GM refuses, you gain 2 action dice.

Signs & Portents III: At Level 19, if the GM refuses, you gain 3 action dice.

Path of the Devoted: At Levels 3, 5, 7, 9, 11, 13, 15, 17, and 19, you take a Step along any 1 of your Alignment's Paths.

Bonus Feat: At Levels 4, 8, 12, 16, and 20, you gain 1 additional Chance or Style feat.

Masks of God: At Levels 6, 9, 12, 15, and 18, you may choose one of the following abilities. Each of these abilities may be chosen only once.

- *Benediction:* You extend divine blessings to close friends. The error ranges of checks made by allies within Close Quarters decrease by 1 (minimum 1).
- *Congregation:* You gain the Followers feat *(see page 98),* the NPC group consisting of Worshippers *(see page 248).* You may gain the Followers feat a second time later, as your character options allow.
- *Exemplar:* You're an ideal of your faith. The threat ranges of checks you make with your Alignment's skills increase by 1.

Table 1.13: The Priest

Level	BAB	Fort	Ref	Will	Def	Init	Lifestyle	Legend	Special
1	+0	+1	+0	+1	+2	+0	+1	+1	Acolyte, *devout*
2	+1	+2	+0	+2	+3	+0	+2	+2	Signs & portents I
3	+2	+2	+1	+2	+3	+1	+2	+3	Path of the devoted
4	+3	+2	+1	+2	+4	+1	+2	+3	Bonus feat
5	+3	+3	+1	+3	+5	+1	+3	+4	Path of the devoted
6	+4	+3	+2	+3	+6	+2	+3	+5	Masks of God
7	+5	+4	+2	+4	+6	+2	+4	+6	Path of the devoted
8	+6	+4	+2	+4	+7	+2	+4	+6	Bonus feat
9	+6	+4	+3	+4	+8	+3	+4	+7	Masks of God, path of the devoted
10	+7	+5	+3	+5	+9	+3	+5	+8	Saved! I (Will)
11	+8	+5	+3	+5	+9	+3	+5	+9	Path of the devoted, signs & portents II
12	+9	+6	+4	+6	+10	+4	+6	+9	Bonus feat, masks of God
13	+9	+6	+4	+6	+11	+4	+6	+10	Path of the devoted
14	+10	+6	+4	+6	+12	+4	+6	+11	Divine intervention
15	+11	+7	+5	+7	+12	+5	+7	+12	Masks of God, path of the devoted
16	+12	+7	+5	+7	+13	+5	+7	+12	Bonus feat
17	+12	+8	+5	+8	+14	+5	+8	+13	Path of the devoted
18	+13	+8	+6	+8	+15	+6	+8	+14	Masks of God
19	+14	+8	+6	+8	+15	+6	+8	+15	Path of the devoted, signs & portents III
20	+15	+9	+6	+9	+16	+6	+9	+15	Bonus feat, saved! II (Fortitude)

- *Fell Hand:* You're a conduit of divine wrath. When attacking with your ritual weapon, you benefit from the All-Out Attack and Cleave Basics feats *(see page 87).*
- *High Priest:* Your piety has earned you the flock's respect and admiration. The Disposition of any NPC sharing your Alignment improves by 5.
- *Perceptive:* Your Wisdom score rises by 1.
- *Rebuke:* You're an instrument of divine spite. Characters you successfully Turn also suffer an amount of divine damage equal to your Resolve bonus; those targeted who make their Will saves suffer half this damage (rounded down). You may only choose this ability if you may Turn.
- *Sacred Turning:* Choose a Type from the following list: animal, beast, construct, elemental, fey, horror, ooze, outsider, plant, spirit, or undead. Once per combat you may Turn characters of this Type or an opposing Alignment *(see page 309).*
- *Sacred Weapon:* You're a divine champion, your ritual weapon possessing extraordinary gifts. You may not be disarmed when wielding your ritual weapon. Also, when the weapon is lost or destroyed it's replaced at the start of the next scene.
- *Visitation:* Once per adventure, you may spend 10 minutes in prayer to summon your Alignment's avatar *(see page 309).* The avatar is a standard character with a Threat Level equal to your Class Level and remains until dismissed or until the end of the scene, whichever comes first.

Saved! I: Your divine bond infuses your party with piercing judgment. At Level 10, your Wisdom score rises by 1. Also, when you or a hero who can see and hear you makes a Will save and the result is less than your Wisdom score, the result becomes equal to your Wisdom score.

Saved! II: At Level 20, your Wisdom score rises by 1 more (total increase 2), and this ability also applies to Fortitude saves.

Divine Intervention: You may call upon your gods for direct assistance. At Level 14, once per adventure, you may cast the Wish II spell without making a Spellcasting check, spending spell points or completing the Quest Subplot *(see page 151).*

SAGE

A deep well of knowledge, but more importantly a fountain of wisdom and guidance, the Sage has the practical know-how to help any party reach its goals. He's flexible and adaptable, always ready with a trick or word of advice, and he can dabble in the techniques of almost any class, filling in where needed.

Depending on your campaign, a Sage could be...

- A scholarly noble tempering book learning with hard-earned practical experience
- A born leader with infectious good spirits
- A cocky know-it-all who's almost as good as he thinks — and inspires others to the same high standard
- A village wise-man guiding his small kinship to greatness
- A royal librarian searching the world for lost tales

Party Role: Backer/Wildcard. You forge your party into a tight-knit, well-oiled machine, ready to face any challenge, and can assume almost any secondary role as needed.

CLASS FEATURES

Favored Attributes: Intelligence, Wisdom

Class Skills: Crafting, Disguise, Haggle, Investigate, Medicine, Notice, Ride, Search, Sense Motive, Tactics

Skill Points: 6 + Int modifier per level (×4 at Career Level 1)

Vitality: 9 + Con modifier per level

Starting Proficiencies: 4

CORE ABILITY

Breadth of Experience: Choose 4 skills. They become Sage class skills for you and you gain 2 ranks in each.

CLASS ABILITIES

Wise Counsel: Your insight lets you supplement your colleagues' victories and make up for their failings. At Level 1, so long as a teammate can hear or see you when he makes an attack, skill check, save, or damage roll, you may spend and roll 1 action die to boost his result. You always roll this die and add your own action die modifiers; the teammate's die type and modifiers are ignored. No single roll may benefit from more than 1 action die from *wise counsel,* even if multiple Sages are present.

Assistance I: Your guidance can accelerate any undertaking, though at some risk. At Level 2, you may increase the error range of an ally's skill check by 1 to reduce the time it takes to 1/2 normal (rounded up, minimum 5 minutes). You may assist only 1 ally at a time and you may not perform any non-free actions when using this ability.

This ability may not be used with Downtime checks.

Assistance II: At Level 11, you may increase the error range of an ally's skill check by 2 to reduce the time it takes to 1/4 normal (rounded up, minimum 1 minute).

Assistance III: At Level 19, you may increase the error range of an ally's skill check by 3 to reduce the time it takes to 1/10 normal (rounded up, minimum 1 round).

Best of the Best: Your knowledge of your companions' strengths and weaknesses lets you perfectly blend their talents. At Level 3, once per scene when you or a teammate who can see or hear you makes a skill check, they may apply the highest available skill bonus among you.

At Levels 5, 7, 9, 11, 13, 15, 17, and 19, you may use this ability 1 additional time per scene.

Cross-Training: Your constant study of heroes lets you pick up some of their abilities along the way. At Levels 4, 8, 12, 16, and 20, you may choose 1 of the following Base Class abilities. You may choose most abilities only once but when 2 or more grades follow an ability name you may take it multiple times, gaining 1 grade each time it's taken.

- *Assassin: Hand of death; cold read 1/session; quick on your feet 1/session; unspoken name +1*
- *Burglar: Very, very sneaky; evasion I; bonus feat; uncanny dodge I*
- *Captain: Right-hand man; master and commander I; battle-planning I; take command +1*
- *Courtier: With a word; gifts and favors I; obligations; eloquence*
- *Explorer: Tomb raider; bookworm I (1/2 time); bonus feat; uncanny dodge I*
- *Keeper: Man of reason; trade secrets (1 skill); bright idea 1/session; bonus feat*
- *Lancer: Born in the saddle; mettle I; bonus feat; bred for war*
- *Mage: Subtle and quick to anger; arcane might; bonus feat*
- *Priest: Acolyte; signs & portents I; path of the devoted (1 Step); bonus feat*

- *Scout: Stalker; rough living +2; bonus feat; sneak attack +1d6*
- *Soldier: Fight on ×2; fortunes of war I; armor use I*

Spell points are *not* granted, limiting a cross-trained character without additional spellcasting ability to Level 0 spells. Neither is Alignment, effectively rendering *acolyte* and *devoted* useless to anyone without an Alignment from another character option.

You may *not* choose an ability you already have, and if you later gain an ability you've chosen here you do *not* gain it a second time; instead, you make a new *cross-training* choice to replace the former one.

When a cross-trained ability uses Class or Caster Level to determine its effect, it is considered to be 4.

If the GM excludes a Base Class from play, then you lose access to its *cross-training* abilities; likewise, if the GM approves additional Base Classes, new options become available.

Hand of Fate: Your thoughtful nature lets you make your own luck. At Level 6, once per adventure, you may spend 10 minutes planning to gain 1 temporary Chance feat of your choice until the end of the current adventure.

At Levels 12 and 18, you may use this ability 1 additional time per adventure.

Take Heart: In times of greatest need it falls to you to inspire your companions to greatness. At Level 9, once per dramatic scene, you may spend a full action in powerful speech. You and each teammate who can see or hear you immediately recovers to 1/2 their maximum vitality (rounded up).

At Level 15 you may use this ability twice per dramatic scene.

Proven Worth: You bring out the best in yourself and your party. At Level 10, you and each teammate's starting action dice increase by 1. No character's starting action dice may increase by more than 3 as a result of this ability, no matter how many Sages are involved.

At Level 20, you and each teammate's starting action dice increase by an additional 1 (total increase 2 dice).

Serendipity: You're a wellspring of good fortune — people, lucky breaks, and bouts of inspiration come to your rescue just when they're needed most. At Level 14, once per session during any time of crisis, the GM may, without prompting from you, introduce something to help your team. Examples include the appearance of a contact, the introduction of a major hint, a 4-die Complication that plagues your team's opponents, or an automatic success with a skill check (even if the character is untrained or doesn't make a skill check).

Alternatively, once per session, you may ask to use this ability to request a 4-die Perk *(see page 366)*.

SCOUT

Few endure the wilds as casually as the Scout and none but he truly *thrive.* He's as comfortable atop northern glaciers as deep in swamp lakes, fearing nothing in nature — not weather or beasts, not even the threatening promise of empty night. He can live off the land almost indefinitely and employs wild, unpredictable tactics most "civilized" adventurers never even consider.

Table 1.14: The Sage

Level	BAB	Fort	Ref	Will	Def	Init	Lifestyle	Legend	Special
1	+0	+1	+1	+1	+0	+1	+1	+1	*Breadth of experience*, wise counsel
2	+1	+2	+2	+2	+1	+1	+2	+2	Assistance I
3	+2	+2	+2	+2	+1	+2	+2	+3	Best of the best 1/scene
4	+3	+2	+2	+2	+2	+2	+2	+3	Cross-training
5	+3	+3	+3	+3	+2	+3	+3	+4	Best of the best 2/scene
6	+4	+3	+3	+3	+2	+4	+3	+5	Hand of fate (1 feat)
7	+5	+4	+4	+4	+3	+4	+4	+6	Best of the best 3/scene
8	+6	+4	+4	+4	+3	+5	+4	+6	Cross-training
9	+6	+4	+4	+4	+4	+5	+4	+7	Best of the best 4/scene, take heart 1/scene
10	+7	+5	+5	+5	+4	+6	+5	+8	Proven worth (1 die)
11	+8	+5	+5	+5	+4	+7	+5	+9	Assistance II, best of the best 5/scene
12	+9	+6	+6	+6	+5	+7	+6	+9	Cross-training, hand of fate (2 feats)
13	+9	+6	+6	+6	+5	+8	+6	+10	Best of the best 6/scene
14	+10	+6	+6	+6	+6	+8	+6	+11	Serendipity
15	+11	+7	+7	+7	+6	+9	+7	+12	Best of the best 7/scene, take heart 2/scene
16	+12	+7	+7	+7	+6	+10	+7	+12	Cross-training
17	+12	+8	+8	+8	+7	+10	+8	+13	Best of the best 8/scene
18	+13	+8	+8	+8	+7	+11	+8	+14	Hand of fate (3 feats)
19	+14	+8	+8	+8	+8	+11	+8	+15	Assistance III, best of the best 9/scene
20	+15	+9	+9	+9	+8	+12	+9	+15	Cross-training, proven worth (2 dice)

Depending on your campaign, a Scout could be...

- A military forward reconnoitering ahead of a massive army
- A bounty hunter seeking escaped mages
- The only guide to have escaped a band of frost giants and their snowy mountain gauntlet
- A grizzled monster hunter stalking creatures of nightmare in dungeons and deep jungles
- A canny tunnel denizen using guerilla warfare to protect a non-human enclave from folk incursions

Party Role: Combatant/Solver. You stand out away from the hustle-bustle of cities, taking advantage of terrain and finding strategy where others find impediment. Better yet, you extend many of your most powerful abilities to the rest of your party, keeping them one step ahead in rough country.

CLASS FEATURES

Favored Attributes: Wisdom, Dexterity, Constitution

Class Skills: Acrobatics, Athletics, Blend, Medicine, Notice, Resolve, Ride, Sneak, Survival, Tactics

Skill Points: 6 + Int modifier per level (×4 at Career Level 1)

Vitality: 9 + Con modifier per level

Starting Proficiencies: 4

CORE ABILITY

Trailblazer: Your presence ensures that everyone survives even the most hostile environments. Once per scene as a free action, you may temporarily grant your teammates 1 of your Terrain feats until the end of the scene.

CLASS ABILITIES

Stalker: At Level 1, each time you fail a Survival or Tactics check and don't suffer an error, you still succeed as long as the check DC (or your opponent's check result) is equal to or less than your Class Level + 20. If several grades of success are possible, you achieve only the lowest possible positive result.

If you gain this ability for either skill from two or more classes, add together your levels in all classes granting the ability when determining its effect.

Rough Living: Your time in the wild has toughened you. At Level 2, you gain a +2 bonus to Defense, as well as with saves prompted by the environment.

At Levels 11 and 19, these bonuses increase by an additional +2 (to +4 at Level 11 and +6 at Level 19).

Bonus Feat: At Levels 3, 5, 7, 9, 11, 13, 15, 17, and 19, you gain 1 additional Ranged Combat or Terrain feat.

Sneak Attack: At Level 4, you gain an additional die of sneak attack damage.

At Levels 8, 12, 16, and 20, you gain another additional die of sneak attack damage.

Huntsman: At Levels 6, 9, 12, 15, and 18, you may choose 1 of the following abilities. Each of these abilities may be chosen only once.

- *Darkvision I:* You ignore the effects of dim and faint light.
- *Expertise:* Choose one skill: Acrobatics, Athletics, Blend, Medicine, Notice, Resolve, Ride, Sneak, Survival, or Tactics. Taking 10 with this skill doesn't take twice as long and taking 20 takes only 10 times as long.
- *Keen Senses:* Your visual, hearing, and scent range increments increase by 20 ft.
- *Killing Blow:* It costs you 1 fewer action dice to activate a critical hit against an animal, elemental, fey, ooze, or plant (minimum 0).
- *Master Handler:* You're considered to have 5 additional ranks in Survival when training animals. This may cause you to exceed your maximum skill rank for these activities.

Table 1.15: The Scout

Level	BAB	Fort	Ref	Will	Def	Init	Lifestyle	Legend	Special
1	+0	+2	+2	+0	+1	+2	+0	+0	Stalker, *trailblazer*
2	+1	+3	+3	+0	+1	+3	+0	+1	Rough living +2
3	+2	+3	+3	+1	+2	+4	+1	+1	Bonus feat
4	+3	+4	+4	+1	+2	+5	+1	+1	Sneak attack +1d6
5	+3	+4	+4	+1	+3	+5	+1	+1	Bonus feat
6	+4	+5	+5	+2	+4	+6	+2	+2	Huntsman
7	+5	+5	+5	+2	+4	+7	+2	+2	Bonus feat
8	+6	+6	+6	+2	+5	+8	+2	+2	Sneak attack +2d6
9	+6	+6	+6	+3	+5	+9	+3	+2	Bonus feat, huntsman
10	+7	+7	+7	+3	+6	+10	+3	+3	Master tracker 1/session
11	+8	+7	+7	+3	+7	+10	+3	+3	Bonus feat, rough living +4
12	+9	+8	+8	+4	+7	+11	+4	+3	Huntsman, sneak attack +3d6
13	+9	+8	+8	+4	+8	+12	+4	+3	Bonus feat
14	+10	+9	+9	+4	+8	+13	+4	+4	Overrun 1/session
15	+11	+9	+9	+5	+9	+14	+5	+4	Bonus feat, huntsman
16	+12	+10	+10	+5	+10	+15	+5	+4	Sneak attack +4d6
17	+12	+10	+10	+5	+10	+15	+5	+4	Bonus feat
18	+13	+11	+11	+6	+11	+16	+6	+5	Huntsman
19	+14	+11	+11	+6	+11	+17	+6	+5	Bonus feat, rough living +6
20	+15	+12	+12	+6	+12	+18	+6	+5	Master tracker 2/session, sneak attack +5d6

- *Rough Riding:* Your vehicle or mount ignores Speed penalties from terrain *(see page 371)*.
- *Sprint:* In combat, your Speed increases by 10 ft.
- *Trail Signs:* You suffer no penalties for Speed when making Track checks.
- *Trophy Hunter:* You can drop even the biggest game with a single attack. When you attack an animal, your threat range increases by 3.
- *Turning:* Your pleasant relationship with the natural world is... discretionary. Choose a Type from the following list: animal, elemental, fey, ooze, or plant. Once per combat you may Turn characters of this Type *(see page 223)*.

Master Tracker: You frequently have uncanny insight about your prey. At Level 10, once per session when you make a successful Track check, you also gain 1 clue about the target *(see page 335)*.

At Level 20, you may use this ability twice per session.

Overrun: You know the first few seconds of any fight are critical. At Level 14, once per session at the start of combat, you may declare that you're "overrunning." While overrunning, if one of your attacks or a teammate's kills an opponent or knocks them unconscious, the attacker may immediately make an additional attack with the same weapon against another opponent. This continues until you and your teammates gain a combined number of additional attacks equal to your Class Level.

SOLDIER

The Soldier inhabits a bloody twilight realm of endless warfare, slashing and crushing his way from one bitter struggle to the next. Even when at relative "peace" he's always preparing, always on the lookout for the next fight, and this vigilance is part of what makes him such a godsend to fellow adventurers. Nothing levels the field of battle like a well-honed Soldier, except perhaps two Soldiers.

Depending on your campaign, a Soldier could be...

- A veteran legionnaire bearing decades of war scars
- A plucky young squire seeking to prove himself through feats of arms and daring
- A martial arts master committed to enlightenment through the perfection of his fighting technique
- A tribal warrior defending his people from ancient foes
- A gladiatorial champion, calling for any and all takers

Party Role: Combatant. You're the ultimate general warrior. With strong fighting stats and abilities, you're the perfect complement to any party that regularly brawls. You're not initially the best at any particular aspect of battle (though you can easily reach that goal); rather, you're strong in all categories.

CLASS FEATURES

Favored Attributes: Strength, Dexterity, Constitution (though not always in that order)

Class Skills: Athletics, Crafting, Intimidate, Notice, Resolve, Search, Survival, Tactics

Skill Points: 4 + Int modifier per level (×4 at Career Level 1)

Vitality: 12 + Con modifier per level

Starting Proficiencies: 6

CORE ABILITY

Accurate: Your finely honed physique is your deadliest weapon. Each time you spend 1 action die to boost an attack check, you roll and add the results of 2 dice (e.g. at Career Level 1, 1d4 becomes 2d4).

CLASS ABILITIES

Fight On: At Levels 1, 3, 5, 7, 9, 11, 13, 15, 17, and 19, you gain 1 additional Basic, Melee, Ranged, or Unarmed Combat feat or 2 additional proficiencies.

Fortunes of War I: You stand fast in battle, especially when the pressure's on. At Level 2, you gain Damage Reduction 1. During dramatic scenes, this DR increases to 2.

Fortunes of War II: At Level 11, your Damage Reduction increases to 2 (4 during dramatic scenes).

Fortunes of War III: At Level 19, your Damage Reduction increases to 3 (6 during dramatic scenes).

Armor Use I: At Level 4, you gain a +1 bonus to Defense while wearing armor and receive a 20% discount when purchasing armor.

Armor Use II: At Level 8, this Defense bonus increases to +2 and this discount increases to 25%.

Armor Use III: At Level 12, this Defense bonus increases to +3 and this discount increases to 30%.

Armor Use IV: At Level 16, this Defense bonus increases to +4 and this discount increases to 35%.

Armor Use V: At Level 20, this Defense bonus increases to +5 and this discount increases to 40%.

Weapon Specialist: Your knowledge of weapons in which you're trained is expansive and precise. At Levels 6, 9, 12, 15, and 18, you may choose 1 of the following abilities. Each of these abilities may be chosen only once.

- *Certainty:* Your error range with proficient attacks decreases by 2 (minimum 0).
- *Decisive Attack:* Once per round when holding a weapon in which you're proficient, you may make 1 free attack against a standard character.
- *Killer Instinct:* You inflict 2 additional damage with proficient attacks.
- *Master Weaponsmith:* You're considered to have 5 additional ranks in Crafting when building, improving, or repairing weapons in which you're proficient. This may cause you to exceed your maximum skill rank for these activities.

- *Most Deadly:* It costs you 1 fewer action dice to activate critical hits with proficient attacks (minimum 0).
- *One Step Ahead:* You gain a +1 dodge bonus to Defense and DR 1 against attacks with weapons in which you're proficient.
- *Rugged Weapons:* When you're holding a weapon in which you're proficient and it must make a Damage save, you may roll twice, keeping the result you prefer.
- *Shrewd Buyer:* You receive a 20% discount when purchasing weapons in which you're proficient.

Portable Cover I: You make the most of terrain, even improvising cover from objects kicked, knocked, or thrown into the path of incoming attacks. At Level 10, you and each ally within 10 ft. is considered to have 1/4 cover at all times, even when standing in the open. This benefit is lost while you're *flat-footed.*

Portable Cover II: At Level 20, this ability grants 1/2 cover and affects allies within 15 ft.

Table 1.16: The Soldier

Level	BAB	Fort	Ref	Will	Def	Init	Lifestyle	Legend	Special
1	+1	+1	+0	+2	+1	+1	+0	+1	*Accurate*, fight on
2	+2	+2	+0	+3	+1	+1	+0	+1	Fortunes of war I
3	+3	+2	+1	+3	+2	+2	+1	+2	Fight on
4	+4	+2	+1	+4	+2	+2	+1	+2	Armor use I
5	+5	+3	+1	+4	+3	+3	+1	+3	Fight on
6	+6	+3	+2	+5	+4	+4	+2	+3	Weapon specialist
7	+7	+4	+2	+5	+4	+4	+2	+4	Fight on
8	+8	+4	+2	+6	+5	+5	+2	+4	Armor use II
9	+9	+4	+3	+6	+5	+5	+3	+5	Fight on, weapon specialist
10	+10	+5	+3	+7	+6	+6	+3	+5	Portable cover I (1/4)
11	+11	+5	+3	+7	+7	+7	+3	+6	Fight on, fortunes of war II
12	+12	+6	+4	+8	+7	+7	+4	+6	Armor use III, weapon specialist
13	+13	+6	+4	+8	+8	+8	+4	+7	Fight on
14	+14	+6	+4	+9	+8	+8	+4	+7	One in a million 1/session
15	+15	+7	+5	+9	+9	+9	+5	+8	Fight on, weapon specialist
16	+16	+7	+5	+10	+10	+10	+5	+8	Armor use IV
17	+17	+8	+5	+10	+10	+10	+5	+9	Fight on
18	+18	+8	+6	+11	+11	+11	+6	+9	Weapon specialist
19	+19	+8	+6	+11	+11	+11	+6	+10	Fight on, fortunes of war III
20	+20	+9	+6	+12	+12	+12	+6	+10	Armor use V, portable cover II (1/2)

One in a Million: You turn nearly any battlefield opportunity into savage amounts of pain. At Level 14, once per session, you may make 1 attack check, Fortitude save, or Strength- or Constitution-based skill check, automatically scoring a natural 20. This roll is a threat and may be activated as a critical success. You may not be forced to re-roll this natural 20.

ALCHEMIST (EXPERT)

Philosopher of the world, the body, and the soul, the Alchemist applies scientific methods and magical energy to transform, purify, and empower simple materials. The height of his art is to turn this knowledge inward so he might rise above his mortal imperfections.

Depending on your campaign, an Alchemist could be...

- A prosperous magician scouring the wild for rare ingredients
- A military researcher whose efforts empower whole armies
- A traveling monk retracing the footsteps of ancient immortals
- A secretive medicine-man whose concoctions spell life or death for the braves of his tribe
- A sun-priest gathering the blessings of open sky and sacred waters

Party Role: Backer. With ready access to high-quality elixirs and a modest selection of support spells and effects, you thrive in the company of others.

CLASS FEATURES

Requirements: *Sorcery* campaign quality, Crafting 6+ ranks, Medicine 4+ ranks, Alchemy Basics feat

Favored Attributes: Intelligence, Constitution

Caster: Each level in this class increases your Casting Level by 1.

Class Skills: Crafting, Haggle, Impress, Investigate, Medicine, Notice, Prestidigitation, Ride, Search, Survival

Skill Points: 6 + Int modifier per level

Vitality: 9 + Con modifier per level

CORE ABILITY

Dancing Waters: You discover the hidden potential of alchemical creations. When you benefit from an elixir, you also gain a bonus d6 action die. Unless used, this action die is lost at the end of the scene.

CLASS ABILITIES

Way of the Crucible: At Level 1, you may purchase ranks in the Spellcasting skill, learn Compass, Conversion, and Creation spells, and cast Level 0 spells you know. Also, when you fail a Spellcasting check to cast a spell of these Disciplines, no spell points are spent on the attempt.

If you already possess this ability from another class, you instead gain an additional Spellcasting feat.

Potent Elixir I: At Level 2, the Casting Level of each elixir you create that produces a spell effect increases by 2. Also, the duration of each Boost Attribute potion you create increases by 2 minutes.

Potent Elixir II: At Level 7, the Casting Level of each elixir you create that produces a spell effect increases by an additional 2 (total 4). Also, the duration of each Boost Attribute potion you create increases by an additional 2 minutes (total 4 minutes).

Circle of Power I: At Level 3, you may cast Level 1 and lower spells you know.

Circle of Power II: At Level 5, you may cast Level 2 and lower spells you know.

Circle of Power III: At Level 7, you may cast Level 3 and lower spells you know.

Circle of Power IV: At Level 9, you may cast Level 4 and lower spells you know.

Alchemical Purity: At Level 4, each elixir you create gains the distilled upgrade at no additional cost.

Bonus Feat: At Levels 4 and 8, you gain an additional Gear or Spellcasting feat.

Alchemical Harmony: Your creations blend more effectively. At Level 6, you and each teammate may benefit from up to 3 oils or potions you've created per scene.

Transmutation: At Level 8, you may spend 1 spell point to transform an elixir you've created into a different elixir you can create of equal or lower value. This does not change when the elixir spoils.

Transmogrification: At Level 10, each of your attributes rises by 1 and you age at 1/10 the normal rate. Also, you and each adjacent teammate may roll each save twice, keeping the result you prefer.

BEASTMASTER (EXPERT)

The Beastmaster understands and bonds with creatures in ways that are incomprehensible to ordinary men. Though often viewed as a savage and untamed warrior, his gifts are undeniable — not only does he guide exceptional "pets" as an extension of his mind and blades, he can directly channel their raw spiritual and physical might, gaining incredible powers.

Depending on your campaign, a Beastmaster could be...

- A monster handler leading horrific beasts into the fray
- A sophisticated animal doctor sharing an innate connection with his wards
- A cunning thief whose tiny pets snatch valuables he can't acquire on his own
- A totem warrior blessed with powerful spirit companions
- A wyrm rider who fights as one with his mighty steed

Table 1.17: The Alchemist

Level	BAB	Fort	Ref	Will	Def	Init	Lifestyle	Legend	SP	Abilities
1	+0	+2	+0	+1	+1	+0	+2	+1	1	*Dancing waters*, way of the crucible
2	+1	+3	+0	+2	+1	+0	+3	+1	2	Potent elixir I
3	+1	+3	+1	+2	+2	+1	+3	+2	3	Circle of power I
4	+2	+4	+1	+2	+2	+1	+4	+2	4	Alchemical purity, bonus feat
5	+2	+4	+1	+3	+3	+1	+4	+3	5	Circle of power II
6	+3	+5	+2	+3	+4	+2	+5	+3	6	Alchemical harmony
7	+3	+5	+2	+4	+4	+2	+5	+4	7	Circle of power III, Potent elixir II
8	+4	+6	+2	+4	+5	+2	+6	+4	8	Transmutation, bonus feat
9	+4	+6	+3	+4	+5	+3	+6	+5	9	Circle of power IV
10	+5	+7	+3	+5	+6	+3	+7	+5	10	Transmogrification

Party Role: Specialist. You're an expert wilderness survivalist, protecting your party when they're away from home. You're also an unparalleled animal trainer, commanding many specialized helpers.

CLASS FEATURES

Requirements: Ride 6+ ranks, Survival 4+ ranks, Animal Partner feat

Favored Attributes: Charisma, Wisdom, Constitution

Class Skills: Acrobatics, Athletics, Impress, Intimidate, Medicine, Notice, Ride, Sense Motive, Sneak, Survival

Skill Points: 6 + Int modifier per level

Vitality: 9 + Con modifier per level

CORE ABILITY

Beast Kin: You share a deep and intuitive bond with animals. When you spend an action die to boost your Animal Partner's checks, you roll and add the results of 2 dice (e.g. at Career Level 6, 1d6 ecomes 2d6).

CLASS ABILITIES

Exotic Partner I: You have a knack for taming exceptional and exotic beasts. At Level 1, a single Animal Partner's maximum XP value increases by 10. Also, your exotic partner may have the Beast, Horror, Ooze, Plant, and Undead Types.

Exotic Partner II: At Level 5, your exotic partner's maximum XP value increases by 20 more (total bonus 30), and you may alternately divide its total XP value between two Animal Partners if you prefer.

Exotic Partner III: At Level 9, your exotic partner's maximum XP value increases by 20 more (total bonus 50), and you may alternately divide its total XP value between up to three Animal Partners if you prefer.

Man and Beast: You can use your companions' abilities as if they're your own. At Level 2, once per session as a 1-minute action, you may choose 1 NPC quality except *class ability, damage defiance, feat,* or *veteran* with an XP value of 3 or less belonging to any of your Animal Partners. You gain this NPC quality until the end of the scene.

At Level 7, you may use this ability twice per session.

Bonus Feat: At Levels 3 and 7, you gain an additional Unarmed Combat or Terrain feat.

Pack Alpha: At Level 4, at the start of each round, you may give an adjacent Animal Partner one of your half actions, or vice-versa.

At Level 10, at the start of each round, you may give an adjacent Animal Partner two of your half actions, or vice-versa.

Sic 'em, Boy!: At Level 4, at the start of each scene, you may grant your Animal Partners 1 of your Unarmed Combat or Terrain feats until the end of the scene.

At Level 8, you may share a combined total of 2 Unarmed Combat and Terrain feats with Animal Partners in each scene.

Life Bond: At Level 6, as a full action, you may transfer up to 1/2 your remaining vitality to your Animal Partner (rounded down), or vice-versa. This may not increase either character's vitality points beyond their normal maximum.

Red in Fang and Claw: At Level 8, so long as your Animal Partner can see or hear you, it costs you 1 fewer action dice to activate its critical hits (minimum 0).

Table 1.18: The Beastmaster

Level	BAB	Fort	Ref	Will	Def	Init	Lifestyle	Legend	Special
1	+1	+1	+1	+0	+1	+2	+0	+1	*Beast kin*, exotic partner I
2	+2	+2	+2	+0	+1	+3	+0	+1	Man and beast 1/session
3	+3	+2	+2	+1	+2	+4	+1	+2	Bonus feat
4	+4	+2	+2	+1	+2	+5	+1	+2	Pack alpha (half action), sic 'em, boy (1 feat)
5	+5	+3	+3	+1	+3	+5	+1	+3	Exotic partner II
6	+6	+3	+3	+2	+4	+6	+2	+3	Life bond
7	+7	+4	+4	+2	+4	+7	+2	+4	Bonus feat, man and beast 2/session
8	+8	+4	+4	+2	+5	+8	+2	+4	Red in fang and claw, sic 'em, boy (2 feats)
9	+9	+4	+4	+3	+5	+9	+3	+5	Exotic partner III
10	+10	+5	+5	+3	+6	+10	+3	+5	Pack Alpha (2 half actions/1 full action)

EDGEMASTER (EXPERT)

The Edgemaster indulges the art of death, painting in blood and sculpting the fear of his enemies. His instrument is his weapon, an extension of his very being, and together they accomplish the impossible and bring down the undefeatable.

Depending on your campaign, an Edgemaster could be...

- A burly berserker often felling his foes with a single overwhelming blow
- A grizzled master seeking a pupil to learn the lethal secrets of his arsenal
- A graceful sword dancer amazing crowds with death-defying performances
- A warrior prodigy respected as the greatest duelist of his tribe
- An elite blade-weaver converting precise rhythm into devastating attacks

Party Role: Combatant/Backer. You view combat as a performance, every swing and thrust a calculated step toward ultimate victory. It isn't enough to merely win the day, however — not when others can learn from your decisions.

CLASS FEATURES

Requirements: Charisma 13+, All-Out Attack feat, Wrestling Basics feat

Favored Attributes: Strength (melee) or Dexterity (ranged), Charisma

Class Skills: Acrobatics, Athletics, Bluff, Intimidate, Notice, Prestidigitation, Sense Motive, Survival

Skill Points: 4 + Int modifier per level

Vitality: 12 + Con modifier per level

CORE ABILITY

Swordplay: Once per round, you may spend an action die to make a free melee attack.

CLASS ABILITIES

Carve: At Level 1, when you Anticipate, Disarm, Distract, Feint, Taunt, or Tire an adjacent opponent, you may also inflict lethal damage equal to your Charisma modifier (minimum 1).

Display of Arms I: At Level 2, you may substitute Prestidigitation in place of Impress when making Influence checks. You also gain the Cheap Shot trick *(see page 221)*.

Display of Arms II: At Level 7, you may substitute Prestidigitation in place of Resolve when attempting to Tire. You also suffer no penalty with attack checks when making a Cheap Shot.

1,000 Blades: At Level 3, once per adventure as a free action, you may gain 1 temporary "Basics" or "Mastery" Melee Combat feat until the end of the adventure.

At Level 7, you may use this ability twice per adventure.

Study the Stance: At Level 4, you and each teammate who can see or hear you gain a +2 bonus with checks to resist being Feinted, Grappled, Taunted, and Tripped.

Swagger I: At Level 4, each time one of your melee attacks kills or knocks an opponent unconscious, you may spend your next half action posturing (e.g. holding your axe menacingly overhead, flicking the blood from your blade, etc.). Thereafter, you or one teammate who can see or hear you gains a bonus d4 action die. Unless used by the end of the combat, all but 1 of these dice are lost.

Swagger II: At Level 8, posturing grants a d6 action die and all but 2 of these dice are lost at the end of the combat.

Table 1.19: The Edgemaster

Level	BAB	Fort	Ref	Will	Def	Init	Lifestyle	Legend	Special
1	+1	+0	+1	+0	+1	+1	+1	+1	Carve, *swordplay*
2	+2	+0	+2	+0	+1	+1	+2	+2	Display of arms I
3	+3	+1	+2	+1	+2	+2	+2	+3	1,000 blades 1/adventure
4	+4	+1	+2	+1	+2	+2	+2	+3	Study the stance, swagger I
5	+5	+1	+3	+1	+3	+3	+3	+4	Blade dance I
6	+6	+2	+3	+2	+4	+4	+3	+5	Deadly blow
7	+7	+2	+4	+2	+4	+4	+4	+6	Display of arms I, 1,000 blades 2/adventure
8	+8	+2	+4	+2	+5	+5	+4	+6	Master's touch I, swagger II
9	+9	+3	+4	+3	+5	+5	+4	+7	Blade dance II
10	+10	+3	+5	+3	+6	+6	+5	+8	Effortless cut

Blade Dance I: At Level 5, you gain a +1 morale bonus with skill checks against opponents who've suffered damage from your melee attacks in the current combat.

Blade Dance II: At Level 9, this bonus increases to +2.

Deadly Blow: At Level 6, you may spend 1 round to prepare a deadly blow. During your next melee Standard Attack your opponent is considered *flat-footed,* your weapon's threat range increases by 4, and the weapon automatically inflicts its maximum possible damage (sneak attack damage, action dice, and other variable bonuses are still rolled). Your deadly blow is lost if you move before using it.

Master's Touch I: At Level 8, you may add 2 tricks to each attack. Also, you may apply unarmed tricks to melee attacks and vice-versa.

Effortless Cut: At Level 10, once per round when making a melee attack, you may roll twice, keeping the result you prefer.

PALADIN (EXPERT)

More than a holy warrior, the Paladin is a recognized symbol of his faith or a chosen champion of a great power. He's revered as a hero for much more than slaying great evils and saving the day, though he frequently enjoys a little admiration for those triumphs as well.

Depending on your campaign, a Paladin could be...

- A generous champion whose good humor and kindness bring comfort to all around him
- A black-hearted fiend spreading misery and despair for his own twisted pleasure
- A thoughtful judge whose steady hand upholds the law of the land
- A free spirit inspiring others to greatness
- A mysterious wanderer who lifts the yoke of oppression and vanishes as unexpectedly as he arrived

Party Role: Wildcard/Combatant. Your role is shaped by your beliefs, though your willingness to fight for them always shines through.

CLASS FEATURES

Requirements: *Miracles* campaign quality, Alignment, Charisma 15+, Bandage feat

Favored Attributes: Strength, Charisma

Caster: Each level in this class increases your Casting Level by 1.

Class Skills: Impress, Intimidate, Medicine, Notice, Resolve, Sense Motive, Alignment skills

Skill Points: 6 + Int modifier per level

Vitality: 9 + Con modifier per level

CORE ABILITY

Lay on Hands: Your rousing presence helps others stay in the fight. You may Mend a character one additional time per day (or 2 additional times per day if they share your Alignment).

CLASS ABILITIES

Smite the Indifferent: At Level 1, when you spend and roll an action die to boost damage against an opponent with a lower Charisma score, you may replace the action die's result with 1/2 your Career Level (rounded up). This may not cause the die to explode.

Stand in Judgment I: The meek shall inherit your faith. At Level 2, you may spend a full action passing judgment on a single adversary within line of sight. Choose Fortitude, Reflex, or Will saves. The opponent suffers a morale penalty with saves of the chosen type equal to your Strength modifier (minimum 1). This penalty lasts until the end of the scene or until you pass judgment on a different adversary. You may use this ability a number of times per scene equal to your starting action dice.

Stand in Judgment II: At Level 7, if you kill or knock a judged adversary unconscious, you recover vitality equal to your Class Level.

Path of the Crusader: At Levels 3, 5, 7, and 9, you take a Step along any 1 of your Alignment's Paths. All Steps from this ability must be taken along a single Path until you complete it, at which point future Steps from this ability may only be taken along a single new Path.

Heritage Revealed: You're a powerful icon to your people. At Level 4, you gain a "Heritage" Species feat (e.g. Angelic Heritage, Elemental Heritage, etc.), ignoring "Level 1 only" prerequisites.

Battle Planning I: At Level 4, you gain 2 of the following battle plans. You may begin each combat with 1 battle plan already in effect and may enact a new one as a full action. Each plan's benefits last until the end of the current combat or until you enact a different battle plan. A battle plan grants you and each teammate who can see or hear you a +2 morale bonus with the following rolls and values.

- *Crush Them!:* Melee and unarmed attack checks
- *Fire at Will!:* Ranged attack checks
- *Guard Yourselves!:* Defense
- *I Want Them Alive!:* Subdual damage rolls
- *No Prisoners!:* Lethal damage rolls
- *Press On!:* Base Speed (morale bonus × 5 ft.)
- *Stand Fast!:* Vitality (morale bonus × target's Career Level)
- *Steady Now!:* Saves

Battle Planning II: At Level 8, you gain 2 additional battle plans (total 4).

Gallantry: At Levels 6 and 10, your Strength and Charisma scores each rise by 1.

Take Heart: In times of greatest need it falls to you to inspire your companions to greatness. At Level 8, once per dramatic scene, you may spend a full action in powerful speech. You and each teammate who can see or hear you immediately recovers to 1/2 their maximum vitality (rounded up).

State of Grace: You rise to every occasion like a true hero. At Level 10, during dramatic scenes, you gain a bonus with saves equal to your Charisma modifier and Damage Reduction equal to your Strength modifier (minimum 1).

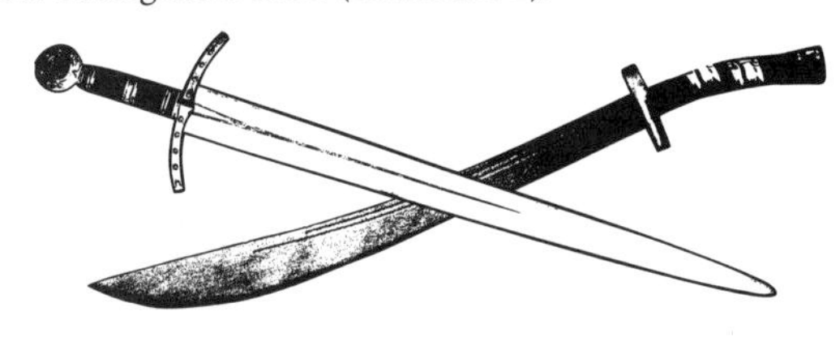

Table 1.20: The Paladin

Level	BAB	Fort	Ref	Will	Def	Init	Lifestyle	Legend	Special
1	+0	+2	+0	+2	+1	+1	+0	+1	*Lay on hands*, smite the indifferent
2	+1	+3	+0	+3	+1	+1	+0	+1	Stand in judgment I
3	+2	+3	+1	+3	+2	+2	+1	+2	Path of the crusader
4	+3	+4	+1	+4	+2	+2	+1	+2	Battle planning I, heritage revealed
5	+3	+4	+1	+4	+3	+3	+1	+3	Path of the crusader
6	+4	+5	+2	+5	+4	+4	+2	+3	Gallantry +1
7	+5	+5	+2	+5	+4	+4	+2	+4	Path of the crusader, stand in judgment II
8	+6	+6	+2	+6	+5	+5	+2	+4	Battle planning II, take heart! 1/dramatic scene
9	+6	+6	+3	+6	+5	+5	+3	+5	Path of the crusader
10	+7	+7	+3	+7	+6	+6	+3	+5	Gallantry +2, state of grace

RUNE KNIGHT (EXPERT)

A martial mage of the first order, the Rune Knight inscribes weapons with rare forms of arcane script, imbuing them with mystical powers. Though many of his kind favor melee weapons, particularly blades, he can inscribe anything: bows, hurled weapons, even pistols and other exotic armaments.

Depending on your campaign, a Rune Knight could be...

- A war wizard using spells in the first onslaught, then wading in with rune-carved blades
- A pistoleer using enchanted guns to launch devastating blasts off the bow of his pirate ship
- A student of secrets blending the arcane and martial arts, recently bestowed the arms of his faith
- A hunter of the occult crafting his enemies' sorcerous blood into his weapons
- A bowman and monstrous student of dark arts whose blood-magic drips from every arrow

Party Role: Combatant. Your enhanced arsenal, unique fighting abilities, and a moderate complement of spells, make you a powerful addition to any adventuring party.

CLASS FEATURES

Requirements: *Sorcery* campaign quality, Spellcasting 4+ ranks, Resolve 6+ ranks, Favored Gear (any 1 weapon) feat

Favored Attributes: Intelligence, Strength (melee) or Dexterity (ranged), Charisma

Caster: Each level in this class increases your Casting Level by 1.

Class Skills: Acrobatics, Athletics, Crafting, Intimidate, Notice, Resolve, Ride, Sneak

Skill Points: 4 + Int modifier per level

Vitality: 12 + Con modifier per level

CORE ABILITY

Battle Mage: When you spend an action die to boost a Spellcasting check or an attack check with a Favored Weapon, you gain the same boost with your next check of the other type. Unless used by the end of your next Initiative Count, this bonus is lost.

CLASS ABILITIES

Rune-Carved: At Levels 1, 5 and 9, you may inscribe a Favored Weapon with 2 runes. Thereafter, as a free action when you hit with an inscribed Favored Weapon but before rolling damage, you may spend a spell point to apply 1 inscribed rune's benefit to the attack.

- *Flaming Rune:* The attack inflicts fire damage instead of its normal damage.
- *Flaying Rune:* The attack gains the *keen* quality equal to your Class Level.
- *Gouging Rune:* The action die cost to activate a critical hit decreases by 1 (minimum 0).
- *Leeching Rune:* You gain vitality equal to 1/2 the attack's damage (rounded up).
- *Lightning Rune:* The attack inflicts electrical damage instead of its normal damage.
- *Seeking Rune:* Roll the damage twice, keeping the result you prefer.
- *Slicing Rune:* The attack gains the *armor-piercing* quality equal to your Class Level.

- *Smashing Rune:* The attack inflicts force damage instead of its normal damage.
- *Thundering Rune:* The attack inflicts sonic damage instead of its normal damage.
- *Weeping Rune:* The attack inflicts acid damage instead of its normal damage.

Warcasting I: At Level 2, a Favored Weapon counts as a mage's pouch for you.

Warcasting II: At Level 7, your Spellcasting threat range increases by 2 while wielding a Favored Weapon.

Circle of Power I: At Level 3, you may cast Level 1 and lower spells you know.

Circle of Power II: At Level 7, you may cast Level 2 and lower spells you know.

Signature Weapon: At Level 4, you gain the Signature Gear feat *(see page 98).*

Spell Breach: Your attacks leave targets vulnerable to deadly magical blows. At Level 4, once per opponent per scene when you hit with a Favored Weapon, the target suffers a penalty equal to your Class Level with his next save against a spell effect. This penalty lasts until the end of the scene.

Spell Parry: You dodge spells with the fluid grace of a master swordsman. At Level 6, once per round while wielding a Favored Weapon and not *flat-footed,* you may substitute your Reflex save bonus when making a Fortitude or Will save against a spell. This does not change the type of save being made.

Blooding Rune: Your weapon saps life force from your enemies and converts it to raw magical power. At Level 8, each time you score a critical hit against an adversary with a Favored Weapon, you gain 2 spell points. Unless used by the end of the combat, these spell points are lost.

Trademark Weapon: At Level 8, you gain the Trademark Gear feat *(see page 98).*

Spell Strike: At Level 10, once per round when you hit with a Favored Weapon, you may immediately attempt a Spellcasting check with a Casting Time of up to 1 full action as a free action. This does not increase the number of spells you may normally cast per round.

SWASHBUCKLER

(EXPERT)

Dashing, daring, and dangerous, the Swashbuckler embodies style on and off the battlefield. His high-flying, death-defying displays of swordsmanship and bravery regularly carry the day (and night), commanding the admiration of friends, the ire of enemies, and the hearts of swooning fans. Though the Swashbuckler exhibits preternatural skill with light blades, he isn't simply a fighter — he's the original action hero, cutting down foes with a sharp tongue as often as a flashing blade.

Depending on your campaign, a Swashbuckler could be...

- A debonair masked avenger with a lustful passion for life
- A courageous musketeer risking it all for honor and love
- A dread pirate battling rodents of unusual size
- A chieftain's son forgiven his excesses in light of his ready charm and trusted blade
- A riverboat captain swinging through riggings and maidens' windows with equal ease

Party Role: Talker/Combatant. While your fighting skills are excellent, you really stand out when you can parley — especially with those you've amazed with your exploits!

CLASS FEATURES

Requirements: Charisma 13+, Acrobatics 6+ ranks, Fencing Basics feat

Favored Attributes: Charisma, Dexterity

Class Skills: Acrobatics, Athletics, Bluff, Disguise, Impress, Notice, Prestidigitation, Resolve, Ride, Tactics

Skill Points: 6 + Int modifier per level

Vitality: 9 + Con modifier per level

CORE ABILITY

Show-Off: Your Panache increases by 1. Also, at Level 1 and for each Class Level thereafter, you gain 1 additional skill point that must be spent on Acrobatics or Impress.

Table 1.21: The Rune Knight

Level	BAB	Fort	Ref	Will	Def	Init	Lifestyle	Legend	SP	Abilities
1	+0	+1	+2	+0	+2	+0	+0	+1	1	*Battle mage,* rune-carved (2 runes)
2	+1	+2	+3	+0	+3	+0	+0	+1	2	Warcasting I
3	+2	+2	+3	+1	+3	+1	+1	+2	3	Circle of power I
4	+3	+2	+4	+1	+4	+1	+1	+2	4	Signature weapon, spell breach
5	+3	+3	+4	+1	+5	+1	+1	+3	5	Rune-carved (4 runes)
6	+4	+3	+5	+2	+6	+2	+2	+3	6	Spell parry
7	+5	+4	+5	+2	+6	+2	+2	+4	7	Circle of power II, warcasting II
8	+6	+4	+6	+2	+7	+2	+2	+4	8	Blooding rune, trademark weapon
9	+6	+4	+6	+3	+8	+3	+3	+5	9	Rune-carved (6 runes)
10	+7	+5	+7	+3	+9	+3	+3	+5	10	Spell strike

Table 1.22: The Swashbuckler

Level	BAB	Fort	Ref	Will	Def	Init	Lifestyle	Legend	Special
1	+0	+0	+1	+1	+2	+1	+0	+1	Rapier wit, *show-off*
2	+1	+0	+2	+2	+3	+1	+0	+2	Legendary swordsman I
3	+2	+1	+2	+2	+3	+2	+1	+3	Bonus feat
4	+3	+1	+2	+2	+4	+2	+1	+3	"All for one…," perfect form
5	+3	+1	+3	+3	+5	+3	+1	+4	Bonus feat
6	+4	+2	+3	+3	+6	+4	+2	+5	Tally ho!
7	+5	+2	+4	+4	+6	+4	+2	+6	Bonus feat, legendary swordsman II
8	+6	+2	+4	+4	+7	+5	+2	+6	Letter of marque, only mostly dead
9	+6	+3	+4	+4	+8	+5	+3	+7	Bonus feat
10	+7	+3	+5	+5	+9	+6	+3	+8	"…And one for all!"

CLASS ABILITIES

Rapier Wit: Your raucous displays aren't only designed to win battles but hearts as well. At Level 1, when you kill or knock an adversary unconscious, you may improve the Disposition of each character within line of sight by 4 for this scene. You may target each character no more than twice per scene with this ability.

Legendary Swordsman I: At Level 2, you gain the Fencing Mastery feat *(see page 88)*. Also, your Heroic Renown increases by 1.

Legendary Swordsman II: At Level 7, you gain the Fencing Supremacy feat. Also, your Heroic Renown increases by an additional 1 (total increase 2).

Bonus Feat: At Levels 3, 5, 7, and 9, you gain an additional Chance or Style feat.

"All for One...": When in need, you can exploit a diverse network of romantic conquests, toadies, and fawning admirers. At Level 4, once per adventure as a full action, you may produce a free Support Favor with a Reputation value equal to your Career Level *(see page 189)*.

Perfect Form: Pizzazz and luck are integral to a "gentleman's war." At Level 4, your Chance and Style feats count as Melee Combat feats when fulfilling prerequisites and requirements or determining the effects of any ability.

Tally Ho!: Your incredible acrobatic skill supplements your extraordinary swordsmanship. At Level 6, after you make a successful Acrobatics check, you may immediately make a free attack with a 1-handed weapon.

Letter of Marque: You're so charming you can get away with murder — *literally.* At Level 8, once per adventure as a full action, you may produce a free Pardon (Major Crime) Favor for yourself only *(see page 189)*.

Only Mostly Dead: You have a handy way of surviving life-or-death situations in improbable ways: washing up on a deserted island after your ship sinks, landing on a conveniently placed cliff at the edge of a bottomless pit, being mistaken for a cannibal tribe's god rather than its dinner... At Level 8, each time you die outside of combat, you may instead sacrifice 1 rank of Heroic Renown to Cheat Death with a Petty fate *(see page 384)*. The loss of Renown represents damage to your reputation as rumors of your death spread and jealous rivals and enemies take advantage of your absence.

"...And One for All!": At Level 10, during dramatic scenes, your threat range with attack and skill checks and that of each teammate increase by 2. No character's threat range may increase by more than 5 as a result of this ability, no matter how many Swashbucklers are involved.

STEP 7: INTERESTS

Your character is more than a collection of numbers. He's a person with opinions, quirks, and... interests. Interests let you round out your character with hobbies, regional curiosity, job experience, pastimes, and other personal pursuits, forming a background you can draw upon and expand when roleplaying.

Fantasy Craft features three types of Interests**: Alignment, Languages,** and **Studies.**

Alignment: If your campaign features Alignments, you may use an Interest to gain one *(see page 308)*. You may have only 1 Alignment at a time, though it may consist of multiple choices. Your choice of Alignment might represent a belief (e.g. in a god), a philosophy (e.g. animism), a moral outlook (e.g. Chaotic Good), kinship with a powerful force (e.g. born under an auspicious star), or a combination of these things. The particular Alignment choices and the effects they have in play available in your game depend on the setting. Check with your GM for a list of the available options.

Languages: Each additional Language counts as 1 Interest. You can read and write any language you know unless you intentionally choose not to, perhaps as a way of expanding your character's background.

Studies: Each Interest not defined as an Alignment or a Language is a Study — something your character takes time to learn about. A Study can focus on a nation or region, a culture, a celebrated adventurer, a religion, a monster, an adversary, or anything else you and the GM feel is appropriate.

Each Study should be broad enough to find periodic use in the setting and story but narrow enough not to enter every conversation. Because of their flexibility, you and the GM must agree on all your Studies before they enter play.

Studies have a number of effects in play.

- When you and the GM agree that a Study relates to a skill check, you gain a +1 bonus with that check.
- When you and the GM agree that a Study relates to a Knowledge check *(see page 66)*, you gain 1 additional hint about the topic after making the check.
- When you and an NPC share a Study, you gain a +1 bonus with skill checks made to improve the NPC's Disposition.

No combination of Studies may grant a character more than a +2 bonus or 2 extra hints with any check.

STARTING INTERESTS

You start out with your native Language, a Study in your native culture or homeland, and 2 additional Interests of your choice. You gain additional Interests as shown on Table 1.4: Career Level *(see page 27)*. You may give up an Interest at any time, though you permanently lose the 'slot' — the interest is *not* replaced.

STEP 8: CHARACTER SHEET

Now it's time to fill in all the other blanks on your character sheet!

Melee/Unarmed Attack Bonus: Add this to unarmed and melee attack rolls. It's equal to your base attack bonus + Strength modifier and may be negative.

Ranged Attack Bonus: Add this to ranged attack rolls. It's equal to your base attack bonus + Dexterity modifier and may be negative.

Fortitude Save Bonus: Add this to saving throws to resist physical attacks and threats. It's equal to your base Fortitude bonus + Constitution modifier and may be negative.

Reflex Save Bonus: Add this to saving throws to evade explosions and certain traps, and when you react to unexpected events. It's equal to your base Reflex bonus + Dexterity modifier and may be negative.

Will Save Bonus: Add this to saving throws to resist mental attack and threats. It's equal to your base Will bonus + Wisdom modifier and may be negative.

Defense: This gauges how difficult it is for others to hit you. It's equal to 10 + your base Defense bonus + Dexterity modifier.

Initiative Bonus: Add this to Initiative rolls. It's equal to your base Initiative bonus + Dexterity modifier and may be negative.

Reputation: This represents your standing in the world. You begin play with Reputation equal to your Career Level × 10 and gain more from each adventure you complete. You may spend Reputation to gain Prizes and other benefits *(see page 186)*.

CHAPTER 2: LORE

There are moments when all that's precious hangs in the balance, when the mountains tremble, the skies swoon, and the fates themselves are breathless. These are moments when history is at hand, when an intrepid band of heroes stands to become legend. Yet first they must prevail, which is rarely a simple thing. Three of the greatest tools at their disposal are discussed here: action dice, skills, and feats. With this mighty lore in hand any character can master his destiny and bring fell history to its knees.

ACTION DICE

Heroes frequently get themselves into seemingly impossible binds, yet they just as frequently manage to save the day. They defy the odds, evade deadly attacks at the last possible moment, find the strength to push on when it looks like they're down for the count, and generally benefit from uncanny fortune. In *Fantasy Craft*, such thrilling twists of fate are made possible with action dice.

Each character starts each session with a pool of action dice, as shown on Table 1.4: Career Level *(see page 27)*. Additional action dice may be gained from various character options, and as GM rewards for playing in character, taking chances (especially heroic ones), furthering the story, solving problems, entertaining the group, and otherwise improving everyone's experience *(for more information about action die rewards, see page 365)*.

Action dice may be spent in any of the following ways. Unless a rule says otherwise (such as the Sage's *wise counsel* ability), characters may only use these options on themselves.

There's no reason to hoard action dice — all action dice not spent by the end of each gaming session are lost.

1. BOOST A DIE ROLL

A character may spend 1 action die to boost each attack check, skill check, Knowledge check, or saving throw he makes. He may also spend 1 action die to boost each of his lethal, stress, or subdual damage results. The choice to boost may be made *after* the dice are rolled, so long as the outcome has not yet been described.

When boosting, an action die "explodes" when it rolls the highest natural number possible (e.g. a 6 on a d6). The player rolls the action die again, adding the new result to the previous one. An action die may explode multiple times, resulting in an extremely high boost.

Example: Brungil rolls a 6 on a d6 action die. He rolls it again, getting a 6, and a third time getting a 4. The total boost is 16.

An action die may only be spent to boost a check or result when dice are rolled. Thus, a character may *not* boost a skill check when he takes 10 or 20.

2. BOOST YOUR DEFENSE

At the start of any combat round, a character may spend 1 action die to boost his Defense by 2 for a number of rounds equal to the die's result. This action die may explode as described in Option 1. A character may only benefit from one action die boost to Defense at any time and the result of a new die spent to boost Defense replaces the old one, even if it's lower.

3. ACTIVATE A THREAT

When a character scores a threat with an attack or skill check, he may spend 1 or more action dice to activate it as a critical hit or success *(see pages 207 and 65, respectively)*. The choice to activate must be made before additional (e.g. damage) dice are rolled and/or the outcome is described.

4. ACTIVATE AN OPPONENT'S ERROR

When an opponent within a character's line of sight suffers an error with an attack or skill check, the character may spend 1 or more action dice to activate it as a critical miss or failure *(see pages 208 and 65)*. The choice to activate must be made before additional dice are rolled and/or the outcome is described.

5. HEAL YOUR CHARACTER

This option is covered in Chapter 5: Combat *(see page 212)*.

SKILLS

In his journeys, a hero does more than fend off the ravening legions of evil — he smooth-talks city guards, explores ancient crypts, and creeps through heavily guarded areas. All these actions are resolved with skills, which represent general aptitude with common tasks. This aptitude is measured in **ranks**.

BUYING SKILL RANKS

Skill ranks are bought and improved with points granted by classes. A character may improve his skill ranks each time he gains a level, though he may *only* buy ranks in Origin and class skills *(see pages 9 and 28)*. Each rank costs 1 skill point. The maximum number of ranks a character may possess in any skill is equal to his Career Level + 3.

In the unlikely event that a character cannot spend all the skill points he earns between levels, excess points are lost.

SKILL BONUS

A character's bonus with a skill is equal to his ranks in it + his modifier with the skill's key attribute (which may be negative). For a list of key attributes and other information, consult Table 2.1: Purchasing Skills *(see page 64)*. The GM may change a skill's key attribute whenever he feels a different one is more appropriate to the situation, meaning that a player's skill bonus may change for certain attempts.

SKILL CHECKS

When a character uses a skill, he makes a "skill check," rolling 1d20 and adding his appropriate skill bonus to obtain a **skill check result**. If the result equals or exceeds the attempt's **Difficulty Class or "DC"** (which generally falls between 10 for a relatively simple action and 60 for an extremely tricky one), the character succeeds; otherwise, he fails. A character may only retry a failed check when the GM determines it's plausible (e.g. retrying an Acrobatics check to jump at a tournament might be fine, but leaping across a chasm doesn't offer much chance for a fresh effort).

Skill checks should only be made when the GM believes there is or should be a chance of failure — anything less and the character succeeds automatically.

UNTRAINED SKILL USE

A character with no ranks in a skill is considered "untrained." He may attempt checks with the skill but his result cannot exceed 15 and his error range increases by 2.

SKILL CHECK MODIFIERS

A number of modifiers may apply to skill checks. Some are "named," falling into one of the following categories, and others are "unnamed." Unnamed bonuses stack but only the highest individual bonus and the highest individual penalty from each named category apply to each skill attempt.

- **Discretionary:** The GM can apply a –4 to +4 modifier to represent circumstances not covered by an existing rule. For example, he might apply +2 when a character makes an Impress check after a moving comment, or –4 when trying to direct a horse into a pitch black cave (–1) to escape trebuchet attacks falling nearby (–3). The GM is encouraged to use discretionary modifiers to make any skill attempt more interesting.
- **Insight:** Origins, class abilities, and feats offer these bonuses, which represent keen understanding of skill techniques.
- **Gear:** Gear and magic items trigger these modifiers.
- **Magic:** Spells and magic items impose these modifiers.
- **Morale:** Class abilities are responsible for most morale modifiers, which showcase confidence under pressure.
- **Synergy:** The GM may determine that one other skill complements the character's attempt. For example, a character might benefit from Bluff when distracting a character to pick his pocket, an activity covered by Prestidigitation. If the character has at least 4 ranks in the supporting skill, he gains a +2 bonus.

Table 2.1: Purchasing Skills

Skill	Key Attribute	Basic Skill Feat	Class Skills											
Base Classes			Asn	Brg	Cpt	Ctr	Exp	Kpr	Lnc	Mge	Prs *	Sge	Sct	Sol
Acrobatics	Dex	Robber	—	X	—	—	—	—	—	—	—	—	X	—
Athletics	Str	Athlete	—	X	X	—	X	—	X	—	—	—	X	X
Blend	Cha	Pickpocket	X	—	—	—	X	—	—	—	—	—	X	—
Bluff	Cha	Actor	X	X	—	X	—	X	—	X	—	—	—	—
Crafting	Int	Trader	X	X	—	—	—	X	—	X	—	X	—	X
Disguise	Cha	Spy	X	—	—	—	—	—	—	—	—	X	—	—
Haggle	Wis	Trader	—	X	—	X	X	X	—	—	—	X	—	—
Impress	Cha	Actor	—	—	X	X	—	X	X	X	X	—	—	—
Intimidate	Wis	Officer	X	—	X	X	—	—	X	X	X	—	—	X
Investigate	Wis	Investigator	—	X	—	X	X	X	—	X	—	X	—	—
Medicine	Int	Healer	—	—	X	—	—	X	—	X	X	X	X	—
Notice	Wis	Spy	X	X	X	X	X	X	X	X	X	X	X	X
Prestidigitation	Dex	Pickpocket	X	X	—	X	X	—	—	X	—	—	—	—
Resolve	Con	Athlete	X	—	X	X	X	X	X	X	X	—	X	X
Ride	Dex	Horseman	—	X	X	X	X	—	X	X	—	X	X	—
Search	Int	Investigator	—	X	—	—	X	X	—	X	—	X	—	X
Sense Motive	Wis	Healer	X	—	X	X	—	X	—	X	X	X	—	—
Sneak	Dex	Robber	—	X	—	—	—	—	—	—	—	—	X	—
Survival	Wis	Horseman	—	—	X	—	X	X	X	—	—	—	X	X
Tactics	Int	Officer	X	X	X	—	—	X	X	—	—	X	X	X

Expert Classes			Alch	Bstm	Edge	Pldn *	Rknt	Swsh
Acrobatics	Dex	Robber	—	X	X	—	X	X
Athletics	Str	Athlete	—	X	X	—	X	X
Blend	Cha	Pickpocket	—	—	—	—	—	—
Bluff	Cha	Actor	—	—	X	—	—	X
Crafting	Int	Trader	X	—	—	—	X	—
Disguise	Cha	Spy	—	—	—	—	—	X
Haggle	Wis	Trader	X	—	—	—	—	—
Impress	Cha	Actor	X	X	—	X	—	X
Intimidate	Wis	Officer	—	X	X	X	X	—
Investigate	Wis	Investigator	X	—	—	—	—	—
Medicine	Int	Healer	X	X	—	X	—	—
Notice	Wis	Spy	X	X	X	X	X	X
Prestidigitation	Dex	Pickpocket	X	—	X	—	—	X
Resolve	Con	Athlete	—	—	—	X	X	X
Ride	Dex	Horseman	X	X	—	—	X	X
Search	Int	Investigator	X	—	—	—	—	—
Sense Motive	Wis	Healer	—	X	X	X	—	—
Sneak	Dex	Robber	—	X	—	—	X	—
Survival	Wis	Horseman	X	X	X	—	—	—
Tactics	Int	Officer	—	—	—	—	—	X

X *denotes a class skill.*

* The Paladin and Priest may also purchase ranks in their Alignment skills *(see page 309).*

TAKING 10 AND TAKING 20

Sometimes a character doesn't want to chance failure so he takes his time. In this case he can "take 10," which requires twice the normal time. He does *not* roll 1d20 when making the skill check; instead, his result is calculated as if he'd rolled a natural 10.

Example: Lorelei has an Acrobatics skill bonus of +8 and faces a jump with a DC of 15. She chooses to take twice as long to set her result to 18 and automatically succeed.

Alternately, a character might have all the time in the world and want to take advantage of it. In this case he can "take 20," which requires twenty times the normal time. As with taking 10 there is no roll; the result is calculated as if he'd rolled a natural 20.

Example: Lorelei has a meager Impress skill bonus of +4 when she finds herself fortuitously snowed in at a prince's home. She decides to take her time wooing him, taking 20 for a total result of 24. With any luck it's high enough to turn his head.

In both cases there was no roll, so the character may *not* spend an action die to boost the result. Also, a character taking 10 or 20 may not score a threat nor be activated as a critical success *(see right)*.

A character may not take 10 or 20 when distracted or endangered, nor may he do so when the GM determines that the element of chance is unavoidable. This option is also unavailable when making opposed, cooperative, and team checks *(see page 66)*.

MULTI-TASKING

Sometimes a character must split his attention between multiple skill attempts — stabilizing a wounded friend while balancing on a precarious surface, for instance, or scanning a house for clues while listening for signs that the owner is lying to him. A character may split his attention between no more than two skill checks at a time and the GM must determine that any combination of skill checks is plausible. When multi-tasking, a character suffers a –5 penalty with *both* checks and his error range with each increases by 2.

SPECIAL SKILL RESULTS

Every skill check has an **error range** and a **threat range**, which are natural die results that trigger special skill results. Unless otherwise specified, a skill check has an error range of 1 and a threat range of 20, though character options, gear choices, and other effects may modify these base values. Bonuses expand the range of natural die rolls that trigger an error or threat, and penalties scale them back. Modifiers may not eliminate error and threat ranges.

Example: A character's error range with a particular skill check increases by 2 and his threat range increases by 1. Unless other modifiers are in play, the check has an error range of 1–3 and a threat range of 19–20.

THREATS AND CRITICAL SUCCESSES

When a skill check succeeds *and* the character rolls a natural number within his threat range (an actual roll of the number on a d20), he scores a threat — a potential critical success. To gain the benefits of a critical success, the character simply spends 1 or more action dice as listed in the skill description. No more than 4 action dice may be spent to activate any critical success. When no cost is listed a character only needs to spend 1 action die to gain the benefit.

The GM could alternately apply effects of his own, let the skill user describe what happens, or even poll the other players for suggestions, especially if he thinks the result will be more interesting or make more sense in the current circumstances. This also costs 1–4 action dice based on the outcome. Most critical successes should have descriptive and mechanical components, and most of the time they should contribute to the ongoing fun and action of the scene rather than ending either.

1 Action Die: Brungil scores a critical success with Sneak while evading a group of roving goblins in an enemy fortress. Rather than have him skip straight to the heart of the complex (thus ending the scene), the GM has the goblins pass unwittingly by his concealed position. Brungil may blindside the mob, benefiting from a successful Ambush *(see page 83)*. Also, he maps a quarter of the area.

2 Action Dice: The goblins are so oblivious to Brungil's presence that he can follow them back to the barracks, learning much about the fortress defenses. Any character with this information gains a +2 bonus with Blend, Sneak, and Tactics checks made inside the fortress during the next 24 hours. Also, Brungil maps about half the complex.

3 Action Dice: Not only can Brungil sneak into the barracks, he can spend 1 hour sabotaging the armory stockpiles to increase the error range of every goblin weapon by 2 and decrease the DR of all goblin armor by 2. He also maps all but the area's most heavily guarded areas.

4 Action Dice: Brungil completes his map of the stronghold and may set successful Ambushes in any four locations of his choice. He can also scrawl an irritating message at a strategic location, allowing him to target the goblin's warlord with a Taunt action when he emerges later in the adventure.

Special Note: A threat scored by a standard NPC may only become a critical success if the NPC possesses the *treacherous* quality *(see page 235)*.

ERRORS AND CRITICAL FAILURES

When a skill check fails *and* the character rolls a natural number within his error range (an actual roll of the number on a d20), or when a skill result is negative, the character suffers an error — a potential critical failure. He only suffers the effects of the critical failure, however, if his *opponent* — commonly the GM

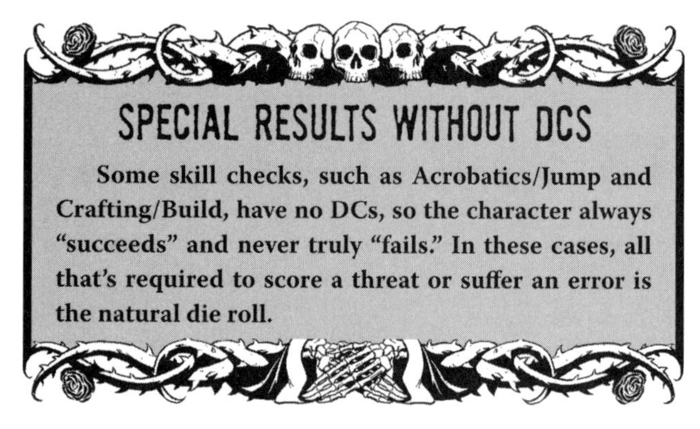

SPECIAL RESULTS WITHOUT DCS

Some skill checks, such as Acrobatics/Jump and Crafting/Build, have no DCs, so the character always "succeeds" and never truly "fails." In these cases, all that's required to score a threat or suffer an error is the natural die roll.

— spends 1 or more action dice as listed in the skill description. No more than 4 action dice may be spent to activate any critical failure. When no cost is listed, the opponent only needs to spend 1 action die to trigger the effect.

Critical failures are generally left to the GM's discretion. The potential pitfall here is using a critical failure to punish the character — true failure is oppressive and demoralizing. A better option is to use the failure to stack the odds a little higher against the character and maybe his entire party. This offers more things for the characters to do and enhances the overall story. Here are some examples of what might happen if Brungil's Sneak check resulted in a critical failure instead.

1 Action Die: The goblins notice Brungil and attack. The sound of battle attracts a second mob of goblins in 1d6 rounds.

2 Action Dice: The stronghold's alarm horns sound at the start of the second round of battle. Even if Brungil makes it out of his current bind he suffers a –2 penalty with all Blend, Sneak, and Tactics checks in the fortress until the goblins lower their guard.

3 Action Dice: The alarm doesn't sound but one goblin that Brungil didn't spot — that the GM didn't initially describe and that Brungil's player doesn't know about — slips out of sight before his companions attack. The goblin watches the fight and trails Brungil through the fortress afterward, studying him. Every five to ten minutes as Brungil continues through the fortress the GM makes a secret Notice check to see if the hero spots his pursuer. If he does he can try to capture or kill the goblin but if the creature remains hidden for at least three consecutive checks he returns to his superiors and reports his findings. For the rest of the adventure the threat range of every adversary in the fortress increases by 2 when targeting Brungil with attack and skill checks.

4 Action Dice: Brungil drops his least valuable silver-economy item in an attempt to recover. Both goblin squads are alerted and the alarm sounds but the GM isn't done. The item is found 1d4 hours later, allowing the goblin shamans to track Brungil's precise location for the rest of the scene. If Brungil returns to his party, he and his friends may soon find themselves with some unexpected visitors...

OPPOSED CHECKS

When a character competes against someone else with a skill, he makes an "opposed check." All involved make a standard skill check with the most relevant skill (e.g. Athletics for everyone in a foot race, Bluff for a lying character and Sense Motive for the listener, etc.), and the character with the highest result wins. Equal results tie unless this provides no clear result, in which case the winner is the character with the highest skill bonus. If this still ties, a random die roll determines the winner.

COOPERATIVE CHECKS

When multiple characters work together to perform a task, they make a "cooperative check." One character becomes the **leader** and all others become **helpers**. A maximum of 5 helpers may assist each skill check. The leader makes a standard skill check against the full DC and then each helper makes the same check against a DC of 15. For each helper who succeeds, the leader's result increases by 1, and for each helper who scores a critical success the leader's result increases by 2. If any of the helpers suffers a critical failure, however, the entire task is ruined and must be started again. The leader's total result — after all helper bonuses are applied — determines the cooperative check's outcome.

TEAM CHECKS

Sometimes several characters perform a single task together and individual success is irrelevant — when Bluffing, for example, even one failure can expose everyone involved. Other times several characters making the same check, or even a cooperative check, unfairly tips the odds in the characters' favor (even a few characters can practically ensure success with Notice or Search, for instance). In either of these cases the group should make a "team check." This works like a standard skill check, except that *only one character makes the check for the entire team.*

- If every member of the team must succeed to reap the benefit (e.g. the Bluff), the character with the *lowest* skill bonus makes the check.
- If only one character must succeed for the entire team to reap the benefit (e.g. the patrol), the character with the *highest* skill bonus makes the check.

When two or more characters qualify, the team chooses which makes the check.

KNOWLEDGE CHECKS

Character knowledge differs from player knowledge and what a character knows can often mean the difference between victory and defeat, or life and death. When a character's knowledge is in question he makes a "Knowledge check." The player rolls 1d20 and adds his Int modifier + the total number of Studies he knows *(see page 61)*. He has the knowledge in question if his result beats the DC listed on Table 2.2: Knowledge Checks *(see page 67)*.

When the character possesses 4 or more ranks in a related skill, he may ask for a synergy bonus, though the GM may refuse if he feels the skill isn't directly relevant. When a Knowledge check result logically translates to an in-game benefit (e.g. realizing details about an opponent's fighting style during a fight), treat the information like a related Study.

COMPLEX TASKS

It can often help the flow and drama of the game to break a task into smaller steps, each a separate skill check. This prolongs the action and sustains tension over multiple die rolls, and also keeps any single roll from ending the fun in what should be a complex encounter. When skill checks are grouped together like this they're called "Complex Tasks."

Crawling inside a huge clockwork monster to disable it from within is an excellent example of a Complex Task, with steps including Acrobatics (to get inside), Search (to find the critical bits of machinery), and Prestidigitation (to disable each in turn). Another great example is rifling through stacks of scrolls and journals in a trapped tomb, looking for the way out before poison gas floods the chamber. In this second case Investigate might be used repeatedly — not to determine success but whether the team finds the answer in time.

A Complex Task consists of 2 or more **Challenges**, each a step in the process and a skill check that must succeed for the task to continue. The GM may make all of a task's Challenges clear at the start or he might keep each secret until it's reached. Each Challenge attempt takes a certain amount of time, which may or may not match the time required for any listed check using the skill. Complex Tasks can also have a time limit, like the previously mentioned tomb search, which makes every check all that much more vital to ultimate victory.

Each successful skill check clears the current Challenge and moves the action to the next. Each failure yields no progress and increases the current Challenge's error range by 2 (as the pressure mounts and the seeds of doubt take hold). A critical success, or **breakthrough**, clears 2 Challenges instead of 1, while a critical failure, or **setback**, rolls the action back by 1 Challenge per action die spent.

Success with the last Challenge completes the task. Conversely, the task fails if a critical failure drops the number of cleared Challenges below 0 or if a time limit runs out before the last Challenge is completed.

MIX N' MATCH SKILLS

***Fantasy Craft* addresses the most common things characters may want to do, but what about all the other tasks? Fortunately, those looking to customize the rules have a couple powerful tools at their disposal.**

First, consider making a skill check with a different key attribute. For example, a Sneak check could be made with Wisdom when a character is trying to second-guess where an opponent will be watching. An Intimidate check could draw from Strength when the character threatens physical violence. Constitution could power Athletics during a marathon, and when a character's endurance is in question.

Second, there's the Knowledge check *(see page 66)*. Appraisal is a Knowledge check with a Haggle synergy (because after all, if you can effectively buy and sell, you know how to assess value). Navigation and weather prediction are both Knowledge checks with a Survival synergy, and diagnosis is a Knowledge check with a Medicine synergy. The same is true of item damage, which benefits from a Crafting synergy.

Most skills can be used in many new ways. Looking to learn a character's Disposition? Sounds like a Sense Motive check. Need to draw an accurate map? Survival with Intelligence is probably your best bet. A game of chess might be handled with an opposed Tactics check, where cards might involve Bluff opposed by Sense Motive. Random games of chance, such as dice, are probably best resolved without skills, as you can rarely get better at them, though betting patterns and strategies may indicate otherwise.

Ultimately, the *Fantasy Craft* skill system is as flexible as you want it to be. The checks on the printed page are the ones we feel are most universal and commonplace but even they're subject to your preference. Experiment with new combinations and ideas. See what works best for you and before you know it you'll settle into your own perfect rhythm.

Table 2.2: Knowledge Checks

Obscurity	DC
Common (e.g. laws in local area, info about brigands and monsters seen often on local roads)	10
Uncommon (e.g. laws in neighboring areas, info about brigands and monsters seen occasionally on local roads)	15
Rare (e.g. laws in distant lands, info about brigands and monsters that keep away from civilized areas)	20
Obscure (e.g. laws of uncommon brigands and monsters and info about their leaders)	25
Presumed Lost (e.g. laws of ancient gods, info about unique creatures of myth and legend)	30

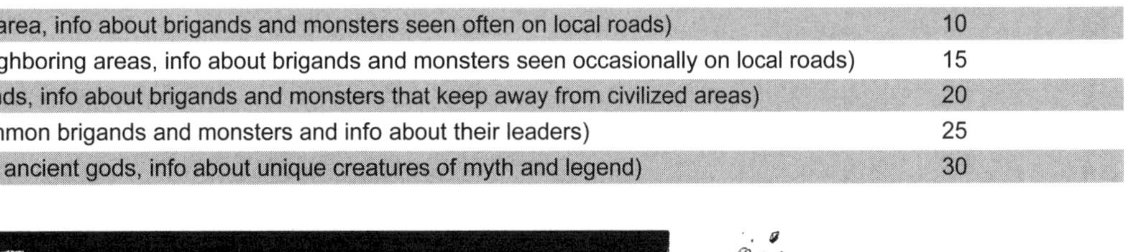

Complex Tasks are a powerful cinematic tool but they work best when lavished with detail unique to the situation. Describing each step, breakthrough, and setback independently of the others — even when they're conceptually and mechanically identical — offers a frame of reference for what the characters are doing and invests the players more heavily in the event. It also keeps them from getting bored. Story-critical Complex Tasks can also be prepped as part of the adventure, giving the GM plenty of time to make them as interesting as possible. However, when they crop up in play improvisation is the watchword of the day — everyone, GM and players alike, should have the chance to get involved *(for more guidance, see page 338)*.

DOWNTIME

In games that take place over long periods (such as full campaigns), the characters often spend a good deal of time *not* adventuring. They visit towns and cities between forays into local dungeons. They travel on ships and in caravans for weeks at a time. Eventually, they may even enjoy a well-earned vacation at home. In *Fantasy Craft,* these periods are called "Downtime."

Downtime offers a fair and quick way for the characters to accomplish things in periods that typically happen "off screen" without the need for complex bookkeeping that might otherwise throw off the momentum of the game. It also allows for fully open-ended play, where adventures overlap with intermittent breaks or the characters drive the plot instead of responding to it.

Downtime can happen whenever at least several hours pass without obvious story development or challenge for the characters. Only the GM may declare Downtime and when he does he must also declare a window of time the characters can fill with Downtime activities. The declared window may not be the actual window the GM has planned — surprise events may shorten or lengthen it — but it's the period the characters *expect* to be free. For instance, a party helping to defend a fortress may receive word that the enemy isn't expected for a full week and plan accordingly, only to find hostile forces amassing outside five days later. The expected Downtime of 1 week shortens to 5 days and less is accomplished as a result.

Downtime exists *outside* the typical flow of an adventure. During this period, characters may not use abilities or other character options with a limited number of uses per scene, adventure, or session. Likewise, unless Downtime marks a break between adventures or scenes, these abilities and options do not refresh, nor do action dice.

DOWNTIME CHECKS

Each character may only productively pursue one activity (make one skill check) during each period of Downtime, no matter how long the period is. Multiple characters may jointly undertake the same activity (make a cooperative check), but this does not allow them to split their attention (make more than one skill check as a group). This limit is arbitrary but practical; though characters live rich, full lives at all times, Downtime doesn't simulate every personal project. Rather, it focuses on the one major activity highlighting each span of loose time, like a montage in a fantasy movie or a brief paragraph in an adventure novel.

Fantasy Craft features several Downtime checks, though the GM may introduce more. Most of these are handled with specific skills: Crafting, Medicine, Resolve, and Survival *(see their individual skill descriptions for details).* Two additional checks allow characters to earn money or Reputation with any plausible skill — though the GM may always decline, preferably with a good reason supported by or expanding the story. For example, a character might be able to use Acrobatics to make some silver as a street performer in one town, only to find that another town's standoffish citizens or draconian laws make it impossible. A high Ride skill might win over a local noble with a fondness for horses, yielding Reputation for the character — unless a recent outbreak of disease decimated the local herd. As usual, the GM should always strive to be fair in ruling what skills may be used to generate money or Reputation, but at the same time he should try to keep the game interesting, diverse, and challenging for everyone.

When a character uses a skill to make money or Reputation, he makes one of two checks.

- *Earn Income:* Before rolling the character names one activity he's performing to earn money, which must be supported by one skill he intends to use. The GM may deny the check based on local opportunity, in which case the player or GM may discuss alternatives. This check has no DC; instead, the character's result is cross-referenced with the available Downtime on Table 2.3: Earning Income and Reputation *(see page 69).* A critical success yields an additional 50% (rounded up) and a critical failure yields 50% less (rounded down). The character's Prudence is immediately applied to the money earned *(see page 153).*
- *Foster Good Will:* Before rolling the character names one activity he's performing to earn Reputation, which must be supported by one skill he intends to use. The GM may deny the check based on local opportunity, in which case the player or GM may discuss alternatives. This check has no DC; instead, the character's result is cross-referenced with the available Downtime on Table 2.3: Earning Income and Reputation. A critical success yields an additional 50% (rounded up) and a critical failure yields 50% less (rounded down).

A character may not take 10 or 20 with either of these checks. Also, he may not spend action dice to boost his result. contacts and assistants may become helpers when these checks are made cooperatively but they may not become leaders.

Table 2.3: Earning Income and Reputation

Result	Per Day	Per Week	Per Month
		Downtime*	
Up to 15	1s/—	10s/0	50s/0
16–25	3s/—	30s/0	150s/1
26–35	6s/—	60s/1	300s/2
36–45	10s/—	100s/1	500s/3
46+	15s/—	150s/1	750s/4

* Money earned is to the left of the slash and Reputation earned is to the right. Multiply the amount listed by the number of days, weeks, or months spent making the check. A character may earn one or the other during each Downtime, *not both.*

DOWNTIME TRAVEL

Lengthy travel frequently takes place during Downtime, letting the GM and players dedicate as much or as little attention to the journey as desired. Speed, encounters, and other facets of travel are found in Chapter 7 *(see page 371),* and with GM permission a relatively calm trip may allow for a Downtime check.

SKILL DESCRIPTIONS

Each skill's most common key attribute is listed in parentheses next to its name. Suggested Knowledge checks follow a general overview, along with any other information pertinent to all the skill's uses. Individual checks and their required times round out the presentation.

ACROBATICS (DEX)

Leaping across pit traps, carefully navigating dangerous terrain, and somersaulting through combat are all ways to use the Acrobatics skill, which measures trained physical agility.

Knowledge: Dexterity-based fighting techniques; available paths over shaky or uneven terrain, around or through obstacles

BALANCE (1 HALF ACTION)

With success against the DC listed on Table 2.4: Balancing *(see right),* the character may move across a precarious surface at up to 1/2 his Speed (rounded up).

With a critical success, the character may move up to his full Speed. With a critical failure, the GM may choose one of two effects: either the character freezes, unable to move until he makes a successful full-action Resolve check against the failed check DC, or the character falls in a random direction *(per the Deviation Diagram, see page 216)* and becomes *sprawled.*

All distance traversed using this check counts against the character's movement for the round.

Table 2.4: Balancing

Surface/Circumstances	DC/DC Modifier
Uneven floor (up to 30° angle)	10
Uneven floor (30–60° angle)	15
Uneven floor (greater than 60° angle)	25
Narrow walkway (9–12 in. wide)	10
Narrow walkway (5–8 in. wide)	15
Narrow walkway (less than 4 in. wide)	25
Buckled, rolling, sagging, or shaking surface	+4
Slippery surface, or up to knee-deep water	+10
Character attacked once or more during previous or current round	+10

BREAK FALL (1 FREE ACTION)

With success (DC 20), a falling character lands on his feet and suffers 1/2 damage from the fall (rounded down, minimum 1 per 10 ft. fallen); otherwise, he suffers full damage and becomes *sprawled.*

With a critical success, the character suffers only 1/4 damage from the fall (rounded down, minimum 1 per 10 ft. fallen) *and* he may immediately reposition 1 square from his landing spot per action die spent. With a critical failure, the character suffers an additional 1 point per die rolled per action die spent.

JUMP (1 HALF ACTION)

A character may not Jump with a heavy load or while wearing full armor. Also, he must move at least 10 ft. to perform a running jump.

This check has no DC; instead, with a running horizontal jump, the character clears a number of feet equal to his check result + 5 (to a maximum of his height × 6). With a standing jump the character clears 1/2 this distance (to a maximum of his height × 2), and with a high jump he clears 1/8 this distance (to a maximum of his height), in both cases rounding down. These values are based on a Speed of 30; for other Speeds, calculate proportionately (e.g. with a Speed of 40, the character jumps 1/3 farther).

With a critical success, the character leaps the maximum possible distance. With a critical failure, the character clears the distance indicated by his result and becomes *sprawled,* suffering 1d6 subdual damage.

A character who fails to clear a pit or other gap may fall in, suffering additional effects. All distance jumped counts against the character's movement for the round.

TUMBLE (1 HALF ACTION)

A character may use this check to weave around or through enemy-occupied squares in combat *(see page 204).* While tumbling, a character may move up to his Speed.

If the character *tumbles* through one or more enemy-occupied squares, his DC is 20 + 5 per enemy adjacent to or in his path (including the first); otherwise, his DC is 10 + 5 per enemy

adjacent to or in his path (including the first). With success, the character moves the full distance; otherwise, he stops at the first empty square adjacent to an enemy and becomes *flat-footed.*

With a critical success, the character may attack 1 target adjacent to his tumble per action die spent (though he may not attack any individual target more than once). With a critical failure, the character stops at the first empty square adjacent to an enemy, becoming *sprawled,* and each adjacent enemy gains 1 free attack against him.

ATHLETICS (STR)

Unlike Acrobatics, this skill represents a character's ability to harness brute muscle. It's used to perform feats of speed and endurance rather than grace and accuracy.

Knowledge: Strength-based fighting techniques; sports and physical game rules and information

CLIMB (1 HALF ACTION)

With success against the DC listed on Table 2.5: Climbing *(see below),* the character may move across a vertical surface at up to 1/4 his Speed (rounded up). This base climbing Speed rises to 1/2 the character's Speed with climber's gear *(see page 159).* Per the GM, some surfaces may be impossible to climb without gear.

With a critical success, the character may move up to twice his base climbing Speed. With a critical failure, the GM may choose one of two effects: either the character freezes, unable to move until he makes a successful full-action Resolve check against the failed check DC, or the character falls in a random available direction *(per the Deviation Diagram, see page 216).* In the latter case the character may catch himself with another Climb check (DC equal to the failed check DC + 10), ending his fall at a random point chosen by the GM; otherwise, he impacts the ground and becomes *sprawled.*

At the end of each hour a character climbs, he must make a Fortitude save (DC 10 + 5 per previous save) or suffer 1d6 subdual damage. Damage reduction has no effect on this damage and it doesn't heal until the character rests for as much time as he spent climbing.

All distance moved using this check counts against the character's movement for the round.

Table 2.5: Climbing

Surface/Circumstances	DC/DC Modifier
Common hand- and footholds/opportunities to brace	10
Infrequent hand- and footholds/opportunities to brace	15
Rare hand- and footholds/opportunities to brace	25
Frequent chances to rest	–4
Unstable surface	+4
Slippery surface	+10
Per character dragged (max. 2)	+4
Character attacked once or more during previous or current round	+10

PUSH LIMIT (1 FREE ACTION)

With success (DC 20), the character may choose one of the following benefits.

- +5 to Ground Speed for 1 minute; for every 5 by which the result beats the DC the character may choose to either boost his Ground Speed by an additional 5 or increase the push duration for 1 additional minute
- +1 MPH to Travel Speed for 1 hour; for every 5 by which the result beats the DC the character may either boost his Travel Speed by an additional 1 MPH or increase the push duration for 1 additional hour
- +2 to Strength (for encumbrance *only*) for 1 minute; for every 5 by which the result beats the DC the character may choose to either boost his encumbrance Strength by an additional 2 or increase the push duration for 1 additional minute

At the end of every minute/hour a character pushes, he suffers 1d6 subdual damage per +2 to encumbrance Strength or +1 MPH to Travel Speed or +5 to Ground Speed, respectively. Damage reduction has no effect on this damage and it doesn't heal until the character rests for as much time as he pushed.

With a critical success, each of the character's chosen push benefits doubles and he only suffers 1/2 the resulting subdual damage (rounded up). With a critical failure, the character suffers 1d6 subdual and 1d6 lethal damage with no benefit.

SWIM (1 HALF ACTION)

With success against the DC listed on Table 2.6: Swimming *(see below),* the character may move across or through water at up to 1/4 his Speed (rounded up).

With a critical success, the character may move up to twice his base swimming Speed. With a critical failure, the GM may choose one of two effects: either the character freezes, unable to move until he makes a successful full-action Resolve check against the failed check DC, or the character slips beneath the surface and must begin holding his breath *(see page 217).*

A character can tread water without a skill check for a number of hours equal to his Constitution score; at the start of each hour thereafter, he must make a Fortitude save (DC 10 + 5 per previous save) or begin to drown *(see page 217).*

Table 2.6: Swimming

Water Conditions/Circumstances	DC/DC Modifier
Calm water	10
Rough water	15
Stormy water	25
Frequent chances to rest	–4
Per character dragged (max. 2)	+4
Character attacked once or more during previous or current round	+10

At the end of each hour a character swims or treads water, he must make a Fortitude save (DC 10 + 5 per previous save) or suffer 1d6 subdual damage. Damage reduction has no effect on this damage and it doesn't heal until the character rests for as much time as he spent swimming.

All distance traversed using this check counts against the character's movement for the round.

BLEND (CHA)

This skill is used to *subconsciously* avoid detection — it comes into play whenever it's important to know whether observers see, hear, or otherwise sense a character who isn't intentionally trying to escape discovery. For this reason, Blend is commonly used when the *Game Master*, rather than the player, initiates such a skill check. Frequently, the GM will make Stealth checks without the player's knowledge.

Knowledge: Local ethnicities, nationalities, walking and riding patterns, and other trends useful in keeping out of sight; mannerisms, words, and other actions that fail to attract attention

STEALTH (1 FREE ACTION)

With success against an observer's Notice or Search *(see pages 78 and 81)*, the character becomes *hidden* from the observer (if he wasn't already); otherwise, the observer becomes alert to the character (and potentially his location, if the GM thinks it's apparent). A number of modifiers apply to this check, as shown on Table 2.7: Blending, Sneaking, and Concealing *(see below)*.

With a critical success, the character fades completely into the background — the error ranges of Notice and Search checks to detect him increase by 2 per action die spent. With a critical failure, every observer who might notice the character does —

Table 2.7: Blending, Sneaking, and Concealing

Circumstances	Check Modifier
Ambient Light and Noise* (see also page 218)	
No light (e.g. pitch black) or extreme noise (e.g. battlefield)	+4
Faint light (e.g. moonlight) or heavy noise (e.g. passing wagon)	+2
Dim light (e.g. dawn, dusk, or torchlight) or moderate noise (e.g. busy tavern)	+0
Bright light (e.g. daylight) or faint noise (e.g. nearby conversation)	–2
Intense light (e.g. Glow II spell) or no noise (e.g. dead of night)	–4
Scenery	
Dense *and* obscuring scenery	+4
Dense scenery (e.g. thick forest) *or* obscuring scenery (e.g. snow mounds)	+2
Unremarkable scenery	+0
Sparse scenery (e.g. barren forest) *or* revealing scenery (e.g. dry leaves)	–2
Sparse *and* revealing scenery	–4
Species	
Close to surrounding group (e.g. elf in crowd of humans)	–2
Similar to surrounding group (e.g. dwarf in crowd of elves)	–4
Unlike surrounding group (e.g. ogre in crowd of dwarves)	–10
Wildly different from surrounding group (e.g. drake in crowd of ogres)	Impossible
Size	
Character is smaller than observer	+4 per Size category difference
Character is larger than observer	–4 per Size category difference
Senses	
Character is *blinded* **or** *deafened*	–2
Character is *blinded* **and** *deafened*	–4
Observer is *blinded* **or** *deafened*	+4
Observer is *blinded* **and** *deafened*	Automatic success
In the current round, the character also...	
Whispers	+0
Talks	–2
Screams	–4
Moves up to 1/2 his Speed (rounded down)	+0
Moves faster than 1/2 his Speed, up to his full Speed	–4
Moves faster than his full Speed (e.g. Runs)	–10
Makes a quiet attack (e.g. sap against leather armor)	–2
Makes a noisy attack (e.g. quarter staff against chainmail)	–4
Makes a loud attack (e.g. steel sword against platemail)	–10

* A separate modifier is applied for each of these circumstances (light and noise).

likely at an inopportune moment — and the character may not escape detection again until he moves out of the observer's sight and earshot.

The GM determines the frequency of Stealth checks, based primarily on the needs and challenges of the story. They may come up as often as once per minute or even once per round in a tense scene; other times they may only come up once every ten minutes, once an hour, or even less often.

BLUFF (CHA)

This skill is used to lie. Other deceptions are handled with Disguise and Crafting (for forgeries).

Language: When a character shares no common tongue with the target of a Bluff check, his error range increases by 4.

Knowledge: Common deceptions (e.g. famous military ploys, popular grifts); "tells" (subconscious signs that betray lies); things people want (and want to hear), based on their background

LIE (1 FULL ACTION)

With success against an observer's Sense Motive *(see page 81)*, the character's falsehood is believed. A number of modifiers apply to this check, as shown on Table 2.8: Bluffing *(see below)*, and as outlined in the Disposition section *(see page 373)*.

With a critical success, the character fully owns the lie — the error ranges of Sense Motive checks to see through it increase by 2 per action die spent. With a critical failure, the observer becomes skeptical of everything the character says, preventing further Lie checks until the end of this scene, until the observer's Attitude improves *(see page 373)*, or until the GM determines that the circumstances have changed enough to warrant a new Lie check.

CRAFTING (INT)

Every object across the great and civilized lands — from the humblest bauble to the most respected work of timeless art, from the simplest blade to the most powerful artifact of destruction — is forged with skilled hands. The art of building takes a lifetime to master, but unveils treasures that in all the world stand unique — for a time.

Focuses: When a character gains his first rank in Crafting and for every 4 full ranks he gains in total, he learns 1 focus from the following list: Carving (bone objects), Carpentry (wood objects), Chemistry (chemical objects, like gunpowder and explosives), Cooking (food), Inscription (documents, including books and paintings), Metalworking (metal objects), Pharmacy (medical supplies and poisons), Pottery (clay and ceramic objects), Stonecutting (stone objects), Tailoring (cloth and leather objects). The GM may add additional focuses as the campaign warrants. Each Crafting skill check uses only 1 focus (making primarily metal armor uses only Metalworking, for example, even if the resulting item has leather parts), and all checks made without the appropriate focus are untrained *(see page 63)*.

Tools: A character without the corresponding kit for the focus he's using is considered untrained even when he has Crafting ranks *(see page 63)*. With access to a crafting workshop, a character's threat range increases by 3.

Magic Items: Forging magic items, potions, and scrolls requires extremely rare and potent training in the form of feats, abilities, or other character options. Two examples include the Alchemist class *(see page 52)* and several Gear feat chains *(see page 96)*.

Knowledge: Crafting techniques (by focus); material and object strengths and weaknesses (by focus); famous creations (including famous artifacts and works of art)

BUILD OR IMPROVE OBJECT (DOWNTIME)

Before rolling the character names a single specific object he wishes to make or improve and the GM names a focus that covers it. The current Downtime must be at least as long as the chosen object's Minimum Crafting Time and the character must have a combined Crafting skill bonus + Career Level of at least the object's total Complexity (including upgrades).

This check has no DC; instead, the character's result is cross-referenced with the amount of Downtime on Table 2.9: Crafting *(see page 73)*. A critical success yields an additional 50% (rounded up) and a critical failure yields 50% less (rounded down). Should the character have any raw materials the GM feels are appropriate to the task *(see page 356)*, he may apply some or all of their value towards to this total. He may also spend coin to increase the total, though the combined value of applied raw materials and coin cannot exceed the original amount rolled (i.e. the character may not do better than double his total with raw materials and coin).

If the total Crafting Value after all modifications is equal to or higher than the desired object's cost, the character builds as many of the object as the Value can buy. Any leftover Value is converted to coin or added to the character's Reputation. At the GM's discretion, the character may "bank" Value toward a particularly

Table 2.8: Bluffing

Lie is...	Check Modifier
Believable (e.g. "Lord Bloodpyre's surrender demands are... *steep*.")	+10
Plausible (e.g. "He's an ogre. Of *course* those are human teeth.")	+4
Unremarkable (e.g. "I wouldn't look in there.")	+0
Questionable (e.g. "Here's a gold piece, no strings attached.")	–4
Suspect (e.g. "Reward? Maidens and treasure aren't really our bag.")	–10

Table 2.9: Crafting

Result	Downtime* Per Day	Per Week	Per Month
Up to 15	1s/—	10s/0	50s/0
16–25	3s/—	30s/0	150s/1
26–35	6s/—	60s/1	300s/2
36–45	10s/—	100s/1	500s/3
46+	15s/—	150s/1	750s/4

* Silver Crafting Value is to the left of the slash and Reputation is to the right. Multiply the amount listed by the number of days, weeks, or months spent making the check. A character may earn one or the other during each Downtime, *not both.*

large or complex item but this significantly increases bookkeeping and is only recommended for advanced games. If banking is allowed and the character abandons a crafting enterprise before it's completed, he may sell the parts off for 1/2 the Value banked toward the item to date (rounded down), or convert the same Value to raw materials *(see page 356).*

COUNTERFEIT (DOWNTIME)

This works like a Build check, except that when the object is ready an observer can make a Notice or Search check to realize it's a fake. This check's DC is equal to 10 + the forger's total bonus with the Crafting skill.

DISMANTLE (VARIES)

This check breaks an item down, producing raw materials *(see page 356).* An item must be inactive (or in the case of locks and traps, Disabled) before it may be Dismantled.

Dismantling an item takes a number of hours equal to the item's Complexity divided by 5 (rounded up). With success against the item's Complexity, the item is destroyed and the character gains raw materials of an appropriate type equal to 1/2 the item's value (rounded down).

With a critical success, the character gains raw materials equal to the item's value. With a critical failure, the item is destroyed but the character gains no raw materials.

IMPROVISE (1 FULL ACTION)

A character may only improvise items with a Complexity of 5D or 7D and may not attempt this check in a barren location (e.g. a prison cell or a desert). The GM must approve all Improvise checks before the roll is made (some items simply can't be improvised and certain situations prevent certain attempts).

With success against the item's Complexity, the character gains an improvised version of the item that lasts until the end of the scene or until it suffers damage, whichever comes first. All checks made with the item are untrained and the error ranges of all checks made with the item increase by 2.

With a critical success, this untrained limitation is lifted. With a critical failure, the character may not attempt to improvise the same item during this scene.

REPAIR (DOWNTIME)

This works like a Build check, except that each item is repaired at 1/2 the cost to build it (rounded down).

DISGUISE (CHA)

With this skill a character can change his appearance, or that of someone else. He can adjust features, add or conceal distinguishing marks, and alter basic body shape with padding and belts. He can mimic a specific person or just change his appearance to avoid detection. Disguise does not let a character act like someone else — that's handled with the Bluff skill.

Tools: A character without actor's props *(see page 159)* is considered untrained even when he has Disguise ranks. With access to an actor's workshop, a character's threat range increases by 3.

Knowledge: Clothing styles by region or locale; plant and animal parts that can be used as pigment; how to use a backpack to mimic a hump; how to affect a limp to walk with a concealed sword or short staff

Table 2.10: Disguises

Disguise changes...	Preparation *	Check Modifier
Small details (e.g. clothes, scars)	2d6 minutes	+0
Moderate details (e.g. skin color or texture)	3d6 minutes	–2
Large details (e.g. accent, walk)	4d6 minutes	–4
Height (up to 5% taller or shorter) **	+2d6 minutes	–4
Weight (up to 5% heavier or lighter) **	+2d6 minutes	–4
Species, close resemblance (e.g. elf posing as human) **	+1d6 minutes	–2
Species, similar resemblance (e.g. dwarf posing as elf) **	+2d6 minutes	–4
Species, little resemblance (e.g. ogre posing as dwarf) **	+4d6 minutes	–10
Species, no resemblance (e.g. drake posing as ogre)	Impossible	Impossible
Gender **	+2d6 minutes	–4
Age (per category of difference) **	+1d6 minutes	–2

* With actor's props *(see page 159)* or similar materials this time drops to 1/2 (rounded down).

** Requires actor's props

MASK (VARIES)

It takes time to build any disguise, as shown on Table 2.10: Disguises *(see page 73).*

This check has no DC; instead, the character's result becomes the DC for Notice and Search checks, which are made whenever the character draws attention or does something out of place for his disguise, or whenever the GM feels an observer's suspicion is raised. A number of modifiers apply to the character's Mask result, as shown on Table 2.10. The disguise holds up until an observer's result beats the character's, at which point the observer knows the character isn't the person he appears to be.

With a critical success, the disguise is near-perfect — the error ranges of Notice and Search checks to see through it increase by 2 per action die spent. With a critical failure, every observer who might see through the disguise does — likely at an inopportune moment — and the character may not adopt a new disguise until he moves out of the observer's sight and earshot.

HAGGLE (WIS)

Merchants are the heart and soul of the vast and thriving economies of the world. They supply armies, equip assassins, and make or break kingdoms at the drop of a coin, yet they never let their eye stray from their greatest ambition: profit.

Language: When a character shares no common tongue with the target of a Haggle check, his error range increases by 4.

Knowledge: Item values (on the open and black markets); where to find items (legally and illegally); negotiating tactics

BARGAIN (1 MINUTE)

With success against another character's Bargain result, a negotiator adjusts the asking price of an item or group of items up or down, as shown on Table 2.11: Bargaining *(see below).* Bargain checks are subject to Disposition (i.e. each negotiator's result is modified by his Disposition toward the other). Only one Bargain check is made per sale, though either party still may walk away after the new price is set.

With a buyer critical success, the sale price is set at 25% the item's street value, while a critical failure sets the price at 300% of street value. These results are inverted for a seller (300% of street value with a critical success and 25% street value with a critical failure).

Table 2.11: Bargaining

Check Result	Sale Price
Buyer wins by 10+	50% of asking price
Buyer wins by 7–9	60% of asking price
Buyer wins by 4–6	80% of asking price
Buyer wins by 1–3	90% of asking price
Tie	100% of asking price
Seller wins by 1–3	110% of asking price
Seller wins by 4–6	120% of asking price
Seller wins by 7–9	140% of asking price
Seller wins by 10+	150% of asking price

The costs listed in Chapter 4 represent common market prices, including vendor markup. When anyone other than a vendor sells an item, the asking price is automatically set to 1/2 the item's listed cost (rounded up). Selling restricted and illegal items is dangerous and buyers must first be enticed with a successful Impress/Persuade check *(see below).*

IMPRESS (CHA)

A delicate touch, a subtle word, or a brilliant performance at just the right time can change the course of history; indeed they have, as evidenced in the epic sagas of the ancient masters.

Language: When a character shares no common tongue with the target of an Impress check, his error range increases by 4.

Knowledge: Ways to invoke loyalty, confidence, and pride; how to thrive in trusting environments (e.g. functional families, uplifting faiths, and intimate courts with strong, positive personalities); famous moving speeches, art, and literature

INFLUENCE (1 MINUTE)

This check is used to nurture one character's opinion of another (either the acting character or another person he's endorsing or slandering). Influencing someone takes more time than Browbeating them but the effects are more profound. Influence checks are subject to Disposition *(see page 373).*

With success against a target's Resolve, one of the target's Disposition modifiers shifts up or down, as the acting character prefers, by an amount equal to 1/2 the difference between the results (rounded down).

With a critical success, the target's Attitude may adjust up to twice during the current scene. With a critical failure, the target closes off and may not be targeted by Influence checks again during this scene.

A character may be the target of multiple Influence checks during a single scene, though only one from each other character. Also, only the highest single shift in either direction applies (being the focus of the target's attention).

PERSUADE (1 MINUTE)

With success against a target character's Resolve, the target performs 1 action or supports 1 of the character's actions. A number of modifiers apply to this check, as shown on Table 2.12: Persuasion and Coercion *(see page 75),* and as outlined in the Disposition section *(see page 373).* A player character or villain may spend 1 action die to ignore a successful Persuade check targeting them.

With a critical success, a standard character supports the character's actions for the rest of the scene (a player character or villain must spend 3 action dice or perform/support 1 action). With a critical failure, the target closes off and may not be targeted by Persuade checks again during this scene. If the character is urging the target to commit a crime, the authorities may also be alerted.

A character may *not* be Persuaded to endanger any life (including his own), though he *may* be Coerced to do so *(see page 76)*.

INTIMIDATE (WIS)

In sharp contrast to Impress, the Intimidate skill is used to bully and malign, to threaten and demean. It's not quite as effective but when you need to adjust someone's Attitude in a hurry, there's no better option.

Language: When a character shares no common tongue with the target of an Intimidate check, his error range increases by 4.

Knowledge: Ways to invoke allegiance, fear, and anxiety; how to thrive in destructive environments (e.g. dysfunctional families, corrupting faiths, and isolating courts with callous, remote personalities); historical acts of terrorism and oppression

BROWBEAT (1 FULL ACTION)

This check is used to force a change in one character's opinion of another (either the acting character or another person he's endorsing or slandering). Browbeating someone is less effective than Influencing them, but it's also faster. Starting Disposition modifiers have no impact on this check.

With success against a target's Resolve, one of the target's Disposition modifiers shifts up or down, as the acting character prefers, by an amount equal to 1/4 the difference between the results (rounded down).

With a critical success, the target's Attitude may adjust up to twice during the current scene. With a critical failure, the target closes off and may not be targeted by Browbeat checks again during this scene.

A character may be the target of multiple Browbeat checks during a single scene, though only one from each other character. Also, only the highest single shift in either direction applies (being the focus of the target's attention).

Impressing and Intimidating Crowds

Sometimes it's important to sway or compel several targets at once. This works similarly to a team check *(see page 66)*. In the case of a mob with no clear leader, use the lowest Resolve bonus of any character in the crowd; otherwise, use the skill bonus of the most influential leader. Any results targeting the crowd affect every character in it.

***Example:* Lord Bloodpyre approaches a small band of nomadic goblins with an offer to split the spoils of a local village. The goblins are known to fiercely distrust strangers, so before he attempts to Coerce them he speaks to them in terms they'll understand — he Browbeats them. The goblin's leader, Witherbred, steps forward to speak for the others. Bloodpyre's Intimidate opposes Witherbred's Resolve.**

***Example:* Brungil addresses a group of angry villagers who've misinterpreted the blood on his weapons as that of their friends and family, whom he tried to save from a savage band of goblins. The villagers are disorganized and have no leader so Brungil's attempt to Persuade them of his innocence opposes the lowest Resolve in the mob.**

People don't like being abused and intimidation has consequences. At the end of the scene, the target's Attitude toward the character worsens by 1 grade, even if the Browbeat check is successful.

Table 2.12: Persuasion and Coercion

Proposition	Check Modifier *
Apparent Risk	
None	+4/+2
Slight (e.g. may prompt ridicule or social sanction)	+0/+0
Moderate (e.g. may prompt mild retribution or minor criminal charges)	–2/–4
Extreme (e.g. may prompt severe retribution or major criminal charges)	–4/–10
Deadly (e.g. may prompt attacks on target or their friends and family)	–10/–15
Apparent Incentive (e.g. bribes)	
Incredible (e.g. target's income for a year or offer of equal personal value)	+10/+4
Extreme (e.g. target's income for a month or offer of equal personal value)	+4/+2
Moderate (e.g. target's income for a week or offer of equal personal value)	+0/+0
Slight (e.g. target's income for a day or offer of equal personal value)	–2/–4
None	–4/–10

* The modifier before the slash applies to Persuade checks and the modifier after the slash applies to Coerce checks.

COERCE (1 FULL ACTION)

With success against a target character's Resolve, the target performs 1 action or supports 1 of the character's actions. A number of modifiers apply to this check, as shown on Table 2.12: Persuasion and Coercion *(see page 75)*. A player character or villain may spend 1 action die to ignore a successful Coerce check targeting them.

With a critical success, a standard character supports the character's actions for the rest of the scene (a player character or villain must spend 3 action dice or perform/support 1 action). With a critical failure, the target closes off and may not be targeted by Coerce checks again during this scene. If the character is urging the target to commit a crime, the authorities may also be alerted.

People don't like being used and intimidation has consequences. At the end of the scene, the target's Attitude toward the character worsens by 1 grade, even if the Coercion check is successful.

INVESTIGATE (WIS)

Power and secrets beckon, waiting to be unearthed by savvy adventurers with sharp eyes and keen intellect. This skill is crucial in their excavation, informing where to look, what to seek, and how to use what's found.

Language: When a character shares no common tongue with the target of an Investigate check, his error range increases by 4.

Knowledge: Common codes, riddles, and ruses; alphabets and symbols; common lines of questioning; famous libraries and vaults

CANVASS (VARIES)

This check is used to gather information from the local populace. Before rolling the character names a single specific subject he's investigating (such as a local cult or a recent crime). The GM may deny the check based on local opportunity, in which case the character may propose alternate lines of questioning. The time required and DC for a Canvass check is based on population density, as shown on Table 2.13: Canvassing *(see below)*. This check is also subject to Disposition *(see page 373)*.

This check has no DC; unless the character suffers a critical failure, he automatically gains 1 clue as shown on Table 2.13. With a critical success, he gains the clue in half the listed time. With a critical failure, the locals close off and may not be targeted by Canvass checks again during this scene. If the questions focus on dangerous or hostile forces, these persons or groups may also become aware of the character's inquiries and respond accordingly...

DECIPHER (VARIES)

This check is used to solve any puzzle, from the word clue left behind by a mocking villain to the code used by an elusive thieves' guild to the gem-and-clockwork portal constructed by a wandering tribe of tinkering pech. Puzzles often hide traps and locks, requiring a character to Decipher before he can Disable *(see page 79)*. Many puzzles are Complex Tasks *(see page 67)*, demanding the character locate various clues or unravel pieces of the greater mystery before solving the whole.

The GM should tailor each puzzle for the story in which it appears and ideally make solving it an unfolding adventure. The previously mentioned word clue, for example, might involve letters inscribed on the tatters of provincial flags mutilated during a peace accord at the kingdom's capital city — arranging the letters in the order that the ambassadors of each province arrived at the capital spells out the name of a chambermaid who's unwittingly delivering diseased bedding to the chambers of the royals. In this scenario, finding the letters is just the beginning. Likewise, the thieves' code could be a substitution alphabet cross-referencing the dates of the guild's greatest heists with the values of each take, and thus investigating the guild helps to decrypt the code. The pech portal might demand a gem from each of the tribe's settlements, all of which are long buried, trap-laden, and monster-infested.

Table 2.13: Canvassing

Population	Canvass Check Time	Check Modifier
None (No inhabitants; abandoned ruins, wilderness)	1d6 days	–20
Rural (1–50 inhabitants; small farm, frontier settlement)	4d6 hours	–10
Sparse (51–200 inhabitants; village, isolated hamlet)	2d6 hours	–5
Average (201–1000 inhabitants; town, independent outpost)	1d6 hours	0
Dense (1001–5000 inhabitants; large town, castle)	1d4 hours	+5
Urban (6001–25,000 inhabitants; city, port)	1d4 hours	+10
Sprawling (25,001+ inhabitants; capital city, bazaar)	1d6 hours	+20
Primary inhabitants are adversaries	×2	–10

Result	Clue Gained
Up to 15	Dubious (e.g. area where cult operates or rough description of criminal with no distinguishing characteristics)
16–30	Fruitful (e.g. location of cult's latest raid or distinguishing mark on criminal's body)
31–45	Illuminating (e.g. location of cult figure's home or detailed description of criminal)
46+	Revelatory (e.g. location of cult's temple or eyewitness account of the crime)

Table 2.14: Puzzles

Difficulty	Time	DC
Trivial	1d6 rounds	10
Challenging	1d6 minutes	15
Grueling	4d6 minutes	25
Maddening	1d6 hours	40

A puzzle is best roleplayed, though there isn't always the time or inspiration to develop one that's stimulates the players without stumping them. When a skill check is desired, the time and DC are based on the puzzle's difficulty, as shown on Table 2.14: Puzzles *(see above)*. Success finds the solution, while failure increases the error range of future attempts by 2 per action die spent.

With a critical success, the attempt takes half the listed time (rounded down). With a critical failure, the character is stumped and may not attempt to Decipher the same puzzle again during this scene.

IDENTIFY (VARIES)

Adventuring is a dangerous career. Beyond the myriad adversaries that must be put down, the wild and hostile creatures defending their homes and hunting grounds, the traps, treachery, and the very environment itself, characters must keep a wary eye on their loot. Is that a Righteous Sword of Holy Vengeance or a Backbiting Barb of Betrayal? Many found items are a mystery until they're used — or identified. This check offers a safe if not speedy alternative to discovering an item's true nature the hard way.

Identifying an item takes a number of minutes equal to the item's Complexity (if non-magical), or a number of hours equal to its Reputation Cost (if magical). This value also acts as this check's DC (note that the value is likely known only to the GM when this check is made). With success, the character accurately identifies the item, including all statistics. With failure, the error ranges of future attempts increase by 2 per action die spent.

With a critical success, the attempt takes half the listed time (rounded down). With a critical failure, the character is stumped and may not attempt to Identify the same item again during this scene.

RESEARCH (VARIES)

Rummaging through stacks of dusty tomes in a long-forgotten library, pouring over battle manuals in a warlord's training hall, and tracing the history of a dead civilization through glyphs scrawled on a jungle temple's walls — all these are examples of Research in action. Sometimes the GM will build Research checks directly into an adventure, as a necessary step forward (e.g. finding a scroll the characters need to defeat a lich); other times, a player may Research a topic when he has details but can't piece them together *(in this way a Research check becomes the inverse of a Game Master hint — see page 366)*.

A Research check's DC and the time needed to make the check are based on the information sought and where the character looks for it, as shown on Table 2.15: Researching *(see below)*. Success yields a clue, while failure increases the error range of future attempts by 2 per action die spent.

With a critical success, the attempt takes half the listed time (rounded down). With a critical failure, the character is stumped and may not attempt to Research the same topic again during this scene.

Some Research checks are doomed to failure — looking for a clue that doesn't exist, for instance. The GM is under no obligation to inform the players when a clue isn't available, before or after the check; the only true confirmation is success (and not even that if the GM decides to keep the DC secret).

Table 2.15: Researching

Circumstances	Time	DC
Research Area		
Single book, scroll, tablet, etc.	1d6 hours	10
Several books, scrolls, tablets, etc.	2d6 hours	15
Dozens of books, scrolls, tablets, etc.	4d6 hours	20
Hundreds of books, scrolls, tablets, etc.	1d6 days	25
Thousands of books, scrolls, tablets, etc.	4d6 days	30
Well organized	×1/2 base time *	–4
Disorganized	2 × base time *	+4
Desired information is...		
Linked to all other topics in area	×1/4 base time	–10
Linked to most other topics in area	×1/2 base time	–4
Linked to some other topics in area	Base time	+0
Linked to a few other topics in area	2 × base time	+4
Linked to no other topics in area	4 × base time	+10

* Applied *before* the desired information modifier

MEDICINE (INT)

Sooner or later every adventurer gets hurt. The lucky ones recover on their own; others are doomed to die without the caring hands of a trained healer. Fortunately, the weaknesses of flesh and bone are well understood, as are the ways to repair them.

Cross-Species Medicine: It's difficult to treat a character whose biology varies from common folk: –2 for animals and beasts; –4 for fey, horrors, oozes, and plants; and –10 for elementals, outsiders, spirits, and undead. Constructs may benefit from any of the following checks using the Crafting skill in place of Medicine.

Tools: A character without a doctor's bag *(see page 159)* is considered untrained even when he has Medicine ranks. With access to a doctor's workshop, a character's threat range increases by 3.

Knowledge: Anatomy (by species); poisons and diseases (natural and magical); herbs, drugs, and treatments; effective bedside manner

CALM (1 MINUTE)

This check may only be made in a peaceful location. With success (DC 15), the character heals 1 stable character of 2d6 stress damage. With a critical success, the target heals 4d6 stress damage. With a critical failure, the target suffers 1d6 stress damage. A character may only be targeted by 1 Calm check per day.

MEND (1 MINUTE)

With success (DC 15), the character heals 1 stable target of 2d6 damage (if the target's a special character, this is split evenly between subdual, vitality, and wound points and the patient distributes any uneven excess). With a critical success, the target heals 4d6 damage. With a critical failure, the target suffers 1d6 lethal damage. A character may only be targeted by 1 Mend check per day.

STABILIZE (1 FULL ACTION)

This check is used to stabilize a dying or poisoned character, staving death off long enough for more substantial treatment. It can be used two ways.

- *Stabilize Dying Character:* With success (DC 15), the character stabilizes 1 dying special character at 0 wound points (unconscious). With a critical success, the target wakes up and recovers 1d6 wound points. With a critical failure, the target dies. This check may not target a standard character.
- *Stabilize Poisoned Character:* With success against the save DC, the character freezes 1 poison victim's current Incubation Period for 2 hours — long enough for a Treatment check. With a critical success, the poison's Incubation Period freezes for 4 hours. With a critical failure, the stabilizing character is exposed to the poison.

TREATMENT (DOWNTIME)

This check is used to speed an injured character's recovery and treat serious maladies. With 2 hours of Downtime, a character can perform one of the following treatments. A character may only be targeted by 1 Treatment check per day.

- *Speed Natural Healing:* With success (DC 15), the character doubles 1 special character's natural healing rate for the day. With a critical success, the target's natural healing rate is tripled for the day. With a critical failure, the target suffers 1d6 lethal damage. This check may not target a standard character.
- *Treat Attribute Impairment:* With success (DC 15 + 5 per point of impairment with 1 attribute), the character heals 1 character of 1d4 points of temporary impairment or 1 point of permanent impairment. With a critical success, the character heals all temporary impairment or 1d4 points of permanent impairment. With a critical failure, the character inflicts 1 point of permanent impairment. In all cases, the target becomes *sickened* for 1d6 days after the treatment.
- *Treat Critical Injury:* With success (DC 20), the character decreases 1 critical injury's healing time by 1 month. With a critical success, the injury's healing time decreases by 2 months. With a critical failure, the injury's healing time increases by 2 months. In all cases, the target becomes *sickened* for 1d6 days after the treatment.
- *Treat Poison or Disease:* With success against the save DC, the character grants a +2 bonus with Fortitude saves against the contagion. With a critical success, the victim fully recovers at the end of the current Incubation Period. With a critical failure, the character is exposed to the contagion. This check may be performed up to 5 times per victim, with cumulative bonuses.

Example: Brungil falls victim to a carnivorous plant's venom. His companion, Gholin, makes a successful Treat Poison check against the venom's save DC, granting Brungil a +2 bonus with Fortitude saves against the disease. Sadly, Brungil still fails his next save against the contagion, so Gholin makes another Assist Recovery check. Once again he's successful, granting Brungil another +2 (for a total of +4). Unless Brungil manages a successful save or dies, this process may continue until Gholin affords Brungil the maximum +10 bonus against the disease. Thereafter, poor Brungil's on his own.

NOTICE (WIS)

This skill is used to *subconsciously* detect things — it comes into play whenever it's important to know whether the character sees, hears, or otherwise senses important details without looking for them. For this reason, Notice is commonly used when the *Game Master*, rather than the player, initiates such a skill check. Frequently, the GM will make Awareness checks without the player's knowledge.

Knowledge: Suspicious clothing, shapes, and actions that portend an imminent threat; terrain and shadows where enemies can hide or ambush

AWARENESS (1 FREE ACTION)

With success against a check result to obscure something (most often with the Blend, Disguise, Prestidigitation, or Sneak skill), the character becomes alert to the deception; otherwise, it becomes *hidden* from him. A character may only become alert to things he can see or hear and each Awareness check suffers a –2 penalty per visual or hearing increment beyond the first between the observer and the target. The character gains a +2 bonus if he's moderately familiar with the thing being obscured or its current location (e.g. he sees or visits it every week), or a +4 bonus if he's intimately familiar (e.g. he sees or visits it every day).

With a critical success, the character remains alert to the deception until the end of the current scene or until the GM determines that the circumstances have changed enough to warrant a new Awareness check. With a critical failure, the deception falls into the character's "blind spot" until the end of the current scene and is only detected before then if someone else points it out.

The GM determines the frequency of Awareness checks, based primarily on the needs and challenges of the story. They may come up as often as once per minute or even once per round in a tense scene; other times they may only come up once every ten minutes, once an hour, or even less often.

PRESTIDIGITATION (DEX)

A favorite of thieves and gamblers, Prestidigitation is used to conceal actions and items. Some of its most popular applications are disabling traps, picking pockets, and conveying secret messages by gesture.

Knowledge: Trap components and ways to bypass and disable them; flashy tricks (e.g. pulling a coin from behind the ear and "knowing someone's card"); pickpocket techniques

CONCEAL ACTION (1 FREE ACTION)

With success against an observer's Notice or Search *(see pages 78 and 81),* the character conceals one of his actions from view; otherwise, the observer becomes alert to the action. If the action involves an item, it must be at least 2 Sizes smaller than the character. A number of modifiers apply to this check, as shown on Table 2.7: Blending, Sneaking, and Concealing *(see page 71).*

With a critical success, the character's action fades completely into the background — the error ranges of Notice and Search checks to detect it increase by 2 per action die spent. With a critical failure, every observer who might notice the action does — likely at an inopportune moment — and the character may not conceal further actions until he moves out of the observer's sight and earshot.

DISABLE (VARIES)

This check disables an item, deactivating and/or neutralizing it. It's commonly used to open locks and bypass traps. A character without thieves' tools *(see page 160)* is considered untrained even when he has Prestidigitation ranks.

Disabling an item takes a number of full actions equal to the item's Complexity divided by 10 (rounded up). Some locks and traps are Disabled as Complex Tasks, as shown on Table 4.8: Locks & Traps *(see page 161).* With success against the item's Complexity, the item is disabled and must be armed or activated again before it may be triggered. A Disabled item may be Dismantled *(see page 73).*

With a critical success, the item is disabled in half the time (rounded up). With a critical failure, the trap may be triggered *(see page 160)* and the character may not attempt to bypass the same item again during this scene.

STASH (1 HALF ACTION)

This check is used to hide an item on a person or in a location. There is no DC; instead, the character's result becomes the DC for Notice and Search checks, which are made whenever someone searches the person or area where the item is stashed, or when the GM feels an observer might stumble onto the item. A number of modifiers apply to this check, as shown on Table 2.7: Blending, Sneaking, and Concealing *(see page 71).* The stash result holds up until an observer's result beats the character's, at which point the observer finds the item.

With a critical success, the hiding place is near-perfect — the error ranges of Notice and Search checks to see through it increase by 2 per action die spent. With a critical failure, every observer who might find the item does — likely at an inopportune moment — and the character may not attempt to Stash the item again until he moves out of the observer's sight and earshot.

Table 2.16: Concentrating

Circumstances	DC Modifier
Distraction	
Mild (e.g. missed with an attack, adjacent shouting or chanting, 1-die Nature's Fury Complication)	+4
Moderate (e.g. up to 10 damage, explosion within 60 ft., 2-die Nature's Fury Complication)	+10
Extreme (e.g. 11–25 damage, explosion within 30 ft., 3-die Nature's Fury Complication)	+15
Incredible (e.g. 26+ damage, explosion within 10 ft., 4-die Nature's Fury Complication)	+20
Character is...	
Bleeding	+4
Fatigued	+4 per grade
Flanked	+4
Shaken	+4 per grade

RESOLVE (CON)

Keeping one's cool under pressure — especially during intense situations like combat — can turn the tide of battle. It can ensure focus while casting a critical spell, steady hands while stabilizing a dying ally, or quick thinking while disabling a trap. Resolve is also helpful during Downtime, allowing a character to make the most of his repose.

Knowledge: Leisure spots (raucous and serene, by region); meditation techniques and ways to ignore pain

CONCENTRATE (1 FREE ACTION)

A character must make 1 Concentrate check per round when the GM determines that his current action(s) are threatened by one or more distractions. With success (DC 10), the character's action(s) continue without pause; otherwise, he must start them again from scratch. A number of modifiers apply to this check, as shown on Table 2.16: Concentrating *(see above)*.

With a critical success, the character's current actions may not be interrupted again. With a critical failure, the character is unable to attempt the same actions again until away from the distraction(s) for at least 1 minute.

RELAX (DOWNTIME)

With at least 10 minutes to indulge in soothing activities in a peaceful location, a stable character can attempt to hasten his stress damage recovery. With success (DC 15), the character's stress damage healing rate doubles for the next hour. With a critical success, the character's stress damage healing rate triples for the next hour. With a critical failure, the character suffers 1d6 stress damage. A character may only attempt 1 Relax check per day.

RIDE (DEX)

The Ride skill is used to control any mount or vehicle.

Focuses: When a character gains his first rank in Ride and for every 4 full ranks he gains in total, he learns 1 focus from the following list: Air Vehicles, Flying Mounts, Land Vehicles, Riding Mounts, Swimming Mounts, Water Vehicles. The GM may add additional focuses as the campaign warrants. Each Ride skill check uses only 1 focus and all checks made without the appropriate focus are untrained *(see page 63)*.

Knowledge: Mount species and vehicle types, plus their capabilities and limits; stunts and tricks; trade and travel routes (safest and fastest, by region)

MANEUVER (1 HALF ACTION)

Most of the time, no skill check is required to control a mount or vehicle. This check comes into play when the character attempts a risky maneuver, especially during combat or another dangerous situation.

A character may make a Maneuver check to perform any Acrobatics or Athletics check except Climb or Tumble while on a mount or using a vehicle, applying the additional modifiers shown on Table 2.17: Maneuvers *(see page 81)*. Certain animals may not be able to perform certain maneuvers, depending on their NPC qualities *(see page 230)*. A mounted character's statistics merge with those of the animal *(see page 215)* and these combined stats are used when determining the effects of any maneuver.

With success, the mount or vehicle performs the desired check; otherwise, the character loses control and must make another half action Maneuver check (DC 20) to regain it. An out-of-control animal is directed by the GM, while an out-of-control self-propelled vehicle moves its current Speed in a random direction, per the Deviation Diagram *(see page 216)*. If this causes the vehicle to travel opposite its original course, it spins in place and comes to a stop at the end of the current round.

The effects of critical success or failure are also determined by the desired check, though the GM may alternately spend 2 action dice to cause the mount or vehicle to crash into the scenery, suffering 1d6 lethal damage per 10 ft. of current Speed. Each character on the mount or in the vehicle also suffers this damage — or half as much, rounded down, with a successful Reflex save (DC 15).

An animal allowed to roam freely uses its own Acrobatics and Athletics skill bonuses but the GM, rather than the player, determines its actions and movement.

Table 2.17: Maneuvers

Circumstances	Check Modifier
Check Attempted	
Acrobatics/Balance	–4
Acrobatics/Break Fall	–10
Acrobatics/Jump	+0
Athletics/Push Limit	+0
Athletics/Swim	–4 (unless the animal is native to water)
Takes animal within 10 ft. of open flame	–10
Takes animal though open flame	–20
Maneuvering Room	
Open (e.g. open plain, quiet road, wide canyon)	+4
Close (e.g. shallow stream, village street, narrow canyon)	+0
Crowded (e.g. light forest, quiet city street, courtyard)	–4
Tight (e.g. jungle, busy city street, cave or large dungeon hall)	–10
Animal is...	
Moving faster than 1/2 its Speed (rounded down)	–4
Wild *(see page 169)*	–10

Example: Brungil directs his pony to make a running horizontal Jump onto a rising drawbridge. He needs to clear 15 ft. to avoid an unfortunate dip in the moat below (currently filled with flaming oil). His Maneuver check result is 17, but he suffers a –10 penalty due to the close fire. This translates to 12 ft. of distance. Happily, the pony has a Speed of 40 ft. (1/3 higher than that of an average human), so it clears an additional 4 ft. (for a total of 16 ft.) — just enough to clear the bridge and prepare for a charge into the garrison's militia.

Example: Hours after leaving Lord Bloodpyre's cherished shaman totem a smoldering husk in the courtyard of one of his garrisons, Brungil is still being pursued by the ogre's cavalry. He needs to press his pony as hard as he can to make it safely back to Valespire. Sounds like an Athletics/Push Limit check. He scores a critical success with a Maneuver result of 26, which isn't further modified (Brungil's technically moving across open terrain but his mount is also moving faster than 1/2 its Speed). This offers him either +4 MPH to Speed for 1 hour or +2 MPH to Speed for 2 hours. He opts for the greater immediate Speed, planning to Push his pony again when it runs out. He'll owe the little beast a special treat when they make it home safely.

SEARCH (INT)

This skill is used to *deliberately* detect things — it comes into play whenever it's important to know whether the character sees, hears, or otherwise senses important details while looking for them. For this reason, Search is commonly used when the *player*, rather than the GM, initiates such a skill check.

Knowledge: Effective hiding places and diversions; the first places people look for things; how to search an area without anyone knowing you were there; ways to hide traps and caches

PERCEPTION (1 FULL ACTION)

With success against a check result to obscure something (most often with the Blend, Disguise, Prestidigitation, or Sneak skills), the character becomes alert to the deception; otherwise, it becomes *hidden* from him. A character may only become alert to things he can see or hear and each Awareness check suffers a –2 penalty per visual or hearing increment beyond the first between the observer and the target. The character gains a +2 bonus if he's moderately familiar with the thing being obscured or its current location (e.g. he sees or visits it every week), or a +4 bonus if he's intimately familiar (he sees or visits it every day).

With a critical success, the character remains alert to the deception until the end of the current scene or until the GM determines that the circumstances have changed enough to warrant a new Perception check. With a critical failure, the deception falls into the character's "blind spot" until the end of the current scene and is only detected before then if someone else points it out.

The GM determines the frequency of Perception checks, based primarily on the needs and challenges of the story. They may come up as often as once per minute or even once per round in a tense scene; other times they may only come up once every ten minutes, once an hour, or even less often.

SENSE MOTIVE (WIS)

This skill is used to detect lies. Seeing through disguises and spotting forgeries are covered by the Notice and Search skills.

Knowledge: Common deceptions (e.g. famous military ploys, popular grifts); "tells" (subconscious signs that betray lies); things people want (and want to hear), based on their background

DETECT LIE (1 FREE ACTION)

With success against a Bluff result *(see page 72)*, the character sees through the lie. Disposition has no impact on this check.

With a critical success, the character gains a keen sense of the target and automatically sees through his lies until the end of the current scene or until the GM determines that the circumstances have changed enough to warrant a new Detect Lie check. With a critical failure, the character buys into the falsehood until the end of the current scene and is only alerted before then if someone else points it out.

SNEAK (DEX)

This skill is used to *deliberately* avoid detection — it comes into play whenever it's important to know whether observers see, hear, or otherwise sense a character who's trying to escape discovery. For this reason, Sneak is commonly used when the *player*, rather than the GM, initiates such a skill check.

Knowledge: Effective hiding places and diversions; the first places people look for things; how to search an area without anyone knowing you were there; ways to hide traps and caches

HIDE (1 FULL ACTION)

With success against an observer's Notice or Search *(see pages 78 and 81)*, the character becomes *hidden* from the observer (if he wasn't already); otherwise, the observer becomes alert to the character (and potentially his location, if the GM thinks it's apparent). A number of modifiers apply to this check, as shown on Table 2.7: Blending, Sneaking, and Concealing *(see page 71)*.

As part of a Hide check, the character may move up to his full Speed, though doing so makes him easier to detect, as shown on Table 2.7.

With a critical success, the character fades completely into the background — the error ranges of Notice and Search checks to detect him increase by 2 per action die spent. With a critical failure, every observer who might notice the character does — likely at an inopportune moment — and the character may not escape detection again until he moves out of the observer's sight and earshot.

The GM determines the frequency of Hide checks, based primarily on the needs and challenges of the story. They may come up as often as once per minute or even once per round in a tense scene; other times they may only come up once every ten minutes, once an hour, or even less often.

SURVIVAL (WIS)

A character at one with nature can make his home almost anywhere, at least in the short term. He's also a master at animal husbandry and the most dangerous of all games — hunting sentient prey.

Knowledge: Plants and animals (by region); animal behavior; geography and navigation (by region); trail signs; weather prediction

BREED ANIMAL (DOWNTIME)

A character may breed any animal with a male and female of the species. Many common fantasy mounts are provided on Table 4.15: Mounts *(see page 170)*. The character must have a combined Survival skill bonus + Career Level of at least the animal's Breeding value.

With success (DC 20), the parent animals couple and the mother gives birth to standard NPC offspring after the duration shown in the Table 4.15 Breeding column. A critical success yields special NPC offspring and a critical failure results in complications that prevent the same parents from coupling again.

FORAGE (4 HOURS)

With success against the DC listed on Table 2.18: Foraging *(see below)*, the character finds adequate shelter for natural healing, as well as enough perishable food and water for his party for 1 day (like any other perishable, this food and water spoils at the end of the adventure). With failure, no food or water is found and natural healing decreases to 1/2 normal (rounded down).

With a critical success, the character finds perishable food, water, and shelter for the next week, or until the party moves into new terrain. With a critical failure, the party can't Forage again for 1 week within 20 miles of their current location.

Table 2.18: Foraging

Circumstances	DC/DC Modifier
Check Attempted	
Fertile (forest/jungle)	10
Harsh (aquatic, caverns/mountains, swamp)	15
Barren (arctic, desert, plains)	20
Travel Speed	
Per Push Limit benefit	+4

TRACK (VARIES)

This check is used to hunt, regardless of the prey. Outdoors, a character makes 1 Track check per mile; indoors, the distance per check decreases to 100 ft. The GM may call for additional checks when the conditions of the hunt change (e.g. when the prey backtracks or tries to hide his trail, when the prey's trail crosses another, when it starts to rain, etc.).

With success against a target's Blend or Sneak result, as appropriate, the character remains on the target's trail; otherwise, he loses it. The character permanently loses a trail if he fails 2 Track checks in a row. A number of modifiers apply to this check, as shown on Table 2.19: Tracking *(see page 83)*.

Table 2.19: Tracking

Circumstances	Check Modifier
Hunter	
Moving faster than 1/2 Speed (rounded down)	–2
Moving faster than full Speed	–4
Prey	
Smaller than Medium	–2 per Size
Larger than Medium	+2 per Size
Moving faster than 1/2 Speed (rounded down)	+2
Moving faster than full Speed	+4
Bleeding	+4
Terrain	
Soft (e.g. sand, mud, snow)	+4
Yielding (e.g. loose dirt, wet grass, gravel)	+2
Firm (e.g. lawn, field, forest, thick rug, dusty floor)	+0
Hard (e.g. rock, cobblestones, hardwood floor)	–2
Age/Condition of Trail	
Per day since trail was left	–2 (max. –10)
Per hour of rain or snow since trail was left	–2 (max. –10)

With a critical success, the character covers twice the expected distance (i.e. 2 miles outdoors or 200 ft. indoors), while the prey remains at the same Speed. With a critical failure, the character permanently loses the prey.

TRAIN ANIMAL (DOWNTIME)

To train an animal, a character must have a combined Survival skill bonus + Career Level of at least the animal's Training value, as shown on Table 4.15: Mounts *(see page 170)*.

With a successful 1-month check (DC 20), the character trains a wild animal. A trained animal can be ridden, accepts commands, and may receive advanced training. With a critical success, the animal is trained and automatically gains 1 advanced training benefit. With a critical failure the character turns the animal against him and may not attempt to train it again in the current year.

Advanced training also involves a 1-month Train Animal check (DC 20). With success, the animal gains 1 of the following benefits.

- *Attribute Training:* +1 to any attribute
- *Combat Training:* +1 to any Trait grade (Initiative, Attack, Defense, Resilience, or Health)
- *NPC Quality:* Any 1: *Beguiling, bright, cagey, charge attack, favored foes* (1 enemy), *fearless, feral, ferocity, frenzy I (frenzy II* and *frenzy III* cannot be trained), *improved stability, knockback, light sleeper, menacing threat, monstrous attack* (1 grade), *monstrous defense* (1 grade), *natural attack* (any 1 the animal can perform but doesn't have, or improving any 1 it already has by 1 grade), *rend, swift attack, tough* (1 grade), *treacherous, tricky* (any 1 trick the animal can perform), *unnerving*
- *Skill Training:* +1 to any Signature Skill grade (Acrobatics, Athletics, Blend, Intimidate, Notice, Resolve, Search, Sense Motive, Sneak, Survival, or Tactics)
- *Speed Training:* +5 ft. to any Speed the animal already has

With a critical success, the animal gains 2 benefits. With a critical failure, the animal reaches its peak for the moment and may not receive further advanced training in the current year.

An animal may gain each advanced training benefit no more than 4 times, and no training may raise any score above the maximum allowed during normal NPC creation. The GM may determine that certain animals can't gain certain benefits.

TACTICS (INT)

Study any famed warlord and it becomes clear they all share a common trait — the ability to leverage the odds in their favor. Through insightful observation and careful planning they elevate battle to an art form, delivering death blows while their opponents are still scrambling for their sheaths.

Knowledge: Military history, ranks, signals, insignia, and etiquette; famous battle strategies; strategic game theory (e.g. chess, go)

AMBUSH (1 MINUTE)

The roll for an Ambush check is not made when the ambush is prepared, but rather when it's sprung.

With success against a target character or group's Notice, Search, or Sense Motive (as appropriate), a surprise round happens with the targets unaware of your party *(see page 203)*.

With a critical success, each member of your party also gains 1d6 sneak attack damage per action die spent *(see page 211)*. This sneak attack damage applies only during the surprise round. With a critical failure, each member of your party suffers an Initiative penalty of –2 per action die spent.

OUTMANEUVER (1 MINUTE)

With success against a target character's Tactics, the target's error range increases by 2 during all opposed checks until the end of the current scene.

With a critical success, the target's error range increases by an additional 1 per action die spent. With a critical failure, your error range increases by 1 per action die spent until the end of the current scene.

A character may be targeted with this check only once per scene.

FEATS

Feats let you customize your character, granting special abilities or bonuses to existing abilities. Characters may gain feats from 3 sources.

- Specialty grants 1 feat *(see page 21).*
- Career Level grants several feats *(see page 27).*
- Class sometimes grants either a choice of feats or a specific feat.

PREREQUISITES

When a character gains his choice of feats (generally from level or a class), he must meet all of a feat's prerequisites before he can take it. Many feats have other, often less powerful feats as prerequisites, ensuring that characters gain access to more advanced abilities as they specialize.

Example: Brungil is interested in the Rage Supremacy feat. He must acquire both Rage Basics and then Rage Mastery before he may take the Rage Supremacy feat.

When a character gains a specific feat, that feat's prerequisites are waived. If the character already has the feat, he instead chooses 1 feat from the same feat tree as described above.

Example: Tanan has the Armor Basics feat (a Basic Combat feat). When he gains Level 2 of the Lancer class, it grants him the Armor Basics feat again. He gets to choose another Basic Combat feat but must meet the prerequisites of any feat he chooses.

If a character loses one or more prerequisites for a feat — due to attribute penalties, for example — he keeps the feat but may not benefit from it or use its abilities until he regains all of its prerequisites.

RESTRICTED AND TEMPORARY FEATS

Sometimes feats come with a catch.

RESTRICTED FEATS

Sometimes a feat suffers from specific limitations (e.g. a feat's abilities may only apply to attacks with a specific weapon, or to skill checks with a specific item). Such a feat is "restricted" and while it may be used to meet the prerequisites of other feats any limitations that apply to it also apply to each feat for which it's a prerequisite. Also, a restricted feat may never be used to meet expert class requirements.

Example: Gholin gains the *fell hand* ability from his Priest class, which grants him the benefits of the All Out Attack and Cleave Basics feats when using his ritual weapon (a war hammer). Gholin later uses this Cleave Basics feat to gain Cleave Mastery but he may *only* use Cleave Mastery with his war hammer.

TEMPORARY FEATS

A temporary feat only lasts for a limited period of time. A character must meet all prerequisites for a temporary feat before he may take it, and he can't gain any temporary feat with the same name as a feat he already has.

Temporary feats may be used to meet the prerequisites of other temporary feats but may never be used to meet the prerequisites for any permanent feat, or to meet expert class requirements.

EDGE

Special characters sometimes build momentum, called Edge, and can use it to pull off amazing results that standard characters can only look upon with awe. Each special character may accumulate up to 5 Edge at one time and all Edge is lost at the end of each combat. Edge may be spent to use certain exclusive tricks, actions, and abilities.

FEAT TREES

Fantasy Craft groups feats into categories called 'trees.' Each tree includes a range of feats relating to one area of heroic expertise.

Basic Combat Feats ***(pages 85–87)*****:** Focus on combat fundamentals and tactics

Melee Combat Feats ***(pages 87–91)*****:** Focus on melee weapons

Ranged Combat Feats ***(page 92)*****:** Focus on ranged weapons

Unarmed Combat Feats ***(pages 93–94)*****:** Focus on martial arts and natural attacks

Chance Feats ***(page 94–95)*****:** Focus on extraordinary luck — good for you and bad for others

Covert Feats ***(pages 95–96)*****:** Focus on stealth, evasion, and subterfuge

Gear Feats ***(pages 96–99)*****:** Focus on equipment

Skill Feats ***(pages 99)*****:** Focus on skill use and character advancement

Species Feats ***(pages 99–105)*****:** Focus on heritage and unusual racial abilities

Spellcasting Feats ***(pages 105–107)*****:** Focus on spell use

Style Feats ***(pages 107–108)*****:** Focus on savoir-faire and social interaction

Terrain Feats ***(pages 108–109)*****:** Focus on using the environment to your advantage

FEAT DESCRIPTIONS

After its title and flavor summary, a feat description includes some or all of these entries.

Prerequisites: You must meet these requirements before you can take the feat.

- *Level 1 only:* The feat may only be gained during character creation (at Career Level 1). You do not lose the feat after gaining additional levels.
- *Species:* The feat may only be gained if your Species is listed.
- *Casting Level 1+:* The feat may only be taken if you have at least 1 level in a class that grants Casting Levels.

Benefit: This describes how the feat affects you and/or what it allows you to do. When a feat ability requires a numerical advantage (e.g. "2-to-1"), you may only use it if together you, your teammates, and your allies *physically* outnumber your opponents by at least the listed ratio. A feat may also grant one or more of the following.

- *Grapple Benefit:* A benefit you may choose with a successful Grapple action *(see page 219)*.
- *Stance:* A stance you can assume *(see page 204)*.
- *Trick:* A trick you can use in the listed circumstances or with the listed action or gear *(see page 221)*.

Special: This entry lists important information not covered elsewhere in the feat description.

BASIC COMBAT FEATS

Every combatant can benefit from this broad array of essential martial training.

ARMOR BASICS

You're quite comfortable in armor.

Benefit: While you wear armor, its Defense penalty drops by 1, its ACP drops by 1, and its Speed penalty drops by 5 ft. (in all cases, minimum 0).

ARMOR MASTERY

You instinctively protect vulnerable spots.

Prerequisites: Armor Basics

Benefit: While you wear armor, its DR increases by 1 and you may not be targeted with Coup de Grace actions.

ARMOR SUPREMACY

You're as comfortable in armor as a turtle in his shell.

Prerequisites: Armor Mastery

Benefit: While you wear armor, its DR increases by an additional 1 (total 2) and you're immune to sneak attack damage.

CHARGING BASICS

You sometimes hurl yourself into the enemy, unleashing devastating fury.

Benefit: Your Speed increases by 5 ft. and you gain a trick.

Charge (Run Trick): You may make 1 free attack at any point during your movement (ignoring adjacency for that attack only). You may use this ability a number of times per combat equal to your starting action dice.

CHARGING MASTERY

You're a raging, slashing bull on the battlefield.

Prerequisites: Charging Basics

Benefit: When you Charge, you may make up to 2 free attacks, each at any point during your movement.

CHARGING SUPREMACY

You're the moving center of a sticky red haze.

Prerequisites: Charging Mastery

Benefit: While Charging, you may roll damage twice, keeping the result you prefer.

COMBAT FOCUS

Your sense of timing is deadly accurate.

Benefit: You may double one of your attribute bonuses for a single attack, damage roll, or save. You may use this ability a number of times per scene equal to the number of Basic Combat feats you have.

COMBAT INSTINCTS

You react instinctively to fresh opportunities.

Benefit: Once per round when an adjacent opponent attacks you and misses, you gain a free attack against him. If this attack hits, it inflicts only 1/2 damage (rounded up).

COMBAT VIGOR

You shrug aside even punishing blows.

Benefit: You gain 1 additional vitality per Career Level and you lose 2 *fatigued* grades at the end of each scene (rather than the normal 1).

CONTEMPT

You haven't the time for lesser foes!

Benefit: Once per round, you may make a free attack against a standard character. You may use this ability a number of times per combat equal to your starting action dice.

ELUSIVE

You deftly avoid many attacks.

Benefit: At the start of your Initiative Count you may accept a penalty with your attack and skill checks of up to –4 to gain an equal dodge bonus to your Defense until the start of your next Initiative Count.

EXPERT DISARM

That's *your* weapon now...

Benefit: You gain a +4 bonus with Disarm attack checks and when you successfully disarm an opponent you may either choose the square in which his weapon lands or (if you're adjacent to the opponent) catch and arm the weapon as a free action. Also, you don't become *flat-footed* when you fail a Disarm action.

GREAT FORTITUDE

You're one tough customer.

Benefit: Your base Fortitude save bonus increases by +3. You also gain 4 extra wound points.

IRON WILL

Your strength of will is legendary.

Benefit: Your base Will save bonus increases by +3. Also, once per scene as a free action, you may shrug off 1 *fatigued* or *shaken* grade.

LIGHTNING REFLEXES

You have the speed and grace of a mighty predator!

Benefit: Your base Reflex save bonus increases by +3. You may also roll twice when making Initiative checks, keeping the result you prefer.

QUICK DRAW

You juggle weapons like witty people juggle quips.

Benefit: Twice per round, you may Handle an Item as a free action.

SNAKE STRIKE

It's worth it just for the shock that creeps across their bloody faces.

Prerequisites: Quick Draw

Benefit: Once per opponent per combat, as a free action, you may draw 1 weapon you haven't used during the current combat and use it to Feint 1 opponent. With success, your attacks inflict 1 die of sneak attack damage until end of the current round.

SURGE OF SPEED

Your moments *count.*

Benefit: Once per round you may take 1 additional non-attack half action as a free action. You may use this ability a number of times per session equal to your starting action dice.

TWO-WEAPON FIGHTING

You fight most effectively with weapons in both hands.

Benefit: At the start of your Initiative Count when you're armed with two 1-handed weapons you may accept a –2 penalty with your attack and skill checks until the start of your next Initiative Count. Once during your current Initiative Count you may take a half action to make 1 Standard Attack with each of those weapons.

TWO-WEAPON STYLE

It's like each hand — and weapon — has a mind of its own.

Prerequisites: Two-Weapon Fighting

Benefit: At the start of your Initiative Count when you're armed with two 1-handed weapons you may accept a –5 penalty with your attack and skill checks until the start of your next Initiative Count. Once during your current Initiative Count you may take a full action to make 2 Standard Attacks with each of those weapons. If any of your attacks miss this round, you become flat-footed at the end of your current Initiative Count.

WOLF PACK BASICS

Controlled chaos is your best friend.

Benefit: You gain an additional +2 bonus when attacking a *flanked* opponent (total +4).

WOLF PACK MASTERY

You spot every opening.

Prerequisites: Wolf Pack Basics

Benefit: You inflict 1 die of sneak attack damage when attacking a *flanked* opponent. Also, an opponent becomes *flanked* when you and any teammate are both adjacent to him in any configuration.

WOLF PACK SUPREMACY

You don't leave much for the next guy. You're greedy that way.

Prerequisites: Wolf Pack Mastery

Benefit: Your threat range increases by 1 and you inflict 1 additional die of sneak attack damage when attacking a *flanked* opponent (total 2 sneak attack dice).

MELEE COMBAT FEATS

Skill at arms is amongst the most common and important advantages a fantasy adventurer can nurture.

ALL-OUT ATTACK

You hit hard. *Really* hard.

Benefit: At the start of your Initiative Count you may accept a penalty with your attack and skill checks of up to –4 to gain an insight bonus with melee damage rolls equal to twice that number until the start of your next Initiative Count. If any of your attacks miss this round, you become *flat-footed* at the end of your current Initiative Count.

AXE BASICS

The bite of your axe isn't limited to the reach of your arm.

Prerequisites: Edged forte

Benefit: When you wield an axe it gains *hurl* and you gain a stance.

Punish the Defiant (Stance): Opponents who haven't moved since your Initiative Count last round are denied their Dexterity bonus to Defense against your melee attacks.

AXE MASTERY

First the shield, then the squishy thing behind it!

Prerequisites: Axe Basics

Benefit: When you wield a 1-handed axe it gains *bleed* and when you wield a 2-handed axe its gains *guard* +2. Also, you gain a trick.

Sundering Chop (Axe Attack Trick): Your attack also inflicts the same damage on 1 piece of gear on the target's person (your choice).

AXE SUPREMACY

Mortal man or mighty oak — your sweeping blade cuts them all down with ease.

Prerequisites: Axe Mastery

Benefit: Your Strength score rises by 1 and you gain a trick.

Cleave in Twain (Axe Attack Trick): If your target is a standard character with a lower Strength score than yours, he immediately fails his Damage save (damage isn't rolled). You may use this trick once per round.

CLEAVE BASICS

With just a taste of blood, your blade's thirst becomes legendary.

Benefit: Once per round, when one of your melee attacks kills an opponent or knocks him out, you may immediately make another Standard Attack with the same weapon as a free action.

CLEAVE MASTERY

You cut through foes like gory stacks of cordwood.

Prerequisites: Cleave Basics

Benefit: Your melee threat range against standard characters increases by 1. Also, you may use your Cleave Basics feat ability any number of times per round.

CLEAVE SUPREMACY

There is naught but a bloody trail of splintered bone and gristle in your wake.

Prerequisites: Cleave Mastery

Benefit: You activate melee critical hits against standard characters for 1 less action die (minimum 0). Also, each time one of your melee attacks kills an opponent or knocks him out, you may move 5 ft. before taking the additional attack, so long as the total distance you travel each round does not exceed your Speed.

CLUB BASICS

You *definitely* bring the beat down.

Prerequisites: Blunt forte

Benefit: Each of your club attacks may inflict your choice of lethal or subdual damage instead of the weapon's normal damage (no penalty or damage decrease occurs). Also, you gain a stance.

Driving Stance (Stance): Each time you hit an adjacent opponent with a melee attack, they're pushed 5 ft. away from you (assuming there's an empty square behind them). If they're pushed, you may move into the square they previously occupied.

CLUB MASTERY

One look at you and people start to recall urgent appointments elsewhere.

Prerequisites: Club Basics

Benefit: When holding a readied club you gain a +4 gear bonus with Intimidate checks. Also, you gain a trick.

Brained (Club Attack Trick): This trick may only be used when inflicting subdual damage. If the target fails his save against subdual damage, he instead fails 2 saves.

CLUB SUPREMACY

You're like an earthquake — a thunderous, explosive, unstoppable force of nature.

Prerequisites: Club Mastery

Benefit: When you wield a 1-handed club it gains *lure* and when you wield a 2-handed club its Reach increases by 1. Also, you gain a trick.

Earth Shaker (Club Trip Trick): You may Trip as a full-action, targeting all opponents within 10 ft. You roll only once while each opponent rolls to resist separately.

DARTING WEAPON

Your strikes are almost too fast to follow.

Benefit: At the start of your Initiative Count when you're armed with a single melee weapon, you may accept a –2 penalty with your attack and skill checks until the start of your next Initiative Count. Once during that round you may take a half action to make 2 Standard Attacks with that weapon.

FENCING BASICS

Your swift movements offer no respite.

Prerequisites: Edged forte

Benefit: Once per round, you may make a free attack with a fencing blade against an adjacent *flat-footed* character. You inflict only 1/2 normal damage with this attack (rounded up). Also, you gain a stance.

Work the Line (Stance): Each time an adjacent opponent attacks you and misses, you may move 5 ft. and draw the opponent into the square you previously occupied. Also, each time an adjacent opponent moves away from you, you may immediately move into the square he just left.

FENCING MASTERY

Your attackers pay in blood — and tears.

Prerequisites: Fencing Basics

Benefit: Each of your fencing blade attacks may inflict your choice of lethal or stress damage instead of the weapon's normal damage (no penalty or damage decrease occurs). Also, you gain a trick.

En Garde! (Fencing Blade Total Defense Trick): Each opponent who moves into a square adjacent to you must make a Reflex save (DC 10 + your Dex modifier + the number of Melee Combat feats you have) or be automatically hit by your fencing blade.

FENCING SUPREMACY

You play with your foes like a cat... until you get bored. Then you do that *other* thing cats do.

Prerequisites: Fencing Mastery

Benefit: Your Dexterity score rises by 1 and you gain a trick.

Touche! (Fencing Blade Attack Trick): If your target is a standard character with a lower Dexterity score than yours, he immediately fails his Damage save (damage isn't rolled). You may use this trick once per round.

FLAIL BASICS

Usually there's a blur, and then a thunk, and then the fight's over.

Prerequisites: Blunt forte

Benefit: Once per round you may make a free attack with a flail against an adjacent *flat-footed* character. You suffer a –4 penalty with this attack. Also, you gain a stance.

Whirling Serpent (Stance): You gain a bonus with your melee attack checks and damage rolls equal to the number of successful melee attacks you made last round. Opponents may not Anticipate your actions and you may not take move actions (though you may still take Bonus 5-ft. Steps as normal).

FLAIL MASTERY

Your approach is simple: speed, versatility, and an unbelievable number of strikes!

Prerequisites: Flail Basics

Benefit: You may use a flail to perform club or garrote tricks. Also, you gain a trick.

Thresher Spin (Flail Attack Trick): If this attack hits it counts as 2 melee hits made this round. You may use this trick up to twice per round.

FLAIL SUPREMACY

In your hands the humble flail can topple kings.

Prerequisites: Flail Mastery

Benefit: Once per round you may immediately make a free attack with a flail against an opponent who moves into a square adjacent to you. You suffer a –4 penalty with this attack. Also, you gain a trick.

Leaping Arc (Flail Attack Trick): You may substitute your Acrobatics (Dex) bonus in place of your melee attack bonus. If the attack misses you become *flat-footed* at the end of your Initiative Count. You may use this trick as many times per combat as you have Melee Combat feats.

FLASHING WEAPON

That blur across their vision? Yeah, that's your weapon.

Prerequisites: Darting Weapon

Benefit: At the start of your Initiative Count when you're armed with a single melee weapon, you may accept a –5 penalty with your attack and skill checks until the start of your next Initiative Count. Once during your current Initiative Count you may take a full action to make 4 Standard Attacks with that weapon. If any of your attacks miss this round, you become *flat-footed* at the end of your current Initiative Count.

GREATSWORD BASICS

You handle even the largest of blades like a delicate dance partner.

Prerequisites: Edged forte

Benefit: When you wield a greatsword it gains *guard +2*. Also, you gain a stance.

Overpowering Force (Stance): When you use a 2-handed melee weapon to hit an opponent who hasn't moved since your Initiative Count last round, you inflict the weapon's maximum damage (sneak attack damage and other random bonuses are rolled normally). You may not take move actions (though you may still take 5-ft. Bonus Steps as normal).

GREATSWORD MASTERY

Even the largest of blades is like a graceful feather to you.

Prerequisites: Greatsword Basics

Benefit: You may use a greatsword to perform hammer and sword tricks. Also, you gain a trick.

Blade Wall (Greatsword Total Defense Trick): Each opponent who tries to move into a square adjacent to you must make a Will save (DC 10 + your Str modifier + the number of Melee Combat feats you have) or end their movement in the previous square.

GREATSWORD SUPREMACY

You sweep foes aside like a deranged windmill.

Prerequisites: Greatsword Mastery

Benefit: Your Strength score rises by 1 and you gain a trick.

Spiral Cutter (Greatsword Attack Trick): You may make a single attack check with a –4 penalty against every character within 10 ft. You become *flat-footed* at the end of your Initiative Count. You may use this trick once per round.

HAMMER BASICS

Your crushing blows reshape the battlefield.

Prerequisites: Blunt forte

Benefit: When you wield a hammer it gains *AP 2* and you gain a stance.

Turn the Millstone (Stance): Each time you hit an adjacent opponent with a 2-handed melee weapon, you may also move them into any empty square adjacent to you.

HAMMER MASTERY

Castle walls? Castle guards? Meh. Same difference.

Prerequisites: Hammer Basics

Benefit: You inflict double damage when attacking objects or scenery with a hammer. Also, you gain a trick.

Bone Crusher (Hammer Attack Trick): The target must also make a Fortitude save (DC 10 + your Str modifier + the number of Melee Combat feats you have) or suffer 1 point of temporary Con impairment. This may not lower the target's Constitution score below 6.

HAMMER SUPREMACY

At this point every foe starts to look like a nail.

Prerequisites: Hammer Mastery

Benefit: Your Constitution rises by 1 and you gain a trick.

Splatter (Hammer Attack Trick): If the target is a standard character with a lower Constitution score than yours, he immediately fails his Damage save (damage isn't rolled). You may use this trick once per round.

KNIFE BASICS

You're done with the fight before most folks know it's started.

Prerequisites: Edged forte

Benefit: All knives on your person are considered armed at all times. Also, you gain a stance.

Wicked Dance (Stance): Your 1-handed melee attacks inflict 2 additional dice of sneak attack damage. You may not take move actions (though you may still take 5-ft. Bonus Steps as normal).

KNIFE MASTERY

It's easier to whittle people than twigs — and more fun.

Prerequisites: Knife Basics

Benefit: Once per round you may Feint an opponent that you've hit with a knife this round as a free action. You suffer a –4 penalty with the Prestidigitation check. Also, you gain a trick.

Blade Flurry (Knife Attack Trick): If you hit by 4 or more, you inflict the knife's damage an additional time. If you hit by 10 or more, you inflict the knife's damage two additional times. In both cases, roll separately each time you inflict damage.

KNIFE SUPREMACY

Hamstrings, kidneys, and throats — when slashing at people, it's good to have a little variety.

Prerequisites: Knife Mastery

Benefit: Your knife attacks inflict 1 die of sneak attack damage. Also, you gain a trick.

Shank! (Knife Attack Trick): If the target is a standard character with a lower Intelligence score than yours, he immediately fails his Damage save (damage isn't rolled). You may use this trick once per round.

POLEARM BASICS

One foot of steel, eight feet of death!

Prerequisites: Edged forte

Benefit: When you wield a polearm it gains *hook.* Also, you gain a stance.

Spinning Shield (Stance): You gain DR against bow and hurled weapon damage equal to the number of Melee Combat feats you have.

POLEARM MASTERY

When you put them down, they don't get back up.

Prerequisites: Polearm Basics

Benefit: Once per round you may immediately make a free polearm attack against an opponent who moves into a square adjacent to you. You inflict only 1/2 damage with this attack (rounded up). Also, you gain a trick.

Topple and Gut (Polearm Trip Trick): You also inflict your polearm's damage.

POLEARM SUPREMACY

Experience has its perks, among them not getting tooled.

Prerequisites: Polearm Mastery

Benefit: Your Wisdom score rises by 1. Also, you gain a trick.

Skull Crack (Polearm Attack Trick): If the target is a standard character with a lower Wisdom score than yours, he immediately fails his Damage save (damage isn't rolled). You may use this trick once per round.

SHIELD BASICS

Shoulder to shoulder or leading the charge, your shield shines at the front of every battle line.

Prerequisites: Blunt forte

Benefit: You gain a +4 gear bonus when Bull Rushing with an armed shield. Also, you gain a stance.

Phalanx Fighting (Stance): Each adjacent ally gains a +1 bonus to Defense and Reflex saves. This bonus increases to +2 when you wield a weapon with *guard +2* or higher. The maximum bonus a character may gain from allies in this stance is +4.

SHIELD MASTERY

Your cunning shield-work turns every blade and punishes every lapse.

Prerequisites: Shield Basics

Benefit: When you wield a shield the *armor-piercing* and *keen* qualities of attacks targeting you decrease by the number of Melee Combat feats you have. Also, you gain a trick.

Shield Slam (Shield Attack Trick): This trick may only be used when inflicting subdual damage. If the target fails his save against subdual damage, he's also *stunned* for 1 round.

SHIELD SUPREMACY

You're a one-man fortress.

Prerequisites: Shield Mastery

Benefit: When you wield a shield its *guard* quality increases by +2. Also, you gain a trick.

Throw Them Back! (Shield Total Defense Trick): Each opponent who tries to move into a square adjacent to you must make a Fortitude save (DC 10 + your Str modifier + the number of Melee Combat feats you have) or end their movement in the previous square.

SPEAR BASICS

You like to keep one hand free for more important things — like mocking your opponent.

Prerequisites: Edged forte

Benefit: When you wield a 1-handed spear its Reach increases by 1 and when you wield a 2-handed spear its gains *bleed.* Also, you gain a stance.

Monkey's Grip (Stance): You may wield a single 2-handed melee weapon with one hand.

SPEAR MASTERY

Sometimes brute force actually *is* the answer.

Prerequisites: Spear Basics

Benefit: You may use a spear to perform staff and polearm tricks. Also, you gain a trick.

Falling Lightning (Spear Attack Trick): You may substitute your Athletics (Str) bonus for your melee attack bonus. If the attack misses you become *flat-footed* at the end of your Initiative Count. You may use this trick as many times per combat as you have Melee Combat feats.

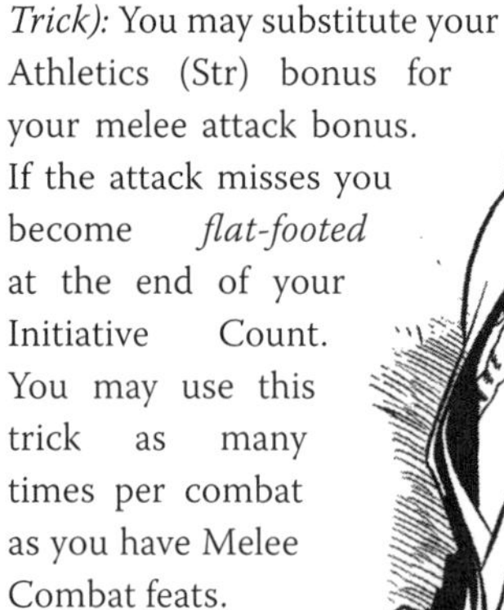

SPEAR SUPREMACY

What do shish kebabs and your enemies have in common?

Prerequisites: Spear Mastery

Benefit: When you wield a spear it gains *hurl.* Also, you gain a trick.

Run Through (Spear Bull Rush Trick): You also inflict double your spear damage. You may use this trick as many times per combat as you have Melee Combat feats.

STAFF BASICS

Some people call it a "stick." You call it "insurance."

Prerequisites: Blunt forte

Benefit: When you wield a staff its Reach increases by 1. Also, you gain a stance.

Whirling Guard (Stance): Standard characters cannot *flank* you.

STAFF MASTERY

Arm's length is for amateurs! Now, the length of a small tree...

Prerequisites: Staff Basics

Benefit: When you wield a staff it gains *guard +2.* Also, you gain a trick.

Wall of Branches (Staff Total Defense Trick): Each opponent who tries to move into a square adjacent to you must make a Reflex save (DC 10 + your Str modifier + the number of Melee Combat feats you have) or end their movement in the previous square.

STAFF SUPREMACY

Even if they get through your makeshift rotary shield, you're rarely still there to greet them.

Prerequisites: Staff Mastery

Benefit: While holding an armed staff you gain a +4 gear bonus with Tumble and Jump checks. Also, you gain a trick.

Guardian's Circle (Staff Total Defense Trick): You gain DR against melee and unarmed attacks equal to the number of Melee Combat feats you have.

SWORD BASICS

Not everyone sees a sword's true flexibility and depth. Pity them.

Prerequisites: Edged forte

Benefit: Once per round as a free action, you may Anticipate an opponent that you've hit with a sword this round. You suffer a –4 penalty with the Sense Motive check. Also, you gain a stance.

Martial Spirit (Stance): You gain a +1 bonus with melee attack checks and a +3 bonus with melee damage rolls.

SWORD MASTERY

The risks and rewards of battle are laid bare before you.

Prerequisites: Sword Basics

Benefit: You may use a sword to perform polearm or spear tricks. Also, you gain a trick.

Bury the Blade (Sword Attack Trick): If you hit by 4 or more, your attack gains *keen 10.*

SWORD SUPREMACY

It's sometimes called the Prince of Arms. In your hands it's the King of War.

Prerequisites: Sword Mastery

Benefit: Your sword attacks inflict +1 damage per 2 your attack check exceeds the target's Defense. Also, you gain a trick.

Think Ahead (Sword Attack Trick): You may substitute your Sense Motive (Wis) bonus for your melee attack bonus. If the attack misses you become *flat-footed* at the end of your Initiative Count. You may use this trick as many times per combat as you have Melee Combat feats.

WHIP BASICS

The whip really *is* an extension of your arm.

Prerequisites: Blunt forte

Benefit: While holding a readied whip, you may Handle Items and Tire characters within your Reach. Also, you gain a stance.

Vicious Intensity (Stance): If you made no attacks last round you gain a +2 bonus with melee attack checks and damage rolls this round.

WHIP MASTERY

Come into my parlor, said the spider...

Prerequisites: Whip Basics

Benefit: When you wield a whip its Reach increases by 1. Also, you gain a trick.

Entwine (Whip Attack Trick): If the target is your Size or smaller, he's also pulled into the nearest empty square adjacent to you and targeted by a Trip action using your attack result.

WHIP SUPREMACY

You spin a web of pain and surprise.

Prerequisites: Whip Mastery

Benefit: Each of your whip attacks may inflict your choice of lethal, stress, or subdual damage instead of the weapon's normal damage (no penalty or damage decrease occurs). Also, you gain a trick.

Thrash (Whip Attack Trick): If the target fails his save against stress damage, he instead fails 2 saves.

RANGED COMBAT FEATS

It's not chivalrous but no one can deny that bow and hurled weapon mastery doesn't change the face of battle.

ANGRY HORNET

Your arrows fly with lethal fleetness.

Benefit: At the start of your Initiative Count when you're armed with a bow or thrown weapon you may accept a –2 penalty with your attack and skill checks until the start of your next Initiative Count. Once during your current Initiative Count you may take a half action to make 2 Standard Attacks with that weapon. You may not use this ability with weapons that have the *load* quality.

BOW BASICS

Your aim is true and your arrows fatal.

Prerequisites: Bows forte

Benefit: When you wield a bow it gains *AP 2* and you gain a stance:

Deadshot (Stance): You gain a +2 bonus with ranged weapon attacks and damage. You may not move while in this stance (though you may still take 5-ft. Bonus Steps as normal).

BOW MASTERY

In your hands, a bow can deliver the wrath of the gods.

Prerequisites: Bow Basics

Benefit: When you wield a bow its maximum range increases by 4 increments (e.g. from ×6 to ×10). Also, you gain a trick.

Eagle Eye (Bow Attack Trick): You may substitute your Search (Wis) bonus for your ranged attack bonus. If the attack misses you become *flat-footed* at the end of your Initiative Count. You may use this trick as many times per combat as you have Ranged Combat feats.

BOW SUPREMACY

You exploit your bow in ways undreamt of by…less *creative* archers.

Prerequisites: Bow Mastery

Benefit: When you wield a bow it gains *spike* and you gain a trick.

Multi-Shot (Bow Attack Trick): Using this trick fires 3 arrows or bolts. If you hit by 4 or more, you inflict your ammunition's damage an additional time. If you hit by 10 or more, you inflict your ammunition's damage two additional times. In both cases, roll separately each time you inflict damage.

BLACKENED SKY

Your enemies fight in the shade.

Prerequisites: Angry Hornet

Benefit: At the start of your Initiative Count when you're armed with a bow or thrown weapon you may accept a –5 penalty with your attack and skill checks until the start of your next Initiative Count. Once during that round you may take a full action to make 4 Standard Attacks with that weapon. If any of your attacks miss this round, you become *flat-footed* at the end of your current Initiative Count. You may not use this ability with weapons that have the *load* quality.

BULLSEYE

Dead center on the target. Dead center.

Benefit: At the start of your Initiative Count you may accept a penalty with your attack and skill checks of up to –4 to gain an equal insight bonus to ranged damage until the start of your next Initiative Count. If any of your attacks miss this round, you become *flat-footed* at the end of your current Initiative Count.

HURLED BASICS

Your hurled attacks always find their mark.

Prerequisites: Hurled forte

Benefit: Your Strength modifier is doubled when calculating thrown weapon damage. Also, you gain a stance.

Zen Shot (Stance): Your target's cover worsens by 2 grades (e.g. 1/2 cover becomes no cover). You may not move while in this stance (though you may still take Bonus 5-ft. Steps as normal).

HURLED MASTERY

Your control and accuracy of hurled attacks is almost supernatural.

Prerequisites: Hurled Basics

Benefit: When you wield a 1-handed thrown weapon it gains *return* and when you wield a 2-handed thrown weapon it gains *AP 4*. Also, you gain a trick.

Staple (Thrown Weapon Attack Trick): With a hit, your target must take a Reflex save (DC 10 + your Dex modifier + the number of Ranged Combat feats you have) or become *entangled* for 1 round.

HURLED SUPREMACY

A high-pitched whistle is usually the last thing your targets hear.

Prerequisites: Hurled Mastery

Benefit: Once per round as a free action, you may Feint or Trip an opponent that you've hit with a thrown weapon this round. You suffer a –4 penalty with the Prestidigitation or Acrobatics check. Also, you gain a trick.

Ricochet (Thrown Weapon Attack Trick): If you hit by 4 or more, you also inflict the weapon's damage on 1 adjacent character of your choice.

UNARMED COMBAT FEATS

Brawlers, pugilists, and martial arts masters can become legendary living weapons of the battlefield.

KICKING BASICS

Your foes better watch your hands *and* your feet.

Prerequisites: Unarmed forte

Benefit: You don't become *flat-footed* when you fail Trip attempts. Also, you gain a stance.

Shifting Footwork (Stance): When you make an unarmed attack, your target's Dodge bonuses decrease to 1/2 normal (rounded down). You may also move 5 ft. each time you hit an opponent with an unarmed attack.

KICKING MASTERY

In the ring, in the dojo, or on the street, you've always got the moves to finish the job.

Prerequisites: Kicking Basics

Benefit: Your unarmed attacks gain *AP 2* and you gain a trick.

Guillotine Kick (Unarmed Attack Trick): If you hit by 4 or more, you inflict your unarmed damage one additional time (rolling damage separately for each). If the attack misses, you become *sprawled.* You may use this trick once per round.

KICKING SUPREMACY

Your fight-ending flourishes are spectacular.

Prerequisites: Kicking Mastery

Benefit: When you hit a single opponent with an unarmed attack and the square on the opposite side of your target is empty, you may immediately move into that square. Also, you gain a trick.

Hurricane Kick (Unarmed Attack Trick): You may make a single attack check against every adjacent character. Each target hit suffers 1/2 your unarmed damage (rounded up) and is pushed 5 ft. away from you (assuming there's an empty square behind them). You may use this trick as many times per combat as you have Unarmed Combat feats.

MARTIAL ARTS

You're a living weapon, delivering deadly blows with your bare hands.

Prerequisites: Unarmed forte, Str 13+, Dex 13+

Benefit: Your unarmed attacks inflict 2 additional damage and gain +1 threat range. Also, you may choose one attribute, substituting that attribute's modifier in place of Dexterity when calculating Defense, and in place of Strength when making unarmed attack checks.

MASTER'S ART

Your fighting skills are the stuff of legend.

Prerequisites: Martial Arts

Benefit: Your unarmed attacks inflict 2 more damage (total 4) and gain an additional +1 threat range (total +2). Also, you may substitute the attribute chosen for Martial Arts in place of Dexterity when calculating Initiative, and in place of Strength when making unarmed damage rolls.

RAGE BASICS

The fury of a caged beast lurks within you.

Benefit: You gain a +2 morale bonus with Intimidate checks. Also, you gain a stance.

Berserk Stance (Stance): Your Strength and Constitution scores rise by 3 each. You may not make skill checks while in this stance (but you may still oppose them as normal). When you leave this stance you become *fatigued.*

RAGE MASTERY

Your frenzy is the stuff of nightmares.

Prerequisites: Rage Basics

Benefit: While in Berserk Stance you may make Intimidate checks and your Strength and Constitution scores rise by an additional 2 each (total 5 each).

RAGE SUPREMACY

Though tamed, your beast hasn't lost its bite.

Prerequisites: Rage Mastery

Benefit: You may make skill checks in Berserk Stance. Also, if you take a half action to change stance or return to normal stance, you don't become *fatigued.*

TWO-HIT COMBO

...and the hits just keep on coming!

Benefit: At the start of your Initiative Count you may accept a –2 penalty with your attack and skill checks until the start of your next Initiative Count. Once during that round you may take a half action to make 2 unarmed Standard Attacks.

WARRIOR'S GRACE

You fist-falls are an avalanche of pain.

Prerequisites: Two-Hit Combo

Benefit: At the start of your Initiative Count you may accept a –5 penalty with your attack and skill checks until the start of your next Initiative Count. Once during that round you may take a full action to make 4 unarmed Standard Attacks. If any of your attacks miss this round, you become *flat-footed* at the end of your current Initiative Count.

WRESTLING BASICS

You prefer to tackle opponents at close range.

Prerequisites: Unarmed forte

Benefit: You gain a +1 bonus to Defense against adjacent opponents. Also, you gain a stance.

Open Stance (Stance): Once per round when you have 2 hands free and an opponent misses you with a melee or unarmed attack, you may immediately Grapple or Trip him as a free action. You may not take move actions (though you may still take 5-ft. Bonus Steps as normal).

WRESTLING MASTERY

Bulk up, beat down!

Prerequisites: Wrestling Basics

Benefit: The lower of your Strength or Constitution scores rises by 1. Also, you gain a trick.

Clothesline (Unarmed Attack Trick): Your target must also make a Fortitude save (DC equal to the damage inflicted after DR and Resistances) or become *sprawled.*

WRESTLING SUPREMACY

Lights out!

Prerequisites: Wrestling Mastery

Benefit: You may Coup de Grace *pinned* characters and gain a trick.

Piledriver (Unarmed Trip Trick): You also inflict double your unarmed damage and an equal amount of flash and bang damage. If you fail this Trip check, you become *sprawled.* You may use this trick as many times per combat as you have Unarmed Combat feats.

CHANCE FEATS

Some characters display extraordinary luck, often without their conscious control.

ADVENTURER'S LUCK

You're every party's best friend.

Benefit: Each time your party rolls for treasure you may roll twice, keeping both results. This benefit only applies once per Treasure roll, no matter how many characters possess this feat.

ALL IN

Never tell me the odds!

Prerequisites: Special character only

Benefit: You gain 1 Edge each time you roll a natural 20 on a skill check against an adversary. You may spend 4 Edge before making a skill check to increase both its threat and error ranges by 4.

BLACK CAT

Strange and unfortunate accidents plague your enemies.

Benefit: Once per character per scene, as a free action, you may raise the target's error ranges by 2 for the rest of the scene. You may use this ability a number of times per session equal to the number of Chance feats you have.

CLOSE CALL

That... That was a close one.

Prerequisites: Special character only

Benefit: You gain 1 Edge each time you spend an action die to boost a save. You may spend 3 Edge to automatically succeed with a failed save.

FORTUNATE

The odds are always in your favor.

Benefit: At the beginning of each session you gain a number of bonus d4 action dice equal to the number of Chance feats you have.

FORTUNE FAVORS THE BOLD

"I'll take my chances" is your favorite strategy.

Benefit: When you roll an action die, the result increases by 2.

FORTUNE'S FOOL

Sometimes you snatch victory from the very jaws of defeat.

Benefit: Each time you suffer a critical failure you gain a bonus d4 action die. You may use this ability a number of times per session equal to the number of Chance feats you have.

JINX

You're a walking disaster area — for your enemies.

Prerequisites: Black Cat

Benefit: While targeting a character with your Black Cat feat, you may activate his errors for 1 less action die (minimum 0).

LADY LUCK'S SMILE

If you're consistently lucky, is it really luck?

Benefit: When you roll an action die, it explodes on its highest or second highest natural result (e.g. 5–6 on a d6, 9–10 on a d10, etc.).

LUCKY BREAK

One inch to the left and that would have been *bad.*

Prerequisites: Special character only

Bonus: You gain 2 Edge at the beginning of each scene. Once per round when an attack hits you by 1 or less, you may spend 1 Edge to cause the attack to miss.

TOUGH LUCK

Your enemies never catch a break.

Prerequisites: Jinx

Benefit: While targeted by your Black Cat feat, a character must spend 1 additional action die to activate each critical hit or success.

COVERT FEATS

Every group, no matter how blunt-minded, must sneak around on occasion, relying on surprise, stealth, and precision to carry the day. These feats elevate that strategy to an exact science.

AMBUSH BASICS

You frequently benefit from the element of surprise.

Benefit: You require only 2 rounds to make a Tactics/Ambush check. Also, your attacks inflict an additional die of sneak attack damage.

AMBUSH MASTERY

Your blows rattle opponents to their core.

Prerequisites: Ambush Basics

Benefit: You may convert damage without suffering the normal –4 attack penalty *(see page 209)*. Also, when you inflict subdual damage on a *flat-footed* opponent, he doesn't lose the *flat-footed* condition.

AMBUSH SUPREMACY

They never see *you* coming.

Prerequisites: Ambush Mastery

Benefit: If you take 10 minutes to make a Tactics/Ambush check, your threat range increases by 4. Also, your attacks inflict an additional die of sneak attack damage (total 2 dice).

FEROCITY BASICS

You *always* go for the kill.

Benefit: When rolling sneak attack damage, you inflict +1 damage per die. Also, once per round, you may take a half action to Coup de Grace a *helpless* character.

FEROCITY MASTERY

That's going to leave a mark!

Prerequisites: Ferocity Basics

Benefit: You gain a trick.

Crippling Strike (Attack Trick): Choose 1 of the target's attributes. With a hit, the attack inflicts 1/2 damage and the opponent suffers a –4 penalty with attack and skill checks using the attribute for the rest of the scene. With a miss, you become *flat-footed.* Each character may suffer from only 1 successful Crippling Strike per scene.

FEROCITY SUPREMACY

You're as ruthless as they come.

Prerequisites: Ferocity Mastery

Benefit: Your melee attacks gain *keen 4*. Also, when you inflict a critical injury *(see page 208)*, you may shift your Table of Ouch result up or down by 1 result (e.g. if you score a broken limb injury, you may alternately choose head trauma or internal rupture).

GARROTE BASICS

You turn a simple cord into a deadly weapon.

Prerequisites: Unarmed forte

Benefit: When you're armed with a garrote, any opponent you pin immediately begins to suffocate. This continues until the pin is broken, you release them, or they die. Also, you gain a stance.

Wraith of the Battlefield (Stance): You gain a +4 bonus with Sneak checks made during combat.

GARROTE MASTERY

They may thrash and they may whimper but none of that will prevent the inevitable.

Prerequisites: Garrote Basics

Benefit: While armed with a garrote you gain a +4 gear bonus with unarmed Disarms. Also, you gain a grapple benefit.

Choke Out (Garrote Grapple Benefit): The target suffers 1 point of temporary Strength impairment. This may not decrease the target's Strength score to less than 6.

GARROTE SUPREMACY

Snap. Crackle. Pop!

Prerequisites: Garrote Mastery

Benefit: If you're armed with a garrote you don't become *flat-footed* when Grappling. Also, you gain a grapple benefit.

Neck Breaker (Garrote Grapple Benefit): If the target is a standard character with a lower Strength score than yours, he immediately fails 1 Damage save (damage isn't rolled).

GHOST BASICS

You're swift, silent, and difficult to pin down.

Benefit: Your Sneak check movement penalties decrease to 1/2 (rounded down). Also, you may move up to double your Speed while making a Hide check.

GHOST MASTERY

You use every available advantage when hiding.

Prerequisites: Ghost Basics

Benefit: Your Sneak check ambient light, noise, and scenery penalties decrease to 1/2 (rounded down). Also, you may make Hide checks without any apparent place to hide (e.g. in an open field with low grass, in a bare room, etc.).

GHOST SUPREMACY

You move like a specter, effortlessly slipping from shadow to shadow.

Prerequisites: Ghost Mastery

Benefit: Your Sneak check penalties for being *blinded, deafened,* or making an attack decrease to 1/2 (rounded down). Also, while *hidden,* you may not be targeted with Perception checks.

MISDIRECTION BASICS

You keep even the most ferocious enemies off balance and off guard.

Benefit: Your threat range with attacks against special characters increases by 1. You also count as 3 additional characters when determining numerical advantage.

MISDIRECTION MASTERY

When *you* set someone up, they fall hard.

Prerequisites: Misdirection Basics

Benefit: Once per combat, you and each teammate may make a free attack against a single *flat-footed* special character. You may not take this action during a surprise round.

MISDIRECTION SUPREMACY

You never miss critical moments and always use them to maximum effect.

Prerequisites: Misdirection Mastery

Benefit: When you use your Misdirection Mastery feat, you and each teammate who hits may also choose one of the following benefits.

- Inflict 2 dice of sneak attack damage
- Recover 2d6 vitality
- Gain 1 bonus d6 action die

MOBILITY BASICS

You're always in just the right place during combat.

Benefit: You may make turns freely during a Run and don't become *flat-footed* afterward. Also, when you take a Total Defense action, you may take 2 Standard Move actions.

MOBILITY MASTERY

Duck and weave, duck and weave!

Prerequisites: Mobility Basics

Benefit: Each time you perform a Standard Move or Run, you gain a +2 dodge bonus to Defense until the start of your next Initiative Count.

MOBILITY SUPREMACY

They never see you coming, or leaving.

Prerequisites: Mobility Mastery.

Benefit: Your base Speed increases by 10 ft.

GEAR FEATS

Making the most of the party's equipment is vital out in the untamed wild.

ALCHEMY BASICS

You've harnessed the ancient and elusive art of making elixirs.

Prerequisites: Crafting (Chemistry) focus

Benefit: You may create elixirs on Table 4.10 using the Crafting (Chemistry) skill. GM approval is required before any elixir may be crafted and additional tasks may need to be undertaken (e.g. if the GM determines that exotic tools or materials are needed). Restrictions may be also applied by the setting and laws of magic in the land *(see page 318).*

ALCHEMY MASTERY

You've unearthed the formulae for many rare and curious elixirs.

Prerequisites: Alchemy Basics

Benefit: You learn 10 new elixir recipes, each based on a spell with a level of 3 or less. Elixirs based on spells have a cost of 25s (Level 0, Complexity 12D), 50s (Level 1, Complexity 15D), 100s (Level 2, Complexity 18D), or 200s (Level 3, Complexity 21W).

ALCHEMY SUPREMACY

Your brewing ability rivals the greatest distillers in the land.

Prerequisites: Alchemy Mastery

Benefit: You learn 10 new elixir recipes, each based on a spell with a level of 5 or less. Elixirs based on these new spell levels have a cost of 400s (Level 4, Complexity 24W) and 800s (Level 5, Complexity 27W).

BANDAGE

You know how to tend hurts in the field.

Benefit: You gain Medicine as an Origin Skill and your Medicine checks are trained even when you lack a doctor's bag. When you have a doctor's bag you may Mend each character one additional time per day.

CHARM BINDING BASICS

You can capture new power in physical form, creating or augmenting magic items.

Benefit: Choose 2 Charms and randomly roll 2 more, re-rolling exact duplicates *(see Table 4.32, page 195).* You may create magic items using these Charms and the Crafting skill (applying the focus most appropriate to the item's material or construction). You may only include an Essence if you have Essence Binding Basics *(see page 97).* Each crafted magic item's level is equal to yours and its Reputation cost may not exceed your total Crafting bonus + Career Level. GM approval is required before any magic item may be crafted and additional tasks may need to be undertaken (e.g. if the GM determines that exotic tools or materials are needed). Restrictions may also be applied by the setting and laws of magic in the land *(see page 318)*.

CHARM BINDING MASTERY

As an artisan magic crafter you may redirect or even redefine an item's power.

Prerequisites: Charm Binding Basics

Benefit: Choose 1 additional Charm and randomly roll 1 more (total 6). You may also replace a magic item's existing Charm by Crafting the difference in Reputation costs (min. 1).

CHARM BINDING SUPREMACY

You can create the most sought after items in the realm.

Prerequisites: Charm Binding Mastery

Benefit: Choose 1 additional Charm and randomly roll 1 more (total 8). Also, after completing 1 Subplot of the GM's choice, you may create 1 artifact with up to 3 Charms (and up to 3 Essences if you have the appropriate Essence Binding feats).

CRAFTING BASICS

You're a true craftsman, forging items of exceptional quality and beauty.

Prerequisites: Crafting 1+ ranks

Benefit: Choose 1 of your Crafting focuses. When creating items of this type, you produce double the normal silver value. Also, the maximum Complexity you may create using this focus increases by the number of Gear feats you have.

Special: You may take this feat multiple times, choosing a different focus each time. Each feat has a separate name (e.g. Crafting Basics (Chemistry), Crafting Basics (Pottery), etc.).

CRAFTING MASTERY

Your broad knowledge and experience lets you complete projects with consistency and grace.

Prerequisites: Crafting Basics

Benefit: Choose 1 of your Crafting Basics feats. When creating items of this type, you produce triple the normal silver value and you may incorporate coin and raw materials worth up to double this value.

Special: You may take this feat multiple times, choosing a different Crafting Basics feat each time (e.g. Crafting Mastery (Chemistry), Crafting Mastery (Pottery), etc.).

CRAFTING SUPREMACY

Your exhaustive knowledge lets you create complex masterpieces with incredible swiftness.

Prerequisites: Crafting Mastery

Benefit: Choose 1 of your Crafting Mastery feats. When creating items of this type, you produce quadruple the normal silver value.

Also, the minimum Downtime required for items of this type decreases by 1 step, to a minimum of D (i.e. Y becomes M, M becomes W, and W becomes D). This does not impact the silver value generated.

Special: You may take this feat multiple times, choosing a different Crafting Mastery feat each time (e.g. Crafting Supremacy (Chemistry), Crafting Supremacy (Pottery), etc.).

ESSENCE BINDING BASICS

You can draw magic from the substance of an item, awakening its primal force.

Benefit: Choose 2 Essences and randomly roll 2 more, re-rolling exact duplicates *(see Table 4.32, page 195)*. You may create magic items using these Essences and the Crafting skill (applying the focus most appropriate to the item's material or construction). You may only include a Charm if you have Charm Binding Basics *(see page 96)*. Each crafted magic item's level is equal to yours and its Reputation cost may not exceed your total Crafting bonus + Career Level. GM approval is required before any magic item may be crafted and additional tasks may need to be undertaken (e.g. if the GM determines that exotic tools or materials are needed). Restrictions may also be applied by the setting and laws of magic in the land *(see page 318)*.

ESSENCE BINDING MASTERY

You can awaken new magical properties, sometimes in previously identified items.

Prerequisites: Essence Binding Basics

Benefit: Choose 1 additional Essence and randomly roll 1 more (total 6). You may also replace a magic item's existing Essence by Crafting the difference in Reputation costs (min. 1).

ESSENCE BINDING SUPREMACY

Your talent for rousing an item's innate power approaches art.

Prerequisites: Essence Binding Mastery

Benefit: Choose 1 additional Essence and randomly roll 1 more (total 8). Also, after completing 1 Subplot of the GM's choice, you may create 1 artifact with up to 3 Essences (and up to 3 Charms if you have the appropriate Charm Binding feats).

FAVORED GEAR

You're practiced — and protective — of one piece of equipment.

Benefit: Choose 1 specific piece of gear you own. Each time you spend an action die to boost a skill or attack check with it, roll 2 dice and add *both* to the result. Also, the item can't be destroyed with a critical miss or failure (though it may still be destroyed by damage). You may switch the item that gains this benefit each time you level.

FOLLOWERS

Several folk or creatures have sworn to serve you.

Prerequisites: Player character only, Charisma 13+

Benefit: You may summon your followers once per adventure during a non-Dramatic scene. There are a number of them equal to your Charisma modifier + 3. They act as a group and share the same statistics, each of them having an XP value no greater than 20 + 5 × the number of permanent Gear feats you have. You may choose your followers from the Rogues Gallery *(see page 244)* or build an original NPC with GM approval. Followers may not possess temporary feats.

Your followers are standard characters with a Threat Level equal to your Career Level minus 4 (minimum 1). They gain no action dice but you may spend your action dice on their behalf. Your followers may not control additional characters.

Followers assist you and your party either with 1 task or until the end of the following scene, whichever comes first (you must define their use when they're summoned). Of course, circumstances may dictate that followers can't or shouldn't leave when their generosity runs out, in which case they leave at the first reasonable opportunity and your Reputation decreases by 1 per additional scene the followers help.

Followers may help with Downtime checks but may not make Downtime checks of their own.

If any of your followers die or are dismissed, you lose 1 Reputation per individual lost (they're replaced in the following adventure).

Special: You may not gain this feat as a temporary feat.

MORE FOLLOWERS

Your following is growing in strength and commitment.

Prerequisites: Followers

Benefit: The number of followers you control increases to your Charisma modifier + 10 and their maximum XP value increases to 30 + 5 × the number of permanent Gear feats you have. Also, you lose only 1 Reputation per 2 individuals lost.

Special: You may not gain this feat as a temporary feat.

PACKRAT

Your collection puts others to shame.

Benefit: You may keep 2 additional Prizes.

SCRIBING BASICS

You've learned how to create scrolls.

Prerequisites: Caster Level 1+, Crafting (Inscription) focus

Benefit: You may create scrolls of spells you know of up to Level 3. GM approval is required before any scroll may be crafted and additional tasks may need to be undertaken (e.g. if the GM determines that exotic tools or materials are needed). Restrictions may be also applied by the setting and laws of magic in the land *(see page 318)*.

SCRIBING MASTERY

Your library of self-scribed scrolls may now include spells not available on the open market.

Prerequisites: Scribing Basics

Benefit: You may create scrolls of spells you know of up to Level 5. These previously unavailable scrolls have a cost of 400s (Level 4, Complexity 24W) and 800s (Level 5, Complexity 27W).

SCRIBING SUPREMACY

Your scrolls unleash such mighty forces as to rock the foundations of the world.

Prerequisites: Scribing Mastery

Benefit: You may create scrolls of spells you know of up to Level 7. These previously unavailable scrolls have a cost of 1,600s (Level 6, Complexity 30M) and 3,200s (Level 7, Complexity 33M).

SCROLL CASTING

You read *between* the lines.

Prerequisites: Crafting (Inscription) focus

Benefit: You may substitute your Crafting skill bonus in place of Spellcasting when casting from a scroll. The scroll's effects are determined as if your Caster Level is equal to your Career Level minus 2 (minimum 1).

SIGNATURE GEAR

Your tools never let you down when it counts.

Prerequisites: Favored Gear

Benefit: At the start of each scene you may roll 1d20 and set it aside. Once during this scene you may make 1 skill or attack check with your favored gear using that d20 instead of rolling. You may not activate a threat scored with this check or spend action dice to boost its result.

TRADEMARK GEAR

Your tools are gaining a reputation for saving your ass.

Prerequisites: Signature Gear

Benefit: At the start of each scene you gain a d6 action die that may only be spent to boost a skill or attack check, or activate a threat, using your favored gear. This die is discarded at the end of the scene. Also, any time the item fails a Damage save, you may spend 1 Reputation to re-roll. You may do this only once per save.

YEOMAN'S WORK

You're disciplined with money and focused in your labors.

Benefit: You gain +3 Prudence.

SKILL FEATS

Heroes frequently exceed their limits. These feats celebrate that phenomenon.

BASIC SKILL MASTERY

Your ability starts where the 'experts' leave off.

Benefit: Choose one of the following pairs. You gain a +2 insight bonus and a threat range of 19–20 with those skills.

Actor: Bluff & Impress
Athlete: Athletics & Resolve
Healer: Medicine & Sense Motive
Horseman: Ride & Survival
Investigator: Investigate & Search
Officer: Intimidate & Tactics
Pickpocket: Blend & Prestidigitation
Robber: Acrobatics & Sneak
Spy: Disguise & Notice
Trader: Crafting & Haggle

Special: You may take this feat multiple times, choosing a different pair each time. Each feat has a separate name (e.g. Basic Skill Mastery (Athlete), Basic Skill Mastery (Horseman), etc.).

EXCEPTIONAL SKILL MASTERY

Your aptitude is seasoned with experience.

Prerequisites: Basic Skill Mastery

Benefit: Choose 1 of your Basic Skill Mastery feats. You gain a +3 insight bonus and a threat range of 18–20 with those skills. Once per scene, you may also re-roll a check with either of those skills.

Special: You may take this feat multiple times, choosing a different Basic Skill Mastery feat each time. Each feat has a separate name (e.g. Exceptional Skill Mastery (Athlete), Exceptional Skill Mastery (Horseman), etc.).

I CAN SWIM

You're full of surprising talents.

Prerequisites: Player character only

Benefit: You don't have to spend your skill points immediately when you level. Instead, you may 'reveal' your skills, spending skill points to purchase ranks at any time during play (not to exceed your maximum rank for each skill). All unspent skill points *must* be spent before you gain your next level.

LEGENDARY SKILL MASTERY

Your skills are known far and wide.

Prerequisites: Exceptional Skill Mastery

Benefit: Choose 1 of your Exceptional Skill Mastery feats. You gain a +4 insight bonus and a threat range of 17–20 with those skills. Also, you may activate critical successes with those skills for 1 less action die (minimum 0).

Special: You may take this feat multiple times, choosing a different Exceptional Skill Mastery feat each time. Each feat has a separate name (e.g. Legendary Skill Mastery (Athlete), Legendary Skill Mastery (Horseman), etc.).

PRODIGAL SKILL

Your gift can only be described as genius.

Benefit: Choose 1 skill described in this chapter. It becomes an Origin skill for you and your maximum rank with it increases to your Career Level + 6.

TALENTED

Your skill mastery often takes people by surprise.

Prerequisites: Basic Skill Mastery

Benefit: Choose 1 of your Basic Skill Mastery feats. You may spend 1 skill point to purchase 1 rank in both skills at the same time (not to exceed your maximum skill rank for either skill).

WELL-ROUNDED

You've dabbled in many different fields.

Benefit: You may always purchase the first five ranks for each skill in this chapter, even if they aren't Origin or class skills for you. Typical skill rank maximums still apply.

SPECIES FEATS

Some characters embrace their unusual heritage, working to develop the special abilities of their race.

ABIDE IN DARKNESS

Your exposure to the roots of the world makes you resistant to lesser magic.

Prerequisites: *Sorcery* campaign quality, *darkvision II* NPC quality

Benefit: You gain Spell Defense equal to 10 + your Career Level + your starting action dice. This Spell Defense decreases by 4 in bright light and by 10 in intense light or direct sunlight (minimum 0).

AGILE FLYER

You're most at home in the air.

Prerequisites: Winged flight *(see page 227)*

Benefit: You gain Acrobatics as an Origin skill and don't suffer the typical error range penalties associated with flying *(see page 227)*.

ANGELIC HERITAGE

Divine forces have touched your family line, gifting you with fine features and unusual grace.

Prerequisites: Level 1 only

Benefit: The higher of your Wisdom or Charisma scores rises by 1, you gain Acid Resistance 5, and your Appearance bonus increases by +1. When taking the Basic Skill Mastery feat you have access to a new skill pair: Savior (Notice & Tactics). However, you're also an Outsider *(see page 227)* and vulnerable to various effects and potentially higher damage from some sources.

ANGELIC LEGACY

Your unearthly heritage continues to shine through in your every word and deed. You may even embrace your heritage completely, becoming like an angel in form and speech.

Prerequisites: Human, Angelic Heritage

Benefit: The lower of your Wisdom or Charisma scores rises by 1, your Acid Resistance increases to 10, and you gain Cold Resistance 10.

You may choose to grow feathered wings once, when you level, gaining winged flight 60 ft. *(see page 227)*. If you do, your starting action dice decrease by 1 and you become uncomfortable telling falsehoods, suffering a –5 penalty with Bluff checks.

DEVILISH HERITAGE

Pacts with the wicked forces have indelibly stained your family tree.

Prerequisites: Level 1 only

Benefit: The higher of your Dexterity or Intelligence scores rises by 1 and you gain Fire Resistance 5 and Gore I *(see page 235)*. When taking the Basic Skill Mastery feat you have access to a new skill pair: Deceiver (Bluff & Sneak). However, you're also an Outsider *(see page 227)* and vulnerable to various effects and higher damage from some sources.

DEVILISH LEGACY

Your path may have been paved with good intentions but they've clearly been forsaken. Another step and you'll reveal your dark destiny to all.

Prerequisites: Human, Devilish Heritage

Benefit: The lower of your Dexterity or Intelligence scores rises by 1, your Fire Resistance increases to 10, and you gain Electricity Resistance 10.

You may choose to grow bat wings once, when you level, gaining winged flight 60 ft. *(see page 227)*. If you do, your starting action dice decrease by 1 and you grow less caring for the wellbeing of others, suffering a –5 penalty with Medicine checks.

DRACONIC HERITAGE

You're a descendant of mighty dragons, feared and admired by all.

Prerequisites: Level 1 only

Benefit: You gain *thick hide 3* and are always considered to have a mage's pouch *(see pages 13 and 159, respectively)*. When taking the Basic Skill Mastery feat you have access to a new skill pair: Conqueror (Impress & Tactics).

DRACONIC LEGACY

Your ancestry's draconic promise manifests fully in you.

Prerequisites: Saurian or Human, Draconic Heritage

Benefit: The higher of your Strength or Intelligence scores increases by 1. You may also breathe fire and select feats as if you're a Drake *(see page 9)*.

You may choose to grow leathery wings once, when you level, gaining winged flight 60 ft. *(see page 227)*. If you do, your starting action dice decrease by 1 and you find it difficult to subdue your imperious nature, suffering a –5 penalty with Blend checks.

EASTERN HORDE

Unafraid of the dawning sun, the Skull Tribes can strike anywhere at any time.

Prerequisites: Goblin or Orc, Level 1 only

Benefit: Your Ground Speed increases by 5 ft. You also lose *light-sensitive* and suffer exactly 1 point per damage die when making a Push Limit check (damage isn't rolled).

ELEMENTAL HERITAGE

Your ancestors were closely tied to primal forces of the world.

Prerequisites: Level 1 only

Benefit: Choose an element.

- *Crystal:* Your unarmed and natural attacks gain *bleed* and you gain 2 Panache. However, you also gain *Achilles heel (sonic)* *(see page 230).*
- *Darkness:* You gain *darkvision II, light-sensitive* *(see pages 233 and 234),* and a +4 bonus with Sneak checks.
- *Dust/Sand:* You gain Unarmed Resistance 5 and a +2 bonus with Prestidigitation checks. However, your Charisma score drops by 1.
- *Earth:* You gain DR 2/Blunt and *sterner stuff* *(see page 234).* However, your Speed decreases by 5 ft. (minimum 10 ft.).
- *Fire:* You gain Fire Resistance 5 and may convert your unarmed damage to fire damage without suffering the normal –4 attack penalty. However, you also gain *Achilles heel (cold).*
- *Ice:* You gain Cold Resistance 5 and may convert your unarmed damage to cold damage without suffering the normal –4 attack penalty. However, you also gain *Achilles heel (fire).*
- *Lava:* You gain Heat Resistance 5 and *grueling combatant* *(see page 233).* However, you also gain *Achilles heel (cold).*
- *Light:* You gain Divine Resistance 5 and *night-blind* *(see page 234),* and may convert your unarmed damage to flash damage without suffering the normal –4 attack penalty.
- *Lightning:* You gain Electrical Resistance 5 and may convert your unarmed damage to electrical damage without suffering the normal –4 attack penalty. However, you also suffer a –2 penalty with Will saves.
- *Metal:* You gain Edged Resistance 5 and a +2 bonus with Resolve checks. However, you also suffer a –2 penalty with Reflex saves.
- *Mist/Smoke:* You gain Ranged Resistance 5 and a +2 bonus with Blend checks. However, you also suffer a –2 penalty with Fortitude saves.
- *Water:* You gain Blunt Resistance 5 and a +2 bonus with Acrobatics checks. However, you also gain *Achilles heel (electricity).*
- *Wind:* You gain Falling Resistance 5 and your Speed increases by 5 ft. However, your Size is considered 1 category smaller during Bull Rushes, Grapples, and Trips.
- *Wood:* You gain DR 2/Edged and attribute impairment you suffer drops by 1. However, you also gain *Achilles heel (fire).*

ELEMENTAL LEGACY

More and more you embrace your element, perhaps enough to feel your birth species slipping…

Prerequisites: Drake, Giant, or Human; Elemental Heritage

Benefit: Your highest attribute rises by 1 and your lowest attribute drops by 1. Also, all numerical benefits of your Elemental Heritage feat (positive and negative) are doubled (i.e. if you have Elemental Heritage (Earth), your Damage Reduction becomes 4/Blunt and your Speed decreases by 10 ft. instead of 5 ft.).

You may choose to embrace your elemental nature once, when you level, gaining the Elemental Type *(see page 226).* If you do, your starting action dice decrease by 1 and you become easier to spot unless trying to hide, suffering a –5 penalty with Blend checks.

FAERIE HERITAGE

The wilds have touched your soul and may one day claim it as their own…

Prerequisites: Non-fey, Level 1 only

Benefit: The higher of your Dexterity or Charisma scores rises by 1 and you gain a +4 bonus with opposed Bluff checks. You always have enough food and water for yourself, so long as you're located within 10 miles of nature. Also, when taking the Basic Skill Mastery feat you have access to a new skill pair: Eldritch (Impress & Sneak). However, you're also a Fey *(see page 227)* and vulnerable to various effects and potentially higher damage from some sources.

FAERIE LEGACY

It seemed a dream when you dined in the courts of Underhill and tasted the nectar of the fair folk — but dream or no, it has marked you forever.

Prerequisites: Human or Pech, Faerie Heritage

Benefit: The higher of your Dexterity or Charisma scores rises by 1 and your bonus with opposed Bluff checks increases by an additional 6 (for a total of +10).

You may choose to grow shimmering insect-like wings once, when you level, gaining winged flight 60 ft. *(see page 227).* If you do, your starting action dice decrease by 1 and you find it hard to fathom the motivations of others, suffering a –5 penalty with Sense Motive checks.

FARSTRIDE FOLK

Like the first rays of morning, you fearlessly fling yourself toward the unknown.

Prerequisites: Pech, Level 1 only

Benefit: You gain Stress Resistance 4 and a +1 morale bonus with Fortitude, Reflex, and Will saves. However, at the start of each session, the GM gains 1 extra action die that may only be spent to activate an error you suffer when making an attack or skill check.

FAST FLYER

You dart through the air with effortless ease.

Prerequisites: Winged flight *(see page 227)*

Benefit: Your winged flight Speed increases by 40 ft. and you gain a +1 dodge bonus to Defense while flying.

FIRE BRAVE

You're among the rarest breed of ogre: the *ohni,* the shape-shifting spawn of demons.

Prerequisites: Ogre, Level 1 only, Charisma 13+

Benefit: You gain Fire Resistance 10 and ignore Species and Size penalties with Disguise checks. You also lose *reviled* and gain Gore I *(see page 235).*

FIRE ELDER

Your diabolical heritage fully permeates your being, warping your body and granting you mastery of arcane power.

Prerequisites: Spellcasting 1+ ranks, Fire Brave

Benefit: You become an Outsider *(see page 227)* with Spell Defense equal to your Intimidate (Str) bonus. Your Intelligence score rises by 2 but your Constitution score drops by 2. Each time you gain 1 or more ranks in the Intimidate skill, you also gain an equal number of ranks in the Spellcasting skill. This may not increase your Spellcasting skill beyond its maximum rank.

FLOATER

Your design includes the ability to hover.

Prerequisites: Unborn, Level 1 only

Benefit: You lose *Achilles heel (electricity)* and gain *flight 20 ft.* *(see page 227),* though you may rise no higher than 20 ft. above the ground.

Special: When you gain this feat you may reduce any of your attributes by 2 to gain an additional Species feat with the prerequisite "Level 1 only."

GREATER BREATH

Your breath lays waste to huge swaths of territory.

Prerequisites: Drake

Benefit: Your breath weapon becomes a 40-ft. line, 20-ft. cone, or 15-ft. sphere (your choice).

GREAT HORDE

The Blood Tribe stands at the center — the very heart — of the Black Blood armies.

Prerequisites: Goblin or Orc, Level 1 only

Benefit: You also gain Stress Resistance 4 and 20 Reputation that must immediately be spent to create or improve a Goblin or Orc contact. This contact doesn't count against the maximum number of Prizes you may keep.

GUTS

You can push yourself harder than most and shake off incredible damage.

Benefit: You gain a +4 bonus with Push Limit checks and suffer only 1/2 the normal penalty to Strength and Dexterity when *fatigued.* Also, when you Cheat Death, you may return to play at the start of the next scene *(see page 384).*

HART NATION

The wood elves of the Hart Nation are among the most elusive and cunning of the elven peoples.

Prerequisites: Elf, Level 1 only

Benefit: The DCs of Tracking checks to follow your trail increase by 10, your Dexterity score rises by 2, and when taking the Basic Skill Mastery feat you gain a new skill pair you may choose: Wood-Elf (Sneak & Survival). However, your Intelligence score drops by 2.

HART NOBLE

Patrolling the edge of their lands, Hart archers know best how to make intruders feel unwelcome.

Prerequisites: Bow forte, Hart Nation

Benefit: You include your Ranged Combat and Species feats in the number of Covert feats you have (when that number is used). You also gain a trick.

Flustering Shot (Bow Attack Trick): The target must also resist a Distract action with the attack result as the DC.

HIDDEN PROMISE

You're destined for great things.

Prerequisites: Level 1 only

Benefit: Your lowest attribute rises by 2 (your choice in the case of a tie).

HILL-BORN

Not every stone is buried deep in the Earth; Hill-Born dwarves dwell above the ground, traveling far and wide in search of adventure and illumination.

Prerequisites: Dwarf, Level 1 only

Benefit: You gain a +1 bonus with all attack and skill checks you make during Dramatic scenes. Also, you gain 2 additional Studies and when taking the Basic Skill Mastery feat you have access to a new skill pair: Hill-Dwarf (Haggle & Ride).

HILL-CLAN

You've shared meals and conversations in many exotic lands.

Prerequisites: Hill-Born

Benefit: You gain 2 additional Languages and 20 Reputation that must immediately be spent to create or improve a contact.

JUNGLE CLUTCH

The *khamai* are secretive tree-dwellers with a luminescent hide that changes color to match their surroundings.

Prerequisites: Saurian, Level 1 only

Benefit: You gain a +2 bonus with Climb checks and are always considered to have climber's gear. Also, you may temporarily gain *chameleon I* as a 1 minute action, matching the surrounding terrain *(see page 231)*. This camouflage is lost when you sleep or replace it with a new terrain.

JUNGLE CREST

As a khamai ages, his body adapts into that of a deadly hunter, with huge rotating eyes and a long and sticky tongue he can use to snare prey.

Prerequisites: Jungle Clutch

Benefit: You may no longer be *flanked* and you may Handle Items and start Grapples within 10 ft, moving the target into your square.

LAVA-BORN

You hail from the fiery depths of the world, where the stones glow with the heat of the First Dwarf's forge.

Prerequisites: Dwarf, Level 1 only

Benefit: You gain Fire and Heat Resistance 5 and each time you inflict lethal damage with an unarmed or melee attack you may convert it to heat damage without suffering the normal –4 attack penalty.

LAVA-CLAN

Flowing rivers of molten stone surround your home. Sometimes, they entrust you with their secrets.

Prerequisites: Lava-Born

Benefit: Your Speed increases by 5 ft. and you gain a +1 bonus to Defense. Also, when you spend an action die to boost unarmed or melee damage, you may convert it to fire damage.

MAKE ME A STONE

This simple prayer means endurance in your culture and it was chanted at your birth.

Prerequisites: Dwarf

Benefit: You gain a +2 bonus with saving throws made during a Dramatic scene and may recover vitality points and wounds during a Refresh action even if attacked before rolling your action die.

MANY-ARMED

You have multiple arms and the coordination to use them.

Prerequisites: Rootwalker or Unborn, Level 1 only

Benefit: You may simultaneously hold and arm up to six 1-handed, four 1-handed and one 2-handed, or two 1-handed and two 2-handed weapons or objects. Also, each round that you hold no more than this, you may Handle an Item as a free action. You also gain a +1 bonus with skill checks made as part of a Grapple action per two of your hands that are free (maximum +3).

This feat does *not* grant additional attacks.

Special: When you gain this feat you may reduce any of your attributes by 2 to gain an additional Species feat with the prerequisite "Level 1 only."

MANY-LEGGED

You have multiple legs.

Prerequisites: Rootwalker or Unborn, Level 1 only

Benefit: You have more than 2 legs and gain *improved stability* and Trample I *(see pages 234 and 235)*.

Special: When you gain this feat you may reduce any of your attributes by 2 to gain an additional Species feat with the requirement "Level 1 only."

MIGHTY BREATH

Your breath weapon is exceptionally deadly.

Prerequisites: Greater Breath

Benefit: Your Constitution score rises by 1 and your breath weapon inflicts an additional 1d6 damage.

NATIVE FEROCITY

You use your natural weapons to deadly effect.

Prerequisites: At least 1 natural attack *(see page 235)*

Benefit: Each of your natural attacks improves by 1 grade (i.e. Gore III becomes Gore IV). You may also activate critical hits with natural attacks for 1 less action die (minimum 0) a number of times per combat equal to your starting action dice.

NEW LEAF

You're a rare breed of rootwalker, sharing the sap of the world's mightiest trees.

Prerequisites: Rootwalker, Level 1 only

Benefit: Choose a breed.

- *Evergreen:* You hail from the frozen wastes. You gain Cold Resistance 10 and 2 additional Studies.
- *Ironwood:* You bend before no wind or man. You gain *sterner stuff* and *thick hide 3 (see page 13).*
- *Mistbranch:* You emerge from deep forests to defend the saplings. You gain Slam II *(see page 235)* and the Relentless Attack trick *(see page 222)*.
- *Purewood:* Your pure sap has special healing powers. You gain *regeneration 1* and you're always considered to have a doctor's bag.

- *Skybranch:* You tower above others, inspiring them to greatness. You may purchase Heroic Renown for 20 Reputation per rank. Also, once per scene, you may speak to 1 of your teammates for 1 minute to grant them a +1 morale bonus with saving throws until the end of the current scene.
- *Sunleaf:* Your roots have thickened in scorching sands and boiling oases. You gain Heat Resistance 10 and lose *Achilles heel (fire)*.
- *Tangleroot:* The clinging vines that extend from your body can snare enemies. You gain a +2 bonus with Grapple checks. Also, adjacent opponents must make a Reflex save (DC 15) at the beginning of their Initiative Count or become *entangled* for 1 round.
- *Whitebark:* The beauty and pride of your breed is legendary. Your Appearance bonus increases by +1 and you may purchase Noble Renown for 20 Reputation per rank.

NORTHERN HORDE

The Bone Tribes sweep through the night, reminding the weak why they should fear the dark.

Prerequisites: Goblin or Orc, Level 1 only

Benefit: You gain *darkvision II (see page 233)*, and you gain a +2 morale bonus to attack checks in faint or no light *(see page 218)*.

OWL NATION

The mighty Owls, favored children of the starry skies, stand aloof and alone; even other elves find them somewhat… prickly.

Prerequisites: Elf, Level 1 only

Benefit: You gain *darkvision I (see page 233)* and your Intelligence score rises by 2. However, the Disposition of any character who's aware of your species and doesn't share your native culture worsens by 10.

OWL NOBLE

The most gifted of the star-elves can weave the light of the heavens into useful forms.

Prerequisites: Owl Nation

Benefit: You gain 3 additional Crafting focuses and the lower of your Intelligence or Wisdom scores rises by 2 (your choice in the case of a tie).

QUICK-FINGER FOLK

Smaller than their fellow pech, the Quick-Fingers have a knack for machinery that makes them welcome in almost any town.

Prerequisites: Pech, Level 1 only

Benefit: Your Intelligence score rises by 2 but your Strength score drops by 2. You gain 1 additional Crafting focus and when taking the Basic Skill Mastery feat you have access to a new skill pair: Tinker (Crafting & Prestidigitation).

QUICK HEALER

You recover very quickly from injury.

Prerequisites: Guts

Benefit: You heal vitality points and wounds, and lose stress and subdual damage, at twice the normal rate.

SEA BRAVE

You and your twisted *fomhoire* kin have long wandered the turbulent oceans, raiding and conquering the weak.

Prerequisites: Ogre, Level 1 only

Benefit: You gain *aquatic II (see page 230)* and Claw I (*venomous* — weakening poison). You also suffer a –2 penalty with Charisma-based skill checks.

SEA ELDER

Like the seas of your birth, your form has twisted with age.

Prerequisites: Sea Brave

Benefit: You gain the Horror Type *(see pages 227)*.

SOUTHERN HORDE

The Fang Tribes keep the black lore of the orcs, some of it mysterious, some deadly.

Prerequisites: Goblin or Orc, Level 1 only

Benefit: Your Intelligence score rises by 1 and you gain 4 ranks in the Crafting skill (not to exceed your maximum ranks). You gain a 20% discount when purchasing poisons.

SPECIAL CONSTRUCTION

Unlike most of your 'kin,' your body is composed of special materials that set you apart.

Prerequisites: Unborn, Level 1 only

Benefit: Choose a construction.

- *Brass:* Your alloy flesh is amazingly resistant to arcane forces. You gain Spell Defense 20.
- *Clay:* Formed of earth and blessed with life, you're a terror to your foes. You gain *sterner stuff (see page 235)* and your *Achilles heel (electricity)* becomes *Achilles heel (fire)*. Also, each time you suffer 10 or more damage from a melee attack you may attempt to Disarm the attacker as a free action.
- *Clockwork:* As a sophisticated machine, you possess uncanny speed and precision. Your Speed increases by 10 ft., you gain a +2 bonus with Initiative checks, and you lose *lumbering*.
- *Flesh:* You're crafted from multiple cadavers and imbued with great strength — and greater rage. You may be healed with both Crafting and Medicine checks, and your *Achilles heel (electricity)* becomes *Achilles heel (fire)*. Your Strength-based damage rolls inflict 1 additional damage, and each time an opponent attacks you and misses, he suffers 2 stress damage.
- *Gem:* Your body is rough-hewn from razor sharp minerals. You gain *natural defense (lethal damage) (see page 234)*.
- *Granite:* You're living stone and nearly impossible to move. You gain Damage Reduction 2 and *improved stability*.

- *Living Metal:* Your steely "flesh" is the product of bizarre alchemy and magic, forged for war and destruction. Your wounds heal normally, the lower of your Strength or Constitution scores rise by 1, and you gain 2 additional proficiencies.

SPIDER NATION

The heartlands of the Spider Nations are hidden deep underground, offering solace to generations of elves driven from the surface by chance, natural disaster, and war (sometimes even by their own kin). These elusive "dark elves" tend to have either very pale or very dark complexions, pitiless demeanors, and sinister reputations.

Prerequisites: Elf, Level 1 only

Benefit: You gain *darkvision II* and *light-sensitive (see pages 233 and 234)*, as well as a 50% discount when purchasing poison. Also, the lower of your Intelligence or Charisma scores rises by 1 (your choice in the case of a tie), and when taking the Basic Skill Mastery feat you have access to a new skill pair: Dark Elf (Sneak & Spellcasting). However, the Disposition of any character who's aware of your species and doesn't share your native culture worsens by 10.

SPIDER NOBLE

Certain dark elves who directly serve their wretched gods are physically transformed to better please them.

Prerequisites: Spider Nation

Benefit: Your lower trunk and legs transform into those of a massive spider, making you a Large (2×2, Reach 1) fey (though you continue to use Medium Scale weapons). Your Ground Speed increases by 10 ft. and the DCs of your Climb checks decrease to 1/2 normal (rounded up).

STONE BRAVE

Your people are the nigh-invincible *trul*, the most terrifying of all ogres.

Prerequisites: Ogre, Level 1 only

Benefit: You gain *regeneration 1 (see page 234)* and you gain a +2 bonus to saves against poison and disease. Also, when taking the Basic Skill Mastery feat you have access to a new skill pair: Bone-Chewer (Athletics & Intimidate). However, you're also *light-sensitive (see page 234)*, and you suffer a –2 Appearance penalty.

STONE ELDER

Age makes you even bigger, tougher, and more simple-minded.

Prerequisites: Stone Brave

Benefit: Your *regeneration 1* becomes *regeneration 2*, and your Reach increases by 1. However, your Intelligence score drops by 2.

SWAMP CLUTCH

The cave-dwelling *effet* have soft, quick-healing bodies adapted for survival in the cold, dark places of the world.

Prerequisites: Saurian, Level 1 only

Benefit: You gain a +2 bonus with Swim checks and *aquatic I (see page 230)*. You also gain *regeneration 1* though only while completely submerged in water *(see page 234)*. Finally, you also gain *Achilles heel (heat)*.

SWAMP CREST

The poisonous hides of alpha *effet* ensure they can protect their tribes from the many predators that stalk their subterranean homeland.

Prerequisites: Swamp Clutch

Benefit: You gain *natural defense (lethal damage) (see page 234)*.

TRUESCALE

You're well adapted to your natural hunting grounds.

Prerequisites: Drake, Level 1 only

Benefit: Choose a terrain: aquatic, arctic, caverns/mountains, desert, forest/jungle, indoors/settled, plains, or swamp. You suffer no Size penalty with Blend checks in this terrain. Finally, choose a damage type: acid, cold, electrical, fire (AP 4), flash, force, sonic, or stress. Your breath weapon inflicts this type of damage instead of fire (AP 0).

UNEARTHLY SPLENDOR

You exemplify the breathtaking beauty and poise of your kind.

Prerequisites: Fey

Benefit: Your Appearance bonus increases by +1 and the lower of your Dexterity or Charisma scores rises by 1 (your choice in the case of a tie).

Special: You may choose this feat up to 3 times.

WESTERN HORDE

When night falls, the Iron Tribe settles in for prolonged siege.

Prerequisites: Goblin or Orc, Level 1 only

Benefit: You gain *thick hide 3 (see page 13)*.

SPELLCASTING FEATS

Purveyors of the arcane and divine are constantly discovering new heights of magical power.

BLESSED

Your unwavering faith has enlightened you.

Prerequisites: *Miracles* campaign quality, Alignment *(see page 61)*

Benefit: You take the first Step along one of your Paths. You may cast spells granted by this Step with a Casting Level of 1.

CASTING BASICS

Your spellcasting ability shows remarkable promise.

Benefit: You gain a +2 insight bonus and a threat range of 19–20 with Spellcasting checks.

CASTING MASTERY

Your command of spellcasting is precise and practiced.

Prerequisites: Casting Basics

Benefit: You gain a +3 insight bonus and a threat range of 18–20 with Spellcasting checks. Also, once per scene, you may re-roll a Spellcasting check.

CASTING SUPREMACY

Your spells impress even the most jaded mentor.

Prerequisites: Casting Mastery

Benefit: You gain a +4 insight bonus and a threat range of 17–20 with Spellcasting checks. Also, you may activate Spellcasting critical successes for 1 less action die (minimum 0).

DOUBLE CAST

You fling a surprising amount of magic around when the pressure's on.

Prerequisites: Spellcasting 1+ ranks

Benefit: You may cast a second spell during a round if you have sufficient remaining actions.

You may use this ability a number of times per session equal to your starting action dice.

THE GIFT

Though not a Mage, you were born with an extraordinary gift to work your will on the world... in small ways.

Prerequisites: Level 1 only

Benefit: You know and may cast a number of Level 0 spells equal to your Intelligence modifier (minimum 2) with a Casting Level of 1. You may automatically cast these spells a total number of times per scene equal to your starting action dice.

HIDDEN SPELLS

You can cast spells without muttering or gesturing.

Prerequisites: Spellcasting 1+ ranks

Benefit: Your Spellcasting checks are not obvious. You make no sound while casting and may cast even when you can't speak.

SPELL CONVERSION: AREA

You shape spells like a sculptor shapes clay.

Prerequisites: Casting Level 1+

Benefit: You gain 2 tricks.

Confine Area (Spellcasting Trick): When casting a spell with an Area, you may double the Casting Time and reduce its Area to 1 character or object to reduce the spell's level by 1 (minimum 1).

Expand Area (Spellcasting Trick): When casting a spell with an Area, you may pay 3 additional spell points to increase each of the area's measurements by 100%.

SPELL CONVERSION: CASTING TIME

You command one of the greatest spell components: time.

Prerequisites: Casting Level 1+

Benefit: You gain 2 tricks.

Careful Casting (Spellcasting Trick): When casting a spell with a Casting Time of 1 half action or more, you may increase the Casting Time to 10 times standard to reduce the spell's level by 1 (min. 1).

Quick Casting (Spellcasting Trick): When casting a spell with a Casting Time of 1 round or less, you may pay 3 additional spell points to reduce the Casting Time to 1 free action. This action may be taken occur during your Initiative Count.

SPELL CONVERSION: DISTANCE

You can fling spells over great distances and tap superior forces at close range.

Prerequisites: Casting Level 1+

Benefit: You gain 2 tricks.

Concentrated Spell (Spellcasting Trick): When casting a spell with a Distance other than Personal, Touch, or Unlimited, you may double the Casting Time and reduce the Distance to Touch to reduce the spell's level by 1 (minimum 1).

Reaching Spell (Spellcasting Trick): When casting a spell with a Distance other than Personal, Touch, or Unlimited, you may pay 1 additional spell point to increase the spell's Distance by 100%.

SPELL CONVERSION: DURATION

You can prolong practiced effects or take your time to achieve greater heights of magical power.

Prerequisites: Casting Level 1+

Benefit: You gain 2 tricks.

Burst Spell (Spellcasting Trick): When casting a spell with a Duration other than Concentration, Instant, or Permanent, you may double the Casting Time and reduce the Duration to 1/2 standard (rounded down) to reduce the spell's level by 1 (min. 1).

Lasting Spell (Spellcasting Trick): When casting a spell with a Duration other than Concentration, Instant, or Permanent, you may pay 1 additional spell point to increase the spell's Duration by 100%.

SPELL CONVERSION: EFFECT

You can unleash the full fury of well-known spells and cast lesser versions of spells typically beyond your training.

Prerequisites: Casting Level 1+

Benefit: You gain 2 tricks.

Focus Spell (Spellcasting Trick): When casting a spell with one or more variable effects, you may double the Casting Time and reduce each of the spell's variable effects to 1/2 standard (rounded down) to reduce the spell's level by 1 (minimum 1).

Power Spell (Spellcasting Trick): When casting a spell with one or more variable effects, you may pay 3 additional spell points to increase each of the spell's variable effects to its maximum value (as if you'd rolled the highest total possible with all random dice).

SPELL LIBRARY

You pick up new spells everywhere you go.

Prerequisites: Spellcasting 1+ ranks

Benefit: You learn a number of additional spells equal to your Lifestyle.

SPELL POWER

You're an arcane battery, a wellspring of magical power.

Prerequisites: Casting Level 1+

Benefit: You gain an additional number of spell points at the start of each scene equal to your starting action dice.

STYLE FEATS

Personality and charm yield great and bounteous rewards.

COMELY

You always turn heads.

Benefit: Your Charisma score rises by 1. You also gain a +2 bonus with Impress checks but suffer a –2 penalty with Blend and Disguise checks.

ELEGANT

Your appeal is timeless.

Prerequisites: Comely

Benefit: Your Appearance bonus increases by +1 and your Comely bonus and penalty increase to 3 each.

ENCHANTING

No one forgets your face.

Prerequisites: Elegant

Benefit: Your Charisma score rises by 1 more (total +2) and your Comely bonus and penalty increase to 4 each.

EXTRA CONTACT

It's all about who you know...

Prerequisites: Player character only

Benefit: You gain an additional contact with a Reputation value of 30 or less who doesn't count against the number of Prizes you may keep.

Special: You may not gain this as a temporary feat.

EXTRA HOLDING

...and where you live. That too.

Prerequisites: Player character only

Benefit: You gain an additional holding with a Reputation value of 30 or less that doesn't count against the number of Prizes you may keep.

Special: You may not gain this as a temporary feat.

GLINT OF MADNESS

There's something deeply disturbing about you. Maybe it's the growling. Or the frothing.

Benefit: You inflict 1d10 stress damage when you Threaten an opponent. Also, once per round when one of your attacks renders an opponent unconscious or dead, you may immediately Threaten another opponent as a free action.

MARK

You can size anyone up at a glance.

Benefit: Once per character per scene, as a free action, you may learn the total bonuses of 3 skills belonging to a character in your line of sight.

PERSONAL LIEUTENANT

Someone's *always* got your back.

Prerequisites: Player character only

Benefit: You control a non-animal NPC with an XP value no greater than 50 + 5 × the permanent Style feats you have. You may choose your lieutenant from the Rogues Gallery or Bestiary *(see pages 244 and 253)* or build an original NPC with GM approval. Your lieutenant may not possess temporary feats.

Your lieutenant is a special character with a Threat Level equal to your Career Level minus 4 (minimum 1). He gains no action dice but you may spend your action dice on his behalf. Your lieutenant may not control additional characters.

If your lieutenant dies or is dismissed, you lose Reputation equal to your Career Level (he's replaced in the following adventure).

Special: You may not gain this feat as a temporary feat.

REPARTEE BASICS

You navigate intricate social webs with hollow promises and sincere lies.

Benefit: The error ranges of Sense Motive checks targeting you increase by your Charisma modifier (minimum +1). You also gain a trick.

Silver Tongue (Distract Trick): Your target's Wisdom score also drops by 1 until the end of the scene (minimum 6). You may use this trick a number of times per scene equal to the number of Style feats you have.

REPARTEE MASTERY

You can demolish pride and confidence with a few well-chosen words.

Prerequisites: Repartee Basics

Benefit: You gain a +2 bonus with Bluff Checks and a trick.

Painful Secrets (Threaten Trick): Your target also loses the ability to spend action dice for a number of rounds equal to the number of Style feats you have.

REPARTEE SUPREMACY

Your soul-piercing declarations stop people dead in their tracks.

Prerequisites: Repartee Mastery

Benefit: Your Lifestyle rises by 1 and you gain a trick.

Staggering Pronouncement (Distract Trick): Also, your target may not take attack actions until he's attacked or the scene ends. You may use this trick once per scene.

TERRAIN FEATS

The land can be as great a weapon as the strongest blade.

ANIMAL PARTNER

He followed you home and now he's going to keep you.

Prerequisites: Player character only

Benefit: You control an animal NPC with an XP value no greater than 50 + 5 × the permanent Terrain feats you have. You may choose your partner from the Bestiary *(see page 253)* or build an original NPC with GM approval. Your partner may not possess temporary feats.

Your partner is a special character with a Threat Level equal to your Career Level minus 4 (minimum 1). It gains no action dice but you may spend your action dice on its behalf. Your partner may not control additional characters.

If your partner dies or is dismissed, you lose Reputation equal to your Career Level (he's replaced in the following adventure).

Special: You may not gain this feat as a temporary feat.

BATTLEFIELD TRICKERY

You use simple traps to disable your foes.

Benefit: When you successfully Ambush one or more characters, you may choose a number of them up to the number of Terrain feats you have. Each target chosen suffers the effects of a successful Cheap Shot trick (no attack is made and no damage is rolled).

BUSHWHACK BASICS

You like to start fights with a little something special.

Benefit: When you have a 2-to-1 or better advantage, your Ambush effects last 3 rounds (beyond the surprise round).

BUSHWHACK MASTERY

You dominate attention during brawls.

Prerequisites: Bushwhack Basics

Benefit: Once per round when you have a 2-to-1 or better advantage, you may Taunt or Distract as a free action.

BUSHWHACK SUPREMACY

You keep the enemy bunched up and pinned down.

Prerequisites: Bushwhack Mastery

Benefit: When you have a 2-to-1 or better advantage, the Speed of each opponent within your line of sight drops to 1/2 normal (rounded up).

COORDINATED ATTACK

Your guidance dramatically improves your teammates' combat prowess.

Benefit: Once per round as a full action, you may direct a teammate who can see and hear you to make an immediate Standard Attack.

COORDINATED MOVE

Your complex synchronized assaults are devastating.

Prerequisites: Coordinated Attack

Benefit: Once per round as a full action, you may direct a teammate who can see and hear you to make an immediate Feint, Reposition, or Standard Move.

COORDINATED STRIKE

You direct battles like a conductor directs orchestra.

Prerequisites: Coordinated Move

Benefit: Once per round as a full action, you may direct up to 2 teammates who can see and hear you to each make an immediate Standard Attack or Standard Move.

THE EXTRA MILE

You go to extreme lengths to make sure everyone comes back alive.

Benefit: Once per adventure, you may choose a single teammate who has died during a standard scene. If you have the teammate's body at the end of the scene, he Cheats Death with a Petty fate *(see page 384)*.

HORDE BASICS

You overwhelm enemies with sheer numbers.

Benefit: You and each teammate gain 1/4 personal cover when you have a 2-to-1 advantage, and 1/2 personal cover when you have a 3-to-1 or greater advantage.

HORDE MASTERY

You drive enemies before you and crush them beneath your allies' heels.

Prerequisites: Horde Basics

Benefit: Once per round when you have a 2-to-1 or greater advantage, you and each teammate may Pummel as a half action.

HORDE SUPREMACY

When you show up in force, you show up in *force!*

Prerequisites: Horde Mastery

Benefit: When you have a 2-to-1 or greater advantage, you and each teammate gain a +3 morale bonus to Close Quarters attack damage.

NIGHT FIGHTING

Vision isn't your most critical sense.

Benefit: Unless *deafened,* you ignore the *blinded* condition when targeting any character within 20 ft. You also gain *darkvision I.*

PATHFINDER BASICS

You exploit the environment to great advantage.

Benefit: Choose a terrain, gaining the following benefits. Also, you may always act during surprise rounds and your Travel Speed increases by 2 MPH while in this terrain.

- *Aquatic:* You may hold your breath twice as long and you gain a +2 bonus with Swim checks.
- *Arctic:* You gain Cold Resistance 5 and a +2 bonus with Balance checks.
- *Caverns/Mountains:* You gain Falling Resistance 5 and a +2 bonus with Climb checks.
- *Desert:* You gain Heat Resistance 5 and you require 1/2 your normal fluids *(see page 217)*.
- *Forest/Jungle:* You gain a +2 bonus with Sneak checks.
- *Indoors/Settled:* You gain Sneak Attack Resistance 5.
- *Plains:* You gain a +2 bonus with Notice checks.
- *Swamp:* You gain a +2 bonus with saves against disease and poison.

Special: You may take this feat multiple times, choosing a different terrain each time. Each feat has a separate name (e.g. Pathfinder (Aquatic), Pathfinder (Plains), etc.).

PATHFINDER MASTERY

You're one with your chosen environment, surviving there even against all odds.

Prerequisites: Pathfinder Basics

Benefit: When in one of your Pathfinder terrains, you gain a +4 gear bonus with Blend and Survival checks, and a +2 gear bonus with saves.

PATHFINDER SUPREMACY

You're the master of your domain.

Prerequisites: Pathfinder Mastery

Benefit: All numerical benefits of your Pathfinder Basics feat are doubled (i.e. if you have Pathfinder Basics (Swamp), you gain a +4 bonus with saves against disease and poison).

CHAPTER 3: GRIMOIRE

Magic exists just below the skin of the world, a primal force waiting to be harnessed. Some characters are "casters," able to tap this force to create a wide variety of effects called "spells." Casters fall into two categories.

ARCANE CASTERS

Arcane casters appear in campaigns with the *sorcery* quality *(see page 325)*. Through study and ritual, they learn to direct magic by will alone, choosing their spells and casting them with precision. They're flexible and versatile but also fallible, squandering precious power when they lose control.

Known Spells: When an arcane caster gains his first Casting Level he immediately learns a number of spells of any level equal to his Wisdom score + his Spellcasting ranks. Depending on the nature of magic in the setting *(see page 314)*, these spells may be chosen or randomly rolled on Table 3.2: Spells *(see page 114)*. Once learned, spells may not be exchanged.

When a caster's Wisdom or Spellcasting ranks permanently increase, he learns an equal number of spells.

The method in which spells are gained is left intentionally undefined so it may be fit the needs of the setting. It may involve research, training, or spells may simply "come to" casters.

Knowing a spell does *not* automatically convey the ability to cast it — the limits of arcane spellcasting are set by class.

Losing and Regaining Known Spells: Should an arcane caster's known spells decrease — temporarily or permanently — he chooses which spells are lost. Should this number later increase again the caster must relearn the lost spells before he can gain new ones. Lost spells may be relearned in any order.

Spell Points: An arcane caster invokes spells by spending spell points, which he gains from a number of sources (primarily class). He pays spell points equal to a spell's level each time he tries to cast it (and doesn't regain them even if his Spellcasting check fails). Spell points are fully recovered at the start of each scene with one exception: if any of the caster's spells with a Duration other than Permanent are still in effect from a previous scene, those spell points are *not* recovered, even if the spell's Duration ends during the current scene.

DIVINE CASTERS

Priests and other divine casters appear in campaign with the *miracles* quality *(see page 324)*. They serve as conduits of great forces or divine will, walking pre-set devotional Paths that grant them a variety of magic effects, including a small number of reliable spells they can cast without fail.

Alignment and Paths: The Paths a divine caster may walk are dictated by his god, ethos, or beliefs (i.e. his Alignment). Steps are taken in order along each Path and each Step grants specific abilities that may or may not include spells *(see page 310)*. These abilities may not be exchanged.

When a divine caster invokes a spell granted by a Path, he does not make a Spellcasting check; rather, the spell is automatically cast, as if he'd rolled a Spellcasting result exactly equal to the DC required to cast the spell. When a divine caster invokes an attack spell, the spell is cast as if he'd rolled a Spellcasting result equal to the target's Defense or the Spellcasting DC, whichever is higher *(see Table 3.1: Spellcasting, page 112)*.

When invoking a spell gained from a Path, a divine caster may apply a single Spellcasting trick without paying spell points, but he must still take the Casting Time and pay the spell's Preparation Cost (if any).

Losing and Regaining Alignment and Steps: Should a divine caster lose or change his Alignment or Steps along a Path — temporarily or permanently — he loses all associated abilities and spells. Regaining the Alignment or Steps restores these abilities and spells *(see Crisis of Faith, page 381)*.

Spell Points: A divine caster doesn't gain spell points and doesn't need them to cast spells; instead, spell abilities granted by Paths are generally limited to 1 use per scene *(see page 310)*.

THE SCHOOLS OF MAGIC

Spells are grouped into 8 Schools, each consisting of 3 Disciplines. Each School represents an iconic approach to magic seen in myth, folklore, and fiction, while each Discipline focuses on a set of related effects and activities. Each spell is part of only 1 Discipline.

For an even more robust experience, check out *Spellbound*, available soon in print and PDF.

Channeler: This highly combative School taps and controls primal forces.

- *Energy:* Creates surges of fire, light, and sound, mostly in the form of powerful destructive spells
- *Force:* Generates invisible mass the caster can shape and direct at will
- *Weather:* Manipulates the environment, particularly the atmosphere

Conjuror: This School makes and controls the building blocks of the physical world.

- *Compass:* Alters time, speed, position, and size
- *Conversion:* Changes the shape and properties of matter
- *Creation:* Creates matter from nothing

Enchanter: This intimate School grants dominion over life in all its myriad forms.

- *Charm:* Influences the minds and emotions of others
- *Healing:* Repairs and refreshes the body and mind
- *Nature:* Sways plants and animals

Preserver: This School focuses on protecting and liberating places and people.

- *Glory:* Invokes righteous fury, promoting excellence and victory in battle
- *Seals:* Forms magical glyphs and impediments
- *Warding:* Prevents and deflects harm

Prophet: This School teaches about the worlds beyond ours, as well as what ours might become.

- *Blessing:* Reveals cosmic splendor, raising the body, mind, and spirit
- *Calling:* Channels and summons from the fringes of this world, and beyond
- *Foresight:* Predicts and manifests the future

Reaper: Rooted in suffering and death, this School promotes pain, fear, and corruption.

- *Affliction:* Brings lasting suffering, commonly as curses
- *Necromancy:* Explores the veil between death and undeath
- *Shadow:* Harnesses the power of darkness

Seer: This School offers unique insights about the mechanics of the known world.

- *Artifice:* Exposes and transforms the inner workings of machines, magic items, and spells
- *Divination:* Gleans details about the past and present
- *Word:* Derives power from language

Trickster: This School makes truth of untruth.

- *Illusion:* Projects false images and feelings
- *Secrets:* Invents lies and reveals truths
- *Shapeshifting:* Transforms the body

SPELLCASTING (INT)

Mages and other arcane casters can spend skill points to purchase ranks in the Spellcasting skill, which is only available to characters with a Casting Level of 1 or higher. Spellcasting operates like any other skill.

Tools: A caster without a mage's pouch is considered untrained even when he has Spellcasting ranks *(see page 63)*. With access to a mage's workshop, a caster's threat range increases by 3.

Knowledge: Magic Schools and Disciplines; casting techniques; spell components

SPELLCASTING (VARIES)

An arcane caster makes this check to cast spells he knows and may use (it's possible for a caster to learn spells without having the ability to use them). Each caster may make only 1 Spellcasting check per round and he must be able to speak aloud to do so. Spellcasting is an obvious action and clearly visible to anyone with line of sight to the caster; to conceal an attempt, the caster must also make a Prestidigitation check opposed by Notice.

To make a Spellcasting check, the caster spends spell points equal to the desired spell's level + any additional points required for tricks and other effects. He takes the spell's Casting Time and compares his result to the DC listed on Table 3.1: Spellcasting Checks *(see below)*. With success, the spell is cast and its effect occurs. With failure, the spell is not cast and has no effect (a sentient target feels a hostile force or tingle but cannot deduce the nature or origin of the sensation).

With a critical success, the caster regains the spell points spent to cast the spell. With a critical failure, his confidence is shaken and he suffers a –5 penalty with Spellcasting checks until he succeeds with a Spellcasting check or until the end of the current scene, whichever comes first.

Table 3.1: Spellcasting Checks

Spell Level	DC
0	13
1	16
2	19
3	22
4	25
5	28
6	31
7	34
8	37
9	40

ATTACK SPELLS

When a spell is used to attack, either as part of the spell description (e.g. "long range attack") or due to the situation (e.g. the target tries to avoid a "touch" spell), the Spellcasting result is also the attack result. Spell attacks that inflict damage share the Spellcasting check's threat range. With a critical success, the caster may choose to either regain the spell points spent to cast the spell **or** cause the spell to inflict a critical hit on the original target — not both.

Ranged spell attacks deviate from the first target with a miss *(see page 214)*. For this purpose each range increment is equal to 1/10 the spell's maximum range (rounded up).

SPELL DEFENSE

Certain characters and objects possess Spell Defense, which makes it more difficult to target them with spells. When a target has Spell Defense, the Spellcasting result must also equal or exceed the Spell Defense or the spell fails.

COUNTERED AND SUPPRESSED SPELLS

Various effects can counter or suppress spells.

- A *countered* spell's effect and Duration end. If this occurs during the Spellcasting check, the spell is still considered to have been cast but its effect and Duration end before they begin.
- A *suppressed* spell's effect pauses but its Duration continues. The effect resumes if any Duration remains when the suppression ends.

SPELL DESCRIPTIONS

Each spell description has some or all of these entries.

LEVEL

A spell's level ranges from 0 to 9 and defines its relative power. The spell's Discipline follows its level, as may one or more of these terms.

Air: This spell cannot be cast underwater or in a vacuum.

Aligned: The caster must possess an Alignment to cast this spell and the spell gains the caster's Alignment when it's cast. Depending on the nature of Alignment in the setting, the spell may oppose one or more other Alignments *(see page 309)*.

Curse: This spell cannot be countered or suppressed. It may only be removed with a Lift Curse spell *(see page 135)*.

Darkness (opposes Light): When a damaging Darkness spell targets an undead character, that character instead heals the same amount. Also, magic darkness blocks darkvision.

Earth: This spell cannot be cast in mid-air.

Fire: This spell cannot be cast underwater. Also, any effect or item generated by the spell is suppressed when submerged.

Ice: When this spell's effect happens underwater, an ice block forms across the Area with a Damage save bonus equal to the caster's Casting Level + the Spell Level. Any character caught in this area becomes *pinned* in the ice block (Athletics check DC 20 to escape).

Light (opposes Darkness): When a healing Light spell targets an undead character, that character instead suffers the same amount of damage.

Lightning: When this spell's effect happens underwater, the Distance becomes Personal and the Area becomes an explosive sphere with a blast increment of 2 squares. Everyone in the Area suffers the effect, including the caster.

Silence (opposes Sonic)

Sonic (opposes Silence): This spell may not be cast in a vacuum.

Water: This spell cannot be cast in mid-air.

When two opposing spells occupy the same Area, the spell with the lower Casting Level + Spell Level is countered. When these values are equal, both spells are countered.

CASTING TIME

Most spells have a Casting Time of 1 free, 1 half, or 1 full action. With a longer Casting Time, the effect happens at the start of the caster's first Initiative Count after the casting is complete.

In all cases, the caster makes the Spellcasting check at the moment casting is complete and chooses targets, Area, effect, and other facts of the spell at that time.

DISTANCE

This is the maximum distance at which the effect may be placed.

Personal: The effect happens at the caster.

Touch: The effect happens at a character, object, or piece of scenery the caster touches. Unless the Distance is also Personal, the caster may not place the effect on himself.

Close: The effect may happen at any distance up to 50 ft. from the caster.

Local: The effect may happen at any distance up to 250 ft. from the caster.

Remote: The effect may happen at any distance up to 1,000 ft. from the caster.

Unlimited: The effect may happen anywhere in the caster's current setting (per the GM).

Short Range: The effect travels from the caster up to 50 ft. away.

Medium Range: The effect travels from the caster up to 250 ft. away.

Long Range: The effect travels from the caster up to 1,000 ft. away.

AREA

When a spell's Area is larger than 1 character or object, it's centered on 1 square and consists of a size and shape (e.g. "20 ft. sphere" or "15 ft. cube"). The size is always in feet and represents volume, distance, or radius as noted in the spell description. The caster may decrease a spell's size during casting but not after.

Caster-Defined: The spell's Area may take any shape, so long as each square is adjacent to at least 1 other square (e.g. if the size is 40 ft. the caster may choose any 8 connected squares).

Cone: The spell's Area is a quarter-circle pointed away from the caster in a direction of his choice *(see page 214)*.

Cube: The spell's Area is a square around the target.

Line: The spell's Area is a straight line from the target square in a direction of the caster's choice.

Penetrating: The spell affects targets even through cover (up to Damage save +20).

Pillar: The spell's Area is a vertical pillar whose bottom is a circular shape centered on the target.

Sphere: The spell's Area is a sphere around the target *(see page 214)*.

Wall: The spell's Area is a barrier through a row of squares. It may wind and curve as the caster likes.

DURATION

Most spells have a fixed Duration measured in rounds, minutes, hours, or other common increments, though there are a few exceptions.

Instant: The effect happens and winks out in a fraction of an instant.

Permanent: The effect lingers until the spell is countered.

Concentration: The effect lasts as long as the caster concentrates (taking no other actions).

Concentration, up to Duration: The effect lasts as long as the caster concentrates, up to the listed Duration.

Concentration + Duration: The effect lasts as long as the caster concentrates and for a Duration thereafter.

Dismissible: The effect lasts for a Duration or until the caster voluntarily wills it to end (as a free action). A dismissible effect immediately ends when the caster is killed.

Enduring: A Permanency spell may be cast on the effect.

Variable Duration: The effect lasts a random amount of time (e.g. "1d4 hours"). The GM rolls the Duration secretly so the caster doesn't know how long the spell will last.

SAVING THROW

When a target can make a saving throw to avoid some or all of the effect, the saving throw DC is 10 + the caster's Charisma modifier + the caster's number of Spellcasting feats. Any target may willingly accept a spell's effect, making no saving throw.

Unattended objects cannot make saving throws and are automatically affected by spells cast on them. Carried objects suffer the same effects as characters holding or wearing them.

Disbelief: The character may instead make a Sense Motive (Wis) check to save against the effect.

Negates: With success, the spell has no effect.

Negates Scene: With success, the spell has no effect and the target is immune to the spell for the rest of the scene.

Partial: With success, the effect is lessened as described.

Half: With success, the effect drops to 1/2 (rounded down).

Harmless: The spell is usually beneficial but a target may attempt a saving throw if he likes.

Repeatable: With failure, the target may spend 1 half action during each subsequent round to try again.

Terminal: The effect is catastrophic and frequently game-ending. In the interest of fairness, special characters gain a +4 bonus with their save. This bonus increases to +8 for a villain.

Table 3.2: Spells

Die Result	Spell Level	d4 Result 1	2	3	4
1	Level 0	Create Water	Endure Elements	Glow I	Read Magic
2		Dancing Lights	Expeditious Retreat	Magic Vestment I	Touch of Light
3		Detect Alignment	Feather Fall	Orient Self	Water Walk
4		Detect Secret Doors	Flare	Polar Ray I	Whispers
1	Level 1	Alarm	Control Weather I	Insight	Ray of Enfeeblement
2		Animate Dead I	Cure Wounds I	Jump	Scare I
3		Bless	Deathwatch	Mage Scribe I	Scrye I
4		Call from Beyond I	Detect Magic	Magic Aura	Shatter
5		Cause Wounds I	Disguise Self	Magic Missile	Shield
6		Charm Person I	Divine Favor	Magic Stone	Sleep I
7		Color Spray	Entangle	Magic Weapon I	Tinker I
8		Command I	Entropic Shield	Nature's Ally I	True Strike I
9		Concealing Countryside I	Identify I	Pass without Trace	Unseen Servant
10		Conjure Elemental I	Illusionary Image I	Protection from Alignment	Winter's Domain I
1	Level 2	Align Weapon	Darkness I	Insanity I	Righteous Aura
2		Arcane Lock	Deadly Draft I	Knock	Scare II
3		Blindness/Deafness	Death Knell	Levitate	Scorching Ray
4		Blur	Detect Emotion	Living Library I	Silence
5		Brawn I	Dominate Undead I	Locate Object	Shield Other
6		Calm Emotions	Goodberry	Mage Armor	Status I
7		Cause Wounds II	Gust of Wind	Mirror Images	Tinker II
8		Chill Storm I	Hold Animal	Obscure Object	Water Walk, Mass
9		Consecrate	Hold Person	Resist Energy	Wild Side I
10		Cure Wounds II	Illusionary Image II	Restoration I	Wit I
1	Level 3	Animate Dead II	Cure Wounds III	Keen Edge	Slow
2		Bestow Curse	Darkness II	Lift Curse I	Shape Stone
3		Call from Beyond II	Fireball I	Magic Vestment II	Speak with the Dead
4		Call Lightning I	Fly I	Nature's Ally II	Tiny Shelter
5		Cause Wounds III	Glow II	Neutralize Poison	Tongues I
6		Charm Person II	Glyph of Protection I	Prayer	Verdure
7		Confounding Images	Haste	Scrye II	Wall of Wind
8		Control Weather II	Heroism I	Searing Ray	Water Breathing
9		Conjure Elemental II	Illusionary Image III	See Invisible	Wish I
10		Counter Magic I	Invisibility	Sleep II	Zone of Truth
1	Level 4	Air Walk	Detect Traps	Illusionary Image IV	Resilient Sphere I
2		Brawn II	Devotion Hammer	Lightning Bolt I	Restoration II
3		Castigate I	Dimension Door	Mage Scribe II	Rusting Grasp
4		Cause Wounds IV	Divine Power	Magic Weapon II	Spell Immunity I
5		Chill Storm II	Elemental Shield	Mantle of the Mundane	True Strike II
6		Concealing Countryside II	Flawless Fib	Move Water	Wall of Fire
7		Cure Wounds IV	Freedom of Movement	Phantasmal Killer	Wall of Ice
8		Detect Lies	Geas	Polar Ray II	Wit II
1	Level 5	Animate Dead III	Cone of Cold	Light's Grace	Scrye III
2		Brawn I, Mass	Conjure Elemental III	Living Library II	Teleport I
3		Call from Beyond III	Control Weather III	Mark of Justice	True Seeing
4		Call Lightning II	Cure Wounds I, Mass	Move Earth	Wall of Counter Magic
5		Cause Wounds I, Mass	Fly II	Natural Attunement	Wall of Stone
6		Charm Person III	Heal	Nature's Ally III	Wild Side II
7		Cloudkill	Illusionary Image V	Power Word: Harm	Winter's Domain II
8		Command II	Insanity II	Resurrection I	Wit I, Mass

1	Level 6	Anti-Magic Field I	Find the Path	Illusionary Image VI	Repelling Wave I
2		Blindness/Deafness, Mass	Glyph of Protection II	Lift Curse II	Status, Mass
3		Brawn III	Harm	Lightning Bolt II	Tongues II
4		Cause Wounds II, Mass	Heroes' Feast	Permanency	Tree Walk
5		Cure Wounds II, Mass	Heroism II	Power Word: Recall	Wish II
6		Disintegrate	Identify II	Quake Touch	Wit III
1	Level 7	Animate Dead IV	Counter Magic II	Fire Storm	Regenerate
2		Call from Beyond IV	Cure Wounds III, Mass	Hindsight	Resurrection II
3		Cause Wounds III, Mass	Deadly Draft II	Nature's Ally IV	Scrye IV
4		Charm Person IV	Dominate Undead II	Phase Door	Shadow Walk
5		Control Weather IV	Finger of Death	Project Presence	Sunlight I
6		Conjure Elemental IV	Fireball II	Purge	Teleport II
1	Level 8	Brawn IV	Invisibility, Mass	Polar Ray III	Scintillating Pattern
2		Castigate II	Iron Body	Power Word: Stun	Spell Immunity II
3		Cause Wounds IV, Mass	Living Library III	Protection from Spells	Sunlight II
4		Cure Wounds IV, Mass	Maze	Repelling Wave II	War Cry
5		Earthquake	Mind Blank	Resilient Sphere II	Wild Side III
6		Insanity III	Pinpoint	Sacred Aura	Wit IV
1	Level 9	Animate Dead V	Control Weather V	Heroism III	Resurrection III
2		Anti-Magic Field II	Conjure Elemental V	Lift Curse III	Scrye V
3		Call from Beyond V	Counter Magic III	Nature's Ally V	Time Stop
4		Charm Person V	Heal, Mass	Power Word: Kill	Wish III

Expanding Your Grimoire: Adding spells to your setting's arcane lexicon is easy. Just add rows to any Spell Level in sets of 2, increasing the die type rolled to randomly generate spell effects (e.g. adding 2 rows to Level 4 raises the die type rolled to a d10). If you're adding less than 8 spells, re-roll empty results. Want an even easier solution? Pick up *Spellbound*, available soon in print and PDF. *Spellbound* presents complete grids with hundreds of spells in uniform Schools, each grouped for easy random results.

PREPARATION COST

This powerful spell requires special preparation and costs the caster Reputation (i.e. he calls in favors to obtain materials or set the stage, or he just ignores his friends and associates to give the spell the attention it requires). The caster always pays a spell's Preparation Cost, even if he casts the spell using a scroll, magic item, or other source.

If the Spellcasting check fails, no Reputation is spent.

EFFECT

Every spell's effect is unique.

AIR WALK

Level: 4 Compass (Air)

Casting Time: 1 half action

Distance: Personal or Touch

Duration: 10 minutes per Casting Level

Effect: One character can tread on air as if walking on solid ground. He can move upward or downward at a 45-degree angle, the former at 1/2 his Speed (rounded up).

ALARM

Level: 1 Seals

Casting Time: 1 half action

Distance: Close

Area: 20 ft. penetrating sphere

Duration: 2 hours per Casting Level (dismissible, enduring)

Effect: The Area is protected by either an audible or mental alarm (your choice) that is triggered whenever a corporeal character enters the Area without saying the pre-set password aloud. The audible alarm can be heard at up to 60 ft., while the mental alarm can only be heard by you (and only if you're within 1 mile of the Area).

ALIGN WEAPON

Level: 2 Word (Aligned)

Casting Time: 1 half action

Distance: Touch

Duration: 1 minute per Casting Level

Effect: 1 melee weapon or 50 ammo gains your Alignment.

ANIMATE DEAD I

Level: 1 Necromancy

Casting Time: 1 round

Distance: Close

Duration: 1 minute per Casting Level (dismissible, enduring)

Effect: You animate the remains of 1 dead character as a standard NPC with a Threat Level equal to your Casting Level.

- *Skeleton:* A skeleton may be created from mostly intact bones, whether flesh remains or not.
- *Zombie:* A zombie may only be created from a mostly intact corpse (including muscle).

With GM approval, you may modify your choice, apply the Skeletal or Risen template template to an NPC from the Rogues Gallery *(see page 244)*, or build a new NPC, so long as it has the Undead Type and a maximum XP value of 40.

An animated skeleton or zombie cannot animate or summon other characters and becomes inert when killed or when this spell ends (whichever comes first). Certain spells and other effects can render animated dead inert earlier.

The skeleton or zombie may not act during the round it appears. Thereafter it follows your commands to the best of its ability. In the absence of instructions the skeleton or zombie falls under the GM's control, though it continues to serve you as best it perceives it can (e.g. attacking whatever seems to be your enemy, bringing you things it thinks will help you, etc.).

Skeleton I (Medium Undead Walker — 36 XP): Str 10, Dex 10, Con 10, Int 10, Wis 10, Cha 10; SZ M (Reach 1); Spd 30 ft. ground; Init II; Atk II; Def III; Res IV; Health II; Comp I; Skills: Acrobatics II, Notice III; Qualities: *Damage defiance (edged), damage immunity (bows), ferocity*

Attacks/Weapons: Claw I (dmg 1d6 lethal; threat 20) or Bite I (dmg 1d8 lethal; threat 18–20), as appropriate to the remains + any weapons carried in life (so long as they don't increase the skeleton's XP value above 40)

Zombie I (Medium Undead Walker — 36 XP): Str 10, Dex 10, Con 10, Int 10, Wis 10, Cha 10; SZ M (Reach 1); Spd 30 ft. ground; Init II; Atk III; Def III; Res IV; Health II; Comp I; Skills: Athletics IV, Blend III, Notice IV, Survival III; Qualities: *Devour, lumbering, monstrous defense I, shambling*

Attacks/Weapons: Claw I (dmg 1d6 lethal; threat 20; qualities: *grab*) or Bite I (dmg 1d8 lethal; threat 18–20; qualities: *grab*), as appropriate to the remains + any weapons carried in life (so long as they don't increase the zombie's XP value above 40)

ANIMATE DEAD II

Level: 3 Necromancy

Effect: As Animate Dead I, except that you gain 1 skeleton or zombie (max. 60 XP) or 2 skeletons or zombies (max. 40 XP each).

Skeleton II (Medium Undead Walker — 56 XP): Str 10, Dex 12, Con 12, Int 10, Wis 10, Cha 10; SZ M (Reach 1); Spd 30 ft. ground; Init IV; Atk III; Def IV; Res VI; Health IV; Comp I; Skills: Acrobatics II, Notice IV; Qualities: *Damage defiance (edged), damage immunity (bows), ferocity, rend*

Attacks/Weapons: Claw II (dmg 1d6+1 lethal; threat 19–20; qualities: *finesse*) or Bite II (dmg 1d8+1 lethal; threat 17–20; qualities: *finesse*), as appropriate to the remains + any weapons carried in life (so long as they don't increase the skeleton's XP value above 60)

Zombie II (Medium Undead Walker — 56 XP): Str 12, Dex 10, Con 12, Int 10, Wis 10, Cha 10; SZ M (Reach 1); Spd 30 ft. ground; Init III; Atk IV; Def IV; Res VI; Health IV; Comp I; Skills: Athletics V, Blend IV, Notice IV, Survival IV; Qualities: *Devour, monstrous defense I, shambling*

Attacks/Weapons: Claw II (dmg 1d6+1 lethal + debilitating poison; threat 19–20; qualities: *grab*) or Bite II (dmg 1d8+1 lethal + debilitating poison; threat 17–20; qualities: *grab*), as appropriate to the remains + any weapons carried in life (so long as they don't increase the zombie's XP value above 60)

ANIMATE DEAD III

Level: 5 Necromancy

Effect: As Animate Dead I, except that you gain 1 skeleton or zombie (max. 80 XP), 2 skeletons or zombies (max. 60 XP each), or 4 skeletons or zombies (max. 40 XP each).

Skeleton III (Medium Undead Walker — 76 XP): Str 10, Dex 14, Con 14, Int 10, Wis 10, Cha 10; SZ M (Reach 1); Spd 30 ft. ground; Init V; Atk IV; Def V; Res VII; Health VI; Comp II; Skills: Acrobatics IV, Notice IV; Qualities: *Damage defiance (edged), damage immunity (bows), ferocity, rend, tough I*

Attacks/Weapons: Claw III (dmg 2d6+2 lethal; threat 19–20; qualities: *finesse*) or Bite III (dmg 2d8+2 lethal; threat 17–20; qualities: *finesse*), as appropriate to the remains + any weapons carried in life (so long as they don't increase the skeleton's XP value above 80)

Zombie III (Medium Undead Walker — 76 XP): Str 14, Dex 10, Con 14, Int 10, Wis 10, Cha 10; SZ M (Reach 1); Spd 30 ft. ground; Init IV; Atk V; Def V; Res VII; Health VI; Comp II; Skills: Athletics VI, Blend IV, Notice V, Survival IV; Qualities: *Devour, monstrous defense I, shambling, tough I*

Attacks/Weapons: Claw III (dmg 2d6+2 lethal + debilitating poison; threat 19–20; qualities: *grab*) or Bite III (dmg 2d8+2 lethal + debilitating poison; threat 17–20; qualities: *grab*), as appropriate to the remains + any weapons carried in life (so long as they don't increase the zombie's XP value above 80)

ANIMATE DEAD IV

Level: 7 Necromancy

Effect: As Animate Dead I, except that you gain 1 skeleton or zombie (max. 100 XP), 2 skeletons or zombies (max. 80 XP each), 4 skeletons or zombies (max. 60 XP each), or 8 skeletons or zombies (max. 40 XP each).

Skeleton IV (Medium Undead Walker — 96 XP): Str 10, Dex 16, Con 16, Int 10, Wis 10, Cha 10; SZ M (Reach 1); Spd 30 ft. ground; Init VI; Atk V; Def VI; Res VIII; Health VII; Comp III; Skills: Acrobatics IV, Notice IV; Qualities: *Class ability (Sage: assistance I), damage defiance (edged), damage immunity (bows), ferocity, rend, tough I*

Attacks/Weapons: Claw III (dmg 2d6+3 lethal; threat 19–20; qualities: finesse) **and** Bite III (dmg 2d8+3 lethal; threat 17–20; qualities: finesse), as appropriate to the remains + any weapons carried in life (so long as they don't increase the skeleton's XP value above 100)

Zombie IV (Medium Undead Walker — 96 XP): Str 16, Dex 10, Con 16, Int 10, Wis 10, Cha 10; SZ M (Reach 1); Spd 30 ft. ground; Init V; Atk V; Def V; Res VIII; Health VII; Comp III; Skills: Athletics VI, Blend IV, Notice V, Survival IV; Qualities: *Class ability (Sage: assistance I), devour, monstrous defense I, shambling, tough I*

Attacks/Weapons: Claw III (dmg 2d6+3 lethal + debilitating poison; threat 19–20; qualities: grab) **and** Bite III (dmg 2d8+3 lethal + debilitating poison; threat 17–20; qualities: grab), as appropriate to the remains + any weapons carried in life (so long as they don't increase the zombie's XP value above 100)

ANIMATE DEAD V

Level: 9 Necromancy

Effect: As Animate Dead I, except that you gain 1 skeleton or zombie (max. 120 XP), 2 skeletons or zombies (max. 100 XP each), 4 skeletons or zombies (max. 80 XP each), 8 skeletons or zombies (max. 60 XP each), or 16 skeletons or zombies (max. 40 XP each).

Skeleton V (Medium Undead Walker — 116 XP): Str 10, Dex 18, Con 18, Int 10, Wis 10, Cha 10; SZ M (Reach 1); Spd 30 ft. ground; Init VII; Atk VI; Def VII; Res VIII; Health VIII; Comp IV; Skills: Acrobatics V, Notice V; Qualities: *Class ability (Sage: assistance I), damage defiance (edged), damage immunity (bows), ferocity, rend, tough I, treacherous*

Attacks/Weapons: Claw IV (dmg 2d6+4 lethal; threat 19–20; qualities: *finesse*) **and** Bite IV (dmg 2d8+4 lethal; threat 17–20; qualities: *finesse*), as appropriate to the remains + any weapons carried in life (so long as they don't increase the skeleton's XP value above 120)

Zombie V (Medium Undead Walker — 116 XP): Str 18, Dex 10, Con 18, Int 10, Wis 10, Cha 10; SZ M (Reach 1); Spd 30 ft. ground; Init VI; Atk VI; Def VI; Res VIII; Health VIII; Comp IV; Skills: Athletics VI, Blend V, Notice V, Survival V; Qualities: *Class ability (Sage: assistance I), devour, killing conversion, monstrous defense I, shambling, tough I*

Attacks/Weapons: Claw IV (dmg 2d6+4 lethal + debilitating poison; threat 19–20; qualities: *grab*) **and** Bite IV (dmg 2d8+4 lethal + debilitating poison; threat 17–20; qualities: *grab*), as appropriate to the remains + any weapons carried in life (so long as they don't increase the zombie's XP value above 120)

ANTI-MAGIC FIELD I

Level: 6 Artifice

Casting Time: 1 half action

Distance: Personal

Area: 10 ft. penetrating sphere

Duration: 10 minutes per Casting Level (dismissible)

Effect: An invisible field surrounds you, suppressing all spells and magic items within — including yours. This spell may not be countered.

ANTI-MAGIC FIELD II

Level: 9 Artifice

Casting Time: 1 minute

Area: 1,000 ft. penetrating sphere

Duration: 1 day (dismissible, enduring)

Preparation Cost: 4

Effect: As Anti-Magic Field I, except as noted.

ARCANE LOCK

Level: 2 Seals

Casting Time: 1 half action

Distance: Touch

Duration: Permanent

Effect: One portal or object is magically locked, the Prestidigitation DC required to open it increasing by 10. You may open the portal or object normally.

BESTOW CURSE

Level: 3 Affliction (Curse)

Casting Time: 1 half action

Distance: Touch

Duration: 1 day per Casting Level (dismissible, enduring)

Saving Throw: Will negates

Effect: You curse the target, inflicting one of the following effects.

- 4 temporary impairment with 1 attribute (minimum 1)
- –2 penalty with attack checks, skill checks, and saves
- 25% chance at the start of each Initiative Count that the character loses 1 half action

Alternately, you may invent a curse of your own, though it requires GM approval and shouldn't be any more powerful than these options.

BLESS

Level: 1 Blessing

Casting Time: 1 half action

Distance: Personal

Duration: 1 minute per Casting Level

Effect: You and each ally within 50 ft. when the spell is cast gain a +1 morale bonus with attack checks and Will saves.

BLINDNESS/DEAFNESS

Level: 2 Affliction (Curse)
Casting Time: 1 half action
Distance: Touch
Duration: 1 round per Casting Level (dismissible, enduring)
Saving Throw: Fortitude negates (terminal)
Effect: The target is *blinded* or *deafened,* as you choose.

BLINDNESS/DEAFNESS, MASS

Level: 6 Affliction (Curse)
Distance: Personal
Area: 30 ft. penetrating cone
Effect: As Blindness/Deafness I, except affecting a number of characters in the Area up to your Casting Level.

BLUR

Level: 2 Illusion
Casting Time: 1 half action
Distance: Personal or Touch
Duration: 1 minute per Casting Level (dismissible)
Effect: One character's outline appears blurred, shifting and wavering. Attacks directed at him suffer a –4 penalty.

BRAWN I

Level: 2 Blessing
Casting Time: 1 full action
Distance: Personal or Touch
Duration: 1 minute per Casting Level (dismissible)
Effect: The character gains a +3 magic bonus to your choice of Strength, Dexterity, or Constitution.

BRAWN II

Level: 4 Blessing
Effect: As Brawn I, except the magic bonus increases to +5.

BRAWN III

Level: 6 Blessing
Effect: As Brawn I, except the magic bonus increases to +7.

BRAWN IV

Level: 8 Blessing
Effect: As Brawn I, except the magic bonus increases to +9.

BRAWN I, MASS

Level: 5 Blessing
Area: 50 ft. sphere
Effect: As Brawn I, except that it affects a number of characters in the Area up to your Casting Level.

CALL FROM BEYOND I

Level: 1 Calling
Casting Time: 1 round
Distance: Close
Duration: 1 minute per Casting Level (dismissible, enduring)
Effect: You summon 1 of the following outsiders as a standard NPC with a Threat Level equal to your Casting Level. With GM approval, you may modify your choice, choose an outsider from the Bestiary *(see page 253)*, or build a new NPC, so long as it has the Outsider Type, a maximum XP value of 40, and matches your Alignment (if any).

The servant's nature should match your magic style. It could be a religious icon sent to aid you, an otherworldly being bound by an ancient pact, or something else entirely.

A summoned character cannot summon other characters and is banished when killed or when the spell that summoned it ends (whichever comes first). Certain spells and other effects can banish a summoned character earlier. A banished character's body and possessions dissolve in 1d4 rounds.

The outsider may not act during the round it appears. Thereafter it follows your commands to the best of its ability. In the absence of instructions it falls under the GM's control, though it continues to serve you as best it perceives it can (e.g. advisors offer wisdom, brawlers attack whatever seems to be your enemy, servitors bring you things they think will help you, etc.).

Advisor I (Medium Outsider Flyer/Walker — 36 XP): Str 12, Dex 10, Con 10, Int 14, Wis 14, Cha 10; SZ M (Reach 1); Spd 30 ft. winged flight, 30 ft. ground; Init II; Atk II; Def III; Res III; Health II; Comp VII; Skills: None; Qualities: *Class ability (Keeper: bright idea II), natural spell (Detect Magic, Identify I, Read Magic, Whispers)*

Attacks/Weapons: Dagger (dmg 1d6+1 lethal; threat 19–20; qualities: *bleed, hurl*)

Brawler I (Large Outsider Walker — 36 XP): Str 15, Dex 12, Con 12, Int 12, Wis 10, Cha 10; SZ L (2×2, Reach 2); Spd 40 ft. ground; Init II; Atk IV; Def IV; Res II; Health IV; Comp I; Skills: None; Qualities: *Contagion immunity, menacing threat*

Attacks/Weapons: Broad axe (dmg 1d12+2 lethal; threat 19–20; qualities: *AP 2, massive*)

Servitor I (Tiny Outsider Flyer/Walker — 36 XP): Str 12, Dex 14, Con 10, Int 12, Wis 10, Cha 10; SZ T (Reach 1); Spd 40 ft. winged flight, 20 ft. ground; Init IV; Atk II; Def II; Res III; Health II; Comp II; Skills: Acrobatics III, Sneak III, Spellcasting II; Spells: Detect Magic, Ray of Enfeeblement; Qualities: *Light-sensitive, spell defense I*

Attacks/Weapons: Claw I (dmg 1d3+1 lethal; threat 20)

CALL FROM BEYOND II

Level: 3 Calling

Effect: As Call from Beyond I, except that you gain 1 outsider (max. 60 XP) or 2 outsiders (max. 40 XP each).

Advisor II (Medium Outsider Flyer/Walker — 56 XP): Str 12, Dex 10, Con 10, Int 16, Wis 16, Cha 10; SZ M (Reach 1); Spd 40 ft. winged flight, 30 ft. ground; Init IV; Atk II; Def IV; Res III; Health II; Comp VIII; Skills: None; Qualities: *Class ability (Captain: battle planning II (I want them alive!, no prisoners!, stand fast!, steady now!); Keeper: bright idea II), contagion immunity, darkvision II, natural spell (Detect Magic, Identify I, Read Magic, Whispers)*

Attacks/Weapons: Dagger (dmg 1d6+1 lethal; threat 19–20; qualities: *bleed, hurl*)

Brawler II (Large Outsider Walker — 56 XP): Str 16, Dex 14, Con 16, Int 12, Wis 10, Cha 10; SZ L (2×2, Reach 2); Spd 40 ft. ground; Init II; Atk V; Def V; Res II; Health V; Comp I; Skills: None; Qualities: *Contagion immunity, damage reduction 1, darkvision II, menacing threat, superior jumper II, unnerving*

Attacks/Weapons: Broad axe (dmg 1d12+3 lethal; threat 19–20; qualities: *AP 2, massive*)

Servitor II (Tiny Outsider Flyer/Walker — 56 XP): Str 12, Dex 16, Con 10, Int 12, Wis 10, Cha 10; SZ T (Reach 1); Spd 60 ft. winged flight, 20 ft. ground; Init IV; Atk II; Def II; Res III; Health II; Comp III; Skills: Acrobatics IV, Sneak IV, Spellcasting III; Spells: Detect Magic, Pass without Trace, Ray of Enfeeblement; Qualities: *Chameleon I (caverns/mountains), contagion immunity, darkvision II, improved sense (hearing), light-sensitive, spell defense II*

Attacks/Weapons: Claw I (dmg 1d3+1 lethal; threat 20)

CALL FROM BEYOND III

Level: 5 Calling

Effect: As Call from Beyond I, except that you gain 1 outsider (max. 80 XP), 2 outsiders (max. 60 XP each), or 4 outsiders (max. 40 XP each).

Advisor III (Medium Outsider Flyer/Walker — 76 XP): Str 12, Dex 10, Con 10, Int 18, Wis 18, Cha 12; SZ M (Reach 1); Spd 40 ft. winged flight, 30 ft. ground; Init IV; Atk II; Def IV; Res III; Health II; Comp VIII; Skills: None; Qualities: *Class ability (Captain: battle planning II (I want them alive!, no prisoners!, stand fast!, steady now!); Keeper: bright idea II), contagion immunity, darkvision II, natural spell (Detect Magic, Identify I, Read Magic, Whispers)*

Attacks/Weapons: Dagger (dmg 1d6+1 lethal; threat 19–20; qualities: *bleed, hurl*), Perplexing Riddle (baffling attack II: 30 ft. aura; Will DC 15 or become *baffled* for 2d6 rounds)

Brawler III (Large Outsider Walker — 76 XP): Str 18, Dex 14, Con 18, Int 12, Wis 10, Cha 10; SZ L (2×2, Reach 2); Spd 40 ft. ground; Init II; Atk VI; Def VI; Res IV; Health VI; Comp I; Skills: None; Qualities: *Contagion immunity, damage reduction 1, darkvision II, menacing threat, superior jumper II, unnerving*

Attacks/Weapons: Broad axe (dmg 1d12+4 lethal; threat 19–20; qualities: *AP 2, massive*), Terrifying Roar (frightening attack II: 30 ft. cone; Will DC 15 or become *frightened* for 2d6 rounds)

Servitor III (Tiny Outsider Flyer/Walker — 76 XP): Str 12, Dex 18, Con 10, Int 12, Wis 10, Cha 10; SZ T (Reach 1); Spd 60 ft. winged flight, 20 ft. ground; Init V; Atk III; Def III; Res V; Health III; Comp IV; Skills: Acrobatics V, Sneak V, Spellcasting IV; Spells: Detect Magic, Locate Object, Pass without Trace, Ray of Enfeeblement; Qualities: *Chameleon I (caverns/mountains), contagion immunity, darkvision II, improved sense (hearing), light-sensitive, spell defense II*

Attacks/Weapons: Claw III (dmg 2d3+1 lethal; threat 19–20; qualities: *bleed*), Irritating Flit (enraging attack II: Will DC 15 or become *enraged* for 2d6 rounds)

CALL FROM BEYOND IV

Level: 7 Calling

Effect: As Call from Beyond I, except that you gain 1 outsider (max. 100 XP), 2 outsiders (max. 80 XP each), 4 outsiders (max. 60 XP each), or 8 outsiders (max. 40 XP each).

Advisor IV (Medium Outsider Flyer/Walker — 96 XP): Str 12, Dex 10, Con 10, Int 20, Wis 20, Cha 12; SZ M (Reach 1); Spd 40 ft. winged flight, 30 ft. ground; Init IV; Atk II; Def II; Res III; Health III; Comp IX; Skills: None; Qualities: *Bright I, class ability (Captain: battle planning IV (crush them!, fire at will!, I want them alive!, no prisoners!, stand fast!, steady now!), virtues of command I; Keeper: bright idea II), contagion immunity, darkvision II, natural spell (Detect Magic, Identify I, Read Magic, Whispers)*

Attacks/Weapons: Dagger (dmg 1d6+1 lethal; threat 19–20; qualities: *bleed, hurl*), Perplexing Riddle (baffling attack III: 30 ft. aura; Will DC 20 or become *baffled* for 3d6 rounds)

Brawler IV (Huge Outsider Walker — 96 XP): Str 20, Dex 16, Con 20, Int 12, Wis 10, Cha 10; SZ H (6×6, Reach 3); Spd 50 ft. ground; Init IV; Atk VII; Def VI; Res V; Health VII; Comp I; Skills: None; Qualities: *Contagion immunity, damage reduction 2, darkvision II, dread, menacing threat, superior jumper II, unnerving*

Attacks/Weapons: Broad axe (dmg 1d12+5 lethal; threat 19–20; qualities: *AP 2, massive*), Terrifying Roar (frightening attack III: 30 ft. cone; Will DC 20 or become *frightened* for 3d6 rounds)

Servitor IV (Tiny Outsider Flyer/Walker — 96 XP): Str 12, Dex 20, Con 10, Int 12, Wis 10, Cha 10; SZ T (Reach 1); Spd 60 ft. winged flight, 20 ft. ground; Init VI; Atk IV; Def III; Res V; Health IV; Comp V; Skills: Acrobatics VI, Prestidigitation VI, Sneak VI, Spellcasting V; Spells: Detect Magic, Haste, Locate Object, Pass without Trace, Ray of Enfeeblement; Qualities: *Chameleon II (caverns/mountains), contagion immunity, darkvision II, improved sense (hearing), light-sensitive, regeneration 1, spell defense II*

Attacks/Weapons: Claw III (dmg 2d3+1 lethal; threat 19–20; qualities: *bleed*), Irritating Flit (enraging attack III: Will DC 20 or become *enraged* for 3d6 rounds)

CALL FROM BEYOND V

Level: 9 Calling

Effect: As Call from Beyond I, except that you gain 1 outsider (max. 120 XP), 2 outsiders (max. 100 XP each), 4 outsiders (max. 80 XP each), 8 outsiders (max. 60 XP each), or 16 outsiders (max. 40 XP each).

Advisor V (Medium Outsider Flyer/Walker — 116 XP): Str 12, Dex 10, Con 10, Int 22, Wis 22, Cha 12; SZ M (Reach 1); Spd 30 ft. ground, 40 ft. winged flight; Init V; Atk II; Def III; Res IV; Health III; Comp IX; Skills: None; Qualities: *Bright II, class ability (Captain: battle planning IV (crush them!, fire at will!, I want them alive!, no prisoners!, stand fast!, steady now!), virtues of command I; Keeper: bright idea II), contagion immunity, darkvision II, natural spell (Detect Emotion, Detect Magic, Identify I, Read Magic, Status, Tongues I, Whispers)*

Attacks/Weapons: Dagger (dmg 1d6+1 lethal; threat 19–20; qualities: *bleed, hurl*), Perplexing Riddle (baffling attack IV: 30 ft. aura; Will DC 25 or become *baffled* for 4d6 rounds)

Brawler V (Huge Outsider Walker — 116 XP): Str 22, Dex 18, Con 22, Int 12, Wis 10, Cha 10; SZ H (6×6, Reach 3); Spd 50 ft. ground; Init V; Atk VIII; Def VIII; Res V; Health VIII; Comp I; Skills: Intimidate V; Qualities: *Contagion immunity, damage reduction 3, darkvision II, dread, menacing threat, superior jumper II, unnerving*

Attacks/Weapons: Broad axe (dmg 1d12+6 lethal; threat 19–20; qualities: *AP 2, massive*), Terrifying Roar (frightening attack IV: 30 ft. cone; Will DC 25 or become *frightened* for 4d6 rounds)

Servitor V (Tiny Outsider Flyer/Walker — 116 XP): Str 12, Dex 22, Con 12, Int 12, Wis 10, Cha 10; SZ T (Reach 1); Spd 60 ft. winged flight, 20 ft. ground; Init VII; Atk IV; Def IV; Res VI; Health V; Comp V; Skills: Acrobatics VII, Prestidigitation VII, Sneak VII, Spellcasting VI; Spells: Detect Magic, Haste, Locate Object, Pass without Trace, Ray of Enfeeblement, Searing Ray; Qualities: *Contagion immunity, darkvision II, improved sense (hearing), invisibility, light-sensitive, regeneration 1, spell defense II*

Attacks/Weapons: Claw III (dmg 2d3+1 lethal; threat 19–20; qualities: *bleed*), Irritating Flit (enraging attack IV: Will DC 25 or become *enraged* for 4d6 rounds)

CALL LIGHTNING I

Level: 3 Weather (Lightning)

Casting Time: 1 full action

Distance: Local

Area: 60 ft. sphere

Duration: 1 minute per Casting Level

Effect: Once per round, you may spend 1 half action to call a local lightning strike in the Area *(see page 369)*. You may call 1 strike per 2 Casting Levels (maximum 8).

CALL LIGHTNING II

Level: 5 Weather (Lightning)

Distance: Remote

Effect: As Call Lightning I, except you may call 1 local or near strike per Casting Level (maximum 12). You may also call one or more direct strikes, though each reduces the number of local or near strikes by 4.

CALM EMOTIONS

Level: 2 Charm

Casting Time: 1 half action

Distance: Local

Area: 20 ft. penetrating sphere

Duration: Concentration, up to 1 round per Casting Level (dismissible)

Saving Throw: Will negates (terminal)

Effect: Characters in the Area are pacified, losing all morale bonuses and penalties, as well as the *enraged* condition (if any of them have it). They also lose the will to fight, becoming unable to make attacks or indulge in other aggressive behavior. This spell ends when any affected character is attacked or otherwise accosted.

CASTIGATE I

Level: 4 Word (Aligned, Sonic)

Casting Time: 1 full action

Distance: Close

Area: 20 ft. penetrating sphere

Duration: Instant

Saving Throw: Will half

Effect: Your faith shakes those with an opposing Alignment to the core, inflicting 1d6 divine damage per 2 Casting Levels (maximum 10d6).

CASTIGATE II

Level: 8 Word (Aligned, Sonic)

Area: 60 ft. penetrating sphere

Saving Throw: Will half (damage)

Effect: As Castigate I, except targets also become *sprawled.*

CAUSE WOUNDS I

Level: 1 Shadow (Darkness)

Casting Time: 1 full action

Distance: Touch

Duration: Instant

Saving Throw: Will half

Effect: Your target suffers 10 lethal damage.

CAUSE WOUNDS II

Level: 2 Shadow (Darkness)

Effect: As Cause Wounds I, except your target suffers 20 lethal damage.

CAUSE WOUNDS III

Level: 3 Shadow (Darkness)

Effect: As Cause Wounds I, except your target suffers 30 lethal damage.

CAUSE WOUNDS IV

Level: 4 Shadow (Darkness)

Effect: As Cause Wounds I, except your target suffers 40 lethal damage.

CAUSE WOUNDS I, MASS

Level: 5 Shadow (Darkness)

Distance: Close

Effect: As Cause Wounds I, except it affects a number of characters up to your Casting Level.

CAUSE WOUNDS II, MASS

Level: 6 Shadow (Darkness)

Distance: Close

Effect: As Cause Wounds II, except it affects a number of characters up to your Casting Level.

CAUSE WOUNDS III, MASS

Level: 7 Shadow (Darkness)

Distance: Close

Effect: As Cause Wounds III, except it affects a number of characters up to your Casting Level.

CAUSE WOUNDS IV, MASS

Level: 8 Shadow (Darkness)

Distance: Close

Effect: As Cause Wounds IV, except it affects a number of characters up to your Casting Level.

CHARM PERSON I

Level: 1 Charm

Casting Time: 1 half action

Distance: Close

Duration: 1 hour per Casting Level

Saving Throw: Will negates (terminal)

Effect: The Disposition of 1 character who shares a Type with you increases by 5. A character is only swayed by the largest single Disposition modifier from a spell at any time. This spell ends when the affected character is attacked or otherwise accosted.

CHARM PERSON II

Level: 3 Charm

Effect: As Charm Person I, except the target's Disposition increases by 10.

CHARM PERSON III

Level: 5 Charm

Effect: As Charm Person I, except the target's Disposition increases by 15.

CHARM PERSON IV

Level: 7 Charm

Effect: As Charm Person I, except the target's Disposition increases by 20.

CHARM PERSON V

Level: 9 Charm

Effect: As Charm Person I, except the target's Disposition increases by 25.

CHILL STORM I

Level: 2 Weather (Ice)

Casting Time: 1 full action

Distance: Remote

Area: 200 ft. per Casting Level sphere

Duration: 1 round per 2 Casting Levels (enduring)

Effect: Light snow blankets the Area, increasing Defense by 2, decreasing visual range increments by 20 ft., and inflicting 1d4 cold damage per round.

CHILL STORM II

Level: 4 Weather (Ice)

Effect: As Chill Storm I, except boosting Defense by 3 and decreasing visual range increments by 30 ft. As a half action, you may end this spell early to rain hail down on the Area, inflicting 3d6 lethal damage.

Cloudkill

CLOUDKILL

Level: 5 Creation (Air)

Casting Time: 1 half action

Distance: Local

Area: 20 ft. penetrating sphere

Duration: 1 minute per Casting Level (dismissible)

Saving Throw: Fortitude negates (death), Fortitude half (Con impairment)

Effect: The Area floods with poisonous fog. Each standard character must make a Fortitude save or die when entering and at the start of each round they remain, while each special character suffers 1d4 temporary Constitution impairment when entering and at the start of each round they remain (Fort save for 1/2, rounded down). The cloud harms on contact, so holding one's breath doesn't help, but characters immune to poison are unaffected.

The cloud may be stationary or move 10 ft. away from you each round (choose when the spell is cast). Its vapors are heavier than air and sink, even pouring down through openings. The cloud can't penetrate liquids. Wind disperses it in 4 rounds and a tornado disperses it immediately. The cloud burns away in 2 rounds when exposed to 20+ fire damage.

COLOR SPRAY

Level: 1 Illusion

Casting Time: 1 half action

Distance: Personal

Area: 15 ft. cone

Duration: Instant

Saving Throw: Will negates (disbelief)

Effect: A vivid cone of clashing colors springs forth from your hand. Anyone in the Area is *blinded* for 1d4 rounds and *stunned* for 1 round.

Blinded and sightless creatures are unaffected by *color spray.*

COMMAND I

Level: 1 Word

Casting Time: 1 free action

Distance: Close

Duration: 1 round

Saving Throw: Will negates scene

Effect: One character immediately performs 1 Movement Action of your choice to the best of his ability.

COMMAND II

Level: 5 Word

Duration: 1 round per Casting Level

Effect: As Command I, except that up to 1 character per Casting Level perform 1 action each.

CONCEALING COUNTRYSIDE I

Level: 1 Nature

Casting Time: 1 half action

Distance: Personal

Duration: 1 hour per Casting Level (dismissible)

Effect: Your surroundings bend and weave, conspiring to mask your presence from others and granting you a +4 magic bonus with Blend and Sneak checks. This spell may only be cast in areas with significant plant life.

CONCEALING COUNTRYSIDE II

Level: 4 Nature

Distance: Personal or Touch

Area: 15 ft. penetrating sphere

Effect: As Concealing Countryside I, except a number of characters up to 1/2 your Casting Level gain the bonus, which increases to +10. The spell ends if any of these characters move outside the Area.

CONE OF COLD

Level: 5 Weather (Ice)

Casting Time: 1 half action

Distance: Personal

Area: 60 ft. cone

Duration: Instant

Saving Throw: Reflex half

Effect: Bitter frost shoots from your fingertips, inflicting 1d6 cold damage per Casting Level (maximum 12d6).

CONFOUNDING IMAGES

Level: 3 Illusion

Casting Time: 1 half action

Distance: Close

Duration: 1 round per Casting Level

Saving Throw: Will negates

Effect: One character may not make free attacks targeting you. He also suffers a –2 penalty with attack checks targeting you and a –2 penalty to his Defense against your attacks.

CONJURE ELEMENTAL I

Level: 1 Creation (Air, Earth, Fire, or Water)

Casting Time: 1 round

Distance: Close

Duration: 1 minute per Casting Level (dismissible, enduring)

Effect: You summon 1 of the following elementals as a standard NPC with a Threat Level equal to your Casting Level. With GM approval, you may modify your choice, choose an elemental from the Bestiary *(see page 253)*, or build a new NPC, so long as it has the Elemental Type and a maximum XP value of 40.

The appearance of this servant should match your style of magic. At the GM's discretion, it could take the form of any species, though this choice has no effect on the NPC's stats. The NPC is always composed entirely of the spell's element.

A summoned character cannot summon other characters and is banished when killed or when the spell that summoned it ends (whichever comes first). Certain spells and other effects can banish a summoned character earlier. A banished character's body and possessions dissolve in 1d4 rounds.

The elemental may not act during the round it appears. Thereafter it follows your commands to the best of its ability. In the absence of instructions the elemental falls under the GM's control, though it continues to serve you as best it perceives it can (e.g. attacks whatever seems to be your enemy, brings you things it thinks will help you, etc.).

Air Elemental I (Small Elemental Flyer — 36 XP): Str 10, Dex 12, Con 10, Int 6, Wis 10, Cha 10; SZ S (Reach 1); Spd 40 ft. flight; Init III; Atk III; Def III; Res III; Health III; Comp II; Skills: Acrobatics IV; Qualities: *Achilles heel (electricity), blindsight, damage defiance (sonic), tricky (Shove)*

Attacks/Weapons: Slam I (dmg 1d4+1 subdual; threat 20; qualities: *finesse, trip*)

Earth Elemental I (Small Elemental Burrower/Walker — 36 XP): Str 12, Dex 8, Con 12, Int 6, Wis 10, Cha 10; SZ S (Reach 1); Spd 30 ft. burrow, 30 ft. ground; Init I; Atk II; Def II; Res III; Health III; Comp I; Skills: Athletics II; Qualities: *Achilles heel (sonic), banned action (Swim, Tumble), charge attack, damage reduction 1, darkvision II, improved stability, lumbering, tough I*

Attacks/Weapons: Slam I (dmg 1d4+1 lethal; threat 20; qualities: *AP 2*)

Fire Elemental I (Small Elemental Flyer — 36 XP): Str 10, Dex 12, Con 10, Int 6, Wis 10, Cha 10; SZ S (Reach 1); Spd 40 ft. flight; Init II; Atk IV; Def II; Res II; Health II; Comp I; Skills: Tactics II; Qualities: *Achilles heel (cold), banned action (Swim), damage immunity (fire), grueling combatant, natural defense (fire)*

Attacks/Weapons: Slam I (dmg 1d4+1 fire; threat 20; qualities: *finesse, keen 4*)

Water Elemental I (Small Elemental Walker — 36 XP): Str 14, Dex 10, Con 10, Int 6, Wis 10, Cha 10; SZ S (Reach 1); Spd 20 ft. ground; Init II; Atk II; Def I; Res II; Health II; Comp I; Skills: Athletics III; Qualities: *Achilles heel (cold, heat), blindsight, damage defiance (bows, edged), grappler, improved stability, knockback, superior swimmer VIII*

Attacks/Weapons: Slam I (dmg 1d4+2 subdual; threat 20)

CONJURE ELEMENTAL II

Level: 3 Creation (Air, Earth, Fire, or Water)

Effect: As Conjure Elemental I, except that you gain 1 elemental (max. 60 XP) or 2 elementals (max. 40 XP each).

Air Elemental II (Medium Elemental Flyer — 56 XP): Str 10, Dex 14, Con 10, Int 6, Wis 10, Cha 10; SZ M (Reach 1); Spd 60 ft. flight; Init IV; Atk III; Def III; Res III; Health IV; Comp III; Skills: Acrobatics V; Qualities: *Achilles heel (electricity), blindsight, damage defiance (sonic), feat (Mobility Basics), knockback, tricky (Shove)*

Attacks/Weapons: Slam II (dmg 1d6+2 subdual; threat 19–20; qualities: *finesse, trip*), Blasting Wind (sprawling attack I: 20 ft. cone; Fort DC 10 or become *sprawled*)

Earth Elemental II (Medium Elemental Burrower/ Walker — 56 XP): Str 14, Dex 8, Con 14, Int 6, Wis 10, Cha 10; SZ M (Reach 1); Spd 30 ft. burrow, 30 ft. ground; Init I; Atk II; Def IV; Res III; Health IV; Comp I; Skills: Athletics II, Search I; Qualities: *Achilles heel (sonic), banned action (Swim, Tumble), charge attack, damage reduction 1, darkvision II, improved stability, lumbering, tough I*

Attacks/Weapons: Slam I (dmg 1d6+2 lethal; threat 20; qualities: *AP 2*), Shifting Earth (slowing attack I: 30 ft. aura; Fort DC 10 or become *slowed* for 1d6 rounds)

Fire Elemental II (Medium Elemental Flyer — 56 XP): Str 10, Dex 14, Con 10, Int 6, Wis 10, Cha 10; SZ M (Reach 1); Spd 60 ft. flight; Init III; Atk IV; Def II; Res III; Health III; Comp II; Skills: Search III, Tactics II; Qualities: *Achilles heel (cold), banned action (Swim), damage defiance (lethal), damage immunity (fire), fearsome, grueling combatant, natural defense (fire)*

Attacks/Weapons: Slam I (dmg 1d6+2 fire; threat 20; qualities: *finesse, keen 4*), Ignition (fire damage attack I: 5 ft. blast; dmg 1d4 fire per 2 TL, Ref DC 10 for 1/2 damage)

Water Elemental II (Medium Elemental Walker — 56 XP): Str 16, Dex 10, Con 10, Int 6, Wis 10, Cha 10; SZ M (Reach 1); Spd 20 ft. ground; Init II; Atk II; Def III; Res III; Health III; Comp II; Skills: Athletics IV; Qualities: *Achilles heel (cold, heat), blindsight, damage defiance (bows, edged), grappler, improved stability, knockback, natural spell (Move Water), superior swimmer VIII*

Attacks/Weapons: Slam I (dmg 1d6+3 subdual; threat 20; qualities: *grab*), Riptide (stunning attack II: Will DC 15 or become *stunned* for 2d6 rounds)

CONJURE ELEMENTAL III

Level: 5 Creation (Air, Earth, Fire, or Water)

Effect: As Conjure Elemental I, except that you gain 1 elemental (max. 80 XP), 2 elementals (max. 60 XP each), or 4 elementals (max. 40 XP each).

Air Elemental III (Medium Elemental Flyer — 76 XP): Str 12, Dex 16, Con 12, Int 6, Wis 10, Cha 10; SZ M (Reach 1); Spd 80 ft. flight; Init IV; Atk III; Def V; Res III; Health IV; Comp II; Skills: Acrobatics V, Search III; Qualities: *Achilles heel (electricity), blindsight, critical surge, damage defiance (lethal, sonic), feat (Mobility Basics, Mobility Mastery), knockback, tricky (Shove)*

Attacks/Weapons: Slam II (dmg 1d6+3 subdual; threat 19–20; qualities: *finesse, trip*), Blasting Wind (sprawling attack II: 20 ft. cone; Fort DC 15 or become *sprawled*)

Earth Elemental III (Medium Elemental Burrower/ Walker — 76 XP): Str 16, Dex 8, Con 16, Int 6, Wis 10, Cha 10; SZ M (Reach 1); Spd 30 ft. burrow, 30 ft. ground; Init I; Atk IV; Def V; Res III; Health VI; Comp I; Skills: Athletics III, Notice III, Search II; Qualities: *Achilles heel (sonic), banned action (Swim, Tumble), charge attack, damage reduction 2, darkvision II, improved stability, lumbering, monstrous defense I, tough I*

Attacks/Weapons: Slam I (dmg 1d6+3 lethal; threat 20; qualities: *AP 2*), Shifting Earth (slowing attack I: 30 ft. aura; Fort DC 10 or become *slowed* for 1d6 rounds)

Fire Elemental III (Medium Elemental Flyer — 76 XP): Str 12, Dex 16, Con 12, Int 6, Wis 10, Cha 10; SZ M (Reach 1); Spd 80 ft. flight; Init VI; Atk VII; Def II; Res IV; Health III; Comp II; Skills: Search III, Tactics II; Qualities: *Achilles heel (cold), banned action (Swim), damage defiance (lethal), damage immunity (fire), fearsome, grueling combatant, natural defense (fire), tough I*

Attacks/Weapons: Slam I (dmg 1d6+3 fire; threat 20; qualities: *finesse, keen 4*), Ignition (fire damage attack I: 5 ft. blast; dmg 1d4 fire per 2 TL, Ref DC 10 for 1/2 damage)

Water Elemental III (Medium Elemental Walker — 76 XP): Str 14, Dex 10, Con 12, Int 6, Wis 10, Cha 10; SZ M (Reach 1); Spd 20 ft. ground; Init III; Atk II; Def III; Res III; Health III; Comp III; Skills: Athletics III; Qualities: *Achilles heel (cold, heat), blindsight, damage immunity (bows, edged), grappler, improved stability, knockback, natural spell (Mass Water Walk, Move Water), superior swimmer VIII*

Attacks/Weapons: Slam I (dmg 1d6+2 subdual; threat 20; qualities: *grab, reach +1*), Riptide (stunning attack II: Will DC 15 or become *stunned* for 2d6 rounds)

CONJURE ELEMENTAL IV

Level: 7 Creation (Air, Earth, Fire, or Water)

Effect: As Conjure Elemental I, except that you gain 1 elemental (max. 100 XP), 2 elementals (max. 80 XP each), 4 elementals (max. 60 XP each), or 8 elementals (max. 40 XP each).

Air Elemental IV (Large Elemental Flyer — 96 XP): Str 12, Dex 16, Con 12, Int 6, Wis 10, Cha 10; SZ L (2×2, Reach 2); Spd 100 ft. flight; Init VI; Atk III; Def VI; Res III; Health IV; Comp II; Skills: Acrobatics V, Search III; Qualities: *Achilles heel (electricity),* *blindsight, critical surge, damage defiance (lethal, sonic), feat (Mobility Basics, Mobility Mastery), knockback, tricky (Shove)*

Attacks/Weapons: Slam II (dmg 1d8+3 subdual; threat 19–20; qualities: *finesse, trip*), Blasting Wind (sprawling attack II: 20 ft. cone; Fort DC 15 or become *sprawled*), Dust Cloud (blinding attack I: 40 ft. aura; Will DC 10 or become *blinded* for 1d6 rounds)

Earth Elemental IV (Large Elemental Burrower/Walker — 96 XP): Str 18, Dex 8, Con 16, Int 6, Wis 10, Cha 10; SZ L (2×2, Reach 2); Spd 40 ft. burrow, 30 ft. ground; Init II; Atk V; Def VI; Res IV; Health VI; Comp I; Skills: Athletics VII, Notice III, Search II; Qualities: *Achilles heel (sonic), banned action (Swim, Tumble), charge attack, damage reduction 2, darkvision II, improved stability, lumbering, monstrous defense I, tough I*

Attacks/Weapons: Slam II (dmg 1d8+4 lethal; threat 19–20; qualities: *AP 4*), Rift Strike (sprawling attack II: 40 ft. beam; Fort DC 15 or become *sprawled*), Shifting Earth (slowing attack I: 30 ft. aura; Fort DC 10 or become *slowed* for 1d6 rounds)

Fire Elemental IV (Large Elemental Flyer — 96 XP): Str 12, Dex 16, Con 12, Int 6, Wis 10, Cha 10; SZ L (2×2, Reach 2); Spd 80 ft. flight; Init VI; Atk VII; Def III; Res VI; Health III; Comp II; Skills: Search III, Tactics III; Qualities: *Achilles heel (cold), banned action (Swim), damage defiance (lethal), damage immunity (fire), fearsome, grueling combatant, natural defense (fire), tough I*

Attacks/Weapons: Slam III (dmg 2d8+3 fire; threat 19–20; qualities: *finesse, keen 4*), Heat Wave (heat damage attack I: 30 ft. aura; dmg 1d4 heat per 2 TL, Ref DC 10 for 1/2 damage), Ignition (fire damage attack I: 5 ft. blast; dmg 1d4 fire per 2 TL, Ref DC 10 for 1/2 damage)

Water Elemental IV (Large Elemental Walker — 96 XP): Str 18, Dex 10, Con 14, Int 6, Wis 10, Cha 10; SZ L (2×2, Reach 2); Spd 20 ft. ground; Init III; Atk IV; Def III; Res V; Health V; Comp III; Skills: Athletics IV, Search IV; Qualities: *Achilles heel (cold, heat), blindsight, damage immunity (bows, edged), grappler, improved stability, knockback, natural spell (Mass Water Walk, Move Water), superior swimmer VIII, tough I*

Attacks/Weapons: Slam III (dmg 2d8+4 subdual; threat 19–20; qualities: *grab, reach +1*), Drown (Swallow II: dmg 1d12+4 lethal; notes: Grapple benefit — Small and smaller only), Riptide (stunning attack II: Will DC 15 or become *stunned* for 2d6 rounds)

CONJURE ELEMENTAL V

Level: 9 Creation (Air, Earth, Fire, or Water)

Effect: As Conjure Elemental I, except that you gain 1 elemental (max. 120 XP), 2 elementals (max. 100 XP each), 4 elementals (max. 80 XP each), 8 elementals (max. 60 XP each), or 16 elementals (max. 40 XP each).

Air Elemental V (Large Elemental Flyer — 116 XP): Str 12, Dex 18, Con 12, Int 6, Wis 12, Cha 12; SZ L (2×2, Reach 2); Spd 100 ft. flight; Init VIII; Atk V; Def VII; Res IV; Health V; Comp III; Skills: Acrobatics V, Search IV; Qualities: *Achilles heel (electricity), blindsight, critical surge, damage immunity (lethal, sonic), feat (Mobility Basics, Mobility Mastery), knockback, tricky (Shove)*

Attacks/Weapons: Slam III (dmg 2d8+4 subdual; threat 19–20; qualities: *finesse, trip*), Blasting Wind (sprawling attack III: 20 ft. cone; Fort DC 20 or become *sprawled*), Dust Cloud (blinding attack II: 40 ft. aura; Will DC 15 or become *blinded* for 2d6 rounds)

Earth Elemental V (Large Elemental Burrower/Walker — 116 XP): Str 18, Dex 8, Con 16, Int 6, Wis 10, Cha 10; SZ L (2×2, Reach 2); Spd 40 ft. burrow, 30 ft. ground; Init II; Atk V; Def VII; Res IV; Health VII; Comp I; Skills: Athletics VIII, Notice III, Search II; Qualities: *Achilles heel (sonic), banned action (Swim, Tumble), charge attack, damage reduction 4, darkvision II, improved stability, lumbering, monstrous defense II, tough I*

Attacks/Weapons: Slam III (dmg 2d8+4 lethal; threat 19–20; qualities: *AP 4*), Rift Strike (sprawling attack III: 40 ft. beam; Fort DC 20 or become *sprawled*), Shifting Earth (slowing attack II: 30 ft. aura; Fort DC 15 or become *slowed* for 2d6 rounds)

Fire Elemental V (Large Elemental Flyer — 116 XP): Str 14, Dex 16, Con 12, Int 6, Wis 10, Cha 10; SZ L (2×2, Reach 2); Spd 80 ft. flight; Init VI; Atk VII; Def III; Res VI; Health III; Comp II; Skills: Search IV, Tactics IV; Qualities: *Achilles heel (cold), banned action (Swim), damage defiance (lethal), damage immunity (fire), fearsome, feat (Combat Focus, Combat Instincts), grueling combatant, natural defense (fire), tough I*

Attacks/Weapons: Slam IV (dmg 2d8+3 fire; threat 18–20; qualities: *finesse, keen 4*), Heat Wave (heat damage attack II: 30 ft. aura; dmg 1d4 heat per 2 TL, Ref DC 15 for 1/2 damage), Ignition (fire damage attack II: 15 ft. blast; dmg 1d4 fire per 2 TL, Ref DC 15 for 1/2 damage)

Water Elemental V (Large Elemental Walker — 116 XP): Str 20, Dex 10, Con 16, Int 6, Wis 10, Cha 10; SZ L (2×2, Reach 2); Spd 20 ft. ground; Init IV; Atk V; Def IV; Res III; Health VI; Comp III; Skills: Athletics IV, Search IV; Qualities: *Achilles heel (cold, heat), blindsight, damage immunity (bows, edged), feat (Ferocity Basics, Ferocity Mastery, Ferocity Supremacy), grappler, improved stability, knockback, natural spell (Mass Water Walk, Move Water), superior swimmer X, tough I*

Attacks/Weapons: Slam III (dmg 2d8+5 subdual; threat 19–20; qualities: *grab, reach +1*), Drown (Swallow III: dmg 2d12+5 lethal; notes: Grapple benefit — Small and smaller only), Riptide (stunning attack II: Will DC 15 or become *stunned* for 2d6 rounds)

CONSECRATE

Level: 2 Word (Aligned)
Casting Time: 1 half action
Distance: Touch
Area: 20 ft. sphere
Duration: 1 hour per Casting Level
Effect: This spell anoints an Area, countering Consecrate spells with an opposing Alignment. Undead and outsiders with the same Alignment gain a +2 magic bonus with Morale checks, attack checks, damage, and saves, while those with an opposing Alignment suffer an equivalent penalty (–2 with these checks, damage, and saves). If the Area contains an altar, shrine, or other permanent fixture dedicated to your Alignment, these modifiers are doubled. You cannot consecrate an area with a similar fixture of a faith other than your own.

Characters may not be summoned into an Area consecrated with the opposed alignment.

CONTROL WEATHER I

Level: 1 Weather (Air)
Casting Time: 1 full action
Distance: Personal
Area: 200 ft. per Casting Level sphere
Duration: 24 hours
Effect: One cold/heat wave, dust/fog/rain/snow, or wind effect with an action die cost of 1 occurs in the Area *(see page 369)*. If desired, you may create an "eye" of calm weather up to 80 ft. in diameter around you. The effect builds over 1d6 minutes after casting. Your choice may change with a full action, the new effect building over the next 1d6 minutes.

CONTROL WEATHER II

Level: 3 Weather (Air)
Area: 400 ft. per Casting Level sphere
Effect: As Control Weather I, allowing any effect with an action die cost up to 2.

CONTROL WEATHER III

Level: 5 Weather (Air)
Area: 600 ft. per Casting Level sphere
Effect: As Control Weather I, allowing any effect with an action die cost up to 3 (or any two effects with a cost of 1).

CONTROL WEATHER IV

Level: 7 Weather (Air)
Area: 800 ft. per Casting Level sphere
Effect: As Control Weather I, allowing any effect with an action die cost up to 4 (or any two effects with a cost of 2).

CONTROL WEATHER V

Level: 9 Weather (Air)
Area: 1,000 ft. per Casting Level sphere
Effect: As Control Weather I, allowing any two effects with a cost of 3 or any three effects with a cost of 1.

COUNTER MAGIC I

Level: 3 Warding
Casting Time: 1 full action
Distance: Touch
Duration: Instant
Effect: You counter one spell effect whose Casting Level + Spell Level is equal to or less than your Casting Level + 3. Some effects may not be countered, as noted in their descriptions.

COUNTER MAGIC II

Level: 7 Warding
Distance: Personal
Area: 15 ft. penetrating sphere
Effect: As Counter Magic I, except that it affects a total number of Spell Levels equal to your Casting Level × 3 and counters effects whose Casting Level + Spell Level is equal to or less than your Casting Level + 7. Spells are countered in order from the caster outward.

COUNTER MAGIC III

Level: 9 Warding
Area: 30 ft. penetrating sphere
Effect: As Counter Magic II, except that it targets every spell effect in the Area and counters effects whose Casting Level + Spell Level is equal to or less than your Casting Level + 9.

CREATE WATER

Level: 0 Creation (Water)
Casting Time: 1 half action
Distance: Close
Duration: Instant
Effect: You create up to 2 gallons of drinkable water per Casting Level. If desired, the water may appear in any open container within the Distance.

CURE WOUNDS I

Level: 1 Healing (Light)
Casting Time: 1 full action
Distance: Touch
Duration: Instant

Saving Throw: Will half (damage vs. undead)

Effect: You heal 10 damage on a standard character, or 10 vitality or 1 wound on a special character (your choice).

CURE WOUNDS II

Level: 2 Healing (Light)

Effect: As Cure Wounds I, except you heal 20 damage on a standard character, or 20 vitality or 3 wounds on a special character (your choice).

CURE WOUNDS III

Level: 3 Healing (Light)

Effect: As Cure Wounds I, except you heal 30 damage on a standard character, or 30 vitality or 6 wounds on a special character (your choice).

CURE WOUNDS IV

Level: 4 Healing (Light)

Effect: As Cure Wounds I, except you heal 40 damage on a standard character, or 40 vitality or 10 wounds on a special character (your choice).

CURE WOUNDS I, MASS

Level: 5 Healing (Light)

Distance: Close

Effect: As Cure Wounds I, except you heal a number of characters up to your Casting Level.

CURE WOUNDS II, MASS

Level: 6 Healing (Light)

Distance: Close

Effect: As Cure Wounds II, except you heal a number of characters up to your Casting Level.

CURE WOUNDS III, MASS

Level: 7 Healing (Light)

Distance: Close

Effect: As Cure Wounds III, except you heal a number of characters up to your Casting Level.

CURE WOUNDS IV, MASS

Level: 8 Healing (Light)

Distance: Close

Effect: As Cure Wounds IV, except you heal a number of characters up to your Casting Level.

DANCING LIGHTS

Level: 0 Energy (Light)

Casting Time: 1 half action

Distance: Local

Area: 60 ft. sphere

Duration: 1 minute (dismissible, enduring)

Effect: Up to 4 lantern-like lights, 4 glowing spheres, or 1 faint, vaguely humanoid shape appear, each illuminating a 10 ft. radius. The lights can instantly move anywhere in the Area and wink out of existence if they leave. While one or more of them is within 5 ft., you gain a +1 gear bonus with Conceal Action checks and Diversions.

DARKNESS I

Level: 2 Shadow (Darkness)

Casting Time: 1 half action

Distance: Touch

Area: 20 ft. penetrating sphere

Duration: 10 minutes per Casting Level (dismissible)

Effect: One target object radiates overwhelming darkness, eliminating ambient and other non-magical light in the Area. This effect is suppressed while the object is completely covered by any solid material.

DARKNESS II

Level: 3 Shadow (Darkness)

Area: 60 ft. penetrating sphere

Duration: 1 day per Casting Level (dismissible, enduring)

Effect: As Darkness I, except as noted.

DEADLY DRAFT I

Level: 2 Weather (Ice)

Casting Time: 1 half action

Distance: Close

Area: 25 ft. long line, 10 ft. wide

Duration: 3 rounds

Saving Throw: Fortitude half

Effect: The Area fills with a chill wind, inflicting a cumulative 1d6 cold damage (e.g. 1d6 during Round 1, 2d6 during Round 2, and 3d6 during Round 3).

DEADLY DRAFT II

Level: 7 Weather (Ice)

Duration: 1 round per 2 Casting Levels

Effect: As Deadly Draft I, except as noted.

DEATH KNELL

Level: 2 Necromancy

Casting Time: 1 half action

Distance: Touch

Duration: 1 hour

Effect: You touch an ally, teammate, or adversary who died in the current or previous round, draining their dwindling life force and gaining a +1 bonus to Strength and Casting Level. You may cast this spell only once on each corpse and the maximum bonus you may gain from it is +5.

DEATHWATCH

Level: 1 Necromancy
Casting Time: 1 half action
Distance: Personal
Area: 30 ft. penetrating cone
Duration: 10 minutes per Casting Level
Effect: You instantly know the type and state (alive, dead, or wounded) of each character you can see in the Area.

DETECT ALIGNMENT

Level: 0 Divination
Casting Time: 1 half action
Distance: Personal
Area: 60 ft. penetrating cone
Duration: Concentration + 1 minute per Casting Level (dismissible)
Effect: You sense aligned characters and objects. You may learn the Alignment of a character or object you sense with a successful Knowledge check (DC 15).

DETECT EMOTION

Level: 2 Divination
Casting Time: 1 half action
Distance: Personal
Area: 60 ft. penetrating cone
Duration: Concentration + 1 minute per Casting Level (dismissible)
Saving Throw: Will negates scene
Effect: You sense the Dispositions of characters. You may identify the focus of a sensed character's attention with a successful Knowledge check (DC 15).

DETECT LIES

Level: 4 Divination
Casting Time: 1 half action
Distance: Personal
Area: 60 ft. penetrating cone
Duration: Concentration + 1 minute per Casting Level (dismissible)
Saving Throw: Will negates scene
Effect: You sense lies. You may determine whether a specific person in the Area is lying with a successful Knowledge check (DC 15).

DETECT MAGIC

Level: 1 Divination
Casting Time: 1 half action
Distance: Personal
Area: 60 ft. penetrating cone
Duration: Concentration + 1 minute per Casting Level (dismissible)
Effect: You sense magic and magical characters and objects. You may learn the Discipline of any spell you sense with an additional Knowledge check (DC 15).

DETECT SECRET DOORS

Level: 0 Secrets
Casting Time: 1 half action
Distance: Personal
Area: 60 ft. penetrating cone
Duration: Concentration + 1 minute per Casting Level (dismissible)
Effect: You sense concealed and secret doors and areas. You may identify the method of opening a door or portal you sense with a successful Knowledge check (DC 15).

DETECT TRAPS

Level: 4 Secrets
Casting Time: 1 half action
Distance: Personal
Area: 60 ft. penetrating cone
Duration: Concentration + 1 minute per Casting Level (dismissible)
Effect: You sense mechanical traps with a Stash result up to your Casting Level + 20. You may identify the method of disabling a trap you sense with a successful Knowledge check (DC 15).

DEVOTION HAMMER

Level: 4 Force (Aligned)
Casting Time: 1 half action
Distance: Local
Area: 20 ft. sphere
Duration: Instant
Saving Throw: Will half (damage), Will negates (condition)
Effect: An explosion of power smites all characters who don't share your Alignment in the Area, leaving them *stunned* for 1d6 rounds. Each target with an opposing Alignment suffers 1d8 force damage per 2 Casting Levels (maximum 10d8), and each other character suffers 1d4 force damage per 2 Casting Levels (maximum 10d4).

DIMENSION DOOR

Level: 4 Compass
Casting Time: 1 full action
Distance: Personal or Touch
Duration: Instant
Saving Throw: Will negates
Effect: You instantly move to any location within 1,000 ft. and may bring along 1 willing character per 3 Casting Levels. All transported characters must be touching each other and at least 1 of them must be touching you.

If any character arrives in a square occupied by solid material, the character and the material each suffer 1d6 lethal damage and the character appears in a random adjacent and unoccupied square. If no adjacent squares are unoccupied, the character reappears back where he was before the spell was cast.

DISGUISE SELF

Level: 1 Shapeshifting
Casting Time: 1 half action
Distance: Personal
Duration: 10 minutes per Casting Level (dismissible)
Effect: Your look and that of your immediate possessions changes, granting you a Disguise result equal to your Spellcasting result (minimum 20). Your appearance reverts if you're knocked unconscious or killed before the spell ends.

DISINTEGRATE

Level: 6 Compass
Casting Time: 1 half action
Distance: Medium range attack
Duration: Instant
Saving Throw: Fortitude half (terminal)
Effect: One character suffers 1d10 damage per Casting Level (maximum 14d10). If the target's wounds drop to 0 or below as a result, he and his belongings are destroyed.

Alternately, Disintegrate destroys and annihilates objects and scenery within a 10 ft. cube, even if it's magical. Only artifacts resist this effect.

DIVINE FAVOR

Level: 1 Glory
Casting Time: 1 half action
Distance: Personal
Duration: 1 minute
Effect: You gain a magic bonus with attack and damage rolls equal to 1/3 your Casting Level (rounded up).

DIVINE POWER

Level: 4 Glory
Casting Time: 1 half action
Distance: Personal
Duration: 1 round per Casting Level
Effect: Your base attack bonus becomes equal to your Career Level, you gain a +5 magic bonus to Strength, and you gain DR equal to your Casting Level against the next attack that hits you.

DOMINATE UNDEAD I

Level: 2 Necromancy
Casting Time: 1 round
Distance: Close
Duration: 1 minute per Casting Level
Saving Throw: Will negates scene (terminal) *(see Effect)*
Effect: You compel a single standard undead character who can hear you to obey your verbal instructions (even if he doesn't understand your language). A character with an Intelligence score of 5 or less automatically fails this save and only understands basic commands: "come here," "go there," "fight," "stand still," and so on. A character with an Intelligence score of 6 or higher remembers the spell and may seek retribution later. Issuing a command that places the character in personal jeopardy immediately grants him another Will save and issuing a suicidal command immediately ends the spell. The spell also ends if you, a teammate, or an ally attacks the character.

You may only have a single Dominate spell in effect at any given time.

DOMINATE UNDEAD II

Level: 7 Necromancy
Duration: 1 hour per Casting Level (dismissible)
Effect: As Dominate Undead I, except you may control a number of standard undead characters up to 1/2 your Casting Level (rounded down).

EARTHQUAKE

Level: 8 Conversion (Earth)
Casting Time: 1 half action
Distance: Remote
Area: 80 ft. penetrating sphere
Duration: 1 round
Saving Throw: Reflex half (dmg), Reflex negates (conditions)
Effect: An intense but highly localized tremor occurs, inflicting 8d6 lethal damage on all scenery, characters, and objects on the ground. Characters also become *sprawled* and are *stunned* for 1d6 rounds.

ELEMENTAL SHIELD

Level: 4 Energy (Fire or Ice)
Casting Time: 1 half action
Distance: Personal
Duration: 1 round per Casting Level (dismissible)
Effect: Fire or ice covers you, reducing incoming damage of the other element to 1/2 normal (rounded down). Also, anyone who hits you with an unarmed or melee attack that doesn't have the *reach* quality suffers 1d6 fire or cold damage + 1 per 2 Casting Levels (maximum +10).

ENDURE ELEMENTS

Level: 0 Warding
Casting Time: 1 half action
Distance: Personal or Touch
Duration: 24 hours
Effect: One character and his carried gear suffer no harm from hot and cold environments. This spell offers no protection against fire damage or temperature-based attacks.

ENTANGLE

Level: 1 Nature

Casting Time: 1 half action

Distance: Remote

Area: 40 ft. penetrating sphere

Duration: 1 minute per Casting Level (dismissible)

Saving Throw: Reflex partial (repeatable)

Effect: Plant life wraps and twists around characters in the Area and those who enter, leaving Large and smaller victims *entangled* and unable to move until they make their save.

This spell may only be cast in areas with vegetation.

Entangle

ENTROPIC SHIELD

Level: 1 Warding

Casting Time: 1 half action

Distance: Personal

Duration: 1 minute per Casting Level (dismissible)

Effect: You're surrounded by an aura of distorted space that inflicts a –4 penalty with incoming ranged attacks.

EXPEDITIOUS RETREAT

Level: 0 Compass

Casting Time: 1 half action

Distance: Personal

Duration: 1 minute (dismissible)

Effect: You gain a +20 ft. magic bonus to your Speed when Running.

FEATHER FALL

Level: 0 Force

Casting Time: 1 free action (may be cast anytime, even during another character's Initiative Count)

Distance: Close

Area: 30 ft. sphere

Duration: 1 round per Casting Level

Effect: A number of freefalling characters and objects up to to your Casting Level descend at 60 ft. per round, suffering no damage if they land during the Duration.

FIND THE PATH

Level: 6 Divination

Casting Time: 1 minute

Distance: Personal or Touch

Duration: Instant

Effect: The target learns the shortest, most direct physical route to a specified destination, even if it winds around corners or through concealed or tight spaces (but not impossible ones — the spell always reveals a route the target can traverse). This spell does reveal traps but not how to disable them, nor does it reveal adversaries and other hostile characters along the route.

FINGER OF DEATH

Level: 7 Affliction

Casting Time: 1 half action

Distance: Close

Duration: Instant

Saving Throw: Fortitude partial (terminal)

Effect: If the target fails his save he immediately dies; otherwise he suffers 3d6 damage + 1 per Casting Level. Constructs, elementals, spirits, and undead are unaffected by this spell.

FIREBALL I

Level: 3 Energy (Fire)

Casting Time: 1 half action

Distance: Medium range attack

Area: 20 ft. sphere

Duration: Instant

Saving Throw: Reflex half

Effect: A bead of flame roars from your palm and may travel through any Small or larger opening. At detonation, the fireball inflicts 1d6 fire damage (AP 5) per 2 Casting Levels (maximum 8d6).

FIREBALL II

Level: 7 Energy (Fire)

Effect: As Fireball I, inflicting 1d6 fire damage (AP 5) per Casting Level (maximum 16d6). Also, you may delay the detonation by up to 5 rounds.

FIRE STORM

Level: 7 Energy (Fire)
Casting Time: 1 round
Distance: Local
Area: 10 ft. per Casting Level caster-defined
Duration: Instant
Saving Throw: Reflex half

Effect: Flames engulf the Area, inflicting 1d4 fire damage (AP 5) per Casting Level (maximum 16d4).

FLARE

Level: 0 Energy (Light)
Casting Time: 1 half action
Distance: Close
Area: 20 ft. sphere
Duration: Instant
Saving Throw: Fortitude negates

Effect: A burst of light appears, forcing all characters in the Area who can see it to make a Fortitude save or suffer a –1 magic penalty with attack checks for 1d6 rounds.

FLAWLESS FIB

Level: 4 Secrets
Casting Time: 1 half action
Distance: Personal
Duration: 10 minutes per Casting Level (dismissible)

Effect: You gain a +10 magic bonus with Bluff checks and Spell Defense equal to your Casting Level + 15 against spells that force you to speak the truth or reveal that you're lying.

FLY I

Level: 3 Force
Casting Time: 1 half action
Distance: Personal or Touch
Duration: 1 minute per Casting Level

Effect: One character gains the ability to fly at a Speed of 45 ft. (with up to a light load) or 30 ft. (with a heavy load); a character with a heavier load cannot fly. The target may ascend at 1/2 this Speed and descend at twice this Speed. Because the target isn't anchored while flying, his Size is considered 2 categories smaller when resisting Bull Rush and Grapple actions.

If the target is still airborne when the spell ends or is countered or suppressed, he immediately falls.

FLY II

Level: 5 Force
Duration: 1 hour per Casting Level

Effect: As Fly I, except that the target gains a flying Speed of 60 ft. (with up to a light load) or 40 ft. (with a heavy load).

FREEDOM OF MOVEMENT

Level: 4 Shapeshifting
Casting Time: 1 half action
Distance: Personal or Touch
Duration: 10 minutes per Casting Level

Effect: The target can move and make melee and unarmed attacks normally, even while under the influence of movement-impeding magic and similar effects. Also, the target can't be grappled.

GEAS

Level: 4 Charm (Curse)
Casting Time: 1 round
Distance: Close
Duration: 1 day per Casting Level (dismissible, enduring)
Saving Throw: Will negates (terminal)

Effect: You compel a single character who can hear and understand you to follow a specific set of instructions, or to refrain from a specific set of actions. You cannot direct the target to commit suicide or perform acts that would result in certain death.

If the target is prevented from obeying the instructions for 24 hours, he suffers 2 temporary impairment with each attribute. This impairment increases by 2 per day he's prevented from obeying (maximum penalty of 8 to each, to a minimum score of 1 in each). This impairment is lost when the target is once again able to obey.

This spell ends when dismissed, when the target completes the instructions, or when the Duration ends, whichever comes first.

GLOW I

Level: 0 Energy (Light)
Casting Time: 1 half action
Distance: Touch
Area: 30 ft. sphere (bright light) + 30 ft. sphere (dim light)
Duration: 10 minutes per Casting Level (dismissible)

Effect: The target glows, lighting the Area. This effect moves with the target and is concealed if the target is covered.

GLOW II

Level: 3 Energy (Light)
Area: 60 ft. sphere (intense light) + additional 60 ft. sphere (bright light) + additional 60 ft. sphere (dim light)

Effect: As Glow I, except as noted.

GLYPH OF PROTECTION I

Level: 3 Seals
Casting Time: 10 minutes
Distance: Touch
Area: 1 object or up to 5 ft. × 5 ft. per Casting Level penetrating caster-defined
Duration: Permanent (dismissible)
Saving Throw: Reflex half (damage) or as triggered spell
Preparation Cost: 2
Effect: You create a magical trap safeguarding an object or area. You define the trap's trigger, which is typically when a character opens or touches the object, or enters the area, but it can be further refined by intruder Alignment, species, Type, and/or physical characteristics (such as height and weight). You may also establish a verbal password that disables the trap. An object or area may only be protected by one magical trap at a time.

Finally, you may apply one of two protective glyphs.

Blast Glyph: When triggered, the trap inflicts 1d8 damage per 2 Casting Levels (max. 5d8) to all characters within 5 ft. You may set the damage type as acid, cold, fire, force, electricity, or sonic.

Spell Glyph: When triggered, the trap automatically casts a harmful spell (up to Level 3) that you know. The spell's Area, if any, is centered on the intruder. Spell effects are determined using your Casting Level when the glyph is placed. If a Spellcasting check is called for, it's equal to your Spellcasting bonus + 10. If the spell summons characters, they appear as close as possible to the intruder and attack.

GLYPH OF PROTECTION II

Level: 6 Seals
Preparation Cost: 5
Effect: As Glyph of Protection I, except that a blast glyph inflicts up to 10d8 damage and a spell glyph can store a single spell up to Level 6.

GOODBERRY

Level: 2 Nature
Casting Time: 1 half action
Distance: Touch
Duration: 1 day per Casting Level
Effect: You gain 2d6 magical berries that each operate as any 1 food the eater desires (the choice is made when the berry is consumed). The berries spoil when the Duration ends.

GUST OF WIND

Level: 2 Weather (Air)
Casting Time: 1 half action
Distance: Personal
Area: 60 ft. long line, 15 ft. wide
Duration: 1 round
Effect: Unanchored characters and objects are hit by a Huge Bull Rush result equal to the Spellcasting result.

HARM

Level: 6 Necromancy (Darkness)
Casting Time: 1 half action
Distance: Touch
Duration: Instant
Saving Throw: Will half
Effect: You flood 1 character with negative energy, inflicting 10 points of damage per Casting Level (maximum 150). This cannot reduce a special character's wounds to less than 1.

HASTE

Level: 3 Compass
Casting Time: 1 half action
Distance: Close
Duration: 1 round per Casting Level
Effect: One character gains 1 additional half action per round and a +1 magic bonus with attack checks and Reflex saves. Each character may be targeted by only 1 Haste spell at a time.

This spell counters Slow.

HEAL

Level: 5 Healing
Casting Time: 1 full action
Distance: Touch
Duration: Instant
Effect: One character recovers from disease, poison, and attribute impairment, and loses 3 conditions of your choice.

HEAL, MASS

Level: 9 Healing
Casting Time: 1 full action
Distance: Close
Effect: As Heal, except targeting a number of characters up to your Casting Level.

HEROES' FEAST

Level: 6 Creation
Casting Time: 10 minutes
Distance: Close
Duration: 12 hours
Effect: You serve up a great magical feast, including a magnificent table and chairs, servants, and food and drink for 1 character per Casting Level. The feast takes 1 hour to consume and fully sustains each character for the day. It also cures all disease, removes the *sickened* condition, and grants DR 10 against the next hit that each character suffers during the current scene. For the next 12 hours each character also becomes immune to poison and gains a +1 morale bonus with attack checks and Will saves.

If the feast is interrupted for any reason, the spell is ruined and the characters gain no benefit.

HEROISM I

Level: 3 Blessing
Casting Time: 1 half action
Distance: Touch
Duration: 10 minutes per Casting Level
Effect: One character gains a +2 morale bonus with attack checks, saves, and skill checks. He also gains Spell Defense 20 against Shadow spells.

HEROISM II

Level: 6 Blessing
Effect: As Heroism I, except the bonus is +4 and the Spell Defense is 30.

HEROISM III

Level: 9 Blessing
Effect: As Heroism I, except the bonus is +6 and the Spell Defense is 40.

HINDSIGHT

Level: 7 Divination
Casting Time: 10 minutes
Distance: Personal
Area: 20 ft. sphere
Duration: Concentration + 1 minute per Casting Level
Preparation Cost: Varies *(see Effect)*
Effect: You project your vision and hearing back in time at your current location. You may observe events in real time or skim them at up to 60 times their normal rate (e.g. observing a minute in a second). The maximum time you may project back is 24 hours per 1 Preparation Cost.

HOLD ANIMAL

Level: 2 Nature
Casting Time: 1 half action
Distance: Local
Duration: 1 round per Casting Level (dismissible)
Saving Throw: Will negates (repeatable, terminal)
Effect: One animal becomes *paralyzed.*

HOLD PERSON

Level: 2 Charm
Casting Time: 1 half action
Distance: Local
Duration: 1 round per Casting Level (dismissible)
Saving Throw: Will negates (repeatable, terminal)
Effect: One character who shares a Type with you becomes *paralyzed.*

IDENTIFY I

Level: 1 Artifice
Casting Time: 8 hours
Distance: Touch
Duration: Instant
Preparation Cost: 1
Effect: You learn whether an object is magical (and if so what it does, how to activate it, and any remaining charges).

IDENTIFY II

Level: 6 Artifice
Casting Time: 1 full action
Duration: 3 rounds
Preparation Cost: 3
Effect: As Identify I, except targeting 1 object per round.

ILLUSIONARY IMAGE I

Level: 1 Illusion
Casting Time: 1 half action
Distance: Remote
Area: 10 ft. per Casting Level penetrating cube
Duration: Concentration + 1 round
Saving Throw: Will negates (disbelief)
Effect: You create a visual illusion of any size and shape. The illusion doesn't exhibit sound, smell, texture, or temperature but it can move and animate, so long as it remains entirely in the Area.

ILLUSIONARY IMAGE II

Level: 2 Illusion
Duration: Concentration + 2 rounds
Effect: As Illusionary Image I, except the illusion may include minor sounds (but not speech).

ILLUSIONARY IMAGE III

Level: 3 Illusion
Duration: Concentration + 3 rounds
Effect: As Illusionary Image II, except the illusion may include speech, smell, and non-damaging heat.

ILLUSIONARY IMAGE IV

Level: 4 Illusions
Duration: 1 minute per Casting Level (dismissible)
Effect: As Illusionary Image III, except the illusion may follow a script, eliminating the need for you to concentrate.

ILLUSIONARY IMAGE V

Level: 5 Illusion
Duration: Special *(see Effect)*
Effect: As Illusionary Image IV, except the illusion remains dormant until a trigger of your choice occurs (typically someone entering or approaching the Area), after which it lingers for 1 round per Casting Level. The trigger must rely on things that can be seen, heard, smelled, or felt in the Area.

ILLUSIONARY IMAGE VI

Level: 6 Illusion

Duration: Permanent

Effect: As Illusionary Image V, except the illusion is permanent. You may control the illusion while concentrating, leave, and return to concentrate and control it again. The illusion resumes its script when you're away.

INSANITY I

Level: 2 Charm

Casting Time: 1 full action

Distance: Touch

Duration: 1 round per Casting Level

Saving Throw: Will negates (repeatable)

Effect: One character behaves randomly for the Duration. At the start of the target's Initiative Count each round, roll 1d20 and consult Table 3.3: Insanity.

Table 3.3: Insanity

Result	Behavior
1–2	Character is unaffected
3–8	Character becomes *stunned*
9–14	Character becomes *frightened* of the caster
15–20	Character becomes *enraged*

INSANITY II

Level: 5 Charm

Distance: Local

Duration: 1 minute per Casting Level

Effect: As Insanity I, except targeting 1 character and all other characters adjacent to him.

INSANITY III

Level: 8 Charm (Curse)

Distance: Local

Duration: 1 day per Casting Level (dismissible, enduring)

Saving Throw: Will negates (terminal)

Effect: As Insanity I, except as noted.

INSIGHT

Level: 1 Divination

Casting Time: 1 minute

Distance: Personal

Duration: Instant

Effect: You gain a GM hint relating to the goals of the current scene. This spell may only be cast once per scene.

INVISIBILITY

Level: 3 Secrets

Casting Time: 1 half action

Distance: Personal or Touch

Duration: 1 minute per Casting Level (dismissible)

Effect: One character or object weighing no more than 100 lbs. per Casting Level become *invisible*. Gear carried by a target character also becomes *invisible*, though items dropped or put down become visible again. Items picked up disappear if tucked into an invisible character's clothing or bags.

This spell ends when the target character makes an attack.

INVISIBILITY, MASS

Level: 8 Secrets

Distance: Remote

Effect: As Invisibility, except targeting a combined number of characters and objects up to your Casting Level. The effect is mobile with the group and the spell ends when anyone in the target group attacks. Individuals in the group cannot see each other.

The spell also ends for any individual who moves more than 400 ft. from the nearest other member of the group. If only two individuals are affected, the one moving becomes visible. If both are moving away from each other, they both become visible.

IRON BODY

Level: 8 Shapeshifting

Casting Time: 1 half action

Distance: Personal

Duration: 1 minute per Casting Level

Preparation Cost: 5

Effect: Your body becomes living iron, making you a construct with DR 15 and Slam III. Your Strength score rises by 6 and you suffer only 1/2 fire and acid damage (rounded up). However, your Dexterity score drops by 6, your Speed drops to 1/2 normal (rounded up), and you suffer a –8 Armor Check Penalty *(see page 173)*. Your weight is multiplied by 10.

JUMP

Level: 1 Shapeshifting

Casting Time: 1 half action

Distance: Touch

Duration: 1 minute per Casting Level (dismissible)

Effect: One character gains a magic bonus with Jump checks equal to 3 × your Casting Level (maximum +30). Also, his Jump distances aren't limited by his height.

KEEN EDGE

Level: 3 Conversion

Casting Time: 1 half action

Distance: Local

Duration: 10 minutes per Casting Level

Effect: One edged weapon or 50 hurled ammo becomes magically sharp, gaining a +2 magic bonus to threat range.

KNOCK

Level: 2 Force
Casting Time: 1 half action
Distance: Touch
Duration: Special *(see Effect)*
Effect: One door, lock, container, or restraint is opened or released if your Spellcasting result beats its Complexity. Alternately, one Arcane Lock is suppressed for 1 minute per Casting Level.

LEVITATE

Level: 2 Force
Casting Time: 1 half action
Distance: Personal or Close
Duration: 1 minute per Casting Level (dismissible)
Saving Throw: Will negates (harmless)
Effect: Once per round as a half action, you may vertically move 1 unanchored character or object weighing up to 100 lbs. per Casting Level at a Speed of 20 ft. You may not move the target horizontally but a target character may propel himself along an available surface at 1/2 his Speed (rounded up).

A levitated character who attacks finds himself increasingly unstable, suffering a cumulative –1 penalty (–1 with the first attack, –2 with the second, and so on, to a maximum of –5). He may spend 1 full round to stabilize himself, negating this penalty.

LIFT CURSE I

Level: 3 Blessing
Casting Time: 1 half action
Distance: Touch
Duration: Instant
Effect: One character or object loses curses with a Casting Level + Spell Level equal to or less than your Casting Level + 3.

LIFT CURSE II

Level: 6 Blessing
Effect: As Lift Curse I, except removing curses with a Casting Level + Spell Level equal to or less than your Casting Level + 6.

LIFT CURSE III

Level: 9 Blessing
Effect: As Lift Curse I, except removing curses with a Casting Level + Spell Level equal to or less than your Casting Level + 9.

LIGHTNING BOLT I

Level: 4 Weather (Lightning)
Casting Time: 1 half action
Distance: Personal ranged attack
Area: 100 ft. + 10 ft. per Casting Level line
Duration: Instant
Saving Throw: Reflex half
Effect: You discharge powerful electrical energy across the Area, inflicting 1d6 electrical damage per 2 Casting Levels (maximum 10d6).

LIGHTNING BOLT II

Level: 6 Weather (Lightning)
Area: 10 ft. per Casting Level caster-defined
Effect: As Lightning Bolt I, except the first target hit suffers 1d6 electrical damage per Casting Level (maximum 14d6), and each target hit thereafter suffers 4 less damage than the target before him.

LIGHT'S GRACE

Level: 5 Blessing (Light)
Casting Time: 1 half action
Distance: Personal or Touch
Duration: 1 minute per Casting Level
Effect: One character gains 25 Resistance against damage from Darkness spells.

LIVING LIBRARY I

Level: 2 Divination
Casting Time: 1 half action
Distance: Personal
Duration: 1 hour per Casting Level
Effect: You gain a +2 magic bonus with Research checks. As a half action, you may end this spell early to gain a +2 magic bonus with a single Knowledge check.

LIVING LIBRARY II

Level: 5 Divination
Effect: As Living Library I, except that you gain a +4 magic bonus with Research checks and may end the spell early to gain a +4 magic bonus with a single Knowledge check.

LIVING LIBRARY III

Level: 8 Divination
Effect: As Living Library I, except that you gain a +10 magic bonus with Research checks and may end the spell early to gain a +10 magic bonus with a single Knowledge check.

LOCATE OBJECT

Level: 2 Divination
Casting Time: 1 minute
Distance: Unlimited
Duration: 1 hour per Casting Level
Effect: You sense the direction of a familiar object, or the nearest object of a general type (e.g. sword, coin, jewel, etc.).

MAGE ARMOR

Level: 2 Force
Casting Time: 1 half action
Distance: Personal or Touch
Duration: 1 hour (dismissible)
Effect: An invisible but tangible field of force surrounds the target, granting him a +4 gear bonus to Defense.

MAGE SCRIBE I

Level: 1 Word
Casting Time: Varies *(see Effect)*
Distance: Touch
Duration: Permanent (dismissible)
Effect: You create script and images on any surface at the rate of 1,000 words or 1 image per hour, or copy an existing document at the rate of 1,000 words or 1 image per minute. The words may be written in any language you know other than arcane script *(see pages 61 and 142)*.

MAGE SCRIBE II

Level: 4 Word
Effect: As Mage Scribe I, except you may embed 1 of your Interests into the script. The next character without the Interest who reads the text in full gains the Interest until the end of the current adventure. The script may only transfer the Interest once; thereafter, it acts as described in Mage Scribe I.

MAGIC AURA

Level: 1 Secrets
Casting Time: 1 half action
Distance: Touch
Duration: 1 day per Casting Level (dismissible)
Saving Throw: Will negates (disbelief)
Effect: When identified *(see pages 77 and 133)*, one item weighing up to 5 lbs. per Casting Level may appear non-magical, magical with Essence(s) and Charm(s) of your choice, or the target of a spell you choose.

MAGIC MISSILE

Level: 1 Force
Casting Time: 1 half action
Distance: Short range
Duration: Instant
Effect: You may fire 3 missiles at targets you can see, each missile inflicting 1d6 force damage.

MAGIC STONE

Level: 1 Conversion (Earth)
Casting Time: 1 half action
Distance: Touch
Duration: 1 hour (dismissible)
Effect: You transmute up to 3 pebbles into magic hurled ammunition, each inflicting a different type of damage.

MAGIC VESTMENT I

Level: 0 Conversion
Casting Time: 1 full action
Distance: Touch
Duration: 1 minute per Casting Level (dismissible)
Effect: You imbue a set of clothes, a piece of armor, or a shield with a +1 magic bonus to Defense.

MAGIC VESTMENT II

Level: 3 Conversion
Duration: 1 hour (dismissible)
Effect: As Magic Vestment I, except that it grants a +1 magic bonus per 4 Casting Levels.

MAGIC WEAPON I

Level: 1 Conversion
Casting Time: 1 full action
Distance: Touch
Duration: 1 minute per Casting Level (dismissible)
Effect: You grant a weapon or 50 ammo a +1 magic bonus with attack checks and damage rolls. You can't cast this spell on natural attacks, extraordinary attacks, or unarmed attacks.

MAGIC WEAPON II

Level: 4 Conversion
Duration: 1 hour (dismissible)
Effect: As Magic Weapon I, except that it grants a +1 magic bonus per 4 Casting Levels.

MANTLE OF THE MUNDANE

Level: 4 Artifice
Casting Time: 1 full action
Distance: Touch
Duration: 1 round per Casting Level
Saving Throw: Will negates
Effect: All magic bonuses affecting one character and all adjacent characters and objects decrease by 1 per 5 Casting Levels (minimum 1).

MARK OF JUSTICE

Level: 5 Seals (Curse)
Casting Time: 10 minutes
Distance: Touch
Duration: 1 day per Casting Level (dismissible, enduring)
Effect: You draw an indelible mark on a character and identify an action that triggers it. When the character performs the action, the mark curses him, targeting him with a successful Bestow Curse spell *(see page 117)*.

MAZE

Level: 8 Compass
Casting Time: 1 half action
Distance: Close
Duration: 10 minutes
Effect: You imprison one character in a labyrinthine gap between worlds. The spell ends early if the character makes a successful 1-minute Knowledge check (DC 15 + your Casting Level), or if the character is targeted with a successful spell that transfers him back to this world.

At the character's return, he appears at his previous location, or in the nearest unoccupied square.

MIND BLANK

Level: 8 Secrets
Casting Time: 1 half action
Distance: Close
Duration: 24 hours
Saving Throw: Will negates (harmless)
Effect: One character's thoughts and emotions can't be read. Also, the character can't be magically observed in his location and Divination spells targeting him automatically fail.

MIRROR IMAGES

Level: 2 Illusion
Casting Time: 1 half action
Distance: Personal
Duration: 1 minute per Casting Level (dismissible)
Effect: You create multiple illusory copies of yourself, masking your true location. You create 1d4 copies + 1 per 3 Casting Levels (maximum 8). The copies spread out but each remains within 5 ft. of either you or another copy at all times. The copies mimic your actions as you take them. They can pass through each other and you through them, though they feel solid to others.

It's impossible to visually discern you and the copies from each other so a random target is determined each time someone engages any of you. Each copy has a Defense of 10 + your Dexterity modifier and immediately vanishes when hit.

MOVE EARTH

Level: 5 Conversion (Earth)
Casting Time: 1 full action
Distance: Remote
Duration: Permanent
Effect: For every 10 minutes you concentrate (to a maximum of 1 hour), you reshape a different flat patch of soil (e.g. clay, dirt, loam, or sand). Each patch may be up to your Casting Level × 10 ft. on a side and up to 10 ft. deep. The reshaping forms wavelike crests and troughs but has no impact on stone and can't dramatically reform the land. Trees, buildings, rock formations, and other solid landmarks are unaffected outside elevation and relative topography. You cannot use this spell to tunnel and it's too slow to trap or bury others. Its primary uses are digging moats, reshaping rivers, and adjusting terrain contours before a battle (collapsing embankments, moving hillocks, shifting dunes, and the like).

MOVE WATER

Level: 4 Conversion (Water)
Casting Time: 1 full action
Distance: Remote
Duration: Concentration, up to 1 hour
Effect: You reshape or redirect a cubic volume of liquid up your Casting Level × 10 ft. on a side and may hold it in any shape, even against gravity. You can pull air through the surface of the liquid to form breathable air pockets. You can also create whirlpools, eddies, and other natural currents in the liquid, requiring a successful Swim or Ride check (DC 20 + your Casting Level) to avoid or escape.

NATURAL ATTUNEMENT

Level: 5 Nature
Casting Time: 10 minutes
Distance: Personal
Duration: Instant
Preparation Cost: 3
Effect: You become one with nature, gaining knowledge of the surrounding region (out to 1 mile per Casting Level). You gain 3 hints about the terrain, animals, plants, minerals, bodies of water, the general state of the natural setting, and the presence of unnatural characters (constructs, horrors, and undead).

This spell may only be cast once per scene.

NATURE'S ALLY I

Level: 1 Nature
Casting Time: 1 round
Distance: Close
Duration: 1 minute per Casting Level (dismissible, enduring)
Effect: You summon 1 of the following animals as a standard NPC with a Threat Level equal to your Casting Level. With GM approval, you may modify your choice, choose an animal from the Bestiary *(see page 253)*, or build a new NPC, so long as it has the Animal Type and a maximum XP value of 40.

The precise nature of this servant should match your style of magic. At the GM's discretion, it could be a temporary familiar, a spirit guide, an arcane creation, or something else entirely.

A summoned character cannot summon other characters and is banished when killed or when the spell that summoned it ends (whichever comes first). Certain spells and other effects can banish a summoned character earlier. A banished character's body and possessions dissolve in 1d4 rounds.

The animal may not act during the round it appears. Thereafter it follows your commands to the best of its ability. In the absence of instructions the animal falls under the GM's control, though it continues to serve you as best it perceives it can (e.g. avians scout the area, mounts get you to safety, predators attack whatever seems to be your enemy, etc.).

Avian I (Tiny Animal Flyer/Walker — 36 XP): Str 10, Dex 12, Con 10, Int 4, Wis 12, Cha 6; SZ T (Reach 1); Spd 50 ft. winged flight, 10 ft. ground; Init III; Atk II; Def II; Res II; Health II; Comp —; Skills: Acrobatics II, Notice II, Search II; Qualities: *Cagey II, darkvision I, improved sense (hearing, vision), rend*

Attacks/Weapons: Gore I (dmg 1d3 lethal; threat 19–20; qualities: *bleed*), Talon I (dmg 1d3 lethal; threat 20)

Mount I (Large Animal Any — 36 XP): Str 14, Dex 10, Con 12, Int 2, Wis 10, Cha 8; SZ L (1×2, Reach 1); Spd 40 ft. ground or 40 ft. swim or 40 ft. burrow or 40 ft. flight; Init III; Atk III; Def IV; Res IV; Health III; Comp —; Skills: Athletics IV, Notice III, Sense Motive II; Qualities: *Superior traveler I*

Attacks/Weapons: Kick or Slam or Talon I (dmg 1d8+2 lethal; threat 20)

Predator I (Small Animal Any — 36 XP): Str 14, Dex 14, Con 12, Int 6, Wis 12, Cha 10; SZ S (Reach 1); Spd 40 ft. ground or 40 ft. swim or 40 ft. burrow or 40 ft. flight; Init III; Atk IV; Def II; Res II; Health II; Comp —; Skills: Notice II, Search II; Qualities: *Superior runner II*

Attacks/Weapons: Bite I (dmg 1d6+2 lethal; threat 18–20), Claw I (dmg 1d4+2 lethal; threat 20)

NATURE'S ALLY II

Level: 3 Nature

Effect: As Nature's Ally I, except that you gain 1 animal (max. 60 XP) or 2 animals (max. 40 XP each).

Avian II (Small Animal Flyer/Walker — 56 XP): Str 10, Dex 14, Con 10, Int 4, Wis 12, Cha 6; SZ T (Reach 1); Spd 70 ft. winged flight, 10 ft. ground; Init III; Atk III; Def III; Res III; Health III; Comp —; Skills: Acrobatics III, Notice III, Search III, Survival II; Qualities: *Cagey II, darkvision I, improved sense (hearing, vision), light sleeper, rend, tricky (Ragged Wound)*

Attacks/Weapons: Gore II (dmg 1d4 lethal; threat 18–20; qualities: *bleed*), Talon I (dmg 1d4+2 lethal; threat 20; qualities: *finesse*)

Mount II (Large Animal Any — 56 XP): Str 16, Dex 10, Con 14, Int 2, Wis 10, Cha 8; SZ L (1×2, Reach 1); Spd 60 ft. ground or 60 ft. swim or 60 ft. burrow or 60 ft. flight; Init III; Atk IV; Def IV; Res V; Health IV; Comp —; Skills: Athletics V, Notice III, Sense Motive III; Qualities: *Improved stability, superior traveler II, tough I*

Attacks/Weapons: Kick or Slam or Talon II (dmg 1d8+3 lethal; threat 19–20; qualities: *keen 4*)

Predator II (Medium Animal Any — 56 XP): Str 16, Dex 16, Con 12, Int 6, Wis 12, Cha 10; SZ M (Reach 1); Spd 40 ft. ground or 40 ft. swim or 40 ft. burrow or 40 ft. flight; Init IV; Atk V; Def II; Res II; Health II; Comp —; Skills: Acrobatics II, Notice II, Search II, Tactics II; Qualities: *Fearsome, superior runner II, swarm*

Attacks/Weapons: Bite II (dmg 1d8+3 lethal; threat 17–20; qualities: *AP 2*), Claw II (dmg 1d6+3 lethal; threat 19–20)

NATURE'S ALLY III

Level: 5 Nature

Effect: As Nature's Ally I, except that you gain 1 animal (max. 80 XP), 2 animals (max. 60 XP each), or 4 animals (max. 40 XP each).

Avian III (Small Animal Flyer/Walker — 76 XP): Str 12, Dex 16, Con 10, Int 4, Wis 14, Cha 6; SZ S (Reach 1); Spd 70 ft. winged flight, 10 ft. ground; Init IV; Atk IV; Def IV; Res IV; Health IV; Comp —; Skills: Acrobatics V, Notice IV, Search IV, Survival III; Qualities: *Cagey II, darkvision I, improved sense (hearing, vision), light sleeper, rend, tricky (Ragged Wound)*

Attacks/Weapons: Gore III (dmg 2d4+1 lethal; threat 18–20; qualities: *bleed*), Talon II (dmg 1d4+3 lethal; threat 19–20; qualities: *finesse*)

Mount III (Large Animal Any — 76 XP): Str 18, Dex 10, Con 16, Int 2, Wis 10, Cha 8; SZ L (1×2, Reach 1); Spd 60 ft. ground or 60 ft. swim or 60 ft. burrow or 60 ft. flight; Init IV; Atk V; Def V; Res V; Health V; Comp —; Skills: Athletics VI, Notice III, Sense Motive III; Qualities: *Condition immunity (fatigued), improved stability, knockback, superior traveler II, tough I*

Attacks/Weapons: Kick or Slam or Talon II (dmg 1d8+4 lethal; threat 19–20; qualities: *keen 4*), Trample I (dmg 1d10+4 lethal; threat 20; notes: Medium and smaller only, Fort (DC equal to damage) or become *sprawled*)

Predator III (Medium Animal Any — 76 XP): Str 18, Dex 18, Con 12, Int 6, Wis 12, Cha 10; SZ M (Reach 1); Spd 50 ft. ground or 50 ft. swim or 50 ft. burrow or 50 ft. flight; Init IV; Atk V; Def II; Res II; Health II; Comp —; Skills: Acrobatics II, Notice II, Search II, Tactics II; Qualities: *Fearsome, feat (Wolfpack Basics, Wolfpack Mastery), superior runner II, swarm, tough I*

Attacks/Weapons: Bite III (dmg 2d8+4 lethal; threat 17–20; qualities: *AP 2*), Claw III (dmg 2d6+4 lethal; threat 19–20; qualities: *trip*)

NATURE'S ALLY IV

Level: 7 Nature

Effect: As Nature's Ally I, except that you gain 1 animal (max. 100 XP), 2 animals (max. 80 XP each), 4 animals (max. 60 XP each), or 8 animals (max. 40 XP each).

Avian IV (Small Animal Flyer/Walker — 96 XP): Str 14, Dex 18, Con 10, Int 4, Wis 14, Cha 6; SZ S (Reach 1); Spd 70 ft. winged flight, 10 ft. ground; Init V; Atk V; Def V; Res V; Health V; Comp —; Skills: Acrobatics VI, Notice V, Search V, Survival IV; Qualities: *Cagey II, darkvision I, improved sense (hearing, vision), light sleeper, monstrous attack, rend, tricky (Ragged Wound)*

Attacks/Weapons: Gore IV (dmg 2d4+2 lethal; threat 16–20; qualities: *bleed*), Talon III (dmg 2d4+4 lethal; threat 18–20; qualities: *finesse*)

Mount IV (Large Animal Any — 96 XP): Str 18, Dex 12, Con 18, Int 2, Wis 10, Cha 8; SZ L (1×2, Reach 1); Spd 80 ft. ground or 80 ft. swim or 80 ft. burrow or 80 ft. flight; Init V; Atk VI; Def VI; Res V; Health VI; Comp —; Skills: Athletics VII, Intimidate V, Notice IV, Sense Motive III; Qualities: *Condition immunity (fatigued), improved stability, knockback, superior traveler II, tough II*

Attacks/Weapons: Kick or Slam or Talon III (dmg 2d8+4 lethal; threat 19–20; qualities: *keen 4*), Trample II (dmg 1d10+4 lethal; threat 19–20; notes: Medium and smaller only, Fort (DC equal to damage) or become *sprawled*)

Predator IV (Large Animal Any — 96 XP): Str 20, Dex 20, Con 12, Int 6, Wis 12, Cha 10; SZ L (1×2, Reach 1); Spd 50 ft. ground or 50 ft. swim or 50 ft. burrow or 50 ft. flight; Init V; Atk VI; Def III; Res III; Health III; Comp —; Skills: Acrobatics II, Notice II, Search II, Tactics III; Qualities: *Fearsome, feat (Wolfpack Basics, Wolfpack Mastery), superior runner III, swarm, tough II*

Attacks/Weapons: Bite IV (dmg 2d10+5 lethal; threat 16–20; qualities: *AP 2*), Claw IV (dmg 2d8+5 lethal; threat 18–20; qualities: *trip*)

NATURE'S ALLY V

Level: 9 Nature

Effect: As Nature's Ally I, except that you gain 1 animal (max. 120 XP), 2 animals (max. 100 XP each), 4 animals (max. 80 XP each), 8 animals (max. 60 XP each), or 16 animals (max. 40 XP each).

Nature's Ally

Avian V (Small Animal Flyer/Walker — 116 XP): Str 16, Dex 20, Con 10, Int 4, Wis 16, Cha 6; SZ S (Reach 1); Spd 80 ft. winged flight, 10 ft. ground; Init VI; Atk VI; Def VI; Res VI; Health V; Comp —; Skills: Acrobatics VII, Notice VI, Search VI, Survival VI; Qualities: *Bright, cagey II, critical surge, darkvision I, improved sense (hearing, vision), light sleeper, monstrous attack, rend, tricky (Ragged Wound)*

Attacks/Weapons: Gore IV (dmg 2d4+3 lethal; threat 16–20; qualities: *bleed*), Talon III (dmg 2d4+5 lethal; threat 18–20; qualities: *finesse*)

Mount V (Large Animal Any — 116 XP): Str 20, Dex 14, Con 20, Int 2, Wis 10, Cha 8; SZ L (1×2, Reach 1); Spd 80 ft. ground or 80 ft. swim or 80 ft. burrow or 80 ft. flight; Init VI; Atk VII; Def VI; Res V; Health VII; Comp —; Skills: Athletics VII, Intimidate V, Notice III, Sense Motive III; Qualities: *Condition immunity (fatigued), damage reduction 1, fearless, improved stability,* knockback, *superior traveler II, tough II*

Attacks/Weapons: Kick or Slam or Talon III (dmg 2d8+4 lethal; threat 19–20; qualities: *keen 4*), Trample III (dmg 2d10+5 lethal; threat 19–20; notes: Medium and smaller only, Fort (DC equal to damage) or become *sprawled*), Rearing Threat (frightening attack II: Will save DC 15 or become *frightened* for 2d6 rounds)

Predator V (Large Animal Any — 116 XP): Str 20, Dex 20, Con 14, Int 6, Wis 12, Cha 10; SZ L (1×2, Reach 1); Spd 50 ft. ground or 50 ft. swim or 50 ft. burrow or 50 ft. flight; Init VI; Atk VII; Def IV; Res IV; Health IV; Comp —; Skills: Acrobatics II, Notice IV, Search IV, Tactics IV; Qualities: *Fearsome, feat (Coordinated Attack, Misdirection Basics, Wolfpack Basics, Wolfpack Mastery), superior runner III, swarm, tough II*

Attacks/Weapons: Bite V (dmg 3d10+5 lethal; threat 16–20; qualities: *AP 2*), Claw V (dmg 3d8+5 lethal; threat 18–20; qualities: *trip*)

NEUTRALIZE POISON

Level: 3 Healing

Casting Time: 1 half action

Distance: Touch

Duration: 10 minutes per Casting Level

Saving Throw: Will negates

Effect: Poison within 1 character or an object measuring up to 1 cubic ft. per Casting Level is rendered harmless. For the spell's Duration, a targeted character becomes immune to poison and a targeted character or item that can produce or convey poison loses that ability.

OBSCURE OBJECT

Level: 2 Secrets

Casting Time: 1 half action

Distance: Touch

Duration: 8 hours (dismissible)

Effect: You mask 1 object weighing up to 100 lbs. per Casting Level. The object can't be magically observed in its location and Divination spells targeting it automatically fail.

ORIENT SELF

Level: 0 Divination

Casting Time: 1 half action

Distance: Personal

Duration: Instant

Effect: You sense the direction of north from your current position and gain a +1 magic bonus with Knowledge checks made to navigate from your current location.

PASS WITHOUT TRACE

Level: 1 Secrets

Casting Time: 1 half action

Distance: Personal or Touch

Duration: 1 hour per Casting Level (dismissible)

Effect: Track checks made to locate one character per Casting Level automatically fail.

PERMANENCY

Level: 6 Artifice

Casting Time: 1 minute

Distance: Personal or Touch

Duration: Instant

Preparation Cost: 20 × target spell's Level (minimum 20)

Effect: One "enduring" spell becomes permanent and cannot be countered. Your Casting Level must exceed the target spell's Level by 8 for you to cast this spell.

PHANTASMAL KILLER

Level: 4 Shadow

Casting Time: 1 half action

Distance: Local

Duration: Instant

Saving Throw: Will negates (disbelief), Fortitude partial (death, terminal)

Effect: You create an illusory creature out of one character's worst nightmares. Only that character can see the creature and he may attempt to save or disbelieve its existence. With success, the spell ends; otherwise the character must make a Fortitude save or die. With success against this second save, the character suffers 3d6 stress damage.

You cannot cast this spell on constructs, elementals, spirits, or undead.

PHASE DOOR

Level: 7 Compass

Casting Time: 1 half action

Distance: Touch

Area: 10 ft. per 5 Casting Levels penetrating caster-defined

Duration: 1 week (dismissible, enduring)

Effect: You create an extra-dimensional corridor across or through the Area with open 10 ft. × 10 ft. doorways at both ends. You disappear when inside the corridor, reappearing when you exit. The corridor is likewise invisible and may overlap with solid matter, allowing you to move freely through walls, hills, and other obstacles.

Any number of other characters may enter or pass through the corridor but only with your permission. You can also set a word, phrase, or action to allow entry when you're not present.

PINPOINT

Level: 8 Divination

Casting Time: 10 minutes

Distance: Unlimited

Duration: Instant

Saving Throw: Will negates scene

Effect: You learn the exact location of a familiar character or object.

POLAR RAY I

Level: 0 Weather (Ice)

Casting Time: 1 half action

Distance: Personal range attack

Area: 15 ft. line

Duration: Instant

Saving Throw: Reflex half

Effect: You release a spray of freezing air across the Area, inflicting 1d6 cold damage.

POLAR RAY II

Level: 4 Weather (Ice)

Area: 75 ft. line

Effect: As Polar Ray I, except inflicting 1d6 cold damage per Casting Level (maximum 10d6).

POLAR RAY III

Level: 8 Weather (Ice)

Area: 150 ft. line

Effect: As Polar Ray I, except inflicting 1d6 cold damage per Casting Level (maximum 18d6).

POWER WORD: HARM

Level: 5 Word

Casting Time: 1 free action

Distance: Close

Duration: Instant

Effect: You and a character of your choice suffer 1d6 lethal damage per Casting Level (maximum 12d6), even if they can't hear you.

POWER WORD: KILL

Level: 9 Word

Casting Time: 1 free action

Distance: Close

Duration: Instant

Preparation Cost: 10

Effect: You and a special character of your choice each suffer enough damage to kill them, even if they can't hear you.

POWER WORD: RECALL

Level: 6 Word

Casting Time: 1 free action

Distance: Close

Duration: Instant

Effect: You and a character of your choice are teleported to one of your residences, even if they can't hear you. All objects the two of you carry or wear are teleported as well.

POWER WORD: STUN

Level: 8 Word

Casting Time: 1 free action

Distance: Close

Duration: Instant

Effect: You and a character of your choice become *stunned* for 2d4 rounds, even if they can't hear you.

PRAYER

Level: 3 Blessing

Casting Time: 1 half action

Distance: Close

Area: 40 ft. penetrating sphere

Duration: 1 round per Casting Level

Prayer

Effect: You and each teammate and ally gain a +1 morale bonus with attack checks, damage rolls, skill checks, and Will saves, while each of your foes suffers a –1 morale penalty with those rolls.

PROJECT PRESENCE

Level: 7 Illusion

Casting Time: 1 half action

Distance: Local

Duration: 1 round per Casting Level (dismissible)

Effect: You create an illusory version of yourself that mimics your actions (including speech) unless you spend 1 half action concentrating to direct separate actions. You may cast any spell from the projected image and may spend 1 half action concentrating to adopt its senses in place of your own (or vice-versa). This spell ends if the illusory you moves out of your sight.

PROTECTION FROM ALIGNMENT

Level: 1 Warding (Aligned)
Casting Time: 1 half action
Distance: Touch
Duration: 1 minute per Casting Level (dismissible)
Effect: One character is surrounded by a magical barrier that moves with him. The barrier grants a +2 gear bonus to Defense and with saves against attacks with an opposing Alignment or made by characters with an opposing Alignment. This bonus increases to +4 against outsiders with an opposing Alignment.

PROTECTION FROM SPELLS

Level: 8 Warding
Casting Time: 1 half action
Distance: Touch
Duration: 10 minutes per Casting Level
Preparation Cost: 5
Effect: One character per 4 Casting Levels gains a +8 magic bonus with saves prompted by spells.

PURGE

Level: 7 Word (Aligned)
Casting Time: 1 half action
Distance: Personal
Area: 40 ft. penetrating sphere
Duration: Instant
Saving Throw: Will half (damage), Will negates (condition, terminal)
Effect: Characters with an opposing Alignment are *sickened* for 1d6 minutes and standard characters with an opposing Alignment suffer 3d6 divine damage. Summoned characters with an opposing Alignment are banished.

QUAKE TOUCH

Level: 6 Energy (Sonic)
Casting Time: 1 round
Distance: Touch
Duration: 1 round per Casting Level (dismissible)
Effect: Each piece of scenery you touch suffers 1d6 sonic damage per Casting Level (maximum 14d6).

RAY OF ENFEEBLEMENT

Level: 1 Affliction
Casting Time: 1 half action
Distance: Short range attack
Duration: 1 minute per Casting Level
Effect: You inflict 1 temporary Strength impairment per 2 Casting Levels, rounded up (to a minimum Strength of 4).

Arcane Script

Like thieves, spies, and other secretive sorts, spellcasters have developed their own private language. Though it appears "magical" to outsiders, arcane script is in fact just ordinary words. Mages weave messages into the fabric of their spells, translate them into code derived from complex arcane formulae, turn them *invisible*, and visibly jumble them with mystical "logic-locks," among other methods. There are only so many ways to code messages, even for spellcasters, making it possible for others experienced with magic to decipher them, which is all that the Read Magic spell does.

Reading arcane script conveys a message. This message has no power and triggers no magic, even when it's woven into a spell. Arcane script is completely unintelligible to those without ranks in the Spellcasting skill, appearing to them to be just another component in the elusive art of magic.

READ MAGIC

Level: 0 Word
Casting Time: 1 full action
Distance: Personal
Duration: Instant
Effect: You decipher the arcane script on one object or in one area and may thereafter read it without issue *(see above).*

REGENERATE

Level: 7 Healing
Casting Time: 1 minute
Distance: Touch
Duration: 2d6 rounds
Preparation Cost: 1
Effect: One character heals from all critical injuries and regains all severed body parts. This process takes the spell's full Duration and no benefit is gained if the spell is interrupted before then.

This spell has no effect on constructs, elementals, spirits, or undead.

REPELLING WAVE I

Level: 6 Force
Casting Time: 1 half action
Distance: Personal
Area: 40 ft. cone
Duration: Instant

Effect: A wave of energy pushes unanchored characters and objects up to Large Size 40 ft. away from you, inflicting 1d8 force damage + 1 per Casting Level (maximum +14). Larger and anchored characters and objects suffer half this amount (rounded down).

REPELLING WAVE II

Level: 8 Force

Area: 60 ft. sphere

Effect: As Repelling Wave I, except pushing characters and objects up to Huge Size 60 ft. away from you, inflicting 1d12 force damage + 1 per Casting Level (maximum +18).

RESILIENT SPHERE I

Level: 4 Force

Casting Time: 1 half action

Distance: Close

Duration: 1 round per Casting Level (dismissible)

Saving Throw: Reflex negates (terminal)

Effect: An airtight globe of force encloses 1 character up to Large Size. During each round, the globe absorbs damage inflicted on the target equal to your Casting Level + 30. The character may not leave the sphere and the sphere may not be damaged, though it may be annihilated.

RESILIENT SPHERE II

Level: 8 Force

Effect: As Resilient Sphere I, except that once per round as a half action you may move the sphere — and the character within — up to 30 ft.

RESIST ENERGY

Level: 2 Warding

Casting Time: 1 half action

Distance: Personal or Touch

Duration: 10 minutes per Casting Level

Effect: One character or object gains Acid, Cold, Electrical, Fire, Heat, or Sonic Resistance equal to your Casting Level (your choice).

RESTORATION I

Level: 2 Healing

Casting Time: 1 minute

Distance: Touch

Duration: Instant

Effect: One character heals 1 *fatigued* grade and 1d4 impairment with 1 attribute of your choice.

RESTORATION II

Level: 4 Healing

Preparation Cost: 1

Effect: One character heals all *fatigued* grades and attribute impairment.

RESURRECTION I

Level: 5 Blessing

Casting Time: 10 minutes

Distance: Touch

Duration: Instant

Preparation Cost: 60

Effect: You restore life to a dead character whose body is whole and present, whose soul is free and willing to return, and

Resurrection

who's been dead no longer than 1 day per Casting Level. The character wakes with 1 wound point and vitality points equal to his Career or Threat Level. Any attributes of 0 are set to 1. Poisons and diseases in his system are neutralized but any critical injuries remain.

RESURRECTION II

Level: 7 Blessing

Preparation Cost: 100

Effect: As Resurrection I, except it may target a character who's been dead for 1 year per Casting Level. Also, the target's body may be mostly destroyed, so long as you have at least some remains (e.g. a fingernail, hair, etc.). The character wakes with full wounds and vitality, no longer suffering from critical injuries or impairment.

RESURRECTION III

Level: 9 Blessing

Distance: Close

Preparation Cost: 150

Effect: As Resurrection II, except it may target a character who's been dead for 5 years per Casting Level, and whose body has been fully destroyed.

RIGHTEOUS AURA

Level: 2 Word (Aligned)

Casting Time: 1 half action

Distance: Personal

Duration: 1 hour per Casting Level

Effect: You gain a +2 magic bonus with Intimidate checks made against characters with an opposing Alignment. As a half action, you may end this spell early to gain a +6 magic bonus with a single Intimidate check made against a character with an opposing Alignment.

RUSTING GRASP

Level: 4 Affliction

Casting Time: 1 half action

Distance: Touch

Area: 5 ft. sphere

Duration: 1 round per Casting Level

Effect: Each round, non-living, non-magical metal in the Area you touch is destroyed, becoming rusted, pitted, and worthless. Touching a metallic character inflicts 25 points of lethal damage that ignores Damage Reduction.

SACRED AURA

Level: 8 Warding (Aligned)

Casting Time: 1 half action

Distance: Close

Duration: 1 round per Casting Level (dismissible)

Saving Throw: Fortitude negates (harmless)

Effect: One charactrer gains a flickering aura and 3 effects.

- +4 magic bonus to Defense and with saves
- Spell Defense 25 against spells with an opposing Alignment cast by characters with an opposing Alignment
- When an adjacent opponent with an opposing Alignment attacks the character, he must make a Fortitude save or suffer 1d4 temporary Strength impairment and become *blinded* for 1d6 rounds.

SCARE I

Level: 1 Shadow

Casting Time: 1 half action

Distance: Close

Duration: Instant

Saving Throw: Special *(see Effect)*

Effect: One character becomes *frightened* for 1d6 rounds. With a successful Will save, he becomes *shaken* instead.

This spell has no effect on undead.

SCARE II

Level: 2 Shadow

Distance: Local

Effect: As Scare I, except affecting up to 1 character per 3 Casting Levels.

SCINTILLATING PATTERN

Level: 8 Illusion

Casting Time: 1 half action

Distance: Close

Area: 20 ft. penetrating sphere

Duration: Concentration + 1d6 rounds

Saving Throw: Will negates (disbelief)

Effect: An oddly compelling pattern of colored lights floods the Area, drawing the attention of those within. Characters in the Area who can see must make a Will save or fall unconscious (if Career or Threat Level 6 or lower), become *stunned* (if Career or Threat Level 7–12), or become *baffled* (if Career or Threat Level 13+). This effect lasts 1d6 rounds.

SCORCHING RAY

Level: 2 Energy (Fire)

Casting Time: 1 half action

Distance: Short range attack

Duration: Instant

Effect: You fire 3 rays at targets you can see, each inflicting 1d4 fire damage (AP 5) per 2 Casting Levels (maximum 6d4).

SCRYE I

Level: 1 Divination
Casting Time: 10 minutes
Distance: Remote
Duration: 1 minute per Casting Level (dismissible)
Effect: You project your vision and hearing to 1 fixed, familiar location. While projecting, you cannot see and hear from your body.

SCRYE II

Level: 3 Divination
Distance: Personal
Effect: As Scrye I, except that you may alternately project your vision and hearing through a 1 in. diameter invisible sensor that appears next to you. While projecting you may move the sensor with a flying Speed of 30 ft. (otherwise it hovers in place).

SCRYE III

Level: 5 Divination
Effect: As Scrye II, except that while projecting you may also cast spells up to Level 3 as if you're located at your point of view.

SCRYE IV

Level: 7 Divination
Saving Throw: Will negates
Effect: As Scrye I, except you may alternately project your vision and hearing through 1 character you can see (or 1 character you know if you have a personal effect belonging to them).

SCRYE V

Level: 9 Divination
Effect: As Scrye II or IV (your choice), except that while projecting you may also cast spells up to Level 8 as if you're located at your point of view.

SEARING RAY

Level: 3 Energy (Light)
Casting Time: 1 half action
Distance: Medium range attack
Duration: Instant
Effect: Light emits from your open palm, inflicting 1d8 lethal damage per 2 Casting Levels (maximum 8d8). This attack ignores dodge bonuses to Defense and has AP 10.

SEE INVISIBLE

Level: 3 Divination
Casting Time: 1 half action
Distance: Personal
Duration: 10 min. per Casting Level (dismissible, enduring)
Effect: You clearly see *invisible* characters and objects as translucent shapes.

SHADOW WALK

Level: 7 Shadow (Darkness)
Casting Time: 1 half action
Distance: Personal or Touch
Duration: 1 hour per Casting Level (dismissible)
Saving Throw: Will negates
Effect: You and a number of allies up to your Casting Level may step partially into any available shadow within your line of sight and move in a single direction or toward a specific location at 50 MPH. Your course must take you through shadows that are touching or separated by no more than 10 ft. of faint or dim ambient light.

It's difficult to perceive details from the material world while traveling through shadows and there's no guarantee you'll arrive where you want; unless you succeed with a Survival check (DC 15 with a synergy bonus from Spellcasting), you wind up a number of miles equal to the difference in a random direction, per the Deviation Rules *(see page 214)*.

Upon arrival, you rise through the nearest available shadow. Should a shadow be eliminated while you're moving through it, you're ejected through the nearest remaining shadow.

SHAPE STONE

Level: 3 Conversion (Earth)
Casting Time: 1 half action
Distance: Touch
Duration: Instant
Effect: You reshape an existing piece of stone up to 10 cubic ft. + 1 cubic ft. per Casting Level. While you can make crude coffers, doors, and the like, fine detail and moving parts aren't possible.

SHATTER

Level: 1 Energy (Sonic)
Casting Time: 1 half action
Distance: Close
Area: 1 square
Duration: Instant
Saving Throw: Reflex negates (damage)
Effect: All characters and objects in the Area up to 1 lb. made of crystal, glass, ceramic, porcelain, or a similar substance are destroyed. Each heavier character and object of the same composition suffers 1d6 sonic damage per 2 Casting Levels (maximum 4d6).

SHIELD

Level: 1 Force
Casting Time: 1 half action
Distance: Personal
Duration: 1 minute per Casting Level (dismissible)
Effect: An invisible, mobile disk of force hovers in front of you, granting you 1/2 personal cover and negating Magic Missiles cast at you.

SHIELD OTHER

Level: 2 Glory
Casting Time: 1 half action
Distance: Close
Duration: 1 hour per Casting Level (dismissible)
Preparation Cost: 1

Effect: One character gains a +1 magic bonus to Defense and saves, and suffers only 1/2 incoming damage (rounded down). The remainder is transferred to you, ignoring DR and Resistances.

This spell ends if the character moves more than 50 ft. from you.

SILENCE

Level: 2 Secrets (Silence)
Casting Time: 1 half action
Distance: Remote
Area: 20 ft. penetrating sphere
Duration: 1 minute per Casting Level (dismissible)
Saving Throw: Will negates

Effect: Complete silence prevails in the Area. Sounds aren't heard, whether they originate within or outside, or simply pass through. This effect is stationary when cast on a location or moves with a character.

SLEEP I

Level: 1 Charm
Casting Time: 1 round
Distance: Close
Area: 10 ft. penetrating sphere
Duration: 1 round per Casting Level
Saving Throw: Will negates (repeatable, terminal)
Effect: Characters in the Area fall asleep.

SLEEP II

Level: 3 Charm
Area: 20 ft. penetrating sphere
Effect: As Sleep I, except as noted.

SLOW

Level: 3 Compass
Casting Time: 1 half action
Distance: Close
Duration: 1 round per Casting Level
Saving Throw: Fortitude negates
Effect: One character is *slowed*. This spell counters Haste.

SPEAK WITH THE DEAD

Level: 3 Necromancy
Casting Time: 10 minutes
Distance: Close
Duration: 1 minute per Casting Level
Saving Throw: Will negates

Effect: You grant a semblance of life and intellect to a corpse with an intact head and may ask it up to 1 question per 2 Casting Levels. Unless the corpse's Alignment was the same as yours, it may make a Will save to resist your questions, remaining silent. The corpse only knows what it knew during life, including the languages it spoke (if any), and can't converse outside these specific questions. Answers are usually brief, cryptic, or repetitive.

You may only cast this spell once on each corpse.

SPELL IMMUNITY I

Level: 4 Warding
Casting Time: 1 full action
Distance: Personal or Touch
Duration: 10 minutes per Casting Level

Effect: One character gains Spell Defense 50 against 1 specific spell per 4 Casting Levels you have. Each spell must be Level 4 or lower.

Each character can only be the target of a single Spell Immunity spell at a time.

SPELL IMMUNITY II

Level: 8 Warding
Effect: As Spell Immunity I, except chosen spells may be up to Level 8.

STATUS

Level: 2 Divination
Casting Time: 1 half action
Distance: Close
Duration: 1 hour per Casting Level
Saving Throw: Will negates (harmless)
Effect: You remain mentally aware of one character's relative position, damage, and conditions.

STATUS, MASS

Level: 6 Divination
Effect: As Status, except targeting a number of characters up to your Casting Level.

SUNLIGHT I

Level: 7 Energy (Light)
Casting Time: 1 half action
Distance: Short range attack

Duration: Instant

Saving Throw: Reflex half (damage), Reflex negates (condition)

Effect: You fire dazzling beams of intense light at 5 targets you can see. Each beam inflicts 4d6 lethal damage (doubled against undead) and forces a Reflex save to avoid becoming *blinded* for 1d6 rounds (undead automatically fail this save).

SUNLIGHT II

Level: 8 Energy (Light)

Distance: Long

Area: 80 ft. sphere

Effect: As Sunlight I, inflicting 1d6 lethal damage per Casting Level (maximum 18d6).

TELEPORT I

Level: 5 Compass

Casting Time: 1 half action

Distance: Personal or Touch

Duration: Instant

Effect: You and one additional willing character per 3 Casting Levels are transported up to 100 miles per Casting Level. You must have visited the destination before and characters may not be overloaded. All characters must be in physical contact with each other and at least 1 of them must be in physical contact with you.

Teleportation is not an exact science; unless you succeed with a Survival check (DC 20 with a synergy bonus from Spellcasting), you wind up a number of miles equal to the difference in a random direction, per the Deviation rules *(see, page 214)*.

TELEPORT II

Level: 7 Compass

Effect: As Teleport I, except you may transport yourself and companions across any distance. You need not have visited the destination before but you must have a reliable description of it. Also, the Survival check DC drops to 15.

TIME STOP

Level: 9 Compass

Casting Time: 1 half action

Distance: Personal

Duration: Instant

Preparation Cost: 10

Effect: Time speeds up for you, making it appear that others are frozen around you. You are free to act for 1d6 rounds of your time, though you can't target other characters with attacks or spells, nor may you move or harm them or anything they carry. Harmful spells that last after Time Stop ends affect others as normal. Fire, heat, cold, gas, and other persistent sources of damage affect you during each of your rounds as normal.

TINKER I

Level: 1 Artifice

Casting Time: 1 half action

Distance: Touch

Duration: Instant

Effect: You repair a broken object weighing up to 1 lb. Alternately, you manipulate the inner workings of a construct, repairing or inflicting 1d8 damage + 1 per Casting Level (maximum +5).

TINKER II

Level: 2 Artifice

Effect: You repair a broken object weighing up to 1 lb. per Casting Level or 1 destroyed object weighing up to 1 lb. Alternately, you repair or inflict 2d8 damage + 1 per Casting Level (maximum +10).

TINY SHELTER

Level: 3 Force

Casting Time: 1 half action

Distance: Personal

Area: 20 ft. sphere

Duration: 2 hours per Casting Level (dismissible)

Effect: An opaque sphere of force appears around you, protecting against Nature's Fury Complications up to 3 dice (a 4-die Nature's Fury Complication immediately destroys it). The hut's exterior is a simple dome of any color you choose but its interior walls are transparent, allowing occupants to see outside. Its interior is always 70° F and provides dim light at your command.

The spell ends if you leave the shelter.

TONGUES I

Level: 3 Word
Casting Time: 1 full action
Distance: Personal or Touch
Duration: 10 minutes per Casting Level (enduring)
Effect: The target may speak, understand, read, and write 1 language of your choice except arcane script *(see pages 61 and 142)*. He must still decipher any codes present.

TONGUES II

Level: 6 Word
Duration: 10 min. per Casting Level
Effect: As Tongues I, except that the target grasps *all* non-magical languages.

TOUCH OF LIGHT

Level: 0 Healing (Light)
Casting Time: 1 full action
Distance: Personal or Touch
Duration: Instant
Saving Throw: Will negates (undead damage)
Effect: One standard character heals 1 damage or one special character heals 1 vitality.

TREE WALK

Level: 6 Nature
Casting Time: 1 half action
Distance: Personal
Duration: 1 hour per Casting Level
Effect: You can enter a tree and, as a full action, shift inside any other living tree of the same type within 1 mile (you automatically sense all other trees of the same type within that distance). Exiting also takes 1 full action, even if you're forced out when the spell ends. Should you remain in a tree until it's cut or burned down, you perish as well.

Tongues I

TRUE SEEING

Level: 5 Divination
Casting Time: 1 half action
Distance: Personal or Touch
Duration: 1 minute per Casting Level
Saving Throw: Will negates (harmless)
Preparation Cost: 2
Effect: The target sees through illusions, darkness, invisibility, concealment, and other visual effects created by spells and magic items.

TRUE STRIKE I

Level: 1 Divination
Casting Time: 1 half action
Distance: Personal
Duration: Special *(see Effect)*
Effect: The defenses of those around you are laid bare. If your next attack check is made before the end of the next round, you gain a +6 magic bonus and your error range decreases by 2 (minimum 0).

TRUE STRIKE II

Level: 4 Divination
Effect: As True Strike I, except the bonus is +10 and you cannot suffer an error.

UNSEEN SERVANT

Level: 1 Force
Casting Time: 1 half action
Distance: Close
Duration: 1 hour per Casting Level

Effect: An invisible, mindless, shapeless force appears next to you, ready to perform simple tasks at your command. It has a Strength score of 5, a Ground Speed of 15 ft., and may exert 20 lbs. of force. It can perform physical skill checks with a DC up to 15 and similar menial labors (fetching things, opening doors and containers, holding chairs, cleaning, mending, etc.). It cannot attack or make saving throws, nor can it perform any action that requires an attack check or saving throw. It may only perform 1 action at a time.

The servant disappears if it suffers 6 or more points of damage.

VERDURE

Level: 3 Nature
Casting Time: 1 full action
Distance: Special *(see Effect)*
Area: Special *(see Effect)*
Duration: Instant

Effect: One effect occurs in an area with at least marginal vegetation (your choice).

- *Enrich:* Plants of your choice within half a mile grow twice as fast and crops of your choice within the same distance produce double the normal yield. This effect lasts 1 year.
- *Inhibit:* Plants of your choice within half a mile grow half as fast and crops of your choice within the same distance produce half the normal yield. This effect lasts 1 year.
- *Prune:* Plants of your choice within 1,000 ft. shrink and/or vanish, forming settled terrain.
- *Thicken:* Plants of your choice within 1,000 ft. become thick and overgrown, forming jungle terrain. Within this area Speed drops to 5 ft. for characters up to Medium Size and to 10 ft. for larger characters.

This spell has no effect on plant characters and may counter itself.

WALL OF COUNTER MAGIC

Level: 5 Warding
Casting Time: 1 full action
Distance: Local
Area: 20 ft. long per Casting Level wall, 20 ft. tall, 1 ft. thick
Duration: Concentration + 1 round per Casting Level (dismissible, enduring)

Effect: An invisible curtain springs into existence, countering spell effects that pass through it with a Casting Level + Spell Level equal to or less than your Casting Level + 5. Some effects may not be countered, as noted in their descriptions. The curtain is immune to damage but may be countered.

WALL OF FIRE

Level: 4 Energy (Fire)
Casting Time: 1 full action
Distance: Local
Area: 20 ft. long per Casting Level wall, 20 ft. tall, 1 ft. thick
Duration: Concentration + 1 round per Casting Level (dismissible, enduring)
Saving Throw: Reflex half

Effect: A curtain of fire springs into existence, inflicting a –2 penalty with Notice and Search checks made through the flames. Each character and object in or moving through the curtain suffers 2d6 fire damage +1 per Casting Level (maximum +10). If 20 points of its fire damage are extinguished, a single-square hole is punched through, reforming in 10 minutes.

WALL OF ICE

Level: 4 Weather (Ice)
Casting Time: 1 full action
Distance: Local
Area: 20 ft. long per Casting Level wall, 20 ft. tall, 1 ft. thick
Duration: Concentration + 1 round per Casting Level (dismissible, enduring)
Saving Throw: Reflex partial (new position)

Effect: A curtain of ice springs into existence, pushing characters and objects into adjacent squares (with a successful Reflex save, a character may wind up on the side of his choice; otherwise, you choose his new location). The curtain provides total cover and inflicts a –6 penalty with Notice and Search checks made through the ice. If it suffers 20 damage a single-square hole is punched through, reforming in 10 minutes.

WALL OF STONE

Level: 5 Creation (Earth)
Casting Time: 1 half action
Distance: Local
Area: 20 ft. long per Casting Level wall, 20 ft. tall, 1 ft. thick
Duration: Concentration + 1 round per Casting Level (dismissible, enduring)
Saving Throw: Reflex partial (new position)

Effect: A curtain of rock rises from the ground, pushing characters and objects into adjacent squares (with a successful Reflex save, a character may wind up on top or on the side of his choice; otherwise, you choose his new location). The curtain can be crudely shaped to produce crenellations along its upper edge, granting 1/4 cover to any kneeling behind. Characters cannot be attacked through the curtain. It has DR 5 and if it suffers 20 damage a single-square hole is punched through, reforming in 10 minutes.

WALL OF WIND

Level: 3 Weather (Air)

Casting Time: 1 full action

Distance: Local

Area: 20 ft. long per Casting Level wall, 20 ft. tall, 1 ft. thick

Duration: Concentration + 1 round per Casting Level (dismissible, enduring)

Effect: A curtain of wind springs into existence, flinging each character and unanchored object up to Medium Size 1d6 squares in a random direction and inflicting 2d6 falling damage + 1 per Casting Level, maximum +8 (with a successful Acrobatics check vs. double the spell save DC, a character may choose his direction and decrease the distance and damage by 1/2, rounded down). This check is also required to pass through or linger inside the curtain. Arrows, bolts, hurled weapons, and gases cannot pass through the curtain.

WAR CRY

Level: 8 Energy (Sonic)

Casting Time: 1 half action

Distance: Personal

Area: 100 ft. + 10 ft. per Casting Level cone

Duration: Instant (damage), 1 minute per Casting Level (bonus)

Saving Throw: Fortitude half (damage)

Effect: Your fearsome battle shout inflicts 1d8 sonic damage per 2 Casting Levels to each opponent in the Area. Each hero who hears it gains a +1 morale bonus with attack checks and Will saves, and recovers lost vitality points equal to his Career or Threat Level.

WATER BREATHING

Level: 3 Shapeshifting (Water)

Casting Time: 1 half action

Distance: Personal or Touch

Duration: Special *(see Effect)*

Effect: Up to 10 characters can breathe water and air interchangeably. This spell's Duration is (2 hours per Casting Level) divided by the number of characters targeted (e.g. if your Casting Level is 10 and you target 5 characters, the spell's Duration is 4 hours).

WATER WALK

Level: 0 Compass (Water)

Casting Time: 1 half action

Distance: Personal or Touch

Duration: 1 minute per Casting Level

Effect: One character can tread on fluid as if walking on solid ground. If the character submerges for any reason, he rises 60 ft. per round until standing on the surface.

WATER WALK, MASS

Level: 2 Compass (Water)

Distance: Close

Effect: As Water Walk, except you may target a number of characters equal to your Casting Level.

WHISPERS

Level: 0 Word (Sonic)

Casting Time: 1 free action

Distance: Local

Duration: 1 minute

Effect: Your conversation with up to one character per Casting Level becomes a series of faint whispers, inaudible to others. All characters in the conversation must be within the spell's Distance and sound must be able to travel between them, though they needn't see each other.

WILD SIDE I

Level: 2 Shapeshifting

Casting Time: 1 free action

Distance: Personal or Touch

Duration: 1 minute per Casting Level

Effect: One willing character gains bestial features and your choice of a Bite I, Claw I, Gore I, Tail Slap I, Talon I, or Trample I natural attack.

WILD SIDE II

Level: 5 Shapeshifting

Effect: As Wild Side I, except the natural attack is Grade III.

WILD SIDE III

Level: 8 Shapeshifting

Effect: As Wild Side I, except the natural attack is Grade V.

WINTER'S DOMAIN I

Level: 1 Weather (Ice)

Casting Time: 1 full action

Distance: Personal

Area: 20 ft. sphere

Duration: Concentration + 1 round per Casting Level (dismissible)

Effect: All Fire effects with a Casting Level + Spell Level equal to or less than your Casting Level + 1 are suppressed.

WINTER'S DOMAIN II

Level: 5 Weather (Ice)

Casting Time: 1 free action

Effect: As Winter's Domain I, except suppressing Fire effects with a Casting Level + Spell Level equal to or less than your Casting Level + 5.

WISH I

Level: 3 Word

Casting Time: 1 full action

Effect: Your desire is made reality — one carefully phrased wish is fulfilled to the best of the Game Master's ability. Take heed, however! Even wishes have their limits. Your wish must be grammatically correct and may invoke no more than 1 effect. Also, poorly phrased wishes can go awry, producing unexpected results. The GM is the ultimate arbiter of what wishes can achieve and what specific wishes yield, though some common Wish I effects follow.

- Cast a single spell up to Level 3 (the wisher paying its Preparation Cost, if any)
- Create an item costing up to 10,000s or 10 Reputation, or upgrade an existing item at up to half that amount
- Undo the effect of a single spell up to Level 3 or a single action of any character up to Level 6
- Undo a single event that occurred in the last minute

Wishes are among the most powerful magic in all creation and should only be introduced with great care. For every wish you desire, you must first complete a Quest Subplot customized to the nature of wishes in the campaign world and story *(see page 383)*.

This spell cannot be countered.

WISH II

Level: 6 Word

Effect: As Wish I, except with these common effects.

- Cast a single spell up to Level 6 (the wisher paying its Preparation Cost, if any)
- Create an item costing up to 25,000s or 25 Reputation, or upgrade an existing item at up to half that amount (rounded up)
- Undo the effect of a single spell up to Level 6 or a single action of any character up to Level 12
- Undo a single event that occurred in the current scene

WISH III

Level: 9 Word

Effect: As Wish I, except with these common effects.

- Cast a single spell up to Level 9 (the wisher paying its Preparation Cost, if any)
- Create an item costing up to 50,000s or 50 Reputation, or upgrade an existing item at up to half that amount
- Undo the effect of a single spell up to Level 9 or a single action of any character up to Level 18
- Undo a single event that occurred in the current adventure

WIT I

Level: 2 Blessing

Casting Time: 1 full action

Distance: Personal or Touch

Duration: 1 minute per Casting Level (dismissible)

Effect: The character gains a +3 magic bonus to your choice of Intelligence, Wisdom, or Charisma.

WIT II

Level: 4 Blessing

Effect: As Wit I, except the magic bonus increases to +5.

WIT III

Level: 6 Blessing

Effect: As Wit I, except the magic bonus increases to +7.

WIT IV

Level: 8 Blessing

Effect: As Wit I, except the magic bonus increases to +9.

WIT I, MASS

Level: 5 Blessing

Area: 50 ft. sphere

Effect: As Wit I, except that it affects a number of characters in the Area up to your Casting Level.

ZONE OF TRUTH

Level: 3 Charm

Casting Time: 1 half action

Distance: Close

Area: 20 ft. penetrating sphere

Duration: 1 minute per Casting Level

Saving Throw: Will negates (repeatable)

Effect: All characters in the Area find it difficult to deliberately lie, suffering a penalty with Bluff checks equal to your Casting Level + 3.

CHAPTER 4: FORGE

As a character forges his destiny he also masses a growing fortune — not only in coin of the realm but also precious treasure and powerful artifacts. His lifestyle improves as well, as his means allow for finer garments, more prestigious accessories, and larger holdings with better facilities. Perhaps most importantly of all, he earns a name for himself, renown he can barter for favors and other perks beyond the value of gold. Because in the end, a hero is worth more than what he owns — for good or ill, he's measured just as much by his deeds and legacy.

This chapter focuses on equipment, magic items, reputation, and related rules. Here you'll learn how to outfit for adventure and what you can expect from the spoils of victory. It all starts with the cornerstones of the *Fantasy Craft* gear system: Coin and Lifestyle.

COIN

The first measure of your riches is the coin you own. The basic monetary unit in *Fantasy Craft* is the **silver piece** (often abbreviated as 's' after the number of coins). All gear prices are listed in silver pieces and other coins and trade goods (such as gems, precious metal ingots, rare spices and commodities) are valued in silver as well. Your setting might substitute another base unit, such as steel in a world where it's a rare metal, or rice koku in feudal Japan, in which case everything should scale against the new base unit (with potential adjustments based on supply and demand). More information is available in the World Building section of Chapter 7 *(see page 317)*.

Coin (or the local equivalent) is used to purchase gear, services, and conduct day-to-day business in civilized parts of the world. It's often a reward for taking on heroic tasks and can be found on defeated bandits, monsters, and other enemies. Your supply of coin will rise and fall throughout your career and there's no "right" amount to have at any point in play. Still, most heroes tend to go through money like water, the lure of coin putting them squarely on the path to adventure.

Coin is divided into 2 categories, each recorded separately on your character sheet.

- *Coin in Hand:* This includes all the money you've acquired in the current adventure. You can spend coin in hand freely.

- *Stake:* This consists of all the money you've put away over time for major purchases and times of need. You may only pull money from your stake while in a city or visiting your home.

At the end of each adventure you can transfer a certain amount of your coin in hand into your stake. The rest is automatically spent during Downtime, frittered away on pleasures and covering expenses not expressly taken into account by the rules (e.g. day-to-day living, entertainment, personal debts, and the like). The amount you can transfer into your stake after each adventure is determined by your Prudence *(see below).*

GETTING STARTED

A new character starts with a stake of 100 silver × his Career Level.

LIFESTYLE

The second measure of your riches is Lifestyle, which determines both your general style and your knack for handling money. Lifestyle is a score divided between *Panache* and *Prudence.* Each time your Lifestyle rises by 1 you may invest that point in either of these two (but not both), choosing whether to live it up or plan for the future. Likewise, each time your Lifestyle falls by 1 you must also reduce your Panache or Prudence by 1. You gain Lifestyle from your class and may gain bonuses from certain character options, including Origin and feats.

PANACHE

Your Panache score summarizes your ability to present yourself with flair and elegance. As your Panache increases, you gain a growing Appearance bonus and modest sums of spending money.

Appearance: Each time you make a Charisma-based skill check targeting another character, you gain a +1 bonus with your check per point that your Appearance bonus exceeds the target's Appearance bonus. Your Appearance bonus may improve through character options and various items and services (a bath, grooming, and laundry). *For more information, see pages 156 and 168.*

Income: This is your monthly take from properties, businesses, scams, and other monetary endeavors. You earn the listed silver at the end of each month, and may collect it at the start of each adventure or any Downtime lasting 1 month or more.

PRUDENCE

Your Prudence reflects how disciplined you are with your time and money. As your Prudence increases, you reap greater lasting rewards from your adventures and Downtime efforts.

Money Saved/Earned: This is the maximum percentage of coin in hand you may transfer into your stake at the end of each adventure. This percentage is also used when earning money during Downtime *(see page 68).*

GETTING STARTED

You begin with Panache and Prudence scores of 0. You may distribute any Lifestyle gained from Origin, class, and feats as you like. Finally, you gain or lose Lifestyle equal to your Charisma modifier. This cannot reduce your Panache or Prudence below 0.

Example: Aaron is a Level 1 Courtier with a Charisma score of 16. He starts with 0 Panache and 0 Prudence but gains 3 Lifestyle from his Charisma modifier and another 2 from his class. He increases his Panache to 1 and applies the rest of his Lifestyle to Prudence. He starts play with Panache 1, Prudence 4, and a total Lifestyle of 5.

Table 4.1: Panache Benefits

Panache	Appearance Bonus	Income
0	+0	—
1	+0	10s
2	+1	20s
3	+1	30s
4	+1	40s
5	+2	50s
6	+2	60s
7	+2	70s
8	+3	80s
9	+3	90s
10	+3	100s
11	+4	110s
12	+4	120s

Table 4.2: Prudence Benefits

Prudence	Money Saved/Earned
0	15%
1	20%
2	25%
3	30%
4	35%
5	40%
6	45%
7	50%
8	55%
9	60%
10	65%
11	70%
12	75%

CARRYING CAPACITY

You can only carry what your body frame and Strength allow. To determine your carrying limits, also known as **encumbrance,** cross-reference your Strength score and the total weight of all items carried, including armor and weapons, on Table 4.3: Carrying Capacity *(see below)*. A character with a Light Load suffers no modifiers. Other loads have the following effects.

Heavy Load: Your Defense decreases by 2, you suffer a –2 penalty with physical skill checks, and you move at only 1/2 Speed (rounded up).

Overloaded: Your Defense decreases by 5, you suffer a –5 penalty with physical skill checks, and you can't move at all, not even with a Bonus 5-ft. Step.

Table 4.3: Carrying Capacity

Strength Score	Light Load	Heavy Load	Overloaded
1	Up to 5 lbs.	6 to 15 lbs.	16+ lbs.
2	Up to 10 lbs.	11 to 30 lbs.	31+ lbs.
3	Up to 15 lbs.	16 to 45 lbs.	46+ lbs.
4	Up to 20 lbs.	21 to 60 lbs.	61+ lbs.
5	Up to 25 lbs.	26 to 75 lbs.	76+ lbs.
6	Up to 30 lbs.	31 to 90 lbs.	91+ lbs.
7	Up to 35 lbs.	36 to 105 lbs.	106+ lbs.
8	Up to 40 lbs.	41 to 120 lbs.	121+ lbs.
9	Up to 45 lbs.	46 to 135 lbs.	136+ lbs.
10	Up to 50 lbs.	51 to 150 lbs.	151+ lbs.
11	Up to 60 lbs.	61 to 180 lbs.	181+ lbs.
12	Up to 70 lbs.	71 to 210 lbs.	211+ lbs.
13	Up to 80 lbs.	81 to 240 lbs.	241+ lbs.
14	Up to 90 lbs.	91 to 270 lbs.	271+ lbs.
15	Up to 100 lbs.	101 to 300 lbs.	301+ lbs.
16	Up to 120 lbs.	121 to 360 lbs.	361+ lbs.
17	Up to 140 lbs.	141 to 420 lbs.	421+ lbs.
18	Up to 160 lbs.	161 to 480 lbs.	481+ lbs.
19	Up to 180 lbs.	181 to 540 lbs.	541+ lbs.
20	Up to 200 lbs.	201 to 600 lbs.	601+ lbs.
21	Up to 250 lbs.	251 to 750 lbs.	751+ lbs.
22	Up to 300 lbs.	301 to 900 lbs.	901+ lbs.
23	Up to 350 lbs.	351 to 1,050 lbs.	1,051+ lbs.
24	Up to 400 lbs.	401 to 1,200 lbs.	1,201+ lbs.
25	Up to 450 lbs.	451 to 1,350 lbs.	1,351+ lbs.
+5	×2	×2	×2

Size: These weights are for Medium characters. When determining limits for bigger and smaller characters, decrease the Strength score by 2 per Size category below Medium or increase the score by 5 per Size category above Medium (e.g. a Huge character with a Strength of 12 determines carrying capacity as if his Strength is 22).

You can dead-lift or -lower up to twice your maximum heavy load but cannot move while doing so. You can push or drag up to twice your maximum heavy load at 1/4 Speed (rounded down), or clear up to 3 × your maximum heavy load in rubble or brush per minute (each square may be filled with 2,000 lbs. of loose debris or half that amount of brush).

Encumbrance limits may be improved with a Push Limit check *(see page 70)*.

GEAR

Gear includes all the items common enough to (usually) be purchased with coin, and is divided into five categories: **General Equipment, Supplies, Transportation, Armor,** and **Weapons.** The items in each category have their own particular stats but the following entries appear on most Gear tables.

Name: The item's name. When a number follows the name, the item is sold in lots of that size.

Effect: A brief summary of the item's game effect. Full rules are provided in each item's description.

SZ/Hand: The item's Size and the number of hands needed to ready the item (when appropriate).

Const(ruction): The item's durability, Damage save bonus, and number of Damage saves *(see page 155)*.

Comp(lexity): A number from 1 to 50 noting the skill required to craft the item *(see page 72)*, and a letter code indicating the minimum amount of continuous Downtime needed to craft the item (D for 1 day, W for 1 week, M for 1 month, or Y for 1 year).

Weight: The item's weight. When items are purchased in bundles, as with arrows, this is the weight of a single item.

Era: The earliest Era in which the item is likely to appear: Primitive, Ancient, Feudal, Reason, or Industrial *(see page 305)*.

Cost: The item's base value in silver pieces.

While the gear tables cover most common adventuring gear they're not a comprehensive catalogue of everything *possible* in a setting. The GM may occasionally need to introduce new items to support the plot or the players' ingenuity, in which case he should devise stats by comparison with listed gear. A new item's stats should always be recorded in case it's needed again.

UPGRADES

Items can be customized with upgrades, which are listed at the end of a gear table when they're available. These modifications allow for hundreds of variations on each item, improving or worsening quality and various stats. In particular armor and weapons can be upgraded to produce unique creations, making a hero's arms and appearance a distinct part of his legend.

Table 4.4: Gear Availability

Population	Haggle Check Time	Availability Modifier
None (No inhabitants; abandoned ruins, wilderness)	1d6 days	–20
Rural (1–50 inhabitants; small farm, frontier settlement)	4d6 hours	–10
Sparse (51–200 inhabitants; village, isolated hamlet)	2d6 hours	–5
Average (201–1000 inhabitants; town, independent outpost)	1d6 hours	0
Dense (1001–5000 inhabitants; large town, castle)	1d4 hours	+5
Urban (6001–25,000 inhabitants; city, port)	1d4 hours	+10
Sprawling (25,001+ inhabitants; capital city, bazaar)	1d6 hours	+20
Primary inhabitants are adversaries	×2	–10

Each upgrade may be added to an item only once. Also, no combination of upgrades may increase an item's Complexity above 50; such items may only be introduced by the GM.

Upgraded items tend to (dramatically) multiply an item's cost.

Example: A hollow, durable, masterwork music box costs 469s. As seen on Table 4.6 *(see page 158),* a music box has a cost of 75s. The 3 upgrades multiply this by a total of 525% (100% for durable, 25% for hollow, and 400% for masterwork).

AVAILABILITY

Your search for adventure may lead you far and wide, from tiny villages to bustling cities, and the same gear may not be available everywhere. Some areas might be too remote for anything but the basics, or the locals might refuse to sell to "outsiders." At his discretion, the GM may impose limited availability, asking characters to make a check to find desired gear. Alternately, he could simply rule that certain items are unavailable in the setting *(see page 318).*

When availability is limited, the party names the item(s) they're after and make a team Haggle check, taking the time and applying the modifiers listed on Table 4.4: Gear Availability *(see above).* Sellers are found offering each item with a Complexity score up to the Haggle result; all other items are unavailable in the area at this time.

DAMAGE

An item's Damage save bonus determines how well it resists damage. Most items with stats already have a Damage save bonus but for those that don't, and for scenery such as chairs, doors, windows, consult Table 4.5: Item Damage Saves *(see right).*

When an item or piece of scenery takes damage, it makes a Damage save against a DC of 10 + 1/2 the damage inflicted (rounded down). With success, the item or scenery may suffer scratches, dings, and other cosmetic flaws but there's no mechanical effect. An item that fails the number of saves listed on Table 4.5 is broken and must be repaired before it can be used again *(see page 73).* When scenery is broken, a hole is punched through it large enough to accommodate a character of smaller Size. An item or piece of scenery that fails twice the listed number of saves is ruined beyond repair. At best, a ruined item or scenery may be scavenged for raw materials *(see page 356).*

Unlike damage inflicted to a standard NPC, item damage does not linger or accumulate. Items and scenery save against each damage value independently.

The following special rules apply to attacks against items.

- Attacks with the *armor-piercing* or *keen* qualities add those modifiers to the damage inflicted on an item.
- When an item fails a save against damage with a blast increment *(see page 214),* it fails 1 additional save per 10 points of difference between the result and the DC (e.g. a save result of 16 against a DC of 34 translates to a total of 2 failed saves).
- With a critical hit, the number of saves failed, if any, is doubled (e.g. an item that would suffer 2 failed saves from an attack instead suffers 4 failed saves with a critical hit).

Table 4.5: Item Damage Saves

Construction/Scale	Damage Save Bonus	Number of Saves
Construction		
Brittle (paper, ice, glass, sand)	+0	—
Soft (cloth, dirt, leather)	+5	—
Hard (bone, metal, stone, wood)	+10	—
Size/Thickness		
Nuisance (N) or up to 1 in. thick	–4	1
Fine (F) or 2 in. thick	–2	1
Diminutive (D) or 3 in. thick	+0	1
Tiny (T) or 6 in. thick	+2	1
Small (S) or 9 in. thick	+4	2
Medium (M) or 1 ft. thick	+6	2
Large (L) or 2 ft. thick	+8	3
Huge (H) or 3 ft. thick	+10	4
Gargantuan (G) or 6 ft. thick	+12	6
Colossal (C) or 9 ft. thick	+15	8
Enormous (E) or 12 ft. thick	+20	10
Vast (V) or 15+ ft. thick	+25	12

GENERAL EQUIPMENT

This category includes adventuring tools (or "kits," which are used to perform various skill checks), as well as minor items that characters often find useful.

GOODS

Goods are essential survival equipment — lanterns, load-bearing gear, and other handy devices that can mean the difference between life and death for a stalwart adventurer.

GOOD DESCRIPTIONS

Astrolabe: These sturdy moon and star charts act as early calendars, indicating the day, month, and year.

Axe, hand: A dull axe made to split wood. It may also be used as an improvised hatchet *(see pages 73 and 179).*

Backpack: The wearer's Strength score is considered 2 higher for carrying capacity.

Bandolier: This wide leather belt can carry up to 20 ready-to-fire black powder rounds. It reduces the *load* quality of black powder weapons by 2.

Blanket/Bedroll: These items offer the user Cold Resistance 4.

Block and Tackle: This portable set of hooks, pulleys, and rope is used by treasure hunters and sailors to lift heavy loads. Block and tackle takes 5 minutes to set up. A user's Strength score is considered 4 higher for lifting *(see page 154).*

Brand: Commonly used to mark cattle and slaves. With a Coup de Grace action, this item permanently scars flesh with a specific mark.

Canteen/Waterskin: This item can hold 2 quarts of liquid.

Chain: This 10-ft. heavy working chain can bear 2,000 lbs. A character bound with chain may escape with a successful 1-minute Prestidigitation check (DC 25).

Chest, Large: In the Feudal and later eras, this sturdy wood and leather chest may be shod with metal and feature a lockable latch. It can hold coin and/or 1 Small item, 2 Tiny, 4 Diminutive, and so on, up to a combined weight of 100 lbs.

Chest, Small: As a large chest, except that it can hold 1 Tiny item, 2 Diminutive, 4 Fine, and so on, and up to a combined weight of 50 lbs.

Compass/Sextant: This magnetic, solar, or lunar compass helps a traveler stay on course, telling direction and granting a +2 gear bonus with Knowledge checks to navigate.

Flag/Standard: This item can strike fear or awe into observers, granting a +2 gear bonus with Impress checks against allies and Intimidate checks against adversaries.

Firesteel/Tinderbox: A character may use this item to start a fire in 1 round.

Fishing Pole/Net: This item grants a +2 gear bonus with Forage checks when fishing.

Game: Dice, playing cards, chess, and other amusements can help a hero relax, granting a +2 gear bonus with Relax checks.

Garrote: The wielder may silence a *held* or *pinned* opponent as a free action.

Glasses/Goggles: This eyewear has tinted lenses or narrow eyeslits, granting the wearer Flash Resistance 4.

Grappling Hook: When attached to rope, this item grants a +2 gear bonus with Climb checks.

Grooming Case: This item improves the user's Appearance bonus by +1. This bonus doesn't stack with the grooming service *(see page 168).*

Hammer, Tool: This crafting tool is good for pounding things, including opponents as an improvised mallet *(see pages 73 and 177).*

Holy Book: The words in these pages are a profound comfort to the like-minded, granting a +2 gear bonus with Calm and Relax checks when the reader shares the text's Alignment. A character may spend 8 hours preparing a sermon from a holy text, then spend 1 hour reading the sermon aloud to grant the same bonus to all who can hear him and share the text's Alignment.

Holy Symbol: A vessel of divine faith, this item increases the Will save DC of the user's Turn actions by 2 *(see page 223).*

Hourglass/Sundial: These devices accurately keep time.

Jar/Jug: This container can hold coin and/or 1 Fine or 2 Nuisance items, up to a combined weight of 5 lbs. Alternately, it can hold 2 quarts of liquid.

Lantern, Bullseye: This item works like a modern flashlight, focusing light through a small opening on the front. It shines dim light in a 75-ft. cone and consumes 1 pint of oil per 4 hours of use.

Lantern, Candle: This delicate paper lantern uses candles rather than oil. It shines faint light in a 30-ft. radius and consumes 1 candle per hour of use.

Lantern, Hooded: This lantern's hood can be lowered to cover its light without putting it out. It shines dim illumination in a 50-ft. radius and consumes 1 pint of oil per 4 hours of use.

Lanyard: This cord attaches another item to the user's wrist or belt, preventing it from leaving his square even when it's dropped or disarmed.

Magnet: This item can attract and hold 2 lbs. of metal.

Magnifying Glass: This item makes a Fine or smaller item appear 1 Size larger to the user.

Manacles: A character bound with manacles may escape with a successful 1-minute Str or Dex check (DC 25).

Map, Average: When trekking through the depicted area, the user's Travel Speed increases by 1 MPH and he gains a +2 gear bonus with Survival checks to avoid getting lost.

Map, Detailed: As an average map plus information about monsters, treasure, and other local features, granting a +2 gear bonus with Knowledge checks about the area.

Mirror: Great for signaling to distant friends and reflecting gaze attacks *(see page 223).*

Music Box: This delicate clockwork device may be wound up to play a single tune.

Musical Instrument: Lutes, lyres, fiddles, pipes, and other instruments can raise spirits — and very occasionally, tame savage beasts.

Pick/Shovel: When a character uses a pick or shovel, his Strength score is considered 4 higher for clearing rubble *(see page 154).* This item may also be used as an improvised fighting pick *(see pages 73 and 177).*

Pipe: Puffing on a packed pipe for 1 minute grants a +2 gear bonus with Concentrate checks for the current scene.

Pocket Watch: Popular with wealthy nobles and merchants, this device keeps accurate time.

Pole, 10-ft.: This ubiquitous adventuring item grants a +2 gear bonus with Jump checks and can be used to trigger traps. It can also be used as an improvised long staff *(see pages 73 and 177).*

Pouch: This container can hold up to 50 coins and weighs 1 lb. per 25 coins held.

Purse: This container can hold up to 200 coins and weighs 1 lb. per 25 coins held.

Ring, Poison: The wearer may expose a target with a successful Standard Unarmed Attack that inflicts at least 1 damage after Damage Reduction and Resistance are applied. This item may hold 1 dose of poison.

Rope, Hemp: This 50-ft. rope can bear 1,000 lbs. A character bound with hemp rope may escape with a successful 1-minute Prestidigitation check (DC 20).

Rope, Silk: This light and compact 50-ft. rope can bear 750 lbs. A character bound with hemp rope may escape with a successful 1-minute Pretidigitation check (DC 25).

Sack, Large: This container can hold coin and/or 1 Small item, 2 Tiny, 4 Diminutive, and so on, up to a combined weight of 25 lbs.

Sack, Small: As a large sack, except that it can hold 1 Tiny item, 2 Diminutive, 4 Fine, and so on, and up to a combined weight of 10 lbs.

Saddlebags: When wearing saddlebags, an animal's Strength score is considered 2 higher for carrying capacity.

Saw: When a character uses a saw, his Strength score is considered 4 higher for clearing brush *(see page 154).* This item may also be used to cut wood.

Seal/Signet Ring: This item bears an image that may be pressed into hot wax to seal a document. This image is often a coat of arms, monogram, or other personal symbol.

Scale, Hand: The simple device accurately measures weight.

Skis: When moving on snow or ice, skis increase the wearer's ground Speed by 10 ft. While wearing skis, a character suffers a –2 gear penalty with attacks and physical skill checks that require his legs.

Snowshoes: When a character wearing snowshoes suffers a Ground Speed penalty for moving on snow and ice, that penalty drops to 1/2 (rounded down).

Spyglass: This device doubles the user's vision increment.

Tent: This item offers the user Heat and Cold Resistance 4. A tent can house 4 Medium characters, 8 Small, 16 Tiny, and so on.

Umbrella: This portable shade keeps you dry in the rain and offers Heat Resistance 4 while outdoors.

Whistle: This item's squeal can be heard a mile away outdoors and 500 ft. away indoors.

GOOD UPGRADES

Durable: The item is constructed with extra care or heavier materials, ensuring it can stand up to rough treatment. The number of Damage saves the item may fail before being broken increases by 1.

Hollow: False-bottomed bottles and hidden pockets are a favorite of thieves and other sneaky characters. A hollow item may contain another at least 2 Size categories smaller than itself. Finding this hidden compartment requires a successful Notice or Search check (DC 20).

Masterwork: The item is masterfully crafted and performs with few mishaps. Error ranges with checks made using the item decrease by 1.

Table 4.6: Goods

Name	Effect	SZ/Hand	Const	Comp	Weight	Era	Cost
Astrolabe	Accurately tells day, month, and year	T/2h	Hard 2	12M	10 lbs.	Ancient	75s
Axe, hand	Chops wood; improvised hatchet	T/2h	Hard 2	5W	2 lbs.	Primitive	5s
Backpack	+2 Str for carrying capacity	Special */—	Soft 2	5D	3 lbs.	Primitive	10s
Bandolier	–2 *load* quality (black powder weapons)	Special */—	Soft 2	5D	1 lb.	Reason	20s
Blanket/bedroll	Cold Resistance 4	Special */—	Soft 1	5D	3 lbs.	Primitive	5s
Block and tackle	+4 Str for lifting	M/2h	Hard 3	7W	25 lbs.	Ancient	10s
Brand	Permanently marks target with Coup de Grace	S/1h	Hard 2	5D	3 lbs.	Ancient	5s
Canteen/waterskin	Holds 2 quarts of liquid	T/1h	Soft 1	5D	1/2 lb. **	Primitive	5s
Chain	10 ft. long; max load 2,000 lbs; escape DC 25	S/2h	Hard 4	10W	10 lbs.	Ancient	10s
Chest, large	Holds 1 Small or more smaller items (max. 100 lbs.)	M/2h	Hard 3	10W	20 lbs.	Ancient	20s
Chest, small	Holds 1 Tiny or more smaller items (max 50 lbs.)	S/2h	Hard 2	10W	10 lbs.	Ancient	15s
Compass/sextant	Tells direction; +2 gear bonus with Knowledge to navigate	F/1h	Brittle 1	12M	1 lb.	Ancient	40s
Flag/standard	+2 gear bonus with Impress (ally) or Intimidate (adversary)	M/2h	Soft 2	10W	12 lbs.	Ancient	40s
Firesteel/tinderbox	Starts fire in 1 round	D/2h	Hard 1	7D	1/2 lb.	Ancient	8s
Fishing pole/net	+2 gear bonus with Forage when fishing	S/1h	Hard 1	7D	4 lbs.	Ancient	5s
Game	+2 gear bonus with Relax	D/1h	Hard 1	7W	1 lb.	Primitive	10s
Garrote	Silences a *held* or *pinned* target as a free action	D/2h	Soft 1	5D	1/10 lb.	Primitive	1s
Glasses/goggles	Flash Resistance 4	T/—	Brittle 1	10W	1/2 lb.	Primitive	20s
Grappling Hook	+2 gear bonus with Climb when using rope	T/1h	Hard 2	7D	4 lbs.	Ancient	12s
Grooming case	+1 to user's Appearance bonus	D/1h	Brittle 1	5D	2 lbs.	Ancient	8s
Hammer, tool	Pounds things; improvised mallet	T/1h	Hard 2	5D	5 lbs.	Primitive	5s
Holy book	+2 gear bonus with Calm and Relax (same Alignment); may be used to prepare a sermon	T/2h	Soft 2	12M	3 lbs.	Feudal	150s
Holy symbol	+2 to Will save DCs of user's Turn actions	T/1h	Hard 2	12D	1 lb.	Primitive	75s
Hourglass/sundial	Accurately keeps time	T/1h	Brittle 1	7W	3 lbs.	Ancient	15s
Jar/jug	Holds 1 Fine or 2 Nuisance items (max. 5 lbs.) or 2 quarts of liquid	T/1h	Brittle 1	5D	1 lb. **	Ancient	3s
Lantern, bullseye	Dim light (50-ft. cone); uses oil	T/1h	Brittle 2	10D	3 lbs.	Feudal	30s
Lantern, candle	Faint light (30-ft. radius); uses candles	T/1h	Brittle 1	5D	1 lb.	Ancient	8s
Lantern, hooded	Dim light (50-ft. radius); may be covered; uses oil	T/1h	Brittle 1	7D	2 lbs.	Ancient	20s
Lanyard	Attached item remains in user's square	D/—	Soft 1	5D	1/2 1b.	Feudal	1s
Magnet	Attracts and holds up to 2 lbs. of metal	T/1h	Hard 3	10W	1 lb.	Ancient	10s
Magnifying Glass	Makes Fine or smaller item appear 1 Size larger to user	T/1h	Brittle 2	12W	1/2 lb.	Feudal	40s
Manacles	Escape DC 25	D/2h	Hard 3	10W	2 lbs.	Ancient	20s
Map, average	+1 MPH and +2 for navigation in mapped area	T/2h	Brittle 1	10D	1/10 lb.	Primitive	5s
Map, detailed	As average map and +2 with Knowledge in area	T/2h	Brittle 1	10W	1/10 lb.	Ancient	30s
Mirror	Signals distant friends; reflects gaze attacks	D/1h	Hard 1	7W	1/2 lb.	Ancient	25s
Music box	Plays 1 song	T/1h	Brittle 2	15M	1 lb.	Reason	75s
Musical instrument	Used in musical performance	S/2h	Brittle 2	12W	5 lbs.	Primitive	50s
Pick/shovel	+4 Str for clearing rubble; improvised fighting pick	S/2h	Hard 2	5D	5 lbs.	Ancient	5s
Pipe	+2 gear bonus with Concentrate (current scene)	D/1h	Hard 1	5D	1/10 lb.	Primitive	5s
Pocket watch	Accurately keeps time	F/1h	Brittle 1	15M	1/10 lb.	Reason	150s

Name	Effect	SZ/Hand	Const	Comp	Weight	Era	Cost
Pole, 10-ft.	+2 gear bonus with Jump; triggers traps; improvised long staff	M/2h	Hard 2	5D	5 lbs.	Primitive	5s
Pouch	Holds 50 coins	D/—	Soft 1	5D	Special	Primitive	2s
Purse	Holds 200 coins	T/—	Soft 1	5D	Special	Primitive	5s
Ring, poison	Target exposed with successful Standard Unarmed Attack that inflicts at least 1 point of damage	N/1h	Hard 1	12W	1/10 lb.	Ancient	30s
Rope, hemp	50 ft. long; max load 1,000 lbs; escape DC 20	S/2h	Soft 2	7W	10 lbs.	Primitive	6s
Rope, silk	50 ft. long; max load 750 lbs.; escape DC 25	S/2h	Soft 2	10W	5 lbs.	Ancient	20s
Sack, large	Holds 1 Small or more smaller items (max. 25 lbs.)	S/1h	Soft 1	5D	1/2 lb.	Primitive	3s
Sack, small	Holds 1 Tiny or more smaller items (max. 10 lbs.)	T/1h	Soft 1	5D	1/4 lb.	Primitive	1s
Saddlebags	+2 Str for carrying capacity	Special */—	Soft 2	5D	5 lbs.	Ancient	10s
Saw	Cuts wood; +4 Str for clearing brush	S/2h	Hard 2	7W	2 lbs.	Ancient	5s
Seal/signet ring	Seals document with hot wax image	N/—	Hard 1	10W	1/10 lb.	Feudal	40s
Scale, hand	Accurately measures weight	S/1h	Hard 1	12D	2 lbs.	Ancient	35s
Skis	+10 ft. ground Speed on snow and ice; –2 gear penalty with certain attacks and checks	Special */2h	Hard 2	7D	10 lbs.	Ancient	8s
Snowshoes	1/2 ground Speed penalty on snow and ice	Special */—	Hard 2	7D	3 lbs.	Primitive	10s
Spyglass	Doubles vision increment	T/1h	Hard 2	12W	3 lbs.	Feudal	100s
Tent	Heat and Cold Resistance 4	L/—	Soft 2	10W	15 lbs.	Primitive	10s
Umbrella	Heat Resistance 4	S/1h	Soft 2	10W	3 lbs.	Ancient	5s
Whistle	Signal 1 mile (outdoors) or 500 ft. (indoors)	D/1h	Hard 1	7D	1/10 lb.	Primitive	2s
Good Upgrades							
Durable	+1 failed Damage save before item is broken	—/—	+1	+2	+10%	Primitive	+100%
Hollow	May contain item 2 or more Sizes smaller	—/—	—	+5	—	Ancient	+25%
Masterwork	–1 error range with skill checks involving item	—/—	—	+5	—	Ancient	+400%

* This item is 1 Size category smaller than the user.

** This item's weight increases by 5 lbs. when full of liquid

KITS

Kits are collections of tools used in conjunction with various skill checks, as shown on Table 4.7: Kits *(see page 160)*. Kits have a variety of effects as seen in Chapter 2.

With the exception of climber's gear and thieves' tools, a larger version of each kit, called a "workshop," provides further benefit. Workshops are sometimes found in towns and other parts of the game world *(see page 319)*, and may be added to a character's holdings *(see page 192)*.

KIT DESCRIPTIONS

The exact contents of each kit and workshop are left up to the Game Master, though some basics are provided as an overview.

Actor's Props: Clothing, cosmetics, and accessories used to build disguises.

Carpenter's Kit: Tools, fasteners, polishes and dyes, and other items used in carpentry.

Carver's Kit: Tools, paints, and other items used in bone carving.

Chemist's Kit: Burners, glassware, binding agents, and other items used in chemistry.

Climber's Gear: Ropes, spikes, small mallet, and other climbing aids.

Cook's Kit: Pots and pans, utensils, herbs, and other cooking accoutrements.

Doctor's Bag: Bandages, splints, salves, scalpels, and other items for performing first aid and surgery.

Mage's Pouch: Arcane talismans, exotic compounds, animal parts, and other spellcasting components.

Pharmacist's Kit: Grinding tools, chemicals, and charts for preparing medicines and poisons.

Potter's Kit: A small wheel, wires, and racks for creating stoneware.

Scribe's Kit: Canvases, scrolls, pens, ink, and other writing implements.

Table 4.7: Kits

Name	Skill Checks/Effect	SZ/Hand	Const	Comp	Weight	Era	Cost
Actor's props	Disguise/Mask	T/2h	Soft 2	7D	5 lbs.	Primitive	15s
Carpenter's kit	Crafting (Carpentry)	S/2h	Hard 2	7W	10 lbs.	Primitive	15s
Carver's kit	Crafting (Carving)	D/2h	Hard 1	7D	3 lbs.	Primitive	12s
Chemist's kit	Crafting (Chemistry)	T/2h	Brittle 2	12W	10 lbs.	Ancient	20s
Climber's gear	Athletics/Climb	T/2h	Hard 2	7W	8 lbs.	Ancient	15s
Cook's kit	Crafting (Cooking)	T/2h	Hard 2	5D	10 lbs.	Primitive	10s
Doctor's bag	Medicine (all checks)	D/2h	Soft 1	10W	2 lbs.	Primitive	20s
Mage's pouch	Spellcasting (all checks)	D/2h	Hard 1	12W	4 lbs.	Primitive	20s
Pharmacist's kit	Crafting (Pharmacy)	D/2h	Brittle 1	10W	4 lbs.	Ancient	20s
Potter's kit	Crafting (Pottery)	S/2h	Hard 2	5D	15 lbs.	Primitive	10s
Scribe's kit	Crafting (Inscription)	D/2h	Brittle 1	7W	2 lbs.	Primitive	20s
Smith's kit	Crafting (Metalworking)	S/2h	Hard 2	7W	12 lbs.	Ancient	15s
Stonecutter's kit	Crafting (Masonry)	T/2h	Hard 2	5W	10 lbs.	Primitive	15s
Tailor's kit	Crafting (Tailoring)	T/2h	Soft 2	5D	3 lbs.	Primitive	10s
Thieves' tools	Prestidigitation/Disarm	D/2h	Hard 1	10W	1 lb.	Ancient	20s
Kit Upgrades							
Beast	May be used by beasts	—/—	—	+5	—	Primitive	+200%
Durable	+1 failed Damage save before kit is broken	—/—	+1	+2	+10%	Primitive	+100%
Masterwork	–1 error range with skill checks involving kit	—/—	—	+5	—	Ancient	+400%

Smith's Kit: A miniature anvil, tongs, and other tools for working metal.

Stonecutter's Kit: Chisels, hammers, polishing rags, and other tools for working stone.

Tailor's Kit: Needles, thread, patches, and patterns for creating clothes and other textile goods.

Thieves' Tools: Picks, shims, and levers for disabling locks and traps.

KIT UPGRADES

Beast: The kit may be used by a creature without hands or fine manipulators (e.g. it may be shrugged or tipped into place, or maneuvered with teeth).

Durable: The kit is built with extra care or heavier materials, ensuring it can stand up to rough treatment. The number of Damage saves it may fail before being broken rises by 1.

Masterwork: The kit is expertly crafted, performing with few mishaps. Error ranges with checks made using it decrease by 1.

LOCKS & TRAPS

Unlike security devices found in dungeons and other areas, the items in this section are man-portable tools used for securing personal property and trapping animals. Samples of classic location traps can be found in Chapter 7 *(see page 338).*

Arming (locking) a lock is a Handle Item action. Hiding a trap is a 10-minute Stash action. Arming a trap requires 10 minutes, a trigger (installer's choice with GM's approval), and a target chosen from the options on Table 4.8: Locks & Traps *(see page 161).* When a character triggers a trap, he must make a successful Reflex save (DC 15) or suffer the listed effect.

An armed lock or trap is Disabled with the Prestidigitation skill *(see page 79).* This is sometimes a Complex Task involving the number of Challenges shown on table 4.8. A disabled lock or trap may be Dismantled *(see page 73).*

LOCK & TRAP DESCRIPTIONS

Combination Lock: This sophisticated lock uses tumblers with codes rather than keys, making it much harder to Disable.

Crushing Trap: The trap dumps or swings heavy objects onto the target, knocking him off his feet.

Explosive Trap: Mines, shrapnel-blasting booby traps, and exploding runes are all examples of explosive traps.

Fear Trap: Gory wards or blasphemous symbols turn weak-willed targets away without physical harm.

Jaw Trap: Also known as a bear trap, this device snaps closed, clamping the target in the trap's metal teeth.

Net Trap: Popular with slavers and big game hunters, this trap is spread across the ground or hung from trees, rising up around or dropping down upon the unwary and unfortunate.

Padlock: This common lock employs a key and tumblers.

Pinlock: This early, simple lock uses wood pins or lengths of rope instead of tumblers.

Pit Trap: A trench or chute disguised with leaf litter, a false floor, or sometimes an illusion.

Projectile Trap: This trap hurls darts, arrows, or other deadly projectiles.

Snare Trap: Ropes tied to springs or tree branches grab their victim by a limb and prevent their escape.

Spike Trap: Sharpened stakes or rocks swing or spike up out of the ground, impaling the victim.

Table 4.8: Locks & Traps

Name	Effect	Target	Challenges	SZ/Hand	Const	Comp	Weight	Era	Cost
Locks									
Combination lock	—	1 object	3	T/2h	Hard 3	15W	2 lbs.	Reason	30s
Padlock	—	1 object	2	T/2h	Hard 2	12W	1/2 lb.	Feudal	20s
Pinlock	—	1 object	1	T/2h	Hard 1	7D	1/2 lb.	Ancient	10s
Traps									
Crushing trap	3d8 subdual damage, *sprawled*	2×2 area or 1 object	1	M/2h	Hard 2	10D	20 lbs.	Primitive	25s
Explosive trap	3d6 explosive damage (*blast 1*)	1×1 area or 1 object	2	S/2h	Hard 1	15W	2 lbs.	Reason	50s
Fear trap	3d8 stress damage, *frightened* 1d6 rounds	2×2 area or 1 object	1	M/2h	Soft 1	10D	10 lbs.	Primitive	40s
Jaw trap	2d8 lethal damage, *bleeding, slowed*	1×1 area	1	S/2h	Hard 2	10W	5 lbs.	Feudal	25s
Net trap	*Entangled*	3×3 area	1	M/2h	Soft 3	7D	10 lbs.	Primitive	10s
Pit trap	2d6 falling damage	2×2 area	1	M/—	Hard 3	5D	—	Primitive	5s
Projectile trap	2d6 ranged lethal damage	2×2 area or 1 object	1	M/2h	Hard 1	12D	4 lbs.	Ancient	10s
Snare trap	No movement actions	2×2 area or 1 object	1	M/2h	Soft 2	7D	3 lbs.	Primitive	5s
Spike trap	3d6 lethal damage	2×2 area or 1 object	1	M/2h	Hard 2	7D	8 lbs.	Primitive	10s
Lock & Trap Upgrades									
Bigger area	Area is doubled	×2	—	+1 Size	—	+2	×2	Primitive	+100%
Complex mechanism	+5 to Disarm and Dismantle DCs	—	—	—	—	+2	—	Ancient	+200%
Durable	+1 failed Damage save before lock or trap is broken	—	—	—	+1	+2	+10%	Primitive	+100%
Hair trigger	+2 to trap's Reflex save DC	—	—	—	—	+5	—	Ancient	+50%
More damage	+2 damage dice	—	—	—	—	+5	—	Primitive	+100%
Poison	Exposed to poison	—	—	—	—	+2	—	Primitive	+50%
Second trigger	1/2 damage with successful Reflex save	—	—	—	—	+2	—	Ancient	+100%
Unusual damage	Trap inflicts different damage type	—	—	—	—	+5	—	Ancient	+100%
Unusual mechanism	+1 Challenge to Disarm	—	+1	—	—	+5	—	Ancient	+50%

LOCK & TRAP UPGRADES

Bigger Area: The trap affects a larger area — and potentially more targets.

Complex Mechanism: The lock or trap uses a unique key, chemical trigger, or other sophisticated mechanism that makes disabling it and taking it apart much harder.

Durable: The lock or trap is constructed with extra care or heavier materials, ensuring it can stand up to rough treatment. The number of Damage saves it may fail before being broken increases by 1.

Hair Trigger: The trap's trigger is extraordinarily sensitive and more difficult to avoid.

More Damage: The trap features deadlier armaments or methods (such as spikes in a pit trap or logs bashing into those caught in a jaw trap), inflicting 2 additional dice of damage.

Poison: The trap employs spikes, needles, gas vents, or other ways to poison victims.

Second Trigger: The trap has a second trigger, making it harder to evade. Even with a successful Reflex save, the victim suffers 1/2 the trap's damage (rounded down).

Unusual Damage: The trap inflicts damage through unconventional means, such as spiked balls in a crushing trap or acid filling a pit.

Unusual Mechanism: The lock or trap's interior workings are unique, frustrating would-be raiders.

SUPPLIES

Supplies are items consumed with use, such as food, fuel, poisons, and medicine. A new column on Supply tables — Uses — indicates the number of times an item may be used, or the duration it lasts, before it's fully spent.

CONSUMABLES

Medical supplies, fuels, and other disposables are some of the most common carried by adventurers.

CONSUMABLE DESCRIPTIONS

Balm: This soothing concoction takes the sting out of minor injuries, doubling a character's vitality recovery for 1 day.

Bandages: Sterile strips of cloth, boiled leaves, and other antiseptics negate the *bleeding* condition.

Body Paint: Several versions of this item are available, one per terrain: aquatic, arctic, caverns/mountains, desert, forest/jungle, indoors/settled, plains, or swamp. For the scene in which it's applied, body paint grants a +2 gear bonus with Blend checks in corresponding terrain.

Candles: A candle shines faint light in a 30-ft. radius for 1 hour. It can also seal documents and fuel candle lanterns.

Chalk: A stick of chalk or chunk of soft stone or charcoal can be used to write on any surface. The inscription may be wiped away with water and fades eventually, commonly at the end of the adventure.

Ink, Common: Simple inks made of natural dies or animal fluids can permanently write on paper and flesh.

Ink, Invisible: Inscriptions in this ink can't be seen until the surface is heated over or near a fire, after which they're permanently visible.

Leeches: Popular with bloodletters, leeches quickly counter swelling and other fatiguing injuries, doubling a character's subdual damage recovery.

Oil, Pint: Oil is most commonly used as lantern fuel but can also become an improvised hurled weapon with no threat range and a range increment of 10 ft. × 3 *(see page 205)*. With a hit, the target suffers 2d6 fire damage.

Ointment: This early antibiotic grants a character 1 re-roll for each failed disease save for 1 day.

Paper, Sheaf: Paper is used to make most books, scrolls, and other documents.

Salve: This gummy paste is applied to clean deep cuts, doubling a character's wound recovery for 1 day.

Smelling Salts: These crystals emit a powerful odor that shocks the system, immediately waking any character whose wounds are above 0.

Table 4.9: Consumables

Name	Effect	Uses	SZ/Hand	Const	Comp	Weight	Era	Cost
General Consumables								
Body paint	+2 gear bonus with Blend in 1 terrain (current scene)	3	T/2h	Soft 1	5D	1/4 lb.	Primitive	4s
Candles (5)	Faint light (30-ft. radius)	1 hour	D/1h	Soft 1	5D	1/10 lb.	Ancient	1s
Chalk	Writes on any surface	5	F/1h	Brittle 1	7D	1/4 lb.	Primitive	2s
Ink, common	Writes on paper, hide, or flesh	20	F/1h	Brittle 1	7D	1/4 lb.	Ancient	2s
Ink, invisible	Inscription is invisible until heated	5	F/1h	Brittle 1	15D	1/4 lb.	Feudal	10s
Oil, pint	Fuels devices; 2d6 fire damage	4 hours	T/1h	Brittle 1	12D	1 lb.	Ancient	1s
Paper, sheaf	Used to make books, scrolls, and other documents	10	T/1h	Brittle 1	5D	1/2 lb.	Ancient	5s
Torches (5)	Dim light (30-ft. radius); 1d4 fire damage	1 hour	T/1h	Soft 1	5D	1 lb.	Primitive	2s
Medical Supplies								
Balm *	Heal vitality at twice normal rate (1 day)	3	T/2h	Soft 1	10D	1 lb.	Primitive	12s
Bandages	Negates *bleeding* condition	10	T/2h	Soft 1	5D	1/2 lb.	Ancient	3s
Leeches	Heal subdual damage at twice normal rate	4 hours	F/1h	Brittle 1	7M	1/2 lb.	Ancient	10s
Ointment *	1 re-roll per failed save vs. disease (1 day)	3	F/1h	Brittle 1	12D	1/4 lb.	Ancient	15s
Salve *	Heal wounds at twice normal rate (1 day)	3	T/2h	Soft 1	10D	1 lb.	Ancient	12s
Smelling Salts	Wakes 1 target	3	F/1h	Brittle 1	10D	1/4 lb.	Reason	5s
Tonic *	1 immediate save vs. poison	3	F/1h	Brittle 1	12D	1/4 lb.	Ancient	10s

* You may benefit from this item only once per day.

Tonic: This foul-tasting drink grants a character an immediate save against 1 poison plaguing the character. If the save fails, the poison continues per its original timetable.

Torches: This handy adventuring tool casts dim light out to 30 ft. and may be used as an improvised melee weapon, inflicting 1d4 fire damage with each hit *(see page 210)*.

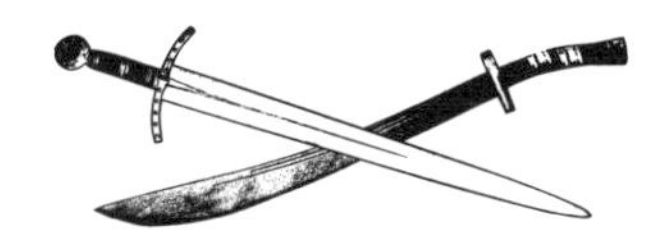

ELIXIRS

Elixirs are alchemical or magical concoctions that, depending on the campaign, might take the form of bottled liquids, herbs, fetishes, or other consumables. They come in three varieties: **oils,** which are poured, rubbed, or crushed on a target; **potions,** which are ingested; and **vials,** which can be used as an oil or thrown as a hurled weapon. Applying oil or drinking a potion is a Handle Item action while attacking with a vial is a Standard Ranged Attack with no threat range and a range increment of 10 ft. × 3.

Table 4.10: Elixirs

Name	Effect	SZ/Hand	Const	Comp	Weight	Era	Cost
Oils							
Blessing	As Bless spell	T/1h	Brittle 1	12D	1/4 lb.	Primitive	50s
Blurring	As Blur spell	T/1h	Brittle 1	15D	1/4 lb.	Primitive	100s
Consecrating	As Consecrate spell	T/1h	Brittle 1	15D	1/4 lb.	Primitive	100s
Mage armor	As Mage Armor spell	T/1h	Brittle 1	15D	1/4 lb.	Primitive	100s
Magic weapon	As Magic Weapon I spell	T/1h	Brittle 1	12D	1/4 lb.	Primitive	50s
Obscuring	As Obscure Object spell	T/1h	Brittle 1	15D	1/4 lb.	Primitive	100s
Purifying	Cleanses food and drink of disease and poison	T/1h	Brittle 1	12D	1/4 lb.	Primitive	50s
Repairing	As Tinker I spell	T/1h	Brittle 1	12D	1/4 lb.	Primitive	50s
Resistance	As Resist Energy spell	T/1h	Brittle 1	15D	1/4 lb.	Primitive	100s
Restoration	As Restoration I spell	T/1h	Brittle 1	15D	1/4 lb.	Primitive	100s
Sanctifying	As Lift Curse I spell	T/1h	Brittle 1	21W	1/4 lb.	Primitive	200s
Wilding	As Wild Side I spell	T/1h	Brittle 1	15D	1/4 lb.	Primitive	100s
Potions							
Boost attribute	+1d4 to preset attribute for 1d6 minutes	T/1h	Brittle 1	18W	1/4 lb.	Primitive	150s
Confidence	Heals 3d6 stress damage	T/1h	Brittle 1	12D	1/4 lb.	Primitive	50s
Darkvision	Negates effects of dim and faint light for 1 hour	T/1h	Brittle 1	9D	1/4 lb.	Primitive	25s
Healing	Heals all damage (standard character) or 1d4 wounds (special character)	T/1h	Brittle 1	12D	1/4 lb.	Primitive	50s
Invisibility	As Invisibility spell	T/1h	Brittle 1	21W	1/4 lb.	Primitive	200s
Love	Improves Disposition by 15 (current scene)	T/1h	Brittle 1	12D	1/4 lb.	Primitive	50s
Mana	Returns 1d6 spell points	T/1h	Brittle 1	15D	1/4 lb.	Primitive	100s
Refreshing	Heals 3d6 subdual damage	T/1h	Brittle 1	12D	1/4 lb.	Primitive	50s
Striking	As True Strike I spell	T/1h	Brittle 1	12D	1/4 lb.	Primitive	50s
Sustaining	Feeds character for 1 day	T/1h	Brittle 1	9D	1/4 lb.	Primitive	25s
Tongues	As Tongues I spell	T/1h	Brittle 1	18W	1/4 lb.	Primitive	200s
Vitality	Heal 2d6 vitality	T/1h	Brittle 1	9D	1/4 lb.	Primitive	25s
Vials							
Acid, strong	2d6 acid damage	T/1h	Brittle 1	12W	1/4 lb.	Primitive	30s
Acid, weak	1d6 acid damage	T/1h	Brittle 1	10W	1/4 lb.	Primitive	12s
Animating	As Animate Dead I spell	T/1h	Brittle 1	18W	1/4 lb.	Primitive	200s
Anointed	2d6 divine damage (opposing Alignment)	T/1h	Brittle 1	12W	1/4 lb.	Primitive	25s
Hold person	As Hold Person spell	T/1h	Brittle 1	15W	1/4 lb.	Primitive	100s
Shattering	As Shatter spell	T/1h	Brittle 1	12W	1/4 lb.	Primitive	50s
Weather	As Control Weather I spell	T/1h	Brittle 1	18W	1/4 lb.	Primitive	200s
Elixir Upgrades							
Cocktail	Combines effects of 2 elixirs of the same type	—	—	Special	—	Ancient	Special
Distilled	Elixir doesn't spoil	—	—	+10	—	Ancient	+400%
Gas	Affects all in target 2 × 2 area	—	—	+2	—	Ancient	+100%

Elixirs may be used in combat and have a variety of effects as shown on Table 4.10: Elixirs *(see page 163)*. When an elixir produces a spell effect, its Casting Level is 4. All saves against an elixir's effects have a DC of 14. A character or object only benefits from the first oil and first potion he uses each day, though he suffers the full effect of all vials used against him.

To craft elixirs, a character must possess the Alchemy Basics feat *(see page 96)*.

Elixirs spoil at the end of the adventure.

ELIXIR DESCRIPTIONS

Acid Vial: A character or item hit with this vial suffers the listed acid damage.

Animating Vial: A corpse hit with this vial suffers the effect of an Animate Dead I spell, falling under the control of the attacker.

Anointed Vial: A character or item whose Alignment opposes that of the vial contents (determined when the vial is made) suffers 2d6 divine damage.

Blessing Oil: A character treated with this oil benefits from a Bless spell.

Blurring Oil: A character treated with this oil benefits from a Blur spell.

Boost Attribute Potion: A character who drinks this potion gains a +1d4 magic bonus with 1 attribute (determined when the potion is made) for 1d6 minutes.

Confidence Potion: A character who drinks this potion heals 3d6 stress damage.

Consecrating Oil: The area treated is subject to a Consecrate spell.

Darkvision Potion: A characters who drinks this potion ignores penalties from dim and faint light for 1 hour.

Healing Potion: A character who drinks this potion recovers all damage (if standard) or 1d4 wounds (if special).

Hold Person Vial: A character hit with this vial suffers the effect of a Hold Person spell.

Invisibility Potion: A characters who drinks this potion benefits from an Invisibility spell.

Love Potion: When a character drinks this potion and fails a Will save (DC 14), his Disposition toward the next character he sees increases by 15 until the end of the current scene.

Mage Armor Oil: A character or item treated with this oil benefits from a Mage Armor spell.

Magic Weapon Oil: A weapon treated with this oil benefits from a Magic Weapon I spell.

Mana Potion: A character who drinks this potion recovers 1d6 spell points.

Obscuring Oil: An item treated with this oil benefits from an Obscure Object spell.

Purifying Oil: Up to 7 uses of food and/or drink may be treated with this oil, cleansing them of disease and poison.

Refreshing Potion: A character who drinks this potion heals 3d6 subdual damage.

Repairing Oil: An item treated with this oil benefits from a Tinker I spell.

Resistance Oil: A character or item treated with this oil benefits from a Resist Energy spell (damage type determined when the oil is made).

Restoration Oil: A character treated with this oil benefits from a Restoration I spell.

Sanctifying Oil: A character treated with this oil benefits from a Lift Curse I spell.

Shattering Vial: An item hit with this vial suffers the effect of a Shatter spell.

Striking Potion: A character who drinks this potion benefits from a True Strike I spell.

Sustaining Potion: A character who drinks this potion is fed for 1 day.

Tongues Potion: A character who drinks this potion benefits from a Tongues I spell.

Vitality Potion: A character who drinks this potion recovers 2d6 vitality.

Weather Vial: The area hit is subject to a Control Weather I spell.

Wilding Oil: A character treated with this oil benefits from a Wild Side I spell.

ELIXIR UPGRADES

Cocktail: The elixir has the combined effects of 2 different elixirs of the same type (e.g. confidence and healing). A cocktail's Complexity is equal to the higher of the two + 10, and its cost is the sum of the two + 25 silver.

Distilled: This elixir never spoils.

Gas: The elixir is a dust or vapor that affects all characters and objects in a 2 square × 2 square area.

Table 4.11: Food & Drink

Name	Effect	Uses	SZ/Hand	Const	Comp	Weight	Era	Cost
Animal feed *	Feeds 1 animal for 1 day	7	S/2h	Hard 1	5D	20 lbs.	Primitive	5s
Booze *	Decreases *shaken* condition by 1 grade	3	T/1h	Brittle 1	7W	2 lbs.	Ancient	15s
Coffee/tea	+1 gear bonus with Ref saves (8 hours)	3	T/1h	Soft 1	7D	1/2 lb.	Ancient	10s
Food, comfort	+1 gear bonus to Will saves (8 hours)	3	T/2h	Soft 1	5D	5 lbs.	Primitive	10s
Food, filling	+1 gear bonus to Fort saves (8 hours)	3	T/2h	Soft 1	7D	10 lbs.	Primitive	10s
Food, fresh	Negates *sickened* condition	3	T/2h	Brittle 1	10D	3 lbs.	Primitive	15s
Food, hearty	Decreases *fatigued* condition by 1 grade	3	T/2h	Soft 1	10D	5 lbs.	Primitive	10s
Meal, common	Feeds 1 character for 8 hours	3	T/2h	Soft 1	7D	2 lbs.	Primitive	1s
Rations *	Feeds 1 character for 1 day	7	T/2h	Hard 1	5D	5 lbs.	Primitive	5s
Spices *	Doubles gear bonus or condition grade decrease	3	F/1h	Hard 1	15W	1/4 lb.	Ancient	25s
Spirits *	Negates *frightened* condition	3	T/1h	Brittle 1	12W	2 lbs.	Ancient	15s

* These items spoil slowly enough that tracking when they go bad is pointless. They remain with the character until consumed or discarded.

FOOD & DRINK

A character must eat and drink to avoid starvation and thirst *(see page 217)*. He can also indulge in good meals and strong drink to raise his spirits, gaining a variety of helpful effects as shown on Table 4.11: Food & Drink *(see above)*. Other than nourishment, the listed effects are only gained for eating and drinking outside combat (when the character can savor the experience without distraction). Also, a character only benefits from the first food and the first drink he consumes each day.

Except for animal feed, rations, booze, and spirits, left over food and drink spoils at the end of each adventure.

FOOD & DRINK DESCRIPTIONS

Animal Feed: Grain, preserved plants, hay, straw, and other fodder can keep an animal healthy during long trips through the wilderness.

Booze: A hefty mug of ale, glass of mead, or draught of beer is a great way to unwind, decreasing the character's *shaken* condition by 1 grade.

Coffee/Tea: The power of caffeine stimulates a character's reflexes, granting a +1 gear bonus with Reflex saves for 8 hours.

Food, Comfort: Homemade delicacies remind a hero of the good things in life, granting a +1 gear bonus with Will saves for 8 hours. It also counts as 1 common meal.

Food, Filling: A meal loaded with all the trimmings can fortify a character, granting a +1 gear bonus with Fortitude saves 8 hours. It also counts as 1 common meal.

Food, Fresh: Fruits and vegetables can settle upset stomachs and cure illness, negating the *sickened* condition.

Food, Hearty: Meals loaded with fats and proteins can refresh a character, decreasing his *fatigued* condition by 1 grade.

Meal, Common: Offered at inns and some taverns, common meals vary widely depending on region, available ingredients, and the whim of the cook.

Rations: Jerky, biscuits, and other trail foods are the perfect way to stay fed away from the comforts of civilization.

Spices: Seasonings can personalize food or drink, doubling its gear bonuses or condition grade decrease.

Spirits: Hard liquors and moonshine are great for calming rattled nerves, negating the *frightened* condition.

POISONS

Favored by assassins, devious courtiers, and other malicious sorts, poison is a powerful, often lethal tool in the wrong hands. Poisons are liquid by default but gas versions are available with an upgrade *(see Table 4.12: Poisons, page 166)*. Liquid poison may be applied to food, drink, an Edged weapon or one with the *poisonous* quality, or any item built to contain poison with a Handle Item action *(for more on poisons, see page 216)*.

Only 1 dose of poison may be applied to a weapon not built to contain more, and 1 dose is consumed with each hit using a poisoned weapon, even if the target isn't exposed (a target hit with a poisoned weapon is only exposed if he suffers 1 or more damage after Damage Reduction and Resistance are applied). Poison damage ignores Damage Reduction.

To allow for unique toxins in each setting, *Fantasy Craft* names poisons according to their effects. GMs and players are encouraged to flesh each toxin out before it enters play, applying details appropriate to the world and story.

POISON DESCRIPTIONS

Agonizing: Victims feel like their blood is on fire, suffering stress damage.

Baffling: This strange poison muddles a victim's mind.

Blinding: Often derived from venom, this poison blinds victims.

Deafening: Victims hear intense ringing or suddenly lose their hearing.

Table 4.12: Poisons

Name	Effect	Incubation	Uses	Comp	Weight	Era	Cost
Agonizing poison	2d6 stress damage	1 minute	3	15D	1/10 lb.	Primitive	50s
Baffling poison	*Baffled* for 1 Incubation Period	1 hour	3	15D	1/10 lb.	Primitive	75s
Blinding poison	*Blinded* for 1 Incubation Period	1 minute	3	18D	1/10 lb.	Ancient	75s
Deafening poison	*Deafened* for 1 Incubation Period	1 hour	3	15D	1/10 lb.	Ancient	30s
Debilitating poison	2 temporary Constitution impairment	1 hour	3	25D	1/10 lb.	Primitive	50s
Disorienting poison	2 temporary Dexterity impairment	1 hour	3	25D	1/10 lb.	Primitive	50s
Enraging poison	*Enraged* for 1 Incubation Period	1 minute	3	15D	1/10 lb.	Primitive	50s
Intoxicating poison	2 temporary Wisdom impairment	1 hour	3	25D	1/10 lb.	Primitive	50s
Knockout poison	Unconscious for 1 Incubation Period	1 minute	3	20D	1/10 lb.	Ancient	60s
Lethal poison	1 failed Damage save (standard character) or –2 wounds (special character)	1 minute	3	20D	1/10 lb.	Primitive	60s
Maddening poison	2 temporary Charisma impairment	1 hour	3	25D	1/10 lb.	Primitive	50s
Necrotic Poison	2d6 lethal damage	1 minute	3	12D	1/10 lb.	Primitive	50s
Numbing poison	2d6 subdual damage	1 minute	3	15D	1/10 lb.	Primitive	50s
Paralyzing poison	*Paralyzed* for 1 Incubation Period	1 minute	3	20D	1/10 lb.	Primitive	75s
Paranoia poison	*Frightened* for 1 Incubation Period	1 minute	3	15D	1/10 lb.	Primitive	60s
Putrid poison	*Bleeding* for 1 Incubation Period	1 minute	3	12D	1/10 lb.	Primitive	20s
Sickening poison	*Sickened* for 1 Incubation Period	1 minute	3	15D	1/10 lb.	Primitive	30s
Slowing poison	*Slowed* for 1 Incubation Period	1 minute	3	18D	1/10 lb.	Ancient	50s
Stupefying poison	2 temporary Intelligence impairment	1 hour	3	25D	1/10 lb.	Primitive	50s
Weakening poison	2 temporary Strength impairment	1 hour	3	25D	1/10 lb.	Primitive	50s
Poison Upgrades							
Cocktail	Combines effects of 2 poisons	—	—	Special	—	Ancient	Special
Exotic	Tonic has no effect	—	—	+8	—	Ancient	+50%
Fast-Acting	Reduces Incubation Period	—	—	+5	—	Ancient	+100%
Gas	Exposes all in target 2 × 2 area	—	—	+2	—	Ancient	+100%
Persistent	Increases Incubation Period	—	—	+2	—	Ancient	+50%
Concentrated	+2 to save DC	—	—	+2	—	Ancient	+50%
Potent	+4 to save DC	—	—	+4	—	Ancient	+100%
Virulent	+6 to save DC	—	—	+8	—	Ancient	+200%

Debilitating: This wicked poison causes the victim's organs to fail.

Disorienting: This poison upsets a victim's equilibrium.

Enraging: This powerful hallucinogen fills the victim's mind with horrible visions, often sending him into a violent rage.

Intoxicating: Extremely strong spirits and psychotropic drugs can be intoxicating poisons, though just as often they're brewed by alchemists for seductresses and interrogators.

Knockout: This poison is especially popular with kidnappers and night-stalking brigands.

Lethal: Victims suffer excruciating pain, shortness of breath and, unless they overcome the toxin, death.

Maddening: Phantasmal voices and strange visions haunt victims, straining their psyche.

Necrotic: This poison liquefies flesh, usually beginning at the point of exposure.

Numbing: The victim's limbs become leaden and sensations fade.

Paralyzing: Victims become paralyzed, prisoners in their own bodies.

Paranoia: This poison causes irrational, unmitigated fear.

Putrid: Most putrid poisons are devilishly simple, concocted from infected body fluids.

Sickening: Victims suffer intense nausea and disorientation.

Slowing: Nerves in the victim's extremities are deadened, drastically reducing his reaction time.

Stupefying: The victim suffers memory loss.

Weakening: This poison saps the target's strength.

POISON UPGRADES

Cocktail: With each failed save, the poison inflicts the combined effects of 2 different poisons (e.g. knockout and putrid). If the poisons have different Incubation Periods, the cocktail gains the shorter of the two. A cocktail's Complexity is equal to the higher of the two + 10, and its cost is the sum of the two + 25 silver.

Concentrated: The poison's save DC increases by 2.

Table 4.13: Scrolls

Spell Level	SZ/Hand	Const	Comp	Weight	Era	Cost
0	T/2h	Brittle 2	12D	1/10 lb	Ancient	25s
1	T/2h	Brittle 2	15D	1/10 lb	Ancient	50s
2	T/2h	Brittle 2	18D	1/10 lb	Ancient	100s
3	T/2h	Brittle 2	21W	1/10 lb	Ancient	200s
Scroll Upgrades						
Heavy Material	—	Soft 2	+2	1 lb.	Ancient	+10%
Solid Material	—	Hard 2	+5	3 lbs.	Ancient	+25%

Exotic: The poison's strange properties bewilder healers, negating the effects of tonic.

Fast-Acting: The poison's Incubation Period is uncharacteristically short (1 hour becomes 1 minute, and 1 minute becomes 1 round).

Gas: The poison is a dust or vapor that exposes all breathing characters in a 2 square × 2 square area.

Persistent: The poison lingers longer, its Incubation Period longer than expected (1 minute becomes 1 hour, and 1 hour becomes 1 day).

Potent: The poison's save DC increases by 4.

Virulent: The poison's save DC increases by 6.

SCROLLS

Scrolls are one-use "pocket spells," allowing spellcasters to reach beyond their knowledge. They're usually recorded on paper, hide, or stone but they can just as easily be chiseled onto branches, inscribed onto metal plates or armor, painted onto walls, or even worked into sand.

Only a character with the Spellcasting skill may use a scroll and the process is similar to casting a spell, though no spell points are spent. The caster doesn't have to know the spell, nor must he be able to normally cast spells of its level. He spends the Casting Time reading the scroll (minimum 1 full action) and makes a Spellcasting check *(see page 111)*. With success, the spell is cast and the scroll is destroyed. With failure, the spell fails but the scroll is retained and may be used again. A critical failure ruins the scroll.

To craft scrolls, a character must possess the Scribing Basics feat *(see page 98)*.

When desired, the spell a scroll contains may be randomized on Table 3.2: Spells *(see page 114)*.

SCROLL UPGRADES

Heavy Material: The scroll is made of a soft material (e.g. cloth, leather, etc.).

Solid Material: The scroll is made of a hard material (e.g. bone, wood, etc.).

SERVICES

For the weary traveler, a hot meal or a warm bed can be worth a king's ransom. Likewise, the assistance of a surgeon, tailor, guide, or consort may be just what an adventurer needs to win the day. Services are all the things characters hire others to do for them. Since they can't be crafted, the Complexity column on Table 4.14 is replaced with Availability, which is used to determine whether a certain service is offered in the area.

Superior services, such as legal pardons and hired muscle, are Favors secured with Reputation *(see page 187)*.

SERVICE DESCRIPTIONS

Announcement: Town criers, street corner poets, and loose-lipped snitches can be paid to spread a simple one-sentence notice through the local populace in 1 day. This doesn't guarantee that anyone will believe the message — that's up to the GM. To determine randomly whether a specific character believes, the GM can make a Persuade check using the skill bonus of the crier, poet, or snitch.

Bath: Often a rare luxury for adventurers, a bath improves the purchaser's Appearance bonus by +1 for the current scene.

Carousing: Nothing's better for blowing off steam and getting a little perspective than a night out on the town. An evening of carousing heals all accumulated stress damage and grants Stress Resistance 4 for the current scene.

Consort: A welcoming pair of open arms or ears isn't quite as effective as a full night of debauchery but it's enough to take the edge off. Hiring a consort heals 1/2 accumulated stress damage (rounded down), and grants Stress Resistance 2 for the current scene.

Delivery: A courier, mage, or informant delivers a message or item up to Small Size. Couriers are likely to charge more to cross dangerous or rugged terrain and Travel Speeds are modified by terrain *(see page 371)*. The delivery is obvious to observers and subject to the rigors of the road; the GM may spend 2 action dice to waylay the delivery with brigands, monsters, a natural disaster, or another hazard of his device. Each redundant or decoy delivery sent along with the main one increases this cost by 1 action die (maximum 4).

Table 4.14: Services

Service	Effect	Availability	Era	Cost
Community Services				
Announcement	Spreads news to the local population in 1 day	5	Primitive	3s
Bath	+1 to user's Appearance (current scene)	10	Ancient	5s
Carousing, 1 night	Heals all stress damage; Stress Resistance 4 (current scene)	7	Primitive	25s
Consort	Heals 1/2 stress damage (rounded down); Stress Resistance 2 (current scene)	5	Primitive	10s
Delivery, neighboring	Within 50 miles (1 day of travel)	5	Primitive	5s
Delivery, regional	Within 500 miles (1 day per 50 miles of travel)	7	Primitive	25s
Delivery, remote	Over 500 miles (1 day per 50 miles of travel)	10	Ancient	50s
Fortune	Gain 1 free hint	10	Primitive	2s
Grooming	+1 to user's Appearance (current scene)	7	Primitive	3s
Healer visit, short	Benefit from successful Mend check	7	Primitive	10s
Healer visit, extended *	Benefit from successful Treatment check	10	Ancient	10s/day
Item, commissioned	Craftsman builds 1 item	12	Primitive	2 × item
Item, repair	Craftsman repairs 1 item	10	Primitive	1/2 item
Laundry	+1 to user's Appearance (current scene)	5	Primitive	3s
Legal advocate, common	+2 morale bonus with skill checks in a trial	10	Ancient	25s
Legal advocate, respected	+5 morale bonus with skill checks in a trial	15	Ancient	100s
Library access	Assists Research	15	Ancient	5s/day
Scribe	Prepares document	10	Ancient	2s/page
Hired Passage				
Neighboring, per person	Within 50 miles, 1 day of travel	5	Primitive	10s
Regional, per person	Within 500 miles, 1 day per 50 miles of travel	7	Primitive	50s
Remote, per person	Over 500 miles, 1 day per 50 miles of travel	10	Primitive	100s
Lodging (per person or animal)				
Poor	Shelter only, start day fatigued	5	Primitive	1s/day
Common	Dinner included (common meal)	7	Primitive	5s/day
Fancy	As common lodging + breakfast and lunch (common meals)	10	Primitive	10s/day
Luxurious	As fancy lodging + 1 unspiced food or drink	12	Primitive	25s/day
Extravagant	As luxurious lodging + 1 community service (see description)	15	Primitive	100s/day
Stabling, poor	Shelter only, start day *fatigued*	5	Primitive	1s/day
Stabling, common	Feed included	7	Primitive	5s/day
Stabling, veterinary *	As common stabling + successful Mend or Treatment check	12	Primitive	10s/day

* This service may only be used in Downtime.

Fortune: The ramblings of an oracle, seer, or gypsy can provide unique insight in the form of a free hint from the GM.

Grooming: Barbers and attendants help a hero look his best, improving his Appearance bonus by +1 for the current scene. This bonus doesn't stack with the grooming kit *(see page 156)*.

Healer Visit, Short: A quick visit to a bone setter or bloodletter can help a hero get back on his feet. A short healer visit grants the benefits of a successful Mend check.

Healer Visit, Extended: Paying a nurse or healer to keep a watchful eye grants the benefits of a successful Treatment check once per day of the character's stay.

Hired Passage: Purchasing space in a caravan or on a galley ensures mostly reliable and relatively safe travel — mostly. It doesn't guarantee that corrupt guides and porters won't try to take advantage of the party, nor does it protect them from dangerous fellow travelers, but at least they won't get lost *(see page 371)*. If the GM rolls for random travel encounters, there's also a smaller chance that the trip will be rudely interrupted *(see page 372)*.

Item, Commissioned: When an item isn't available, a character can hire a craftsman to build it. It costs twice the item's listed cost and takes a number of (D)ays, (W)eeks, or (M)onths

equal to the item's Complexity divided by 10 (rounded up). No skill checks are made — the craftsman simply produces the item.

Item, Repair: Hiring a craftsman to repair an item costs half the item's listed value (rounded up). It takes a number of days equal to the item's Complexity divided by 10 (rounded up), and restores the item to full operation (no Damage saves failed). No skill checks are made — the craftsman simply repairs the item.

Laundry: Cleaning and repairing an outfit improves the wearer's Appearance bonus by +1 for the current scene.

Legal Advocate: Hired counsel represents a character in the court of the land, whether it be a holy or military tribunal, a judge and jury, or gathering of tribal leaders. This grants the character a +2 or +5 morale bonus with skill checks made in a trial *(see page 320)*.

Library Access: Any respectable library is well organized and contains hundreds of books, making Research checks much easier (of course, the books may or may not have anything to do with the information a character wants). At the GM's discretion, a library in a major city might contain thousands of books or more, and specialize in any topic sensible for the area and its history.

Lodging, Poor: Barns and flophouses are cheap but uncomfortable. A character "enjoying" poor lodging receives only shelter, not food, and starts the next day with the *fatigued I* condition.

Lodging, Common: Common houses, hostels, and space around the hearth at an inn are standard fare for many adventurers. A common dinner is provided with each night's stay.

Lodging, Fancy: A private room at an inn, residence, or guest house offers comfort and solitude, along with three square (common) meals.

Lodging, Luxurious: Rare unless the character is the guest of a noble, successful merchant, or other wealthy benefactor, luxurious lodging offers all the comforts of home — including 1 unspiced option from Table 4.11 *(see page 165)*. The GM may choose the option (based on the nature of the lodging) or let the players choose from a menu.

Lodging, Extravagant: The pinnacle of lavish living, extravagant lodging includes a helpful inn owner or personal assistant who performs or acquires 1 community service other than a commissioned item from Table 4.14 *(see page 168)*. The GM may choose the service offered (based on the nature of the lodging) or let the players choose from options available in the area.

Scribe: A scribe can be hired to write a character's spoken words or duplicate a non-magical document.

Stabling, Poor: Tying a mount, pet, or other animal to a post under an awning is cheap but doesn't do the animal any favors. The animal isn't fed (at least, not by the owner of the lodging), and starts the next day with the *fatigued I* condition.

Stabling, Common: Stabling an animal for the night keeps it warm, dry, and fed for the day.

Stabling, Veterinary: A skilled and caring animal healer can provide the benefit of a short or extended healer visit, and feed guests as well.

TRANSPORTATION

This category includes mounts and vehicles. Hired passage is a service *(see page 168)*.

MOUNTS

Animal descriptions and statistics are located in Chapter 6 *(see page 253)*, and animals are bred and trained with the Survival skill *(see page 83)*. Only a trained animal may be ridden; wild animals refuse to follow commands and buck riders. All mounts listed on Table 4.15 are trained, though a character may find a wild animal and train it with the Survival skill (which is also used to breed animals and improve their statistics).

Unless otherwise specified, a mount is a standard NPC controlled by the GM. It is guided with the Ride skill but otherwise follows the same rules as a character. It can carry 2 characters 1 Size smaller, 4 characters 2 Sizes smaller, 8 characters 3 Sizes smaller, and so on. A mount is subject to encumbrance, including all items and riders it carries.

A mount's Travel Speed in miles per hour is equal to its Speed divided by 10, rounded up *(see page 371)*.

Animals don't have Complexity, so Availability is used to determine whether a certain animal is offered in the area.

MOUNT UPGRADE DESCRIPTIONS

Exceptional Specimen: The mount is a special NPC rather than a standard one.

Training: The mount has already learned 1 or more training benefits *(see page 83)*.

VEHICLES

Like mounts, vehicles are controlled with the Ride skill. A character and his vehicle follow the rules for mounted combat *(see page 215)*. A vehicle's Initiative and saving throw bonuses are +0 and its Defense is listed on Table 4.16: Vehicles *(see page 171)*. Some vehicles can't Run and no vehicle can become *sprawled*. Vehicles suffer all damage from normal hits but with a critical hit the attacker may spend 2 action dice to instead hit an occupant or draft animal (if one is present).

Due to the unique rules for vehicles, Table 4.16 features some different columns.

Speed: The vehicle's Ground Speed, used in combat and movement. When another Speed follows in parentheses, it's the vehicle's Run distance. These values override animal statistics when the vehicle is drawn.

Table 4.15: Mounts

Mount	Breeding	Training	Weight	Availability	Cost
Draft Animals					
Bison	7 (275 days)	12	2,000 lbs.	10	250s
Bull/Ox	5 (275 days)	12	1,800 lbs.	5	200s
Donkey/mule	10 (350 days)	15	400 lbs.	5	100s
Elephant	12 (650 days)	12	10,000 lbs.	10	400s
Goat	7 (150 days)	10	150 lbs.	5	100s
Horse, draft	7 (340 days)	10	1,800 lbs.	5	250s
Llama	7 (325 days)	5	350 lbs.	7	200s
Flying Mounts					
Eagle, giant	15 (80 days)	12	500 lbs.	18	1,200s
Griffon	20 (250 days)	20	500 lbs.	20	2,500s
Hippogriff	20 (350 days)	20	1,000 lbs.	20	1,500s
Pegasus	20 (350 days)	20	1,500 lbs.	20	1,500s
Military Mounts					
Bear	15 (225 days)	12	450 lbs.	12	900s
Rhino	15 (450 days)	12	3,000 lbs.	15	800s
War-horse	15 (340 days)	10	1,500 lbs.	10	750s
War-raptor	18 (80 days, 1d4 chicks)	12	600 lbs.	15	1,500s
Wolf	10 (65 days, 1d6 puppies)	10	150 lbs.	10	500s
Riding Mounts					
Camel	7 (410 days)	15	1,200 lbs.	10	300s
Dog, riding	7 (65 days, 1d6 puppies)	7	100 lbs.	10	200s
Horse, race	15 (340 days)	10	900 lbs.	12	750s
Horse, riding	10 (340 days)	10	1,000 lbs.	7	500s
Pony	7 (340 days)	7	700 lbs.	7	250s
Raptor, riding	12 (80 days, 1d4 chicks)	12	400 lbs.	15	1,000s
Swimming Mounts					
Hippocampus	20 (300 days)	20	700 lbs.	20	2,500s
Turtle, giant	15 (225 days)	15	5,000 lbs.	20	2,000s
Water serpent	15 (150 days)	20	3,000 lbs.	20	2,000s
Mount Upgrades					
Exceptional specimen	—	—	—	+5	+250%
Training	—	—	—	+1 per benefit	+5% per benefit

Travel: The vehicle's Travel Speed in miles per hour *(see page 371)*. As with Ground Speed, this value overrides animal statistics when the vehicle is drawn.

SZ/Def: The vehicle's Size and Defense.

Occ/Load: The number of Medium characters (including driver) and total weight the vehicle may carry.

VEHICLE QUALITIES

Cover: The vehicle offers protection from outside attack, granting the listed cover to occupants. This cover only applies in the vehicle's "open areas," such as a boat's deck, from which an occupant may attack.

Crew: The vehicle requires a minimum number of characters to function.

Draft: The vehicle requires a minimum number of animals or characters as its source of locomotion.

Overrun: The vehicle is designed to ram enemies or run them down. During a Run, the driver may direct the vehicle to Trample as a free action, inflicting the lethal damage listed in parentheses with a hit.

Table 4.16: Vehicles

Name	Qualities/Effect	Speed	Travel	SZ/Def	Occ/Load	Const	Comp	Era	Cost
Air Vehicle									
Balloon	*Cover (1/2)*	20 ft.	10 *	G/7	3/1,000 lbs.	Soft 4	15W	Reason	2,500s
Flying Carpet	—	60 ft.	15	L/15	2/500 lbs.	Soft 3	25W	Ancient	12,000s
Mechanical Wings	—	30 ft. (60 ft.)	3	M/—	1/250 lbs.	Soft 2	20W	Reason	6,000s
Land Vehicles									
Cart	—	20 ft. (40 ft.)	2	L/9	4/1,000 lbs.	Hard 3	5W	Primitive	175s
Chariot	*Draft (1), cover (1/2), overrun (2d6)*	40 ft. (60 ft.)	5	L/10	3/1,000 lbs.	Hard 3	10W	Ancient	450s
Coach	*Draft (2), cover (1/2), overrun (1d6)*	20 ft. (40 ft.)	4	L/9	4/800 lbs.	Hard 3	10W	Feudal	600s
Litter/Palanquin	*Draft (2)*	20 ft.	2	L/9	1/300 lbs.	Soft 3	7W	Ancient	250s
Siege Tower	*Draft (8), cover (full)*	15 ft.	1	G/5	30/8,000 lbs.	Hard 6	12M	Feudal	1,000s
Sled	*Draft (2)*	30 ft. (50 ft.)	5	M/10	2/500 lbs.	Hard 3	10W	Ancient	75s
Stagecoach	*Draft (4), cover (3/4), overrun (3d6)*	30 ft. (50 ft.)	4	L/9	6/2,000 lbs.	Hard 4	12W	Reason	750s
Wagon	*Draft (2), cover (1/4), overrun (2d6)*	20 ft. (40 ft.)	3	L/9	6/1,500 lbs.	Hard 3	7W	Ancient	200s
Water Vehicles									
Barge	*Draft (8)*	10 ft.	1	G/4	20/15 tons	Hard 6	10M	Ancient	1,000s
Canoe	—	20 ft. (40 ft.)	2	L/10	3/800 lbs.	Hard 3	7W	Primitive	100s
Catamaran	*Crew (4)*	30 ft. (50 ft.)	3	H/8	10/2,400 lbs.	Hard 4	10W	Ancient	250s
Frigate	*Cover (1/2), crew (50), overrun (5d6)*	10 ft. (50 ft.)	10 *	E/3	100/25 tons	Hard 10	15Y	Reason	15,000s
Galley	*Cover (1/4), crew (30), overrun (4d6)*	20 ft. (40 ft.)	6 *	C/5	50/15 tons	Hard 7	12Y	Ancient	10,000s
Ironclad	*Cover (3/4), crew (20), overrun (3d6)*	10 ft. (30 ft.)	7	C/3	40/10 tons	Hard 9	20Y	Reason	12,000s
Longship	*Cover (1/2), crew (15)*	20 ft. (40 ft.)	8 *	G/7	30/10 tons	Hard 6	10M	Feudal	5,000s
Raft	—	15 ft.	2	L/8	2/500 lbs.	Hard 3	5D	Primitive	25s
Rowboat	—	20 ft.	3	L/10	4/1,000 lbs.	Hard 3	7W	Ancient	150s
Vehicle Upgrades									
Agile	+2 gear bonus to Defense	—	—	—/+2	—/—	—	+5	Reason	+25%
Armored	+2 gear bonus with Damage saves; +1 save	–5 ft.	–1 (min. 1)	—/—	—/—	+1	+2	Feudal	+25%
Enclosed	+1/4 cover	—	—	—/—	—/—	—	+2	Feudal	+25%
Fast	+2 miles per hour (Travel Speed)	—	+2	—/—	—/—	–1	+2	Ancient	+50%
Hauling	2 × Load, 1/2 Occupancy (rounded down)	—	—	—/—	1/2 / ×2	—	+2	Ancient	+25%
Powered	Removes *draft* quality	—	—	—/—	—/—	—	+5	Feudal	+150%
Sail-borne	Moves by wind power	—	*	—/—	—/—	—	+5	Ancient	+10%
War-built	+2d6 damage during Trample attacks	—	—	—/—	—/—	—	+5	Ancient	+25%

* This vehicle's Speed is altered by the wind — 1/2 normal (rounded down) when moving against it and double when moving with it.

VEHICLE DESCRIPTIONS

Balloon: This early lighter-than-air vehicle lets a small party avoid travel encounters on the ground but it's also at the mercy of the wind.

Barge: This smooth-bottomed, river-going cargo hauler may be pulled by a swimming draft team or float with the current.

Canoe: This light, slender boat is made of hide or wood and guided by paddle.

Cart: This simple draft wagon has one axle and a flat bed for hauling cargo.

Chariot: This early horse-drawn war machine smashes through enemy lines at great speeds.

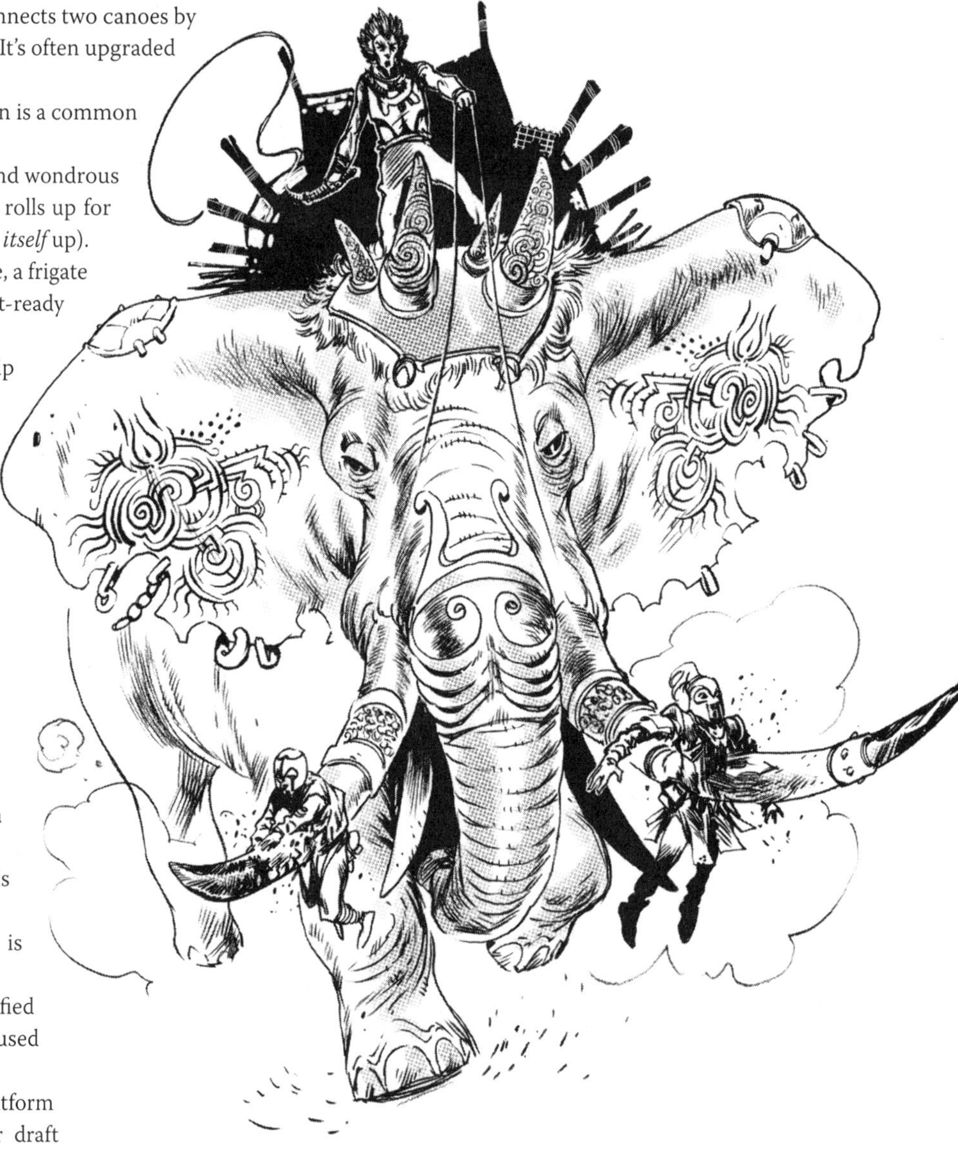

Catamaran: This sea-going vessel connects two canoes by platform, offering much greater stowage. It's often upgraded with a sail.

Coach: This enclosed, two-axle wagon is a common conveyance of nobility and the wealthy.

Flying Carpet: This extremely rare and wondrous vehicle can carry two at great speed and rolls up for easy storage (if sapient, it might even roll *itself* up).

Frigate: The pinnacle of naval warfare, a frigate often bristles with guns and combat-ready mariners.

Galley: This multi-purpose sailing ship is useful in trade and battle.

Ironclad: A seaborne tank, this early metal ship is terrifyingly effective in war.

Litter/Palanquin: This throne or lounging seat is carried on the shoulders of human bearers.

Longship: This small, nimble warship is a favorite of sea raiders and can be carried across land for short distances.

Mechanical Wings: This bizarre mechanical contraption is worn like a backpack and lets the wearer fly like a bird.

Raft: This simple floating platform is guided by paddle, pole, or sail.

Rowboat: This small watercraft is guided by row or sometimes a small sail.

Siege Tower: This massive, fortified tower moves on rollers or wheels and is used to attack enemy fortifications.

Sled: This smooth-bottomed platform is pulled across snow by dogs or other draft animals.

Stagecoach: This heavy wagon is fully enclosed (and often armored), though cargo and the driver usually sit outside.

Wagon: This two-axle cargo hauler is pulled by a single steed or horse team and provides decent cover during poor weather.

VEHICLE UPGRADES

Agile: The vehicle is unusually maneuverable, gaining a +2 gear bonus to Defense. This bonus also extends to the vehicle's driver.

Armored: The vehicle is fitted with armor plates or durable materials, gaining a +2 gear bonus with Damage saves. Also, its total saves increase by 1.

Enclosed: Additional baffles or closures improve occupant cover by 1/4.

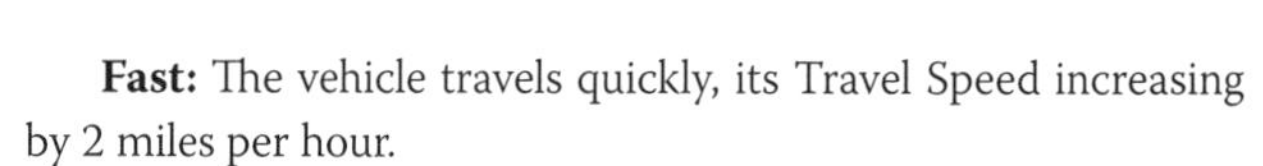

Fast: The vehicle travels quickly, its Travel Speed increasing by 2 miles per hour.

Hauling (min. Occupancy 1): The vehicle's Load is doubled but its Occupancy drops to 1/2 (rounded down).

Powered: The vehicle is fitted with an advanced engine or magical modification that allows it to move without draft animals.

Sail-Borne (water vehicle only): The vehicle is fitted to catch the wind — its Water and Travel Speeds are 1/2 normal (rounded down) when moving against it and doubled when moving with it.

War-Built (ground vehicle only): The vehicle is fitted with a ram, wheel-spikes, or other vicious implements for mowing down enemy infantry. It inflicts +2d6 damage during Trample attacks.

ARMOR

In general, armor reduces mobility and slightly increases the chance of being hit in exchange for reducing incoming damage. Armor is graded by coverage: **partial** (10–40%), **moderate** (50–80%), or **full** (90–100%). The greater the coverage, the more difficult it is for opponents to use certain actions and abilities, including Called Shots *(see page 221)*.

Partial armor covers the torso alone while moderate armor covers both the torso and legs. Light or heavy fittings may be added to armor (not thick hide), adjusting its base values. Heavy fittings also increase the armor's coverage by 1 grade (from partial to moderate, or from moderate to full). For a more detailed but complex armor system, and a greater view of how fittings play into armor, see Descriptive Armor, right.

A character may only wear armor of his exact Size. Armor Size affects cost and weight *(see the footnote on Table 4.17: Armor, page 174)*.

The armor tables feature several different columns.

Damage Reduction (DR): Damage Reduction granted by the armor. This decreases to 1/2 (rounded up) when the wearer is *held, helpless, pinned, sprawled,* or *unconscious.*

Resistances: Damage Resistance granted by the armor.

Defense Penalty (DP): A penalty applied to the wearer's Defense and Reflex saves.

Armor Check Penalty (ACP): A penalty applied to the wearer's physical skill checks.

Speed: A penalty applied to the wearer's Speed (to a minimum of 5 ft.).

Disguise: A modifier to Disguise checks targeting the wearer, whether they're made to conceal the armor or not (it's more difficult to look like someone else, or some specific, when you're weighed down with protective gear). 'Obvious' means the wearer can't be disguised at all.

SHIELDS

Shields are carried by hand and may be used as weapons, so they're described in the weapons section *(see page 177)*.

ARMOR DESCRIPTIONS

Articulated Plate: The pinnacle of armorsmithing excellence, this option adds sliding plates over joints and other areas still exposed by platemail.

Chainmail: Sheets of interlocking metal rings bend like cloth but can absorb blows and prevent cuts.

Hardened Leather: This armor consists of rigid plates of boiled and treated leather. It offers impressive protection but also prevents fluid movement.

Leather: Animal hides and tanned leather are light and flexible but still absorb minor punishment.

Descriptive Armor

These optional rules are a more detailed approach to armor in any historical or fantasy setting. They're entirely compatible with the basic armor section.

- **Partial Armor (Torso Only): Depending on the setting, this might be a breastplate, coat, cuirass, jack, jacket, shirt, or vest.**
- **Moderate Armor (Torso and Legs): This might be a harness, outfit, suit, garb, or armor suit.**

Fittings offer protection for extremities and reinforce critical areas. Up to five fittings may be applied, one protecting each of the following areas.

- **Feet: Armored boots or greaves.**
- **Forearms: Gauntlets, bracers, arm wraps, or heavily armored sleeves.**
- **Head: A cap, coif, helm, helmet, or hood.**
- **Shoulders: Mantle, paldrons, or shoulder guards.**
- **Vitals: Armpit guards, knee guards, a collar, or a gorget.**

If two or three fittings are applied, the armor gains the light fittings modification. Four or five fittings apply the heavy fittings modification.

Example 1: **Taman prepares for battle by donning a platemail breastplate (partial armor), plus greaves and a helmet (two fittings, which qualify as light fittings). His armor applies partial coverage, DR 5 (4 for platemail, +1 for light fittings), Blunt Resistance 1 (platemail), –3 Defense (platemail), –4 ACP (platemail modified by fittings), and –5 ft. Speed (platemail). It's obvious, made of hard materials and must fail 4 saves before it breaks, has a Complexity of 15W, weighs 33 lbs., and costs 430 silver.**

Example 2: **Riss will be out stalking the alleys this evening in a leather cuirass (partial armor), plus matching gloves, boots, mantle, and a hood (four fittings, which qualify as heavy fittings). Her armor applies moderate coverage (because heavy fittings increase the coverage by 1 grade), DR 3 (1 for leather, +2 for heavy fittings), Fire Resistance 3 (leather), –2 Defense (leather modified by fittings), –1 ACP (fittings), and –5 ft. Speed (fittings). Disguise checks targeting her suffer a –6 penalty. The armor is made of soft materials and must 3 saves before it breaks, has a Complexity of 7D, weighs 18 lbs., and costs 95 silver.**

Table 4.17: Armor

Type	DR	Resistances	DP	ACP	Speed	Disguise	Const	Comp	Weight *	Era	Cost *
Partial Armor (torso only)											
Padded	0	Cold 3	–0	–0	—	+0	Soft 2	5D	4 lbs.	Primitive	10s
Leather	1	Fire 3	–1	–0	—	+0	Soft 2	7D	6 lbs.	Primitive	20s
Studded leather	2	—	–1	–0	—	+0	Soft 2	12D	12 lbs.	Ancient	40s
Chainmail	2	Edged 2	–1	–0	–5 ft.	–4	Hard 2	15W	24 lbs.	Feudal	100s
Hardened leather	3	Fire 3	–1	–1	–5 ft.	–2	Soft 3	10W	18 lbs.	Primitive	100s
Scalemail	3	Edged 2	–2	–1	–5 ft.	–8	Hard 3	12W	22 lbs.	Ancient	200s
Platemail	4	Blunt 1	–3	–3	–5 ft.	obvious	Hard 3	15W	27 lbs.	Feudal	400s
Moderate armor (torso and legs)											
Padded	1	Cold 5	–0	–0	—	+0	Soft 3	5W	6 lbs.	Primitive	25s
Leather	2	Fire 5	–1	–0	–5 ft.	+0	Soft 3	7W	10 lbs.	Primitive	50s
Studded leather	3	—	–1	–0	–5 ft.	–2	Soft 3	15W	20 lbs.	Ancient	100s
Chainmail	3	Edged 3	–1	–0	–5 ft.	–6	Hard 3	15W	40 lbs.	Feudal	250s
Hardened leather	4	Fire 5	–1	–1	–5 ft.	–4	Soft 4	10M	32 lbs.	Primitive	250s
Scalemail	4	Edged 3	–2	–1	–5 ft.	obvious	Hard 4	15M	45 lbs.	Ancient	500s
Platemail	5	Blunt 2	–3	–3	–5 ft.	obvious	Hard 4	17M	50 lbs.	Feudal	1,000s
Articulated plate	5	Blunt 2	–2	–2	–5 ft.	obvious	Hard 4	25M	55 lbs.	Reason	1,600s
Fittings											
Light	+1	—	–0	–1	—	–4	+1	—	+6 lbs.	Primitive	30s
Heavy	+2	—	–1	–1	–5 ft.	–6	+1	—	+12 lbs.	Ancient	75s

* These values assume armor for a Medium character. For smaller characters they drop by 50% per Size (rounded down), and for larger characters they increase by 300% per Size.

Barding: In the Feudal and later Eras, barding may be made of any armor. Barding is specific to each species of animal or beast.

Unborn: In any era in which Unborn are present, armor may be built into or removed from their bodies with a successful Build or Improve check against the armor's Complexity + 10.

Padded: This armor consists of layers of padding or quilted fabric. It helps with cold weather but isn't stitched from sturdy enough materials to protect against attacks.

Platemail: This armor strategically places large metal plates over a leather or chainmail undergarment. It offers incredible damage protection but also severely impacts mobility.

Scalemail: This armor consists of an interlocking mesh of metal plates or 'scales' over a leather or padded undergarment. Long, horizontal plates are sometimes used, in which case this armor is called banded or splint mail.

Studded Leather: This improved leather armor adds studs, rings, and other metal pieces to guard against blades. It's sometimes called ringmail.

ARMOR UPGRADES

There are 3 types of armor upgrade: **craftsmanship,** which adjusts the design to a particular culture, technique, or style (in this case, species); **materials,** which change composition; and **customization,** which applies general changes like tailoring, ornamentation, and spiritual blessings.

Each armor may only have 1 craftsmanship and 1 materials upgrade at a time, though any number of customizations may be applied. Also, species craftsmanship is only possible if the species exists in the campaign (check with the GM if you're unsure).

Upgrades may not be applied to fittings and may not decrease any armor penalty below 0.

UPGRADE DESCRIPTIONS

Beast: The armor may be donned and worn by a creature without hands or fine manipulators (e.g. it may be shrugged on or dragged into the creature's body with its teeth).

Blessed: The armor is spiritually charged, offering protection from divine damage.

Ceremonial: The armor is resplendent, sacrificing safety for looks. Ceremonial armor is often worn by nobles.

Crude Materials: Simple, low-quality materials reduce durability but make the armor easier to build.

Cushioned: The armor features extra padding, improving protection against blunt trauma.

Discreet: The armor is close-fit or incorporates clothing, making it easier to disguise.

Drake: Drake-made armors are ostentatious and convey a hint of their magical nature to the wearer.

Dwarf: The durability of dwarven armor is legendary.

Elf: Light and flexible, elven armor is prized by graceful warriors and thieves alike.

Fitted: The armor is fitted for 1 character, decreasing the Defense and Armor Check Penalties by 1 each for him alone.

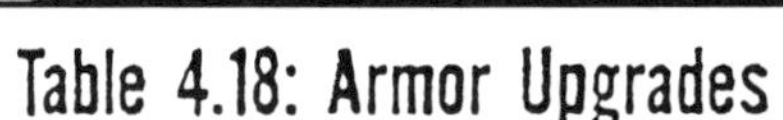

Table 4.18: Armor Upgrades

Name	DR	Effect	DP	ACP	Speed	Disguise	Const	Comp	Weight	Era	Cost
Craftsmanship											
Drake	—	+2 gear bonus with Spellcasting	—	—	—	–4	—	+5	—	Primitive	+200%
Dwarf	+1	—	—	—	—	—	+1 save	+5	—	Primitive	+100%
Elf	—	—	—	+1	+5 ft.	—	—	+5	–50%	Primitive	+200%
Giant	—	+2 to all armor Resistances	—	—	—	—	—	—	—	Primitive	+50%
Goblin	—	—	–1	–1	—	—	—	–5	—	Primitive	–25%
Ogre	—	+2 damage (unarmed/grapple)	—	—	—	–4	—	+2	—	Primitive	+50%
Orc	—	+2 gear bonus with Intimidate	—	—	—	—	—	—	—	Primitive	+50%
Pech	—	—	+1	—	—	+4	—	+2	—	Primitive	+50%
Rootwalker	—	Edged Resistance 2, Fire Resistance 2	—	—	—	—	—	+2	—	Primitive	+50%
Saurian	—	Cold Resistance 2, +2 gear bonus with Sneak in 1 terrain	—	—	—	—	—	+2	—	Primitive	+50%
Unborn	—	Electrical Resistance 4	+1	—	—	—	—	+5	—	Primitive	+200%
Materials											
Crude	—	—	—	—	—	—	–1 save	–2	—	Primitive	–25%
Superior	—	—	—	—	—	—	+1 save	+5	—	Primitive	+100%
Customization											
Beast	—	May be used by beasts	—	—	—	—	—	+5	—	Primitive	+200%
Blessed	—	Divine Resistance 4	—	—	—	—	—	—	—	Primitive	+50%
Ceremonial	–1	+1 to user's Appearance bonus	—	—	—	—	—	+2	–25%	Primitive	+50%
Cushioned	—	Blunt Resistance 2	—	—	—	—	—	+2	—	Ancient	+100%
Discreet	—	Armor is harder to spot	—	—	—	+4	—	+2	—	Feudal	+100%
Fireproofed	—	Fire Resistance 4	—	—	—	—	—	+2	—	Ancient	+50%
Fitted	—	–1 to DP/ACP penalties (owner only)	—	—	—	—	—	+5	—	Ancient	+200%
Insulated	—	Electrical Resistance 4	—	—	—	—	—	+2	—	Feudal	+50%
Lightweight	—	Armor is lightened	—	—	+5 ft.	—	—	+2	–25%	Ancient	+100%
Reinforced	—	Edged Resistance 2	—	—	—	—	—	+2	+25%	Ancient	+100%
Vented	—	Heat Resistance 4	—	—	—	—	—	+2	—	Feudal	+50%
Warm	—	Cold Resistance 4	—	—	—	—	—	+2	—	Primitive	+50%

* A species may apply its smithing techniques to armor made for any character (no matter the character's species).

Fireproofed: The armor incorporates flame-retardant fabrics or is treated to resist flame.

Giant: Armor made by giants shares their bond with the elements, granting protection from many weapons and effects.

Goblin: What goblins lack in resources they make up for in wicked ingenuity. Consequently, their craftsmen smith armor that's perfect for fast and dirty assembly or modification.

Insulated: The armor includes a non-conductive layer of clothing or other materials.

Lightweight: The armor sheds non-essential elements to reduce weight and increase mobility.

Ogre: Spikes, hooks, and studded plates are hallmarks of ogre-crafted armor, granting +2 damage with unarmed attacks and Injure grapple benefits.

Orc: Trophies from fallen enemies enhance the fearsome appearance of orc-made armor, granting a +2 gear bonus with Intimidate checks.

Pech: Seeking comfort in all things, pech build armor to be lightweight and easy to use.

Reinforced: Stiff ribs or metal studs adorn this armor, mitigating damage from cutting attacks.

Rootwalker: Fearing fire and axes above all else, rootwalkers build armor with sturdy, flame-retardant materials.

Saurian: Armor built by saurians retains body heat, keeping the cold-blooded species warm in cold environments. It's also commonly camouflaged.

Superior Materials: Layered metals and fine alloys increase durability but make the armor harder to build.

Unborn: Armor crafted by unborn fits snugly to the body and protects against shocking attacks.

Vented: The armor features cooling vents under the arms and legs. This upgrade is a favorite of desert and jungle denizens, as well as those who travel through them.

Warm: The armor is lined with wool or furs.

WEAPONS

As noted in One- and Two-Handed Weapons, a character may only wield weapons of his Size or smaller *(see page 215)*. Weapons may be scaled up or down in Size with the large-scale and small-scale upgrades *(see page 185)*.

Weapons are grouped by proficiency: Blunt, Edged, Hurled, Bows, Black Powder, and Siege Weapons *(see page 28)*.

The weapon tables feature a few different columns.

Damage (Dmg): The weapon's base damage.

Threat: The weapon's threat range.

Range: The weapon's range increment followed by the maximum number of increments it may be thrown or fired (e.g. a range of "10 ft. × 3" means the weapon may be used to attack a target up to 30 ft. away with a range increment of 10 ft.).

Upgrades for all weapons are collected in one section starting on page 184.

WEAPON QUALITIES

Aligned: The weapon is magically, spiritually, or otherwise aligned and its attacks gain 1 Alignment.

Armor-Piercing (AP): The weapon's attacks ignore the listed Damage Reduction. When a weapon and its ammunition both have this quality, their AP values are combined.

Blast: The weapon's damage tapers off *(see page 214)*.

Bleed: An opponent struck with the weapon must make a successful Fortitude save (DC equal to the damage after DR and Resistances are applied) or begin *bleeding*.

Bludgeon: A character with the Blunt proficiency may use the weapon in melee (dmg 1d6 subdual if 1-handed or 1d8 subdual if 2-handed, threat range 20).

Cavalry: The weapon is designed for mounted use, negating attack penalties while mounted *(see page 215)*.

Cord: The weapon features a safety cord or tether, allowing the character to recover it as a full action. Readying it thereafter requires an additional half action, and weapons with this quality also often need to reloaded after recovery.

Double: This single weapon can be used to repeatedly batter an opponent. The wielder may use 'Two-Weapon' feat abilities with it.

Excruciating: Wounds from this weapon cause terrible pain. An opponent struck with this weapon also suffers 1/2 as much stress damage (after DR and Resistances are applied).

Finesse: The character uses the higher of his Strength or Dexterity modifiers when rolling the weapon's damage.

Grip: The wielder gains a +4 gear bonus to resist Disarm attempts targeting the weapon.

Guard: When armed, the wielder gains the listed gear bonus to Defense. He loses this bonus when *flat-footed, held, helpless, pinned, sprawled,* or unconscious.

Heavy: The wielder may not take Movement actions in the same round he attacks with the weapon.

Hook: The user gains a +2 gear bonus with Disarm actions.

Hurl: A character with the Hurled proficiency may throw this weapon with a range of 15 ft. × 2.

Inaccurate: The wielder suffers a –2 attack penalty with the weapon.

Indirect: The weapon may be fired at squares the wielder can't see with a –5 attack penalty. With a miss, the attack deviates *(see page 214)*.

Keen: The weapon's damage rises by the listed amount when determining critical injuries and massive damage *(see page 208)*.

Lightweight: A character may arm this weapon as if he's 1 Size larger (i.e. a Medium character may arm a Large lightweight weapon).

Load: The weapon is reloaded with the listed number of Handle Item actions.

Lure: The wielder gains a +2 gear bonus with Feint actions. With a ranged attack, he may try to Feint opponents in Close Quarters.

Massive: A character must have a Strength score of 15 or higher to wield this weapon. Also, a smaller opponent who's struck with the weapon must make a successful Fortitude save (DC equal to the damage after DR and Resistances are applied) or become *sprawled*.

Poisonous: The weapon may be poisoned with 1 half action and exposes a target with a hit that inflicts at least 1 damage after Damage Reduction and Resistance are applied. Unless otherwise specified it may carry only 1 dose of poison at a time.

Pummeling: This weapon may Pummel *(see page 220)*.

Reach: A bonus to the wielder's Reach with the weapon.

Return: With a miss, the weapon automatically returns to the wielder at the start of his next Initiative Count (or the wielder's square if he moves before then).

Spread: One character adjacent to the target who is also in the attacker's line of sight without cover (attacker's choice) must make a successful Reflex save (DC equal to the attack result) or suffer 1/2 the damage (rounded down).

Spike: A character with the Edged proficiency may use the weapon in melee (dmg 1d6 lethal if 1-handed or 1d8 lethal if 2-handed, threat range 20).

Stationary: The weapon is so massive it can only be moved in combat when it's mounted on a vehicle. Setting it up independently or preparing it for transport takes 5 minutes.

Trip: The wielder gains a +2 gear bonus with Trip actions. With a ranged attack, the wielder may try to Trip opponents in Close Quarters.

Unreliable: The weapon's error range increases by 2 (e.g. an error range of 1 becomes 1–3).

BLUNT WEAPONS

This category offers non-cutting melee weapons and shields.

BLUNT WEAPON DESCRIPTIONS

Barwhip: Crafted of short metal bars in a long chain (thus its other name: the "spiked chain"), this weapon is designed to flay a target's flesh with every strike.

Table 4.19: Blunt Weapons

Name	Dmg	Threat	Qualities	SZ/Hand	Const	Comp	Weight	Era	Cost
Clubs									
Club	1d8 subdual	20	—	S/2h	Hard 2	5D	3 lbs.	Primitive	5s
Great club	2d6 lethal	20	*Massive*	M/2h	Hard 3	7D	10 lbs.	Primitive	20s
Jitte/sai *	1d6 subdual	20	*Hook*	T/1h	Hard 2	12D	3 lbs.	Ancient	10s
Mace	1d8 lethal	20	*AP 4*	T/1h	Hard 2	10D	5 lbs.	Ancient	20s
Sap	1d6 subdual	19–20	*Finesse, pummeling*	D/1h	Soft 1	7D	2 lbs.	Primitive	2s
Tonfa *	1d6 subdual	20	*Guard +1*	T/1h	Hard 2	7D	3 lbs.	Ancient	10s
War club	1d8 lethal	19–20	*Bleed*	S/1h	Hard 2	10D	6 lbs.	Primitive	20s
Flails									
Flail	1d8 subdual	20	*AP 2*	T/1h	Hard 2	15D	5 lbs.	Primitive	10s
Nunchaku *	1d8 subdual	19–20	*Lure*	T/1h	Hard 2	10D	3 lbs.	Ancient	10s
Scourge	1d8 subdual	20	*Bleed, excruciating*	T/1h	Soft 1	7D	3 lbs.	Primitive	8s
Three-section rod *	1d10 subdual	20	*AP 2*	S/1h	Hard 2	15D	5 lbs.	Feudal	20s
Hammers									
Mallet	1d6 lethal	20	—	T/1h	Hard 2	7D	2 lbs.	Primitive	10s
Maul	2d6 subdual	19–20	*Massive*	M/2h	Hard 2	7D	12 lbs.	Primitive	30s
Pick	1d6 lethal	19–20	*AP 4*	S/2h	Hard 2	10D	5 lbs.	Ancient	10s
War hammer	1d12 subdual	20	*AP 2*	S/2h	Hard 2	12D	5 lbs.	Feudal	20s
Shields									
Buckler	1d3 subdual	20	*Guard +1*	T/1h	Hard 2	7D	4 lbs.	Ancient	20s
Shield, hide	1d3 subdual	20	*Guard +2*	S/1h	Soft 3	7D	6 lbs.	Primitive	10s
Shield, metal	1d4 subdual	20	*Guard +2*	S/1h	Hard 3	7W	8 lbs.	Ancient	20s
Shield, tower	1d4 subdual	—	*Guard +3*	M/1h	Hard 3	10W	12 lbs.	Ancient	40s
Staves									
Staff, long *	1d8 subdual	20	*Reach +1, trip*	M/2h	Hard 2	5D	5 lbs.	Primitive	10s
Staff, quarter	1d8 subdual	20	*Double, trip*	M/2h	Hard 2	5D	4 lbs.	Primitive	5s
Staff, shod	1d8 lethal	19–20	*Double, trip*	M/2h	Hard 2	10W	5 lbs.	Ancient	40s
Staff, short	1d6 subdual	20	*Double, trip*	S/1h	Hard 2	5D	3 lbs.	Primitive	2s
Whips									
Barwhip *	1d8 lethal	19–20	*AP 2, reach +1*	T/1h	Hard 1	15W	10 lbs.	Feudal	15s
Bullwhip	1d6 subdual	20	*Reach +2, trip*	D/1h	Soft 1	5D	3 lbs.	Primitive	5s
Chain	1d6 subdual	20	*Hook, reach +1*	D/1h	Hard 1	12D	5 lbs.	Ancient	10s

* You must have the Blunt forte to be proficient with this exotic weapon.

Buckler: This tiny wrist shield is popular in duels and other fights involving light blades.

Bullwhip: This 10-ft. braided leather whip is most noteworthy for the incredible pain it inflicts and its utility for the resourceful dungeon-delver.

Club: Usually made of heavy or weighted wood, this ubiquitous bludgeon can be found in every society.

Chain: This fighting chain often has weights fixed at each end, letting the wielder entangle weapons and trip opponents.

Great Club: This large club is often studded with iron or rock to inflict grievous damage.

Flail: One to five weights are attached to this weapon's handle by chains or cords, letting the wielder strike with terrific force.

Hide Shield: Typically made of leather stretched across a wooden frame, this shield is often made and decorated by its wearer.

Jitte/Sai: These blunt knife-like weapons have wide-forked cross-guards that can be used to catch and wrench weapons from the attacker's hands. Jitte have one fork while sai have two.

Long Staff: This 8- to 10-ft. staff offers exceptional reach.

Mace: This metal-headed club is often set with spikes or flanges to break armor and bones.

Mallet: This one-handed tool doubles as a fine bludgeon.

Maul: This monstrous two-handed hammer uses a large wooden, stone, or metal head to cleave wood (and opponents) in twain.

Metal Shield: Metal shields come in all shapes and sizes but most are round and made of wood with metal plating to deflect blows and missiles.

Nunchaku: This weapon consists of two wooden handles connected by chain or cord. It's often whirled around the body to confuse opponents and wind up for bone-shattering strikes.

Pick: This mining tool features a long spike on one side, giving it tremendous armor-piercing power.

Quarter Staff: This common weapon is easily disguised as a walking stick.

Sap: A favorite of burglars, the sap is a weighted cloth or leather sack used to knock opponents out, often in a single blow. As an added bonus it's small and easily concealed.

Scourge: This flail-like weapon features leather straps set with barbs that inflict agonizing pain. While the blows look hideous and bleed fiercely, the scourge is commonly used non-lethally as an instrument of discipline.

Shod Staff: This is a quarter staff with one or both ends capped by ridged or knobbed metal.

Short Staff: This staff resembles a cane or other wooden rod and can be wielded in one hand.

Three-Section Rod: This flail is like a nunchaku with a second string and third handle, giving it extra weight and power.

Tonfa: This "pistol grip" club is held along the arm and used to block incoming blows.

Tower Shield: This oblong shield obscures 75% of the body, making it popular with line troops, especially those facing ranks of enemy archers.

War Club: Sometimes known as a "toothed club," this weapon often features a jagged or wedged end to split flesh and skulls.

War Hammer: This two-handed hammer is a common sight on feudal battlefields due to its impressive damage and concussive force.

EDGED WEAPONS

This category includes melee weapons that slice and pierce, such as knives, swords, and polearms.

EDGED WEAPON DESCRIPTIONS

Axe: This ubiquitous tree-cutting tool is also found in the hands of warriors across the land.

Bastard Sword: This versatile weapon can sometimes be unwieldy but its raw power makes it a favorite of barbarians and knights alike.

Battle Axe: This single-bladed, two-handed axe has a 3- to 4-ft. haft for landing powerful strikes.

Boar Spear: This popular hunting weapon, also called a "thrusting spear," features a cross-guard that's useful for deflecting angry boars and sharp blades.

Broad Axe: This weapon has a very heavy head, translating to tremendous force with each swing. Many broad axes have double heads to make them look more imposing.

Cavalry Axe: This one-handed axe features a long handle and semi-circular blade for fighting from horseback.

Claymore: This huge blade, roughly the height of an average wielder, is called a "shield-breaker," though it's just as good at shattering bone.

Cutlass/Saber: These weapons' curved blades let horsemen slice fighters on foot.

Dagger: This weapon is common at all levels of society as a tool for cooking, defense, and larceny.

Double Axe: This long-hafted battle axe has blades at both ends and can be twirled to bring both to bear.

Double Sword: This sword has long, straight blades extending from both ends of its overlong hilt. It's large enough to be mistaken for a staff at a distance.

Fan Blade: A favorite of courtiers, this steel fan has razor-sharp edges and can parry or distract opponents.

Fork/Trident: This pronged spear is favored by mariners and pit fighters for its ability to attack distant targets and tangle opponents' weapons.

Table 4.20: Edged Weapons

Name	Dmg	Threat	Qualities **	SZ/Hand	Const	Comp	Weight	Era	Cost
Axes									
Axe	1d10 lethal	20	*AP 2*	S/1h	Hard 2	10D	4 lbs.	Primitive	20s
Battle axe	1d10 lethal	19–20	*AP 2, trip*	S/2h	Hard 2	12D	6 lbs.	Ancient	30s
Broad axe	1d12 lethal	19–20	*AP 2, massive*	S/2h	Hard 3	10D	12 lbs.	Ancient	45s
Cavalry axe	1d8 lethal	20	*AP 2, cavalry*	S/1h	Hard 2	12D	4 lbs.	Ancient	15s
Double axe	1d10 lethal	20	*AP 2, double*	S/2h	Hard 2	12D	10 lbs.	Ancient	40s
Hatchet	1d6 lethal	20	*AP 2, hurl, trip*	T/1h	Hard 2	7D	2 lbs.	Primitive	8s
Fencing Blades									
Cutlass/saber	1d10 lethal	19–20	*Cavalry, finesse*	S/1h	Hard 2	10W	3 lbs.	Feudal	40s
Ninja-to/sword cane	1d8 lethal	20	*AP 2, finesse*	S/1h	Hard 2	12W	3 lbs.	Feudal	40s
Rapier	1d8 lethal	19–20	*Bleed, finesse*	S/1h	Hard 1	12W	3 lbs.	Reason	30s
Razor sword *	1d8 lethal	18–20	*Finesse, keen 4*	S/1h	Hard 1	15W	4 lbs.	Reason	80s
Scholar's sword	1d8 lethal	20	*Finesse, lure*	S/1h	Hard 2	10W	3 lbs.	Feudal	30s
Knives									
Dagger	1d6 lethal	19–20	*Bleed, hurl*	D/1h	Hard 2	7D	1 lb.	Primitive	15s
Fan blade *	1d6 lethal	20	*Guard +1, lure*	D/1h	Hard 1	10W	1 lb.	Feudal	40s
Hand claw	1d6 lethal	20	*Bleed, grip*	F/1h	Hard 1	7D	1 lb.	Primitive	6s
Hook	1d6 lethal	20	*Hook*	D/1h	Hard 2	5D	1 lb.	Ancient	4s
Long knife/kukri	1d6 lethal	19–20	*Finesse, keen 4*	T/1h	Hard 2	10D	2 lbs.	Ancient	30s
Main gauche *	1d6 lethal	20	*Guard +1, hook*	D/1h	Hard 2	15W	2 lbs.	Reason	30s
Punch dagger	1d6 lethal	19–20	*Finesse, grip*	D/1h	Hard 2	10D	2 lbs.	Feudal	15s
Razor	1d6 lethal	19–20	*Bleed, excruciating, finesse*	F/1h	Hard 1	12D	1/2 lb.	Ancient	5s
Sickle/kama	1d6 lethal	20	*AP 2, trip*	D/1h	Hard 2	7D	2 lbs.	Primitive	6s
Stiletto *	1d4 lethal	18–20	*AP 8, finesse*	D/1h	Hard 1	12D	1/2 lb.	Feudal	20s
Swords									
Bastard sword	1d10 lethal	20	*Massive*	S/1h	Hard 3	10W	6 lbs.	Ancient	60s
Jagged sword	1d8 lethal	20	*Bleed, hook*	S/1h	Hard 1	10W	5 lbs.	Primitive	40s
Katana	1d10 lethal	19–20	*Cavalry, keen 4*	S/1h	Hard 2	15M	4 lbs.	Feudal	80s
Long sword	1d12 lethal	20	—	S/1h	Hard 2	12M	4 lbs.	Feudal	60s
Machete	1d8 lethal	20	*AP 2*	T/1h	Hard 2	10D	2 lbs.	Ancient	15s
Short sword	1d8 lethal	19–20	*Keen 4*	T/1h	Hard 2	12D	2 lbs.	Ancient	25s
Sickle sword	1d8 lethal	19–20	*Hook*	S/1h	Hard 2	12W	3 lbs.	Ancient	40s
Greatswords									
Claymore *	1d12 lethal	19–20	*Massive, reach +1*	M/2h	Hard 3	10W	6 lbs.	Ancient	90s
Double sword	1d10 lethal	20	*Double, hurl*	M/2h	Hard 2	12M	10 lbs.	Feudal	110s
No-dachi/shamshir *	1d12 lethal	19–20	*AP 4, cavalry*	M/2h	Hard 2	12M	8 lbs.	Feudal	120s
Polesword/nagamaki *	1d10 lethal	19–20	*Finesse, guard +1*	M/2h	Hard 2	12M	10 lbs.	Ancient	90s
Zweihander *	1d12 lethal	19–20	*Guard +1, massive*	M/2h	Hard 3	10M	15 lbs.	Reason	100s
Polearms									
Glaive/naginata	1d8 lethal	19–20	*Keen 4, reach +1*	M/2h	Hard 2	10W	8 lbs.	Ancient	40s
Halberd/ji	1d10 lethal	19–20	*AP 4, reach +1*	M/2h	Hard 2	10W	8 lbs.	Feudal	40s
Mancatcher/rake	1d6 subdual	—	*Reach +1, trip*	M/2h	Hard 2	7W	8 lbs.	Ancient	25s
Pole dagger	1d6 lethal	20	*Finesse, reach +1*	M/2h	Hard 2	5D	8 lbs.	Primitive	20s
Scythe *	1d10 lethal	20	*AP 2, trip*	M/2h	Hard 2	7D	10 lbs.	Ancient	15s
Spears									
Boar spear	1d8 lethal	19–20	*Guard +1, reach +1*	M/2h	Hard 3	10W	10 lbs.	Ancient	40s
Fork/trident	1d8 lethal	19–20	*Hook, hurl*	M/1h	Hard 2	10W	6 lbs.	Ancient	30s
Lance *	1d8 lethal	19–20	*AP 4, cavalry, massive, reach +1*	M/1h	Hard 2	7D	10 lbs.	Feudal	25s
Pike	1d8 lethal	20	*Lightweight, reach +2*	L/2h	Hard 2	7D	12 lbs.	Ancient	20s
Throwing spear	1d8 lethal	19–20	*Hurl, reach +1*	M/1h	Hard 2	5D	4 lbs.	Primitive	20s

* You must have the Edged forte to be proficient with this exotic weapon.

** All edged weapons also have the *poisonous* quality.

Glaive/Naginata: This polearm's head consists of a curved blade that buries deep in exposed flesh.

Halberd/Ji: This versatile weapon combines one or two axe heads with a long spike on a 6- to 8-ft. pole.

Hand Claw: This weapon is fixed to the wrist by straps or handles so that the blades project between or over the fingers, cutting the target with a scratching motion.

Hatchet: This versatile hand-axe is balanced for hurling and heavy enough to puncture many armors. Throwing axes and tomahawks share this weapon's stats.

Hook: A maritime tool adapted to warfare, the hook's curved shape and wicked point make it a natural armament.

Jagged Sword: This "sword" is typically a wooden handle spiked with slivers of bone, obsidian, or animal teeth.

Katana: The steel of this masterful sword is folded over itself to create hundreds of layers. This lets it hold a superior edge while remaining flexible enough not to shatter in combat. Its curved blade is ideal for fighting from the saddle.

Lance: This heavy, 10- to 12-ft. spear skewers infantry and forcibly dismounts heavy cavalry.

Long Knife/Kukri: The long knife has a thick spine and keen edge designed to chop brush and flesh. The kukri is similar but has a shorter blade bent at a steeper angle.

Long Sword: With a 3- to 4-ft. double-edged blade and low weight, the long sword is popular with adventurers everywhere.

Machete: Originally a brush-clearing tool, this chopping sword cleaves through light armor with ease.

Main Gauche: Also called a parrying dagger, the main gauche is typically used in the off-hand to deflect blows and disarm.

Mancatcher/Rake: These esoteric polearms have large open heads with barbs to snag clothing or limbs. They're often used to subdue criminals.

Ninja-To/Sword Cane: The classic "ninja sword" is light and straight. In a pinch, it can be used as a survival or climbing tool.

No-dachi/Shamshir: This oversized cutlass has a long handle and huge curved blade. It excels at slicing through armor.

Pike: The incredible reach of this 10- to 15-ft. spear makes it a popular military weapon, at least until the invention of gunpowder.

Pole Dagger: Among the most basic of all polearms, this weapon features a dagger-like blade that extends at a right-angle from a long shaft.

Polesword/Nagamaki: This weapon sits somewhere between a spear and sword, thanks to a blade and handle of equal length.

Punch Dagger: This weapon's handle runs perpendicular to the blade, letting the wielder put the force of his body behind every blow.

Rapier: The thin-bladed rapier is better at wounding a foe's honor than his body, making it a favorite of nobles and duelists.

Razor: In the right hands, this exceedingly sharp blade can become an instrument of abject terror.

Razor Sword: This thin and sharp sword inflicts deep wounds at the expense of durability.

Scholar's Sword: This straight fencing weapon's thin, wagging blade and pommel-sash often confuse and surprise opponents.

Scythe: This wide-bladed polearm threshes through foes like squishy, squealing wheat.

Short Sword: This weapon's small size and keen edge ensure its place at the hips of warriors throughout history.

Sickle/Kama: This simple farming implement became a discreet and deadly bladed weapon in the hands of early peasants and monks. Now it's made and sold by weaponsmiths everywhere.

Sickle Sword: This unusual chopping sword has a semi-circular curve halfway down the blade that's often used to catch enemy weapons. Variants of the sickle sword include the falx, kopesh, and sappara.

Stiletto: This weapon's long, spike-shaped blade easily slips between armor plates and joints.

Throwing Spear: A favorite of warriors and hunters since the dawn of time, the throwing spear is deadly at any range.

Zweihander: Champion of greatswords, the zweihander is fielded by elite infantry to break troop formations and crush heavily armored cavalry.

Table 4.21: Hurled Weapons

Name	Dmg	Threat	Range	Qualities	SZ/Hand	Const	Comp	Weight	Era	Cost
Thrown Weapons										
Atlatl *	Javelin or Spear	19–20	+2 increments	*AP 4, load 1*	S/1h	Hard 2	12D	3 lbs.	Primitive	15s
Blowgun	Dart	20	20 ft. × 3	*AP 2, load 1,* negates *inaccurate* quality	S/2h	Hard 1	10D	1 lb.	Primitive	10s
Bola (3) *	1d6 subdual	19–20	20 ft. × 3	*Cavalry, trip*	S/1h	Soft 2	12D	2 lbs.	Primitive	12s
Boomerang *	1d6 subdual	20	20 ft. × 3	*Lure, return*	S/1h	Hard 2	15D	1lb.	Primitive	9s
Chakram	1d6 lethal	20	20 ft. × 3	*Keen 4*	T/1h	Hard 2	10W	1 lb.	Feudal	25s
Dart (5)	1d4 lethal	20	10 ft. × 3	*Inaccurate, poisonous*	T/1h	Hard 1	5D	1/10 lb.	Primitive	4s
Harpoon	1d8 lethal	18–20	20 ft. × 3	*Bleed, cord*	M/1h	Hard 2	12W	6 lbs.	Primitive	10s
Javelin (3)	1d8 lethal	19–20	30 ft. × 3	—	S/1h	Hard 1	10D	3 lbs.	Ancient	12s
Lasso *	—	—	10 ft. × 2	*Cord, hook, trip*	D/2h	Soft 1	7D	2 lbs.	Feudal	3s
Net (3) *	—	—	10 ft. × 3	*Cord, trip*	S/2h	Soft 2	7W	5 lbs.	Ancient	15s
Rock, large	1d10 lethal	20	10 ft. × 2	*Massive*	S/2h	Hard 3	5D	15 lbs.	Primitive	—
Rock, small	1 subdual	—	15 ft. × 3	—	D/1h	Hard 2	5D	—	Primitive	—
Shuriken (10) *	1d4 lethal	19–20	20 ft. × 2	*Poisonous*	D/1h	Hard 1	10W	1/10 lb.	Feudal	20s
Sling	1d4 subdual	20	60 ft. × 6	*Load 1*	D/1h	Soft 1	5D	1/2 lb.	Primitive	1s
Staff sling	1d6 subdual	19–20	30 ft. × 6	*Load 1*	S/2h	Hard 2	7D	4 lbs.	Ancient	12s
Throwing knife (10)	1d4 lethal	19–20	15 ft. × 3	*Poisonous*	D/1h	Hard 1	7W	1/2 lb.	Feudal	25s
Grenades										
Bomb *	3d6 explosive	20	10 ft. × 3	*Blast 1, inaccurate*	D/1h	Hard 1	15W	2 lb.	Reason	30s
Concussion bomb *	3d6 bang	—	10 ft. × 3	*Blast 1, inaccurate*	D/1h	Hard 1	20W	2 lb.	Reason	10s
Flash bomb (3) *	3d6 flash	—	15 ft. × 3	*Blast 1*	D/1h	Hard 1	15D	1 lb.	Feudal	25s
Greek fire *	3d6 fire	20	10 ft. × 3	*Inaccurate*	D/1h	Hard 1	15D	1 lb.	Feudal	20s

* You must have the Hurled forte to be proficient with this exotic weapon.

HURLED WEAPONS

This category includes weapons that are thrown, as well as primitive grenades.

HURLED WEAPON DESCRIPTIONS

Atlatl: This "weapon" is essentially a long cradle for a javelin or throwing spear. It lets the wielder whip the loaded projectile with much greater force, gaining more range and punching power.

Blowgun: This long tube propels darts with more precision. It's common among assassins and tribal warriors.

Bola: This weapon consists of 2–4 weights on a cord. It's thrown at a target's legs, entangling them.

Bomb: A primitive grenade made of iron or stone, the bomb is most popular in ship-to-ship and siege warfare.

Boomerang: This throwing stick's wing design guides it back to the wielder with a miss.

Chakram: This sharpened steel ring is thrown like a discus and casually saws through flesh on impact.

Concussion Bomb: This bulky, gunpowder-laden grenade stuns and terrifies troops rather than kill them.

Dart: This hand-thrown or blowgun-fired missile is made of a weighted wooden rod sharpened at its end, or topped with a pointy spike.

Flash Bomb: This tiny, hand-thrown explosive often consists of an eggshell filled with alchemical powders. It's common among thieves and assassins, especially when they need to mask an escape.

Greek Fire: The original "sticky bomb," greek fire is a flammable mixture of oil and tar in a glass or clay sphere. It's lobbed at the decks of wooden ships and from the ramparts of assaulted fortresses.

Harpoon: This weapon's wicked point and fine throwing balance make it much more than a seaborne hunting weapon.

Javelin: This small and light spear is specifically designed for throwing. It's often used by skirmishers and light infantry.

Lasso: The simplest of capture devices, this weapon is nothing more than a rope tied with a quick-knot eyelet. Just loop it over the prey and pull.

Net: Like the lasso, the net inflicts no damage, but it's incredibly useful for snaring and slowing enemies.

Rocks: Sometimes enemies are just a stone's throw away. Remind them of it.

Shuriken: "Ninja stars" and sharpened coins are mostly used for distraction and delivering poison.

Sling: Perhaps the simplest of ranged weapons, the sling turns any Fine or smaller object into a weapon with exceptional distance and moderate power.

Staff Sling: This large sling's long handle allows for up to Tiny bullets at the expense of range.

Throwing Knife: While too flimsy for the rigors of hand-to-hand combat, this compact weapon is ideal for finishing off a weakened target.

BOWS

This category includes bows, crossbows, and exotic variants.

BOW DESCRIPTIONS

Arrows and Bolts: Arrows are long, thin missiles fired by bows, and bolts are squatter, heavier rounds fired by crossbows. They share statistics but crossbows can't fire arrows and bows can't fire bolts.

- *Barbed:* This missile features backward hooks that tear open the wound when removed.
- *Bird:* This missile has a heavy blunt tip, rather than a point. It's used to stun small game.
- *Climbing Line:* This heavy missile has a hook near the tail to carry a thin line to its destination.
- *Flaming:* The head of this missile is doused in pitch or oil and set alight before firing.
- *Standard:* This missile's sharpened tip pierces armor and hide.
- *Whistler:* This missile's hollow, fluted tip emits a high pitched whine when aloft. Whistler arrows and bolts are often used to alert nearby allies and troops.

Daikyu: This asymmetrically shaped long bow is easily fired from horseback.

Foot Bow: This early siege weapon's "string" is drawn with the whole body. It may only be fired from the prone position.

Hand Bow: This concealable weapon is almost square when fully drawn.

Hand Crossbow: Favored by thieves and assassins, this pistol-style crossbow is ideal for poison delivery at close range.

Heavy Crossbow: This weapon is cocked with a winch and drives bolts through plate armor.

Light Crossbow: The world's first crossbow, this weapon employs a firing mechanism to boost power and penetration.

Long Bow: This weapon is commonly taller than their shooter and grants a crossbow's penetration without the lengthy reload time.

Reflex Bow: This basic bow is made of treated or laminated wood and strung with tendon, catgut, or cured fibers.

Repeating Crossbow: This crossbow features an ammo hopper and mechanism that fires the bolt, then cocks and loads the next with one action. This weapon is popular in sieges for filling the air with storms of bolts.

Short Bow: Sometimes called a "horse bow," this small weapon is favored by cavalry skirmishers, big game hunters, and outlaws.

Pellet Bow: This weapon fires sling bullets with the power and range of a full sized bow. It's regularly used to hunt small game.

Table 4.22: Bows

Name	Dmg	Threat	Range	Qualities	SZ/Hand	Const	Comp	Weight	Era	Cost
Arrows and Bolts										
Standard (30)	1d6 lethal	—	—	*AP 2, poisonous*	—	Hard 1	7D	1/10 lb.	Primitive	10s
Barbed (20)	1d6 lethal	—	—	*Bleed, poisonous*	—	Hard 1	10D	1/10 lb.	Primitive	10s
Bird (30)	1d6 subdual	—	—	—	—	Hard 1	5D	1/10 lb.	Primitive	8s
Climbing line (5)	1d4 lethal	—	–5 ft.	*Cord*	—	Hard 1	12W	1/10 lb.	Feudal	20s
Flaming (10)	1d6 fire	—	—	—	—	Hard 1	7D	1/10 lb.	Ancient	10s
Whistler (10)	1d4 subdual	—	—	*Lure*	—	Hard 1	10D	1/10 lb.	Ancient	10s
Bows										
Crossbow, hand *	Bolt	20	20 ft. × 6	*Load 3*	T/1h	Hard 1	15W	2 lbs.	Reason	80s
Crossbow, light	Bolt	19–20	50 ft. × 6	*AP 2, load 5*	S/2h	Hard 2	15W	4 lbs.	Feudal	90s
Crossbow, heavy	Bolt	18–20	60 ft. × 6	*AP 5, load 7*	S/2h	Hard 2	15W	8 lbs.	Feudal	120s
Crossbow, repeating	Bolt	20	40 ft. × 6	*Inaccurate, indirect*	S/2h	Hard 2	20W	6 lbs.	Feudal	100s
Daikyu *	Arrow	19–20	40 ft. × 6	*Cavalry*	M/2h	Hard 1	10D	3 lbs.	Feudal	80s
Foot bow *	Javelin	18–20	50 ft. × 6	*AP 4, heavy*	M/2h	Hard 2	10D	6 lbs.	Ancient	60s
Hand bow *	Arrow	20	10 ft. × 6	—	D/2h	Hard 1	10D	1 lb.	Feudal	50s
Long bow	Arrow	19–20	40 ft. × 6	*AP 2*	M/2h	Hard 1	10D	3 lbs.	Feudal	60s
Reflex bow	Arrow	20	30 ft. × 6	—	M/2h	Hard 1	7D	2 lbs.	Primitive	30s
Short bow	Arrow	19–20	20 ft. × 6	*Cavalry*	S/2h	Hard 1	10D	2 lbs.	Primitive	40s
Pellet bow	1d4 subdual	20	20 ft. × 6	*AP 2*	M/2h	Hard 1	10D	2 lbs.	Ancient	30s

* You must have the Bows forte to be proficient with this exotic weapon.

Table 4.23: Black Powder Weapons

Name	Dmg	Threat	Range	Qualities	SZ/Hand	Const	Comp	Weight	Era	Cost
Powder										
Powder & shot (10)	—	—	—	—	D/—	Soft 1	15W	1/4 lb.	Feudal	10s
Sidearms										
Pistol, boarding *	3d6 lethal	19–20	10 ft. × 3	*Load 7, spread*	T/1h	Hard 2	20M	3 lbs.	Reason	95s
Pistol, dueling *	3d4 lethal	18–20	30 ft. × 3	*Load 7, unreliable*	T/1h	Hard 2	30M	2 lbs.	Reason	65s
Pistol, military *	3d6 lethal	18–20	20 ft. × 3	*Bludgeon, load 7, unreliable*	T/1h	Hard 3	25M	3 lbs.	Reason	85s
Pistol, pocket *	3d4 lethal	18–20	10 ft. × 3	*Load 7, unreliable*	F/1h	Hard 2	30M	1 lb.	Reason	75s
Longarms										
Blunderbuss	3d8 lethal	19–20	30 ft. × 3	*Load 7, spread*	S/2h	Hard 3	20M	6 lbs.	Reason	110s
Fire lance	3d6 fire	20	15 ft. × 2	*Load 9, spread*	M/2h	Hard 1	15W	10 lbs.	Feudal	60s
Hand cannon	3d6 lethal	18–20	30 ft. × 6	*Heavy, inaccurate, load 9, massive*	M/2h	Hard 2	15W	12 lbs.	Feudal	80s
Harquebus	3d6 lethal	18–20	30 ft. × 6	*Heavy, inaccurate, load 7, unreliable*	S/2h	Hard 2	15M	10 lbs.	Reason	75s
Long rifle	3d6 lethal	18–20	60 ft. × 6	*Bludgeon, load 7, unreliable*	M/2h	Hard 3	25M	9 lbs.	Reason	125s
Musket	3d6 lethal	18–20	40 ft. × 6	*Load 7, spike, unreliable*	S/2h	Hard 3	20M	8 lbs.	Reason	100s
Musketoon	3d6 lethal	18–20	30 ft. × 6	*Cavalry, load 7, unreliable*	S/2h	Hard 3	20M	6 lbs.	Reason	100s

* You must have the Black Powder forte to be proficient with this exotic weapon.

BLACK POWDER WEAPONS

This category includes the very height of fantasy technology: early firearms.

BLACK POWDER WEAPON DESCRIPTIONS

Blunderbuss: The ancestor of modern shotguns, the blunderbuss looks like a musket or harquebus with a flared barrel. It fires shot, stones, or even bits of scrap metal in a deadly cloud.

Boarding Pistol: This miniature blunderbuss is used for close-quarters and ship-to-ship combat.

Dueling Pistol: This low-caliber military pistol is perfect for avenging slights and upholding one's honor.

Fire Lance: This odd-looking weapon uses an overcharged firework as a deadly Roman candle, belching shrapnel and flames at nearby enemies.

Hand Cannon: Literally a "cannon on a stick," this foot-long brass or iron gun is mounted on a 4- to 6-ft. pole and loaded with a lead ball. It's typically ignited with a smoldering match.

Harquebus: This matchlock predecessor to the musket comes with a stock and barrel. In its class it's comparatively cheap and easy to manufacture.

Long Rifle: This 4.5 to 5.5-ft. long musket is favored by sharpshooters and game hunters. It's sometimes called a jezail.

Military Pistol: This rugged flint- or wheel-lock handgun can double as a cudgel and sees wide use among cavalry and sailors.

Musket: This ubiquitous and temperamental smoothbore gun arms many Age of Reason armies. It employs a flint-, match- or wheel-lock firing mechanism.

Mustketoon: This carbine musket is built to be fired from horseback and is popular in boarding actions.

Pocket Pistol: A favorite of criminals and assassins, this weapon is only helpful at very close ranges.

SIEGE WEAPONS

The original "weapons of mass destruction," weapons in this category are rarely seen off the battlefield, though characters of great size and strength might find new and innovative uses for them...

SIEGE WEAPON DESCRIPTIONS

Arbalest: The heaviest of man-portable crossbows, an arbalest uses a complex winch and steel "string" to fire bolts across amazing distance with incredible force.

Ballista, Light: This oversized crossbow is mounted on a stand and fires oversized bolts at troop formations.

Ballista, Heavy: This massive 9- to 12-ft. crossbow hurls spear-sized bolts at distant targets.

Battering Ram: Often little more than a felled tree swung by its branches, a battering ram crashes through barred doors and shuttered windows. It can, of course, do the same to people.

Table 4.24: Siege Weapons

Name	Dmg	Threat	Range	Qualities	SZ/Hand	Const	Comp	Weight	Era	Cost
Arbalest	Bolt	17–20	125 ft. × 6	*AP 8, heavy, load 9*	M/2h	Hard 3	20W	18 lbs.	Feudal	200s
Ballista, light	3d6 lethal	17–20	75 ft. × 6	*AP 4, load 7, stationary*	L/—	Hard 3	18W	50 lbs.	Ancient	175s
Ballista, heavy	3d8 lethal	17–20	100 ft. × 6	*AP 6, load 9, massive, stationary*	L/—	Hard 3	18W	100 lbs.	Ancient	250s
Battering ram	3d8 lethal	18–20	—	*AP 6, heavy, massive*	L/2h	Hard 4	7D	100 lbs.	Primitive	25s
Cannon, deck *	4d6 lethal	19–20	50 ft. × 6	*Load 7, spread, stationary, unreliable*	M/—	Hard 3	18W	25 lbs.	Reason	300s
Cannon, light *	5d6 lethal	18–20	100 ft. × 6	*Heavy, Inaccurate, load 11, unreliable*	L/2h	Hard 4	12W	100 lbs.	Feudal	500s
Cannon, harpoon *	Harpoon	18–20	30 ft. × 6	*AP 4, load 7, stationary*	M/—	Hard 3	15W	50 lbs.	Reason	250s
Cannon, heavy *	6d6 lethal	18–20	150 ft. × 6	*Inaccurate, load 13, stationary, unreliable*	L/—	Hard 4	12W	200 lbs.	Reason	650s
Catapult	4d6 lethal or fire	18–20	100 ft. × 6	*Indirect, load 13, massive, stationary*	L/—	Hard 3	12W	500 lbs.	Ancient	150s
Flare (1)	1d12 lethal or fire	20	50 ft. × 6	*Load 9, stationary, unreliable*	L/—	Hard 2	15W	30 lbs.	Feudal	20s
Mortar	4d6 explosive	19–20	75 ft. × 6	*Blast 2, indirect, load 11, stationary*	L/—	Hard 3	15W	100 lbs.	Reason	325s
Rocket (1)	3d8 explosive	20	50 ft. × 6	*Blast 1, load 9, stationary, unreliable*	L/—	Hard 2	15W	30 lbs.	Feudal	50s
Springdal	1d6 lethal	17–20	50 ft. × 6	*Blast 1, load 13, stationary*	L/—	Hard 3	18W	400 lbs.	Ancient	200s
Trebuchet	6d6 lethal	19–20	100 ft. × 6	*Indirect, load 11, spread, stationary*	H/—	Hard 4	18M	800 lbs.	Ancient	400s

* You must have the Siege Weapons forte to be proficient with this exotic weapon.

Cannon, Deck: AKA a "swivel gun," this compact weapon fires grapeshot at crew and vulnerable parts of nearby ships.

Cannon, Light: This common cannon is made of cast iron or bronze and found aboard ships and at besieged fortifications.

Cannon, Harpoon: Another maritime development, the harpoon cannon is mounted on vehicles and used to hunt whales, dragons, and other large seafaring creatures.

Cannon, Heavy: This huge, stationary weapon fires foot-thick cannonballs through ship hulls and other hard targets.

Catapult: The tension catapult is a fixture in siege warfare, hurling heavy stones or flaming pitch over walls and cover.

Flare: Fireworks are great for signaling over great distances. They also make moderately effective ranged weapons, especially when you're interested in setting the opposition on fire.

Mortar: This stubby cannon blasts its explosive payloads high in the air, shredding everything in the vicinity.

Rocket: An early gunpowder weapon, the rocket is essentially a giant firecracker; it presents as much risk to the shooter as the enemy.

Springdal: This "arrow catapult" uses a tension mechanism to launch a deadly flight of arrows into advancing troops or nearby ships.

Trebuchet: This terrifying siege engine is essentially a giant sling, using massive counterweights to hurl heavy stones or masonry at the enemy.

WEAPON UPGRADES

As with armor, there are three types of weapon upgrades: **craftsmanship,** which adjusts the weapon's design to match those of a particular culture, technique, or style (in this case, by species); **materials,** which change the weapon's composition; and **customization,** which often adds weapon qualities.

Each weapon may only have 1 craftsmanship and 1 materials upgrade at a time, though any number of customizations may be made. Also, species craftsmanship is only possible if the species is present in the campaign (check with the GM if you're unsure).

WEAPON SCALE

A character may only wield weapons of his Size or smaller. Default weapons Sizes are listed on each table and may be scaled up or down with the large-scale and small-scale upgrades *(see right)*. These upgrades have the following effects.

- When a weapon's Scale increases, its error range increases by 1, its weight increases by 300%, and its Size and damage dice each rise by 1 step (e.g. from Medium to Large and from d6 to d8). If the weapon's damage dice are d12s, it rolls twice that number of d6s instead (e.g. 1d12 becomes 2d6).
- When a weapon's Scale decreases, its error range increases by 1, its weight decreases by 50%, and its Size and damage dice each drop by 1 step (e.g. from Medium to Small and from d6 to d4), to a minimum of d4.

Table 4.25: Weapon Upgrades

Name	Effect	Const	Comp	Weight	Era	Cost
Craftsmanship						
Drake	May be used as a mage's pouch	—	+5	—	Primitive	+200%
Dwarf	+5 gear bonus with weapon's Damage saves	+1 save	+5	—	Primitive	+100%
Elf	+2 gear bonus with Impress	—	+5	–25%	Primitive	+150%
Giant	+2 threat range vs. smaller	—	+2	—	Primitive	+100%
Goblin	+2 points of sneak attack damage	—	–2	–25%	Primitive	+50%
Ogre	Force 1 special adversary or 1 mob to make a DC 15 Morale check *(see page 379)*	—	—	+25%	Primitive	+50%
Orc	Always inflicts lethal damage, target suffers 1 stress damage with a miss	—	+2	—	Primitive	+100%
Pech	Grants Cheap Shot trick *(see page 221)*	—	—	—	Primitive	+100%
Rootwalker	Inflicts subdual damage only	—	—	—	Primitive	+50%
Saurian	Adds *grip* quality; negates underwater combat penalties	—	+2	—	Primitive	+50%
Unborn	–1 weapon Size when not armed	—	+5	—	Primitive	+50%
Material						
Crude	–1 damage (min. 1)	–1 save	–2	—	Primitive	–25%
Superior	+1 damage	+1 save	+5	—	Primitive	+100%
Customization						
Accurate	Removes *inaccurate* quality	—	+5	—	Reason	+100%
Armor-Piercing	Adds *AP 2* quality	—	+2	+25%	Ancient	+50%
Bayonet	Adds *spike* quality	—	+2	—	Reason	+25%
Bleed	Adds *bleed* quality	—	+2	—	Primitive	+50%
Bludgeon	Adds *bludgeon* quality	—	+2	+25%	Primitive	+25%
Cavalry	Adds *cavalry* quality	—	+2	+25%	Feudal	+50%
Cord	Adds *cord* quality	—	—	—	Ancient	+25%
Finesse	Adds *finesse* quality	—	+5	—	Primitive	+100%
Grip	Adds *grip* quality	—	—	—	Primitive	+25%
Hook	Adds *hook* quality	—	+2	—	Ancient	+25%
Hurl	Adds *hurl* quality	—	+5	—	Ancient	+50%
Keen	Adds *keen 4*	—	+5	+25%	Feudal	+50%
Large-scale	Increases weapons Scale by 1 *(see left)*	—	—	+300%	Primitive	+200%
Lure	Adds *lure* quality	—	—	—	Primitive	+25%
Massive	Adds *massive* quality	—	+2	+50%	Primitive	+50%
Poisonous	Adds *poisonous* quality	–1 save	—	—	Ancient	+50%
Reliable	Removes *unreliable* quality	—	+5	—	Reason	+100%
Small-scale	Decreases weapons Scale by 1 *(see left)*	—	—	–50%	Primitive	–25%
Trip	Adds *trip* quality	—	+2	+25%	Primitive	+50%

Unborn: In any era in which Unborn are present, a weapon may be built into or removed from their bodies with a successful Build or Improve check against the weapon's Complexity + 10. Weapons installed in this fashion may not be Disarmed..

UPGRADE DESCRIPTIONS

Accurate: The weapon is rebalanced or retooled, losing the *inaccurate* quality.

Armor-Piercing: The weapon gains a chopping edge or penetrating studs and spikes.

Bayonet (bows and black powder only): The weapon gains a knife extension or other sharpened bit the wielder can thrust at enemies.

Bleed: The weapon gains ragged edges that cause vicious bleeding wounds.

Bludgeon (black powder only): A heavy stock is installed, letting the wielder pound opponents senseless.

Cavalry: The weapon is heavier than normal and balanced for mounted combat.

Cord (hurled and *hurl* quality only): A tether is added, letting the wielder reel the weapon back in after throwing it.

Crude Materials: Simple, low quality materials reduce durability and damage but make the weapon easier to build.

Drake: Drake-made weapons are enchanted and emit faint magical forces that assist spellcasting.

Dwarf: Like most dwarven creations, the weapon can withstand *decades* of abuse.

Elf: An elf-made weapon conveys the deft majesty of the race, its subtle grace aiding with negotiations and other "soft" efforts.

Finesse (blunt, edged, and hurled only): The weapon is light and precise for pinpoint attacks.

Giant: Giants forge weapons that reflect their immense stature, improving the chance of a critical hit.

Grip: The weapon gains a custom grip, making it harder to Disarm.

Goblin: Goblin-made weapons are quick and spiky, helping with ambushes and other times a target is caught off-guard.

Hook (blunt and edged only): A notch or hook is added so the wielder can snag an opponent's weapon.

Hurl (blunt and edged only): This weapon is rebalanced for throwing.

Keen (blunt and edged only): This weapon concentrates force to break bones and rupture vitals. It gains *keen 4.*

Large-Scale: This weapon is increased in size for use by larger wielders.

Lure: The weapon is unusually flexible or uses a bright tassel to mislead opponents in combat.

Massive: The weapon is extremely thick and heavy, making it hard to use but generating tremendous impact with a hit.

Ogre: Ogre-made weapons are adorned with bones and other viscera claimed from their enemies, to give opponents pause.

Orc: Weapons made by orcs are covered in terrifying barbs and ragged edges, ripping flesh and leaving targets rattled even when an attack fails to connect.

Pech: Frequently looking to escape with minimal fuss, Pech build weapons to maim and harry.

Poisonous (blunt and hurled only): Thin spines or spurs are added, along with space for 1 dose of poison.

Reliable: The weapon is built to overcome the weaknesses of its design, negating the *unreliable* quality.

Rootwalker: Weapons forged by Rootwalkers are heavy and blunt, making them the perfect tools for knockout attacks.

Saurian: Saurian-made weapons are flexible and easy to hold, and just as useful when a character is submerged.

Small-Scale: The weapon is reduced in size and weight for smaller combatants.

Superior: Folded steel, adamant, or another material increases the weapon's durability and damage but makes it harder to build.

Trip (blunt and edged only): An additional spur or bar makes the weapon useful for sweeping an opponent's legs out from under him.

Unborn: Weapons crafted by unborn are highly sophisticated and can be collapsed for easy concealment when not in use.

REPUTATION AND PRIZES

Many of the greatest rewards of adventuring are beyond price, their value impossible to gauge in pounds of silver or sacks of gold. These exceptional rewards might be found or claimed (e.g. an abandoned tomb you decide to spruce up and call home), taken from fallen enemies (e.g. a magic relic you take from a defeated foe), or bestowed by a grateful community or patron (e.g. a constable who promises to help you in the future for protecting his town from a raiding party). Regardless of their origin, however, these rewards are *kept* by spending Reputation points, the currency of heroism.

Reputation points are earned for achieving victories during adventures *(see page 342),* and may be spent to increase **Renown** (your standing in various circles). Renown has a variety of effects, among them setting the maximum number of Prizes you can keep at any time. As illustrated in the previous examples, Prizes include **Contacts, Favors, Holdings,** and **Magic Items,** each described in a later section.

GETTING STARTED

A new character's Reputation points are equal to his Career Level × 10. He may spend some or all of this to increase his Renown and, if the campaign allows, buy one or more Prizes; otherwise, a character starts with no Renown or Prizes.

LOSING PRIZES

The spoils of glory are often fleeting: titles can be stripped away, friends can die in battle, territories can be raided or destroyed, and relics can be shattered or stolen. Losing a Prize can be a devastating blow and it takes time for a hero's legend to recover. As with silver, spent Reputation doesn't magically reappear when a Prize is lost; the hero must continue to adventure to gain more. Whether a hero replaces a lost Prize with newly gained Reputation is a choice for tomorrow.

RENOWN

One of the most common uses for Reputation is building Renown, which measures your social standing and public recognition. Renown is key to your progression, representing not only your popularity and title but also your growing legend, which is reflected in the number of Prizes you can keep and the favors you can request.

Renown is a score divided into three tracks: **Heroic** (fame and sway with the people of the world), **Military** (respect and duty paid by armies and police forces), and **Noble** (stature and influence in circles of political power). Optionally, your GM may introduce new Renown tracks unique to the setting and story *(see page 317)*.

Each point of Renown costs 30 Reputation and may be invested in a Renown track of your choice, marking your growing standing in the world. Each Renown track caps out at 10, and Renown may only be purchased between adventures.

THE BENEFITS OF RENOWN

Renown confers a number of benefits, some for total Renown (the sum invested in all Renown tracks), others for Renown in a specific track.

Title: Your Renown in each track grants you a title that's commonly used to describe and refer to you. A list of default titles is found on Table 4.26: Titles *(see right)*, though the GM may develop new ones for your world setting.

Recognition and Reactions: The higher your total Renown, the greater the chance that others have heard of you. Once per scene, you may request that any NPCs who can see and hear to make a team Knowledge check (DC 20), adding 1/2 your total Renown as an insight bonus (rounded down). With success, they recognize you, recalling your name and titles.

Calling in Favors: Your progress along each Renown track also gives you pull within a segment of the populace (the people for Heroic Renown, the armed forces for Military Renown, and the leadership for Noble Renown). This pull lets you spend Reputation to call in a wide variety of Favors *(see below)*.

Keeping Prizes: *You may keep a number of Prizes equal to your total Renown + 1 at the end of each adventure.* If you have more, you must give the excess to other characters or "discard" them (e.g. release a contact from service, relinquish the deed to a holding, or donate a magic item to the town's city guard).

Purchasing Prizes (GM Approval): During Downtime of a week or more, your GM may permit you to "buy" new Prizes with a Reputation cost up to 10 × your total Renown. No actual currency exchanges hands; these Prizes are acquired by pulling strings and taking advantage of relationships. The GM may restrict this option, only allowing certain Prizes, or may not allow the option at all, as appropriate to the setting and story.

Table 4.26: Titles

Rank	Heroic Title	Military Title	Noble Title
1	Swordsman	Squire	Lord
2	Adventurer	Man-at-Arms	Baron
3	Gallant	Corporal	Viscount
4	Champion	Sergeant	Earl
5	Knight Errant	Lieutenant	Margrave
6	Knight	Captain	Marquis
7	Exemplar	Major	Duke
8	Knight Champion	Lieutenant General	Archduke
9	Dragon Slayer	General	Monarch
10	Savior of the Realm	Warlord	Lord Sovereign

FAVORS

Heroes are rarely alone in their journey — they're aided by grateful recipients of their kindness, powerful patrons, close friends, and others. Favors can take many forms, from a noble jailing a knavish member of the court to a bandit providing an out-of-the-way hiding place for the night, from a military captain supporting the party's assault on a fortress to a wizened master providing exotic training, and more. In all cases the characters are putting their names on the line for a Favor, which in game terms translates to spending Reputation for a potent, one-time benefit.

To call in a Favor, you must have the required Renown, devote the minimum Downtime, and spend the Reputation listed on Table 4.27: Favors *(see page 188)*. You must also be in or near a population center or be able to communicate with allies who can plausibly provide the Favor. You may only call in each Favor once per adventure, though you can keep it as a Prize if you'd prefer not to use it immediately. You may only keep 1 of each Favor as a Prize at any time, even if the Favor can grant multiple effects (e.g. you may keep 1 Basic Feat Training Favor and 1 Advanced Feat Training Favor, *but only 1 of each*).

Table 4.27: Favors

Favor	Renown Requirement	Minimum Downtime	Reputation Cost
Blessing — Party receives 1 benefit for the adventure:			
Luck (+1 with action die results)	Heroic 2	—	10
Protection (+1 with Defense and saves)	Heroic 4	—	15
Rage (+1 with attack and damage rolls)	Heroic 6	—	20
Victory (action die cost to activate threats and errors decreases by 1, minimum 0)	Heroic 8	—	25
Combat Training — Character receives 1 proficiency or trick for the adventure	Any 1	W	5
Decree: Alter local law for the scene:			
Holiday (Suspend work and government activity)	Military or Noble 2	D	10
Instate minor law	Military or Noble 4	W	15
Suspend minor law	Military or Noble 6	W	20
Instate major law	Military or Noble 8	W	25
Suspend major law	Military or Noble 10	W	30
Delivery — Safe transport of 1 message or Small item:			
Neighboring (within 50 miles, 1 day of travel)	Any 1	—	5
Regional (within 500 miles, 1 day per 50 miles of travel)	Any 3	—	10
Remote (over 500 miles, 1 day per 50 miles of travel)	Any 5	D	20
Detention: Imprison 1 NPC without trial:			
For 1 day	Military or Noble 4	—	5 + 1/2 Disposition (rounded down)
For 1 week	Military or Noble 6	—	10 + 1/2 Disposition (rounded down)
For 1 month	Military or Noble 8	—	15 + 1/2 Disposition (rounded down)
Indefinitely	Military or Noble 10	—	25 + 1/2 Disposition (rounded down)
Per additional 5 characters detained	+1 (maximum 10)	—	+5
Diversion — Arrange spectacle:			
Minor (observers suffer –2 penalty with Notice and Search checks for 1 minute)	Any 2	—	2
Moderate (observers suffer –4 penalty with Notice and Search checks for 2d6 minutes)	Any 4	—	5
Major (observers suffer –10 penalty with Notice and Search checks for 4d6 minutes)	Any 6	D	10
Event — Draw people to a gathering:			
Small (local protest/private event; 10–100 attendees)	Noble 2	—	5
Medium (speech or ceremony/city-wide event; 100–500 attendees)	Noble 4	D	10
Large (holiday or festival/region-wide event; 500–2000 attendees)	Noble 6	D	15
Massive (king's coronation/national event; 2000–10,000 attendees)	Noble 8	W	20
Feat Training — Character receives 1 temporary feat for the adventure:			
Basic (Any Basics feat or one of the following: Great Fortitude, Iron Will, Lightning Reflexes, and Quick Draw)	Any 3	W	10
Advanced (Any Mastery feat or one of the following: Angry Hornet, Darting Weapon, Two-Hit Combo, and Two-Weapon Fighting/Style)	Any 5	W	20
Expert (Any Supremacy feat or one of the following: All-Out Attack, Bullseye, Contempt, and Surge of Speed)	Any 7	M	30
Harassment — Abuse 1 NPC, inflicting penalties for the scene:			
Emotional abuse (target suffers –2 penalty with Resolve checks and Will saves)	Heroic or Military 3	D	15
Mental abuse (target suffers –2 penalty with Tactics checks and Reflex saves)	Heroic or Military 3	D	15
Physical abuse (target suffers –2 penalty with Athletics checks and Fortitude saves)	Heroic or Military 3	D	15

Favor	Renown Requirement	Minimum Downtime	Reputation Cost
Hirelings — Party gains NPC follower(s) for the scene:			
Standard NPCs (1 mob)	Any 3	D	1/4 XP value (rounded up)
Special NPC (1 character)	Any 5	D	1/4 XP value (rounded up)
Invitation — Party gains access to restricted event, secure location, or protected NPC:			
Private (pivotal stadium game, guard tower, or audience with an influential citizen)	Heroic or Noble 1	—	5 (15 in hostile area)
Privileged (nobles' ball, city court, or audience with a local lord)	Heroic or Noble 3	D	10 (20 in hostile area)
Elite (king's coronation, royal dungeon, or audience with the emperor)	Heroic or Noble 5	D	20 (30 in hostile area)
Language Training — Character gains 1 language for the adventure	Any 1	W	2
Loan — Character borrows money or an item for the adventure	Any 5	D	1 per 1,000s or 2 Reputation value
Pardon — Escape punishment for 1 crime:			
Minor crime	Any 4	—	15
Major crime	Any 8	D	25
Reconnaissance — Party gains information about a character or location:			
Cursory (public information; 1 key detail)	Military 2	D	5
Detailed (private information; 2 key details)	Military 4	D	15
Exhaustive (guarded information; 3 key details)	Military 6	W	20
Meticulous (secret information; 4 key details)	Military 8	W	25
Rumor — Character shifts public Disposition toward 1 character or group for the adventure:			
Calm campaign (+/–10 Disposition)	Noble 2	D	10
Earnest campaign (+/– 15 Disposition)	Noble 4	D	15
Impassioned campaign (+/– 20 Disposition)	Noble 6	W	20
Zealous campaign (+/– 30 Disposition)	Noble 8	W	30
Target is a group	—	—	+10
Safe Haven – Party and its animals gain food and protective shelter for the day:			
Common (shelter + 1 common meal/1 day's feed)	Heroic 2	--	5
Fancy (As common safe haven + 2 additional common meals)	Heroic 4	--	10
Luxurious (As fancy safe haven + 1 unspiced food or drink)	Heroic 6	--	20
Extravagant (As luxurious safe haven + 1 community service *(see extravagant lodging, page 169)*	Heroic 8	--	30
Safe Passage — Party and its animals are safely transported to a destination:			
Neighboring (within 50 miles, 1 day of travel)	Any 2	—	5
Regional (within 500 miles, 1 day per 50 miles of travel)	Any 4	D	10
Remote (over 500 miles, 1 day per 50 miles of travel)	Any 6	W	20
Skill Training — Character receives temporary bonus ranks in 1 skill for the adventure:			
Basic (+2 ranks)	Any 1	W	5
Intermediate (+4 ranks)	Any 3	W	15
Advanced (+6 ranks)	Any 5	M	20
Expert (+8 ranks)	Any 7	M	25
Spellcasting — Character benefits from 1 successfully cast spell:			
Any 1 spell allowed by the GM	Any equal to Spell Level	D	4 × Spell Level
Support — Character benefits from 1 skill check with a set result:			
Result equal to Threat Level	Any 2	—	5
Result equal to Threat Level + 5	Any 4	—	10
Result equal to Threat Level + 10	Any 6	D	15
Result equal to Threat Level + 15	Any 8	W	20
Result equal to Threat Level + 20	Any 10	W	25

The GM determines who can provide each Favor, though you can and should make suggestions, especially among NPCs who've already appeared in the game. To use a Favor you must be able to communicate with the NPC or group providing it. A Favor is lost once it's used, though you may call it in again during a later adventure by spending more Reputation.

Not all Favors of the same type are identical. Safe passage across a quiet area populated with well-meaning folk is a far cry from safe passage across the same distance in hostile wilderness. The GM can and should increase a Favor's cost based on the circumstances. Generally, no Favor should exceed triple the listed cost, even for the most outlandish requests.

As many Favors can potentially upset or derail adventures, the GM may disallow each Favor request by spending 2 action dice, in which case the Reputation spent to call the Favor in is returned. Though not required, the GM should always try to offer a story reason for refusing a Favor (e.g. following this section's initial examples, the knavish court member might enjoy popular support, the bandit might be on the run, the captain's troops might be committed elsewhere, or the wizened master might be on a vision quest).

FAVOR DESCRIPTIONS

Blessing: The party receives a divine mandate or religious endorsement and the corresponding benefit from Table 4.27 for the rest of the adventure. This might involve moral and spiritual support or an actual gift from the gods, depending on the nature of the campaign.

Combat Training: The character receives intense training in new weapons or combat maneuvers, gaining 1 proficiency or trick for the rest of the adventure.

Decree: The law of the land shifts, creating a government-sanctioned holiday, instating a new law, or suspending an existing law for rest of the scene *(see page 319).*

Delivery: A courier, mage, or informant delivers a message or item up to Small Size. Unlike transport bought with silver, the delivery is entirely secret and arrives without incident. Travel Speeds are still modified by terrain, however *(see page 371).*

Detention: An NPC or group is arrested and locked up without trial by the military or local watch. This Favor's Reputation cost is determined by the length of the detention and the Disposition of the military or local watch commander toward the target(s).

Diversion: The character's allies create a spectacle that distracts observers, inflicting a penalty on their Notice and Search checks. A minor diversion might be a staged duel or a carriage accident, a moderate one could be a fire or explosion, and a major one could be a riot or the destruction of an entire building.

Event: The character's allies put on a festival, rally, protest, or other large gathering, summoning a number of NPCs for a period deemed appropriate by the GM.

Feat Training: The character undergoes a crash course to temporarily develop a talent or special ability. He gains one of the listed temporary feats for the rest of the adventure. These feats are exclusive and do *not* grant previous feats in the same chains (i.e. Advanced Feat Training does *not* also grant a Basics feat).

Harassment: The character's allies emotionally hassle an NPC (e.g. undermining or humiliating them), mentally (e.g. keeping them from sleeping or relaxing), or physically (e.g. roughing them up or arranging harmful "mishaps"). This inflicts various penalties with all the target's actions for the rest of the scene.

Hirelings: The party employs a mob of standard NPCs or a single special NPC for the rest of the scene. The NPC(s) may be built from scratch or chosen from the Rogues Gallery *(see page 244).* They're controlled by the GM, have a Disposition of 10, and assist the party in any way that doesn't place them in unreasonable jeopardy. This option covers all the myriad types of hirelings the characters may want, from mercenaries to sages to thieves to guides.

Invitation: The party gains access to a restricted event, secure location, or protected NPC. The invitation lasts for the scene, the event's duration, or until the NPC's patience runs out, whichever comes first.

Language Training: The character is tutored in one foreign tongue and may communicate with it, albeit in a broken fashion, for the rest of the adventure.

Loan: The character borrows an item or money, promising to return it before the end of the adventure. If he reneges, he pays this Favor's Reputation cost again and may gain a Debt Subplot of equivalent value *(see page 382).*

Pardon: The character or 1 other character escapes punishment for 1 crime *(see page 320).*

Reconnaissance: The party taps into a network of scouts, spies, or seers to get a "lay of the land" or "word on the street."

Rumor: The character fires up the local rumor mills, starts a whisper campaign, or uses town gossips to change the public's opinion toward 1 character or group.

Safe Haven: The party "lays low" with standard NPC friends who feed and possibly assist them. The friends also lie to keep the party's location a secret and fight to give the party time to escape should danger intrude on the safe haven. When needed, the GM chooses the friends' stats from the Rogues Gallery *(see page 244).*

Safe Passage: The party is safely escorted or transported to a destination of their choice (no chance of travel encounters).

Skill Training: Friends offer the character special insight into the use of a single skill. He gains the listed ranks in 1 skill for the rest of the adventure.

Spellcasting: The character employs a magic user to cast a spell on his behalf (with a Casting Level equal to the adventure's Threat Level). Due to the powerful and flexible nature of magic, even when it's restricted in the setting *(see page 314),* the GM is advised to carefully consider spellcasting Favors and deny any that might upset the game. Should a spellcasting Favor be denied, it should not become available later without a reasonable story justification.

Support: The character employs an expert or craftsman to perform a single task for them.

CONTACTS

Contacts are fully developed special NPCs who share a personal history and strong bond with a single player character. Unlike other NPCs, a contact is predisposed to like and help the character out of friendship, loyalty, or obligation.

Each contact is a Prize and therefore gained by spending (in this case, leveraging) Reputation, though some character options grant them as well. Not all characters have contacts — deep friendships and abiding trust aren't part of every hero's tale.

To establish a contact, a character may either choose an existing NPC with a minimum Disposition of 16 or create a new one, paying Reputation equal to 1/2 the NPC's base XP value, rounded up *(complete rules for creating NPCs can be found on page 225)*. Contacts may be offered at no cost as an Instant Reward — assuming the characters treat them well *(see page 344)*.

The reason(s) for a contact's support should be determined before the contact enters play, and it's a good idea to note a few additional details about the contact as well. At the very least every contact should have a name and home location. Adding one to three background details (banker to the Crown, owns hundreds of books, former militiaman) and/or one to three personality quirks (jovial, womanizing, afraid of horses) will help the Game Master run the contact in an expected fashion, rather than making them up on the fly when the contact is called upon.

The Game Master must approve each new contact before it enters play, even if the contact is granted by a character option. Like everything in this chapter, contacts shouldn't replace a character's raw ability and the GM should be mindful of ways that contacts might be used — intentionally or accidentally — to circumvent or undermine a campaign's challenge. For instance, a diplomat might be a great contact in a political intrigue game, so long as he doesn't wind up doing all the talking for the party. Generally, contacts should be making the characters' lives a little easier or getting them out of minor binds rather than replacing their need to adventure.

TRUST

A contact's willingness to help is determined by his Trust. In order from lowest to highest, contacts with each level of Trust are called **acquaintances, associates, confederates,** and **partners.** Unless otherwise specified, a newly established contact always begins as an acquaintance.

Table 4.28: Trust

Trust	Persuasion Result
Acquaintance	20
Associate	30
Confederate	40
Partner	50

CALLING ON A CONTACT

Everyone lives somewhere and most people will only travel so far from home — even for friends. A contact's home is set when he's gained and only the GM may change it later (though the player may lobby for a contact to move if it suits the game's story).

Each character may only call on a contact once per scene and each individual contact may only be approached once per adventure. A character may only call upon a contact with whom he can communicate; in a fantasy game, this may often mean that the character must go to the contact to request help.

The purchase of a contact represents kindness the character has extended and the contact is happy to return the favor. When called upon, a contact helps to the best of his ability as if the character had generated the Impress/Persuade result shown on Table 4.28: Trust *(see above)*.

No skill check is required to gain a contact's help, but there's only so much help to go around. When called upon, a contact assists the character and his party either with 1 task or until the end of the following scene, whichever comes first (the player must define both). Of course, the circumstances may dictate that a contact can't or shouldn't leave when his generosity runs out, in which case he leaves at the first reasonable opportunity and the character's Reputation decreases by 1 per additional scene the contact helps.

Contacts may help with Downtime checks but may not make Downtime checks of their own.

IMPROVING A CONTACT

At the end of each adventure during which a contact was called upon, the character may spend 25 Reputation to increase the contact's Trust by 1. Further, with GM approval, the contact's statistics may improve, increasing his XP value by up to 10 at an equal cost in Reputation.

In the event that a contact is killed, abandoned, or otherwise removed from play, the character regains 1/2 his invested Reputation (rounded up). This includes Reputation spent to increase the contact's statistics and Trust but *not* Reputation lost if the contact was forced to linger for more than one scene.

HOLDINGS

Homes, hideouts, houses you rent, and places you squat are all holdings. Each holding is a separate Prize with a Scale ranging from 1 to 12, as shown on Table 4.29: Holding Scale *(see right)*. A holding's Scale determines the maximum number of guests you can host and shelter there (in addition to yourself).

A holding's Reputation cost is also listed on Table 4.29 and additional Reputation may be spent to improve a holding with Assistants, Fortifications, Guards, Rooms, and Tradesmen, as described in the following sections. Holdings may be acquired in any of the ways a magic item can *(see page 193)*.

The Scale of each of your holdings may not exceed the higher of your Panache or Prudence. You may keep any number of holdings at a time but each is a separate Prize. Improvements to one holding have no effect on your other holdings.

Each holding should be tailored to its surroundings and the character's history. Sneaking away to a barge wouldn't make much sense in a desert campaign but a series of appropriated catacombs beneath the capital city could house the same number of characters (and possibly give the party an immediate link to a central spot in the story as well). The more detail you can lavish

Table 4.29: Holding Scale

Scale	Examples	Maximum Guests/ Reputation Cost
1	Room at an inn; storage room on a ship	2
2	Apartment above a shop; private deck on a ship	5
3	Cottage; fishing boat	10
4	Small farm; private dock compound	15
5	Boarding house or small barracks; barge	20
6	Large farm; small caravan	30
7	Hunting lodge; ironclad	40
8	Small manor house; galley	50
9	Large manor house; large caravan	75
10	Large manor house with surrounding compound; frigate	100
11	Mansion; mountain aerie	150
12	Palace; private island	250

on holdings the better; these are places where you and your party should be spending a lot of Downtime, and perhaps even the odd scene or two. They should seem no less special than any other place you visit in your travels.

As with contacts, the GM must approve any holding before it enters play, even if it's granted by a character option.

ASSISTANTS

Holdings may permanently house various NPCs to help you and your guests complete various tasks. Each Assistant grants a bonus with checks made using a single skill. This bonus is determined by the Reputation invested, as shown on Table 4.30: Holding Upgrades *(see page 193)*. An Assistant may be improved between adventures and counts as a guest in the holding. They will not accompany the party outside the holding. The combined bonuses granted by all Assistants at a single holding may not exceed the holding's Scale; when they do (e.g. because of new or improved Assistants), you must dismiss enough Assistants to bring the combined bonuses under this limit.

FORTIFICATIONS

Unwelcome visitors face additional challenges when trying to enter a fortified holding. Entering when the location is secure becomes a Complex Task with DCs and a number of Challenges determined by the Reputation invested, as shown on Table 4.30: Holding Upgrades *(see page 193)*. The specific skills used to overcome each Challenge must be determined and approved before a fortification enters play. Work with the GM to find suitable options (e.g. Athletics to swim across a moat, Investigate or Survival to locate a concealed lair, etc.)

Table 4.30: Holding Upgrades

Reputation Investment	Assistant Bonus	Fortification Challenges	Tradesman Bonus
1	+1	2 (DC 14)	+0
3	+2	3 (DC 18)	+2
6	+3	4 (DC 22)	+4
10	+4	5 (DC 26)	+6
15	+5	6 (DC 30)	+8

GUARDS

Holdings may permanently house defenders to protect it from incursion. Each complement of guards consists of a number of standard NPCs equal to 1/3 the holding's maximum guests (rounded down), and requires a Reputation investment equal to the NPC's XP value. Guards may be built from scratch or chosen from the Rogues Gallery *(see page 244)*, and must be approved by the GM before they enter play. Guards will not accompany the party outside the holding. A holding may benefit from no more than 3 guard complements at a time and each individual guard counts as a guest.

ROOMS

Special rooms can be built into holdings, providing benefits to you and your guests when you're there. Each Room costs 10 Reputation. A holding may only benefit from one of each specific Room (Armory, Actor's Workshop, Carver's Crafting Workshop), and may contain a maximum number of Rooms equal to 1/2 its Scale (rounded up).

Armory: Once per adventure when you or a guest loses or breaks a weapon or armor worth 50s or less, an identical copy may be retrieved from the holding's armory at no cost.

Dressing Room: The Appearance bonus of each character residing at the holding improves by +1.

Escape Passage: This hidden route out of your holding — and the exit, which must be located within 5 miles — may only be found with a successful Search check (DC 25).

Kitchen: Once per adventure, you and each guest gain any 1 unspiced food at no cost.

Library: While at your holding, you and each guest may re-roll 1 Knowledge check per scene.

Prison: This Room may contain a number of prisoners equal to the holding's Scale. They may only leave if released by you, a guest, or someone who defeats the holding's Fortifications and Guards.

Stables: This Room may contain a number of animals equal to the holding's Scale. Once per adventure, each animal at the Stables may be fed for 1 day. Also, the threat range of each Breed Animal or Train Animal check made at a Stables increases by 3.

Throne Room: The Impress threat range of each character residing at the holding improves by 3.

Torture Chamber: The Intimidate threat range of each character residing at the holding improves by 3.

Vault: This hidden Room may only be found with a successful Search check (DC 25) and may only be breached with a successful Prestidigitation check (DC 25). It may contain up to 1,000 lbs. of gear, Prizes, and other items.

Workshop: Any of 13 workshops may be added to a holding, each improving a single skill use *(see page 159 and the corresponding skill descriptions in Chapter 2).*

TRADESMEN

Holdings may permanently house various builders, merchants, and other moneymakers to generate income for you, even when you're not there. Each Tradesman makes a single Downtime check to earn income at the end of each adventure *(see page 68)*, using the length of time since the end of the last adventure and the skill bonus shown on Table 4.30: Holding Upgrades *(see left)*. A Tradesman may be improved between adventures and counts as a guest in the holding. The specific skill each Tradesman uses must be determined before he enters play. Tradesmen will not accompany the party outside the holding. A holding may benefit from no more than 3 Tradesmen.

MAGIC ITEMS

Magic items are a staple of most fantasy settings: legendary swords, ancient stone orbs infused with the spirits of forgotten kings, crumbling scrolls containing powerful secrets of lost arts… These precious and often unique objects grant a seemingly infinite variety of benefits, all the stuff of high fantasy. Even so, not all heroes possess magic items — supernatural objects and tools can be out of character for the self-reliant and superstitious, and other characters may not wish to tarnish their accomplishments with speculation that they couldn't have been earned with skill alone. When kept, magic items become part of a character's growing legend. For this reason each magic item is a Prize and counts toward the maximum number of Prizes permitted by his Renown *(see page 187).*

GAINING AND LOSING MAGIC ITEMS

During an adventure, you might seize magic items from defeated adversaries and captured treasure hordes. You might also find them in dungeons and other locations in the wild. Beneficent patrons and grateful NPCs you've saved might bestow them on you as recompense for a job well done. The GM built these items into the adventure and they're yours to keep without cost. They still count toward your maximum Prizes, however.

If the setting permits, you might decide at some point to craft a magic item, in which case you're sacrificing Downtime — and precious training in the form of the Charm Binding and/or Essence Binding feats *(see pages 96 and 97)* — but you gain the item without further cost.

Then there's "buying" magic items, which is often disallowed (check with the GM before marching off to a vendor). Even the lowliest magic item is essentially priceless, its value impossible to gauge in mere coin. When magic items can be bought, the only currency precious enough to compare is a character's good name among friends and across the world: his Reputation. To "purchase" a magic item, you must pay the item's total Reputation cost, including all Essences and Charms *(see page 195)*. This is true whether the item is actually bought (in a very high-magic campaign where the forces of creation are displayed in shop windows) or leveraged away from its former owner (for example, by burning some of your standing to convince a noble to part with a prized heirloom). Even when this option is allowed, your accumulated Reputation will only carry you so far — you may only "buy" magic items with a Reputation cost up to your Renown × 10.

When magic items can be "bought," they can also be "sold," yielding half their Reputation value (rounded down). You can keep this Reputation (e.g. generating some good will by "gifting" the item to a worthy cause, like the city guard), or apply it toward the cost of a purchased item.

As with any Prize, losing a magic item for any reason — theft, destruction, or misplacing it — yields nothing; it is simply gone.

The GM must approve all magic items before they enter play, whether they're found, seized, crafted, or purchased.

Example: A Career Level 6 metalsmith with the proper Gear feats sets out to create a magic metal shield with the Lesser Vitality Essence and the Lesser Defense Charm — the "Stalwart's Shield" *(see page 201)*. At its initial Level (6), the item has a total Reputation cost of 15. During Downtime, the metalsmith makes Crafting (Metalworking) checks to generate Reputation until he amasses the 15 he needs to complete the shield. At that point he claims the magic item as a Prize at no additional cost.

Later, a young knight is awarded the shield by the head of his family in recognition of his fine exploits and growing prominence in the kingdom. The knight pays 15 Reputation for the shield and adds it to his list of Prizes.

Unfortunately, the knight is soon eaten by a dragon and the shield becomes part of the creature's horde. A decade later, adventurers slay the beast and claim the shield as an adventure reward at no Reputation cost.

USING MAGIC ITEMS

Using a magic item is generally as simple as donning a piece of clothing or wielding an object. Items that require activation may be triggered with a Handle Item action defined by the object's creator (e.g. mental command, manipulating the object, uttering a word or phrase, etc.), and Charms and Essences that don't require activation may likewise be turned on or off with a Handle Item action. Discovering how to trigger a magic item can become part of the play experience and may require specialized research or even completing a new adventure.

Table 4.31: Random Magic Items

d20 Result	Essences and Charms
1–2	1 Lesser Essence
3–4	1 Lesser Charm
5–7	1 Greater Essence
8–10	1 Greater Charm
11–15	1 Lesser Essence & 1 Lesser Charm
16–17	1 Greater Essence & 1 Lesser Charm
18–19	1 Lesser Essence & 1 Greater Charm
20	1 Greater Essence & 1 Greater Charm

BUILDING MAGIC ITEMS

Whether found, seized, crafted, or purchased, every magic item possesses 1 Essence and/or 1 Charm (but no more). An Essence is an effect that's innate to the object or the substance from which it's made, while a Charm is an effect that's imbued or forged into the object when it's awakened (i.e. made magical). The specific Essences that are linked to each object or substance are left to the GM (so they can fit the setting and story), but they can just as easily be left undefined, part of the mystery behind the mojo.

The GM chooses a magic item's Essence and/or Charm when the item is introduced, and will usually build items into the plot of each adventure. When magic items can be crafted, the creator may choose an item's Essence and/or Charm from those he is able to imbue, though GM approval is still required *(see page 318)*. The same is true when shopping (the GM determines what's available in a given market). For those who wish to be surprised, random results are available on Table 4.31: Random Magic Items *(see above)*.

A magic item also has a level ranging from 1 to 20. Like its Essence and/or Charm, an item's level is usually chosen by the GM and should usually be equal to the adventure's Threat Level *(see page 335)*. The level of a crafted magic item is commonly equal to the creator's Career Level *(see page 27)*. Among other things, an item's level is used to determine its Charm Bonus, which is critical when determining Reputation cost.

Example: In the previous example, the weaponsmith was Level 6 when he created the Stalwart's Shield. Thus, the item's level was also 6, which produces a Charm Bonus of +1. The

Table 4.32: Essences and Charms

d20 Result	Essence/Charm	Effect	Reputation Cost *
Lesser Essences			
1	ACP Negation	Armor Check Penalties decrease by 2	3
2	Trained Skill	Untrained penalties ignored when using 1 skill	3
3	Interest	+1 specific Interest	3
4	Proficiency	+1 specific proficiency	4
5	Trick	+1 specific trick or advanced action	4
6–7	NPC Quality	+1 specific NPC quality	6
8	Aligned Damage (melee)	Weapon or melee attacks gain 1 Alignment	4
9	Aligned Damage (unarmed)	Weapon or unarmed attacks gain 1 Alignment	4
10–11	Exotic Damage (melee)	Weapon or melee damage changes type	5
12	Exotic Damage (unarmed)	Weapon or unarmed damage changes type	5
13	Damage Aura	Adjacent attackers suffer 1d6 damage when they hit you	6
14	Damage Resistance	Damage Resistance 4 against 1 damage type or source	8
15	Edge Surge	Trigger item to gain 2 Edge (once per combat)	8
16	Travel Speed	+3 miles per hour (travel only)	10
17	Save Bonus	+1 magic bonus with saves of 1 type	8
18	Vitality	+10 vitality	12
19	Wounds	+4 wounds	10
20	Threat Range	+1 threat range with attacks of 1 type or checks with 1 skill	10
Greater Essences			
1	ACP Negation, Greater	Armor Check Penalties are ignored	5
2–3	NPC Quality, Greater	+1 specific NPC quality	15
4	Aligned Damage (ranged)	Weapon or ranged attacks gain 1 Alignment	5
5	Exotic Damage (ranged)	Weapon or ranged damage changes type	5
6	Damage Aura, Greater	Adjacent attackers suffer 1d10 damage when they hit you	10
7	Damage Resistance, Greater	Damage Resistance 10 against 1 damage type or source	15
8	Damage Reduction	DR 2 against all damage except 1 Aligned	15
9	Edge Surge, Greater	Trigger item to gain 4 Edge (once per combat)	15
10	Travel Speed, Greater	+7 miles per hour (travel only)	20
11	Save Bonus, Greater	+3 magic bonus with saves of 1 type	25
12	Vitality, Greater	+20 vitality	25
13	Wounds, Greater	+10 wounds	25
14–15	Feat	+1 specific feat	20
16	Threat Range, Greater	+2 threat range with attacks of 1 type or checks with 1 skill	20
17	Casting Level Bonus	+2 Casting Level when casting spells of 1 School	20
18–19	Class Ability	Grants 1 cross-training ability *(see page 47)*	20
20	Class Enhancement	Next level's abilities from 1 specific class	25
Lesser Charms			
1–3	Skill Ranks	Extra ranks in 1 skill	4 per rank
4	Storage	Trigger item for extra-dimensional storage	1 per item
5	Defense Bonus	Magic bonus to Defense	8 per +1
6–7	Accuracy Bonus	Magic bonus to attacks with weapon or 1 attack type	8 per +1
8–9	Damage Bonus	Magic bonus to damage with weapon or 1 attack type	10 per +1
10	Bane	Threat range increased against 1 creature type	8 per +1
11–12	Spell Point Bonus	Extra spell points at the start of each scene	8 per point
13–17	Spell Effect (Level 1–5)	Trigger item for 1 spell effect	Spell Level × uses
18–20	Attribute Bonus	Magic bonus to 1 attribute	10 per +1
Greater Charms			
1–3	Skill Ranks, Greater	Extra ranks in 1 skill	4 per rank
4	Storage, Greater	Trigger item for extra-dimensional storage	2 per item
5	Defense Bonus, Greater	Magic bonus to Defense	8 per +1
6–7	Accuracy Bonus, Greater	Magic bonus to attacks with weapon or 1 attack type	8 per +1
8–9	Damage Bonus, Greater	Magic bonus to damage with weapon or 1 attack type	10 per +1
10	Bane	Threat range increased against 1 creature type	8 per +1
11–12	Spell Point Bonus, Greater	Extra spell points at the start of each scene	8 per point
13–17	Spell Effect (Level 6–9)	Trigger item for 1 spell effect	Spell Level × uses × 3
18–20	Attribute Bonus, Greater	Magic bonus to 1 attribute	10 per +1

* The item's overall Reputation cost decreases by 5 (if 1-handed), 10 (if armor or 2-handed), or 20 (if stationary or immobile). This cannot decrease an item's cost below 1/2 (rounded up).

shield's total Reputation cost is 15 because the Lesser Vitality Essence has a cost of 12, its Lesser Defense Charm Bonus of +1 has a cost of 8, and the item is 1-handed, which decreases its overall cost by 5. All these numbers can be found on Table 4.32: Essences and Charms *(see page 195)*.

Every magic item is a single object that conveys its benefit only while whole and unbroken. Most magic items are portable but there's no reason a throne or fountain couldn't be one as well (in fact, these items make great additions to a location the GM wants the players to return to again and again). Magic items can't be combined or merged and even if they're made part of a larger object each individual magic item counts against your maximum Prizes.

Example: A glove has four inlaid gems, each with 1 Essence and 1 Charm. Despite the fact that the glove is a single item it's the gems that are magical and so the glove counts as 4 Prizes.

Except in games where magic is ubiquitous, every item should also have a background, even if it's (initially) unknown to the party. Magic items are special and should have names and history, often linked to their Essences and Charms. When brainstorming these details it's often best to imagine who created the item and why, where they were and what they were doing, and why they needed the item in the first place. Unless the item's still in their possession when the party finds it, you might also consider others who've owned it and the role the item played in their lives. Granting an item this kind of history grounds it in the setting and story, and goes a long way toward making it a memorable facet of play (as opposed to a bundle of bonuses).

ARTIFACTS

Some magic items rise above the rest, becoming synonymous with a character and his exploits. Just as Excalibur to Arthur and Sting to Bilbo, such a pivotal object can become a unique fixture in a hero's life, as integral to his legend as his fellow party members. In *Fantasy Craft* these remarkable items are called "artifacts."

An artifact differs from a traditional magic item in the following ways.

- An artifact may have up to 5 Essences and 5 Charms, all chosen by the GM. Most of the time these will be determined once when the artifact is created and won't change through its lifespan. In a particularly evolving storyline the GM may decide to hold certain Essences and/or Charms back until certain events or actions occur in the game but he should still decide on all of them before the artifact is introduced.
- An artifact's level can advance with that its owner. At any time when a character's Career Level is higher than his artifact's level, he may spend Reputation to increase the artifact's level to match his own. This costs Reputation equal to the character's Career Level × 2.
- Because an artifact is intrinsically linked with its owner, attribute bonuses it grants are considered permanent changes (i.e. they can affect his vitality, wounds, skill points, Lifestyle, etc.).
- Each hero may possess only 1 artifact at a time. Should a character abandon his artifact, he loses Reputation equal to his Career Level. He may regain the same or another artifact at a later time.

Artifacts cannot be purchased or crafted in any way — they're introduced strictly by the GM, usually to satisfy a specific need in the setting or storyline. Typically they're built into an adventure though the GM might occasionally 'awaken' a traditional magic item after it's used extensively in a pivotal adventure. This approach can be particularly satisfying as it emphasizes an item the player already knows and uses. In both cases the artifact becomes an adventure reward.

ESSENCE DESCRIPTIONS

Essences are fixed benefits the magic item or artifact grants regardless of the item's level.

All of an Essence's details — such as the specific Alignment conveyed by Aligned Damage and the specific School affected by Casting Level Bonus — must be chosen when the item is introduced and cannot change. An Essence may be applied to an artifact as many times as there are unique details for that Essence (e.g. Aligned Damage may be applied once per available Alignment). When no details must be chosen, an Essence may only be applied once.

ACP Negation: The item decreases your Armor Check Penalties by 2.

ACP Negation, Greater: The item negates your Armor Check Penalties.

Aligned Damage: If the item is a weapon, attacks with it gain 1 Alignment available in the setting; otherwise, all your attacks of the 1 type (unarmed, melee, or ranged) gain the Alignment.

Casting Level Bonus: If your Casting Level is at least 1, the item increases it by 2 when casting spells of 1 School.

Class Ability: The item grants 1 class ability offered by the *cross-training* ability *(see page 47)*. If you already have the ability, this Essence has no effect.

Class Enhancement: The item is attuned to 1 specific base or expert class. If you have at least 1 level in that class, the item grants the next level's class abilities. You gain *no*

Table 4.33: Magic Item Feats

d20	Feat Tree				
1–3	Basic Combat	*d20 Result*	*Feat*	*d20 Result*	*Feat*
		1	Armor Basics	12	Great Fortitude
		2–3	Charging Basics	13	Iron Will
		4–5	Combat Focus	14	Lightning Reflexes
		5–6	Combat Instincts	15	Quick Draw
		7–8	Combat Vigor	16–17	Surge of Speed
		9	Contempt	18	Two-Weapon Fighting
		10	Elusive	19–20	Wolf Pack Basics
		11	Expert Disarm		
4–5	Melee Combat	*d20 Result*	*Feat*	*d20 Result*	*Feat*
		1–2	All-Out Attack	12	Hammer Basics *
		3	Axe Basics *	13	Knife Basics *
		4–5	Cleave Basics	14	Polearm Basics *
		6	Club Basics *	15	Shield Basics *
		7–8	Darting Weapon	16	Spear Basics *
		9	Fencing Basics *	17	Staff Basics *
		10	Flail Basics *	18–19	Sword Basics *
		11	Greatsword Basics *	20	Whip Basics *
6	Ranged Combat	*d20 Result*	*Feat*	*d20 Result*	*Feat*
		1–5	Angry Hornet	11–15	Bullseye
		6–10	Bow Basics *	16–20	Hurled Basics *
7–8	Unarmed Combat	*d20 Result*	*Feat*	*d20 Result*	*Feat*
		1–4	Kicking Basics	13–16	Two-Hit Combo
		5–8	Martial Arts	17–20	Wrestling Basics
		9–12	Rage Basics		
9–10	Chance	*d20 Result*	*Feat*	*d20 Result*	*Feat*
		1–2	Adventurer's Luck	13–14	Fortune Favors the Bold
		3–5	All In	15–16	Fortune's Fool
		6–7	Black Cat	17–18	Lady Luck's Smile
		8–10	Close Call	19–20	Lucky Break
		11–12	Fortunate		
11–12	Covert	*d20 Result*	*Feat*	*d20 Result*	*Feat*
		1–4	Ambush Basics	10–12	Ghost Basics
		5–7	Ferocity Basics	13–16	Misdirection Basics
		8–9	Garrote Basics *	17–20	Mobility Basics
13–15	Skill	*d20 Result*	*Feat*	*d20 Result*	*Feat*
		1–2	Basic Skill Mastery (Actor)	11–12	Basic Skill Mastery (Officer)
		3–4	Basic Skill Mastery (Athlete)	13–14	Basic Skill Mastery (Pickpocket)
		5–6	Basic Skill Mastery (Healer)	15–16	Basic Skill Mastery (Robber)
		7–8	Basic Skill Mastery (Horseman)	17–18	Basic Skill Mastery (Spy)
		9–10	Basic Skill Mastery (Investigator)	19–20	Basic Skill Mastery (Trader)
16–17	Spellcasting	*d20 Result*	*Feat*	*d20 Result*	*Feat*
		1–3	Casting Basics	11–12	Spell Conversion: Casting Time
		4–5	Double Cast	13–15	Spell Conversion: Distance
		6–8	Hidden Spells	16–18	Spell Conversion: Duration
		9–10	Spell Conversion: Area	19–20	Spell Conversion: Effect
18	Style	*d20 Result*	*Feat*	*d20 Result*	*Feat*
		1–5	Comely	11–15	Mark
		6–10	Glint of Madness	16–20	Repartee Basics
19–20	Terrain	*d20 Result*	*Feat*	*d20 Result*	*Feat*
		1–3	Battlefield Trickery	11–14	Horde Basics
		4–6	Bushwhack Basics	15–17	Night Fighting
		7–10	Coordinated Attack	18–20	Pathfinder Basics

* If the magic item is a weapon or shield, the feat tree corresponds (Axe Basics if an axe, Shield Basics if a shield, etc.).

other benefits from the next level, such as skill points, vitality, base attack bonus, save bonuses, etc. If you have no levels in the class or have reached its maximum level, this Essence has no effect.

Damage Aura: Each time an adjacent opponent hits you with an unarmed or melee attack the item inflicts 1d6 damage (or 1d10 damage for a Greater Damage Aura) of a type listed on Table 4.34: Damage Auras *(see below).*

Table 4.34: Damage Auras

d20 Result	Damage Type
1	Acid
2	Divine
3–4	Electrical
5–6	Fire
7–8	Force
9	Sonic
10	Stress
11	Subdual
12–13	Blunt (subdual)
14–15	Edged (lethal)
16–17	Cold (subdual)
18–19	Heat (subdual)
20	Poison (any 1)

Damage Reduction: The item grants DR 2 against all damage except attacks with 1 Alignment available in the setting.

Damage Resistance: The item grants Damage Resistance 4 (or 10 for Greater Damage Resistance) against 1 damage type listed on Table 4.35: Damage Resistance *(see below).*

Table 4.35: Damage Resistance

d20 Result	Damage Type or Source
1	Acid
2–3	Cold
4	Divine
5–6	Electrical
7–8	Fire
9–10	Force
11–12	Heat
13–14	Sonic
15	Blunt weapons
16	Edged weapons
17	Ranged weapons
18	Natural attacks
19–20	Spells

Edge Surge: Once per combat, the item may be triggered to gain 2 Edge (4 Edge for Greater Edge Surge).

Exotic Damage: If the item is a weapon, its damage shifts to 1 different type; otherwise, all your attacks of 1 type (unarmed, melee, or ranged) inflict 1 alternate damage type.

Feat: The item grants 1 temporary feat listed on Table 4.33: Feats *(see page 197).* If the feat is the first in a chain and you already have it, you instead gain the next feat in the chain you don't already have. If you already have all the feats in the chain, this Essence has no effect.

Interest: The item grants 1 Interest. If you already have the Interest, this Essence has no effect.

NPC Quality: The item grants 1 NPC quality listed on Table 4.36: NPC Qualities *(see below).* If you already have the quality, this Essence has no effect.

Table 4.36: NPC Qualities

d12 result	Lesser NPC Quality	Greater NPC Quality
1	*Always ready*	*Aquatic II*
2	*Aquatic I*	*Beguiling*
3	*Cagey I*	*Blindsight*
4	*Chameleon I*	*Chameleon II*
5	*Charge Attack*	*Superior climber III*
6	*Critical Surge*	*Contagion immunity*
7	*Darkvision I*	*Darkvision II*
8	*Dread*	*Fearsome*
9	*Fast healing*	*Regeneration 2*
10	*Superior jumper II*	*Rend*
11	*Never outnumbered*	*Spell reflection*
12	*Unnerving*	*Tough I*

Proficiency: The item grants 1 proficiency. If you already have the proficiency, you gain the forte. If you already have that, this Essence has no effect.

Save Bonus: The item grants a +1 magic bonus (or a +3 bonus for Greater Save Bonus) with saves of 1 type (Fortitude, Reflex, or Will).

Threat Range: The item increases your threat range by 1 (or 2 for Greater Threat Range) with attacks of 1 type (unarmed, melee, or ranged), or checks with 1 skill.

Trained Skill: The item ensures you're always trained with checks made using 1 skill, even if you lack the proper tools.

Travel Speed: The item grants a +3 MPH magic bonus to the character's Travel Speed (+7 MPH for Greater Travel Speed).

Trick: The item grants 1 trick or advanced action. If you already have it, this Essence has no effect.

Vitality: The item increases your maximum vitality by 10 (or 15 for Greater Vitality).

Wounds: The item increases your maximum wounds by 4 (or 10 for Greater Wounds).

CHARM DESCRIPTIONS

Unlike Essence effects, which are fixed, Charm effects are determined by the item or artifact's level. This ensures that newly found magic items gradually improve over the life of the campaign, and it's the cornerstone for artifact advancement.

As with an Essence, all of a Charm's details must be chosen when the item is introduced and cannot change. Each Charm can be applied as many times as there are unique details for it.

Table 4.37: Charm Bonuses

Level	Lesser Bonus	Greater Bonus
1	+1	+2
2	+1	+2
3	+1	+3
4	+1	+3
5	+1	+3
6	+1	+3
7	+2	+4
8	+2	+4
9	+2	+4
10	+2	+4
11	+2	+5
12	+2	+5
13	+3	+5
14	+3	+5
15	+3	+6
16	+3	+6
17	+3	+6
18	+3	+6
19	+4	+7
20	+4	+7

Accuracy Bonus: If the item is a weapon, it grants a magic bonus with attack checks made using it as shown on Table 4.37: Charm Bonuses *(see above)*; otherwise, all your attacks of 1 type (unarmed, melee, or ranged) gain this bonus.

Attribute Bonus: The item grants a magic bonus to 1 attribute as shown on Table 4.37: Charm Bonuses.

Bane: If the item is a weapon, its threat range increases against 1 creature type as shown on Table 4.37: Charm Bonuses; otherwise, your threat range with all attacks against the creature Type are increased. Creature Type can be chosen or randomly rolled on Table 4.38: Creature Types *(see right)*.

Damage Bonus: If the item is a weapon, it grants a magic bonus to damage against all targets as shown on Table 4.37: Charm Bonuses; otherwise, all your attacks of 1 type (unarmed, melee, or ranged) gain this bonus.

Defense Bonus: The item grants a magic bonus to Defense as shown on Table 4.37: Charm Bonuses.

Table 4.38: Creature Types

d20 Result	Creature Type
1–2	Animal
3–4	Beast
5	Construct
6–7	Elemental
8–9	Fey
10	Folk
11–12	Horror
13	Ooze
14–15	Outsider
16	Plant
17–18	Spirit
19–20	Undead

Skill Ranks: The item grants a number of bonus ranks in 1 skill as shown on Table 4.37: Charm Bonuses. These ranks may exceed your maximum ranks in the skill.

Spell Effect: The item may be triggered to cast 1 spell chosen from the listed level range. This spell may not have a Prep Cost and its level may not exceed that of the item. If desired, this spell may be rolled on Table 3.2: Spells *(see page 114)*. If needed, the Casting Level is equal to the item's level. You need not be a caster to use the item or trigger the spell effect and no Spellcasting check is required. The spell's save DC is calculated using the wielder's stats. Any special requirements — such as completing a Subplot to cast a Wish — must still be satisfied before the spell may be cast. The item may cast the spell a number of times per scene or adventure as shown on Table 4.39: Spell Uses *(see below)*.

Table 4.39: Spell Uses

Item	Spell Level			
Level	1–3	4–5	6–7	8–9
1	1/scene	—	—	—
2	1/scene	—	—	—
3	1/scene	—	—	—
4	1/scene	1/scene	—	—
5	2/scene	1/scene	—	—
6	2/scene	1/scene	1/adventure	—
7	2/scene	1/scene	1/adventure	—
8	3/scene	1/scene	2/adventure	1/adventure
9	3/scene	2/scene	2/adventure	1/adventure
10	3/scene	2/scene	2/adventure	1/adventure
11	3/scene	2/scene	2/adventure	1/adventure
12	4/scene	2/scene	3/adventure	2/adventure
13	4/scene	3/scene	3/adventure	2/adventure
14	4/scene	3/scene	3/adventure	2/adventure
15	5/scene	3/scene	3/adventure	2/adventure
16	5/scene	3/scene	4/adventure	2/adventure
17	5/scene	3/scene	4/adventure	3/adventure
18	5/scene	4/scene	4/adventure	3/adventure
19	6/scene	4/scene	4/adventure	3/adventure
20	6/scene	4/scene	5/adventure	3/adventure

Spell Point Bonus: The item grants a number of bonus spell points per scene as shown on Table 4.37: Charm Bonuses *(see page 199)*.

Storage: The item can contain a number of smaller objects equal to 1/3 its level (rounded up). Each object must be able to fit through an extra-dimensional rift with a diameter equal to the item's longest dimension (e.g. a 4-ft. long sword's rift opens with a 4-ft. diameter). Objects stored in the item weigh nothing until removed. The item must be triggered to deposit or retrieve each object.

Storage, Greater: As Storage, except that the item can store a number of objects of any Size equal to its level.

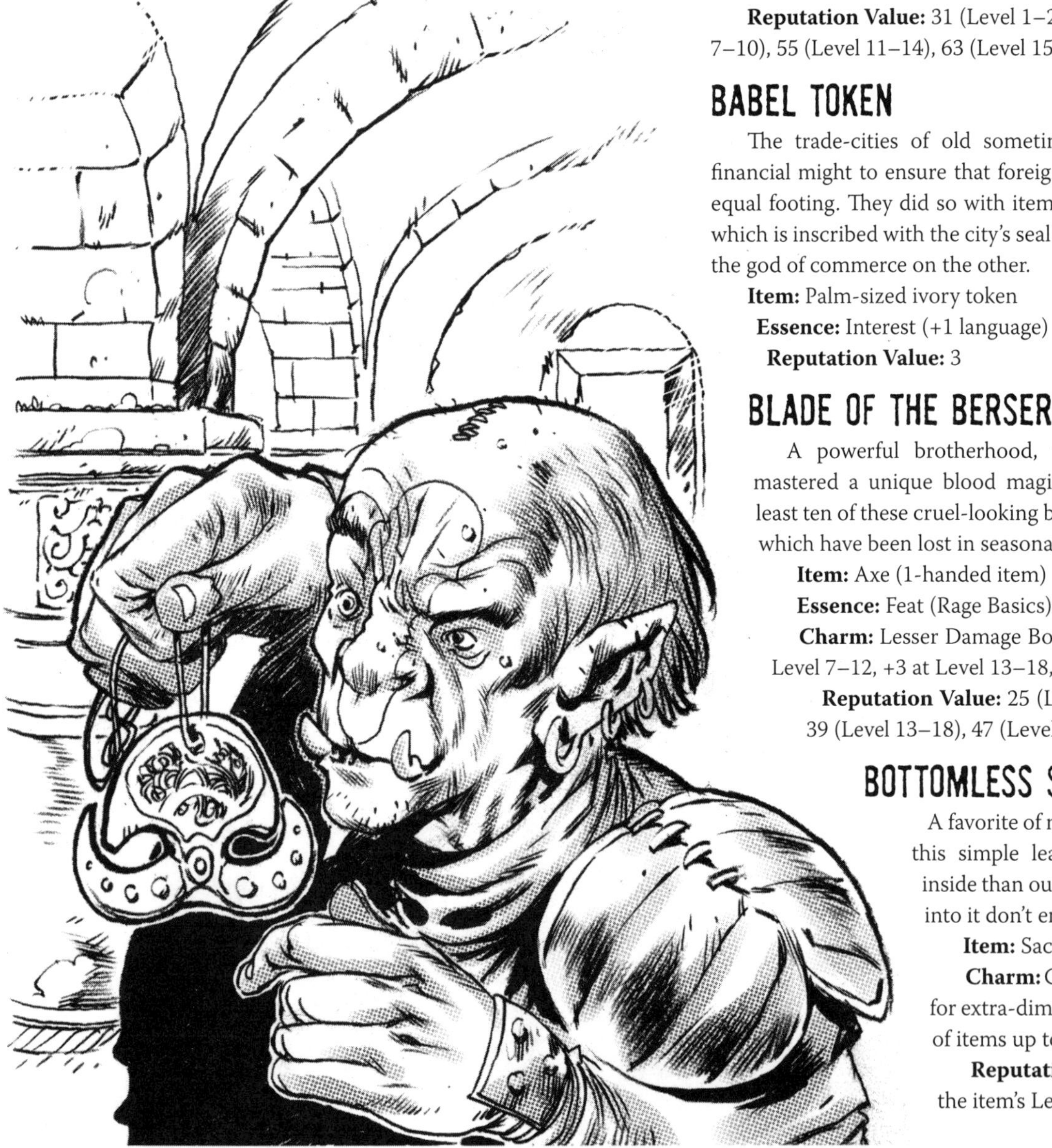

SAMPLE MAGIC ITEMS

Here's a small sampling of magic items possible with this rich and diverse system. Your game will of course benefit from a number created expressly for your setting and story.

ARCHMAGE'S STAFF

A classic symbol of the mage's art, this staff is a symbol of excellence among students of the arcane.

Item: Quarter Staff (2-handed item)

Essence: Class Enhancement (Next level's abilities from Mage class)

Charm: Greater Spell Point Bonus (+2 at Level 1–2, +3 at Level 3–6, +4 at Level 7–10, +5 at Level 11–14, +6 at Level 15–18, +7 at Level 19–20)

Reputation Value: 31 (Level 1–2), 39 (Level 3–6), 47 (Level 7–10), 55 (Level 11–14), 63 (Level 15–18), 71 (Level 19–20)

BABEL TOKEN

The trade-cities of old sometimes had the magical and financial might to ensure that foreign visitors could bargain on equal footing. They did so with items like this small ivory disk, which is inscribed with the city's seal on one side and a prayer to the god of commerce on the other.

Item: Palm-sized ivory token

Essence: Interest (+1 language)

Reputation Value: 3

BLADE OF THE BERSERKER

A powerful brotherhood, the Teeth of the North, mastered a unique blood magic to create these axes. At least ten of these cruel-looking blades were made, several of which have been lost in seasonal raids against gentler folk.

Item: Axe (1-handed item)

Essence: Feat (Rage Basics)

Charm: Lesser Damage Bonus (+1 at Level 1–6, +2 at Level 7–12, +3 at Level 13–18, +4 at Level 19–20)

Reputation Value: 25 (Level 1–6), 31 (Level 7–12), 39 (Level 13–18), 47 (Level 19–20)

BOTTOMLESS SACK

A favorite of merchants and thieves alike, this simple leather sack is vastly larger inside than out. Even better, items slipped into it don't encumber the bearer.

Item: Sack

Charm: Greater Storage (trigger item for extra-dimensional storage — number of items up to item Level, any Size)

Reputation Value: 2–40 (double the item's Level)

BOWL OF STORMS

The prized icon of a fallen sect of sky-worshipers, this broad bronze bowl is carved with alternating images of clear and cloudy skies. It's attached to a solid marble stand deep in their ancestral territory and retains its powers only while it remains in their ruined central temple. In this position, the bowl may be filled with clear water and gently stirred with bare fingers to gain control over the local weather.

Item: Metal bowl (immobile item)

Charm: Lesser Spell Effect (Control Weather III — 1 use per scene at Level 5–8, 2 uses per scene at Level 9–12, 3 uses per scene at Level 13–17, 4 uses per scene at Level 18–20)

Reputation Value: 3 (Level 5–8), 5 (Level 9–12), 8 (Level 13–17), 10 (Level 18–20)

HARLEQUIN'S MASK

A brightly painted expression decorates this simple porcelain domino mask, showcasing or perhaps mocking its effect on the wearer — for behind this false face, a character is inspired to extraordinary feats of daring and reckless displays of bravado!

Item: Mask

Essence: Greater Edge Surge (Trigger item to gain 4 Edge, once per combat)

Charm: Lesser Skill Ranks (Impress — +1 rank at Level 1–6, +2 ranks at Level 7–12, +3 ranks at Level 13–18, +4 ranks at Level 19–20)

Reputation Value: 19 (Level 1–6), 23 (Level 7–12), 27 (Level 13–18), 31 (Level 19–20)

STALWART'S SHIELD

The plain but functional shield once belonged to a junior knight who gave his life defending his lady from a dragon that consumed their procession. The shield's bright face bears the triple scar of the dragon's final, killing stroke.

Item: Metal shield (1-handed item)

Essence: Lesser Vitality (+10 vitality)

Charm: Lesser Defense (+1 at Level 1–6, +2 at Level 7–12, +3 at Level 13–18, +4 at Level 19–20)

Reputation Value: 15 (Level 1–6), 23 (Level 7–12), 31 (level 13–18), 39 (Level 19–20)

TRACKS OF THE CONQUEROR

This carefully drawn map is heavily annotated with the insights and observations of a famous warlord who united the region in the days of old. Even centuries later, Captains can study the map to glean incredible strategic wisdom.

Item: Detailed Map (2-handed item)

Essence: Class Enhancement (Next level's abilities from Captain class)

Reputation Value: 15

SAMPLE ARTIFACTS

Finally, here are two artifacts upon which an entire campaign might hang.

THE BLACK MIRROR

This profane mass of black stone is a rare, reliable portal between the realm of demons and the world of men.

Item: Wall-sized obsidian slab (immobile)

Essences:

- Lesser Damage Resistance (Evil 4)
- Greater Save Bonus (+3 magic bonus with Will saves)
- Greater Vitality (+20 vitality)
- Interest (+1 Study — Demons)

Charms:

- Lesser Spell Effect (Call From Beyond III — 1 use per scene at Level 5–8, 2 uses per scene at Level 9–12, 3 uses per scene at Level 13–17, 4 uses per scene at Level 18–20)
- Greater Spell Effect (Call from Beyond V — 1 use per adventure at Level 8–11, 2 uses per adventure at Level 12–16, 3 uses per adventure at Level 17–20)

Reputation Value: Priceless

FOE-BITER

Once carried by the greatest hero of the west, the mighty hooked spear known as Foe-Biter has an honorable home in the largest of the elven halls. When the enemies of man and elf grow numerous, a great tourney is held among the nation's warriors to choose a new bearer. This hero carries Foe-Biter for 1 year or until he dies in battle.

Item: Fork (1-handed item)

Essences:

- Greater Damage Aura (adjacent attackers suffer 1d10 edged (lethal) damage when they hit you)
- Lesser Save Bonus (+1 magic bonus with Will saves)

Charms:

- Greater Bane (+2 vs. outsiders at Level 1–2, +3 vs. outsiders at Level 3–6, +4 vs. outsiders at Level 7–10, +5 vs. outsiders at Level 11–14, +6 vs. outsiders at Level 15–18, +7 vs. outsiders at 19–20)
- Greater Attribute Bonus (+2 Con at Level 1–2, +3 Con at Level 3–6, +4 Con at Level 7–10, +5 Con at Level 11–14, +6 Con at Level 15–18, +7 Con at 19–20)
- Lesser Spell Effect (Haste — 1 use per scene at Level 1–4, 2 uses per scene at Level 5–7, 3 uses per scene at Level 8–11, 4 uses per scene at Level 12–14, 5 uses per scene at Level 15–18, 6 uses per scene at Level 19–20)

Reputation Value: Priceless

CHAPTER 5: COMBAT

At the very heart of every fantasy odyssey is the fierce, personal struggle of one adventuring party against the world. Over the course of a party's career, it fights through harrowing dungeons, remote wilderness, and all the dark and forgotten corners of cities, vanquishing foes for glory, gold, and occasionally the gratitude of those saved and satisfied. Yet it's not just about the accolades and the rewards — in a truly great *Fantasy Craft* campaign, every battle becomes its own thrilling, memorable experience. Every swing of bone and steel, every speeding arrow shifts the face of the battlefield, and every wound is another chance for victory. Parties dreams of such thrilling encounters, but how do you make them a reality?

The *Fantasy Craft* combat system is streamlined to keep the focus on the characters and their enemies, helping them direct and define the action through a series of fast and furious exchanges. No character is without something to do and everyone contributes to the escalating conflict until the explosive conclusion. It all starts with knowing where everyone is and what they're carrying.

SETTING UP

The circumstances of most fights are determined by the situation leading into them. Someone throw a punch at one of the characters in a tavern? You already know the locale and the positions of two of the combatants, and that both are aware of each other. The characters stumble on a monster in its lair? Whether the monster and characters know about each other has probably been determined by skill checks leading up to the fight, which should inform the characters' locations and how they're approaching the lair (not to mention whether the monster is ready for them when they get there). A party that sets an ambush will be happy to explain what it's got planned...

At the start of each combat, it's the GM's job to answer three questions: Where is everyone? What's everyone carrying? And are any participants unaware of any of the others? Some additional details may also be required, such as the effectiveness of an ambush *(see page 83)*, special terrain *(see page 204)*, and the locations of important items, but those three questions set up the basics. The GM may choose to poll the players about their characters' locations and carried items, especially if they're given an opportunity to act before the combat starts, but he probably shouldn't let them determine their awareness unless they start the fight themselves. Also, when playing without a battle mat, tracking distances between characters is plenty.

THE ORDER OF COMBAT

Each combat is carried out in four steps, as follows.

STEP 1: FLAT FOOTEDNESS

Unless a character intentionally enters a combat after it begins, he begins the fight *flat-footed.* This means that he loses his Dexterity bonus to Defense (if positive), as well as all dodge bonuses to Defense. He might also be vulnerable to a number of special attacks and effects. A character stops being *flat-footed* as soon as he takes any half or full action, or immediately after he's hit.

STEP 2: INITIATIVE

Each character rolls 1d20 and adds his Initiative bonus *(see page 61).* The result is the character's **Initiative Count.** A character cannot score a threat or error with an Initiative check.

The GM may either make one Initiative check for all opponents, or separate the opponents into groups and make an Initiative check for each. The first option makes things run faster, but it can unbalance combat, especially if the opponents' Initiative Count is particularly high or low.

STEP 3: SURPRISE ROUND

If any combatants are unaware of the others, a **surprise round** happens. Each combatant who is aware of one or more other combatants gets to take 1 free action, 1 half action, or 1 full action during this round. A character who takes a full action may not break it into 2 half actions, nor may any character take more than 1 free action during a surprise round.

Surprise round actions occur from highest to lowest Initiative Count and are subject to all standard combat rules.

STEP 4: COMBAT ROUNDS

The remainder of each combat occurs in combat rounds, each of which lasts 6 seconds. During each combat round, characters may act from highest to lowest Initiative Count. When two or more characters' Initiative Counts are equal, the character with the highest Initiative bonus acts first. If both characters' Initiative bonuses are the same as well, the characters each roll 1d20, re-rolling ties, and the character with the highest result acts first throughout the combat.

When a character gets the chance to act, he may take either **1 full action** or **2 half actions** *(for a list of standard actions, see* *page 218).* Most characters may also take a variety of other actions using skills, class and feat abilities, and other character options.

Additionally, if the character doesn't take any Movement action during the round he may take a Bonus 5-ft. Step, moving 5 ft. in any direction *(for more about movement,* *see page 204).*

Finally, he can take any number of **free actions,** which are trivial, effortless activities that don't affect the character's ability to take his full or half actions during the round. Typical free actions include talking, performing simple gestures, and dropping something. The GM may limit the number of free actions a character can take under certain circumstances.

The following general rules apply to actions taken during combat.

- Skill checks may carry over from round to round. For instance, a character may take a half action to move and follow up with a full-action Disable check, in which case the check is resolved at the end of his first half action in the second round. This option is not available for combat actions, which must be completed in the round they begin.

- A character can combine 2 half actions gained from different sources to take 1 full action. All restrictions placed on either or both half actions apply to the resulting full action. For example, if the Surge of Speed feat is combined with another half action to take a full action, that full action may not be an attack.

- Some rules reduce the time it takes to perform an action, but each individual action may only be affected by one such rule at a time.

WHAT'S DIFFERENT?

***Fantasy Craft* is an independent product with everything you need to embark on as many wondrous journeys as you can imagine. Though similar to other d20-style products, it varies in many significant ways and as a general rule any mechanics not expressly included have been removed on purpose. Some of the most common questions are about attacks of opportunity, iterative attacks, and move/attack actions, none of which are featured in *Fantasy Craft.* Instead, this game simply features half and full actions, with characters generally able to take 1 full action or two half actions in a round. Half actions include making an attack or taking a standard move, so a character can usually attack and move, or attack twice, or move twice, in every round. It's all just part of *Fantasy Craft's* fast-paced, heroically cinematic style.**

MOVEMENT

With each Standard Move action *(see page 218),* a character may move a number of feet equal to his Speed, meaning that a character who spends both his half actions during a round moving can cover twice this distance. Most characters possess a Speed of 30 ft., though some may vary due to Species, encumbrance, armor, and other factors. For ease of play, all movement is broken down into 5-ft. increments, so no character may move less than 5 ft. at a time.

Again, if a character doesn't take any Movement action during a round he may take a Bonus 5-ft. Step, moving 5 ft. in any direction. This step may be taken at any time during the character's Initiative Count — before, during, or after any of the character's other actions. Once a character takes a Bonus 5-ft. Step, though, he cannot take any other Movement action during the same round *(for a list of Movement actions, see page 218).*

A character may freely move through areas occupied by allies and teammates but restrictions apply when he's close to opponents.

- A character who's within 5 ft. of an opponent is considered **adjacent** to him.
- Any character who moves into an area adjacent to an opponent must stop moving, unless that opponent is *flat-footed* or unable to attack him.
- While adjacent to one or more opponents, a character may only move by taking a Bonus 5-ft. Step, making a Tumble check *(see page 69),* or taking a Standard Move action in which the first 10 ft. of movement does not leave him adjacent to any opponent.

The GM may sometimes apply Speed modifiers when a character moves through difficult terrain, such as mud, snow, or cluttered areas. Speed modifiers usually consume 10 or even 15 ft. of Speed for every 5 ft. moved. For instance, the GM may determine that a character moving through mud with a Speed of 30 could only move 15 ft. per Standard Move action, or that the same character moving through raging rapids could only move 10 ft. per Standard Move action.

Many groups may find it easier to track characters, movement, and ranges with figures and a battle mat. While this dramatically improves the precision of play and offers great tactile and visual benefits, it's not for everyone and those who prefer to keep things loose should feel free to do so. These rules assume this only so far as to periodically call 5-ft. × 5-ft. areas "squares" for ease of language.

DIAGONAL MOVEMENT (THE "5/10 RULE")

When using a battle mat, diagonal movement between squares covers slightly more distance than movement along an axis. For this reason, players are encouraged to use the 5/10 rule, which consumes 10 ft. of Speed for every other diagonal movement taken during the same round — that is, the *second, fourth, sixth,* and so on.

Example: Brungil has a Speed of 30 ft. and takes two Standard Move actions to move as far as he can diagonally in a single round. He moves a total of 8 squares instead of 12.

This rule can also be used to determine actual distance between characters or objects on a battle mat.

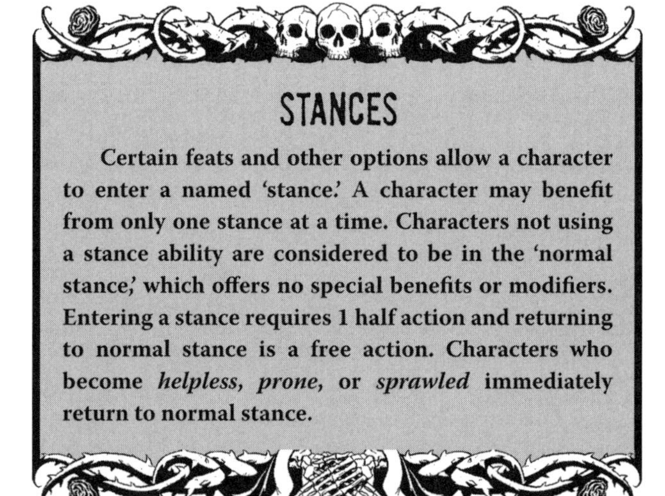

STANCES

Certain feats and other options allow a character to enter a named 'stance.' A character may benefit from only one stance at a time. Characters not using a stance ability are considered to be in the 'normal stance,' which offers no special benefits or modifiers. Entering a stance requires 1 half action and returning to normal stance is a free action. Characters who become *helpless, prone,* or *sprawled* immediately return to normal stance.

ATTACKS

Ultimately, every character's goal in combat is to prevent opponents from hurting him. This typically involves putting them out of commission before they return the favor.

LINE OF SIGHT

A character can only attack things that are in his line of sight (i.e. things he can physically see). A target is considered to be within a character's line of sight if it's within the character's visual range and no obstacles completely obscure it from the character's view. Sometimes a character will only be able to see part of a target, in which case cover comes into play *(see page 214).*

THE STANDARD ATTACK CHECK

When a character tries to hit an opponent, he makes a "Standard Attack check." Each attack check may represent one attack or multiple attacks made during the same amount of time (e.g. it may represent a single weapon swing or a flurry of blows granted by a feat ability).

The player rolls 1d20 and adds his appropriate attack bonus to obtain an **attack check result** *(see page 61 for details about a character's attack bonuses).* If the result equals or exceeds the target's Defense, the character hits and inflicts damage; otherwise, he misses.

RANGE

Each target is located at one of three ranges.

- **Melee Range (Reach):** Targets within a character's Reach are within his Melee Range. A character's Reach is determined by his Species *(see page 9).* Most Medium species have a Reach of 1 square, which means that most of the time only adjacent targets are within a character's Melee Range. Any character within an opponent's Melee Range is considered to be "engaged in melee combat," even if he isn't fighting them.

- **Close Quarters (Beyond Reach, up to 30 ft.):** Targets beyond a character's Melee Range but within 30 ft. are within his Close Quarters Range. A ranged weapon is required to hit these targets.

- **Long Range (More Than 30 ft.):** Targets more than 30 ft. away from a character but still within his weapon's maximum range are within his Long Range.

When a character makes a ranged attack, his weapon or attack will have a **range increment.** Within this distance the character suffers no penalty with his attack check. Beyond this distance, however, he suffers a –2 penalty per full range increment between him and his target.

Example: A long bow has a range increment of 40 ft. When the weapon is fired at a target 110 ft. away, the range modifier is –4.

A ranged weapon is only effective out to a limited number of increments. This limit is noted in the stat line as a multiplier following the range distance.

Example: The long bow's full range increment entry is 40 ft. × 6. It cannot be used effectively past 240 ft.

UNTRAINED ATTACKS

When a character makes an attack without the appropriate proficiency, the attack is "untrained." Any character may make an untrained attack, but he suffers a –4 attack check penalty and his error range increases by 2.

ATTACK CHECK MODIFIERS

A number of modifiers may apply to attacks. Some are "named," falling into one of the following categories, and others are "unnamed." Unnamed modifiers stack but only the highest individual bonus and the highest individual penalty from each named category apply to each attack.

- **Discretionary:** The GM can apply a –4 to +4 modifier to represent circumstances not covered by an existing rule. For example, he might apply a +3 bonus when an attack is made from higher ground (+2) against a target on a slippery surface (+1). The GM is encouraged to use discretionary modifiers to add spice to a lagging combat.

- **Dodge:** Feats and actions offer these modifiers, which represent a keen ability to evade attacks. Unlike all other named modifiers, these *do* stack. However, when a character is *flat-footed,* he loses access to all dodge bonuses.

- **Insight:** Origins, class abilities, and feats offer these modifiers, which represent keen understanding of fighting styles.

- **Gear:** Gear and magic items trigger these modifiers.

- **Magic:** Spells and magic items impose these modifiers.

- **Morale:** Class abilities offer most morale modifiers, which showcase confidence in battle.

- **Size:** A character's Size affects Defense as shown on Table 5.4: Size *(see page 217).*

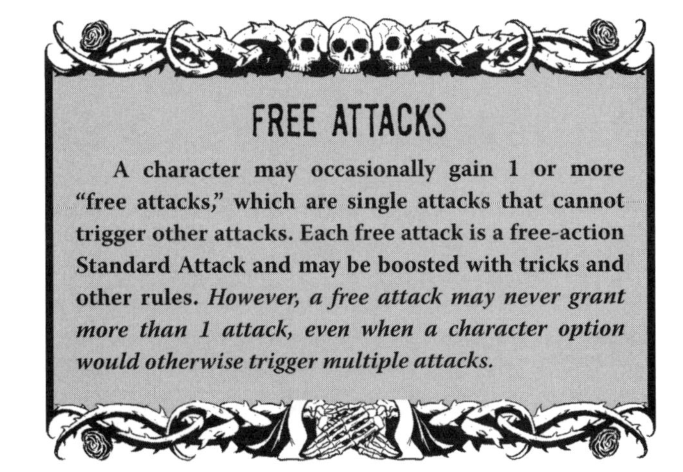

FREE ATTACKS

A character may occasionally gain 1 or more "free attacks," which are single attacks that cannot trigger other attacks. Each free attack is a free-action Standard Attack and may be boosted with tricks and other rules. *However, a free attack may never grant more than 1 attack, even when a character option would otherwise trigger multiple attacks.*

DEFENSE

A character's Defense is equal to 10 + the sum of his class Defense bonuses + his Dexterity modifier.

An object's Defense is equal to 5 + its Size modifier (if stationary), 10 + its Size modifier (if moving), or its holder's total Defense bonus + its Size modifier (if carried).

The Defense of a 5 ft. area (1 square) is 15, whether it's occupied or not.

THE DAMAGE ROLL

When an attack hits, the weapon used determines the damage inflicted.

No Weapon (Unarmed Attack): If the attacker has the Unarmed proficiency, he inflicts 1d4 lethal damage; otherwise, he inflicts 1d3 subdual damage. In both cases, he applies his Strength modifier.

Weapon: The character inflicts the weapon's base damage *(see page 176)*. With a melee attack or a non-explosive hurled attack, he applies his Strength modifier.

Character options, actions, and other effects may modify an attack's damage, which may only drop to 0 due to Damage Reduction or Damage Resistance *(see page 208 and 209)*.

Occasionally, bonuses or multipliers may apply to a character's damage. When 1 or more bonuses and multipliers apply to the same damage total, flat bonuses are applied before multipliers while variable bonuses — i.e. all rolled bonuses — are applied after.

Example: Brungil hits with an attack that inflicts 1d6 lethal damage. He benefits from a +2 bonus to damage as well as 1 die of sneak attack damage and a ×2 multiplier. He rolls a 4 with his lethal damage die and a 3 with his sneak attack damage die, so his total damage is 15: ((4 + 2) ×2) + 3.

INJURY AND DEATH

Fantasy Craft features two types of combatants: **standard** and **special.** Standard characters are easy to kill and generally have fewer statistics because they'll often appear in large numbers for the fun of it, while special characters are important to the plot and represent significant danger to the opposition. Player characters are examples of special characters, as are villains. Monsters and NPCs can be either standard or special, as determined by the GM. More information is available in Chapter 6 *(see page 224)*.

Special characters have **vitality points** and **wound points,** which together measure their ability to remain standing in a fight. Individually, however, these points represent very different things.

- **Vitality Points:** These are a mixture of endurance, luck, and the will to fight, measuring a character's ability to *avoid* injury. Losing vitality does not represent actual physical damage but rather combat fatigue, as it gradually becomes more difficult for the character to avoid being hurt. As a character's vitality drops, he edges closer to exhaustion and the possibility of a nasty wound.

- **Wound Points:** These are a direct measure of a character's remaining vigor, measuring his ability to *sustain* injury. As a character's wounds drop, he acquires abrasions, cuts, and eventually broken bones and worse.

These points simulate the flow of an adventure epic, in which the heroes dive through endless ranks of the enemy before they suffer a single serious hit in a critical battle.

For ease of tracking, standard characters don't have vitality and wounds; rather, they have **Damage saves**, which are used to determine the immediate effects of each hit. Much of the time, standard characters drop out of the fight after failing a single Damage save.

SPECIAL CHARACTER DAMAGE

When a special character suffers damage, it usually reduces his vitality. He suffers no ill effects from damage until his vitality drops to 0, at which point he becomes *fatigued* and any remaining damage reduces his wounds (a character's vitality cannot drop below 0). When a character's wounds reach 0, the character falls unconscious and if there is damage remaining it continues to reduce his wounds below 0. A character dies at –10 wounds and his body is destroyed at –25 wounds.

While a special character's wounds are negative, he's dying and his wounds continue to drop even if he's not attacked. At the start of his Initiative Count during each round, he rolls d%. If the result is equal to or less than his Constitution score, he stabilizes and his wounds return to 0; otherwise, his wounds drop by 1. A dying character may also be stabilized with a successful full action Medicine/Stabilize check (DC 15).

STANDARD CHARACTER DAMAGE

When a standard character suffers damage from any source (or of any type, including stress or subdual), it adds to a single damage total the character's suffered during the current scene. The GM rolls 1d20 and adds the character's Damage save bonus. If the result is equal to or higher than 10 + 1/2 the accumulated damage (rounded down), the character suffers nicks and scratches but no lasting injury; otherwise, he either falls unconscious (if the damage is subdual or stress), or dies (otherwise).

Some standard characters must fail more than 1 Damage save before they're out of the fight, such as those with the *tough* quality *(see page 235)*. Each time one of these characters fails a Damage save, his accumulated damage resets to 0.

SPECIAL ATTACK RESULTS

Every attack has an **error range** and a **threat range,** which are natural die results that trigger special attack results. Unless otherwise specified, an attack has an error range of 1 and a threat range of 20, though character options, weapon choices, and other effects may modify these base values. Bonuses expand the range of natural die rolls that trigger an error or threat, and penalties scale them back. Modifiers may not eliminate error and threat ranges.

Example: A character's error range increases by 2 and his threat range increases by 1. Unless other modifiers are in play, his attacks have an error range of 1–3 and a threat range of 19–20.

THREATS AND CRITICAL HITS

When a character hits with an attack *and* rolls a natural number within his threat range (an actual roll of the number on a d20), he scores a threat — a potential critical hit. To gain the benefits of a critical hit, the character simply spends 1 or more action dice (when an attack hits multiple characters, the attacker chooses which to critically hit, spending 1 or more dice for *each*). This cost is paid separately for *each hit*, even when multiple hits are scored with a single attack or action.

A critical hit has the following effects.

Special Character: The attacker may spend 1 action die to apply the damage directly to the target's wounds, ignoring any remaining vitality. Alternately, if the damage exceeds the target's Constitution score, the attacker may spend 2 action dice to inflict a critical injury, as shown on Table 5.1: The Table of Ouch *(see below)*.

Standard Character or Object: The attacker may spend 1 to 4 action dice to cause the target to automatically fail the same number of Damage saves. In the case of most standard targets, 1 action die is enough to knock them out of the fight *(see Injury and Death, page 206)*.

The GM and players are encouraged to come up with interesting descriptions for critical hits, such as dramatic flourishes, cool maneuvers, and impressive strategic ploys. Critical hits are an excellent way to turn any otherwise mundane combat into something extraordinary.

Special Note: A threat scored by a standard NPC may only become a critical hit if the NPC has the *treacherous* quality *(see page 235)*.

Table 5.1: Table of Ouch

Result	Critical Injury
Up to 35	*Bleeding*
36–40	Battered limb (1d6: 1–3: –2 with actions taken using the arm, 4–6: Speed reduced by 10 ft.)
41–45	Bruised ego (all healing times doubled)
46–50	Head trauma (1d6: 1–3: visual range 1/2 normal (rounded down), 4–6: hearing range 1/2 normal (rounded down))
51–55	Broken limb (1d6: 1–3: lose use of arm, 4–6: Speed reduced by 20 ft.)
56–60	Internal rupture (–3 to highest of Str, Dex, or Con)
61–65	Brain trauma (–3 to highest of Int, Wis, or Cha)
66+	Grave wound (once per hour, Fort save (DC 15) or lose 1 Con; Downtime Medicine check (DC 40) to repair)

ERRORS AND CRITICAL MISSES

When a character misses with an attack *and* rolls a natural number within his error range (an actual roll of the number on a d20), or produces a negative attack check result, he suffers an error — a potential critical miss. He only suffers the effects of the critical miss, however, if his *opponent* — commonly the GM — spends 1 or more action dice.

The GM determines the effects of any critical miss, based on the number of action dice spent (though he can certainly poll the defender or even the other players for ideas). Most critical misses should have a descriptive and mechanical component, and they should be challenging and entertaining rather than debilitating. The goal is not to punish the attacker but rather to insert some new obstacles and interesting elements into the fight. Depriving the party of the one weapon it needs to defeat an enemy is bad form, as is destroying an item the party worked hard to craft or obtain. Having an arrow fly wildly off course to attract more monsters is an excellent option, however, as is wedging a sword in a stone pillar, forcing an Athletics check to wrench it free. If all else fails and nothing comes to mind, simply apply 1d6 stress or subdual damage per action die spent and call it heat-of-battle tension or incidental battle bruising.

1 Action Die: In a fight to save a colony of friendly pixies from several undead rootwalkers, Brungil accidentally smacks the pixie leader with the broad side of his axe. The pixie will be fine, but he's out of the fight for 1 round.

2 Action Dice: In the same fight, Brungil swings too powerfully and loses grip, flinging his axe into one of the rootwalker's branches. He'll have to make a half action Jump or Climb check with a DC of 15 to get it back. (If the GM had spent 3 action dice, the rootwalker could use the weapon to attack Brungil until it's retrieved.)

3 Action Dice: Continuing the example, Brungil overextends himself and drives his axe into the forest earth — which opens up to swallow him! Half the rootwalkers drive their feet through the earth to thrust at him as he tries to climb free, making the Climb check a full round action with a –2 discretionary penalty. The other half can use the same method to attack Brungil but he can't return the favor until he's out of the pit.

4 Action Dice: In a moment of supreme misadventure Brungil's axe... slices through one of the rootwalkers, eliciting a sorrowful moan as brackish sap erupts through the wound. Brungil is covered in the stuff but suffers no other immediate effects. As he'll soon find out, however, he can wash the sap off but the stain remains... and inflicts a –2 morale penalty with all Impress and Haggle checks until Brungil finds and dispatches the dark wizard who created the vile rootwalker army.

ADVANCED DAMAGE

Now that the basics are out of the way, here are a few advanced damage rules.

CRITICAL INJURIES

One of the most effective ways to leave a lasting impression in a fight is to leave the opponent with a little something to remember you by. Critical injuries offer an opportunity for characters to scar, break, and maim the enemy, brutally establishing their battle superiority. Using them is simple. Each time a character suffers 25 or more points of damage in a single hit, he makes a Fortitude save (DC 1/2 the damage suffered, rounded down). With failure, he rolls 1d20 and adds the damage suffered, consulting Table 5.1: The Table of Ouch to find his critical injury *(see page 207)*.

Except for the *bleeding* condition, which heals naturally at the end of the current scene, each critical injury lingers for 1d4 months. This time may be reduced with a successful Treatment check *(see page 78)*.

The GM and players are encouraged to keep track of critical injuries and factor them into subsequent adventures. NPCs might ask about nasty scars and enemies might comment on suspicious limps in the area of wounds they've inflicted, among other scenarios.

MASSIVE DAMAGE

When a character suffers 50 or more points of damage in a single hit, he makes a Fortitude save (DC 1/2 the damage suffered, rounded down). With failure, he dies instantly.

DAMAGE REDUCTION

Gear, abilities, animal and monster hides, and other effects grant Damage Reduction (DR), which allows a target to ignore some or all damage from each hit. When a target with 1 or more points of Damage Reduction suffers damage, the Damage Reduction is subtracted from the damage before it's applied. If this reduces the damage to 0 or lower, any special effects inflicted by the attack are negated as well.

Example: Brungil is hit with a poisoned knife but his armor's Damage Reduction reduces the attack's damage to 0. Brungil takes no damage and is not affected by the poison.

Damage Reduction is sometimes abbreviated as "DR" and weaknesses sometimes follow the full value in parentheses.

Example: A special piece of armor might offer "DR 4/blunt," which means that it offers 4 points of Damage Reduction against everything except blunt weapons.

Finally, when damage possesses the *armor-piercing* quality, the target's DR decreases against the damage by the number listed after the quality *(see page 176)*.

DAMAGE RESISTANCE

Another protection against damage is Damage Resistance, which differs from Damage Reduction in that it affects only one source of damage (see next). Damage Resistance is defined by the GM and may offer protection from virtually anything. Common Resistances include cold (offered by warm clothing), blunt, edged, and other weapons (offered by armor), and various damage types (offered by spells).

Damage Resistance is listed as a source of damage followed by a number (e.g. 'acid 5,' which means "5 points of Damage Resistance against acid damage," or "cold 2," which means "2 points of Damage Resistance against damage inflicted by cold"). When a target with 1 or more points of Damage Resistance suffers damage of the listed type or from the listed source, the Resistance is subtracted from the damage before it's applied. As with Damage Reduction, if this reduces the damage to 0 or lower, any special effects inflicted by the attack are negated as well.

When Damage Resistance and Damage Reduction both apply to the same damage, Damage Reduction is applied first.

DAMAGE TYPES

Adventuring is a wild and untamed profession, bringing characters in contact with many awful situations, not all of which simply harm. Some have other effects, which are handled with damage types. Lethal and subdual are the most common damage types but there are many others.

Each attack or injury may inflict only one type of damage. When more than one damage type applies to an attack (e.g. a flaming sword, which can inflict for either lethal or fire damage), the attacker decides which to apply. Sneak attack damage is the one exception to this rule, as it's a special damage type that augments another.

Damage Conversion: A special case applies when an attack inflicts subdual or lethal damage. In this case, the attacker may choose to convert the damage from one of these types to the other. This decision must be made before the attack roll is made, as a –4 penalty is applied to the check. The resulting damage is converted to the chosen type and reduced to 1/2 normal (rounded up).

Object Damage: Some damage types, such as acid, also damage a character's gear or surroundings. The GM might want to do the same with other damage types, though the option is best reserved for special situations where it might have an impact on the current adventure or the character's personal saga.

ACID DAMAGE

- When an unarmored character suffers acid damage, he suffers the full damage when hit and at the start of his Initiative Count during the following round he suffers 1/2 as much (rounded down). The damage continues to be reduced and applied in this fashion until it reaches 0.
- When an armored character suffers acid damage, compare the acid damage to the armor's DR. If the acid damage is higher, both the character and the armor suffer damage as described above; otherwise, the armor suffers the damage until it fails a single Damage save, at which point both the character and the armor suffer any remaining damage.
- Acid damage can quickly destroy armor. Armor that fails 1 Damage save against acid damage is broken and armor that fails 2 saves is destroyed.

BANG DAMAGE

- Bang damage does not affect objects or characters who are *deafened.*
- Bang damage ignores Damage Reduction.
- Bang damage tapers off *(see Blast, page 214).*
- Bang damage is not applied to the target's vitality and wounds and cannot prompt Damage saves or inflict critical injuries; rather, it becomes a Fortitude save DC for all characters in range. Any character who fails this save becomes stunned for 1 round and *deafened* for 1d6 rounds.

COLD DAMAGE

- Cold damage immediately becomes subdual damage and also has the following effects.
- Cold damage ignores Damage Reduction.
- When cold damage is inflicted by an extreme environment (i.e. a blizzard), an exposed character makes a Survival check (DC 20). With success, he suffers 1d6 subdual damage every four hours; otherwise, he suffers 1d6 subdual damage every hour.

DIVINE DAMAGE

- Divine damage ignores Damage Reduction.
- When a character suffers divine damage he must also make a Will save (DC equal to the damage inflicted) or become *baffled* for 1d6 rounds.

ELECTRICAL DAMAGE

- Electrical damage ignores Damage Reduction.
- When a character suffers electrical damage he must also make a Fortitude save (DC equal to the damage inflicted) or become *sickened* for 1d6 rounds.

EXPLOSIVE DAMAGE

- Explosive damage tapers off *(see Blast, page 214).*
- Each character within range of explosive damage may make a Reflex save (DC equal to the damage inflicted). With success, he suffers only 1/2 the damage (rounded down, minimum 1).
- Each character who suffers more than 20 points of explosive damage from a single attack becomes *sprawled.*

FIRE DAMAGE

- When a character suffers fire damage, he must also make a Reflex save (DC equal to the damage) or catch fire. While burning, a character suffers the fire's full damage at the start of his Initiative Count each round. Further, he must make a Will save (DC equal to the damage) or immediately run as far out of the fire as possible, drop *prone,* and begin rolling to put himself out. While rolling, a character's fire damage drops by 10 per round until the fire is out.
- Each round that a character or object remains on fire, the GM rolls 1d20 and with a result equal to or lower than the damage the fire spreads to the immediate scenery. Unless put out, a scenery fire spreads 5 ft. in a random direction every round, per the Deviation Diagram *(see page 216).*
- Until put out, any fire — whether on a character or scenery — worsens by 1d6 damage per round.
- Putting out a fire by any means — water, blankets, etc. — decreases a fire's damage by 10 points per round.

FLASH DAMAGE

- Flash damage does not affect objects or characters who are *blinded.*
- Flash damage ignores Damage Reduction.
- Flash damage tapers off *(see Blast, page 214).*
- Flash damage is not applied to the target's vitality and wounds and cannot prompt Damage saves or inflict critical injuries; rather, it becomes a Fortitude save DC for all characters in range. Any character who fails this save becomes *blinded* for 1d6 rounds.

FORCE DAMAGE

- Force damage affects *incorporeal* targets *(see page 213).*

HEAT DAMAGE

- Heat damage immediately becomes subdual damage and also has the following effects.
- Heat damage ignores Damage Reduction.
- When heat damage is inflicted by an extreme environment (i.e. a heat wave), an exposed character makes a Survival check (DC 20). With success, he suffers 1d6 subdual damage every four hours; otherwise, he suffers 1d6 subdual damage every hour.

SNEAK ATTACK DAMAGE

- When a character possesses 1 or more dice of sneak attack damage, he may use them to augment the damage of any Standard Attack or Coup de Grace made against a *flat-footed*, *flanked*, or *helpless* target.
- Sneak attack damage only affects characters who can suffer critical hits, who are not *hidden* from the attacker, and whose vitals are within reach.
- If a single attack generates multiple hits, sneak attack damage is only applied to the first hit.

SONIC DAMAGE

- Sonic damage affects all targets, even *deafened* characters, as its vibrations can literally shred skin and organs.
- Sonic damage ignores Damage Reduction.
- Sonic damage tapers off *(see Blast, page 214)*.
- When a character suffers sonic damage he must also make a Fortitude save (DC equal to the damage inflicted) or become *deafened* for 1d6 rounds.

STRESS DAMAGE

- Stress damage doesn't affect objects.
- Stress damage ignores Damage Reduction.
- For ease of use and because stress damage should be as ubiquitous as the GM wants, stress damage is included in very few places in these rules. Rather, the GM may apply stress damage anytime a character suffers any other damage, or at any point when he feels a character is sufficiently unnerved. When applying stress damage on top of other damage, the GM simply decides whether to apply 1/2 as much stress damage (rounded down), or an equal amount (stress damage is encouraged when a character suffers acid or fire damage, for instance, likely equal to the acid or fire damage suffered). When no other damage is present, the GM simply chooses a single die of any type, as appropriate to the situation, and rolls. The result is the stress damage suffered (d12s and d20s should be reserved for only the most soul-crushing experiences).
- Stress damage is not applied to the target's vitality and wounds and cannot inflict critical injuries; rather, it accumulates over time until it wears off.
- Each time a special character suffers stress damage, he must make a Will save (DC 10 + 1/2 his total stress damage, rounded down). With failure, he becomes *shaken* and his total stress damage resets to 0. If he's already *shaken,* the condition worsens by 1 grade *(see page 213)*. With a critical hit, the character is also *stunned* for 1 round (if the Will save succeeds), or *stunned* for 1d6 rounds (otherwise).
- Outside combat or once all sources of anguish are removed, stress damage wears off at the rate of 1 point per 10 minutes.

Example: During a fierce border skirmish between two rival nations, Brungil witnesses a close friend skewered in a hail of arrows. The GM determines this is harrowing enough to justify a d8 of stress damage and rolls, inflicting 4 points. Brungil must make a Will save (DC 12) and scores a result of 15. He manages to press on. Minutes later, enemy reinforcements arrive with a dragon in their ranks and Brungil charges forth, unsure of anything but the fact that the wyrm must fall. Before he even reaches the foot of the beast it unleashes a hellish blast of flame across the friendly troops, reducing many to ash and setting Brungil alight. The GM rules that Brungil suffers as much stress damage as the attack, which inflicts an incredible 22 points of fire damage. Now at 26 points of stress damage, Brungil must make a Will save with a DC of 23 or become *shaken.* If the dragon's attack is a critical hit, Brungil is also *stunned* for 1 round, or 1d6 rounds if he fails his Will save.

SUBDUAL DAMAGE

- Subdual damage doesn't affect objects.
- Subdual damage is not applied to the target's vitality and wounds and cannot inflict critical injuries; rather, it accumulates over time until it wears off.
- Each time a special character suffers subdual damage, he must make a Fortitude save (DC 10 + 1/2 his total subdual damage, rounded down). With failure, he becomes *fatigued* and his total subdual damage resets to 0. If he's already *fatigued*, the condition worsens by 1 grade *(see page 213)*. With a critical hit, the character is also *stunned* for 1 round (if the Fortitude save succeeds), or *stunned* for 1d6 rounds (otherwise).
- Subdual damage can eventually kill. When an unconscious character suffers subdual damage, the character instead suffers the same amount of lethal damage.
- Outside combat or once all sources of physical strain are removed, subdual damage wears off at the rate of 1 point per 10 minutes.

Example: An orc pummels Brungil, inflicting 18 points of subdual damage and forcing him to make a Fortitude save (DC 19). He succeeds with a result of 21. A couple rounds later he's hit for an additional 4 points of subdual damage and has to make another Fortitude save (DC 21). This time he fails with a result of 18. He becomes *fatigued* and his accumulated subdual damage resets to 0. The very next round the orc performs a Tire action on Brungil, inflicting 5 points of subdual damage. Poor Brungil's save result is only 8 — he needed at least a 12 — and so his *fatigued* condition worsens to *fatigued II.* His accumulated subdual damage resets to 0 again, but if he fails three more saves he's down for the count.

HEALING

After a good beating, the party limps back to town hoping to recuperate. Will they heal before their enemies descend on the hapless hamlet looking for some retribution?

NATURAL HEALING

A standard character loses all accumulated damage at the end of every scene.

A special character regains 1 vitality per Career Level per hour of rest, and 1 wound per day of rest, so long as he restricts himself to light activities during that time (i.e. no combat).

In both cases, this healing occurs even if the character possesses 1 or more critical injuries.

An unconscious character wakes after 2d4 hours of sleep.

ASSISTED HEALING

When targeted with a successful Mend check (DC 15), a stable character heals 2d6 damage (if he's a special character, this is split evenly between subdual, vitality, and wounds, with the patient distributing any uneven excess). A character may only be Mended once per day, no matter how many characters are available to attempt perform the check.

An unconscious character may be awakened with a successful Medicine check (DC 10).

SPENDING ACTION DICE TO HEAL

Outside combat, a standard character may spend and roll any number of action dice to reduce his accumulated damage by the total result of the action dice spent.

Outside combat, a special character may spend and roll any number of action dice to regain vitality or wounds. For each action die spent, the character regains an amount of vitality equal to the action die's result and 2 wounds.

During combat, a character must take a Refresh action before he can spend an action die to regain vitality or wounds *(see page 220).*

An unconscious character may not spend action dice to heal.

CONDITIONS

The life of adventurers is never dull. On a disturbingly regular basis they're tested mentally, physically, and spiritually, and the consequences of these assaults are many and varied. Conditions are a way of easily categorizing large numbers of lingering effects that might plague characters.

Conditions are temporary. Sometimes their durations are defined by the rules that inflict them; other times their durations are fixed in the condition text. Regardless of their stated durations, however, all conditions fade at the end of each adventure.

Some conditions are graded, featuring Roman Numerals (e.g. "I–III"). When a character suffers a graded condition he already has, the condition's grade increases by 1. In all other cases, suffering a condition twice at the same time has no effect.

Unless otherwise specified, the effects of all conditions stack.

Baffled (I–V): The character suffers a –2 penalty with all skill checks per grade he suffers. A character loses 1 *baffled* grade at the end of each scene.

Bleeding: The character suffers 1 point of subdual damage at the end of each round. If he takes 1 or more actions during the round, he suffers 1d4 lethal damage instead. This condition heals at the end of the current scene, but may be eliminated earlier with a successful full-round Medicine check (DC 20).

Blinded: The character is *flat-footed* and cannot see anything. He cannot make skill checks that require sight and suffers a –8 penalty with attack checks. Meanwhile, his opponents gain a +2 bonus when attacking him.

Deafened: The character cannot hear anything and cannot make skill checks that require hearing.

Enraged: The character may not make skill checks and

automatically attacks the nearest conscious opponent with his most damaging attack. If no opponent is close enough to attack during the current round, the character turns on the nearest target, even if it's a friend. Once per round, the character may make a Resolve check (DC 20) to calm himself and lose this condition; otherwise it fades at the end of the current scene. In either case, the character falls unconscious immediately after.

Entangled: The character suffers a –2 penalty with attack checks and a –4 penalty with Dexterity-based skill checks. He may not Refresh or Run, and his Speed drops to 1/2 standard (rounded down).

Fatigued (I–IV + special): The character may not Run. Further, his Speed drops by 5 ft., his Strength score drops by 2, and his Dexterity score drops by 2 per grade he suffers (e.g. at *fatigued II*, a character's Speed drops by 10 ft. and his Strength and Dexterity scores drop by 4 each). If a character with *fatigued IV* is *fatigued* again, he instead falls unconscious. A character loses 1 *fatigued* grade at the end of each scene and for each full hour of sleep.

Fixated: The character may not attack or make skill checks and must take at least 1 Standard Move action per round toward the source of his fixation. Once per round, the character may make a Resolve check (DC 20) to regain composure and lose this condition; otherwise it fades at the end of the current scene. This condition is also lost if the character is attacked by an adversary.

Flanked: A character is *flanked* when 2 opponents stand on directly opposite and adjacent sides of him. While flanking a character, an opponent gains a +2 bonus with attack checks against him.

Flat-Footed: The character loses his Dexterity bonus to Defense (if positive), as well as all dodge bonuses to Defense. He may also be targeted with a variety of special effects, such as sneak attack damage. The *flat-footed* condition is lost when the character takes a half or full action, or is successfully attacked.

Frightened: The character may not attack or make skill checks and must take at least 1 Standard Move action per round away from the source of his fear. Once per round, the character may make a Resolve check (DC 20) to regain composure and lose this condition; otherwise it fades at the end of the current scene.

Held: The character is *flat-footed* and may take no non-free actions except an opposed Athletics check to escape the hold. A character who becomes *held* a second time loses this condition and becomes *pinned.*

Helpless: A character is *helpless* when he is unable to defend himself in any way. Attacks against a *helpless* character gain a +4 bonus. Also, the character may be targeted with a Coup de Grace action *(see page 219)*.

Hidden: A character is hidden from those who don't know his location. They may not attack him, nor may they target him with skill checks that require line of sight. When a *hidden* character attacks an oblivious target within Close Quarters, the target is considered *flat-footed* (even if he isn't otherwise).

Any character aware of a *hidden* character's presence may make an opposed full-round Search check vs. the hidden character's Blend or Sneak (GM's choice) and with success the target character loses the *hidden* condition. A character also loses this condition whenever he casts a spell, makes an attack, or takes any obvious action.

Incorporeal: The character cannot be harmed with physical attacks but is affected by force damage and other non-physical attacks as normal. He may pass through solid objects at will, though force fields and other effects block his movement. This condition doesn't convey any special ability to float or fly, and an incorporeal character must hold his breath when his mouth and nose are blocked. Should a character lose this condition while occupying the same space as another character or object, they merge and all characters in the merged mass are immediately killed.

Invisible: When the character moves at least 10 ft. from his starting position as his last action during a round, he becomes *hidden.*

Paralyzed: The character is *flat-footed* and may only take actions that are purely mental.

Pinned: The character is *flat-footed* and may take no actions except an opposed Athletics check to escape the pin (in which case the character becomes *held* instead). He may be bound with 1 free action and may only speak as the pinning character allows. The pinning character may use him as a human shield, gaining 1/2 personal cover. Finally, each adjacent opponent gains a +4 bonus with attacks targeting the character.

Prone: A character is *prone* when he's intentionally lying on the ground. He may not take Movement actions other than Handle Item and Reposition, though he still gains his Bonus 5-ft. Step if he doesn't take a Movement action. The character gains a +2 bonus to Defense against ranged attacks, but also suffers a –2 penalty with melee attacks.

Shaken (I–IV + special): The character may not take 10 or 20. Further, he suffers a –2 penalty with all attack checks, as well as Charisma- and Wisdom-based skill checks, per grade suffered. If a character with *shaken IV* is *shaken* again, he instead falls unconscious. A character loses 1 *shaken* grade at the end of each scene.

Sickened: The character suffers a –2 penalty with all attacks and skill checks, as well as all damage rolls and saves.

Slowed: The character may take only 1 half action during each round. Further, he suffers a –1 penalty with attack checks and Reflex saves, his Defense decreases by 1, and his Speed drops to 1/2 standard (rounded down).

Sprawled: A character is *sprawled* when he's knocked off his feet. He is *flat-footed* and suffers a –2 penalty with all attack checks. This condition is lost when the character Repositions *(see page 220)*.

Stunned: The character is *flat-footed* and may take no actions.

SPECIAL COMBAT RULES

The following sections cover all the various parts of the combat equation that don't fit well among the basic rules, compartmentalized for easy reference and use.

BLAST

Some attacks affect everything within an area, their damage tapering off over distance. This effect is called "blast." Every blast attack has a base area of effect — a **blast increment** — that's measured in 5-ft. squares, and a center square called **Ground Zero,** which is the square where the blast attack lands or from which it erupts (e.g. a bomb's point of impact). Everything and everyone at Ground Zero suffers the blast's full damage. This damage drops by 1/2 (rounded down) within each blast increment out from Ground Zero, until the damage drops below 1 point, at which point it tapers off entirely.

Blast can also take the shape of a cone. The damage still tapers off over distance, though only in one direction.

For examples of circular and conical blast, see below.

COVER

When a character's line of sight to a target is partially blocked, that target benefits from cover. All cover is rated in quarters (1/4 cover, 1/2 cover, 3/4 cover, and total cover) and offers a bonus to the target's Defense from attacks from beyond the cover, as well as Reflex saves made to avoid attacks and damage from beyond the cover, as shown on Table 5.2: Cover *(see page 215).*

At any time, a character may only benefit from the best each of two types of cover: **personal cover** (cover available in his square or gained from gear or character options) and **scenery cover** (cover available from intervening obstacles). These cover values are added together to determine the character's actual cover from attacks and damage.

Example: Brungil squats behind the ruins of a fortress wall (1/4 cover) at the other side of several large trees from an attacker (1/2 cover). He benefits from 3/4 cover against that attacker.

DEVIATION

When a character misses with an attack or weapon that is subject to deviation (such as a thrown vial of acid), the shot deviates a random number of 5-ft. squares from the target. The die rolled to determine this distance is based on the number of range increments between the character and his target, as shown

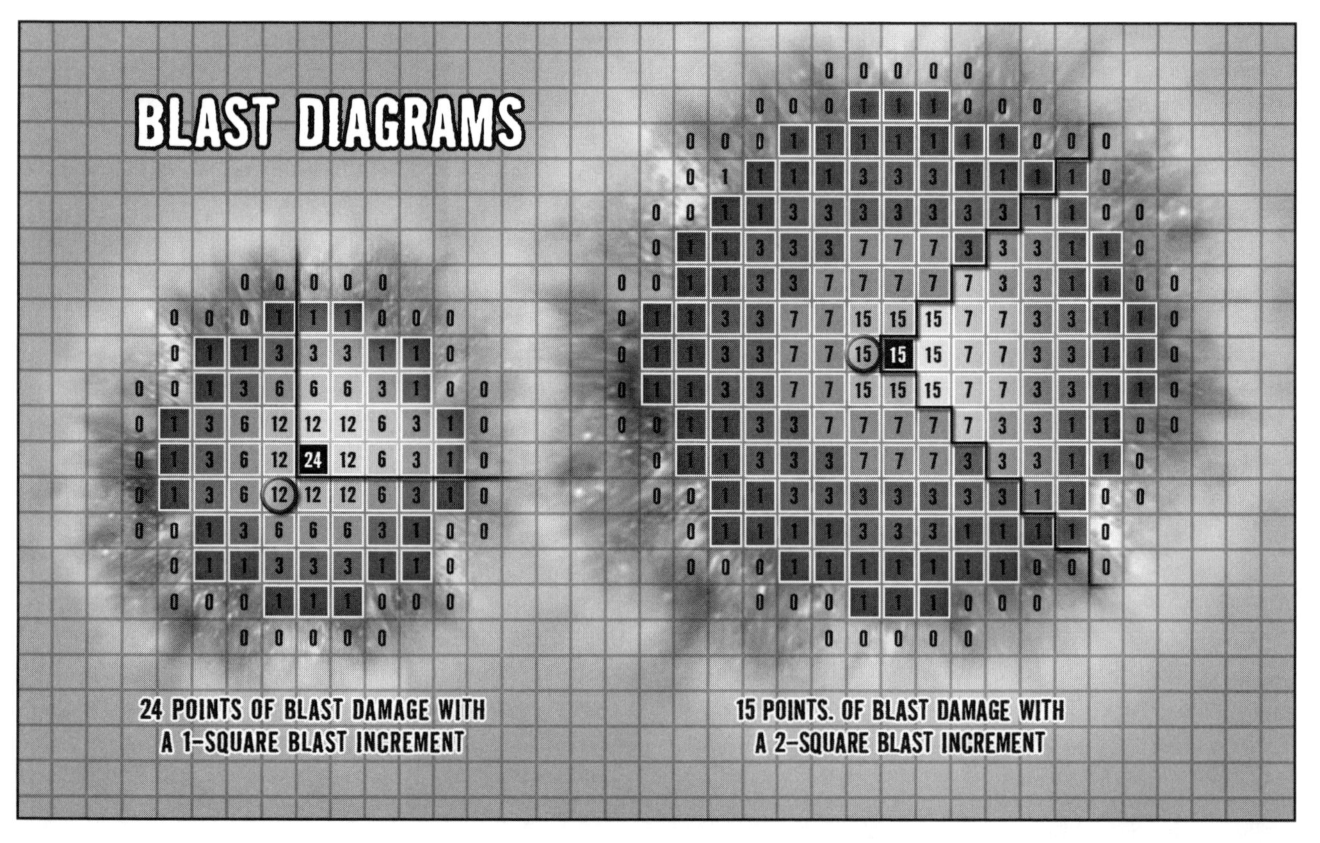

Black squares are Ground Zero. Cone effects are illustrated by areas blocked out with hard black lines and the circled squares behind Ground Zero are the locations of casters when these cone effects are spells.

Table 5.2: Cover

Cover	Examples	Defense Bonus	Reflex Bonus
One-quarter (1/4)	Short wall that protects up to knees	+2	+1
One-half (1/2)	Corner that protects all but half of the torso and head; window that reveals down to waist	+4	+2
Three-quarters (3/4)	Corner or narrow opening that protects all but part of the head	+6	+3
Total	Solid wall that protects entire body	Attack impossible	+4

on Table 5.3: Deviation *(see page 216)*. To determine the direction of deviation, roll 1d8 and consult the Deviation Diagram *(see page 216)*.

If this deviation causes the shot to hit something else, damage is applied as standard.

FALLING

Normally, a character suffers 1d6 lethal damage per 10 ft. fallen (max. 20d6) and automatically becomes *sprawled* when he lands. However, a falling character may make an Acrobatics check (DC 20), and with success he suffers only 1/2 the damage (rounded down, minimum 1 per 10 ft. fallen).

Damage Reduction has no effect on falling damage.

MOUNTED CHARACTERS

The development of cavalry is one of the greatest innovations in the history of warfare. The combined strength and speed of a trained mount with the cunning and weaponry of an experienced rider is a powerful asset on any battlefield, able to casually sweep aside many other combatants. Mounted warfare is similarly devastating in *Fantasy Craft* and in some ways more so, given the possibilities to be had with griffons, drakes, and more!

During combat, a rider and his mount are treated as a single "mounted character." This character's Size is equal to the larger of the pair (usually the mount) and it benefits from all the mount's movement options and Speed values. It uses the lower of the pair's Defense, Initiative, and Saving Throw bonuses but the higher of the pair's Damage Reduction and Resistances. The mounted character's attack and skill bonuses are determined by the half of the pair that performs each action. When it isn't clear whether to use the rider or mount's stats, use those of the mount.

A mounted character may take 1 full action or 2 half actions per round — the mount and rider do *not* act separately or gain additional actions. The mounted character can use these actions to do anything either of the pair can. If only one of the pair is a special character that character makes all decisions, but if both are standard or special characters they must agree on actions taken. When an equal pair can't decide in a reasonable amount of time, they revert to separate characters (one a passenger on the other).

A mounted character's ability to withstand damage is likewise not combined — damage is applied separately to each half of the pair. By default when a mounted character is hit, the rider chooses whether the damage is applied to him or the mount, though the attacker can spend 2 action dice to make the choice instead.

A mounted character suffers a –2 penalty with melee and unarmed attacks, and a –4 penalty with Spellcasting and ranged attacks.

Finally, when fighting a mounted character, an attacker can use a special variant of the Trip action *(see page 221)*. With success, the attacker upsets the mount, which throws the rider. Both characters become *sprawled* and the rider is moved to any unoccupied 5-ft. area adjacent to the mount (his choice). This effect replaces the Trip action's standard benefit. Keep in mind that Trip actions are modified by the relative Size between attacker and target, and that a mounted pair is often the bigger of the two.

Most of these rules also apply when a character uses a vehicle, such as a chariot *(see page 169)*.

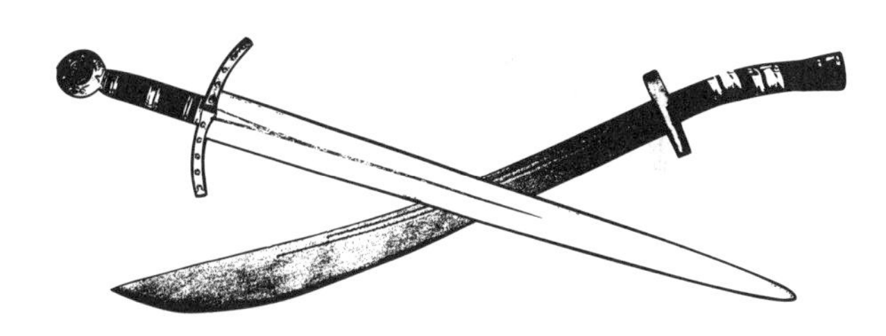

ONE- AND TWO-HANDED WEAPONS

In *Fantasy Craft,* all weapons are either 1-handed or 2-handed. A character may hold one 1-handed weapon in each hand, but this does *not* grant him any additional attacks. Each time he may make an attack, he may use the weapon in either hand.

A character of Medium or larger Size may use a 2-handed weapon with one hand, but suffers a –4 penalty with his attack check. Conversely, a character may hold a 1-handed weapon with both hands, in which case his Strength score increases by 2 when determining damage.

A character may only wield weapons of his Size or smaller. Weapons may be scaled up or down in Size with the large-scale and small-scale upgrades *(see page 184)*.

POISON AND DISEASE

Little compares to the horror of a lurking killer you can't see or fight, stealing your life by the minute. It's every adventurer's worst nightmare: that his body might turn against him, stealing glory to leaving him an enfeebled, withering husk. Poisons and disease can change worlds, killing kings and toppling nations, but they're also some of the most dangerous tools in the GM's adventure toolbox. Most players resent helplessness and outside the hunt for an antidote there isn't much a party can do to combat the spread. Game Masters are advised to keep deadly and disabling contagions in the background most of the time, using them primarily as flavor. When specific effects must be determined, however, here are the rules.

Poisons and diseases can be inhaled, ingested, absorbed through the skin, or applied to weapons. Each has an Incubation Period, during which time it spreads through a character's system. Thereafter, and at the end of each subsequent Incubation Period, he makes a Fortitude save (DC 12). With success, he fights the contagion off entirely; otherwise, he suffers the listed effects. This process continues until the character fights off the contagion or dies. Antidotes are specific to each contagion and spread through the system over a period of time equal to the Incubation Period (during which the character may still have to make another Fortitude save).

Fantasy Craft details common poisons in Chapter 4 *(see page 165)*, and common diseases in Chapter 7 *(see page 341)*.

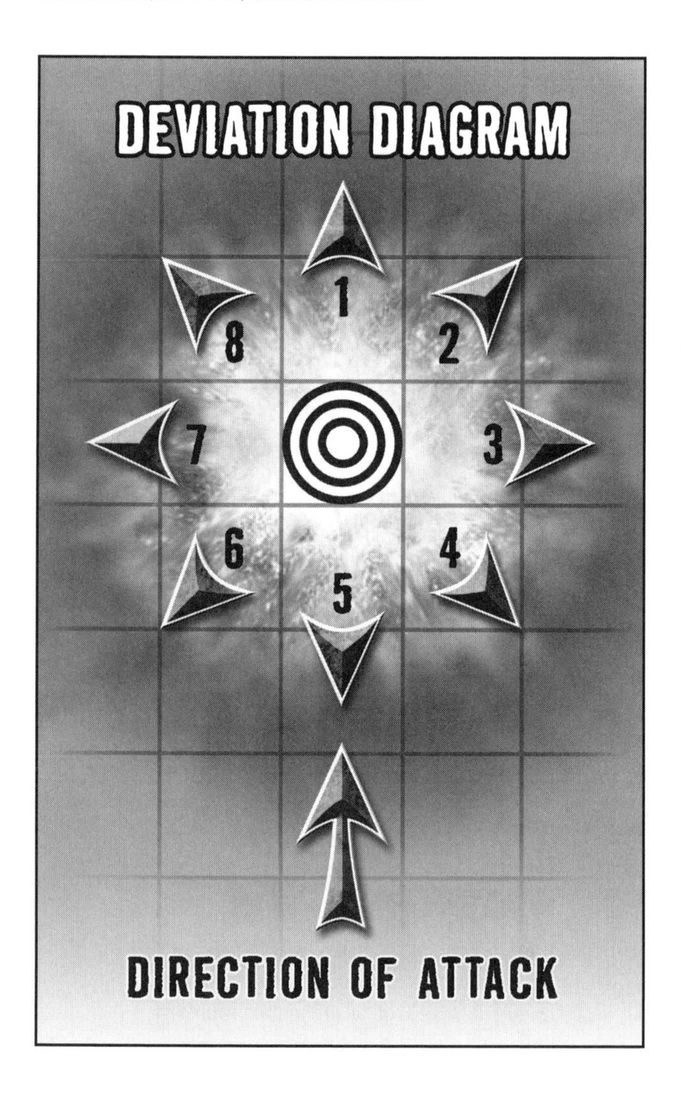

SAVING THROWS

Most of the time when a character resists an effect, he makes a "saving throw," or "save." There are three types of saves, each with its own bonus and uses *(see page 61)*.

Saves are made as directed by the GM or the rules. When a rule calls for a save, the DC and other pertinent information is provided. When the GM calls for a save, he determines the DC based on the relevant rules or the difficulty of resisting the effect, with 15 representing a routine save and 40 representing a nearly impossible one.

The player rolls 1d20 and adds his appropriate save bonus to obtain a saving throw result. If this equals or exceeds the DC, the character resists; otherwise, he suffers the full effect. In most cases, a successful save either negates the effect or reduces it to 1/2 standard, though many other results are possible, as noted in each save description or directed by the GM.

All Reflex saving throws are subject to Defense Penalties from armor *(see page 173)*.

SIZE

The physical profiles of characters, scenery, animals, and objects vary widely but everything in the universe — including weapons — uses the same Size scale, as shown on Table 5.4: Size *(see page 217)*. Size has a couple mechanical effects, as follows.

Defense: This modifier is applied to the Defense of characters and objects. It may not reduce Defense below 1.

Footprint: This is the space a character or object takes up, presented as a range in 5-ft. × 5-ft. squares. A character or object's Footprint determines the maximum number of characters that can attack (no more than one per adjacent square). Creatures and objects of Large or bigger Size likely have unique footprints (e.g. a typical horse has a 1 × 2 footprint). Unique footprints are listed in Chapters 4 and 6 and more may be introduced with ease.

Table 5.3: DEVIATION

Range Increments to Target	1–2	3–4	5–6	7–8	9–10
Deviation Distance	1d2	1d4	1d6	1d8	1d10

Table 5.4: SIZE

Size	Defense	Maximum Footprint	Example Object/Scenery	Example Creature
Nuisance (N)	+16	32 per square	Ring	Housefly
Fine (F)	+8	16 per square	Vial	Sparrow
Diminutive (D)	+4	8 per square	Dagger	Pigeon
Tiny (T)	+2	4 per square	Machete	Eagle
Small (S)	+1	2 per square	Long sword	Goblin
Medium (M)	+0	1 square	Claymore	Human
Large (L)	–1	3 × 3 squares	Ballista	Bear
Huge (H)	–2	6 × 6 squares	Trebuchet	Hydra
Gargantuan (G)	–4	12 × 12 squares	Siege Tower	Ancient Red Dragon
Colossal (C)	–8	25 × 25 squares	Galley	Kraken
Enormous (E)	–16	50 × 50 squares	Frigate	Kaiju Creature
Vast (V)	–32	Larger than 50 × 50 squares	Mansion	Nothing Yet Discovered

Other Effects of Size: Beyond Defense and Footprint, Size impacts a number of statistics and rules, including wounds *(see pages 9 and 230)*, carrying capacity *(see page 154)*, the armor and weapons a character can use *(see pages 173, 176, and 215)*, natural attacks *(see page 237)*, hiding *(see page 71)*, and the use and effects of certain actions *(see page 218)*. NPC Size is handled in its own section *(see page 226)*.

Squeezing: A character may move through a space of at least 1/2 his Footprint (rounded up). While doing so he's *flat-footed*, loses dodge bonuses to Defense, and moves at 1/2 normal Speed (rounded down, to a minimum of 10 ft.).

STARVATION AND THIRST

An active character needs 3 common meals each day *(see page 165)*. At the start of the 4th and each subsequent day a character goes without this minimum sustenance, he makes a Fortitude save (DC 10 + 1 per previous save). With failure, he becomes *fatigued* and suffers 1d6 lethal damage + an additional 1d4 lethal damage per day he's gone without food. The character may not lose the *fatigued* condition until he consumes at least 1 day's necessary nourishment.

Likewise, an active character requires 1 quart of fluids per day, or 2 quarts per day when exposed to any heat over 90° F. At the start of each day a character goes without these minimum fluids, he makes a Fortitude save (DC 10 + 1 per previous save). With failure, he becomes *fatigued* and suffers 1d6 lethal damage + an additional 1d4 lethal damage per day he's gone without fluids. The character may not lose the *fatigued* condition until he drinks at least 1 day's necessary fluids.

SUFFOCATION

A character may hold his breath for a number of rounds equal to his Constitution score. At the start of each round thereafter, he makes a Fortitude save (DC 10 + 1 per previous save). With failure, his vitality drops to 0 (if he's a special character), or he falls unconscious (if he's standard). At the start of his Initiative Count during the following round, the character must start breathing if he's able. If not, his wounds drop to 0 (if he's a special character) and he begins to die regardless of his type.

TERMINAL SITUATIONS

Characters sometimes find themselves in appalling peril. They fall from dizzying heights. They're at the center of firestorms cast down by gods. They find assassins standing beside their beds in the morning, holding knives to their throats. *Fantasy Craft* calls these "Terminal Situations."

Outside combat only, the GM may declare that any situation from which a character cannot logically escape is a Terminal Situation. Until the situation passes, any opponents within Melee Range may spend 1 action die to cause the victim to either fall unconscious or die, as appropriate to the circumstances at hand.

UNDERWATER COMBAT

While underwater, a character possessing 4 or fewer ranks in Athletics suffers a –2 penalty with all attack checks, Reflex saves, and skill checks (except Athletics checks made to swim). Also, the blast increment of any explosive set off underwater is doubled. Swimmers don't suffer these penalties *(see page 227)*.

VISION AND HEARING

A character can see up to 10 visual range increments (each equal to his Wisdom score × 10 ft.), hear up to 10 hearing range increments (each equal to his Wisdom score × 5 ft.), and smell up to 10 scent range increments (each equal to his Wisdom score × 1 ft.). Various character options and circumstances modify these base range increments, as shown on Table 5.5: Vision and Hearing *(see page 218)*.

While conditions reduce a character's vision increment to 0 ft. or below he is *blinded*, and while conditions reduce a character's hearing increment to 0 ft. or below he is *deafened*.

Vision and hearing also affect many skill checks, including Blend and Sneak *(see pages 71 and 82, respectively)*. Ambient light also applies a modifier to Defense, as shown on Table 5.5: Vision and Hearing *(see page 218)*.

Table 5.5: VISION AND HEARING

Circumstance	Visual Increment	Hearing Increment	Defense
Ambient Light			
None (e.g. pitch black)	Drops to 0 ft.	+0 ft.	+8
Faint (e.g. moonlight)	–40 ft.	+0 ft.	+4
Dim (e.g. dawn, dusk, or torchlight)	–20 ft.	+0 ft.	+2
Bright (e.g. daylight)	+0 ft.	+0 ft.	+0
Intense (e.g. Glow II spell)	+40 ft.	+0 ft.	–2
Ambient Noise			
None (e.g. dead of night)	+0 ft.	+20 ft.	—
Faint (e.g. nearby conversation)	+0 ft.	+0 ft.	—
Moderate (e.g. busy tavern)	+0 ft.	–10 ft.	—
Heavy (e.g. passing wagon)	+0 ft.	–20 ft.	—
Extreme (e.g. battlefield)	+0 ft.	–40 ft.	—

ACTIONS

Actions are key to elevating any combat beyond the sum of its parts. They expand combat beyond merely bashing or stabbing and ensure that everyone can contribute. Every action operates a little differently, but they're all equally simple to use. Beneath each action's name line are two items in bold — the number of free, half, or full actions required and the category into which the action falls. There are three categories: Attack, Initiative, and Movement. A character may perform only 1 action at any time.

Some actions may be taken outside combat, as noted in their descriptions and elsewhere in the rules. The GM is also encouraged to call for them anytime they're appropriate.

STANDARD ATTACK

1 Half Action • Attack Action

The character makes 1 attack against 1 target.

STANDARD MOVE

1 Half Action • Movement Action

The character moves up to his Speed in feet.

AIM

1 Half Action • Initiative Action

The character takes a moment to steady his attacks against an opponent. So long as the target does not move more than 5 ft. in any single round, the character gains a +1 bonus with all Standard Attack checks made against him. A character may only aim at 1 target at a time.

ANTICIPATE

1 Half Action • Initiative Action

The character attempts to second-guess an opponent's upcoming actions. With a successful Sense Motive check (DC 10 + the target's base attack bonus), the character gains a Defense dodge bonus against the target's attacks equal to the character's Wisdom modifier (min. +1). This effect lasts for 1 full round.

A character may only benefit from 1 Anticipate Action at any time.

BULL RUSH

1 Full Action • Attack Action

The character attempts to shove an opponent in a straight line. He moves up to his Speed directly toward 1 opponent whose Size may be up to 1 category bigger than his own. When he enters the opponent's square, the characters make an opposed Athletics check. If the bullrusher is mounted or operating a personal vehicle he uses the Ride skill instead. The bigger combatant gains a +2 bonus with this check per Size category of difference between them.

If the bullrusher loses this opposed check, he moves back 5 ft. and becomes *sprawled;* otherwise, his opponent is pushed directly back 5 ft. + an additional 5 ft. per 4 points of difference between the results, after which he becomes *sprawled.* If this path is obstructed, the following occurs.

- An obstructing character makes an Athletics check against the bullrusher's Athletics result. If he wins, all movement ends and the bullrusher becomes *sprawled;* otherwise, the obstructing character becomes *sprawled* in a random adjacent square (using the Deviation Diagram) and the Bull Rush continues past him. With either result, everyone involved suffers the bullrusher's unarmed damage.

- An obstructing object makes a Damage save against the bullrusher's Athletics result. With success, all movement ends and the bullrusher becomes *sprawled;* otherwise, the Bull Rush punches through the obstructing object and continues past it. With either result, the bullrusher and his opponent both suffer the bullrusher's unarmed damage.

COUP DE GRACE

1 Full Action • Attack Action

The character takes advantage of an adjacent and *helpless* opponent's vulnerability. He may knock the opponent unconscious or inflict 1 automatic critical hit against him at no action die cost. If he chooses the second option and the opponent survives, the opponent must also make a Fortitude save (DC 10 + the damage inflicted) or die.

DELAY

1 Free Action • Initiative Action

The character waits to see what other combatants do by voluntarily reducing his Initiative Count by 1. He may take this action a number of times per round equal to his Initiative bonus + 10, at which point he must act or forfeit his chance to act during the current round. Once the character acts, his Initiative Count resets to its value at the start of the round.

DISARM

1 Half Action • Attack Action

The character attempts to disarm an opponent. The opponent must be within the character's Reach (he's unarmed or using a melee weapon), or within Close Quarters (if he's using a ranged weapon). The characters make an opposed Standard Attack check. If either character is holding his weapon with both hands he gains an additional +4 bonus. Also, the character with the bigger weapon gains a +4 bonus per Size category of difference (an unarmed character's "weapon" is 2 Size categories smaller than him). If the character wins, the opponent is disarmed and his weapon lands in an adjacent square (per the Deviation Diagram); otherwise, the disarming character becomes *flat-footed.*

DISTRACT

1 Half Action • Initiative Action

The character tries to draw an opponent's attention, keeping him from reacting quickly. He makes a Bluff (Dex) check opposed by the opponent's Sense Motive. If the character wins, the opponent's Initiative Count drops by 2d6 for this round only; otherwise, the distracting character becomes *flat-footed.*

A character may only be targeted with 1 Distract action during each round.

FEINT

1 Half Action • Attack Action

The character attempts to dupe an adjacent opponent with a false action, leaving him vulnerable to a different one. He makes a Prestidigitation check opposed by the opponent's Notice. If the character wins, his opponent becomes *flat-footed;* otherwise, the feinting character becomes *flat-footed.*

A character may only be targeted with 1 Feint action during each round.

GRAPPLE

1 Full Action • Unarmed/1-Handed Melee Attack Action

The character tries to wrestle an adjacent opponent whose Size may be no larger than 1 category bigger than his own. He steps into the target's square and they make an opposed Athletics check. The **smaller** character gains a +2 bonus per Size category of difference. If the character wins, both combatants remain in the square and the opponent becomes *held*; otherwise, the character is pushed back into his original square and becomes *flat-footed.*

The character may release the opponent at any time as a free action but until he does he remains *flat-footed.* Further, any combatants may move through adjacent squares without restriction. Finally, the only non-free action any grapple participant may take is an opposed full-action Athletics check, with the **bigger** character gaining a +2 bonus per Size category of difference. The winner of this check may pin the opponent or choose 1 Grapple benefit *(see next).*

Up to 2 characters may grapple a smaller opponent, up to 4 characters may grapple an opponent of the same Size, and up to 8 characters may grapple a larger target. In all cases, the cooperative check rules are used to determine the results *(see page 66).*

GRAPPLE BENEFITS

Break Free: The winner escapes or helps another character escape. If *pinned,* the character becomes *held.* If *held,* the character exits the grapple and moves into an unoccupied adjacent square (this option is unavailable when no squares are open).

Disarm: The winner forces 1 grapple opponent to drop 1 weapon in the grapple square.

Handle Item: The winner draws or uses a 1-handed weapon or object, dropping another in the grapple square if he carried one. This item may come from his inventory or that of another character in the grapple, so long as it's readily accessible. This option may be used to unbuckle a character's armor, decreasing its DR to 1/2 standard (rounded down) until the opponent spends 1 half action outside the grapple to adjust it.

Injure: The winner inflicts his unarmed damage or a held 1-handed weapon's damage upon 1 grapple opponent.

Grapple Second Opponent (Held Only): The winner moves the grapple into an adjacent square and targets the second opponent therein with a Grapple action. A character suffers a –4 penalty with all Athletics checks when grappling or holding 2 opponents, and no character may attempt to grapple more than two opponents at a time.

Move: The winner moves the grapple into an adjacent square (if holding an opponent) or up to his Speed (if pinning an opponent).

Screaming Club (Pinned Opponent Only): The winner picks up 1 smaller grapple opponent and uses him to make 1 melee attack. The opponent is treated as a club of his Size and with a hit both the target and the grapple opponent suffer the appropriate damage.

Sprawl: The winner goes *prone* and forces 1 grapple opponent to become *sprawled.*

Throw: The winner tosses 1 grapple opponent into an unoccupied adjacent square, inflicting his unarmed damage + an additional amount of damage equal to his Strength bonus (min. +1). The opponent leaves the grapple and becomes *sprawled.*

Use Opponent's Weapon (Pinned Only): The winner uses a grapple opponent's 1-handed weapon to inflict damage on any 1 character in the grapple (this may be the weapon's owner).

HANDLE ITEM

1 Half Action • Movement Action

The character draws, sheaths, picks up, or manipulates one weapon or object (dropping an item is a free action).

MOUNT/DISMOUNT

Full Action • Movement Action

The character assumes control of a vehicle or trained mount. This requires no skill check if the character is adjacent to the animal or vehicle; otherwise, the character may move up to his Speed to reach the animal or vehicle (as part of this action), but in this case he may only mount or board with a successful Acrobatics check (DC 15).

When a mount is unwilling, the character must target it with a Grapple check. Achieving a *held* result gets the character on the mount, at which point the opposed skill check becomes Survival. Should the character achieve a *pinned* result, the mount calms enough for him to ride it, though the GM may at any time spend 1 action die to remind the mount what it disliked about the proceedings and resume the grapple with the mount *held.* While a mount is resisting, it moves and acts per the GM's discretion and may lead the character through difficult areas to try and buck him.

PUMMEL

1 Full Action • Unarmed Attack Action

The character attempts to beat an adjacent opponent senseless, possibly knocking him unconscious. He makes an unarmed Standard Attack check against the opponent and with a hit he inflicts triple his unarmed damage as subdual damage.

Pummel has a special application outside combat. The subdual damage from the first — and *only* the first — Pummel action against each character made out of combat in each scene is applied normally, except that the target suffers 1 grade of *fatigued* per 5 by which he fails this save *(see page 211).*

Special: This action may *never* inflict lethal damage.

READY

1 Full Action • Initiative Action

The character prepares a half action and a trigger that prompts that action (e.g. attacking the first monster through a door). If the trigger is another character's action, the acting character's Ready action occurs first (e.g. the character attacks the monster *as* it passes through the door, not after). If the trigger doesn't occur during the current round, the character loses any remaining chances to act, and his Ready action and trigger remain active until the start of his Initiative Count during the following round.

REFRESH

1 Full Round • Initiative Action

The character takes a breath and possibly patches up some minor injuries. He cannot be suffering from any conditions to take this action, and he forfeits his chance to act during the current round. Unless he's targeted by 1 or more attacks before the start of his Initiative Count during the following round, the character may at that point spend and roll 1 action die. A special character recovers 2 wounds and an amount of vitality equal to the die's result, while a standard character reduces his accumulated damage by the result. If the character is targeted by any attacks during this period (whether they hit or not), he may *not* spend the die and still loses his chance to act.

A character may spend *only* 1 action die to heal per uninterrupted Refresh action.

REPOSITION

1 Half Action • Movement Action

The character assumes a different position. He stands or drops *prone,* becoming *flat-footed* in the process.

RUN

1 Full Action • Movement Action

The character breaks into a full sprint. If wearing full armor, he may move up to 3× his Speed; otherwise, he may move up to 4× his Speed. A character may only Run in a straight line and becomes *flat-footed* after taking this action.

TAUNT

1 Half Action • Attack Action

The character attempts to goad an opponent into attacking him. The opponent must be within Close Quarters. The characters make an opposed Sense Motive check. If the character wins, the opponent must attack him with his next available action (unless he physically can't); otherwise, the opponent may act freely during his next action but also gains a +1 bonus with his next attack against the character during the current combat.

THREATEN

1 Half Action • Attack Action

The character tries to humiliate an opponent within Close Quarters. The character makes an Intimidate check opposed by the opponent's Resolve. If the character wins, the opponent suffers 1d6 stress damage; otherwise, the opponent gains a +1 bonus with his next attack against the character during the current combat.

TIRE

1 Half Action • Attack Action

The character tries to force an adjacent target onto the defensive. He and his target make an opposed Resolve check. If the character wins, the opponent suffers 1d6 subdual damage that ignores Damage Reduction and Resistances; otherwise, the character becomes *flat-footed.*

TOTAL DEFENSE

1 Full Action • Movement Action

The character focuses exclusively on defending himself. He may take 1 Standard Move action and gains a +4 dodge bonus to Defense for 1 full round.

TRIP

1 Half Action • Attack Action

The character attempts to trip an adjacent opponent whose Size may be no larger than 1 category bigger than his own. The characters make an opposed Acrobatics check. The bigger character gains a +2 bonus per Size category of difference. If the character wins, the opponent becomes *sprawled;* otherwise, the tripping character becomes *flat-footed.*

ADVANCED ACTIONS AND TRICKS

Where standard actions are available to everyone, *advanced* actions are reserved for those who devote special attention to tailoring a personal combat style. They let characters divert weapons training time into developing a customized set of specialized maneuvers. Most of these maneuvers operate like actions, though many also require a character to have a forte with the weapon category to use them.

Also included in this group are "tricks," which are ways to modify actions for various results. You may apply a single trick to any action listed in the trick's description. You may *not* apply more than 1 trick to any action.

Each advanced action or trick costs 1 weapon proficiency *(see page 28).*

ARROW CUTTING

Initiative Action (Forte): The character tries to 'cut a projectile out of the air' the instant before it hits him. While armed with a melee weapon, once per round after the character's been hit by a bow or hurled attack but before damage is rolled, he may make a Reflex save (DC equal to the attack check result). With success, the damage drops to 0 (though any special effects from the attack are still felt). The character may take this action a number of times per combat equal to the number of Melee Combat feats he has (min. 1).

CALLED SHOT

Attack Trick: The character attempts to find a chink in a target's armor. He suffers a –3 attack check penalty if the target is wearing partial armor, a –6 penalty if the target is wearing moderate armor, or a –9 penalty if the target is wearing full armor. With a hit, the attack ignores any Damage Reduction provided by the target's armor.

CHEAP SHOT

Attack Trick: The character attempts to exploit an opponent's obvious weakness. He chooses 1 of the opponent's attributes or the opponent's Speed and makes his attack check, suffering a –4 penalty. With a hit, the opponent suffers a –2 penalty with all attack and skill checks using the chosen attribute, or a –10 ft. penalty to his Speed, until the end of the scene. With a miss, the character becomes *flat-footed.* Each combatant may suffer from only 1 successful Cheap Shot per scene.

FORCED OPENING

Melee Attack Trick (Forte): The character makes a risky attack to spin an opponent about and disorient him. While attacking with a 2-handed melee weapon and not *flat-footed,* the character may increase his error range by 2 to cause the target to become *flanked* for 1 full round. With a miss, the character becomes *flat-footed* at the end of his current Initiative Count.

FULLY ENGAGED

Melee or Unarmed Attack Trick (Forte): The character punishes an opponent who ignores him. When an opponent has been adjacent to the character for at least 1 round and not attacked him since his last Initiative Count, the character may roll damage twice, keeping the result he prefers.

DAUNTING SHOT

Ranged Attack Trick (Forte): The character's shots upset the target's courage. With a hit, in addition to suffering normal damage, the target suffers a –2 morale penalty with attacks targeting the character. This effect lasts until the target successfully attacks the character.

MIX-UP

Trick: The character is full of surprises, calling upon techniques when they're least expected. He chooses one of the following actions when he gains this trick: Anticipate, Bull Rush, Disarm, Distract, Feint, Grapple, Pummel, Taunt, Threaten, Tire, or Trip. Once per round, when the character hasn't taken the chosen action during the last 3 rounds, he may take it and gain a +3 morale bonus with the first attack or skill check it requires.

Special: This trick may be gained multiple times, each time for a different action.

PARRY

Initiative Action (Forte): The character uses his hands or weapon to knock an incoming attack aside. Once per round when the character's not *flat-footed,* after he's been hit by a melee or unarmed attack but before damage is rolled, he may make a Reflex save (DC equal to the attack check result). With success, the damage drops to 0 (though any special effects from the attack are still felt). The character may take this action a number of times per combat equal to the number of Melee Combat feats he has (min. 1).

RAGGED WOUND

Melee Attack Trick (Forte): The character angles for a long, bloody slash. When making an attack, he may increase his error range by 1 and decrease his damage by 2 to grant his weapon the *bleed* quality.

RELENTLESS ATTACK

Attack Trick: The character focuses completely on one opponent, keeping the pressure on until an attack gets through. If the character's last attack was also against the current opponent and missed, he gains a +2 bonus with this attack.

SALT THE WOUND

Attack Trick (Forte): The character uses an opponent's injuries against him. When he attacks an opponent who has the *bleeding* condition, he inflicts an additional 1d6 damage.

SHIELD BLOCK

Initiative Action: The character uses his shield to absorb what might otherwise be a solid hit. Once per round when the character has a readied shield and isn't *flat-footed,* after he's hit by an unarmed or melee attack but before damage is rolled, he may make a Fortitude save (DC equal to the attack check result). With success, the attack's damage drops to 0 (though any special effects from the attack are still felt). The character may take this action a number of times per combat equal to the number of Melee Combat feats he has (min. 1).

SHOVE

Melee or Unarmed Attack Trick (Forte): The character uses an attack's momentum to drive his opponent back. With a hit against a target of equal or smaller Size, the character pushes the target back 5 ft. He may follow to remain adjacent to the target or stay in his current location.

STEADY SHOT

Bow or Hurled Attack Trick (Forte): The character parlays familiarity with his surroundings into a deadly barrage. If he hasn't moved from his current location in the last 2 rounds, he gains a +2 bonus with bow and hurled attack checks.

TRIUMPHANT SWING

Melee Attack Trick: Feeling the tide of battle turning in his favor gives the character the will to fight on. While attacking a special opponent, the character may increase his error range by 3, recovering 1d6 vitality with a hit. With a miss, the character becomes *flat-footed* at the end of his current Initiative Count. The character may use this trick a number of times per combat equal to the number of Melee Combat feats he has (min. 1).

VENOM MASTER

Attack Trick: Poisoned weapons are very dangerous in the character's hands. When he makes an attack with the *poisonous* or *venomous* quality, he may raise his error range by 1 to lower the poison's first Incubation Period to Instant. With a miss, the character becomes *flat-footed* at the end of his current Initiative Count. The character may apply this trick a number of times per combat equal to the number of Covert feats he has (min. 1).

WARDING STRIKE

Melee Attack Trick (Forte): The character claims his ground, daring anyone to force him from it. After one or more hits, the character gains a +2 morale bonus with Fortitude and Reflex saves until he leaves his current square.

WHIRLING STRIKE

Melee Attack Trick: The character attacks with overwhelming speed. While attacking with two or more 1-handed melee weapons, the character may increase his error range by 2 to set the attack's minimum damage to his Dexterity modifier (min. 1), even with a miss. The character may take this action a number of times per combat equal to the number of Melee Combat feats he possesses (min. 1).

RESTRICTED ACTIONS

Finally, restricted actions are available only through specific character options and rules, as noted in their bolded action lines. These actions include powerful Species abilities, benefits of special class training, and more.

GAZE ATTACK

1 Half Action • Ranged Attack Action • Requires Gaze Attack

Gaze attacks are made with just a glance and have many different effects, from petrifying targets to driving them away in fear. They require no proficiency or gear, and ignore Size modifiers to Defense. Gaze attacks may only be made within a distance equal to 1/2 of one visual range increment (rounded up), and automatically miss *blinded, hidden,* and *invisible* targets.

Finally, a special critical failure is possible with any gaze attack: if a mirrored surface is located within the attacker's line of sight when he suffers an error, an opponent may spend 4 action dice to cause the attacker to view his own reflection, suffering the gaze attack's effects. When a gaze attack's target wields a mirror or other smooth reflective surface, this cost decreases to only 1 action die.

A character may only make 1 gaze attack at a time; when he possesses more than one gaze attack, he chooses one each time he takes this action.

SWALLOW

Grapple Benefit • Requires Swallow Natural Attack

With a critical success during a Grapple Athletics check, the character may use 1 Grapple benefit to consume a target 2 or more Sizes smaller than himself, inflicting his Swallow natural attack damage in the process. The grapple ends and the victim is subject to suffocation *(see page 217)*. The victim cannot act except to make an opposed Athletics or attack check to escape. The character suffers a –2 penalty with all attack and skill checks until his new meal escapes or expires (and stops struggling).

Should the victim win an opposed check to escape, he exits the character's gullet, inflicting his unarmed or weapon damage along the way. Until then, however, he suffers the character's Swallow damage at the end of each round.

A character digests 1 swallowed target every 12 hours and may not add a new meal beforehand, though he could voluntarily throw a previous victim up with 1 full action so he could enjoy a new delicacy.

TRAMPLE

1 Full Action • Unarmed Attack Action • Requires Trample Natural Attack

The character moves up to his Speed through areas occupied by targets 2 or more Sizes smaller. He doesn't have to stop when he moves past or through conscious opponents, though he does have to end his movement in an unoccupied area. At the end of the character's movement, he makes a single Trample attack and the result is compared to the Defense of each opponent run over during the move. The second and each subsequent opponent gains a cumulative +2 bonus to defense against this attack (+2 for the second, +4 for the third, and so on). Damage is rolled separately for each opponent hit. Targets hit by this attack must also make a Fortitude save (DC equal to the damage) or become *sprawled.*

TURN

1 Full Action • Attack Action • Requires Turning Ability

'Turning' is the process of willfully or spiritually rebuking a target, attacking its will to fight. Each turning ability targets only 1 Alignment or NPC Type (e.g. construct, undead, etc.), having no effect on other Alignments or Types.

When a character uses a turn ability, each qualifying NPC within 30 ft. makes a Will save (DC 10 + 1/2 the character's Resolve bonus, rounded up). Mobs make only 1 save each for the whole unit. Special characters can partially resist turning actions, gaining a +4 bonus with their save.

With success, a target must move away from the character via the most direct path available, until at least 30 ft. away. With failure, the target becomes *frightened* of the character. These effects last a number of rounds equal to 1d4 + the character's Charisma modifier (min. 1).

WING BUFFET

1 Full Action • Attack Action • Requires Winged Flight Speed

The character flaps his wings vigorously, creating a momentary gale. Each smaller target within a cone facing in a direction of the character's choice and with a length equal to the character's winged flight speed makes a Reflex save (DC equal to the character's Strength score). This DC increases by 4 per Size category of difference. With success, the target is pushed 1 square away from the character. With failure, the target is pushed 1d4 squares away and becomes *sprawled.*

CHAPTER 6: FOES

Nothing defines fantasy gaming quite like its menagerie of memorable opponents: cunning warlords, opportunistic brigands, savage orcs, lumbering trolls, implacable golems, scheming liches, and of course, treasure-hording dragons. This chapter offers a hassle-free way to create any non-player character or monster you can imagine. Gone are arcane processes — this fast and flexible system builds just the right friend or foe, right now! Better yet, *Fantasy Craft* NPCs and monsters automatically scale to match the players' Career Levels, making them useful without modification throughout your entire campaign!

Conversion rules are included so you can make use of all those OGL products you've collected over the years *(see page 295)*, but you can get started with dozens of pre-built friends and foes in the Rogues Gallery and Bestiary *(see pages 244 and 253, respectively)*.

NPC BASICS

Fantasy Craft features two types of non-player characters (NPCs): **standard** and **special.** Standard characters populate the backdrop and rarely contribute significantly to the world or the plot. Few have names. Special characters, on the other hand, are focal points in the setting or story — they always have names and tend to have significant power or authority. They're also harder to kill than standard characters, have access to exclusive abilities, and trigger special rules in and out of combat.

Any NPC may be standard or special *(see page 337)*. The choice is entirely up to the GM, based on the needs of the adventure. To qualify as a special character, an NPC should play an important role in the adventure, pose a significant challenge to the party, or be important to the GM's plans; otherwise, he should probably be standard.

ADVERSARIES

The GM may further define any NPC as an adversary, making the character an antagonist of the story and/or an intended threat to the party. Adversaries trigger various rules and are vulnerable to certain hero abilities. Like all NPCs, they can be standard or special *(see page 337)*.

ROGUES AND MONSTERS

Traditional NPCs (e.g. shopkeepers, town guards, etc.) are presented in the Rogues Gallery *(see page 244)*, while monsters (e.g. kobolds, gelatinous cubes, and dragons) are found in the Bestiary *(see page 253)*. This is merely for convenience, however,

as the same rules are used to build both. They utilize very different options, of course, but they share similar stats and interact with the rest of the game in the same way. Outside the specific rules for each NPC's stats, no special rules are required to use any living being in *Fantasy Craft,* no matter how civilized it is, what it's made of, how many legs it's got, how it sees, or anything else. All that's important is whether each individual NPC is standard or special, and whether it's an adversary or not.

For simplicity, the term "NPC" refers to everything this chapter can create, from people to animals to monsters.

BUILDING AN NPC

Players sometimes use these rules to build followers *(see page 98),* contacts *(see page 191),* and hirelings *(see page 190).* Most of the time, however, this chapter is the province of the GM, who uses it to create all the other people and monsters the party meets and fights.

Building an NPC is a simple process that begins with a blank NPC Record Sheet. You can download one from **www.crafty-games.com** or photocopy page 400 of this book. Then just follow these steps. Detailed instructions are provided for each step beginning on the pages listed in parentheses.

Step 0: Concept *(right)*: Start with the basics. Are you building a person, animal, or monster? They all use the same rules but the choices to be made in later steps are very different. Think a bit about the NPC's appearance, motivations, strengths, and weaknesses. Your initial thoughts should be enough to decide whether the NPC is standard or special, and whether it should be an adversary.

Step 1: Statistics *(page 226)*: Like player characters, NPCs have attributes, skills, initiative and attack bonuses, Defense, saves, and other statistics. Unlike PCs, a streamlined system is used to generate an NPC's stats, making them faster to build and easier to use. This system also produces part of the NPC's total XP value.

Step 2: NPC Qualities *(page 230)*: NPCs also differ from player characters in that they don't gain Origins or class levels. Instead, they have access to "NPC qualities," which grant them special abilities and powers and sometimes assign weaknesses as well. Each quality also has an XP value, which is applied to the base total generated in Step 1.

Step 3: Attacks *(page 235):* NPCs can use dozens of different attacks: weapons, claws, bites, breath weapons, paralyzing gazes, and more. Special attacks are handled in this step and add to the NPC's XP value based on type, strength, range, and upgrades. Weapon-using NPCs are equipped in Step 4.

Step 4: Gear and Treasure *(page 239):* Gear assigned to a player-created NPC increases its total XP value, as the NPC is assumed to be using the gear in the party's favor. Gear and treasure added to a GM-created character, however, has no XP value. This is because anything held by the GM's characters either doesn't affect the PCs (weapons carried by non-combatants, for example), or is seized by the party when the fighting is done (the case with nearly all adversaries). Seized gear and treasure is its own reward and therefore generates no XP.

Step 5: XP Value *(page 240):* This step is only important for adversaries and NPCs the players build. For adversaries, the total XP from Steps 1–3 becomes the adversary's **bounty,** or reward the characters gain for defeating the NPC (in or out of combat). For player-built NPCs, the total XP from steps 1–4 must fall within the amount allotted by the rule granting the follower, contact, or hireling.

All other NPCs — the myriad inhabitants of the world that don't oppose or help the characters — don't need an XP value; the GM simply assigns them whatever stats, qualities, and other features he feels best fits the needs of the setting and story.

STEP 0: CONCEPT

Start with a basic idea: perky sidekick, morose pack laborer, stalwart champion, devious bandit king, rampaging wyvern, mercenary goon, vicious kobold, or whatever's needed. The advice for conceiving player characters is equally helpful here, so it might be a good idea to give that section a read before getting started *(see page 7).* The main difference is that NPCs generally require far less detail — a single paragraph for major personalities and a few words for others is plenty. Focus on the most fundamental or obvious traits. Here's a sample set of questions to get you started.

Visual Cue(s): What is the NPC's most distinctive or memorable feature? Answers might include tribal tattoos, a guttural growl, a pronounced limp, or an "interesting" smell.

Motivation: What does the NPC want? Answers might include money, power, revenge, or adventure. How does this apply to the characters? Does he want to join them? Hunt them? Manipulate them?

Strengths: What does the NPC do well? What are his most common tactics? (The answers to these questions don't necessarily have to be the same.) Answers might include brute force, manipulation, subterfuge, or stealth.

Weaknesses: What are the NPC's shortcomings? Especially if he's an adversary, how can the PCs exploit him? Answers might include cowardice, pride, greed, or vulnerability to a particular situation or type of damage.

NPCs also have Dispositions *(see page 373)*. This value is often pre-set for a player-created NPC but otherwise it's helpful to start thinking about how the NPC views the world and the party. You might already know the NPC well enough to decide but don't worry if you're unsure — Disposition doesn't impact the NPC's XP value and may be set at any point in the process, or even during play for non-pivotal characters.

STEP 1: STATISTICS

An NPC's statistics, or "stats," consist of Size, Type, Mobility, Attributes, Traits, Health, and Signature Skills. They're assigned independently from one another, allowing you to create the character you want without worrying about the effects of any single statistic on the others (though attribute modifiers do impact some of the other stats). There's no rule to determine each stat — it's purely a matter of what "feels" right. Go with your gut and adjust as you get comfortable with how the numbers perform at the table.

SIZE

The full range of options is listed on Table 5.4: Size *(see page 217)*. An NPC's Size doesn't impact his XP value — just run with whatever works best. If you assign a Size larger than Medium, define the NPC's footprint, which can have any dimensions up to the listed maximum.

Example: The GM wants to build an old standby for his campaign, an owlbear. It's a hulking brute the size of a grizzly or an ogre, so the GM makes it Large (footprint 2×2).

Example: Later, the GM builds a character he calls "Fortunado," who initially serves as a friendly rival to the PCs — until it's revealed he's spying on them for the story's Big Bad. Fortunado is an average human, so the GM makes him Medium.

A related stat is Reach. Each NPC starts with a base Reach of 1 (square, or 5 ft.), which adds no XP. This is enough for most NPCs but those with unusual physiology and special abilities may deserve a higher value. Increased Reach increases the NPC's XP value by the same amount.

Example: The owlbear's not particularly long-armed, so the GM keeps its Reach at 1. This adds no XP, so the owlbear's XP starts at 0.

Example: Fortunado's Reach is likewise set to 1. His XP starts at 0 as well.

TYPE

Fantasy worlds are full of creatures that defy conventional classification: acidic slimes lurking in dank dungeons, digesting anything they creep across; dark horrors stalking the night, born in realms without dimension; and lumbering golems of stone and steel that live without souls, animated by their masters' magical will. Even so, every creature falls into a rough category, called a "Type," which defines its fundamental characteristics.

Every NPC has at least one Type and some that straddle the boundaries of physiology have two or more. Most Types add 0 XP but a few offer sufficient advantage to add 5 XP to the character's total value.

Animal (+0 XP): The NPC is non-sapient, relying on base instinct and natural ability to survive. Its Intelligence score may not be higher than 6 and it may not become proficient except with extraordinary and natural attacks. The NPC doesn't have a Competence bonus but it may gain Acrobatics, Athletics, Blend, Intimidate, Notice, Resolve, Search, Sense Motive, Sneak, Survival, and Tactics as Signature Skills. Unless otherwise specified, the GM determines whether any animal is trained. A trained animal can be ridden, accepts commands, and may receive advanced training *(see page 83)*. An animal ages and must eat, sleep, and breathe.

Beast (+0 XP): The NPC resembles and is easily mistaken for an animal but may have any Intelligence score. It lacks hands or other fine manipulators and can't take actions requiring them. It can only use armor, handheld gear, and non-natural weapons specifically modified for its use. A beast ages and must eat, sleep, and breathe.

Construct (+5 XP): The NPC is inorganic or manufactured. It's immune to Intelligence, Wisdom, Charisma, sneak attack, stress, and subdual damage, as well as poison and disease. It can't fall unconscious and never gains the *bleeding, enraged, fatigued, fixated, frightened, paralyzed, shaken,* or *sickened* conditions. The NPC only suffers 1 kind of critical injury — severe internal damage (–4 to random physical attribute) — on a result of 51 or higher. It regains vitality normally but does *not* naturally heal wounds, though it may be Mended with a successful Crafting check using the Medicine rules *(see page 77)*. It becomes inert when reduced below 0 wounds but only "dies" when destroyed (i.e. reduced to –25 wounds or worse). A construct doesn't age and doesn't need to eat, sleep, or breathe.

Elemental (+5 XP): The NPC is a physical incarnation of a natural or primal force, without tissue, organs, or other signs of biological life. It's immune to poison, disease, subdual damage, and sneak attack damage. It can't fall unconscious and never gains the *bleeding, flanked, paralyzed,* or *sickened* conditions. The NPC can't suffer critical injuries and is banished instead of dying. An elemental doesn't age and doesn't need to eat, sleep, or breathe.

Fey (+0 XP): The NPC has a deep supernatural connection to the wilds and is as much a spiritual embodiment of a natural force or location as a creature of flesh and blood. Natural animals refuse to attack the NPC and often flee from it unless they're trained to hunt fey or they're attacked by the NPC or its teammates. A fey doesn't age but must eat, sleep, and breathe.

Folk (+0 XP): The NPC is a tool-using, civilized creature with linguistic skills. It often lives with others of its kind and frequently bonds with other folk species, valuing cultural identity above racial solidarity. A folk character ages and must eat, sleep, and breathe.

Horror (+5 XP): The NPC has an alien appearance or psychology that undermines an observer's psyche. Any character other than one of the NPC's teammates who see it suffers a –3 morale penalty with Will saves. Natural animals refuse to attack the NPC and often flee from it unless they're trained to attack horrors or they're attacked by the NPC or its teammates. The NPC is extremely resilient to injury, gaining a +4 bonus with Fortitude saves. Threat ranges of attacks made against it decrease by 2 and it suffers only 1/2 normal sneak attack damage (rounded down). A horror ages and must eat, sleep, and breathe.

Ooze (+5 XP): The NPC's amorphous, boneless body can twist, compress, and shift in a fluid fashion. Its Size is considered 1 category larger when resisting Bull Rush, Disarm, Grapple, and Trip actions, and up to 2 categories smaller when squeezing into or through confined spaces. The NPC may hold a number of readied items or weapons up to 3 + its Dexterity modifier (minimum 1), but can only use armor specifically designed for an ooze. An ooze doesn't age but must eat, sleep, and breathe.

Outsider (+0 XP): The NPC is an abstract notion or ideal manifesting in the physical world as either flesh and blood or an animate object. If it has an Alignment, its attacks gain that Alignment and it inflicts +2 damage per die against targets with the opposing Alignment. When the NPC dies, it is instead banished. An outsider doesn't age and doesn't have to eat but must sleep and breathe.

Plant (+5 XP): The NPC is an animate plant. It gains the *aquatic I* and *light sleeper* NPC qualities at no additional cost and is immune to diseases, poisons, sneak attack damage, and the *fixated, paralyzed,* and *sickened* conditions. A plant ages and must eat, sleep, and breathe.

Spirit (+5 XP): The NPC is a ghost or otherworldly creature who lingers here by sheer force of will. It may spend 1 full action becoming *incorporeal* and vice-versa, and automatically becomes *incorporeal* if knocked unconscious. When the NPC dies, it is instead banished. A spirit doesn't age and doesn't need to eat, sleep, or breathe.

Undead (+5 XP): The NPC is a supernatural force clothed in the physical or spiritual remains of a once-living creature. It gains the *darkvision I* and *light-sensitive* NPC qualities at no additional cost, can't fall unconscious, and is immune to Constitution damage, subdual and stress damage, diseases, and poisons, as well as the *bleeding, paralyzed, sickened,* and *stunned* conditions. It's also immune to critical injuries other than battered and broken limbs, suffering the former with any result below 30 and the latter with any other result. The NPC suffers damage instead of healing from Light spells and heals instead of suffering damage from Darkness spells. It regains vitality normally but does not naturally heal wounds, though it may benefit from all Medicine checks as normal *(see page 77)*. An undead NPC doesn't age and doesn't need to eat, sleep, or breathe.

Example: The owlbear is a bestial creature, capable of only limited reasoning and intellect. After scanning Types, the GM decides it should be an Animal. This adds 0 to the owlbear's XP (for a total of 0).

Example: Fortunado is a human and so the GM assigns him the Folk Type. His XP value also remains at 0.

MOBILITY

Fundamentally, every NPC is a walker, burrower, flyer, swimmer, or immobile. In all cases but immobile, the NPC's base Speed in his native environment is 30 ft., though you may increase this Speed by adding 1 XP per additional 10 ft. You can decrease this Speed as well though doing so has no impact on XP value.

Walker (+0 XP): The NPC has legs and walks, crawls, or slinks on land. He may make Acrobatics and Athletics checks to Climb, Jump, Run, and Swim (and may gain *the superior climber, superior jumper, superior runner,* and *superior swimmer* qualities to improve these abilities).

Burrower (+0 XP): The NPC tunnels through brittle and soft substances. He can also become a Walker and/or Flyer at 1 XP per 10 ft. of Speed (starting with a base Speed of 0 ft.).

Flyer (+0 XP): The NPC flies using wings or other means (e.g. levitation). While in the air, he makes Maneuver checks with the Acrobatics skill *(see pages 69 and 80)*.

While a winged NPC is in the air, he's considered 1 Size larger for Defense, as well as Blend and Sneak checks. His error ranges with attacks and Spellcasting checks also increase by 2 (or 4 while he hovers).

The NPC can also become a Walker and/or Burrower at 1 XP per 10 ft. of Speed (starting with a base Speed of 0 ft.).

Swimmer (+0 XP): The NPC is legless and may only travel through liquid. He can't Climb but may Jump out of liquid and "Run" through it (and may gain the *superior jumper* and *superior runner* qualities to improve these abilities). He can swim without making Athletics checks. He must regularly surface for air unless he has the *aquatic* quality but suffers no penalties for fighting underwater *(see page 217)*.

Immobile (–5 XP): The NPC is stationary and cannot move (e.g. he's permanently rooted in the terrain or bound by permanent magic).

Example: The GM doesn't think the ungainly owlbear should be any quicker than the average human, so he makes it a Walker with a Ground Speed of 30 ft. (same as a human's base Ground Speed). This adds no XP and the owlbear's value remains at 0.

Example: Fortunado is also a Walker but might need to flee quickly, so the GM assigns a Ground Speed of 40 ft. This brings Fortunado's XP value to 1.

ATTRIBUTES

NPCs have all six basic attributes — Strength, Dexterity, Constitution, Intelligence, Wisdom, and Charisma — and they work just as they do for player characters, except for Lifestyle (which NPCs don't have), and Health *(see right)*. Each attribute starts at 10 (+0 modifier), though they can be increased by adding the same amount to the NPC's XP value. They can be decreased as well, though this has no effect on XP value.

Example: The owlbear is animalistic and reasonably strong, rugged and simple-minded. The GM assigns it Str 14, Dex 10, Con 16, Int 4, Wis 10, and Cha 10, which increases its XP by 10 (+4 for Strength and +6 for Con). This is the first XP added to the owlbear, so its value starts at 10.

Example: Fortunado needs to be impressive as he may wind up squaring off with the party, so the GM assigns him Str 14, Dex 16, Con 16, Int 12, Wis 12, and Cha 16, which translate to 26 XP. This brings Fortunado to 27 XP.

TRAITS

NPCs have five Traits — Initiative, Attack, Defense, Resilience, and Competence — each of which is scored with a Roman Numeral grade ranging from I to X (1 to 10). When the NPC is prepped for play *(see page 240)*, each Trait's grade is cross-referenced with the adventure's Threat Level to determine a numerical bonus, as shown on Table 6.1: NPC Traits *(see page 229)*.

Initiative: The NPC's base Initiative bonus, to which his Dexterity modifier is added.

Attack: The NPC's base attack bonus, to which his Strength modifier is added (for unarmed and melee attacks), or his Dexterity modifier is added (for hurled and ranged attacks).

Defense: The NPC's base Defense bonus, which is added with his Dexterity modifier to a base score of 10 (e.g. with a base Defense bonus of +2 and a Dexterity modifier of +1, the NPC's Defense is 13). Unless the NPC's Size is Medium, it applies a modifier as well *(see page 217)*.

Resilience: The NPC's base save bonus, to which a modifier is added: Dexterity for Reflex saves, Constitution for Fortitude saves, or Wisdom for Will saves.

Competence: The NPC's base skill bonus, to which key attribute modifiers are added for any non-Signature skill check (except Spellcasting, which NPCs may only gain as a Signature skill).

Unlike attribute scores, grades don't necessarily correspond to any human "average," though it might be helpful to double-check the bonus a particular grade generates at the adventure's Threat Level to make sure it doesn't seem too high or low.

Each Trait grade increases the NPC's XP value by the same amount.

Example: An owlbear is tough, hard-hitting, and durable, so the GM assigns Initiative III, Attack VII, Defense IV, and Resilience V (as an Animal, the owlbear can't have a Competence score). This generates a total of 19 XP, bringing the owlbear's value to 29.

Example: For no particular reason other than the GM's fancy, Fortunado gets Initiative II, Attack V, Defense III, Resilience IV, and Competence V. Fortunado's XP value also increases by 19, bringing his value to 46.

HEALTH

As described in Chapter 5, standard characters have Damage save bonuses while special characters have vitality and wounds *(see page 206)*. Both are scored with a Roman Numeral Health grade ranging from I to X (1 to 10).

Standard Character: The NPC's Health grade is cross-referenced with the adventure's Threat Level to determine his base Damage save bonus, to which his Constitution modifier is added. This bonus also increases or decreases by 2 per Size category above or below Medium (minimum +0).

Special Character: The NPC's vitality is equal to his Health grade × the Threat Level × 5, and his wounds are calculated as shown on Table 6.2: NPC Wounds *(see page 230)*.

An NPC's Health grade increases his XP value by the same amount.

Example: The owlbear's a tough customer and gets Health V, bringing its XP value to 34.

Example: The GM assigns Fortunado a Health score of IV, which brings his XP value to 50.

SIGNATURE SKILLS

Most of the time, an NPC makes skill checks with his Competence bonus *(see above)*. When you want an NPC to be especially adept with a particular activity though, you can assign him one or more Signature Skills. Only skills you expect

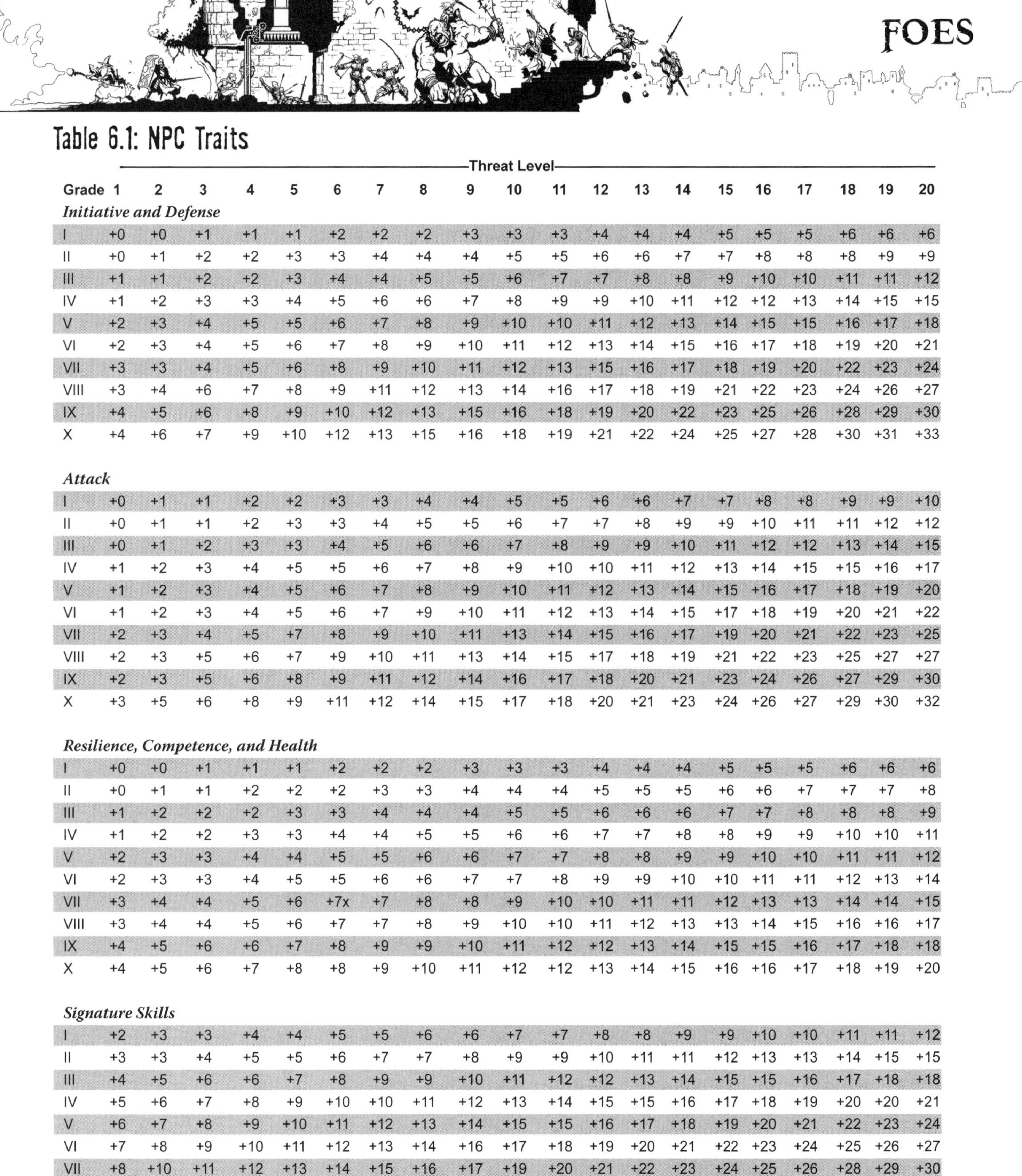

Table 6.1: NPC Traits

	Threat Level																			
Grade	1	2	3	4	5	6	7	8	9	10	11	12	13	14	15	16	17	18	19	20
Initiative and Defense																				
I	+0	+0	+1	+1	+1	+2	+2	+2	+3	+3	+3	+4	+4	+4	+5	+5	+5	+6	+6	+6
II	+0	+1	+2	+2	+3	+3	+4	+4	+4	+5	+5	+6	+6	+7	+7	+8	+8	+8	+9	+9
III	+1	+1	+2	+2	+3	+4	+4	+5	+5	+6	+7	+7	+8	+8	+9	+10	+10	+11	+11	+12
IV	+1	+2	+3	+3	+4	+5	+6	+6	+7	+8	+9	+9	+10	+11	+12	+12	+13	+14	+15	+15
V	+2	+3	+4	+5	+5	+6	+7	+8	+9	+10	+10	+11	+12	+13	+14	+15	+15	+16	+17	+18
VI	+2	+3	+4	+5	+6	+7	+8	+9	+10	+11	+12	+13	+14	+15	+16	+17	+18	+19	+20	+21
VII	+3	+3	+4	+5	+6	+8	+9	+10	+11	+12	+13	+15	+16	+17	+18	+19	+20	+22	+23	+24
VIII	+3	+4	+6	+7	+8	+9	+11	+12	+13	+14	+16	+17	+18	+19	+21	+22	+23	+24	+26	+27
IX	+4	+5	+6	+8	+9	+10	+12	+13	+15	+16	+18	+19	+20	+22	+23	+25	+26	+28	+29	+30
X	+4	+6	+7	+9	+10	+12	+13	+15	+16	+18	+19	+21	+22	+24	+25	+27	+28	+30	+31	+33
Attack																				
I	+0	+1	+1	+2	+2	+3	+3	+4	+4	+5	+5	+6	+6	+7	+7	+8	+8	+9	+9	+10
II	+0	+1	+1	+2	+3	+3	+4	+5	+5	+6	+7	+7	+8	+9	+9	+10	+11	+11	+12	+12
III	+0	+1	+2	+3	+3	+4	+5	+6	+6	+7	+8	+9	+9	+10	+11	+12	+12	+13	+14	+15
IV	+1	+2	+3	+4	+5	+5	+6	+7	+8	+9	+10	+10	+11	+12	+13	+14	+15	+15	+16	+17
V	+1	+2	+3	+4	+5	+6	+7	+8	+9	+10	+11	+12	+13	+14	+15	+16	+17	+18	+19	+20
VI	+1	+2	+3	+4	+5	+6	+7	+9	+10	+11	+12	+13	+14	+15	+17	+18	+19	+20	+21	+22
VII	+2	+3	+4	+5	+7	+8	+9	+10	+11	+13	+14	+15	+16	+17	+19	+20	+21	+22	+23	+25
VIII	+2	+3	+5	+6	+7	+9	+10	+11	+13	+14	+15	+17	+18	+19	+21	+22	+23	+25	+27	+27
IX	+2	+3	+5	+6	+8	+9	+11	+12	+14	+16	+17	+18	+20	+21	+23	+24	+26	+27	+29	+30
X	+3	+5	+6	+8	+9	+11	+12	+14	+15	+17	+18	+20	+21	+23	+24	+26	+27	+29	+30	+32
Resilience, Competence, and Health																				
I	+0	+0	+1	+1	+1	+2	+2	+2	+3	+3	+3	+4	+4	+4	+5	+5	+5	+6	+6	+6
II	+0	+1	+1	+2	+2	+2	+3	+3	+4	+4	+4	+5	+5	+5	+6	+6	+7	+7	+7	+8
III	+1	+2	+2	+2	+3	+3	+4	+4	+4	+5	+5	+6	+6	+6	+7	+7	+8	+8	+8	+9
IV	+1	+2	+2	+3	+3	+4	+4	+5	+5	+6	+6	+7	+7	+8	+8	+9	+9	+10	+10	+11
V	+2	+3	+3	+4	+4	+5	+5	+6	+6	+7	+7	+8	+8	+9	+9	+10	+10	+11	+11	+12
VI	+2	+3	+3	+4	+5	+5	+6	+6	+7	+7	+8	+9	+9	+10	+10	+11	+11	+12	+13	+14
VII	+3	+4	+4	+5	+6	+7x	+7	+8	+8	+9	+10	+10	+11	+11	+12	+13	+13	+14	+14	+15
VIII	+3	+4	+4	+5	+6	+7	+7	+8	+9	+10	+10	+11	+12	+13	+13	+14	+15	+16	+16	+17
IX	+4	+5	+6	+6	+7	+8	+9	+9	+10	+11	+12	+12	+13	+14	+15	+15	+16	+17	+18	+18
X	+4	+5	+6	+7	+8	+8	+9	+10	+11	+12	+12	+13	+14	+15	+16	+16	+17	+18	+19	+20
Signature Skills																				
I	+2	+3	+3	+4	+4	+5	+5	+6	+6	+7	+7	+8	+8	+9	+9	+10	+10	+11	+11	+12
II	+3	+3	+4	+5	+5	+6	+7	+7	+8	+9	+9	+10	+11	+11	+12	+13	+13	+14	+15	+15
III	+4	+5	+6	+6	+7	+8	+9	+9	+10	+11	+12	+12	+13	+14	+15	+15	+16	+17	+18	+18
IV	+5	+6	+7	+8	+9	+10	+10	+11	+12	+13	+14	+15	+15	+16	+17	+18	+19	+20	+20	+21
V	+6	+7	+8	+9	+10	+11	+12	+13	+14	+15	+15	+16	+17	+18	+19	+20	+21	+22	+23	+24
VI	+7	+8	+9	+10	+11	+12	+13	+14	+16	+17	+18	+19	+20	+21	+22	+23	+24	+25	+26	+27
VII	+8	+10	+11	+12	+13	+14	+15	+16	+17	+19	+20	+21	+22	+23	+24	+25	+26	+28	+29	+30
VIII	+9	+11	+12	+13	+14	+16	+17	+18	+19	+21	+22	+23	+24	+26	+27	+28	+29	+31	+32	+33
IX	+10	+12	+13	+14	+16	+17	+18	+20	+21	+22	+24	+25	+26	+28	+29	+30	+32	+33	+34	+36
X	+11	+12	+14	+15	+17	+18	+20	+21	+23	+24	+26	+27	+29	+30	+32	+33	+35	+36	+38	+39

Table 6.2: NPC Wounds

NPC Size	Wounds
Nuisance (N)	1/8 Constitution score (rounded up)
Fine (F)	1/4 Constitution score (rounded up)
Diminutive (D)	1/3 Constitution score (rounded up)
Tiny (T)	1/2 Constitution score (rounded up)
Small (S)	2/3 Constitution score (rounded up)
Medium (M)	Equal to Constitution score
Large (L)	1.5 × Constitution score (rounded up)
Huge (H)	2 × Constitution score
Gargantuan (G)	3 × Constitution score
Colossal (C)	4 × Constitution score
Enormous (E)	5 × Constitution score
Vast (V)	6 × Constitution score

to regularly come into play should get this treatment, as non-critical Signature Skills needlessly bloat XP value.

A non-Folk NPC with a Signature Skill does not suffer a penalty for not using a kit (as he uses the skill through natural ability or has adapted accordingly).

Like a statistic, a Signature Skill is scored with a Roman Numeral grade ranging from I to X (1 to 10), which produces a bonus on Table 6.1 when the NPC is prepped for play. Each Signature Skill grade except Spellcasting must exceed the NPC's Competence grade and increases the NPC's XP value by the same amount.

Example: The GM thinks an owlbear should be an observant stalker of prey, so he gives it Notice IV and Survival IV. This adds 8 XP, bringing the monster's value to 42.

Example: Needing to pull of prolonged deception, Fortunado receives Bluff VII and Impress VI. This adds 13 XP, making his value 63.

Spellcasting is only available to NPCs as a Signature Skill. When an NPC has a Spellcasting grade he knows the same number of spells, and when he's prepped for play he gains double the Threat Level in spell points.

Example: While magical in origin, the owlbear doesn't use magic, so the GM skips Spellcasting.

Example: Fortunado, on the other hand, works for the campaign's Big Bad, which the GM decides is a powerful necromancer. He settles on Fortunado being an adept of the black wizard and assigns Spellcasting II, increasing the NPC's XP value from 63 to 65. Fortunado starts with 2 spells: Command I and Scrye I.

STEP 2: NPC QUALITIES

Qualities alter an NPC's flavor, statistics, and abilities. They can boost combat capability, grant superhuman power, and give mechanical weight to story and campaign decisions. In combination with the rest of the NPC system, even a handful of qualities can generate thousands of different NPCs, making them one of the most powerful tools in the GM's arsenal. It's easy to overdo it though — more than a few qualities and an NPC can become complicated and hard to use. An NPC's XP value can also become unnecessarily bloated, granting too high a reward for defeating it. Except for truly landmark characters, you should probably add no more than 3–5 qualities per standard NPC and no more than 5–7 per special NPC.

Many qualities may be applied multiple times. Any that don't specifically mention this, however, may only be applied once.

Example: The GM wants the owlbear's qualities to reflect both its root species. On the bear side, he assigns *damage reduction 2* (+6 XP), *grappler* (+2 XP), and *fearless I* (+2 XP). Owls have excellent eyesight and deadly claw attacks, so the GM also assigns *improved sense (sight)* and *rend* for an additional 4 XP. All this adds up to an additional 14 XP, bringing the owlbear's value to 56.

Example: In keeping with his desire to keep Fortunado alive, the GM gives him *cagey II* (+2 XP), which lets him automatically succeed with 2 saves per scene. He also adds *class ability (Mage: arcane wellspring I)* for 4 XP, which lets Fortunado cast Level 1 spells without spell points, and for flavor he also adds *class ability (Rune Knight: blooding rune)* for 2 XP. Two additional spells are added with *expanded spellbook* (+2 XP), and the GM rounds Fortunado's package out with *critical surge* (+2 XP) and story-critical (+0 XP). These six qualities add up to 12 additional XP, bringing Fortunado's value to 75.

NPC QUALITY DESCRIPTIONS

Achilles Heel (–2 XP per damage type): When the NPC suffers damage of the specified type *(see page 209)* or source (such as a weapon category, NPC Type, etc.), he also suffers an equal amount of lethal damage.

Always Ready (+2 XP): The NPC may always act in surprise rounds.

Aquatic I (+1 XP): The NPC may hold his breath for a number of minutes equal to 15 × his Constitution score.

Aquatic II (+3 XP): The NPC can't drown, and suffers no penalties when underwater *(see page 217)*.

Attractive (+1 XP per grade): The NPC gains an Appearance bonus of +2 per grade.

Banned Action (+0 XP): The NPC can't take certain attack actions (e.g. Bull Rush, Disarm, etc.) or perform certain skill checks (e.g. Jump, Swim, etc.). These limitations may be psychological, physical, or have a story justification.

Battering (+2 XP): Each time the NPC hits with an unarmed or melee attack, the target also suffers 2 subdual damage.

Beguiling (+2 XP): When the NPC successfully Taunts a character, he may decline the standard result to have his target become *fixated* on him for 1d6 rounds. Special characters may spend 1 action die to cancel this effect and become immune to this ability for the rest of the scene. If an NPC gains this benefit from multiple sources, he may also damage the target once without interrupting his fixation (he may do this only once, no matter how many times he gains the benefit).

Blindsight (+4 XP): The NPC has extraordinarily or supernaturally acute senses that replace his vision. His blindsight operates like vision out to 10 blindsight increments, each equal to his Wisdom score × 10 ft. Within this range he ignores ambient light penalties and cannot be *blinded*. He also sees *hidden* and *invisible* characters and objects without restriction.

Bright (+3 XP per grade): The NPC's threat range with skills increases by 1 per grade.

Burden of Ages: (–4 XP): The NPC's will to live has been worn down by the long ages and he finds it difficult to express the fire of youth. Any effect that heals damage has only 1/2 the normal effect (rounded up).

Cagey (+1 XP per grade): The NPC may automatically succeed with 1 save per scene per grade.

Chameleon I (+2 XP per terrain): The NPC gains a +4 bonus with Stealth and Hide checks in 1 terrain (aquatic, arctic, caverns/mountains, desert, forest/jungle, indoors/settled, plains, or swamp).

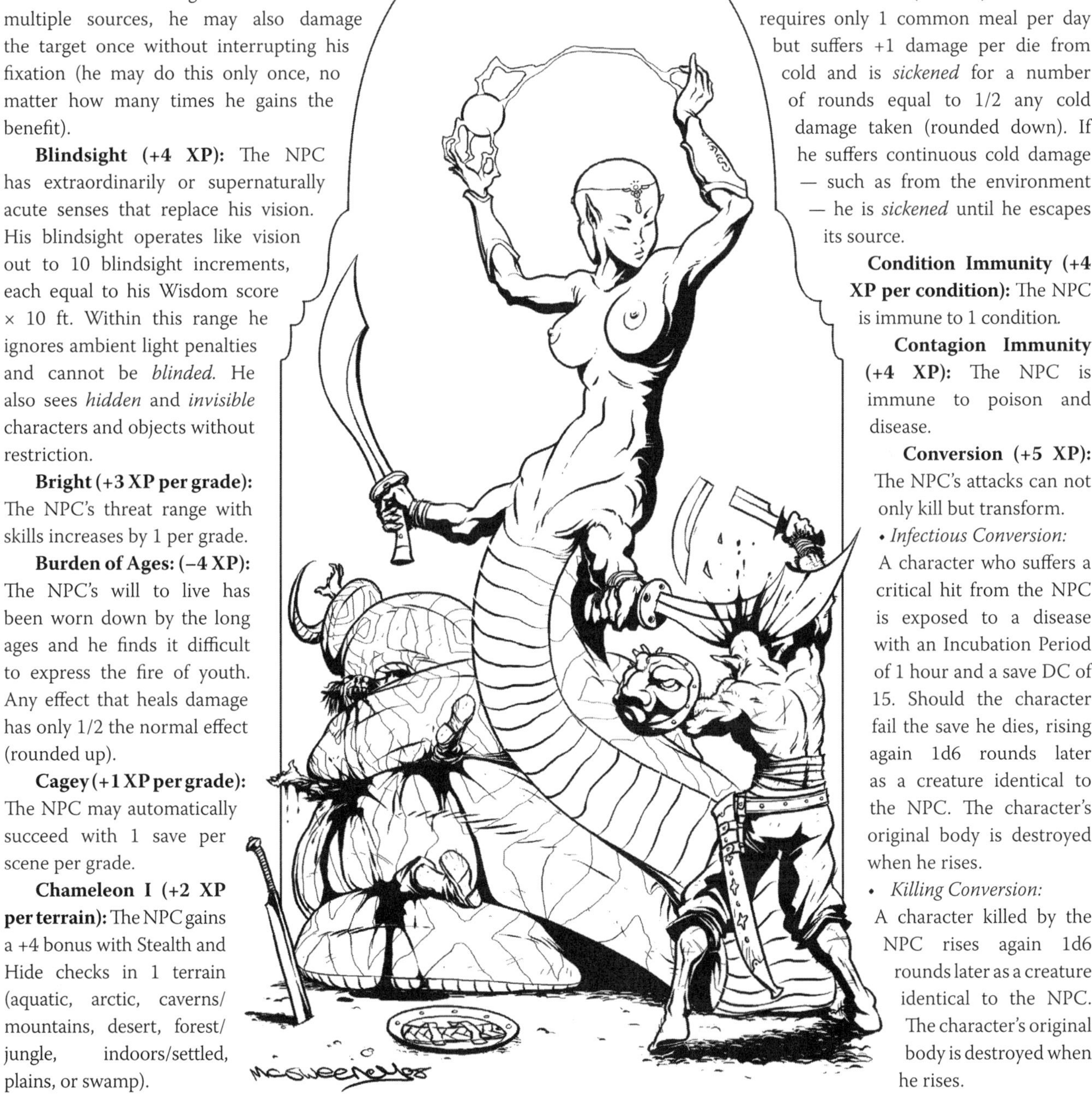

Chameleon II (+4 XP per terrain): The NPC gains a +8 bonus with Stealth and Hide checks while moving and automatically becomes *hidden* when stationary. He also gains 1 die of sneak attack damage during each of the first 3 rounds of combat in the chosen terrain.

Charge Attack (+2 XP): Up to 3 times per combat, the NPC may take a free Standard Move before attacking.

Class Ability (Varies): The NPC gains a class ability from Table 6.3: NPC Class Abilities *(see page 232)*.

Clumsy (–2 XP): The NPC's error ranges increase by 2.

Cold-Blooded (–2 XP): The NPC requires only 1 common meal per day but suffers +1 damage per die from cold and is *sickened* for a number of rounds equal to 1/2 any cold damage taken (rounded down). If he suffers continuous cold damage — such as from the environment — he is *sickened* until he escapes its source.

Condition Immunity (+4 XP per condition): The NPC is immune to 1 condition.

Contagion Immunity (+4 XP): The NPC is immune to poison and disease.

Conversion (+5 XP): The NPC's attacks can not only kill but transform.

- *Infectious Conversion:* A character who suffers a critical hit from the NPC is exposed to a disease with an Incubation Period of 1 hour and a save DC of 15. Should the character fail the save he dies, rising again 1d6 rounds later as a creature identical to the NPC. The character's original body is destroyed when he rises.
- *Killing Conversion:* A character killed by the NPC rises again 1d6 rounds later as a creature identical to the NPC. The character's original body is destroyed when he rises.

Table 6.3: NPC Class Abilities

Class Ability	Class (page number)	XP Value
Adaptable toolbox	Keeper (40)	1
Alchemical harmony	Alchemist (53)	2
"...And one for all!"	Swashbuckler (61)	5
Arcane wellspring I–II	Mage (44)	4 per grade
Armor use I–V	Soldier (51)	2 per grade
Assistance I–III	Sage (47)	1 per grade
Bald-faced lie	Assassin (31)	5
Battle planning	Captain (34)	2 per grade
Benediction	Priest (45)	2
Best of the best	Sage (47)	2 per grade
Black vial	Assassin (31)	2
Blade dance I–II	Edgemaster (56)	2 per grade
Blooding rune	Rune Knight (59)	2
Bloody mess	Burglar (33)	2
Bookworm I–III	Explorer (38)	2 per grade
Born in the saddle	Lancer (42)	2
Bred for war	Lancer (42)	1 per grade
Bright idea	Keeper (40)	1 per grade
Carve	Edgemaster (55)	2
Cold read	Assassin (30)	2 per grade (1/session)
Convincing	Assassin (31)	2
Deadly blow	Edgemaster (56)	5
Devout	Priest (44)	5
Display of arms I–II	Edgemaster (55)	2 per grade
Divine intervention	Priest (46)	10
Effortless cut	Edgemaster (56)	8
Elbow grease	Keeper (40)	2
Evasion I–III	Burglar (32)	2 per grade
Fake it	Assassin (31)	2
Finish him!	Assassin (32)	8
Follow my lead	Assassin (31)	2
Fortunes of war I–III	Soldier (51)	2 per grade
Hand of death	Assassin (30)	2
He did it!	Burglar (33)	2
I'll cut you! I–II	Burglar (33)	2 per grade (*bleeding* and *stunned*)
Instant solution	Keeper (41)	5
Killer instinct	Soldier (51)	1
Killing blow	Scout (49)	1
Last stand	Lancer (42)	8
Lay on hands	Paladin (57)	1
Lifeline	Explorer (39)	5
Look out!	Burglar (33)	2
Man of reason	Keeper (40)	2
Master of magic	Mage (44)	8
Master plan I–II	Courtier (37)	2 per grade
Master rider	Lancer (42)	5 per grade (1/adventure)
Master tracker	Scout (50)	2 per grade (1/session)
Master's touch I	Edgemaster (56)	5
Never outdone	Courtier (37)	8
Notebook	Explorer (39)	2 per grade (1/session)
Offer they can't refuse	Assassin (31)	2
One in a million	Soldier (52)	5
One step ahead	Soldier (51)	2
Only the finest	Courtier (36)	2
Overrun	Scout (50)	5
Portable cover I–II	Soldier (51)	2 per grade
Quick on your feet	Assassin (30)	2
Rebuke	Priest (46)	2
Rough living	Scout (49)	2 per grade (+2)
Rough riding	Scout (50)	1
Rugged weapons	Soldier (51)	2
Rune-carved	Rune Knight (58)	2 per grade (2 runes)
Sacred weapon	Priest (46)	2
Saved! I–II	Priest (46)	2 per grade
Serendipity	Sage (48)	5
Slanderous	Courtier (37)	2
Slippery	Burglar (33)	2
Smite the indifferent	Paladin (57)	2
Sneak attack	Scout (49)	2 per grade
Spell breach	Rune Knight (59)	5
Spell parry	Rune Knight (59)	2
Spell secret	Mage (44)	1 per grade
Spell strike	Rune Knight (59)	8
Sprint	Scout (50)	2
Stalker	Scout (49)	2
Stand in judgment I–II	Paladin (57)	2 per grade
Stash it	Burglar & Keeper (33)	2
State of grace	Paladin (57)	8
Stick close and don't make a sound	Burglar (33)	2
Study the stance	Edgemaster (55)	2
Take command	Captain (35)	2 per grade
Take heart	Sage (48)	5 per grade (1/Dramatic scene)
Take measure	Captain (35)	2 per grade (1/session)
Tally ho!	Swashbuckler (60)	2
Tomb raider	Explorer (38)	2
Trail signs	Scout (50)	2
Transmutation	Alchemist (53)	2
Trophy hunter	Scout (50)	2
Uncanny dodge	Burglar & Explorer (32)	2 per grade
Very, very sneaky	Burglar (32)	2
Virtues of command I–II	Captain (35)	5
Warcasting I–II	Rune Knight (59)	2 per grade
With a word	Courtier (36)	2

Critical Hesitation (–2 XP): The NPC wavers when he suffers a critical hit or failure, becoming *slowed* for 1 round.

Critical Surge (+2 XP): The NPC gains clarity with each critical hit or success, also gaining 1 additional half action.

Damage Defiance (+2 XP per damage type): The NPC suffers only half damage of a single type or from a single source (such as a weapon category, NPC Type, etc.).

Damage Immunity (+5 XP per damage type): The NPC is immune to damage of a single type or from a single source (such as a weapon category, NPC Type, etc.).

Damage Reduction (+3 XP per point): The NPC gains 1 Damage Reduction.

Darkvision I (+1 XP): The NPC ignores penalties from dim and faint light.

Darkvision II (+3 XP): The NPC ignores all ambient light penalties.

Death Throes (+5 XP or +7 XP for a damage type other than lethal): The NPC thrashes about viciously, explodes, or otherwise inflicts damage when killed. His body is destroyed, inflicting 1/2 his base XP value in lethal damage (rounded down) with a blast increment of 1 square.

Devoted (+2 XP per grade — requires *miracles* campaign quality): The NPC takes 1 Step per grade along 1 Path. If he also has an Alignment, he gains its ritual weapon with 1 or more grades and may 2 spend action dice to summon its avatar with 5 or more grades.

Devour (+3 XP): The NPC can feed on the dead, gaining incredible strength. This takes a full action and destroys the target body. The NPC gains a +1 bonus with attack checks, skill checks, and damage rolls for a number of rounds equal to the devoured target's Career or Threat Level.

Diurnal (–1 XP): The NPC is most comfortable during the day, suffering a –4 penalty with attack checks, skill checks, and saves at night and in areas with no light.

Dramatic Entrance (+8 XP): The scene becomes Dramatic when the NPC arrives *(see page 335)*. If the scene is already Dramatic, the GM gains 1 additional action die per player character that may only be spent to support this NPC's actions.

Dread (+2 XP): Each time an opponent attacks the NPC and misses, the opponent suffers 2 stress damage.

Everlasting (+0 XP): Unless the NPC's body is destroyed, he returns to life at the start of the next adventure (though the PCs may not see him for some time after that).

Expanded Spellbook (+1 XP per spell — spellcaster only): The NPC knows 1 additional spell.

Expertise (+2 XP per skill): When the NPC takes 10 with the skill it doesn't take twice as long, and when he takes 20 it takes only 10 times normal.

Fast Healing (+1 XP): The NPC heals damage at twice the standard rate.

Fatal Falls (–1 XP): The NPC suffers +1 falling damage per die. Falling damage also gains the *keen (20)* quality.

Favored Foes (+1 per Type): The NPC's threat range increases by 2 when attacking and making Notice, Sense Motive, and Survival checks targeting standard characters of 1 Type *(see page 226)*.

Fearless I (+2 XP): The NPC gains a +4 bonus with Morale checks.

Fearless II (+4 XP): The NPC is immune to negative Morale effects.

Fearsome (+2 XP): Up to 3 times per scene, as a half action, the NPC can invoke fear in all opponents who can see or hear him. Each target suffers 1d6 stress damage and must make a Will save (DC 20) or become *frightened.*

Feat (+2 XP per feat): The NPC gains 1 feat. He must meet any feat or Species prerequisites but ignores all other prerequisites. A feat may not grant an NPC qualities or statistics it can't otherwise gain.

Feral (+1 XP): Once per combat, at the GM's discretion, the NPC becomes *enraged.*

Ferocity (+3 XP): If the NPC is standard, he may immediately make a free attack when he fails his last Damage save. If he's special, he continues to act normally even when dying.

Frenzy I (+4 XP): The NPC may frenzy once per combat, gaining a number of additional half actions in one round equal to the number of opponents he faces (maximum equal to the total extraordinary and natural attacks he has + 2). These half actions may only be used to attack and may be used to make multiple extraordinary attacks in the same round. Unless the NPC has only 1 attack, each attack must use a different weapon, extraordinary attack, or natural attack than the last.

Example: An NPC facing a dozen opponents has frenzy I, 2 extraordinary attacks, and 1 natural attack. He may use frenzy to gain 5 half actions he may only use to attack. If he uses one of his extraordinary attacks first, he must use his other extraordinary attack or his natural attack second.

Frenzy II (+8 XP): As *frenzy I,* except that the NPC may frenzy 3 times per combat.

Frenzy III (+12 XP): As *frenzy I,* except that the NPC may frenzy once per round.

Grappler (+2 XP): The NPC gains a +2 bonus with Athletics checks made during a Grapple.

Grueling Combatant (+2 XP): Each time an adjacent opponent attacks the NPC and misses, the opponent suffers 2 subdual damage.

Hive Mind (+2 XP): The NPC shares thoughts and reactions with others of his species within 1 mile. He cannot become *blinded, deafened, flanked* or *flat-footed* unless all others of his kind who can see and hear him already suffer the condition.

Honorable (+3 XP): The NPC is immune to incentives, negating those modifiers on Table 2.12: Persuasion and Coercion *(see page 75)*.

Impaired Sense (–1 XP per sense): The NPC's visual, hearing, or scent range is halved (rounded down), and he suffers a –4 penalty with related Awareness and Perception checks.

Improved Carrying Capacity (+0 XP): This NPC's Strength is considered 4 higher for carrying capacity.

Improved Sense (+1 XP per sense): The NPC's visual, hearing, or scent range is doubled and he gains a +4 bonus with related Awareness and Perception checks.

Improved Stability (+2 XP): The NPC is considered 1 Size category larger for carrying capacity, Trample attacks, and resisting Bull Rush and Trip attempts so long as he's standing firmly on the ground and not climbing, flying, or riding.

Interests (+0 XP): The NPC gains any number of Interests.

Invisibility (+8 XP): As a full action, the NPC may become *invisible* or visible again.

Knockback (+2 XP): When the NPC scores a threat with an unarmed or natural attack, he may push the opponent 1 square away per 10 damage inflicted and cause him to become *sprawled.*

Light-Sensitive (–2 XP): Each time the NPC enters a more brightly lit area, he suffers 20 flash damage *(see page 210).*

Light Sleeper (+1 XP): Sleeping is never a Terminal Situation for the NPC.

Lumbering (–2 XP): The NPC suffers a –2 penalty with Reflex saves and becomes *flanked* whenever 2 or more opponents are adjacent to him in any configuration.

Meek (–2 XP): The NPC suffers a –4 penalty with Morale checks.

Menacing Threat (+2 XP): The NPC may Threaten up to 3 opponents at once. He only rolls once for the action while each opponent rolls to resist separately.

Mook (–4 XP): The NPC must have a Heath of I and may not have the *tough* quality. If he's standard, he automatically fails Damage saves. If he's special, he has no vitality.

Monstrous Attack (+3 XP per grade): The NPC's threat range with attacks increases by 1 per grade.

Monstrous Defense (+3 XP per grade): The threat ranges of attacks targeting the NPC decrease by 1 per grade. If this reduces a threat range to less than 20, the attacker may not score a threat.

Natural Defense (+5 XP or +7 XP for a damage type other than lethal): The NPC enjoys natural protection that injures close quarters battlers. Each time a character hits the NPC with an unarmed or melee attack, he must make a Reflex save (DC 15) or suffer 1d6 lethal damage.

Natural Spell (+1 XP per Spell Level): The NPC can reliably produce 1 specific spell effect per scene. This isn't traditional spellcasting — for which the NPC needs the Spellcasting skill — but rather a natural ability that operates in all mechanical ways like a spell and produces the same effect. No Spellcasting check or spell points are required. The spell's save DC is equal to 10 + 1/2 the NPC's Threat Level (rounded up), with a Casting Level equal to the NPC's Threat Level. This quality can be used to replicate hundreds of common monster abilities.

Never Outnumbered (+2 XP): The NPC can never be outnumbered *(see the Benefit description on page 85).*

Night-Blind (+0 XP): The NPC's vision penalties from ambient light are doubled.

Nocturnal (–1 XP): The NPC is most comfortable at night, suffering a –4 penalty with attack checks, skill checks, and saves in during the day and in areas with intense light.

Regeneration (+3 XP per point): The NPC heals 1 point of damage per round (if he's a special character, he chooses whether to heal subdual, vitality, or a wound). Also, his critical injuries heal in 1d4 hours instead of 1d4 months and he is only *sickened* for 1d6 minutes when successfully treated.

Rend (+3 XP): Each time the NPC hits an adjacent opponent, he may make a free attack against the same target.

Repulsive (–1 XP per grade): The NPC gains an Appearance "bonus" of –2 per grade.

Shambling (–4 XP): This NPC may take only 1 half action or 1 full action per round and may not Run or make any free attacks.

Shapeshifter I (+4 XP): With 2 full actions, the NPC can assume the form of another NPC whose Size is within 1 category (e.g. Small to Large if the shapeshifter is Medium). The target's XP may not exceed half the shapeshifter's own (rounded up). The shapeshifter always retains its own Intelligence, Wisdom, and Charisma, as well as this quality. A True Seeing spell reveals the shapeshifter's base form, which he returns to when killed.

Shapeshifter II (+8 XP): As Shapeshifter I, except that the NPC can assume the form of an NPC whose Size is within 2 categories (Tiny to Huge if the shapeshifter is Medium), and whose XP does not exceed the shapeshifter's own.

Shapeshifter III (+12 XP): As Shapeshifter II, except that the NPC can also assume the form of a player character with a Career Level not exceeding the NPC's Threat Level. When copying a PC, the NPC gains a character sheet identical to the victim's.

Spell Defense (+2 XP per grade): The NPC gains Spell Defense equal to 10 + (the grade × 5).

Spell Reflection (+3 XP): Each time the NPC is the target of a successfully cast spell, he may make a Will save (DC 20) to reflect it to another target within 30 ft.

Splitter (+0 XP or +5 XP if the new NPCs mature instantly): The NPC grows exponentially when it feeds.

- *Damage Splitter:* The NPC splits when it suffers a critical injury.
- *Killing Splitter:* The NPC splits when it kills a character whose Career or Threat Level is at least 1/2 its own (rounded up).

In either case, the NPC spends 2 full actions splitting into two separate NPCs, each with Trait grades at 1/2 original (rounded up). Both NPCs keep the original's qualities, including this one, though they can't split again until fully grown. These smaller NPCs mature quickly, their Trait grades each rising by 1 per hour until they reach the full original values.

Stench (+2 XP): Each living character coming within 10 ft. of the NPC must make a Fortitude save (DC 10 + the NPC's Threat Level) or become *sickened* for 1d6 rounds. With success, the character becomes immune for the rest of the scene. Characters accustomed to the NPC's stench are also immune.

Sterner Stuff (+1 XP): The *keen* quality of each attack made against the NPC decreases by 4.

Story-Critical (+0 XP): Once per scene, the NPC may Cheat Death with a Petty fate *(see page 384)*.

Superior Climber (+1 XP per grade — walker only): With a successful Climb check, the NPC moves the resulting distance one additional time per grade (e.g. an NPC with *superior climber III* and a result of 10 ft. moves 40 ft.)

Superior Jumper (+1 XP per grade): With a successful Jump check, the NPC moves the resulting distance one additional time per grade (e.g. an NPC with *superior jumper III* and a result of 10 ft. moves 40 ft.)

Superior Runner (+1 XP per grade): The NPC's Speed multiplier when Running increases by 1 per grade.

Superior Swimmer (+1 XP per grade — walker only): If the NPC is a walker, he moves the resulting distance one additional time per grade with a successful Swim check (e.g. a walker with *swimmer III* and a result of 10 ft. moves 40 ft.).

Superior Traveler (+1 XP per grade): The NPC's Travel Speed increases by 1 MPH per grade.

Swarm (+2 XP): The NPC can make simultaneous attacks with others of his species. A single attack check is made with a bonus equal to the number of NPCs involved. With a hit, the target suffers the attack's base damage only once, but it's multiplied by 1/2 this bonus (rounded down).

Example: Five NPCs of the same species make a swarm attack. They make only 1 attack with a +5 bonus but with a hit they inflict double their base damage.

Swift Attack (+3 XP per extra attack): Once per round, the NPC gains 1 free attack.

Telepathic (+1 XP): The NPC can mentally communicate with intelligent creatures.

Tough (+5 XP per grade): If the NPC is standard, he ignores the effect of 1 failed Damage save per scene per grade. If he's special, he may ignore all damage from a single critical hit once per scene per grade.

Treacherous (+5 XP): If the NPC is standard, he can activate threats as critical hits and successes. If he's special, he may activate threats as critical hits for 1 less action die (minimum 0).

Tricky (+2 XP per trick): The NPC gains 1 trick.

Turning (+4 XP): Once per combat the NPC may Turn characters of 1 Type *(see pages 223 and 226)*.

Turn Immunity (+2 XP): The NPC cannot be Turned.

Unlimited Spell Points (+5 XP): The NPC has an unlimited supply of spell points.

Unnerving (+2 XP): Each time the NPC hits with an unarmed or melee attack, the target also suffers 2 stress damage.

Veteran (+2 XP per grade): The NPC's Threat Level increases by 1 per grade (maximum Threat Level 20).

STEP 3: ATTACKS

NPCs may gain three types of attacks: *weapons*, which are covered in Step 4; *natural attacks*, which include "ordinary" physical weapons like claws and teeth; and *extraordinary attacks* like breath weapons and gaze attacks that inflict damage, conditions, attribute impairment, and other effects, often at range or across an area. Determining how your NPC defends himself is critical in defining his role and how you use him, so his attacks should ideally be informed by his background, statistics, and qualities.

WEAPONS

Folk, humanoids, and other tool-using creatures typically attack with unarmed strikes and weapons. Unless they also possess natural or extraordinary attacks, you can skip this step for them, proceeding to page 239.

NATURAL ATTACKS

Natural attacks include savage bites, lashing tentacles, poisonous stings, and the ability to swallow prey whole! All natural attacks are Standard Unarmed Attacks except where noted, and may not be disarmed.

An NPC may possess more than one natural attack (e.g. a horse may have Bite and Kick attacks), or more than one of the same natural attack (e.g. a hydra with an identical Bite attack for each head). When an NPC has 3 or more natural attacks, he may spend 1 full action to flurry, attacking once with each of his natural attacks.

Each natural attack has a grade ranging from I to V (1 to 5). At Grade I the NPC gains the attack listed on Table 6.4: Natural Attacks *(see page 237)*. At Grades II and IV the threat range increases by 1 each, at Grade III the damage dice double, and at the maximum Grade of V the damage dice triple. Each natural attack added increases the NPC's XP value by 2 per attack grade + 2 per upgrade.

Example: The owlbear rakes its enemies with savage claws. Scanning Table 6.4, the GM decides these are best handled as a Talon attack. Since the owlbear is Large, its Talon attack stats look like this...

- *Grade I:* 1d8 damage, 20 threat range
- *Grade II:* 1d8 damage, 19–20 threat range
- *Grade III:* 2d8 damage, 19–20 threat range
- *Grade IV:* 2d8 damage, 18–20 threat range
- *Grade V:* 3d8 damage, 18–20 threat range

The GM settles on two Grade II Talon attacks with no upgrades, which increases the owlbear's XP value from 56 to 64 (+4 XP for each attack). The owlbear's Strength modifier is applied to these attacks, so they inflict 1d8+2 lethal damage.

Next the GM builds the owlbear's sharp beak, choosing a Bite I attack with no upgrades (1d10+2 lethal damage, threat 18–20). This increases the creature's XP value by 2 more (to 66).

NATURAL ATTACK DESCRIPTIONS

Bite: The NPC inflicts deep wounds with sharp fangs or powerful jaws.

Claw/Kick/Slam/Talon: The most common natural attacks all operate the same, with the NPC striking with arms, feet, hooves, or in some cases the bulk of his body.

Gore: The NPC impales its foes on horns, spikes, or other bony protrusions.

Squeeze: The NPC wraps its limbs or body around its prey, crushing the life out of them. This damage is used in place of the NPC's normal unarmed damage when he uses the Injure Grapple benefit.

Swallow: The NPC engulfs, smothers, or swallows a Grapple opponent, triggering a Restricted Action *(see page 223).*

Tail/Tentacle Slap: The NPC smacks targets with its tail or tentacles.

Trample: The NPC uses its superior bulk to crush or run over its enemies, triggering a Restricted Action *(see page 223).*

NATURAL ATTACK UPGRADE DESCRIPTIONS

Natural attack upgrades often add weapon qualities *(see page 176).*

Aligned: The attack is powered by the NPC's beliefs or designed to smite those with certain convictions, gaining the *aligned* weapon quality.

Alternate Damage: The attack harms in an unusual way (e.g. acid-secreting claws or hooves rimmed with hellfire), its damage type changing to something other than lethal *(see page 210).*

Armor-Piercing: The attack penetrates with diamond-tipped teeth, divinely-graced blows, or other means, gaining the *armor-piercing 2* weapon quality.

Bleed: Savage barbs, supernatural filth, or other nasty surprises keep wounds from healing. The attack gains the *bleed* weapon quality.

Diseased: The attack transmits 1 disease from Table 7.8: Diseases *(see page 341),* exposing any target who suffers 1 or more damage after Reduction and Resistances.

Finesse: The attack is light and nimble, gaining the *finesse* weapon quality.

Grab: The attack latches onto the target with each hit, letting the NPC Grapple the same target as a free action.

Keen: The attack slices or pierces deeply into the foe's body, gaining the *keen 4* weapon quality.

Reach: A long tail, craning neck, or other means increase the NPC's striking range, increasing the attack's Reach by 1.

Trip: Hooked claws or snaring tentacles easily pull opponents off their feet, granting the *trip* weapon quality.

Venomous: The attack transmits 1 poison from Table 4.12: Poisons *(see page 166),* exposing any target who suffers 1 or more damage after Reduction and Resistances.

EXTRAORDINARY ATTACKS

Extraordinary attacks are supernatural or fantastic in nature and range from a dragon's fiery breath to a basilisk's petrifying gaze to a plague demon's sickening aura. Because these versatile attacks can represent literally thousands of different abilities, it's extremely helpful to start with a solid concept. Ask yourself: does the attack inflict damage or affect the target in another way? Does it require physical contact or is it made over range? Does it affect an entire area and if so, what shape and size? Answering these questions ahead of time will greatly smooth the process.

There are two types of extraordinary attacks, as shown on Table 6.5 *(see page 238):* **Damage Attacks,** which inflict various types of damage; and **Save Attacks,** which inflict conditions, drain, and other effects. Like a natural attack, an extraordinary attack has a grade ranging from I to V (1 to 5), which defines its effectiveness.

- *Damage Attacks:* The grade determines the dice used when rolling damage (Grade I is d4, Grade II is d6, Grade III is d8, Grade IV is d10, and Grade V is d12). For example, a Grade IV damage attack inflicts 1d10 damage per 2 NPC Threat Levels.
- *Save Attacks:* The grade determines the save DC (5 + an additional 5 per Grade). For example, a Grade III save attack requires the target make a successful save (DC 20) or suffer the listed effect.

An extraordinary attack can also be enhanced with upgrades and/or an Area *(see Table 6.5).* Each extraordinary attack increases the NPC's XP value by (the attack's grade × the listed cost per grade) + the cost of the attack's upgrades and Area, if any.

Table 6.4: Natural Attacks

Attack (2 XP per Grade)	Damage (by NPC Size)						Threat Range	Qualities/Notes
	T or smaller	S	M	L	H-G	C or larger		
Bite	1d4	1d6	1d8	1d10	1d12	2d8	18–20	—
Claw/Kick/Slam/Talon	1d3	1d4	1d6	1d8	1d10	1d12	20	—
Gore	1d3	1d4	1d6	1d8	1d10	1d12	19–20	*Bleed*
Squeeze	1d6	1d8	1d10	1d12	2d8	2d10	—	Grapple benefit
Swallow *	1d6	1d8	1d10	1d12	2d8	2d10	—	Grapple benefit
Tail/Tentacle Slap	1d4	1d6	1d8	1d10	1d12	2d8	20	*Reach +1*
Trample *	1d4	1d6	1d8	1d10	1d12	2d8	20	—

Natural Attack Upgrades (+2 XP per upgrade)	
Aligned	Attack gains *aligned* weapon quality
Alternate damage	Attack inflicts damage other than lethal
Armor-piercing **	Attack gains *armor-piercing 2* weapon quality
Bleed	Attack gains *bleed* weapon quality
Diseased	Transmits disease if target suffers 1 or more damage after Reduction and Resistances
Finesse	Attack gains *finesse* weapon quality
Grab	With successful hit, NPC may Grapple target as free action
Keen **	Attack gains *keen 4* weapon quality
Reach **	Attack's Reach increases by 1
Trip	Attack gains *trip* weapon quality
Venomous	Transmits poison if target suffers 1 or more damage after Reduction and Resistances

* This attack may only target characters 2 or more Sizes smaller.

** This quality may be added to an attack multiple times.

Example: Working up Fortunado the Traitor, the GM decides that his necromantic master made various… adjustments to him over the years, one of which granted him the ability to breathe fire. The GM makes this a Grade IV fire damage attack with a 30-ft. cone Area. This increases Fortunado's XP by 16 (8 for the Grade IV damage attack, 2 for the alternate damage upgrade, and 6 for the 30 ft. cone Area). Fortunado's XP rises to 91.

Example: Fortunado's master also gave him a grade III slowing beam attack with a 60 ft. range. This increases Fortunado's XP by another 15 (9 for the Grade III slowing save attack and 6 for the 60 ft. beam Area). Fortunado's XP rises to 106.

An NPC may only make 1 extraordinary attack per round. Extraordinary attacks are Standard Unarmed Attacks unless they have an Area and may not be disarmed.

With an Area, an extraordinary attack becomes a single Standard Ranged Attack against all targets therein. Each target hit suffers the attack's damage or must make the attack's save. In the case of a damage attack, the victim may make a Reflex save (DC 5 + an additional 5 per grade) to suffer 1/2 damage (rounded down).

DAMAGE ATTACK DESCRIPTIONS

Damage: The attack hammers the target with 1 die of lethal damage per 2 NPC Threat Levels.

Rotting: The attack rots or decays natural materials, inflicting 1 die of lethal damage per 2 NPC Threat Levels to plant and wood targets only.

Rusting: The attack is corrosive or disintegrating, inflicting 1 die of lethal damage per 2 NPC Threat Levels to metal targets only.

SAVE ATTACK DESCRIPTIONS

Baffling: The attack addles or confuses the victim, scrambling his thoughts. With a failed Will save, he becomes *baffled.*

Blinding: The attack strikes at the target's vision. With a failed Will save, he becomes *blinded.*

Deafening: The attack strikes at the target's hearing. With a failed Will save, he becomes *deafened.*

Draining, Attribute: The attack withers one of the victim's attributes. With a failed Fortitude save, he suffers 1 temporary impairment with a specific attribute.

Draining, Life: The attack siphons the target's life force, transferring it to the NPC. With a failed Fortitude save, he suffers 1 lethal damage per NPC Threat Level, and the NPC immediately heals an equal amount.

Draining, Soul: The attack strikes at the very core of the target's being. With a failed Fortitude save, a standard NPC instantly dies. A special character who fails the save suffers a –10 penalty to his maximum vitality and loses 1 action die. If this reduces his maximum vitality to 0 or less, the target dies. A special character may recover from all soul drain with 8 hours' sleep.

Enraging: The attack fills the target with insane fury, causing him to lash out at nearby friends and foes. With a failed Will save, he becomes *enraged.*

Table 6.5: Extraordinary Attacks

Attack	XP Value	Damage/Effect	Save (DC 5 + 5 per grade)	Threat Range
Damage Attacks				
Damage	2 per grade	1 die lethal per 2 Threat Levels *	**	20
Rotting	2 per grade	1 die lethal per 2 Threat Levels * (plant/wood only)	**	20
Rusting	2 per grade	1 die lethal per 2 Threat Levels * (metal only)	**	20
Damage Attacks Upgrades				
Aligned	+2	Attack gains *aligned* weapon quality	—	—
Alternate damage	+2	Attack inflicts damage other than lethal	—	—
Armor-piercing †	+2	Attack gains *armor piercing 2* weapon quality	—	—
Bleed	+2	Attack gains *bleed* weapon quality	—	—
Diseased	+2	Transmits disease if target suffers 1 or more damage After Reduction and Resistances	—	—
Keen †	+2	Attack gains *keen 4* weapon quality	—	—
Venomous	+2	Transmits poison if target suffers 1 or more damage	—	—
Save Attacks				
Baffling	3 per grade	Target becomes *baffled* for 1d6 rounds per grade	Will	—
Blinding	2 per grade	Target *blinded* for 1d6 rounds per grade	Will	—
Deafening	2 per grade	Target *deafened* for 1d6 rounds per grade	Will	—
Draining, attribute	4 per grade	1 temporary attribute impairment	Fortitude	—
Draining, life	3 per grade	1 lethal damage per Threat Level, NPC heals equal amount	Fortitude	—
Draining, soul	5 per grade	Target dies (standard character) or loses 1 action die and 10 maximum vitality (special character)	Fortitude	—
Enraging	2 per grade	Target *enraged* for 1d6 rounds per grade	Will	—
Entangling	2 per grade	Target *entangled* for 1d6 rounds per grade	Fortitude	—
Fatiguing	3 per grade	Target becomes *fatigued*	Fortitude	—
Frightening	2 per grade	Target *frightened* for 1d6 rounds per grade	Will	—
Paralyzing	4 per grade	Target *paralyzed* for 1d6 rounds per grade	Will	—
Petrifying	5 per grade	Target turned to stone	Fortitude	—
Shaking	3 per grade	Target becomes *shaken*	Will	—
Sickening	2 per grade	Target *sickened* for 1d6 rounds per grade	Will	—
Slowing	3 per grade	Target *slowed* for 1d6 rounds per grade	Will	—
Sprawling	2 per grade	Target becomes *sprawled*	Fortitude	—
Stunning	3 per grade	Target *stunned* for 1d6 rounds per grade	Will	—
Wounding	2 per grade	Target begins *bleeding* for 1d6 rounds per grade	Fortitude	—
Save Attack Upgrades				
Supernatural Attack	+2	Triggered by natural attack, may not have Area	—	—
Area				
Aura	+3 per 10 ft. radius	Per effect	Per effect	Per effect
Beam	+1 per 10 ft. range	Per effect	Per effect	Per effect
Blast	+3 per 5 ft. blast increment (damage attacks only)	Per effect	Per effect	Per effect
Cone	+2 per 10 ft. range	Per effect	Per effect	Per effect
Gaze	+3	Per effect	Per effect	Per effect
Ray	+1 per 20 ft. range	Per effect	Per effect	Per effect

* Damage die determined by grade: I = d4, II = d6, III = d8, IV = d10, V = d12

** If the attack has an Area, it gains a Ref save to reduce the damage by 1/2 (rounded up)

† This quality may be added to an attack multiple times.

Entangling: The attack roots the target in place. With a failed Fortitude save, he becomes *entangled.*

Fatiguing: The attack weakens the target. With a failed Fortitude save, he becomes *fatigued.*

Frightening: The attack fills the target with anxiety and horror. With a failed Will save, he becomes *frightened.*

Paralyzing: The attack causes the target's muscles to lock up. With a failed Will save, he becomes *paralyzed.*

Petrifying: The attack transmogrifies the target's flesh into solid rock. With a failed Fortitude save, he's turned into stone (effectively dying, unless restored through magical means).

Shaking: The attack rattles the target. With a failed Will save, the target becomes *shaken.*

Sickening: The attack fills the target with nausea or vertigo. With a failed Will save, he becomes *sickened.*

Slowing: The attack hampers the target's reaction time. With a failed Will save, he becomes *slowed.*

Sprawling: The attack sends the target reeling or lashes him to the earth. With a failed Fortitude save, he becomes *sprawled.*

Stunning: The attack shocks the target, overwhelming his senses. With a failed Will save, he becomes *stunned.*

Wounding: The attack causes the target to hemorrhage. With a failed Fortitude save, he begins *bleeding.*

UPGRADE DESCRIPTIONS

Extraordinary attack upgrades often add weapon qualities *(see page 176).*

Aligned (damage attacks only): The attack is powered by the NPC's beliefs or designed to smite those with certain convictions, gaining the *aligned* weapon quality.

Alternate Damage (damage attacks only): The attack harms in an unusual way, its damage type changing to something other than lethal *(see page 210).*

Armor-Piercing (damage attacks only): The attack penetrates easily, gaining the *armor-piercing 2* weapon quality.

Bleed (damage attacks only): The attack inflicts injuries that don't heal quickly. It gains the *bleed* weapon quality.

Diseased (damage attacks only): The attack transmits 1 disease from Table 7.8: Diseases *(see page 341),* exposing any target who suffers 1 or more damage after Reduction and Resistances.

Keen (damage attacks only): The attack slices or pierces deeply into the foe's body, gaining the *keen 4* weapon quality.

Supernatural Attack (save attacks with no Area only): One of the NPC's natural attacks is linked to this extraordinary save attack. Once per round when the NPC hits with the natural attack, the target is also automatically hit by the save attack.

Venomous (damage attacks only): The attack transmits 1 poison from Table 4.12: Poisons *(see page 166),* exposing any target who suffers 1 or more damage after Reduction and Resistances.

AREA DESCRIPTIONS

Aura: The attack radiates out in all directions from the NPC, affecting all characters within the listed radius.

Beam: The attack radiates out in a single direction of the NPC's choice, affecting all characters along its path.

Blast (damage attacks only): The attack explodes outward from the NPC with the listed blast increment *(see page 214).*

Cone: The attack radiates out in a cone shape from the NPC *(see page 214).*

Gaze: The attack targets one character who can see the NPC *(see page 223).*

Ray: The attack targets one character the NPC can see.

STEP 4: GEAR AND TREASURE

Players may assign limited gear to NPCs they create (contacts, followers, and hirelings) while GMs may assign any gear they like to their NPCs. Treasure may *only* be assigned to the GM's NPCs.

Gear assigned to player-created NPCs always increases XP value (as it's assumed to be helping the party) while gear and treasure assigned to GM-created NPCs never increases XP value (because it's inconsequential on non-combatants and acts as an additional reward when seized from adversaries).

Kits: NPCs automatically gain kits for their Signature Skills. This has no impact on XP value.

PLAYER-CREATED NPCS

A player may assign any gear to his NPCs so long as each individual piece has a Complexity of 15 or less. The gear increases an NPC's XP value by the total Complexity of all items divided by 10 (rounded up).

Example: Brungil gains a personal lieutenant and assigns a claymore (Complexity 10), partial platemail (Complexity 15), and a bullseye lantern (Complexity 10). The lieutenant's XP value increases by 4.

GM-CREATED NPCS

The GM may assign gear with any Complexity to his NPCs without modifying the XP value. He can do the same with Reputation items and benefits.

Treasure comes in six categories.

- *(A)ny:* Random results from any of the following categories
- *(C)oin:* Money of the realm
- *(G)ear:* Non-magical items with a silver cost
- *(L)oot :* Art, gems, raw materials, and trade goods
- *(M)agic:* Potions, scrolls, and other magic items
- *(T)rophies:* Body parts, jewelry, and other remains (whether they're stripped from the NPC or carried by it)

The GM simply chooses how many rolls the party makes in each category when the NPC is defeated (e.g. 1 Any roll, 2 Coin rolls, and 1 Magic Item roll, which would be listed as "1A, 2C, 1M"). As with gear, treasure doesn't increase the XP value of a GM-created NPC.

Example: The GM doesn't think the owlbear carries much in the way of coin, gear, or magic items, but it's chock full of trophies. He assigns it "2T," which adds 0 XP.

Example: Fortunado, on the other hand, has plenty of gear and treasure. The GM gives him partial leather armor and a claymore, plus a mage's pouch for his Spellcasting Signature Skill. The GM also assigns Fortunado some treasure: 1C, 2G, 1M, and 1T. Despite this haul, Fortunado's XP remains unaffected. Remember that all of this is stuff the party can seize after they defeat the traitor.

See page 344 for details about making Treasure Rolls.

STEP 5: XP VALUE

This last step applies only if you're a player building a follower, contact, or hireling, or the GM building an adversary. In either of these cases, total the XP values from statistics, qualities, and gear. If it's negative, it becomes 0.

FOLLOWERS, CONTACTS, AND HIRELINGS

Make sure the total XP value doesn't exceed the maximum amount allowed by the rule granting you the NPC. If it does, go back and make adjustments as necessary. When you're done, fill out the NPC Record Sheet and check with the GM to make sure it works in the story and setting.

ADVERSARIES

An adversary's XP value becomes its **bounty**. A special adversary's bounty is earned when he's defeated *(see page 337)*. Standard adversaries are a bit more ubiquitous and their bounty is earned once per **mob** that's defeated (a mob being equal in number to the player characters). Fewer standard adversaries add proportionately less XP (rounding up).

Example: The GM introduces owlbears as a standard NPC threat to the region. A party of five characters defeats three of them, which translates to 40 XP (3/5 of the creature's full value of 66 XP).

Example: Several adventures later, after the party has blithely slaughtered a few dozen owlbears, the GM introduces a special NPC, Mother Wisdom Gristleclaw, who seeks to exterminate her cubs' hunters. She has the same XP as a standard owlbear but defeating her yields a bounty of 66 XP.

PREPPING AN NPC FOR PLAY

Each NPC is presented in a standard template, called a "stat block." Before the Threat Level is known, a completed NPC is ready for use in any game with characters having any combination of Career Levels. For loads of examples, check out the Rogues Gallery *(see page 244)* and Bestiary *(see page 253)*. For now, here are our completed owlbear and Fortunado the traitor. Note that the owlbear has no gear so that part of the stat block has been left off. Also note that the XP seen here is just a base and interacts with the Threat Level to determine the actual encounter reward *(see page 342)*.

Owlbear (Large Animal Walker — 66 XP): Str 14, Dex 10, Con 16, Int 4, Wis 10, Cha 10; SZ L (2×2, Reach 1); Spd 30 ft.; Init III; Atk VII; Def IV; Res V; Health V; Comp —; Skills: Notice IV, Survival IV; Qualities: *Damage reduction 2, fearless I, grappler, improved sense (sight), rend*
Attacks/Weapons: Bite I (dmg 1d10+2 lethal; threat 18–20), Talon II × 2 (dmg 1d8+2 lethal; threat 19–20)
Treasure: 2T

Fortunado (Medium Folk Walker — 106 XP): Str 14, Dex 16, Con 16, Int 12, Wis 12, Cha 16; SZ M (Reach 1); Spd 40 ft.; Init II; Atk V; Def III; Res IV; Health IV; Comp V; Skills: Bluff VII, Impress VI, Spellcasting II; Spells: Command I, Scrye I; Qualities: *Cagey II, class ability (Mage: arcane wellspring I; Rune Knight: blooding rune), critical surge, story-critical*
Attacks/Weapons: Claymore (dmg 2d6+2 lethal; threat 19–20; qualities: *massive, reach +1*), Cone of Fire (fire attack IV: 30 ft. cone; dmg 1d10 fire per 2 TL, Ref DC 25 for 1/2 damage), Muscle Cramp (slowing attack III: 60 ft. beam; Will save DC 15 or become *slowed* for 3d6 rounds)
Gear: Fitted partial leather armor (DR 1; Resist Edged 3; DP –1; ACP –0; Spd —; Disguise +0)
Treasure: 1C, 2G, 1M, 1T

Once the Threat Level is known, an NPC's stat block easily generates all the numbers needed for play. Just look up each Grade on Table 6.1 and plug the numbers in. As an example, here's what the two example characters look like at Threat Level 2. Note that Size is factored into Defense and attribute modifiers are factored into Trait and Signature Skill bonuses.

Owlbear (Large Animal Walker — 66 XP): Str 14, Dex 10, Con 16, Int 4, Wis 10, Cha 10; SZ L (2×2, Reach 1); Spd 30 ft.; Init +1; Atk +5 (unarmed and melee) or +3 (hurled and ranged); Def 11; Res +6 (Fortitude) or +3 (Reflex) or +3 (Will); Health +8 if standard or 50 vitality and 24 wounds if special; Comp —; Skills: Notice +6, Survival +6; Qualities: *Damage reduction 2, fearless I, grappler, improved sense (sight), rend*

Attacks/Weapons: Bite I (dmg 1d10+2 lethal; threat 18–20), Talon II × 2 (dmg 1d8+2 lethal; threat 19–20)

Treasure: 2T

Fortunado (Medium Folk Walker — 106 XP): Str 14, Dex 16, Con 16, Int 12, Wis 12, Cha 16; SZ M (Reach 1); Spd 40 ft.; Init +4; Atk +4 (unarmed and melee) or +5 (hurled and ranged); Def 14; Res +5 (Fortitude) or +5 (Reflex) or +3 (Will); Health +5 if standard or 40 vitality and 16 wounds if special; Comp +3; Skills: Bluff +13, Impress +11, Spellcasting +4; Spells: Command I, Scrye I; Qualities: *Cagey II, class ability (Mage: arcane wellspring I; Rune Knight: blooding rune), critical surge, story-critical*

Attacks/Weapons: Claymore (dmg 2d6+2 lethal; threat 19–20; qualities: *massive, reach +1*), Cone of Fire (fire attack IV: 30 ft. cone; dmg 1d10 fire per 2 TL, Ref DC 25 for 1/2 damage), Muscle Cramp (slowing attack III: 60 ft. beam; Will save DC 15 or become *slowed* for 3d6 rounds)

Gear: Fitted partial leather armor (DR 1; Resist Edged 3; DP –1; ACP –0; Spd —; Disguise +0)

Treasure: 1C, 2G, 1M, 1T

And here's what they look like at Threat Level 10. Again, Size is factored into Defense and attribute modifiers are factored into Trait and Signature Skill bonuses.

Owlbear (Large Animal Walker — 66 XP): Str 14, Dex 10, Con 16, Int 4, Wis 10, Cha 10; SZ L (2×2, Reach 1); Spd 30 ft.; Init +6; Atk +15 (unarmed and melee) or +13 (hurled and ranged); Def 17; Res +10 (Fortitude) or +7 (Reflex) or +7 (Will); Health +12 if standard or 250 vitality and 24 wounds if special; Comp —; Skills: Notice +13, Survival +13; Qualities: *Damage reduction 2, fearless I, grappler, improved sense (sight), rend*

Attacks/Weapons: Bite I (dmg 1d10+2 lethal; threat 18–20), Talon II × 2 (dmg 1d8+2 lethal; threat 19–20)

Treasure: 2T

Fortunado (Medium Folk Walker — 106 XP): Str 14, Dex 16, Con 16, Int 12, Wis 12, Cha 16; SZ M (Reach 1); Spd 40 ft.; Init +8; Atk +12 (unarmed and melee) or +13 (hurled and ranged); Def 19; Res +9 (Fortitude) or +9 (Reflex) or +7 (Will); Health +9 if standard or 200 vitality and 16 wounds if special; Comp +7; Skills: Bluff +22, Impress +20, Spellcasting +10; Spells: Command I, Scrye I; Qualities: *Cagey II, class ability (Mage: arcane wellspring I; Rune Knight: blooding rune), critical surge, story-critical*

Attacks/Weapons: Claymore (dmg 2d6+2 lethal; threat 19–20; qualities: *massive, reach +1*), Cone of Fire (fire attack IV: 30 ft. cone; dmg 1d10 fire per 2 TL, Ref DC 25 for 1/2 damage), Muscle Cramp (slowing attack III: 60 ft. beam; Will save DC 15 or become *slowed* for 3d6 rounds)

Gear: Fitted partial leather armor (DR 1; Resist Edged 3; DP –1; ACP –0; Spd —; Disguise +0)

Treasure: 1C, 2G, 1M, 1T

Same NPC scaled to any adventure, whether it's introduced as standard or special. This lets you quickly and easily develop NPCs in advance or even build them "on the fly" during a game. It also lets you include exactly the people and monsters that fit the flavor of the world, regardless of play level. Hit the party with a special ancient dragon at Level 1 or throw formidable standard orcs at them at Level 12. The shackles are off and the sky's the limit!

USING AN NPC

An NPC doesn't have and can't gain any stat, option, or ability unavailable during NPC creation. This includes but isn't limited to Origins, Subplots, and Lifestyle. They can, however, spend Reputation by increasing their XP value by 1/4 the same amount (rounded down).

An NPC's personal Threat Level and Career Level are each equal to the current adventure's Threat Level and his starting action dice, when needed to determine the effectiveness of abilities only, are calculated accordingly (the GM maintains only one actual pool of action dice, as described on page 365). Standard NPCs roll d6 action dice and special NPCs roll 1 die type higher than the highest typically available to player characters.

Example: The GM introduces Fortunado in an adventure with five PCs whose Career Levels range from 10 to 12. The highest action die type among them is d8 so Fortunado rolls d10s.

Rules for NPC injury and healing are found in Chapter 5 *(see pages 207 and 212, respectively).*

TIPS & TRICKS

The *Fantasy Craft* NPC system is wildly flexible, capable of creating lowly peasants or world-destroying monsters — all scaled to properly challenge the party — in just a few minutes. This versatility comes at a price, however, as it's possible (though difficult) to accidentally create NPCs that are unnecessarily lethal or cumbersome. Here are some tips for building fun, effective, and challenging threats for your party.

BUILDING A BETTER MONSTER

Let's start with the "big secret": this system *isn't perfectly balanced.* Devious GMs (and players) *can* game this system by min-maxing stats, abusing qualities, and optimizing attacks. There are a number of reasons for this — the system's plug and play nature demands that countless stats, qualities, and customized attacks work in tandem; simpler, *slightly* less balanced mechanics are much easier and faster to use (a major goal of Mastercraft) — but the upshot is that, as in all RPGs, the GM's judgment is vital to ensuring NPCs are a fun and fair challenge for the characters. It's critical that the final decision about any NPC rest with him.

So, about building that better monster... It starts with a solid concept. Ask some basic questions about its ecology. How large is it? Is it domesticated or wild? Is it sapient or animalistic? What does it eat? Where does it live? Are its abilities magical or mundane? All these questions provide guidelines for stats, qualities, and attacks, even if you're not entirely sure what role the creature will serve in your game.

When you're starting to get a picture of the monster in your mind, ask one of the most critical questions: What are its strengths and weaknesses? Even though the NPC system tends not to reward penalties — a low Speed or attribute score doesn't reduce the NPC's XP value except in a few very specific circumstances — you should still try to *ensure that your monster has weaknesses as well as strengths.* There are no perfect specimens in nature and even if there were, they wouldn't be fun to fight.

Next, a walkthrough of the some of the more complex parts of NPC creation...

MOBILITY

Mobility is fairly self-explanatory: *unless the creature moves in some special way, it's probably a walker.* Burrowers and flyers can become walkers, allowing them to also swim. In the event that you need a walker to swim particularly well, there's the *superior swimmer* quality, which covers most aquatic walkers up to Grade IV. Grades V though VIII are great for legged creatures whose primary method of travel is swimming, or who move through water with the grace and ease of a fish.

It's easy to get carried away with Speeds, particularly in the case of flyers (which we as a modern audience can easily view like jets instead of birds). As a general rule, you should avoid giving any creature — no matter its origin or source of mobility — any Speed over 100 ft. Doing so needlessly bloats the creature's XP and tends to be irrelevant in actual play, boiling down to "anywhere in the combat" every round. If you're worried about the creature being able to cover ground quickly enough out of combat, consider the *superior traveler* quality.

Also, when you want to model clumsy flight and swimming, simply make sure the creature's Competence is relatively low and don't give it Acrobatics (which is used for Maneuver checks) or Athletics (which is used for Swim checks). Conversely, you can add these Signature Skills for deft or lithe climbers, flyers, or swimmers.

STATISTICS

Traits, which are graded from I–X to grant shifting bonuses, can be difficult to gauge. It's hard to tell how well a creature will perform at the table, especially against a diverse group of characters. Fortunately, there's a hidden benchmark built into the system: NPC stats tend to hover around those of player characters at Grades II to V (II being roughly equivalent to low-end PC progressions and V being roughly equivalent to the high end). With this in mind, you can make a number of informed decisions when building any NPC, monster or no. Slower than the slowest hero? Initiative I. Mid-range fighter? Attack III or IV. Hardier than the toughest PC? Resilience VI or above. Remember, you can always go back and revise stats if you're unhappy with the results.

Attributes can easily contribute to XP bloat (i.e. adding XP value without giving the NPC a meaningful advantage in play). They only offer bonuses at even numbers (+1 at 12, +2 at 14, etc.), so odd numbers do nothing but increase XP value by 1 (animals being a notable exception, as they benefit from odd scores during training). Very high or across-the-board attribute bonuses also contribute to bloat and make the NPC harder to use because the GM has to constantly apply modifiers.

Signature Skills are a particular culprit for bloat, as it's easy to envision NPCs having "a little of everything and/or a lot in a few things." It's also easy to forget that they're not player characters. Ultimately, it's better for an NPC to stick to the small number of skills they're likely to use in play: three or less is fine for "average" NPCs, or up to five for "high-functioning" characters. When an NPC must be broadly capable, apply a high Competence grade instead (as seen in summoned Advisors on page 119).

QUALITIES

In a similar vein, *beware of overloading NPCs with qualities.* The Bestiary offers examples as simple as sheep or as complex as the tarasque but in each case qualities have been carefully chosen to flesh out the creature's concept. As mentioned in Step 2, it's important not to pile qualities onto your creation for no reason other than to make it "better." This dilutes the flavor and impact of all the qualities you add, bloats XP, and makes the NPC harder to use.

Defensive qualities can also easily get out of hand, particularly *damage reduction, damage defiance,* and *damage immunity* (especially defiance or immunity to lethal or subdual damage). Keep in mind, *unkillable NPCs aren't fun.* Damage Reduction above 8 essentially renders 75–90% of all mundane weapons useless. Most of the time, you should apply no more than two to three defensive qualities to a creature and make sure they thoroughly support its concept.

ATTACKS

Natural and extraordinary attacks deserve special attention because, while they can be highly effective ways to represent a creature's function, they can also be a fast track to XP bloat. They're attractive to NPC builders because they include lots of interesting effects but again, be careful not to add anything that isn't strictly necessary.

When adding natural attacks, consider the damage grade against the heroes' weapons: Grades I and II are generally comparable to low-damage melee and hurled weapons while Grades III and IV are similar to high-damage melee weapons, black powder weapons, and magic weapons. Grade V attacks can be as effective as artifacts or siege weapons and should be used only in the very rarest of cases. Skim the Bestiary and you'll notice the scarcity of natural attack Grades III and above. This keeps games from turning into arms races and ensures maximum versatility on the battlefield.

Extraordinary attacks are tricky. They replicate an incredible range of supernatural effects but, like monsters, only come into their own with a solid concept. Ask yourself several critical questions.

- *Does the attack inflict damage or do something else?* Unless it inflicts damage you should probably consider a save attack.
- *Is the attack especially damaging or difficult to resist?* If so, a higher grade is in order. This increases damage dice and/or save DCs. If you need an average, apply Grades II or III. Grade I is intentionally mild and Grades IV and V are truly savage.
- *Does the NPC make the attack in melee or at a distance?* An extraordinary attack made in melee often won't have an Area and may gain the *supernatural attack* upgrade so it's triggered by a natural attack hit. At a distance you have to ask yourself...
- *Does the attack affect one target or many?* With a single target at range you're probably looking at a Ray or Gaze attack. For a discriminating Area, consider a Line or Cone. Auras and Blasts should be reserved for truly wide-reaching assaults.

Finally, watch for ways NPC qualities augment a monster's attacks. *Charge attack, rend, swift attack,* and particularly *frenzy* can greatly expand the volume of attacks your beast brings to bear, while *monstrous attack, favored foes,* and *treacherous* vastly improve their lethality. *Grueling combatant, fearsome,* and *unnerving* can wear the enemy down in long combats and specialized qualities like *grappler* and *improved stability* offer narrowly defined advantages with specific attacks.

MAGIC

NPCs gain magic ability in three ways: the Spellcasting Signature Skill, the *natural spell* quality, and the *devoted* quality. *Natural spell* is best for inherent abilities, especially those possessed by animals (though some can also be handled as extraordinary attacks). It's also good for abilities only used infrequently ("once a day" spells in that *other* game). Tool-using and magic-reliant creatures, plus those with formal magic training, are better off with Spellcasting. It requires a skill check to use but offers far more flexibility than *natural spell. Devoted* straddles this divide, granting a discreet bundle of once-per-scene or at-will spells in a themed pattern. It's a good fit for focused magic users and divine casters.

TREASURE

An NPC's treasure can represent how it lives and what it collects, especially if the NPC is a monster (in which case it can also represent the creature's physical makeup: an ooze absorbing things it slides over, for example). Poor monsters and animals might have no treasure, or 1 roll in an appropriate category. Humanoids can have 1–3 rolls but *even very rich and powerful NPCs shouldn't have more than 6.* Weapons, armor, and other gear can and probably should cut into this limit — often, it's treasure enough.

Treasure categories depend greatly on the creature's physiology and proclivities. Trophies are a perfect fit for beasts with valuable hides, ivory, or other highly sought parts. Supernatural monsters sometimes have Magic treasure, while humanoids and tool-users frequently carry Coin and Gear. Wealthy foes, like merchants, liches, and wizards, are likely to have Coin and/or Loot, and creatures with lairs (like dragons) and immobile NPCs (like plants) often tap the Any category. What's important is that an NPC's treasure be that hint of additional flavor showcasing their story; anything more and you risk turning the monster into a goodie piñata for the party.

THE ART OF (NOT) KILLING THE PCS

Because *Fantasy Craft* monsters don't have "levels," it can be difficult to judge their effectiveness against the player characters. Traits, skills, attacks, and other NPC options scale to the Threat Level, but that only toggles each graded statistic in a vacuum. It doesn't take into consideration how the sum of the NPC's parts rates against the party, which is the most important metric when building encounters. Fortunately, there's another number already available for this purpose — the NPC's XP value. You can gauge the threat of *a single special NPC or a mob of standard NPCs with this handy scale.*

Minor Threat (Up to 40 XP): The NPC(s) are pushovers, likely possessing sub-par statistics and very few distinguishing qualities. They offer little challenge to the average adventuring party. *Examples:* Kobold "warriors," small animals, and most NPCs in the Rogues Gallery

Average Threat (41–80 XP): The NPC(s) are a fair-to-middling challenge, with a few useful statistics or abilities.

Given the right circumstances, they might prove a reasonable obstacle for the party. *Examples:* Basilisks, minotaurs, knights, and necromancers

Significant Threat (81–120 XP): The NPC(s) have a number of powerful statistics or unusual qualities that set them apart. The party should be cautious opposing them. *Examples:* Doppelgangers, trolls, and dire animals

Serious Threat (121–160 XP): The NPC(s) are extremely competent, with superior stats and powerful qualities that collectively pose a grave threat to the party's wellbeing. *Examples:* Brain fiends, elder elementals, and many demons

Extreme Threat (161+ XP): The NPC(s) are party killers, best employed rarely or when the heroes are spoiling for a life-or-death battle. *Examples:* Dragons, greater demons, and watchers in the dark

As a rule, *each additional special NPC or mob of standard NPCs increases the threat by one degree* (e.g. from minor to average or from significant to serious).

Insight about choosing the right adversaries (beyond the numbers) can be found on pages 328 and 337. For help balancing encounters during play, see page 363.

ROGUES GALLERY

These NPCs make great contacts, followers, or hirelings. They can also help populate your setting.

Apothecary (Medium Folk Walker — 36 XP): Str 10, Dex 10, Con 10, Int 10, Wis 10, Cha 10; SZ M (1×1, Reach 1); Spd 30 ft. ground; Init I; Atk I; Def IV; Res III; Health III; Comp III; Skills: Crafting IV, Medicine VI, Resolve IV; Qualities: *Expertise (Medicine), feat (Alchemy Basics, Bandage, Basic Skill Mastery (Healer))*

Attacks/Weapons: None

Mounts and Vehicles: Cart (Spd 20 ft. ground (Run 40 ft.); Travel 2; SZ/Def L/9) or none

Gear: Bandages (10), chemist's kit, doctor's bag

Treasure: 1G, 1M

Apprentice (Medium Folk Walker — 24 XP): Str 10, Dex 10, Con 10, Int 10, Wis 10, Cha 10; SZ M (1×1, Reach 1); Spd 30 ft. ground; Init III; Atk II; Def IV; Res IV; Health III; Comp II; Skills: Crafting IV; Qualities: *Feat (Crafting Basics)*

Attacks/Weapons: Dagger (dmg 1d6 lethal; threat 19–20; qualities: *bleed, hurl*)

Mounts and Vehicles: Cart (Spd 20 ft. ground (Run 40 ft.); Travel 2; SZ/Def L/9) or none

Gear: Crafting kit

Treasure: 1G

Artist (Medium Folk Walker — 28 XP): Str 10, Dex 10, Con 10, Int 10, Wis 10, Cha 10; SZ M (1×1, Reach 1); Spd 30 ft. ground; Init IV; Atk II; Def IV; Res II; Health II; Comp III; Skills: Crafting V, Impress V; Qualities: *Class ability (Keeper: adaptable toolbox)*

Attacks/Weapons: Short staff (dmg 1d6 subdual; threat 20; qualities: *double, trip*)

Gear: Crafting kit

Treasure: 2L

Attendant (Medium Folk Walker — 35 XP): Str 10, Dex 10, Con 10, Int 10, Wis 10, Cha 10; SZ M (1×1, Reach 1); Spd 30 ft. ground; Init VI; Atk II; Def III; Res III; Health II; Comp III; Skills: Notice IV, Ride IV, Sense Motive IV; Qualities: *Always ready, class ability (Burglar: look out!)*

Attacks/Weapons: Short sword (dmg 1d8 lethal; threat 19–20; qualities: *keen 4*)

Mounts and Vehicles: Riding horse ground (Spd 50 ft. (Run 250 ft.); Travel 7; SZ/Def L/IV) or none

Gear: Ceremonial partial leather armor (DR 0; Resist Fire 3; DP –1; ACP –0; Spd —; Disguise +0)

Treasure: 1C, 1G

Banker (Medium Folk Walker — 37 XP): Str 10, Dex 10, Con 10, Int 10, Wis 10, Cha 10; SZ M (1×1, Reach 1); Spd 30 ft. ground; Init III; Atk II; Def IV; Res III; Health III; Comp IV; Skills: Haggle VII, Sense Motive VI; Qualities: *Class ability (Courtier: with a word), honorable*

Attacks/Weapons: Sword cane (dmg 1d8 lethal; threat 20; qualities: *AP 2, finesse*)

Mounts and Vehicles: Coach (Spd 20 ft. ground (Run 40 ft.); Travel 4; SZ/Def L/9) or none

Gear: Common ink, sheaf of paper, signet ring, small chest with combination lock

Treasure: 1A, 3C

Barkeep/Tavern Master (Medium Folk Walker — 29 XP): Str 10, Dex 10, Con 12, Int 10, Wis 10, Cha 10; SZ M (1×1, Reach 1); Spd 30 ft. ground; Init II; Atk IV; Def III; Res IV; Health III; Comp I; Skills: Athletics III, Sleight of Hand III; Qualities: *Grappler*

Attacks/Weapons: Club (dmg 1d8 subdual; threat 20)

Gear: Booze (6 uses), Spirits (3 uses)

Treasure: 2C

Bowman (Medium Folk Walker — 32 XP): Str 10, Dex 10, Con 10, Int 10, Wis 10, Cha 10; SZ M (1×1, Reach 1); Spd 30 ft. ground; Init IV; Atk V; Def II; Res II; Health II; Comp I; Skills: Ride III, Search V, Sneak III; Qualities: *Feat (Bow Basics, Bow Mastery), improved sense (sight)*

Attacks/Weapons: Dagger (dmg 1d6 lethal; threat 19–20; qualities: *bleed, hurl*), long bow + 40 standard arrows (dmg 1d6

lethal; threat 19–20; range 40 ft. × 6; qualities: *AP 4, poisonous*)

Gear: Partial leather armor (DR 1; Resist Fire 3; DP –1; ACP –0; Spd —; Disguise +0)

Treasure: 1C

Brigand (Medium Folk Walker — 38 XP): Str 10, Dex 10, Con 10, Int 10, Wis 10, Cha 10; SZ M (1×1, Reach 1); Spd 30 ft. ground; Init V; Atk IV; Def III; Res III; Health IV; Comp II; Skills: Intimidate VI, Ride IV, Tactics IV; Qualities: *Menacing threat, tricky (Cheap Shot)*

Attacks/Weapons: Short sword (dmg 1d8 lethal; threat 19–20; qualities: *keen 4*)

Mounts and Vehicles: Riding horse (Spd 50 ft. ground (Run 250 ft.); Travel 7; SZ/Def L/IV) or none

Gear: Partial leather armor (DR 1; Resist Fire 3; DP –1; ACP –0; Spd —; Disguise +0), saddlebags

Treasure: 1A, 1C

Con Man (Medium Folk Walker — 40 XP): Str 10, Dex 10, Con 10, Int 10, Wis 10, Cha 10; SZ M (1×1, Reach 1); Spd 30 ft. ground; Init IV; Atk II; Def II; Res II; Health II; Comp IV; Skills: Bluff IX, Impress V, Sense Motive V; Qualities: *Attractive I, class ability (Assassin: cold read I; Burglar: he did it!)*

Attacks/Weapons: Sap (dmg 1d6 subdual; threat 19–20; qualities: *finesse*)

Mounts and Vehicles: Coach (Spd 20 ft. ground (Run 40 ft.); Travel 4; SZ/Def L/9) or none

Gear: Booze (1 use), knockout poison (3 uses)

Treasure: 1C, 1L

Craftsman (Medium Folk Walker — 36 XP): Str 10, Dex 10, Con 10, Int 10, Wis 10, Cha 10; SZ M (1×1, Reach 1); Spd 30 ft. ground; Init II; Atk II; Def III; Res III; Health II; Comp III; Skills: Crafting VII, Haggle IV, Resolve IV; Qualities: *Expertise (Crafting), feat (Crafting Basics, Crafting Mastery)*

Attacks/Weapons: Mallet (dmg 1d6 lethal; threat 20)

Gear: Masterwork crafting kit

Treasure: 2G, 1L

Cutpurse (Medium Folk Walker — 41 XP): Str 10, Dex 10, Con 10, Int 10, Wis 10, Cha 10; SZ M (1×1, Reach 1); Spd 30 ft. ground (Run 150 ft.); Init IV; Atk III; Def V; Res II; Health II; Comp II; Skills: Blend VII, Disguise IV, Prestidigitation VII; Qualities: *Class ability (Assassin: quick on your feet 1/session; Burglar: stash it), superior runner I*

Attacks/Weapons: Dagger (dmg 1d6 lethal; threat 19–20; qualities: *bleed, hurl*)

Gear: Thieves' tools

Treasure: 2C

Damsel (Medium Folk Walker — 37 XP): Str 10, Dex 10, Con 10, Int 10, Wis 10, Cha 10; SZ M (1×1, Reach 1); Spd 30 ft. ground; Init I; Atk II; Def IV; Res II; Health II; Comp II; Skills: Impress VIII, Intimidate III, Ride III; Qualities: *Attractive III, honorable, feat (Comely, Repartee Basics)*

Attacks/Weapons: None

Mounts and Vehicles: Riding horse (Spd 50 ft. ground (Run 250 ft.); Travel 7; SZ/Def L/IV) or none

Gear: Lady's favor (love potion, 1 use)

Treasure: None

Devotee (Medium Folk Walker — 31 XP): Str 10, Dex 10, Con 10, Int 10, Wis 10, Cha 10; SZ M (1×1, Reach 1); Spd 30 ft. ground; Init II; Atk III; Def II; Res V; Health II; Comp I; Skills: Impress III, Resolve VI; Qualities: *Devoted II (any Alignment), honorable, interests (Alignment)*

Attacks/Weapons: Ritual weapon

Gear: Holy book

Treasure: None

Entertainer (Medium Folk Walker — 34 XP): Str 10, Dex 10, Con 10, Int 10, Wis 10, Cha 10; SZ M (1×1, Reach 1); Spd 30 ft. ground; Init III; Atk II; Def III; Res II; Health I; Comp III; Skills: Acrobatics IV, Impress VI, Prestidigitation IV; Qualities: *Beguiling, class ability (Burglar: slippery), expertise (Impress)*

Attacks/Weapons: Dagger (dmg 1d6 lethal; threat 19–20; qualities: *bleed, hurl*)

Gear: Disguise kit, musical instrument, torches (5)

Treasure: 1C

Farmer (Medium Folk Walker — 28 XP): Str 10, Dex 10, Con 12, Int 10, Wis 10, Cha 10; SZ M (1×1, Reach 1); Spd 30 ft. ground; Init II; Atk III; Def I; Res IV; Health V; Comp I; Skills: Athletics IV, Crafting IV, Survival IV; Qualities: None

Attacks/Weapons: Scythe (dmg 1d10 lethal; threat 20; qualities: *AP 2, trip*)

Mounts and Vehicles: Wagon (Spd 20 ft. ground (Run 40 ft.); Travel 3; SZ/Def L/9) or none

Gear: Fresh food (3 uses)

Treasure: 1L

Fortune Teller (Medium Folk Walker — 44 XP): Str 10, Dex 10, Con 10, Int 10, Wis 10, Cha 10; SZ M (1×1, Reach 1); Spd 30 ft. ground; Init VII; Atk III; Def V; Res II; Health II; Comp III; Skills: Bluff V, Impress V, Sense Motive VII, Spellcasting II; Spells: Locate Object, Scrye I; Qualities: *Feat (Basic Skill Mastery (Actor), Lady Luck's Smile), spell defense I*

Attacks/Weapons: Dagger (dmg 1d6 lethal; threat 19–20; qualities: *bleed, hurl*)

Mounts and Vehicles: Wagon (Spd 20 ft. ground (Run 40 ft.); Travel 3; SZ/Def L/9) or none

Gear: Mage's pouch

Treasure: 1C, 1L

Goon (Medium Folk Walker — 27 XP): Str 10, Dex 10, Con 10, Int 10, Wis 10, Cha 10; SZ M (1×1, Reach 1); Spd 30 ft. ground; Init III; Atk VI; Def III; Res III; Health I; Comp I; Skills: Athletics IV, Intimidate IV; Qualities: *Feat (Club Basics, Horde Basics, Horde Mastery), mook*

Attacks/Weapons: Club (dmg 1d8 subdual; threat 20)

Gear: Partial leather armor (DR 1; Resist Fire 3; DP –1; ACP –0; Spd —; Disguise +0), booze (1 use)

Treasure: 1C

Guide (Medium Folk Walker — 37 XP): Str 10, Dex 10, Con 10, Int 10, Wis 10, Cha 10; SZ M (1×1, Reach 1); Spd 30 ft. ground; Init IV; Atk II; Def II; Res III; Health IV; Comp II; Skills: Medicine IV, Search IV, Survival VIII; Qualities: *Class ability (Scout: rough living I), superior traveler II*

Attacks/Weapons: Machete (dmg 1d8 lethal; threat 20; qualities: *AP 2*), short bow + 20 standard arrows (dmg 1d6 lethal; threat 19–20; range 20 ft. × 6; qualities: *AP 2, cavalry, poisonous*)

Mounts and Vehicles: Mule (Spd 30 ft. ground (Run 150 ft.); Travel 5; SZ/Def M/III) or riding horse (Spd 50 ft. ground (Run 250 ft.); Travel 7; SZ/Def L/IV)

Gear: Compass, saddlebags, rations (10), torches (5)

Treasure: None

Guild Boss (Medium Folk Walker — 61 XP): Str 10, Dex 10, Con 10, Int 10, Wis 10, Cha 10; SZ M (1×1, Reach 1); Spd 30 ft. ground; Init II; Atk III; Def V; Res III; Health III; Comp V; Skills: Haggle X, Impress VII, Intimidate VII; Qualities: *Class ability (Assassin: offer they can't refuse; Courtier: never outdone; Sage: best of the best I), condition immunity (Baffled)*

Attacks/Weapons: Dagger (dmg 1d6 lethal; threat 19–20; qualities: *bleed, hurl*)

Mounts and Vehicles: Coach (Spd 20 ft. ground (Run 40 ft.); Travel 4; SZ/Def L/9) or none

Treasure: 2A, 2C

Hunter (Medium Folk Walker — 41 XP): Str 10, Dex 10, Con 10, Int 10, Wis 10, Cha 10; SZ M (1×1, Reach 1); Spd 30 ft. ground; Init IV; Atk V; Def III; Res II; Health III; Comp II; Skills: Notice III, Search VI, Sneak III, Survival VI; Qualities: *Class ability (Scout: killing blow, trophy hunter), favored foes (animal)*

Attacks/Weapons: Hatchet (dmg 1d6 lethal; threat 20; qualities: *AP 2, hurl, trip*), reflex bow + 40 barbed arrows (dmg 1d6 lethal; threat 20; range 30 ft. × 6; qualities: *bleed, poisonous*)

Mounts and Vehicles: Riding horse (Spd 50 ft. ground (Run 250 ft.); Travel 7; SZ/Def L/IV) or none

Gear: 2 jaw traps

Treasure: 2T

Knight (Medium Folk Walker — 68 XP): Str 15, Dex 10, Con 10, Int 10, Wis 10, Cha 10; SZ M (1×1, Reach 1); Spd 30 ft. ground; Init IV; Atk VI; Def IV; Res V; Health V; Comp II; Skills: Athletics V, Impress III, Resolve V, Ride V, Tactics III; Qualities: *Class ability (Lancer: master rider I), fearless II, feat (Armor Basics, Charging Basics), honorable*

Attacks/Weapons: Lance (dmg 1d8+2 lethal; threat 19–20; qualities: *AP 4, cavalry, massive, reach +1*), long sword (dmg 1d12+2 lethal; threat 20), metal shield (dmg 1d4+2 subdual; threat 20; qualities: *guard +2*)

Mounts and Vehicles: War horse (Spd 50 ft. ground (Run 250 ft.); Travel 5; SZ/Def L/IV)

Gear: Full plate (moderate platemail with heavy fittings: DR 7; Resist Blunt 2; DP –4; ACP –4; Spd –10 ft.; Disguise obvious)

Treasure: 1C

Laborer (Medium Folk Walker — 27 XP): Str 10, Dex 10, Con 10, Int 10, Wis 10, Cha 10; SZ M (1×1, Reach 1); Spd 30 ft. ground; Init II; Atk IV; Def I; Res II; Health IV; Comp I; Skills: Athletics V, Crafting III, Haggle III; Qualities: *Improved stability*

Attacks/Weapons: Mallet (dmg 1d6 lethal; threat 20)

Gear: Crafting kit

Treasure: 1G

Man-at-Arms (Medium Folk Walker — 36 XP): Str 10, Dex 10, Con 10, Int 10, Wis 10, Cha 10; SZ M (1×1, Reach 1); Spd 30 ft. ground; Init IV; Atk IV; Def III; Res II; Health IV; Comp I; Skills: Athletics III, Intimidate III, Notice III, Tactics III; Qualities: *Class ability (Soldier: rugged weapons), feat (All-Out Attack, Combat Instincts)*

Attacks/Weapons: Glaive (dmg 1d8 lethal; threat 19–20; qualities: *keen 4, reach +1*), metal shield (dmg 1d4+2 subdual; threat 20; qualities: *guard +2*), short sword (dmg 1d8 lethal; threat 19–20; qualities: *keen 4*)

Gear: Partial chainmail with light fittings (DR 3, Resist Edged 2; DP –1; ACP –1; Spd –5 ft.; Disguise –8)

Treasure: 1C

Mercenary (Medium Folk Walker — 43 XP): Str 10, Dex 10, Con 10, Int 10, Wis 10, Cha 10; SZ M (1×1, Reach 1); Spd 30 ft. ground; Init IV; Atk IV; Def V; Res II; Health V; Comp II; Skills: Athletics III, Haggle V, Intimidate V, Tactics III; Qualities: *Always ready, class ability (Scout: sneak attack I), tricky (Called Shot)*

Attacks/Weapons: Dagger × 4 (dmg 1d6 lethal; threat 19–20; qualities: *bleed, hurl*), long sword (dmg 1d12 lethal; threat 20)

Mounts and Vehicles: Riding horse (Spd 50 ft. ground (Run 250 ft.); Travel 7; SZ/Def L/IV) or none

Gear: Partial studded leather armor (DR 2, Resist —; DP –1; ACP –0; Spd —; Disguise –0), game, spirits (1 use)

Treasure: 2C

Merchant (Medium Folk Walker — 33 XP): Str 10, Dex 10, Con 10, Int 10, Wis 10, Cha 10; SZ M (1×1, Reach 1); Spd 30 ft. ground; Init II; Atk I; Def II; Res I; Health IV; Comp III; Skills: Bluff IV, Haggle X, Crafting IV, Sense Motive IV; Qualities: *Expertise (Haggle)*

Attacks/Weapons: Dagger (dmg 1d6 lethal; threat 19–20; qualities: *bleed, hurl*)

Mounts and Vehicles: Wagon (Spd 20 ft. ground (Run 40 ft.); Travel 3; SZ/Def L/9) or none

Treasure: 1A, 2C, 2G

Necromancer (Medium Folk Walker — 53 XP): Str 10, Dex 10, Con 10, Int 10, Wis 10, Cha 10; SZ M (1×1, Reach 1); Spd 30 ft. ground; Init II; Atk II; Def III; Res V; Health V; Comp III; Skills: Intimidate VIII, Medicine V, Resolve V, Spellcasting V; Spells: Animate Dead II, Deathknell, Deathwatch, Dominate Undead I, Speak with Dead; Qualities: *Condition immunity (frightened), feat (Ghost Basics, Glint of Madness), stench*

Attacks/Weapons: Shod staff (dmg 1d8 lethal; threat 19–20; qualities: *double, trip*)

Mounts and Vehicles: Riding horse (Spd 50 ft. ground (Run 250 ft.); Travel 7; SZ/Def L/IV) or none

Gear: Moderate padded armor (DR 1, Resist Cold 5; DP –0; ACP –0; Spd —; Disguise +0), mage's pouch, mana potion

Treasure: 1M, 2T

Nobleman (Medium Folk Walker — 45 XP): Str 10, Dex 10, Con 10, Int 10, Wis 10, Cha 10; SZ M (1×1, Reach 1); Spd 30 ft. ground; Init III; Atk III; Def II; Res V; Health II; Comp III; Skills: Impress V, Intimidate IV, Ride IV, Sense Motive IV; Qualities: *Attractive I, class ability (Courtier: only the finest, with a word), feat (Repartee Basics, Repartee Mastery), tricky (Parry)*

Attacks/Weapons: Dagger (dmg 1d6 lethal; threat 19–20; qualities: *bleed, hurl*), rapier (dmg 1d8 lethal; threat 19–20; qualities: *bleed, finesse*)

Mounts and Vehicles: Riding horse (Spd 50 ft. ground (Run 250 ft.); Travel 7; SZ/Def L/IV) or none

Gear: Ceremonial partial leather armor (DR 0; Resist Fire 3; DP –1; ACP –0; Spd —; Disguise +0)

Treasure: 2C, 1L

Outrider (Medium Folk Walker — 37 XP): Str 10, Dex 10, Con 10, Int 10, Wis 10, Cha 10; SZ M (1×1, Reach 1); Spd 30 ft. ground; Init V; Atk II; Def IV; Res II; Health III; Comp II; Skills: Notice VII, Ride VII, Survival III; Qualities: *Improved sense (sight), light sleeper*

Attacks/Weapons: Cutlass (dmg 1d10 lethal; threat 19–20; qualities: *cavalry, finesse*), lasso (dmg —; threat —; range 10 ft. × 2; qualities: *cord, hook, trip*)

Mounts and Vehicles: Riding horse (Spd 50 ft. ground (Run 250 ft.); Travel 7; SZ/Def L/IV)

Gear: Partial leather armor (DR 1; Resist Fire 3; DP –1; ACP –0; Spd —; Disguise +0)

Treasure: 1C, 1G

Peasant (Medium Folk Walker — 20 XP): Str 10, Dex 10, Con 10, Int 10, Wis 10, Cha 10; SZ M (1×1, Reach 1); Spd 30 ft. ground; Init I; Atk II; Def III; Res IV; Health II; Comp I; Skills: Athletics III, Bluff III, Survival III; Qualities: *Meek*

Attacks/Weapons: Fork (dmg 1d8 lethal; threat 19–20; qualities: *hook, hurl*)

Treasure: None

Scholar (Medium Folk Walker — 33 XP): Str 10, Dex 10, Con 10, Int 10, Wis 10, Cha 10; SZ M (1×1, Reach 1); Spd 30 ft. ground; Init I; Atk I; Def II; Res II; Health II; Comp V; Skills: Investigate VII, Medicine VII; Qualities: *Bright I, class ability (Explorer: bookworm II; Keeper: bright idea I), interests (2 Studies), meek*

Attacks/Weapons: Scholar's sword (dmg 1d8 lethal; threat 20; qualities: *finesse, lure*)

Mounts and Vehicles: Donkey (Spd 30 ft. ground (Run 150 ft.); Travel 5; SZ/Def M/III) or none

Gear: Scribe's kit, astrolabe, magnifying glass

Treasure: None

Servant (Medium Folk Walker — 19 XP): Str 10, Dex 10, Con 10, Int 10, Wis 10, Cha 10; SZ M (1×1, Reach 1); Spd 30 ft. ground; Init II; Atk I; Def III; Res II; Health III; Comp II; Skills: Blend V, Bluff III; Qualities: *Meek*

Attacks/Weapons: None

Treasure: 1G

Strumpet (Medium Folk Walker — 27 XP): Str 10, Dex 10, Con 10, Int 10, Wis 10, Cha 10; SZ M (1×1, Reach 1); Spd 30 ft. ground; Init II; Atk III; Def I; Res II; Health II; Comp I; Skills: Bluff IV, Haggle IV, Impress II, Prestidigitation II; Qualities: *Beguiling, class ability (Courtier: slanderous)*

Attacks/Weapons: Stiletto (dmg 1d4 lethal; threat 18–20; qualities: *AP 8, finesse*)

Gear: Grooming case

Treasure: 1C

Town Drunk (Medium Folk Walker — 19 XP): Str 10, Dex 10, Con 10, Int 8, Wis 10, Cha 8; SZ M (1×1, Reach 1); Spd 20 ft. ground; Init I; Atk IV; Def I; Res III; Health I; Comp —; Skills: Athletics II, Investigate II; Qualities: *Clumsy, feral, frenzy I, stench*

Attacks/Weapons: Club (dmg 1d8 subdual; threat 20)

Gear: Spirits (3 uses)

Treasure: None

Town Crier (Medium Folk Walker — 25 XP): Str 10, Dex 10, Con 10, Int 10, Wis 10, Cha 10; SZ M (1×1, Reach 1); Spd 30 ft. ground; Init II; Atk I; Def III; Res II; Health II; Comp II; Skills: Impress III, Investigation V, Notice III; Qualities: *Expertise (Impress)*

Attacks/Weapons: None

Gear: Hooded lantern

Treasure: 1C

Treasure Hunter (Medium Folk Walker — 56 XP): Str 10, Dex 10, Con 10, Int 10, Wis 10, Cha 10; SZ M (1×1, Reach 1); Spd 30 ft. ground; Init IV; Atk III; Def V; Res V; Health III; Comp II; Skills: Acrobatics IV, Haggle IV, Prestidigitation VII, Search VII; Qualities: *Class ability (Burglar: evasion I; Explorer: tomb raider, uncanny dodge III), fearless I*

Attacks/Weapons: Bullwhip (dmg 1d6 subdual; threat 20; qualities: *reach +2, trip*)

Mounts and Vehicles: Mule (Spd 30 ft. ground (Run 150 ft.); Travel 5; SZ/Def M/III) or none

Gear: Backpack, grappling hook, hemp rope (50 ft.), shovel, thieves' tools, torches (5)

Treasure: 1A, 1L, 1T

Warlord (Medium Folk Walker — 71 XP): Str 15, Dex 10, Con 10, Int 10, Wis 10, Cha 10; SZ M (1×1, Reach 1); Spd 30 ft. ground; Init V; Atk IV; Def IV; Res IV; Health IV; Comp III; Skills: Intimidate VIII, Resolve IV, Tactics VIII; Qualities: *Class ability (Captain: battle planning I (crush them!, press on!), take heart), fearless I, feat (Battlefield Trickery, Coordinated Attack, Coordinated Move), frenzy II, menacing threat*

Attacks/Weapons: Bastard sword (dmg 1d10+2 lethal; threat 20; qualities: *massive*), tower shield (dmg 1d4+2 subdual; threat —; qualities: *guard +3*)

Mounts and Vehicles: War horse (Spd 50 ft. ground (Run 250 ft.); Travel 5; SZ/Def L/IV)

Gear: Moderate scalemail with light fittings (DR 5; Resist Edged 3; DP –2; ACP –2; Spd –5 ft.; Disguise obvious), standard

Treasure: 1A, 2C, 1M

Watchman (Medium Folk Walker — 37 XP): Str 10, Dex 10, Con 10, Int 10, Wis 10, Cha 10; SZ M (1×1, Reach 1); Spd 30 ft. ground; Init V; Atk II; Def II; Res III; Health III; Comp II; Skills: Investigate V, Notice V, Search V; Qualities: *Feat (Basic Skill Mastery (Investigator), Combat Instincts), improved sense (hearing)*

Attacks/Weapons: Club (dmg 1d8 subdual; threat 20), mancatcher (dmg 1d6 subdual; threat —; qualities: *reach +1, trip*)

Gear: Partial hardened leather armor (DR 3; Resist Fire 3; DP –1; ACP –1; Spd –5 ft.; Disguise –2), hooded lantern, manacles, whistle

Treasure: 1C

Wizard (Medium Folk Walker — 56 XP): Str 10, Dex 10, Con 10, Int 14, Wis 10, Cha 14; SZ M (1×1, Reach 1); Spd 30 ft. ground; Init II; Atk II; Def I; Res III; Health II; Comp V; Skills: Investigate VII, Resolve VII, Spellcasting VII; Spells: Cure Wounds I, Identify, Knock, Mage Armor, Magic Missile, Read Magic, Sleep; Qualities: *Class ability (Mage: arcane wellspring I), expertise (Resolve), feat (Casting Basics), spell defense II*

Attacks/Weapons: Quarterstaff (dmg 1d8 subdual; threat 20; qualities: *double, trip*)

Mounts and Vehicles: Riding horse (Spd 50 ft. ground (Run 250 ft.); Travel 7; SZ/Def L/IV) or none

Gear: Mage's pouch, mana potion

Treasure: 2M, 1L

Worshipper (Medium Folk Walker — 25 XP): Str 10, Dex 10, Con 10, Int 10, Wis 10, Cha 10; SZ M (1×1, Reach 1); Spd 30 ft. ground; Init II; Atk II; Def III; Res IV; Health II; Comp II; Skills: Resolve V; Qualities: *Cagey I, class ability (Sage: assistance I), honorable, interests (Alignment)*

Attacks/Weapons: Club (dmg 1d8 subdual; threat 20)

Treasure: None

ROGUE TEMPLATES

The NPCs in the Rogues Gallery are, by default, human. To shift their Species, simply add one of the following templates. For example, a Pech Cutpurse has an XP value of 43, a Size of Small, and a Dexterity score of 12.

DRAKE (+14 XP)

Benefit: The NPC becomes a Large (2×3, Reach 2) Beast Flyer with a winged flight Speed of 40 ft. He also gains *cold-blooded* and Fire Breath (fire damage attack II: 20 ft. beam; dmg 1d6 fire per 2 TL, Ref DC 15 for 1/2 damage), Bite II (dmg 1d10 lethal; threat 17–20), and Claw II (dmg 1d8 lethal; threat 19–20).

DWARF (+11 XP)

Benefit: The NPC's Speed decreases by 10 ft. and his Constitution score rises by 2. He also gains *damage reduction 2, darkvision I,* and *improved stability.* In most cases you should also avoid the Acrobatics and Athletics Signature Skills.

ELF (+2 XP)

Benefit: The NPC's Type changes to Fey, his Speed increases by 10 ft., and his Wisdom score rises by 2. He also gains *attractive I, burden of ages,* and *improved sense (hearing, sight).*

GIANT (+7 XP)

Benefit: The NPC's size increases to Large (2×2, Reach 2) and his Speed increases by 20 ft. He also gains *improved stability* and Trample I (dmg 1d10 lethal; threat 20).

Every Pech's a Snowflake

Some might wonder why NPC species operate a bit differently from their PC counterparts (why a Pech Burglar might have different stats and follow different rules when it's controlled by a player rather than the GM). The obvious reason, of course, is that in order for the NPC system to offer the staggering amount of customization it does, it has to work a little differently than the focused player character rules. There's another reason too: different strains of species have different strengths and weaknesses. They look different and have different specialties. Rather than worry about whether two orcs born on opposite sides of your world should share a talent, embrace the disparity as the sign of a diverse and plausible setting.

GOBLIN (+2 XP)

Benefit: The NPC's Size decreases to Small and his Health increases by 1 grade. He also gains *darkvision I, feat (Ambush Basics),* and *light-sensitive.*

OGRE (+7 XP)

Benefit: The NPC's Size increases to Large (2×2, Reach 1) and his Constitution rises by 2. He also gains *tough I.* In most cases you should also avoid Acrobatics, Impress, and Tactics.

ORC (+4 XP)

Benefit: The NPC's Strength score rises by 2. He also gains *always ready, grueling combatant,* and *light-sensitive.* In most cases you should also avoid Impress, Investigate, and Medicine.

PECH (+2 XP)

Benefit: The NPC's Size decreases to Small and his Dexterity score rises by 2.

ROOTWALKER (+11 XP)

Benefit: The NPC becomes a Large (2×2, Reach 1) Plant. He also gains *Achilles heel (fire), chameleon I (forest/jungle or swamp), condition immunity (bleeding), damage reduction 1, light sleeper,* and *lumbering.*

SAURIAN (+6 XP)

Benefit: One of his attribute score rises by 2 and he gains *aquatic I, cold-blooded,* and *darkvision I.* He also gains Bite I (dmg 1d8 lethal, threat 18–20) and its Tail Slap becomes grade I (dmg 1d8 lethal, threat 20, qualities: reach +1) and Tail Slap II (dmg 1d8 lethal; threat 19–20; qualities: *reach +1*).

UNBORN (+4 XP)

Benefit: The NPC's Type changes to Construct and his Defense, Health and Resilience each increase by 1 grade. However, his Charisma decreases by 2, his Speed decreases by 10 ft., and he gains *Achilles heel (electrical)* and *lumbering.*

BEYOND THE STATS

It's tempting to make NPCs caricatures — after all, many have a life expectancy of a single combat (if that), without much chance for roleplaying beyond a battle cry and a death-rattle. Giving in to this impulse can rob you of valuable opportunities, however. Here are a few ways to spice up your NPCs before sending them into the fray.

WHAT'S IN A NAME?

Nowhere else are names more telling of a character's goals, disposition, or history than in fantasy. Here NPCs are named for important traits, great achievements, and family legacies, any of which can become potential adventure hooks. Sometimes a name can spark ideas before the NPC even appears at the table. For example, it's probably safe to assume that Baron Rakarth Bloodspike, Lord of the Pit is a villain (or at least, a dangerous person). By contrast, Bilbo Appledimple is likely not; in fact, his name pretty obviously indicates he's a humble Pech farmer.

To quickly construct an appropriate name for any NPC in the Rogues Gallery, roll 1d20 and consult Table 6.6: Name by Species *(see page 250)*. Follow the pattern, rolling on Table 6.7: Random Name Generator to fill in the blanks and tweak to taste.

"[Column + Column]" indicates a compound word or two-word name in the order you prefer.

Example: The GM is naming a male dwarf. He rolls a 7 on Table 6.6, which translates to a first name from Column L and a compound last name from Columns E and A. He rolls a 2, 9, and 6 for these, respectively, which means his dwarf's first name is Dalgar and his last can be Hearthcrusher, Hearth Crusher, Crusherhearth, or Crusher Hearth.

Columns K, N, and O are broken into a prefixes and suffixes, or male and female names. "[Column × 2]" in these columns indicates two rolls in the same column, once for the prefix and once for the suffix.

Example: The GM is naming a saurian. He rolls a 2 on Table 6.6, which translates to two rolls in Column O. He rolls a 14 and 19, which means his saurian is either Sserxec or Xylryn.

These tables can generate silly names, of course, so feel free to ignore or re-roll as needed.

Table 6.6: Name by Species

Drake Result	First Name	Last Name	Example
1–6	[Column D + Column B]	—	Lightning-Hide
7–12	[Column G + Column B]	—	Asheart
13–18	[Column H + Column B]	—	Skull Truth
19–20	[Column O × 2]	the [Column A]	Gethyss the Singer

Dwarf Result	First Name	Last Name	Example
1–8	[Column L]	[Column E + Column A]	Sigurd Orewatcher
9–16	[Column L]	[Column E + Column B]	Oddvar Ironmaw
17–18	[Column L]	[Column D + Column J]	Wulf Bowstar
19–20	[Column M]	[Column G + Column A]	Lief Anvil-Eater

Elf Result	First Name	Last Name	Example
1–6	[Column K × 2]	[Column E + Column C]	Rhysil Adamant-Stag
7–12	[Column K × 2]	[Column D + Column B]	Telewyn Seaclaw
13–18	[Column K × 2]	[Column F + Column A]	Naidil Hollow Sworn
19–20	[Column K × 2]	the [Column H + Column J]	Luir Daggerdawn

Giant Result	First Name	Last Name	Example
1–6	[Column M]	[Column D + Column A]	Ronan Hillwalker
7–12	[Column L]	[Column D + Column B]	Hamar Stoneback
13–16	[Column L]	[Column E + Column D]	Tarn Mountaingem
17–20	[Column D + Column A]	the [Column I]	Raintaker the Conqueror

Goblin Result	First Name	Last Name	Example
1–8	[Column N × 2]	—	Bludshak
9–12	[Column N + Column O]	—	Skum Lyth
13–16	[Column N × 2]	the [Column C]	Ogresh the Rat
17–20	[Column N + Column O]	the [Column G]	Morghul the Bane

Human Result	First Name	Last Name	Example
1–6	[Column L or Column M]	[Column H + Column C]	Kell Devil Summer
7–12	[Column L or Column M]	[Column C + Column B]	Seth Monsterheart
13–16	[Column L or Column M]	[Column K × 2]	Geir Alavain
17–20	[Column I] [Column M]	the [Column J]	Bastard Bruce the Axe

Ogre Result	First Name	Last Name	Example
1–7	[Column B + Column A]	—	Wingsworn
8–14	[Column G + Column A]	—	Shadechaser
15–17	[Column I + Column J]	—	Forgemad
18–20	[Column K + Column N]	[Column I + Column B]	Durrond Crestclever

Orc Result	First Name	Last Name	Example
1–8	[Column N × 2]	[Column G + Column J]	Goruk Broken-Lance
9–12	[Column N × 2]	[Column C + Column A]	Yaggit Angeltaker
13–16	[Column N × 2]	[Column H + Column A]	Luthgog Striderking
17–20	[Column N × 2]	the [Column I + Column J]	Gazbrak the Lame Bow

Pech Result	First Name	Last Name	Example
1–5	[Column M]	[Column H + Column F]	Sarah Blue Elm
6–10	[Column L]	[Column E + Column C]	Liva Horse-Slayer
11–15	[Column L]	[Column D + Column F]	Kell Mosscloud
16–20	[Column M]	[Column E + Column F]	Tom Coppervalley

Rootwalker Result	First Name	Last Name	Example
1–5	[Column F + Column B]	—	Needlearms
6–10	[Column G + Column F]	—	River Fouler
11–15	[Column H + Column F]	—	Law of the Root
16–20	[Column D + Column F]	—	Moonleaf

Saurian Result	First Name	Last Name	Example
1–8	[Column O × 2]	—	Ssathmash
9–12	[Column O × 2]	[Column E + Column B]	Lythtek Goldhand
13–16	[Column O × 2]	[Column F + Column A]	Sslalyss Springholder
17–20	[Column O × 2]	[Column D + Column C]	Klatetch Flame-Dragon

Unborn Result	First Name	Last Name	Example
1–4	[Column K + Column O]	—	Grathmus
5–10	[Column H + Column J]	—	Soulsaw
11–15	[Column M]'s	[Column G + Column C]	Scarlett's Jagged Angel
16–20	[Column E + Column C]	[1d20]	Jade Weasel Mk. IX

Table 6.7: Random Name Generator

Result	A. Actions	B. Anatomy	C. Critters	D. Elements	E. Gems
1	Breaker	Arm	Angel	Cloud	Adamant
2	Builder	Back	Boar	Dawn	Bronze
3	Caller	Beard	Crow	Dusk	Copper
4	Chaser	Breath	Devil	Earth	Diamond
5	Cleaver	Claw	Dragon	Fire	Emerald
6	Crusher	Crest	Eagle	Flame	Gem
7	Eater	Eye	Hawk	Frost	Gold
8	Holder	Fang	Horse	Hill	Granite
9	Ruler	Fist	Hound	Lightning	Hearth
10	Scraper	Flesh	Lion	Moon	Iron
11	Seeker	Foot	Man	Mountain	Jade
12	Seer	Hand	Monster	Rain	Mithril
13	Singer	Head	Rat	Sea	Onyx
14	Slayer	Heart	Raven	Sky	Opal
15	Speaker	Hide	Serpent	Star	Ore
16	Strider	Maw	Shark	Stone	Ruby
17	Sworn	Skull	Stag	Storm	Sapphire
18	Taker	Spine	Tiger	Sun	Silver
19	Walker	Tooth	Weasel	Thunder	Steel
20	Watcher	Wing	Wolf	Wind	Tin

Result	F. Nature	G. Negative	H. Positive	I. Titles	J. Tools
1	Branch	Ash	Blue	Bastard	Anvil
2	Elm	Bane	Boon	Bonny	Arrow
3	Flower	Black	Brave	Bloody	Axe
4	Forest	Blood	Dawn	Conquerer	Bow
5	Grass	Bone	Day	Clever	Blade
6	Grove	Broken	Glory	Cruel	Dagger
7	Hollow	Dark	Green	Fat	Edge
8	Leaf	Death	Hero	Flatulent	Forge
9	Moss	Doom	Just	Handsome	Guard
10	Needle	Foul	King	Jolly	Hammer
11	Oak	Fume	Law	Killer	Knife
12	Pine	Grey	Light	Lame	Lance
13	River	Jagged	Oath	Mad	Maul
14	Root	Night	Pure	Magnificent	Saw
15	Spring	Red	Soul	Mighty	Shield
16	Tree	Shade	Spring	One-Eyed	Spear
17	Twig	Shadow	Sun	Randy	Spike
18	Valley	Venom	Summer	Swift	Staff
19	Vine	Vile	Truth	Terrible	Sword
20	Willow	Wither	White	Ugly	Wheel

Result	K. Elvish (Pre/Suff)	L. Dwarven (M/F)	M. Folk (M/F)	N. Orcish (Pre/Suff)	O. Reptilian (Pre/Suff)
1	Aen/-ael	Bjorn/Asta	Aiden/Abby	Blud/-bag	Geth/-chal
2	Ala/-ari	Dalgar/Bodil	Bruce/Bridget	Bruh/-brak	Grath/-chyss
3	And/-eth	Einar/Dagmar	Dirk/Cate	Dirg/-dar	Gyss/-geth
4	Ar/-dil	Fulnir/Emla	Gareth/Daisy	Dur/-dreg	Hyss/-hesh
5	Cas/-eil	Garth/Flos	Gregor/Helen	Gaz/-gar	Kla/-hyll
6	Cyl/-evar	Galinn/Freya	Gustav/Hilda	Gor/-gog	Lath/-kesh
7	El/-ir	Geir/Ginna	Halsten/Ingrid	Goth/-ghul	Lex/-klatch
8	Eln/-mus	Hakon/Gunnhild	Harold/Jessica	Gut/-git	Lyth/-lyss
9	Fir/-oth	Hamar/Haldis	Jack/Linnea	Lor/-grub	Mor/-mash
10	Gael/-rad	Hrothgar/Helga	James/Maggie	Luth/-ok	Nar/-moth
11	Hu/-re	Ivar/Idona	Kirk/Natalia	Mag/-rak	Nyl/-myss
12	Koeh/-riel	Kell/Inge	Lief/Olga	Nar/-rot	Pesh/-resh
13	Laer/-rond	Magne/Liva	Liam/Rebecca	Nug/-ruk	Ssath/-ron
14	Lue/-sar	Oddvar/Norna	Patrick/Raelia	Od/-sarg	Sser/-ryn
15	Nai/-sil	Ranulf/Ragnhild	Robert/Rose	Og/-shak	Ssla/-tetch
16	Rhy/-tahl	Sigurd/Sigrun	Ronan/Sarah	Skum/-sot	Ssyss/-tek
17	Sere/-thus	Snorri/Solveig	Seth/Scarlett	Teg/-tek	Tla/-thyss
18	Tia/-uil	Tarn/Thoris	Steven/Sophia	Was/-thag	Xer/-toss
19	Tele/-vain	Tor/Valda	Tom/Tamara	Wort/-tor	Xyl/-xec
20	Zau/-wyn	Wulf/Unni	William/Violet	Yag/-zod	Xyss/-yss

NPC QUIRKS

You can firmly establish any NPC with a few character quirks: mannerisms, possessions, or appearance tags that help define the character to the audience (in this case, the GM and/or the other players). Great villains are likewise defined by their eccentricities (e.g. Gollum's multiple personalities and obsession with the One Ring, Voldemort's struggles with manifesting in bodily form, and the unearthly beauty and callousness of *The Black Company's* Lady). Just a few distinctive quirks can make an NPC memorable and interesting, not to mention fun to play and encounter. To quickly add some, roll 1d20 up to once per column on Table 6.8: NPC Quirks *(see below).*

Table 6.8: NPC Quirks

Result	Appearance	Mannerisms	Personality	Props
1	Brawny	Facial tic	Brash	Ornate ring
2	Filthy	Overused saying	Cautious	Multiple piercings
3	Lanky	Intoxicated	Bloodthirsty	Trophy or medal
4	Stunning	Stutter	Shifty	Necklace of ears/fingers/teeth
5	Stunted	Booming voice	Fearful	Cool scar
6	Rotund	Gossips	Stormy	Missing limb/digit
7	Ugly	Lisp	Stoic	Huge weapon
8	Refined	Wrings hands	Sorrowful	Lucky charm
9	Immaculate	Poor hygiene	Penitent	Heavily tattooed
10	Noble	Limp	Frantic	Battered armor
11	Military	Fidgets	Talkative	Glasses
12	Flamboyant	Cough/sickness	Haughty	Outrageous hair
13	Poor	Gestures with hands	Learned	Portrait of loved one
14	Impressive	Mumbles to self	Assured	Cane/walking stick
15	Scarred	Tells bad jokes	Impatient	Severe expression
16	Cute	Wheezy voice	Boisterous	Unibrow
17	Sickly	Mute	Grumpy	Distinctive perfume/smell
18	Flushed	Wears distinctive color	Contrary	Fine clothing
19	Scary	Complains constantly	Pessimistic	Easy smile
20	Savage	Hard of hearing	Upbeat	Piercing glare

NPC MOTIVATIONS

You can also round out an NPC by giving him a purpose beyond furthering the adventure's plot. Just like a real person, a good NPC has his own goals, dreams, and aspirations, pursuing them whenever he can. Discovering these motivations not only fleshes the NPC out but gives the players more to work with when interacting with him.

Roll 1d20 and consult Table 6.9: NPC Motivations to get started. The results are written to provide new plot hooks and tasks, should the party wish to explore the NPC's background or try to get involved in his business. As in all things, GMs should reward players who engage with an NPC's background in creative ways, both for their commitment to roleplaying and their willingness to look at the NPC as more than an obstacle on the path to victory.

Table 6.9: NPC Motivations

Result	Motivation
1	*Apotheosis:* The NPC is looking for allies to help him achieve divinity (or the appearance of such).
2	*Conquest:* The NPC seeks champions to help him crush the armies or nation of a rival.
3	*Debt:* The NPC owes a great deal of money to another character and must repay it soon. Perhaps the party can stake him...
4	*Destruction:* The NPC wants to tear down the world and needs rough and ready associates to do his dirty work.
5	*Discovery:* The NPC seeks lost or rare knowledge — but is afraid to search for them alone.
6	*Errand:* The NPC is on a quest and requires the aid of hardy heroes to complete it.
7	*Escape:* The NPC is on the run from bounty hunters or the law and needs help from someone who isn't (at least, not yet).
8	*Greed:* The NPC wants to fill his vaults and coffers and adventurers run into so much treasure…
9	*Justice:* The NPC seeks to right a wrong or capture a law-breaker. Perhaps he could deputize the characters…
10	*Madness:* The NPC is insane, reveling in the manipulation of unwitting pawns.
11	*Peace:* The NPC seeks a simpler life but can't escape his violent circumstances — not without help.
12	*Provider:* The NPC supports friends, family, or perhaps even a whole village, but needs assistance to do so.
13	*Rebellion:* The NPC wants to overthrow or undermine the authorities, perhaps with espionage, perhaps with violent opposition.
14	*Revelation:* The NPC craves spiritual truth through divine insight or contact. The road will be long and fraught with danger…
15	*Revenge:* The NPC wishes to avenge a slight. He's on the lookout for extra hands to exact his single-minded goal.
16	*Salvation:* The NPC longs for redemption after some grievous wrongdoing but knows he cannot find it on his own.
17	*Status:* The NPC longs to increase his standing in society and may identify the characters as likely advocates.
18	*Torment:* The NPC is harassing another with pranks or worse. Maybe the party would be inclined to assist.
19	*Theft:* The NPC desires a secret or protected item but lacks the skills to find or acquire it.
20	*True Love:* The NPC yearns to prove his love to another. Perhaps the party can help this Romeo find his Juliet.

BESTIARY

NPCs in the Bestiary range from the mythical to the mundane — animals, spirits, the monstrous, the horrific, and everything in between. Collectively, they're sometimes called "monsters" as they're very different from the heroic species in *Fantasy Craft* and commonly encountered as foils, foes, and rampaging beasts to be killed and looted. Unlike NPCs in the Rogues Gallery, these creatures aren't available as contacts, hirelings, or followers except with special GM permission.

ANGELS

These luminous beings are the eyes, ears, and hands of beneficent gods, charged with guarding the innocent and punishing the wicked. Though their individual appearance varies wildly and can change between visitations, they're naturally winged humanoids, often with perfect features and a welcoming aura. Depending on their native pantheon, they sometimes have an extra pair of wings, a wreath of flames, or a welcoming aura. They're almost universally scrupulous, honest, and charismatic.

Avenging angels are the enforcers of law, terrifying hunters who track down and slay those endangering the natural order. Their rare yet wrathful arrival is enough to panic even the most stout-hearted evildoers.

Guardian angels are protectors of good and stewards of innocence. They're more healers than warriors, appearing to rescue the pure-hearted and protect places holy to their heavenly masters.

Herald angels are divine messengers, delivering good tidings and stern warnings to the world of men. Their glory is an extension of their unearthly liege, threatening to blind all who look upon them.

Tactics: Angels are beings of pure devotion and duty, never giving up and never violating their gods' decrees. They're fiercely dedicated to their mission and rarely turn from it for any purpose. Though they possess great combat prowess, they always seek peaceful resolution through dialogue before resorting to violence. When they finally engage an enemy, they first Detect Alignment and then invoke Protection against it, shielding themselves against enemies of the faith. Only then do they turn to their mighty melee and ranged attacks, using *devoted* abilities to augment the assault.

Avenging Angel (Large Outsider Flyer/Walker — 177 XP): Str 18, Dex 10, Con 14, Int 10, Wis 18, Cha 18; SZ L (2×2, Reach 1); Spd 60 ft. winged flight, 30 ft. ground; Init V; Atk VII; Def V; Res VIII; Health VII; Comp III; Skills: Acrobatics V, Resolve X, Spellcasting II, Survival V; Spells: Detect Alignment, Protection from Alignment; Qualities: *Class ability (Paladin: smite the indifferent, stand in judgment I), damage defiance (acid, cold, electrical, fire), damage reduction 8, darkvision I, devoted (Order II), feat (Agile Flyer, Cleave Basics, Mobility Basics), honorable, regeneration 5, spell defense IV, telepathic, veteran III*

Attacks/Weapons: Large claymore (dmg 2d8+4 lethal; threat 19–20; qualities: *massive, reach +1*), long bow + 30 standard arrows (dmg 1d6 lethal; threat 19–20; range 40 ft. × 6; qualities: *AP 4, poisonous*), Wrathful Strike (Slam II: dmg 1d8+4 divine; threat 19–20)

Treasure: 2M, 1T

Guardian Angel (Medium Outsider Flyer/Walker — 101 XP): Str 14, Dex 10, Con 12, Int 12, Wis 18, Cha 18; SZ M (1×1, Reach 1); Spd 55 ft. winged flight, 30 ft. ground; Init IV; Atk IV; Def V; Res VI; Health V; Comp IV; Skills: Impress X, Medicine V, Sense Motive V, Spellcasting II; Spells: Detect Alignment, Protection from Alignment; Qualities: *Attractive I, class ability (Paladin: lay on hands; Sage: take heart), devoted (Good II), honorable, spell defense III, telepathic*

Attacks/Weapons: Longsword (dmg 1d12+2 lethal; threat 20), metal shield (dmg 1d4+2 subdual; threat 20; qualities: *guard +2*)

Gear: Blessed breastplate (partial platemail: DR 4; Resist Blunt 1, Divine 4; DP –3; ACP –3; Spd –5 ft.; Disguise: obvious)

Treasure: 2M, 1T

Herald Angel (Medium Outsider Flyer/Walker — 79 XP): Str 10, Dex 10, Con 12, Int 12, Wis 14, Cha 18; SZ M (1×1, Reach 1); Spd 60 ft. winged flight, 30 ft. ground; Init II; Atk III; Def VI; Res IV; Health V; Comp IV; Skills: Impress X, Spellcasting II; Spells: Detect Alignment, Protection from Alignment; Qualities: *Attractive II, class ability (Courtier: with a word; Priest: benediction), devoted (Light II), honorable, telepathic*

Attacks/Weapons: Boar spear (dmg 1d8 lethal; threat 19–20; qualities: *guard +1, reach +1*), Open the Seal (sonic damage attack II: 5 ft. blast increment; dmg 1d6 sonic per 2 TL, Ref DC 15 for 1/2 damage)

Gear: Silver trumpet (masterwork musical instrument)

Treasure: 1M, 1T

ANIMATED OBJECTS

Given life by demonic mischief, spiritual havoc, or ambitious wizards' apprentices, magically animated objects can prove an obnoxious adversary. They're especially dangerous when encountered in groups.

Animated melee weapons include all sorts of hand weapons, ranging from clubs to swords, which attack independent of wielders.

Animated furniture runs the gamut from demonic rocking chairs to maniacal stuffed-moose heads.

Animated vehicles diligently run down their master's foes at maximum overdrive.

Tactics: Being mindless, animated objects never parlay with the party, opting instead for straightforward combat. Animated weapons, as the most ill-tempered and bloodthirsty of the lot, tend to charge in recklessly, while furniture and vehicles are more likely to lie in wait, leveraging their unassuming appearances to launch surprise attacks. All animated objects are universally concerned with ejecting intruders from their premises and only give chase after a fleeing party if expressly directed to by their creators.

Animated Melee Weapon (Small Construct Flyer — 30 XP): Str 10, Dex 10, Con 10, Int 1, Wis 10, Cha 1; SZ S (1×1, Reach 1); Spd 20 ft. flight; Init III; Atk III; Def III; Res II; Health III; Comp I; Skills: None; Qualities: *Blindsight, charge attack*

Attacks/Weapons: Wild slash (Bite I: dmg 1d6 lethal; threat 18–20; qualities: *bleed*)

Treasure: None

Animated Furniture (Medium Construct Walker — 33 XP): Str 10, Dex 10, Con 10, Int 1, Wis 10, Cha 1; SZ M (1×1, Reach 1); Spd 30 ft. ground; Init II; Atk II; Def IV; Res I; Health IV; Comp I; Skills: None; Qualities: *Blindsight, chameleon II (indoors/settled)*

Attacks/Weapons: Slam I (dmg 1d6 subdual; threat 20; upgrades: *trip*)

Treasure: None

Animated Vehicle (Large Construct Walker — 41 XP): Str 10, Dex 10, Con 10, Int 1, Wis 10, Cha 1; SZ L (2×3, Reach 1); Spd 40 ft. ground (Run 240 ft.); Init II; Atk IV; Def IV; Res I; Health IV; Comp I; Skills: None; Qualities: *Blindsight, improved stability, superior runner II, tough I*

Attacks/Weapons: Trample III (dmg 2d10 lethal; threat 19–20; notes: Medium and smaller only, Fort (DC equal to damage) or become *sprawled*)

Treasure: 1L

APES

These omnivores stalk jungles and deep forests, claiming territory, prey, and mates with equal pride and power. They have loose social structures centered upon an alpha male *(see page 286).* Rare albino giants are rumored to exist deep in lost jungles.

Tactics: Given the chance, apes work themselves up for combat, shifting about restlessly until they reach a fever pitch. Their strikes, when they come, are lightning fast and relentlessly brutal.

Ape (Medium Beast Walker — 78 XP): Str 16, Dex 8, Con 12, Int 7, Wis 12, Cha 10; SZ M (1×1, Reach 1); Spd 30 ft. ground; Init III; Atk V; Def III; Res V; Health VI; Comp I; Skills: Athletics IV, Intimidate V; Qualities: *Charge attack, fearsome, improved sense (scent), superior climber I, tough I*

Attacks/Weapons: Bite II (dmg 1d8+3 lethal; threat 17–20), Claw III (dmg 2d6+3 lethal; threat 19–20)

Treasure: 1T

White Ape (Large Beast Walker — 89 XP): Str 20, Dex 10, Con 16, Int 7, Wis 12, Cha 10; SZ L (1×2, Reach 1); Spd 40 ft. ground; Init V; Atk VI; Def III; Res V; Health VII; Comp I; Skills: Athletics V, Intimidate VIII; Qualities: *Charge attack, fearsome, improved sense (scent), superior climber I, tough I*

Attacks/Weapons: Bite III (dmg 2d10+5 lethal; threat 17–20), Claw IV (dmg 2d8+5 lethal; threat 18–20)

Treasure: 2T

BARGHEST

Barghests are twisted fiends born of nightmare, canine demons with fanged, vaguely humanoid faces and smoldering cruel eyes, come to glut themselves on the spirits of the living. They run on all fours, like massive black dogs or wolves, but can speak and possess humanoid hands that let them use tools and weapons. Barghests are consummate predators, cladding themselves in the shape of common folk, spiriting away their prey and consuming them utterly, body and soul.

Tactics: As solitary hunters, barghests prefer trickery and one-on-one combat to old-fashioned dust-ups. They hide within simple cultures and large populations where missing persons aren't likely to be noticed, using their *shapeshifter* ability to take on inconspicuous forms while selecting their prey. When ready, they separate their targets from the herd and spring into action, using Crushing Despair to undermine their quarry's will. A flurry of natural attacks follows as the barghest attempts to subdue the target. Foes that are killed are *devoured,* preparing the barghest for its next hunt.

Should a fight look unwinnable or the prey too tough, barghests quickly break off, using Pass without Trace to cover their tracks.

Barghest (Medium Outsider Walker — 93 XP): Str 14, Dex 12, Con 12, Int 10, Wis 14, Cha 10; SZ M (1×1, Reach 1); Spd 30 ft. ground (Run 150 ft.); Init VIII; Atk V; Def V; Res IV; Health V; Comp V; Skills: Survival VII; Qualities: *Damage reduction 2, darkvision I, devour, feat (Combat Instincts), improved sense (scent), natural spell (Pass Without Trace), shapeshifter I, superior runner I, tough I*

Attacks/Weapons: Bite I (dmg 1d8+2 lethal; threat 18–20), Claw I × 2 (dmg 1d6+2 lethal; threat 20), Crushing Despair (shaking attack II: 30 ft. cone; Will DC 15 or become *shaken*)

Treasure: 2A

BASILISK

Basilisks are eight-legged reptilian predators best described as the offspring of a komodo dragon and a rhino (with a couple extra legs for good measure). Native to warm deserts and savannahs, they spend their days soaking up the heat so they can hunt at night. They're as slow-witted as they are slow-moving but widely feared for their most deadly ability: a glance that can transform flesh to stone. They're also highly prized as pets by wealthy nobles, conniving thieves, and savvy wizards. The brave souls who train basilisks find them to be lazy and slow to learn, but reap great rewards when it's time to sell... provided they've not joined the local statuary.

Tactics: A basilisk's behavior is very much like that of any large lizard — languid, even indifferent, at least until their burrow or eggs are threatened. Pairs of basilisks mate for life (decades) and hunt together in the late afternoon and twilight hours. Not surprisingly, they commonly open combat with Petrifying Gazes, hoping to consume their stony prey at their leisure. If this fails they fall back on their Bite, though they're just as likely to let the prey escape so they can wait for other meals to stumble into their laps.

Basilisk (Medium Animal Walker — 76 XP): Str 14, Dex 8, Con 16, Int 2, Wis 10, Cha 10; SZ M (1×1, Reach 1); Spd 20 ft. ground; Init II; Atk VII; Def IV; Res VI; Health IV; Comp —; Skills: Sneak V, Survival III; Qualities: *Cold-blooded, damage reduction 4, darkvision II, feat (Great Fortitude, Pathfinder Basics (desert)), improved sense (scent)*

Attacks/Weapons: Bite I (dmg 1d8+2 lethal; threat 18–20; upgrades: *keen 4*), Petrifying Gaze (petrifying attack II: 50 ft. gaze; Fort DC 15 or be turned to stone)

Treasure: 1A, 1T

BEARS

These massive woodlands predators are opportunists, feeding on meat, carrion, and anything else they can get their paws on.

Tactics: Bears are not overtly dangerous unless their homes or cubs are threatened; then they're ferocious fighters, shredding opponents with powerful swipes with their vicious claws.

Bear (Medium Animal Walker — 68 XP): Str 16, Dex 8, Con 12, Int 3, Wis 12, Cha 10; SZ L (1×2, Reach 1); Spd 30 ft. ground (Run 150 ft.); Init III; Atk V; Def III; Res V; Health VI; Comp —; Skills: Athletics IV, Intimidate V, Notice IV; Qualities: *Grappler, menacing threat, superior runner I, tough I*

Attacks/Weapons: Bite II (dmg 1d10+3 lethal; threat 17–20), Claw II (dmg 1d6+3 lethal; threat 19–20), Squeeze II (dmg 1d10+3 subdual; notes: Grapple benefit)

Treasure: 1T

Grizzly Bear (Large Animal Walker — 85 XP): Str 20, Dex 8, Con 16, Int 3, Wis 12, Cha 10; SZ L (1×2, Reach 1); Spd 30 ft. ground (Run 150 ft.); Init III; Atk VI; Def IV; Res VI; Health VII; Comp —; Skills: Athletics V, Intimidate VI, Notice IV; Qualities: *Grappler, menacing threat, superior runner I, tough I*

Attacks/Weapons: Bite III (dmg 2d10+5 lethal; threat 17–20), Claw III (dmg 2d8+5 lethal; threat 19–20), Squeeze III (dmg 1d12+3 subdual; notes: Grapple benefit)

Treasure: 2T

BRAIN FIEND

Slender and pallid, these terrifying humanoids wear disturbing garments tailored from blackened skin. Their faces are little more than masses of writhing tentacles sprouting from between deep, soulless black eyes. Brain fiends enslave intelligent beings they can overpower, forcing them into back-breaking servitude before eventually splitting their skulls and devouring the grey matter within.

Tactics: Brain fiends are sadistic creatures with immense mental and magical ability. They're keen schemers who employ slaves and less-intelligent pawns to harass intruders and wage war on one another. They only show themselves at times of greatest leverage and when foes are least able to counter their overwhelming attacks.

When seeking prey or slaves, a fiend begins with Detect Emotions to get a read on its targets. It follows with Mind Howl to suppress the opposition and Command II to drive away powerful defenders. Assuming this offers the fiend a clear advantage it moves in for the kill, grappling with its facial tentacles and crushing the unfortunate victim until he passes out. A Coup de Grace dispatches the enemy, at which point the fiend can feed on his warm brain.

Should a fight go against a fiend, it behaves as any self-respecting mastermind, abandoning the field with Levitate or Teleport I.

Brain Fiend (Medium Horror Walker — 145 XP): Str 10, Dex 14, Con 10, Int 18, Wis 16, Cha 14; SZ M (1×1, Reach 1); Spd 25 ft. ground; Init VI; Atk III; Def IV; Res III; Health III; Comp V; Skills: Athletics VII, Notice VI, Sense Motive VI, Sneak VI, Spellcasting IV; Spells: Command II, Detect Emotion, Levitate, Teleport I; Qualities: *Damage reduction 1, grappler, spell defense III, telepathic, treacherous, veteran II*

Attacks/Weapons: Facial Tentacles × 4 (Slam I: dmg 1d6 lethal; threat 20; upgrades: *grab*), Squeeze V (dmg 3d10 subdual; notes: Grapple benefit), Mind Howl (stunning attack II, 60 ft. cone; Will DC 15 or become *stunned* for 2d6 rounds)

Gear: Moderate leather armor (DR 2; Resist Fire 5; DP –1; ACP –0; Spd –5 ft.; Disguise +0)

Treasure: 2A, 2M

BUGBEAR

Bugbears are muscular, hairy humanoids a bit taller than a man. They have broad ears, ochre hides, protruding fangs, and beady red eyes. Many sport simple but intricately interwoven tattoos on their arms, chests, and faces as a sign of prestige. Bugbear clans are commonly found in foothills and badlands where they thrive as raiders and marauders. Their clothing and weapons speak to these predilections, as they're often jury-rigged from local fashions or cobbled together from mismatched armors.

Some scholars suggest that bugbears may be hybrids of goblin and ogre, though most shudder to imagine the technical details of such a union.

Tactics: Bugbears are greedy and covetous pillagers with a great love of shiny and useful acquisitions. The capture of a finely crafted weapon or suit of armor inevitably leads to a brawl within the clan. When they put aside these mercenary instincts, however, they're excellent mob fighters, springing from ambush to issue severe beatings. Bugbears have a taste for folk flesh but they also know they can ransom living captives; besides, they can always seize ransoms and score some new vittles in the process.

Bugbear (Medium Folk Walker — 49 XP): Str 14, Dex 10, Con 12, Int 10, Wis 10, Cha 9; SZ M (1×1, Reach 1); Spd 30 ft. ground; Init III; Atk IV; Def II; Res IV; Health IV; Comp II; Skills: Athletics III, Notice III, Survival III; Qualities: *Damage reduction I, darkvision I, feat (Ambush Basics, Club Basics, Pathfinder Basics (mountains)), improved sense (hearing), swarm, veteran I*

Attacks/Weapons: Mace (dmg 1d8+2 lethal; threat 20; qualities: *AP 4*), hide shield (dmg 1d3+2 subdual; threat 20; qualities: *guard +2*), Net (dmg —; threat —; range 10 ft. × 3; qualities: *cord, trip*)

Gear: Partial leather armor with light fittings (DR 2; Resist Fire 3; DP –1; ACP –1; Spd —; Disguise –4)

Treasure: 1A, 1G

BULETTE

Essentially bottomless stomachs wrapped in plated ovoid shells, bulettes are fearless, voracious "landsharks" known for their insatiable appetites and their bony crests, which rise above the soil just before they emerge beneath their quarry. Bulettes live to eat everything that moves. Their long bodies are evolved for subterranean and surface life, being tapered like torpedoes, protected with large boney plates, and supported by squat but powerful legs that let them jump many times their own height.

Tactics: Bulettes are mercifully solitary creatures that hunt much like a dumb cat, relying on high Speed and their *superior jumper* ability to pounce on prey, or lying in wait a few feet below the surface and springing forth to attack. Only truly serious wounds drive bulettes off — most are simply too dim and single-minded to see the end coming. Wise adventurers know that fighting a bulette head-to-head is a quick path to an extremely painful death in its acidic gullet, and stick to ranged attacks whenever possible.

Bulette (Huge Animal Burrower/Walker — 113 XP): Str 18, Dex 12, Con 14, Int 2, Wis 10, Cha 6; SZ H (2×4, Reach 1); Spd 10 ft. burrow, 50 ft. ground; Init IV; Atk VII; Def V; Res VIII; Health VI; Comp —; Skills: Acrobatics VI, Athletics III, Notice III; Qualities: *Blindsight, damage reduction 4, darkvision II, fearless II, improved sense (scent), superior jumper III, tough I*

Attacks/Weapons: Bite III (dmg 2d12+4 lethal; threat 17–20), Claw II × 2 (dmg 1d10+4 lethal; threat 19–20; upgrades: *AP 2*), Swallow III (dmg 4d8+4 acid; notes: Grapple benefit — Medium and smaller only)

Treasure: 1A, 2T

BURROWING BEHEMOTH

Burrowing behemoths are among the most fiercely territorial subterranean creatures in the world. Bane of miners and prospectors, these bipedal beetles prowl the caves and crags of the deep earth, on constant watch for intruders looking to steal the precious ore upon which they feed. They sabotage mining operations by attacking equipment, digging deep pit traps, and leading predators to the camps. When these tactics fail, they engage directly, employing savage hooks and mandibles capable of punching through plate steel, plus terrifying glares that incite madness and paranoia.

Tactics: Despite their buggish appearance, burrowing behemoths are exceptionally clever, exploiting their knowledge of the underworld to sneak up on and ambush prey. They favor bite and claw attacks to selectively remove the most vulnerable threats, but always seize opportunities to direct their Confusing Gaze at cowering or clumped enemies. Teams of behemoths often work together, with one creature luring adventurers toward ambushes in narrow passages and precipices where escape is impossible.

Burrowing Behemoth (Large Horror Burrower/Walker — 97 XP): Str 16, Dex 10, Con 14, Int 10, Wis 10, Cha 10; SZ L (2×2, Reach 2); Spd 20 ft. burrow, 20 ft. ground; Init III; Atk IV; Def II; Res VI; Health IV; Comp II; Skills: Athletics V, Notice V; Qualities: *Blindsight, damage reduction 4, feat (Pathfinder Basics (caverns/mountains)), superior climber II, tough I*

Attacks/Weapons: Bite III (dmg 2d10+3 lethal; threat 17–20; upgrades: *AP 2*), Claw II × 2 (dmg 1d8+3 lethal; threat 19–20; upgrades: *AP 2*), Confusing Gaze (enraging attack II: 50 ft. gaze; Will DC 15 or become *enraged* for 2d6 rounds)

Treasure: 2L, 1T

CAMEL

Perhaps the most widely recognized desert denizens, camels are highly adapted to life in arid regions. Despite their sometimes mean temperament, they're highly valued by anyone who has to cross the wastes.

Tactics: While camels may spit or nip to show displeasure, they actually have few defenses against large predators. They attempt to flee from any serious danger.

Camel (Large Animal Walker — 40 XP): Str 14, Dex 10, Con 15, Int 2, Wis 10, Cha 10; SZ L (1×2, Reach 1); Spd 30 ft. ground; Init II; Atk II; Def II; Res V; Health IV; Comp —; Skills: Athletics IV, Notice II, Survival II; Qualities: *Feat (Pathfinder Basics (desert)), improved stability, meek, superior traveler II*

Attacks/Weapons: Kick I (dmg 1d8+2 subdual; threat 20)

Treasure: None

CHAOS BEAST

Chaos Beasts are churning amalgams of disparate body parts, horrific imitations of natural life that defy all rational logic. In their "natural" states, they appear as roiling blobs of faintly glowing flesh, rippling with the anarchy of constant and unknowable change. As they touch organic beings, however, they appropriate parts of the victims, their bodies warping and churning into a riot of new shapes. One moment, a chaos beast may appear as a man with a tentacle arm and a dog's head projecting form his midriff, the next it might become a giant slug with children's faces for antennae and the horns of a stag.

Tactics: Thanks to their exceptional mobility (a high Acrobatics skill coupled with the Elusive and Mobility Basics feats), plus incredible toughness (a high Resilience, immunity to *paralyzing* and *stunning* effects, a –3 penalty to opponent threat range from *monstrous defense*, spell defense 20, *and* tough), chaos beasts are terrifying foes. They close and strike with Devolving Touch to prevent foes from escaping, then follow up with Chaos Touch to goad powerful spellcasters and ranged combatants into melee. Chaos beasts are true to the name, quickly tiring of targets. They're easily distracted, sometimes even turning against "allies" without rhyme or reason.

Chaos Beast (Medium Ooze Outsider Walker — 120 XP): Str 12, Dex 10, Con 10, Int 10, Wis 10, Cha 10; SZ M (1×1, Reach 1); Spd 20 ft. ground; Init IX; Atk VII; Def III; Res VII; Health III; Comp IV; Skills: Acrobatics VII, Athletics VI, Sneak V; Qualities: *Condition immunity (paralyzed, stunned), damage immunity (sneak attack), damage reduction 2, darkvision II, feat (Elusive, Mobility Basics), monstrous defense III, spell defense II, tough I, unnerving*

Attacks/Weapons: Claw I (1d6+1 lethal; threat 20), Chaos Touch (enraging attack II: Will save DC 15 or become *enraged* for 2d6 rounds, upgrades: *supernatural attack (claw)*), Devolving Touch (slowing attack II: Will save DC 15 or become *slowed* for 2d6 rounds, upgrades: *supernatural attack (claw)*)

Treasure: 3A

CHIMERA

The solitary chimera is a mishmash of lion, she-goat, and great wyrm, with the heads of all three creatures, a powerful hunting cat's body, large draconic wings, and a long sinuous tail. It's a rare but exceedingly dangerous creature, ill-tempered and happy to work out its aggressions with all its mixed parts: the vicious bite of a lion, the fiery breath of a wyrm, the powerful head butt of a goat, and the predatory instincts of all three. It's known for terrorizing caravans and pilgrims crossing savannahs and broad plains, where it launches deadly strafing attacks and feasts on the charred remains.

Tactics: Despite its large and unwieldy form, the chimeras behaves much like a lion in most instances, seeking to close using *charge attack* and unleash a flurry of attacks with *frenzy I* and *swift attack*. It hopes to quickly take down the slowest and weakest of the herd, securing a meal even if most enemies get away. Being a bit lazy, it's happy to break off when facing superior numbers or fighters.

The chimera has three brains and splits its focus between opponents unless directly threatened. When fully embroiled, it dives in the middle of the scrum and targets a different opponent with each head, though it reserves its breath weapon for crowd control and warding away overwhelming enemies.

Chimera (Large Beast Flyer/Walker — 101 XP): Str 14, Dex 10, Con 16, Int 7, Wis 12, Cha 10; SZ L (2×3, Reach 1); Spd 60 ft. winged flight, 30 ft. ground; Init III; Atk VII; Def III; Res VI; Health V; Comp I; Skills: Notice III, Survival IV; Qualities: *Chameleon I (plains), charge attack, condition immunity (flanked), damage reduction 3, frenzy I, swift attack 1, tough I*

Attacks/Weapons: Goat's Head (Gore I: dmg 1d8+2 lethal; threat 19–20; upgrades: *bleed*), Lion's Head (Bite III: dmg 2d10+2 lethal; threat 17–20), Wyrm's Head (Bite I: dmg 1d10+2 lethal; threat 18–20), Wyrm's Breath (fire damage attack III: 20 ft. cone; dmg 1d8 fire per 2 TL, Ref DC 20 for 1/2 damage)

Treasure: 3T

DARKMANTLE

Darkmantles are highly evolved subterranean opportunists resembling octopoid stalactites. They hang motionless from ceilings until a potential target walks past, at which point they fill the air with inky darkness and float down onto the would-be meal, their thin leather membranes smothering it to death so they can feast on its vital fluids. Darkmantles are relatively harmless on their own but swarms can quickly become a serious threat.

Tactics: Darkmantles rely heavily on ambush and superior numbers. As mentioned, they lead off with Darkness I to cover their approach and lower their target's Defense. Tentacle slaps follow so they can grapple and Squeeze (smother) the target. Swarms of Darkmantles attack like bats, counting on superior numbers to take a target down.

Darkmantle (Small Animal Flyer/Walker — 65 XP): Str 14, Dex 10, Con 10, Int 2, Wis 10, Cha 10; SZ S (1×1, Reach 1); Spd 40 ft. winged flight, 20 ft. ground; Init VI; Atk IV; Def VII; Res V; Health III; Comp —; Skills: Athletics III, Notice IV;

Qualities: *Blindsight, chameleon II (caverns), damage reduction 2, natural spell (Darkness I), swarm*

Attacks/Weapons: Squeeze II (dmg 1d8+2 lethal; notes: Grapple benefit), Tentacle Slap I (dmg 1d6+2 lethal; threat 20; upgrades: *grab, reach +1*)

Treasure: None

DEMONS

Living embodiments of evil, demons are devious, powerful, and completely malign. They come in as many varieties as the depravities of Man and delight is all forms of misery and suffering, both naturally occurring and engineered through their wicked schemes.

Anarchy demons are chaos incarnate, cruel pranksters living to thwart order and peace. They delight in the pain and suffering they cause, relishing their victims' torment.

Plague demons are rotted, emaciated humanoids exuding the stench of death. They spread horrific disease through the mortal realm, deriving perverse glee as charnel houses and the legions of the damned swell with unnatural rot.

Temptress demons take the guise of beautiful women (or men), taunting the opposite sex with intoxicating physical charms. They corrupt with false love and dangerous promiscuity, spoiling minds and bodies in a relentless bid for their lovers' immortal souls.

Tormentor demons are often synonymous with the mortal definition of 'demon.' Massive beasts born to inflict shock and terror, they wear away at the spirit by destroying the body. Torture and brutality are their weapons of choice and their mastery of them is legendary.

Tactics: Demons are brilliant strategists, their minds finely honed by millennia-long gambits. Encounters with them are harrowing games of cat-and-mouse, often preceded by clever and grueling challenges custom-tailored to undermine their target's particular psyche. The greater the anguish they cause before finally relieving an opponent of his harried life, the better.

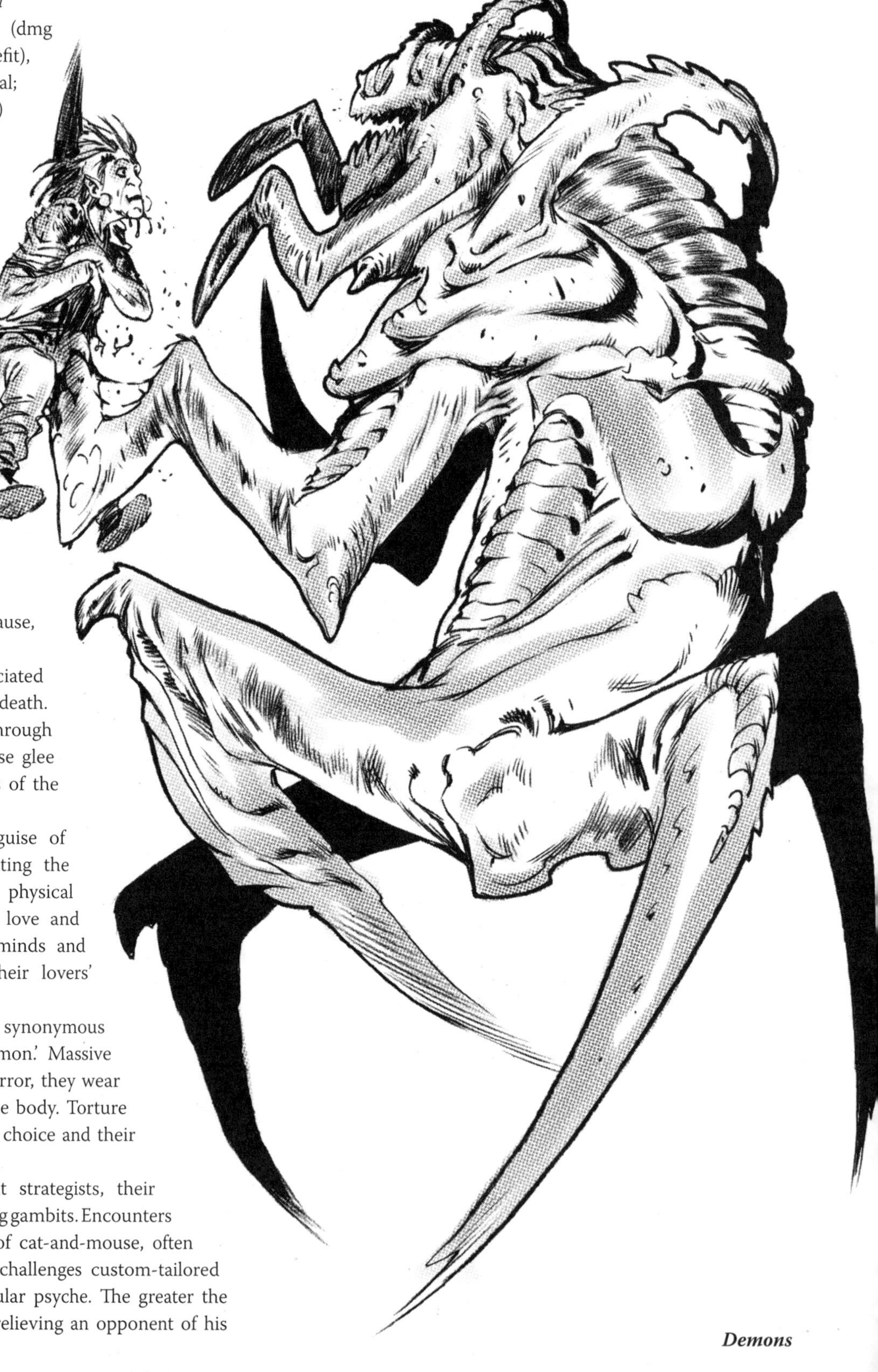

Demons

Anarchy Demon (Medium Outsider Walker — 100 XP): Str 12, Dex 10, Con 14, Int 14, Wis 10, Cha 10; SZ M (1×1, Reach 1); Spd 40 ft. ground; Init IV; Atk V; Def VI; Res V; Health IV; Comp III; Skills: Acrobatics V, Intimidate V, Prestidigitation VIII, Spellcasting V; Spells: Confounding Images, Disguise Self, Entropic Shield, Insanity II, Shatter; Qualities: *Cagey I, class ability (Burglar: evasion II, I'll cut you! I, slippery), contagion immunity, darkvision II, killing splitter*

Attacks/Weapons: Claw II (dmg 1d6+1 lethal; threat 19–20; upgrades: trip), Lethargic Ray (attribute draining attack I: 60 ft. ray; Fort DC 10 or suffer 1 temporary Dex impairment)

Treasure: 1A, 1M

Plague Demon (Medium Outsider Walker — 124 XP): Str 14, Dex 10, Con 18, Int 12, Wis 14, Cha 4; SZ M (1×1, Reach 1); Spd 30 ft. ground; Init II; Atk V; Def IV; Res VIII; Health VII; Comp II; Skills: Athletics V, Blend V, Intimidate X, Spellcasting III; Spells: Cloudkill, Death Knell, Ray of Enfeeblement; Qualities: *Class ability (Burglar: bloody mess), contagion immunity, damage reduction 3, darkvision II, feat (Great Fortitude), grueling combatant, repulsive II, stench, tough II*

Attacks/Weapons: Diseased Slash (Tentacle Slap III: dmg 2d8+2 lethal + bubonic plague; threat 19–20; upgrades: *reach +1, diseased*), Aura of Pestilence (sickening attack III: 30 ft. aura; Will DC 20 or become *sickened* for 3d6 rounds)

Treasure: 1M, 1T

Temptress Demon (Medium Outsider Flyer/Walker — 146 XP): Str 12, Dex 12, Con 10, Int 16, Wis 12, Cha 20; SZ M (1×1, Reach 1); Spd 60 ft. winged flight, 30 ft. ground; Init III; Atk II; Def V; Res VI; Health V; Comp IV; Skills: Bluff IX, Impress IX, Intimidate IX, Sense Motive IX, Spellcasting V; Spells: Calm Emotions, Command II, Detect Emotion, Teleport I, Tongues I; Qualities: *Attractive II, beguiling, class ability (Assassin: bald-faced lie, offer they can't refuse; Courtier: slanderous), contagion immunity, darkvision II, feat (Repartee Basics, Repartee Mastery), shapeshifter II, tough I*

Attacks/Weapons: Trident (dmg 1d8+1 lethal; threat 19–20; qualities: *hook, hurl*), Deadly Kiss (soul draining attack III: Fort DC 20 or die (standard character), lose 1 action die and 10 max. vitality (special character))

Treasure: 2C, 2M

Tormentor Demon (Large Outsider Walker — 164 XP): Str 18, Dex 14, Con 14, Int 14, Wis 10, Cha 12; SZ L (2×2, Reach 2); Spd 40 ft. ground; Init IV; Atk VIII; Def VI; Res VI; Health VI; Comp III; Skills: Intimidate X, Resolve VIII, Spellcasting III; Spells: Cause Wounds II, Darkness I, Insanity II; Qualities: *Contagion immunity, damage immunity (fire, stress), damage reduction 5, devoted (Curses III), dread, feat (Glint of Madness, Whip Basics, Whip Mastery), menacing threat, spell defense IV, tough II, unnerving*

Attacks/Weapons: Large barwhip (dmg 1d10+4 lethal; threat 19–20; qualities: *AP 2, reach +1*), Kick III (dmg 2d8+4 lethal, threat 19–20), Damning Glare (shaking attack IV: 50 ft. gaze; Will DC 25 or become *shaken*)

Treasure: 2A, 2M

DINOSAURS

These massive, primordial reptiles dominate the landscape, dwarfing all but the largest rivals.

Triceratops is a herbivore with an elephantine body and a head crowned by a bony plate and three sharp horns.

Tyrannosaurus Rex is a gigantic eating machine with six inch teeth and tiny useless forearms. It tops the thunder lizard food chain, running quarry down and snatching it up in its powerful jaws.

Velociraptor is one of the most vicious hunters in the wild, using wicked, sickle-clawed feet to take down creatures many times its own size.

Tactics: Most dinosaurs aren't bright, charging into melee and fighting to the death. Velociraptors are a rare exception, hunting in packs, maneuvering carefully to herd and confuse the enemy, and luring weak prey into deadly traps. All dinosaurs act the same after a victory, settling in to consume the carcasses of their kills.

Triceratops (Huge Animal Walker — 88 XP): Str 22, Dex 8, Con 18, Int 1, Wis 10, Cha 8; SZ H (3×4, Reach 2); Spd 30 ft. ground; Init I; Atk VII; Def IV; Res V; Health IX; Comp —; Skills: Notice IV; Qualities: *Charge attack, damage reduction 5, improved sense (scent), tough I*

Attacks/Weapons: Gore III (dmg 2d10+6 lethal; threat 18–20; upgrades: *bleed*), Trample IV (dmg 2d12+6 lethal; threat 18–20; notes: Medium and smaller only, Fort (DC equal to damage) or become *sprawled*)

Treasure: 2T

Tyrannosaurus Rex (Huge Animal Walker — 106 XP): Str 20, Dex 10, Con 16, Int 4, Wis 10, Cha 10; SZ H (2×4, Reach 1); Spd 40 ft. ground (Run 200 ft.); Init IV; Atk VII; Def III; Res V; Health VIII; Comp —; Skills: Athletics II, Search VI, Survival VI; Qualities: *Class ability (Scout: trail signs), damage reduction 3, grappler, impaired sense (scent), superior runner I, tough II, treacherous*

Attack/Weapons: Bite IV (dmg 2d12+5 lethal; threat 16–20; upgrades: *AP 2, grab*), Swallow III (dmg 4d8+5 lethal; notes: Grapple benefit — Medium and smaller only)

Treasure: 1A, 2T

Velociraptor (Medium Animal Walker — 74 XP): Str 14, Dex 14, Con 14, Int 6, Wis 10, Cha 10; SZ M (1×1, Reach 1); Spd 60 ft. ground (Run 300 ft.); Init V; Atk V; Def IV; Res IV; Health V; Comp —; Skills: Acrobatics III, Notice III, Survival IV,

Tactics III; Qualities: *Feat (Bushwhack Basics, Wolf Pack Basics), charge attack, improved sense (scent, sight), superior jumper II, superior runner I*

Attacks/Weapons: Bite I (dmg 1d8+2 lethal; threat 18–20), Rending Talon (Kick III: dmg 2d6+2 lethal; threat 19–20; upgrades: *AP 2, bleed*)

Treasure: 1T

DIRE CREATURES

"Dire" is a monster template and may be applied to any NPC *(see page 288).* For *really* big dire creatures, you might consider applying the Kaiju template instead *(see page 291).*

DOGS

Domesticated wolves can be trained as guardians and attack animals and some smaller folk use dogs as mounts. They often consider owners and trainers part of their "pack," becoming extremely reliable companions as long as they're reasonably well-fed and treated with care and discipline. Unfortunately, others go feral, stalking weaker animals and small folk as food.

Tactics: Dogs commonly go for the throat, especially if an opponent is distracted or prone (hence their Bite's high threat range). Failing that, they try to wear opponents down in anticipation of a killing blow.

Guard Dog (Small Animal Walker — 46 XP): Str 12, Dex 10, Con 10, Int 5, Wis 16, Cha 8; SZ S (1×1, Reach 1); Spd 40 ft. ground; Init VI; Atk IV; Def III; Res III; Health III; Comp —; Skills: Intimidate III, Notice V, Sneak III; Qualities: *Improved sense (hearing, scent), light sleeper*

Attacks/Weapons: Bite II (dmg 1d6+1 lethal; threat 17–20)

Treasure: None

Riding Dog (Medium Animal Walker — 48 XP): Str 16, Dex 10, Con 12, Int 4, Wis 14, Cha 12; SZ S; Spd 50 ft. ground; Init IV; Atk III; Def III; Res III; Health IV; Comp —; Skills: Athletics V, Notice V; Qualities: *Improved sense (scent)*

Attacks/Weapons: Bite II (dmg 1d8+3 lethal; threat 17–20)

Treasure: None

War Dog (Small Animal Walker — 52 XP): Str 12, Dex 10, Con 10, Int 4, Wis 14, Cha 7; SZ S (1×1, Reach 1); Spd 35 ft. ground; Init IV; Atk V; Def III; Res III; Health III; Comp —; Skills: Athletics III, Intimidate IV, Search IV, Tactics III; Qualities: *Feat (Wolf Pack Basics), improved sense (scent)*

Attacks/Weapons: Bite IV (dmg 2d6+1 lethal; threat 16–20; upgrades: *grab*)

Gear: Moderate leather armor barding (DR 2; Resist Fire 5; DP –1; ACP –0; Spd –5 ft.; Disguise +0)

Treasure: None

DOPPELGANGER

These inquisitive shapeshifters lurk in the great civilizations of the world, perfectly imitating other intelligent species. In their native form, doppelgangers are lanky humanoids with crocodile-like eyes, their internal organs clearly visible through translucent skin. They're immensely curious and go to great lengths to ingratiate themselves into society, occasionally murdering and taking their victim's place. This isn't done out of malice but rather to fully immerse themselves in the victim's life, indulging every aspect of their daily routine.

Doppelgangers are greatly feared by governments and secret societies which rely on the strength of their private membership. Some groups regularly purge their ranks, just in case doppelganger spies are present.

Tactics: Exposure is a doppelganger's greatest fear, which is why the creature spends so much time crafting undetectable lies. It augments its fabrications with a keen sense of character (represented by *convincing* and *fake it*) and a complement of mild telepathic abilities (*cold read I* and Detect Emotion). If discovered, the doppelganger heads for an area with dense population and assumes a new form. It uses Mind Blank to foil magical detection and, if necessary, shapeshifts into one of the hunters, perhaps sowing enough doubt in the party to escape before it's identified again.

Doppelganger (Medium Horror Walker — 95 XP): Str 10, Dex 10, Con 10, Int 12, Wis 12, Cha 12; SZ M (1×1, Reach 1); Spd 30 ft. ground; Init III; Atk VII; Def III; Res VIII; Health III; Comp II; Skills: Blend X, Bluff X, Disguise X; Qualities: *Class ability (Assassin: cold read I, convincing, fake it), expertise (Disguise), feat (Basic Skill Mastery (Actor), Iron Will), light sleeper, natural spell (Detect Emotion, Mind Blank), shapeshifter II*

Attacks/Weapons: Slam I (dmg 1d6 lethal; threat 20)

Treasure: 2G

DRAGONS

Dragons are the self-appointed kings of monsterdom, and rightfully so. Rarely does one find such intelligence, magical prowess, raw physical power, and killer instinct in one package.

Fire dragons are the most common and terrifying of their kind, winged scourges belching flame across villages and armies alike. They're proud, petty beasts whose love of gold and power blinds them to all else.

Forest dragons are sinuous, wingless beasts that live in the deepest forests of the world. They crave isolation, though some befriend the faeries and elves that share their arboreal home.

Frost dragons live atop mountains and in polar regions, in deep caves of ice and snow. They're brutish, voracious hunters that feast on herd-beasts and foolish explorers.

Royal dragons are the most civilized of dragonkind, wearing their metallic scales with great pride. Kings, generals, and heroes alike seek their wise counsel, offering riches and high magic in return.

Sea dragons are the largest of their kin, commanding the waves and all within. They're indifferent to the affairs of men, though they respond poorly to those who hunt their whale-herds and make war near their homes.

Storm dragons own the skies, soaring on the great winds as champions stride lands under their protection. Free-spirited and fickle, storm dragons are unpredictable in and out of combat.

Tactics: Dragons are fiercely territorial, self-confident, and utterly unafraid of lesser creatures (read: all but other dragons). Battling them is always an event thanks to *dramatic entrance,* and the stakes are always high with *ferocity, treacherous,* and *veteran* in the mix.

Every dragon has a devastating primary attack — the fire dragon's Fiery Breath, the forest dragon's wicked Bite, the royal dragon's skillful magic, etc. — and uses it to terrorize enemies into submission. When characters press their advantage and get in close, a dragon's numerous natural attacks should quickly make them reconsider their strategy.

Savvy parties know the best way past a dragon is to avoid battle: to sneak past, challenge it with riddles or puzzles, or play on its sympathy or pride. Dragons often live in isolation and sometimes indulge intruders to combat boredom. Sadly, even the loneliest dragon's amusement wanes eventually, leaving most parties with two options: flee or perish.

Fire Dragon (Huge Beast Flyer/ Walker — 243 XP): Str 22, Dex 10, Con 18, Int 14, Wis 16, Cha 14; SZ H (3×5, Reach 2); Spd 140 ft. winged flight; 40 ft. ground; Init III; Atk VI; Def III; Res VI; Health VI; Comp IV; Skills: Athletics X, Haggle V, Intimidate X, Notice V, Resolve V; Qualities: *Achilles heel (cold), damage immunity (fire, heat), damage reduction 7, darkvision I, dramatic entrance, fearsome, ferocity, improved sense (sight), light sleeper,*

Dragons

menacing threat, monstrous defense II, never outnumbered, tough II, treacherous, veteran II

Attacks/Weapons: Fiery Breath (fire damage attack IV: 50 ft. cone; dmg 1d10 fire per 2 TL, Ref Save DC 25 for 1/2 damage), Bite IV (dmg 2d12+6 lethal; threat 16–20; upgrades: *reach +1*), Talon II × 2 (dmg 1d10+6 lethal; threat 19–20), Tail Slap II (dmg 1d12+6 lethal; threat 19–20; upgrades: *reach +1, trip*), Trample III (dmg 2d12+6 lethal; threat 19–20; notes: Medium and smaller only, Fort (DC equal to damage) or become *sprawled*), Wing Slam × 2 (Slam I: dmg 1d10+6 lethal; threat 20)

Treasure: 3A, 3C

Forest Dragon (Huge Beast Flyer/Walker — 222 XP): Str 20, Dex 10, Con 16, Int 14, Wis 14, Cha 14; SZ H (2×5, Reach 2); Spd 120 ft. winged flight, 40 ft. ground; Init IV; Atk VIII; Def VI; Res IX; Health VIII; Comp V; Skills: Acrobatics VI, Impress VI, Intimidate VII, Search VII, Sneak VI, Spellcasting IV; Spells: Pass Without Trace, Sleep, Tree Walk, Verdure; Qualities: *Aquatic I, beguiling, chameleon I (forest/jungle) damage reduction 5, dramatic entrance, never outnumbered, spell defense III, swift attack 1, superior swimmer IV, tough II, treacherous, veteran I*

Attacks/Weapons: Venomous Maw (Bite III: dmg 2d12+5 acid; threat 17–20), Choking Breath (fatiguing attack III: 40 ft. aura; Fort DC 20 or become *fatigued*), Claw II × 2 (dmg 1d10+5 lethal; threat 19–20), Tail Slap II (dmg 1d12+5 lethal; threat 19–20; upgrades: *reach +1, trip*), Trample II (dmg 1d12+5 lethal; threat 19–20; notes: Medium and smaller only, Fort (DC equal to damage) or become *sprawled*)

Treasure: 2A, 2L, 2M

Frost Dragon (Huge Beast Flyer/Walker/Burrower — 197 XP): Str 18, Dex 10, Con 18, Int 10, Wis 10, Cha 10; SZ H (3×4, Reach 2); Spd 200 ft. winged flight, 60 ft. ground, 30 ft. burrow; Init II; Atk X; Def IV; Res X; Health VI; Comp III; Skills: Intimidate VII, Notice VI, Survival V, Tactics IV; Qualities: *Achilles heel (fire, heat), chameleon I (arctic), damage immunity (cold), damage reduction 4, darkvision I, frenzy I, improved sense (scent), natural spell (Wall of Ice), never outnumbered, superior climber II, superior swimmer IV, tough IV, treacherous*

Attacks/Weapons: Freezing Breath (cold damage attack II: 50 ft. cone; dmg 1d6 cold per 2 TL, Ref DC 15 for 1/2 damage), Bite III (dmg 2d12+4 lethal; threat 17–20; upgrades: *AP 2*), Claw II × 2 (dmg 1d10+4 lethal; threat 19–20), Tail Slap I (dmg 1d12+4 lethal; threat 20; upgrades: *reach +1, trip*), Wing Slam × 2 (Slam I: dmg 1d10+4 lethal; threat 20)

Treasure: 2A, 1C, 1L, 1T

Royal Dragon (Huge Beast Flyer/Walker — 256 XP): Str 16, Dex 10, Con 16, Int 18, Wis 16, Cha 16; SZ H (3×6, Reach 1); Spd 200 ft. flight, 60 ft. ground; Init III; Atk VII; Def III; Res X; Health VII; Comp V; Skills: Disguise VI, Impress IX, Investigate VI, Resolve VI, Spellcasting VI; Spells: Bless, Command II, Geas, Mark of Justice, True Seeing, Zone of Truth; Qualities: *Bright II, cagey II, class ability (Captain: virtues of command I), contagion immunity, damage immunity (divine), damage reduction 4, dramatic entrance, light sleeper, monstrous defense I, never outnumbered, shapeshifter II, spell defense IV, spell reflection, superior swimmer IV, tough II, unlimited spell points, veteran IV*

Attacks/Weapons: Radiant Breath (divine damage attack III: 80 ft. beam; dmg 1d8 divine per 2 TL, Ref DC 20 for 1/2 damage), Bite III (dmg 2d12+3 lethal; threat 17–20; upgrades: *reach +1*), Claw II × 2 (dmg 1d10+3 lethal; threat 19–20), Tail Slap III (dmg 2d12+3 lethal; threat 19–20; upgrades: *reach +1*), Trample II (dmg 1d12+5 lethal; threat 19–20; notes: Medium and smaller only, Fort (DC equal to damage) or become *sprawled*)

Treasure: 3A, 3M

Sea Dragon (Gargantuan Beast Swimmer — 184 XP): Str 16, Dex 8, Con 20, Int 8, Wis 12, Cha 8; SZ G (4×8, Reach 2); Spd 80 ft. swim; Init II; Atk VIII; Def V; Res VIII; Health VII; Comp III; Skills: Athletics VI, Search VI, Survival VI; Qualities: *Achilles heel (electrical), aquatic II, charge attack, clumsy, damage immunity (fire), damage reduction 6, dramatic entrance, fearsome, feat (Cleave Basics, Cleave Mastery, Pathfinder Basics (aquatic)), improved stability, never outnumbered, regeneration 5, tough II , treacherous, veteran I*

Attacks/Weapons: Steam Breath (heat damage attack II: 40 ft. cone; dmg 1d6 heat per 2 TL, Ref DC 15 for 1/2 damage), Thundering Lash (Tail Slap IV: dmg 2d12+3 explosive; threat 18–20; upgrades: *reach +1*), Bite V (dmg 3d12+3 lethal; threat 16–20; upgrades: *reach +1*)

Treasure: 2A, 2L, 1T

Storm Dragon (Huge Beast Flyer/Walker/Burrower — 225 XP): Str 18, Dex 10, Con 18, Int 12, Wis 14, Cha 12; SZ H (3×5, Reach 2); Spd 160 ft. winged flight, 40 ft. ground, 20 ft. burrow; Init II; Atk IX; Def V; Res X; Health VII; Comp IV; Skills: Bluff IX, Intimidate IX, Search VIII, Sense Motive VIII, Spellcasting III; Spells: Call Lightning II, Control Weather II, Gust of Wind; Qualities: *Cagey I, damage defiance (cold), damage immunity (electrical), damage reduction 4, dramatic entrance, fearsome, feat (Agile Flyer, Fast Flyer), frenzy II, improved sense (sight), never outnumbered, tough III, treacherous, veteran II*

Attacks/Weapons: Lightning Breath (electrical damage attack IV: 80 ft. beam; dmg 1d10 electrical per 2 TL, Ref DC 25 for 1/2 damage), Bite III (dmg 2d12+4 lethal; threat 17–20), Talon II × 2 (dmg 1d10+4 lethal; threat 19–20), Tail Slap II (dmg 1d12+4 lethal; threat 19–20; upgrades: *reach +1*), Trample II (dmg 1d12+4 lethal; threat 19–20; notes: Medium and smaller only, Fort (DC equal to damage) or become *sprawled*)

Treasure: 3A, 2C

DRAKE

Drakes are handled with a rogue template *(see page 248).* Species feats can be applied for additional archetypes, such as arctic and mountain drakes.

DRIDER

Damned by dark gods to the belly of the world, driders are foul centaur-like beings combining the upper torso of folk (often an elf) with the eyes and hindquarters of a giant venomous spider. Many are acolytes of dark religions, fallen from their masters' "grace" and cursed to wander the depths alone. Driders take particular delight in avenging themselves upon other living things, especially the beautiful.

Tactics: Driders are solitary, cruel predators that hunt with the help of Darkness III, employing Sneak and Phantasmal Killer to knock foes out before they're aware they're a target. Driders carry arrows and blades coated in their own venom, using them to soften enemies up before finishing them off. In melee, they Web and Sting targets, leaving them defenseless so they can toy with them before bleeding them dry.

Drider (Large Horror Walker — 82 XP): Str 12, Dex 12, Con 14, Int 12, Wis 14, Cha 12; SZ L (2×2, Reach 1); Spd 30 ft. ground; Init IV; Atk II; Def II; Res V; Health III; Comp II; Skills: Athletics V, Notice III, Sneak V; Qualities: *Damage reduction 2, darkvision II, devoted (Darkness III), expertise (Athletics), improved stability, repulsive I, superior climber III*

Attacks/Weapons: Kukri × 2 (dmg 1d6+1 lethal; threat 19–20; qualities: *finesse, keen 4*), short bow + 20 barbed arrows (dmg 1d6 lethal + weakening poison; threat 19–20; range 20 ft. × 6; qualities: *bleed, cavalry, poisonous*), Sting (Slam II: 1d8+1 lethal + weakening poison; threat 19–20; upgrades: *venomous*), Web (entangling attack II: Fort DC 15 or become *entangled* for 2d6 rounds)

Gear: Weakening poison (6 uses)

Treasure: 1A, 2G

DWARF

Dwarves are handled with a rogue template *(see page 248).* Species feats can be applied for additional archetypes, such as hill dwarves.

EAGLES

These majestic predatory birds attack prey up to their own size and supplement their diet with carrion when hunting proves difficult. Eagles are difficult to train but fiercely loyal once broken.

Tactics: Eagles swoop down to pluck and peck at foes' faces with sharp talons and beaks.

Eagle (Tiny Animal Flyer/Walker — 46 XP): Str 10, Dex 14, Con 10, Int 2, Wis 14, Cha 6; SZ T (1×1, Reach 1); Spd 60 ft. winged flight, 20 ft. ground; Init II; Atk III; Def III; Res II; Health III; Comp —; Skills: Acrobatics II, Notice IV, Search IV; Qualities: *Improved sense (sight), rend*

Attacks/Weapons: Bite I (dmg 1d4 lethal; threat 18–20; upgrades: *bleed*), Talon I (dmg 1d3 lethal; threat 20)

Treasure: None

Giant Eagle (Large Animal Flyer/Walker — 57 XP): Str 10, Dex 14, Con 10, Int 2, Wis 16, Cha 6; SZ L (2×2, Reach 1); Spd 60 ft. winged flight, 20 ft. ground; Init III; Atk III; Def III; Res III; Health IV; Comp —; Skills: Acrobatics II, Notice IV, Search IV; Qualities: *Feat (Agile Flyer), improved sense (sight), rend*

Attacks/Weapons: Bite I (dmg 1d10 lethal; threat 18–20; upgrades: *bleed, keen 4*), Talon I (dmg 1d8 lethal; threat 20; upgrades: *AP 2*)

Treasure: 1T

ELDER ELEMENTALS

Elder elementals are living embodiments of the primal energies of creation — air, earth, fire, and water. Though their lesser brethren are often summoned *(see page 123),* elders are rarely seen unless the forces of nature are upset or great upheaval has occurred. Even then they walk the world alone, avoiding "materials" (the lesser species) and departing when their unknowable tasks are complete. Only in the Final Days will the elders walk together, burning and crushing the land and all upon it, then blowing and washing the debris away to herald a new age.

Air elementals are living cyclones that dart about with lightning speed. They batter foes with powerful blasts of wind and blinding clouds, laughing as blades pass harmlessly through them.

Earth elementals are plodding piles of rock and soil weighing many tons. They move through and burst forth from the earth, raining blows upon the ground to topple all but the most stable enemies.

Fire elementals are terrifying pyres that move like wildfire, gleefully turning all to ash and ember. Battling these beings is an exhausting affair as heat and licking flames quickly take their toll.

Water elementals are sentient tidal waves, impervious to blades and arrows. They aspire to drown opponents in their mass, drawing the unprepared into their bodies for a quick and panicked death.

Tactics: Elder elementals are tremendously tough and often require special tactics to defeat. Their raw power is frightening but they're not without their weaknesses. They don't comprehend the world the way fleshy species do and fail to consider tactics that extend beyond their elements. An earth elemental would understand to take cover (or make it!), for example, but it wouldn't occur to him to exploit a *bleeding* injury (as he, being made of rock, has no veins or blood). As each is a being of pure force, elementals can't truly be killed (thus the *everlasting* quality), and contentedly pursue their objectives without concern for their physical forms.

Elder Air Elemental (Large Elemental Flyer — 150 XP): Str 12, Dex 20, Con 12, Int 6, Wis 14, Cha 12; SZ L (2×2, Reach 2); Spd 100 ft. flight; Init VIII; Atk VII; Def VII; Res VI; Health V; Comp IV; Skills: Acrobatics V, Search V; Qualities: *Achilles heel (electricity), blindsight, cagey II, class ability (Scout: master tracker II), critical surge, damage immunity (lethal, sonic), everlasting, feat (Mobility Basics, Mobility Mastery), knockback, tough I, tricky (Shove), veteran II*

Attacks/Weapons: Slam IV (dmg 2d8+4 subdual; threat 18–20; upgrades: *finesse, trip*), Blasting Wind (sprawling attack III: 20 ft. cone; Fort DC 20 or become *sprawled*), Dust Cloud (blinding attack III: 50 ft. aura; Will DC 20 or become *blinded* for 3d6 rounds)

Treasure: None

Elder Earth Elemental (Large Elemental Burrower/ Walker — 150 XP): Str 20, Dex 8, Con 18, Int 6, Wis 10, Cha 10; SZ L (2×2, Reach 2); Spd 40 ft. burrow, 30 ft. ground; Init III; Atk V; Def VII; Res VI; Health VII; Comp II; Skills: Athletics VIII, Notice III, Search II; Qualities: *Achilles heel (sonic), banned action (Swim, Tumble), battering, charge attack, class ability (Lancer: last stand), damage reduction 5, darkvision II, everlasting, improved stability, lumbering, monstrous defense II, tough II, veteran II*

Attacks/Weapons: Slam IV (dmg 2d8+5 lethal; threat 18–20; upgrades: *AP 4*), Rift Strike (sprawling attack III: 40 ft. beam; Fort DC 20 or become *sprawled*), Shifting Earth (slowing attack III: 30 ft. aura; Fort DC 20 or become *slowed* for 3d6 rounds)

Treasure: None

Elder Fire Elemental (Large Elemental Flyer — 150 XP): Str 14, Dex 18, Con 12, Int 6, Wis 10, Cha 10; SZ L (2×2, Reach 2); Spd 80 ft. flight; Init VI; Atk VIII; Def VI; Res VI; Health IV; Comp III; Skills: Search V, Tactics V; Qualities: *Achilles heel (cold), banned action (Swim), class ability (Edgemaster: deadly blow), damage defiance (lethal), damage immunity (fire), everlasting, fearsome, feat (Combat Focus, Combat Instincts), grueling combatant, natural defense (fire), tough II, veteran II*

Attacks/Weapons: Slam IV (dmg 2d8+3 fire; threat 18–20; upgrades: *finesse, keen 4*), Heat Wave (heat damage attack III: 40 ft. aura; dmg 1d6 heat per 2 TL, Ref DC 15 for 1/2 damage), Ignition (fire damage attack III: 20 ft. blast; dmg 1d6 fire per 2 TL, Ref DC 15 for 1/2 damage)

Treasure: None

Elder Water Elemental (Large Elemental Walker — 150 XP): Str 20, Dex 10, Con 20, Int 6, Wis 10, Cha 10; SZ L (2×2, Reach 2); Spd 20 ft. ground; Init V; Atk V; Def V; Res IV; Health VI; Comp IV; Skills: Athletics VII, Search IV; Qualities: *Achilles heel (cold, heat), blindsight, class ability (Burglar: evasion II), damage immunity (bows, edged), everlasting, feat (Ferocity Basics, Ferocity Mastery, Ferocity Supremacy), grappler, improved stability, knockback, natural spell (Mass Water Walk, Move Water), never outnumbered, superior swimmer X, tough II, veteran II*

Attacks/Weapons: Slam IV (dmg 2d8+5 subdual; threat 18–20; upgrades: *grab, reach 1*), Drown (Swallow III: dmg 2d12+5 lethal; notes: Grapple benefit — Small and smaller only), Riptide (stunning attack III: 30 ft. beam; Will DC 20 or become *stunned* for 3d6 rounds)

Treasure: None

ELEPHANTS

These massive herd animals generally keep to themselves but can stampede when spooked; their distinctive trumpeting cry is reason enough for even the bravest travelers to clear the way. Trained elephants are powerful allies, assisting in a wide variety of tasks ranging from construction to combat.

Tactics: While only the males possess the deadly tusks so (rightfully) feared in a toe-to-toe fight, any adult elephant can use its immense bulk as a weapon. Better still, they're highly social and naturally form into orderly ranks to protect their flanks (and young). Military generals have been known to use this to their advantage, sending a herd of trampling elephants in ahead of their troops to decimate an enemy's front line.

Elephant (Large Animal Walker — 74 XP): Str 18, Dex 10, Con 13, Int 6, Wis 10, Cha 8; SZ L (2×3, Reach 1); Spd 30 ft. ground (Run 150 ft.); Init I; Atk IV; Def III; Res VI; Health V; Comp —; Skills: Athletics III, Intimidate III, Notice II, Sense Motive II; Qualities: *Damage reduction 2, improved stability, superior runner I, tough I*

Attacks/Weapons:, Kick I (dmg 1d8+4 lethal; threat 20), Slam I (dmg 1d8+4 subdual; threat 20; upgrades: *trip*), Trample III (dmg 2d10+4 lethal; threat 19–20; notes: Medium and smaller only, Fort (DC equal to damage) or become *sprawled*), Tusks (Gore III: dmg 2d8+4 lethal; threat 18–20; upgrades: *bleed, reach +1*)

Treasure: 2T

Mammoth (Huge Animal Walker — 82 XP): Str 18, Dex 10, Con 15, Int 5, Wis 10, Cha 7; SZ H (3×4, Reach 1); Spd 30 ft. ground; Init I; Atk VI; Def IV; Res VI; Health VI; Comp —; Skills: Athletics II, Intimidate III, Notice III; Qualities: *Damage defiance (cold), damage reduction 2, improved stability, tough II*

Attacks/Weapons: Slam II (dmg 1d10+4 subdual; threat 19–20; upgrades: *trip*), Trample III (dmg 2d12+4 lethal; threat 19–20; notes: Large and smaller only, Fort (DC equal to damage) or become *sprawled*), Tusks (Gore II: dmg 1d10+4 lethal; threat 18–20; upgrades: *reach +1*)

Treasure: 3T

FAERIE

The "fair folk" are kin to the natural world, children of forest and field who live beyond the reach of mortal folk. As incarnations of the primordial world, they tend to seem simple and emotional, as quick to befriend as to bewitch. All are exceedingly wary of mortals, as contact with them weakens their ties to nature, eventually dooming them to mortality and corruption.

Sidhe ("shee") are faerie lords who rule over sacred forest glades. They're brides and grooms of the wild, with whom they makes life bloom and prosper.

Spriggan are the strongest and most outgoing of their kind, emerging from the deep wood to steal from — and occasionally fight — outsiders. Their journeys beyond the faerie realms wear upon their glamour, hedging them toward darkness and cruelty.

Sprites are curious, rambunctious and friendly. Many fall in love with the mortal world. Some even choose to live there, stealing human children and replacing them.

Tactics: Faerie are inherently reclusive, taking up arms only to defend their lands from the encroachment of outsiders. Those who venture out into the world rely heavily on trickery, theft, sabotage and misdirection to avoid combat whenever possible. Faerie pressed into battle summon natural animals to their aid and use hit-and-run tactics to buy themselves enough time to escape; only the spriggan seek to draw fights out any longer than absolutely necessary.

Sidhe (Small Fey Walker — 77 XP): Str 10, Dex 12, Con 10, Int 12, Wis 12, Cha 16; SZ S (1×1, Reach 1); Spd 40 ft. ground; Init VII; Atk III; Def II; Res IX; Health II; Comp III; Skills: Blend IV, Spellcasting IV, Survival VII; Spells: Command I, Entangle, Nature's Ally II, Sleep; Qualities: *Attractive II, honorable, natural spell (Dimension Door), invisibility*

Attacks/Weapons: Short sword (dmg 1d8 lethal; threat 19–20; qualities: *keen 4*), Stunning Look (stunning attack I: 60 ft. gaze; Will DC 10 or become *stunned* for 1d6 rounds)

Gear: Fast-acting maddening poison (3 uses), mage armor oil

Treasure: 2M

Faerie

Spriggan (Medium Fey Walker — 63 XP): Str 12, Dex 10, Con 14, Int 10, Wis 14, Cha 12; SZ M (1×1, Reach 1); Spd 40 ft. ground; Init V; Atk IV; Def III; Res V; Health IV; Comp III; Skills: Prestidigitation IV, Sneak IV, Survival VI; Qualities: *Class ability (Burglar: evasion I), darkvision I, favored foes (folk), feat (Charging Basics, Great Fortitude)*

Attacks/Weapons: Gore II (dmg 1d6+1 lethal; threat 19–20; upgrades: *bleed*), javelin × 3 (dmg 1d8+1 lethal; threat 19–20; range 30 ft. × 3)

Gear: Sustaining potion × 2, wilding oil

Treasure: 1G, 1M

ELF

Elves are handled with a rogue template *(see page 248).* Species feats can be applied for additional archetypes, such as wood or dark elves.

Sprite (Diminutive Fey Flyer/Walker — 72 XP): Str 10, Dex 18, Con 10, Int 10, Wis 10, Cha 14; SZ D (1×1, Reach 1); Spd 40 ft. winged flight, 10 ft. ground; Init VI; Atk I; Def IX; Res IV; Health I; Comp II; Skills: Acrobatics VII, Bluff III, Impress III; Qualities: *Chameleon II (forest/jungle), class ability (Burglar: he did it!), feat (Agile Flyer), shapeshifter I*

Attacks/Weapons: Diminutive short bow + 30 standard arrows (dmg 1d4 lethal; threat 19–20; range 20 ft. × 6; qualities: *AP 2, cavalry, poisonous*)

Gear: Fast-acting baffling poison (3 uses)

Treasure: 1M

GHOSTS

"Ghostly" is a monster template, which may be applied to any monster or rogue *(see page 288).*

GHOUL

Ghouls are said to be folk cursed for great transgressions against life — massacre of the innocent, cannibalism, murdering the holy and benign, and worse. Their acts have damned them with endless, unnatural hunger for decaying flesh. Eventually their minds snap and they abandon civilization, becoming as beasts and dressing themselves in the rags of the dead. Immortal foulness brews in them like a poison, seeping into wounds they inflict and sending victims into feverish comas.

Tactics: Ghouls are disgusting creatures haunting catacombs and graveyards, scavenging for fresh corpses to consume. They're often encountered in loose "tribes," like perverse families, which graze cemeteries under cover of darkness. In combat, ghouls lash out with their putrid claws, following with other natural attacks until a target's last breath escapes his lungs.

Ghoul (Medium Undead Walker — 56 XP): Str 10, Dex 12, Con 10, Int 10, Wis 12, Cha 10; SZ M (1×1, Reach 1); Spd 30 ft. ground; Init IV; Atk III; Def III; Res V; Health VI; Comp I; Skills: Sneak III; Qualities: *Feral, improved sense (scent), stench, swarm*

Attacks/Weapons: Bite I (dmg 1d8 lethal; threat 18–20), Ghoul Fever (sickening attack II: Will DC 15 or become *sickened* for 2d6 rounds; upgrades: *supernatural attack (bite)*), Claw I (dmg 1d6 lethal; threat 20), Paralyzing Claw (paralyzing attack I: Will DC 10 or become *paralyzed* 1d6 rounds; upgrades: *supernatural attack (claw)*)

Treasure: 1G, 1T

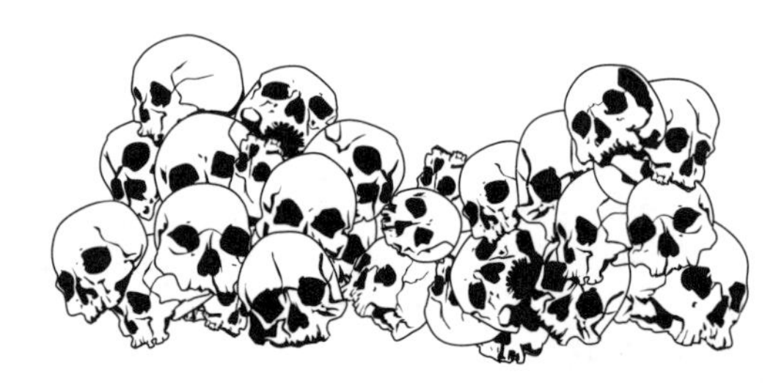

GIANTS

Giants are handled with a rogue template *(see page 248).* Species feats can be applied for additional archetypes, such as hill and storm giants.

GNOLL

The most prolific of the many beastmen races, gnolls are marauding nomadic humanoids with the heads of wild dogs and bodies covered in dirty yellow or reddish-brown fur. They're nocturnal carnivores, wandering the starlit plains and scrublands in search of intelligent creatures to kill (because they scream more), but they're also fond of taking slaves to work in their mines. Occasionally they sell slaves to merchant caravans and kingdoms in need of extra hands, and this is one of the ways in adventurers can track them back to their remote outposts.

Gnoll warbands are motley, noisy packs, held together by a shaman who channels their ancestors' favor. Every gnoll seeks to prove his valor in melee combat and accomplished warriors wear grisly trophies like the scalps and ears of previous kills.

Tactics: Gnolls prefer to attack at night, when darkness covers their approach and adds to the confusion of battle. They announce their bloody intentions with "laughing" war-barks as they flood the sky with whirling bolas. A headlong charge and excessive bloodshed generally follow.

Gnoll (Medium Folk Walker — 23 XP): Str 12, Dex 10, Con 10, Int 8, Wis 10, Cha 8; SZ M (1×1, Reach 1); Spd 30 ft. ground; Init II; Atk IV; Def II; Res I; Health IV; Comp I; Skills: Notice II, Survival II; Qualities: *Darkvision I, nocturnal, improved sense (scent), tricky (Relentless Attack)*

Attacks/Weapons: Axe (dmg 1d10+1 lethal; threat 20; qualities: *AP 4*), hide shield (dmg 1d3+1 subdual; threat 20; qualities: *guard +2*), bola × 3 (dmg 1d6+1 subdual; threat 19–20; range 20 ft. × 3; qualities: *cavalry, trip*)

Gear: Partial studded leather (DR 2; Resist —; DP –1; ACP –0; Spd +0 ft.; Disguise +0)

Treasure: 1C, 1G

Gnoll Shaman (Medium Folk Walker — 36 XP): Str 10, Dex 10, Con 10, Int 8, Wis 12, Cha 8; SZ M (1×1, Reach 1); Spd 30 ft. ground; Init IV; Atk III; Def II; Res II; Health III; Comp I; Skills: Medicine II, Notice II, Survival II, Tactics II; Qualities: *Class ability (Priest: benediction), darkvision I, devoted III (any 1 Path), improved sense (scent), nocturnal, tricky (Relentless Attack)*

Attacks/Weapons: Shod staff (dmg 1d8 lethal; threat 19–20; qualities: *double, trip*)

Gear: Partial studded leather (DR 2; Resist —; DP –1; ACP –0; Spd +0 ft.; Disguise +0)

Treasure: 1C, 1L, 1G

GOBLINS

Goblins are handled with a rogue template *(see page 249).* Species feats can be applied for additional archetypes.

GOLEMS

Golems are the inventions of skilled mages, great philosophers, and wise men — constructs granted the spark of life through arcane or divine means. Each is a unique creation, reflecting the needs and personality of its creator.

Clay golems are formed of soil and blood. Their blows cause deep wounds and horrible bruising.

Flesh golems are a perverse mockery of the living, stitched together with parts from different bodies (and sometimes different species). Some are driven mad with self-loathing, further fueling their destructive power.

Stone golems are sculpted living statues wielding great granite weapons. Their soulless gaze robs targets of their will, preventing escape.

Tactics: Most golems are created as sentinels to guard palaces, laboratories, and other areas important to their makers. They serve mindlessly, capable of only the simplest tasks without direction, which translates to direct and repetitive actions in combat. They can't be swayed, however, and never betray their instructions.

Clay Golem (Large Construct Walker — 78 XP): Str 18, Dex 9, Con 10, Int 8, Wis 10, Cha 1; SZ L (2×2, Reach 2); Spd 25 ft. ground; Init I; Atk III; Def IV; Res I; Health V; Comp I; Skills: None; Qualities: *Damage defiance (Blunt), fatal falls, fearless II, feat (Surge of Speed), regeneration 2, rend, spell defense V, tough I*

Attacks/Weapons: Slam IV (dmg 2d8+4 lethal; threat 17–20), Cursing Wound (wounding attack IV: Fort DC 25 or begin bleeding for 4d6 rounds; upgrades: *supernatural attack (slam)*)

Treasure: 1L

Flesh Golem (Large Construct Walker — 58 XP): Str 16, Dex 8, Con 10, Int 6, Wis 10, Cha 10; SZ L (2×2, Reach 1); Spd 30 ft. ground; Init I; Atk IV; Def III; Res II; Health V; Comp I; Skills: None; Qualities: *Achilles heel (fire), clumsy, damage reduction 3, fearless II, feral, monstrous defense I, repulsive I, spell defense IV, tough I*

Attacks/Weapons: Claw III (dmg 2d8+3 lethal; threat 19–20)

Treasure: None

Stone Golem (Huge Construct Walker — 115 XP): Str 24, Dex 6, Con 14, Int 4, Wis 10, Cha 4; SZ H (4×4, Reach 2); Spd 20 ft. ground; Init I; Atk III; Def V; Res II; Health VI; Comp I; Skills: None; Qualities: *Critical hesitation, damage reduction 6, darkvision II, fearless II, improved stability, knockback, lumbering, spell defense VI, tough II*

Attacks/Weapons: Slam IV (dmg 2d10+7 lethal; threat 18–20), Slowing Stare (slowing attack II: 40 ft. ray; Will DC 15 or become *slowed* for 2d6 rounds)

Treasure: 2L

GORGON

According to legend, these snake-maned terrors were once beautiful but invited the wrath or jealousy of vindictive gods. They're certainly malicious enough for this to be true. Gorgons are cursed walk the world alone, unable to look upon another without turning them to stone. This terrible fate has unhinged them, depriving them of empathy and compassion. Now they relish the hunt, especially the moment they first catch an enemy's eye, as the victim feels his muscles harden and crack…

Given the great fear gorgons inspire, and the swell of heroes that rise up to face them, it's no wonder they keep to themselves. They favor the dim solitude of crypts and deep forests, where their awful visage isn't reviled.

Tactics: Gorgons are canny fighters who greatly prefer ranged combat. They know and resent their value as a hero's trophy and cruelly toy with all who hunt them. Whenever possible they wear attackers down with distant bow shots before closing to deliver a final Petrifying Gaze.

Gorgon (Medium Folk Walker — 71 XP): Str 10, Dex 10, Con 12, Int 10, Wis 16, Cha 12; SZ M (1×1, Reach 1); Spd 30 ft. ground; Init IV; Atk IV; Def II; Res VI; Health II; Comp II; Skills: Bluff III, Disguise IV, Sneak III; Qualities: *Condition immunity (flat-footed), damage reduction 1, darkvision 1, fearsome, feat (Bow Basics), tricky (Daunting Shot)*

Attacks/Weapons: Reflex bow + 30 standard arrows (dmg 1d6 lethal; threat 20; range 30 ft. × 6; qualities: *AP 2, poisonous*), Snakes (Bite I: dmg 1d8 lethal + weakening poison; threat 18–20; upgrades: *venomous*), Petrifying Gaze (petrifying attack II: 80 ft. gaze; Fort DC 15 or be turned to stone)

Gear: Actor's props, weakening poison (6 uses)

Treasure: 2L, 1T

GRIFFONS

These graceful aerial chimera are surprisingly mutable. All varieties have the fore-body and vast wings of a giant eagle but their rear limbs and tails are drawn from many combinations of animals.

Griffons have the hindquarters of a lion. Many have leonine tails, though serpent tails have also been seen.

Hippogriffons have the hindquarters of a horse with a matching tail or the broad-feathered train of a bird. "Hippogriffs" are less temperamental than griffons and easier to saddle as mounts.

Tactics: Griffons of all sorts count on their superior mobility to escape dangerous situations. When forced (or trained) to fight, they snap with powerful beaks during swift fly-by attacks.

Griffon (Large Animal Flyer/Walker — 66 XP): Str 14, Dex 14, Con 12, Int 5, Wis 10, Cha 6; SZ L (1×2, Reach 1); Spd 80 ft. winged flight, 30 ft. ground; Init III; Atk VI; Def III; Res IV; Health V; Comp —; Skills: Acrobatics III, Notice III; Qualities: *Feat (Charging Basics), improved sense (sight), rend, tough I*

Attacks/Weapons: Bite I (dmg 1d10+2 lethal; threat 18–20; upgrades: *bleed, keen 4*), Talon II (dmg 1d8+2 lethal; threat 19–20)

Treasure: 1T

Hippogriffon (Large Animal Flyer/Walker — 65 XP): Str 12, Dex 14, Con 12, Int 5, Wis 12, Cha 8; SZ L (1×2, Reach 1); Spd 100 ft. winged flight, 40 ft. ground (Run 200 ft.); Init III; Atk IV; Def III; Res IV; Health IV; Comp —; Skills: Acrobatics IV, Notice IV; Qualities: *Damage reduction 2, feat (Charging Basics), superior runner I, superior traveler I*

Attacks/Weapons: Bite I (dmg 1d10+2 lethal; threat 18–20; upgrades: *bleed, keen 4*), Kick I (dmg 1d8+1 lethal; threat 20)

Treasure: 1T

HAG

Resembling withered, aged female folk, hags are lesser manifestations of the power of Fate. They're gifted seers with oblique motives and wicked minds, as quick to slay as to provide wise counsel. They love to challenge the worthiness of others and take particular delight in 'testing' heroes with trickery, cryptic prophecy, and outright violence. Those who persevere may gain some small insight about their future, though not always of the type they desire.

Tactics: Hags are exceptional sorcerers wielding ruinous powers of prognostication. Battling them is no mean feat, as they often see enemy actions before they're taken. Their mere presence can spoil fortune like old milk, making it difficult to best them when luck is at all a factor. Hags know and revel in this, of course, and this can be their undoing; some are so busy manipulating their foes that they miss crucial details or overlook flaws in their defenses.

Hag (Medium Outsider Flier/Walker — 131 XP): Str 16, Dex 10, Con 14, Int 16, Wis 12, Cha 10; SZ M (1×1, Reach 1); Spd 60 ft. flight, 30 ft. ground; Init III; Atk VI; Def V; Res VII; Health VI; Comp IV; Skills: Bluff VIII, Crafting V, Sense Motive VIII, Spellcasting VIII; Spells: Bestow Curse, Control Weather I, Disguise Self, Geas, Hold Person, Scare I, Scrye III, Tiny Shelter; Qualities: *Achilles heel (divine), beguiling, bright I, class ability (Assassin: black vial; Mage: spell secret III (Bestow Curse, Disguise Self, Scrye III)), darkvision II, everlasting, feat (Black Cat, Iron Will, Jinx, Tough Luck), repulsive I, spell defense II, spell reflection, tough I, treacherous, veteran II*

Attacks/Weapons: Dagger (dmg 1d6+3 lethal; threat 19–20; qualities: *bleed, hurl*), Evil Eye (stress damage attack II: 60 ft. gaze; dmg 1d6 stress per 2 TL, Ref DC 15 for 1/2 damage)

Gear: Chemist's kit, invisibility potion, love potion, mage's pouch

Treasure: 1A, 3M

Hag

HARPY

Harpies are deceitful, cowardly scavengers, lazily riding the wind in search of lone travelers they can snatch away as an easy meal. They resemble vultures with the chest, head, and arms of a human, and live in aeries on barren rock faces and sea cliffs. Their siren voices sometimes echo out of these warrens, drawing the reckless and the unwary to their doom.

Tactics: Simple-minded and mean-spirited, harpies attack the weakest members of any party, luring them away with beguiling songs. In Close Quarters they hover, whittling the enemy down with arrows until they feel confident they can steal away with at least one or two of their prey.

Harpy (Medium Folk Flyer/Walker — 55 XP): Str 10, Dex 12, Con 10, Int 7, Wis 10, Cha 14; SZ M (1×1, Reach 1); Spd 80 ft. winged flight, 10 ft. ground; Init IV; Atk IX; Def I; Res VI; Health V; Comp I; Skills: Acrobatics III, Search II, Sense Motive III; Qualities: *Beguiling, improved sense (sight)*

Attacks/Weapons: Short bow + 20 barbed arrows (dmg 1d6 lethal; threat 19–20; range 20 ft. × 6; qualities: *bleed, cavalry, poisonous*), Kick II (dmg 1d6 lethal; threat 19–20; upgrades: *bleed*)

Treasure: 1T

HELL HOUND

These great black hounds are composed of brimstone and flame, with glowing red eyes and fetid smoky breath lit by the unholy furnaces burning deep in their bellies. They're believed to be harvesters of the dead, unleashed to issue karmic damnation and run down all found lacking. Their ferocity and diligence is attractive to evil priests and summoners, who sometimes employ them to enact hate and revenge.

Tactics: Hell hounds hunt in packs, driving prey to exhaustion before shredding them limb from limb. They never give up and never tire, driven by evil and possessed of infernal providence. They prefer to divide and conquer, using Flame Breath to cut enemies off from assistance, but indulge their voracious appetites when it comes time for the kill. They pounce on the isolated victim, sinking their fiery teeth deep into its flesh and belching scorching clouds of flame into its innards. Soon only ash and memory remain.

Hell Hound (Medium Animal Outsider Walker — 74 XP): Str 10, Dex 10, Con 10, Int 6, Wis 10, Cha 6; SZ M (1×1, Reach 1); Spd 40 ft. ground; Init VII; Atk VIII; Def IV; Res VIII; Health V; Comp —; Skills: Acrobatics III, Notice IV, Sneak IX, Survival IV; Qualities: *Achilles heel (cold), damage immunity (fire), darkvision II, feat (Wolf Pack Basics), improved sense (scent), nocturnal*

Attacks/Weapons: Fiery Bite (Bite III: dmg 2d8 fire; threat 17–20), Flame Breath (fire damage attack II: 10 ft. cone; dmg 1d6 fire per 2 TL, Ref DC 15 for 1/2 damage)

HIPPOCAMPUS

Also known as "water horses," these creatures combine the upper body of a stallion with the lower body of a great fish or dolphin. They're powerful, graceful swimmers and favored mounts of mermen and other sea-folk.

Tactics: Hippocampi are sturdy and brave but rarely join riders in battle. They prefer to swim out of the enemy's range until their masters once again need them for travel.

Hippocampus (Large Animal Swimmer — 46 XP): Str 12, Dex 12, Con 12, Int 3, Wis 10, Cha 6; SZ L (1×2, Reach 1); Spd 60 ft. swim; Init III; Atk III; Def IV; Res V; Health IV; Comp —; Skills: Acrobatics III, Notice III, Survival III; Qualities: *Aquatic II, superior traveler II*

Attacks/Weapons: Bite I (dmg 1d10+1 lethal, threat 18–20), Tail Slap (dmg 1d10+1 lethal; threat 20; upgrades: *reach +1*)

Treasure: 1T

HOBGOBLIN

Hobgoblins are larger, more disciplined cousins to goblins. Their society is militaristic, clan-based, and male-dominated, headed by warlords favoring battle over diplomacy. Conquest is the cornerstone of their society and when they successfully suppress opposition in a region the clans quickly turn on each other. Hobgoblins are proud warriors, donning colorful regalia and keeping their gear well polished and in good repair.

Tactics: With a strong sense for tactics and a mind for complex battle plans, hobgoblins excel during mass confrontations. They commonly assume military formations, with warriors in the front using shields to protect the halberds behind. Taunting individuals is a quick way to shatter this discipline, however, as hobgoblins are far too proud to let any slight go.

Hobgoblin (Medium Folk Walker — 33 XP): Str 10, Dex 10, Con 12, Int 10, Wis 9, Cha 8; SZ M (1×1, Reach 1); Spd 25 ft. ground; Init III; Atk IV; Def III; Res III; Health III; Comp II; Skills: Intimidate III, Tactics III; Qualities: *Darkvision I, fearless I, feat (Shield Basics), tricky (Fully Engaged)*

Attacks/Weapons: Halberd (dmg 1d10 lethal; threat 19–20; qualities: *AP 4, reach +1*), short sword (dmg 1d8 lethal; threat 19–20; qualities: *keen 4*), metal shield (dmg 1d4 subdual; threat 20; qualities: *guard +2*)

Gear: Partial scalemail with light fittings (DR 4; Resist Edged 2; DP –2; ACP –2; Spd –5 ft.; Disguise –12)

Treasure: 1C, 1G

HOMUNCULUS

Smaller cousins to the golem, homunculi are magical wonders made of alchemical materials and the bodily fluids of a mage. Their features faintly resemble those of their creators, though the messy process of creation distorts them and often leaves them with skins of lead or brass.

Homonculi serve as companions, research assistants, and spies, thriving in these roles because their senses feed unerringly back to their masters. This bond also improves the mage's defenses (*look out!*), and doubles the mage's research ability (via *living library* and cooperative Investigate checks).

Tactics: Sadly, homunculi are fragile and weak, only fighting when absolutely necessary. Their Slumbering Bite is helpful as a defensive tool but should it fail the construct is frequently at the attacker's mercy.

Homunculus (Tiny Construct Flyer/Walker — 54 XP): Str 8, Dex 12, Con 10, Int 10, Wis 12, Cha 7; SZ T (1×1, Reach 1); Spd 40 ft. winged flight, 20 ft. ground; Init IV; Atk IV; Def II; Res III; Health III; Comp II; Skills: Acrobatics III, Blend X, Investigate III, Search III, Spellcasting I; Spells: Living Library I, Read Magic; Qualities: *Cagey I, class ability (Burglar: look out!; Mage: spell secret (Living Library I)), expanded spellbook I, interests (as master), telepathic*

Attacks/Weapons: Slumbering Bite (Bite I: dmg 1d4–1 + knockout poison; threat 18–20; upgrades: *venomous*)

Treasure: None

HORSES

Horses have worked with and alongside folk for centuries, serving as mounts and beasts of burden.

Tactics: Most horses shy away from combat and carefully avoid trampling creatures for fear of damaging their slender ankles. They're also highly temperamental when riled, making them unpredictable in a fight. Trained war horses and sturdy draft beasts are better prepared for the rigors of combat, staying focused and using their hooves to deadly effect.

Donkey (Medium Animal Walker — 43 XP): Str 14, Dex 10, Con 12, Int 4, Wis 10, Cha 6; SZ M (1×1, Reach 1); Spd 30 ft. ground (Run 150 ft.); Init III; Atk II; Def III; Res V; Health III; Comp —; Skills: Athletics IV, Resolve IV; Qualities: *Damage reduction 1, improved sense (scent), improved stability, superior runner I, superior traveler II*

Attacks/Weapons: Kick II (dmg 1d6+2 lethal; threat 19–20)

Treasure: None

Horse, Draft (Large Animal Walker — 42 XP): Str 17, Dex 10, Con 14, Int 4, Wis 10, Cha 8; SZ L (1×2, Reach 1); Spd 40 ft. ground; Init II; Atk III; Def IV; Res V; Health III; Comp —; Skills: Athletics V, Notice III; Qualities: *Improved sense (scent), improved carrying capacity, superior traveler II*

Attacks/Weapons: Kick I (dmg 1d8+3 lethal; threat 20)

Treasure: 1T

Horse, Race (Large Animal Walker — 53 XP): Str 13, Dex 14, Con 12, Int 4, Wis 10, Cha 7; SZ L (1×2, Reach 1); Spd 60 ft. ground (Run 360 ft.); Init III; Atk III; Def V; Res IV; Health IV; Comp —; Skills: Acrobatics IV, Athletics VI, Notice IV; Qualities: *Improved sense (scent), superior runner II, superior traveler I*

Attacks/Weapons: Kick II (dmg 1d8+1 lethal; threat 19–20)

Treasure: 1T

Horse, Riding/Wild (Large Animal Walker — 43 XP): Str 12, Dex 12, Con 12, Int 3, Wis 10, Cha 6; SZ L (1×2, Reach 1); Spd 50 ft. ground (Run 250 ft.); Init III; Atk III; Def IV; Res V; Health III; Comp —; Skills: Athletics V, Notice IV; Qualities: *Improved sense (scent), improved stability, superior runner I, superior traveler II*

Attacks/Weapons: Kick I (dmg 1d8+1 lethal; threat 20)

Treasure: 1T

Horse, War (Large Animal Walker — 55 XP): Str 14, Dex 12, Con 12, Int 4, Wis 10, Cha 6; SZ L (1×2, Reach 1); Spd 50 ft. ground; Init IV; Atk IV; Def IV; Res V; Health III; Comp —; Skills: Athletics V, Notice III; Qualities: *Fearless I, improved stability, tough I*

Attacks/Weapons: Kick III (dmg 2d8+2 lethal; threat 19–20), Trample I (dmg 1d10+2 lethal; threat 20; Medium and smaller only, Fort (DC equal to damage) or become *sprawled*)

Treasure: 1T

Mule (Large Animal Walker — 48 XP): Str 15, Dex 10, Con 12, Int 6, Wis 10, Cha 4; SZ L (1×2, Reach 1); Spd 30 ft. ground; Init III; Atk II; Def III; Res VI; Health III; Comp —; Skills: Acrobatics III, Athletics IV, Notice IV, Resolve III; Qualities: *Damage reduction 1, improved sense (scent), improved stability, superior traveler II*

Attacks/Weapons: Kick I (dmg 1d8+2 lethal; threat 20)

Treasure: None

Pony (Medium Animal Walker — 41 XP): Str 13, Dex 10, Con 12, Int 3, Wis 10, Cha 6; SZ M (1×1, Reach 1); Spd 40 ft. ground (Run 200 ft.); Init III; Atk II; Def IV; Res VI; Health IV; Comp —; Skills: Athletics V, Notice IV; Qualities: *Improved sense (scent), improved carrying capacity, superior runner I, superior traveler III*

Attacks/Weapons: Kick I (dmg 1d6+1 lethal; threat 20)

Treasure: None

Pony, War (Medium Animal Walker — 55 XP): Str 15, Dex 12, Con 12, Int 4, Wis 10, Cha 6; SZ M (1×1, Reach 1);

Spd 40 ft. ground (Run 200 ft.); Init IV; Atk IV; Def III; Res IV; Health IV; Comp —; Skills: Athletics V, Notice III; Qualities: *Fearless I, improved stability, superior runner I, tough I*

Attacks/Weapons: Kick III (dmg 2d6+2 lethal; threat 19–20), Trample I (damage 1d8+2 lethal; threat 20; notes: Small and smaller only, Fort (DC equal to damage) or become *sprawled*)

Treasure: 1T

HYDRA

Hydras are giant reptilian monsters with squat, strong bodies, seven snapping heads on serpentine necks, and the ability to recover from nearly any wound in seconds. They wallow in bogs and swamps, feeding on fish and crocodiles as their poisonous waste slowly voids the land of all life. When there's nothing else to feed upon, hydras make their way onto land, sometimes even venturing into towns and villages in search of another hot meal…

Tactics: A hydra's heads keep it from becoming *flanked* and also ensure it's *always ready* and *never outnumbered.* Its incredible toughness and *regeneration* remove any fear of death the beast might have had, letting it leap into combat without hesitation. A hydra often leads a fight with its *charge attack,* closing so it can take a full action and attack with all seven Bites in one round.

Hydra (Huge Beast Walker — 160 XP): Str 14, Dex 10, Con 16, Int 2, Wis 10, Cha 9; SZ H (3×4, Reach 3); Spd 20 ft. ground; Init III; Atk VII; Def III; Res VI; Health V; Comp I; Skills: Athletics VI, Notice III; Qualities: *Always ready, charge attack, condition immunity (flanked), damage reduction 2, feat (Combat Instincts, Iron Will, Pathfinder Basics (swamp)), improved sense (scent), monstrous defense I, never outnumbered, regeneration 15, superior swimmer II, swift attack 1, tough II*

Attacks/Weapons: Bite II × 7 (dmg 1d12+2 lethal; threat 17–20)

Treasure: 1A, 2T

IMP

Imps are devilish messengers of fallen gods and unspeakable powers, emerging from nether realms to draw power-hungry men into their master's fold. Most present themselves as "servants," offering advice and espionage with no apparent strings attached. An imp's services never come without a price, however, and that price is commonly eternal damnation.

Most imps look like tiny, bat-winged devils with exaggerated features and malicious expressions. They're gleefully mischievous and cunning, staying out of sight until their safety is assured.

Tactics: Imps are self-serving cowards whose only purpose is to deceive and manipulate. They quickly abandon "masters" when the chips are down, using *invisibility* to make for the hills. They might stick around long enough to empty their liege's cupboards of valuables and magic, but only if there's little risk involved.

Should an imp be forced into combat, it turns to sabotage and traps before attacking directly.

Imp (Tiny Outsider Flyer/Walker — 62 XP): Str 12, Dex 10, Con 12, Int 14, Wis 10, Cha 10; SZ T (1×1, Reach 1); Spd 60 ft. winged flight, 20 ft. ground; Init III; Atk V; Def III; Res II; Health II; Comp II; Skills: Acrobatics V, Bluff III, Prestidigitation III, Sneak V; Qualities: *Invisibility, light-sensitive, natural spell (Detect Magic), regeneration 1, spell defense II*

Attacks/Weapons: Claw I (dmg 1d3+1 lethal; threat 20)

Treasure: 1M

KOBOLD

Kobolds are scrawny doglike humanoids standing roughly two to three feet tall. They form tribal communities, often in subterranean warrens surrounded with primitive traps. Despite their small stature, they're malicious and territorial, particularly towards anything their own size (like goblins and pech).

Tactics: Aggressive and underhanded, kobolds attack from ambush whenever possible. When a fight is fully joined, they rely on superior numbers and flanking attacks to *swarm* and overwhelm the enemy. As the odds inevitably turn against them (i.e. drop to less than 2-to-1 in their favor), they usually retreat past their simple traps (at least one per kobold), hoping their enemies will trigger them in the pursuit.

Kobold (Small Folk Walker — 26 XP): Str 9, Dex 10, Con 10, Int 10, Wis 9, Cha 8; SZ S (1×1, Reach 1); Spd 30 ft. ground; Init III; Atk II; Def V; Res III; Health I; Comp I; Skills: Crafting II, Sneak II, Tactics II; Qualities: *Darkvision I, feat (Ambush Basics, Wolf Pack Basics), light-sensitive, mook, swarm*

Attacks/Weapons: Small throwing spear (dmg 1d6–1 lethal; threat 19–20; qualities: *hurl, reach +1*), Sling (dmg 1d4–1 subdual; threat 20; qualities: *load 1*)

Gear: Partial leather armor (DR 1; Resist Fire 3; DP –1, ACP –0, Spd +0 ft., Disguise +0), 1 trap (pit or spike, set near the fight, Notice DC 15 to spot)

Treasure: 1G

Kraken

KRAKEN

Kraken are colossal octopoid creatures that capsize and crush ships, dragging them into the ocean's inky depths. The waves conceal their approach, which is often made in craggy capes and treacherous narrows. Wrapping their thick tentacles around the hull, they use their tremendous bulk to smash vessels against rocks and other obstacles (including other ships), speeding their destruction. Kraken attacks are often preceded by violent storms, leading to old sailing legends that they're a curse inflicted by angry sea gods betrayed their due tribute. Others believe kraken are a manifestation of the sea itself, demanding recompense from those living off the water's bounty.

Tactics: One doesn't "fight" a kraken so much as *parts* of it. Only a small portion of the beast is visible above the surface of the water at any time — usually only its tentacles, which are 40 ft. long and as thick as a man is tall. Once a ship is fully shattered the kraken uses these massive appendages to *grab* bodies and other interesting morsels from the wreckage. This is the most dangerous time for survivors but it's also their greatest chance to seriously injure the monster, placing them close to its main body, as well as its vulnerable mouth and eyes. Until then, kraken are indiscriminate in their thrashing, pummeling and crushing everything with roughly equal attention. The only hope of driving one off is to injure it, inflicting a wound or causing it to fail a Damage save.

Kraken (Colossal Animal Swimmer — 185 XP): Str 22, Dex 10, Con 20, Int 6, Wis 14, Cha 10; SZ C (12×18, Reach 8); Spd 50 ft. swim; Init VI; Atk X; Def III; Res X; Health VII; Comp —; Skills: Athletics VII, Notice VII, Search VII, Tactics V; Qualities: *Aquatic II, amage reduction 7, fast healing, fearsome, grueling combatant, knockback, natural spell (Control Weather III), never outnumbered, rend, tough IV*

Attacks/Weapons: Tentacle Slap II × 2 (dmg 2d8+6 lethal; threat 19–20; upgrades: *bleed, grab, reach +1*), Squeeze II (dmg 2d10+6 lethal; upgrades: *keen 8;* notes: Grapple benefit), Slam I × 4 (dmg 1d12+6 lethal; threat 20)

Treasure: 3A, 3T

LAMIA

Lamia are callous centurions at distant oases and ancient tombs, guardian beasts of the kings of old. They combine the torso of an attractive human with the body of a mighty lion, and possess the ability to concoct mirages and other illusions. They use this ability to lure travelers into their realms so they can bewitch and subjugate them. Lamia are often lonely and view slaves as close companions, though they're wise enough not to let them keep gear or slip out of their sight. They also enjoy riddles and puzzles, trading them with worthy "guests."

Tactics: Lamia are master illusionists and precede all contact with magical trickery. Most use Illusionary Image III to project something of interest (e.g. a caravan or person in distress), then cast Charm Person II or Sleep to weaken the newcomers. They frequently use Disguise Self to change their appearance before they show themselves, potentially with Mirror Images if they feel their prey might retaliate.

Should an encounter turn to violence, lamia rely on their exceptional speed and deadly attacks, supplementing with Stupefying Touch as needed.

Lamia (Large Folk Walker — 89 XP): Str 14, Dex 12, Con 10, Int 10, Wis 12, Cha 10; SZ L (1×2, Reach 1); Spd 60 ft. ground; Init IV; Atk VIII; Def III; Res VII; Health VI; Comp III; Skills: Bluff VII, Search V, Survival V, Spellcasting V; Spells: Charm Person II, Disguise Self, Illusionary Image III, Mirror Images, Sleep; Qualities: *Attractive I, damage reduction 3, darkvision I, feat (Elusive, Pathfinder Basics (desert))*

Attacks/Weapons: Cutlass (dmg 1d10+2 lethal; threat 19–20; qualities: *cavalry, finesse*), Claw I × 2 (dmg 1d8+2 lethal; threat 20), Stupefying Touch (attribute draining attack II: Fort DC 15 or suffer 1 temporary Wis impairment)

Treasure: 2L, 1M

LICH

"Lich" is a monster template, which may be applied to any monster or rogue *(see page 292)*.

LIVESTOCK AND GAME ANIMALS

These simple herbivores dot the landscape as wild game and domesticated livestock.

Bison: These ponderous grazers shouldn't be underestimated. They're fiercely territorial and are known to make seemingly unprovoked attacks against Medium and larger characters.

Cattle/Oxen: These placid creatures are used as food and draft animals. They've been thoroughly domesticated and offer no real threat to anyone, least of all the predators that sometimes prey upon them.

Elk: These large deer are highly sought game. They can be quite dangerous when confronted, goring enemies with spiky, gnarled horns.

Goat/Sheep: These small animals survive in harsh climates by eating every plant they find. Without a large grazing area they quickly strip the land down to bare earth.

Llama: These sure-footed animals are large enough to make good pack animals and are sometimes also used as mounts by Small characters. Their nasty disposition can make them difficult to work with, however, so they're just as often bred exclusively for their wool.

Tactics: Most livestock flees unless cornered, at which point they charge, trying in a blind panic to break free.

Bison (Large Animal Walker — 54 XP): Str 14, Dex 10, Con 14, Int 2, Wis 10, Cha 6; SZ L (2×2, Reach 1); Spd 40 ft. ground; Init V; Atk IV; Def II; Res VI; Health VI; Comp —; Skills: Intimidate III, Notice III; Qualities: *Damage defiance (cold), damage reduction 2, feat (Charging Basics)*

Attacks/Weapons: Gore II (dmg 1d8+2 lethal; threat 18–20; upgrades: *bleed*), Trample I (dmg 1d10+2 lethal; threat 20; notes: Small and smaller only, Fort (DC equal to damage) or become *sprawled*)

Treasure: 1T

Cattle/Oxen (Large Animal Walker — 24 XP): Str 14, Dex 8, Con 10, Int 1, Wis 10, Cha 6; SZ L (1×2, Reach 1); Spd 30 ft. ground; Init II; Atk II; Def I; Res V; Health V; Comp —; Skills: Athletics II, Notice I; Qualities: *Improved stability, meek*

Attacks/Weapons: Slam I (dmg 1d8+2 subdual; threat 20)

Treasure: 1T

Elk (Large Animal Walker — 48 XP): Str 12, Dex 10, Con 10, Int 2, Wis 10, Cha 8; SZ L (1×2, Reach 1); Spd 50 ft. ground (Run 250 ft.); Init III, Atk IV; Def IV; Res IV; Health VI; Comp —; Skills: Acrobatics II, Athletics III, Notice II, Sneak III; Qualities: *Damage reduction 1, feat (Pathfinder Basics (forest/jungle)), improved sense (hearing), superior runner I*

Attacks/Weapons: Gore III (dmg 2d8+1 lethal; threat 18–20; upgrades: *bleed*)

Treasure: 2T

Goat/Sheep (Small Animal Walker — 15 XP): Str 8, Dex 8, Con 8, Int —, Wis 6, Cha 5; SZ S; Spd 30 ft. ground (Run 150 ft.); Init II; Atk II; Def I; Res III; Health IV; Comp —; Skills: Athletics I, Notice I; Qualities: *Meek, superior runner I*

Attacks/Weapons: Slam I (dmg 1d4–1 lethal; threat 20)

Treasure: 1T

Llama (Medium Animal Walker — 38 XP): Str 12, Dex 10, Con 12, Int 3, Wis 10, Cha 2; SZ M (1×1, Reach 1); Spd 30 ft. ground; Init II; Atk III; Def III; Res IV; Health III; Comp —; Skills: Athletics V, Notice V; Qualities: *Damage defiance (cold), feat (Pathfinder Basics (caverns/mountains)), improved sense (scent), superior traveler II*

Attacks/Weapons: Bite I (dmg 1d8+1 lethal; threat 18–20)

Treasure: 1T

MANTICORE

Manticores are bizarre creatures, combining the twisted face of a man, the mane and body of a lion, and huge bat wings with a spike-studded tail resembling a wicked morning star. A single snap of this tail sends a volley of razor-sharp spines toward enemies, punching through hide and leather with ease.

Tactics: Like their distant cousins, the chimera, manticores are primarily aerial hunters, strafing wanderers with spike salvos before mauling them to death with their teeth and claws.

Manticore (Large Beast Flyer/Walker — 87 XP): Str 16, Dex 12, Con 14, Int 7, Wis 10, Cha 9; SZ L (2×2, Reach 1); Spd 40 ft. winged flight, 30 ft. ground; Init IV; Atk V; Def III; Res IX; Health VI; Comp I; Skills: Notice II, Search IV, Survival IV; Qualities: *Damage reduction 3, darkvision I, feat (Bullseye, Charging Basics), improved sense (scent, sight)*

Attacks/Weapons: Bite I (dmg 1d10+3 lethal; threat 18–20), Claws II × 2 (dmg 1d8+3 lethal; threat 19–20), Tail Spikes (lethal damage attack I: 50 ft. beam; dmg 1d4 lethal per 2 TL, Ref DC 10 for 1/2 damage; upgrades: *AP 2*)

Treasure: 2T

MERFOLK

Merfolk are half-elf, half-fish, and beloved shepherds of the sea. They're far more outgoing than most fey, periodically establishing relationships with sea-going communities for trade and mutual protection. They're only roused to war by invasion, over-fishing, and pollution of their waters.

Tactics: When they're on the warpath, merfolk are encountered in battle-schools of five to fifteen raiders accompanied by sharks and other fighting sea creatures. They poison shark-tooth arrows with pufferfish venom and use them to shoot down ranged fighters or watchmen. When the enemy comes into the water, they anchor boats with grappling hooks and use their Conch Horns to deafen and confuse those on board. Despite the ferocity and decisiveness of these assaults, merfolk are rarely above reason; they can be negotiated with and are happy to forgive invaders who agree to respect their territory.

Merfolk (Large Fey Swimmer — 47 XP): Str 10, Dex 10, Con 12, Int 10, Wis 9, Cha 10; SZ L (1×2, Reach 1); Spd 60 ft. swim; Init III; Atk IV; Def II; Res III; Health IV; Comp III; Skills: Athletics VII, Impress IV; Qualities: *Aquatic II, natural spell (Nature's Ally II)*

Attacks/Weapons: Trident (dmg 1d8 lethal; threat 19–20; qualities: *hook, hurl*), light crossbow + 20 standard bolts (dmg 1d6 lethal + agonizing poison; threat 19–20; qualities: *AP 4, load 5, poisonous),* Conch Horn (bang damage attack I: 20 ft. cone; dmg 1d4 bang per 2 TL, Ref DC 10 for 1/2 damage)

Mounts and Vehicles: Hippocampus (Spd 60 ft. swim (Run 240 ft.); Travel 8; SZ/Def L/IV) or none

Gear: Silk rope + grappling hook

Treasure: 1G, 1L

MIMIC

These baffling shapeshifters don't copy people or animals but rather imitate inanimate objects like chairs, beds, and, most vexingly, treasure chests. They're endlessly patient, content to sit utterly still for days or weeks until someone stumbles across them, at which point they unleash a devastating attack with sticky pseudopods.

Tactics: Mimics rely entirely upon the element of surprise, using *chameleon II* to appear as everyday objects of Small and Medium size. When a character comes within striking distance, they Slam and *grab* them, using *sneak attack II* to cripple or knock them out, then follow with Squeeze attacks to crush the life and delicious fluids from their prostrate bodies. Mimics flee (slowly) when overpowered, trying to get around a corner so they can use *chameleon* again.

Mimic (Medium Horror Walker — 82 XP): Str 14, Dex 10, Con 14, Int 10, Wis 10, Cha 10; SZ M (1×1, Reach 2); Spd 10 ft. ground; Init III; Atk VII; Def II; Res VIII; Health IV; Comp II; Skills: Athletics III, Disguise VII, Search III; Qualities: *Chameleon II (indoors/settled), class ability (Scout: sneak attack II), damage immunity (acid), damage reduction 2*

Attacks/Weapons: Slam II (dmg 1d6+2 lethal; threat 19–20; upgrades: *grab*), Squeeze II (dmg 1d10+2 lethal; notes: Grapple benefit)

Treasure: 1A, 2G

MINOTAUR

Minotaurs are bull-headed humanoids clocking in at 8 ft. of rippling muscle. They come from braying herds, where the battle for dominance and mates is endless, so every specimen is a hardened survivor forged by years of savage combat. Most minotaurs continue to wander in herds, though some profit from their incredible sense of direction as scouts and guides (anyone hiring one should be prepared, of course, for constant self-aggrandizing stories about the minotaur's wisdom, strength, skill at arms, and virility).

Tactics: Minotaurs are immensely self-satisfied, supremely confident that they can crush the opposition. They skip pleasantries and happily wade right in, using Berserker Basics and their Charging feats to unleash wicked first strikes with Gore, then chopping at anything that's close with their broad axes. Minotaurs are difficult to drive off, rooted as they are by pride and arrogance.

Minotaur (Large Folk Walker — 65 XP): Str 16, Dex 10, Con 12, Int 7, Wis 10, Cha 8; SZ L (2×2, Reach 2); Spd 30 ft. ground; Init II; Atk VIII; Def III; Res VII; Health V; Comp I; Skills: Notice III, Survival III; Qualities: *Always ready, condition immunity (flat-footed), feat (Charging Basics, Charging Mastery, Rage Basics), fearless I, ferocity, improved sense (scent), natural spell (Orient Self)*

Attacks/Weapons: Large broad axe (dmg 2d6+3 lethal; threat 19–20; qualities: *AP 2, massive*), Gore III (dmg 2d8+3 lethal; threat 19–20; upgrades: *bleed*)

Treasure: 1G, 1T

MONSTROUS INSECTS

Many have aversions to insects but they're largely harmless. That statement's only half true here.

Bleeding Murk: These blood-sucking fliers sweep through villages, leaving nothing but scoured skeletons in their wake.

Fire Beetle: These beetles have hind leg venom sacks filled with glowing liquid that bursts into flame when it comes in contact with open air. They spray sheets of the substance at opponents when threatened.

Tactics: Monstrous insects have little to no sense of self-preservation when roused to battle. They simply attack until one side or the other is dead.

Bleeding Murk (Medium Animal Flyer — 32 XP): Str 10, Dex 10, Con 10, Int 1, Wis 6, Cha 2; SZ M (1×1, Reach 1); Spd. 40 ft. winged flight; Init I; Atk IV; Def II; Res II; Health VI; Comp —; Skills: Notice III; Qualities: *Improved sense (scent), swarm, tough I*

Attacks/Weapons: Devour (soul draining attack I: Fort DC 10 or die (standard character), lose 1 action die and 10 max. vitality (special character))

Treasure: None

Fire Beetle (Tiny Animal Walker — 34 XP): Str 12, Dex 10, Con 12, Int 1, Wis 6, Cha 2; SZ T (1×1, Reach 1); Speed 20 ft. ground; Init II; Atk IV; Def III; Res III; Health III; Comp —; Skills: Notice V; Qualities: *Swarm*

Attacks/Weapons: Fire spray (fire damage attack II: 10 ft. cone; dmg 1d6 fire per 2 TL, Ref DC 15 for 1/2 damage)

Treasure: 1T

Monstrous Insects

MONSTROUS PLANTS

Most plants are content to drink in the sunlight. Others…

Fanged Vase: This massive plant's center stalk is a vase-shaped bulb twice the size of a fully grown man, topped by one to three toothy, flesh-grinding 'flowers.' A broad mat of tentacle-like fronds surrounds the snapping mouths, ready to spring into action when prey approaches.

Slasher Vine: This aggressive plant masquerades as simple decorative ivy. Its dangling creepers hang across walkways and thread though other foliage, hoping to strangle or perhaps even decapitate prey. The slasher vine can (slowly) relocate to better hunting grounds when needed.

Tactics: Monstrous plants have an extremely limited but highly refined set of attacks. They rarely improvise or deviate from basic strategies and given their slow speed or immobility they must kill quickly to survive.

Fanged Vase (Large Immobile Plant — 55 XP): Str 16, Dex 10, Con 10, Int 3, Wis 2, Cha 7; SZ L (3×3, Reach 1); Spd —; Init V; Atk V; Def I; Res III; Health IV; Comp —; Skills: Search III; Qualities: *Blindsight, tough II*

Attacks/Weapons: Swallow I (dmg 1d12+3 lethal; notes: Grapple benefit — Medium and smaller only), Tentacle Slap I × 3 (dmg 1d10+3 lethal; threat 20; upgrades: *grab, reach +2*)

Treasure: 1A, 1G

Slasher Vine (Large Plant Walker — 38 XP): Str 14, Dex 10, Con 10, Int 1, Wis 2, Cha 2; SZ L (3×1, Reach 2); Speed 10 ft. ground; Init II; Atk I; Def I; Res III; Health III; Comp —; Skills: Athletics III, Notice III; Qualities: *Chameleon I (indoors/settled), grappler, improved stability*

Attacks/Weapons: Squeeze III (dmg 2d12+2 lethal; notes: Grapple benefit)

Treasure: 1A

MUMMY

Sometimes the dead can't let go of life. Case in point: mummies, which are the remains of powerful mortals — emperors, high priests, nobles and others of station — risen to reclaim what they possessed before the grave. Mummies retain their former bodies, rotted or desiccated by time or the unholy ceremonies that allowed for their return. Most still wear the wraps or clothes in which they were entombed.

Tactics: Mummies inspire horror in all who encounter them. Aside from the standard resilience of the dead, they possess unnatural toughness and devastating attacks that can quickly cripple a party. Their *fearsome* quality weakens an enemy's resolve, their Pharaoh's Curse impairs spellcasters, and Scarab Swarm occupies the survivors. As a fight wears on mummies Slam, infecting enemies with life-draining Mummy Rot. Should all this prove ineffective they withdraw, using ranged extraordinary attacks to cover their escape.

Mummy (Medium Undead Walker — 74 XP): Str 18, Dex 10, Con 10, Int 10, Wis 12, Cha 12; SZ M (1×1, Reach 1); Spd 20 ft. ground; Init II; Atk IV; Def V; Res V; Health VI; Comp I; Skills: Notice IV; Qualities: *Achilles heel (fire), burden of ages, damage defiance (bows), damage reduction 4, fearsome, tough I, veteran I*

Attacks/Weapons: Mummy Rot (Slam II: dmg 1d6+4 lethal + flesh-eating virus; threat 19–20; upgrades: *diseased*), Pharaoh's Curse (attribute draining attack II: 60 ft. gaze; Fort DC 15 or suffer 1 temporary Cha impairment), Scarab Swarm (slowing attack I: 30 ft. cone; Will DC 10 or become *slowed* 1d6 rounds)

Treasure: 3L

MYRMIDON

Myrmidons are man-sized, sentient ants living in massive hive-cities dug into the surface of the earth. They have manipulating hands and can raise their thoraxes upright, similar to a centaur. Myrmidons are furious builders, tirelessly expanding and reinforcing the hive for an unseen queen.

Encounters with myrmidons are alien experiences. The creatures are matter-of-fact and efficient, ignoring strangers unless they damage the hive or its occupants. Each has limited free will but none enjoy individual identity. Communicating with them is difficult as they only react individually when their basic survival instinct kicks in. When they do speak, all myrmidons in the vicinity turn, talk, and gesture in unison, struggling to get their point across. They refer to themselves in the second person (i.e. "we go to rebuild the tunnel"), speaking in flat, emotionless tones utterly without guile or personality.

Tactics: When the hive mind identifies a threat, every myrmidon in range rushes toward the transgressors, contributing to a frightening flurry of well-coordinated flanking maneuvers and perfectly timed attacks. Individuals attack without regard for their own safety or survival, for only the hive matters. To defy that will is death.

Myrmidon (Medium Folk Walker — 92 XP): Str 12, Dex 14, Con 12, Int 10, Wis 10, Cha 8; SZ M (1×1, Reach 1); Spd 40 ft. ground; Init V; Atk VII; Def IV; Res IX; Health IV; Comp IV; Skills: Athletics VI, Crafting V, Tactics VI; Qualities: *Banned action (Bluff, Impress, Intimidate), contagion immunity, damage reduction 2, fearless I, hive mind, honorable, improved stability, superior jumper II, swarm*

Attacks/Weapons: Bite I (dmg 1d8+1 lethal; threat 18–20), Claw I (dmg 1d6+1 lethal; threat 20), Gore II (dmg 1d6+1 lethal + weakening poison; threat 18¬–20; upgrades: *bleed, venomous*), Chakram × 3 (dmg 1d6+1 lethal; threat 20; range 20 ft. × 3; qualities: *keen 4*)

Treasure: 2G

NAGA

Giant snakes with more-or-less human faces, naga guard sacred places and secrets best left undiscovered. They're extraordinarily sensitive to their environment and their personality reflects whatever they protect — a naga watching over a foul pit of sorcery might become dark-humored and quick-tempered, for example, while another defending a holy temple might become righteous and just. All naga are powerful wizards with keen minds.

Tactics: Naga are curious and ask demanding questions of all they encounter. Occasionally they let visitors through their stations without a fight, but only if they succeed at rigorous tests of strength and willpower. When fighting is the only recourse, naga buy themselves time with *menacing threat* and Command II. They empower themselves with Divine Favor and let loose

with fireballs and venomous bites and spittle. So long as it draws breath, a naga never gives up its sacred duty.

Naga (Large Beast Fey Walker — 75 XP): Str 16, Dex 12, Con 16, Int 12, Wis 14, Cha 14; SZ L (1×3, Reach 2); Spd 40 ft. ground; Init IV; Atk II; Def II; Res V; Health V; Comp V; Skills: Resolve VI, Sense Motive VI, Spellcasting VI; Spells: Command II, Divine Favor, Fireball I, Mirror Images, Ray of Enfeeblement, Righteous Aura; Qualities: *Damage reduction 4, darkvision I, fearless II, feat (Iron Will, Lightning Reflexes), menacing threat, tricky (Venom Master)*

Attacks/Weapons: Bite II (dmg 1d10+3 lethal; threat 17–20 + necrotizing poison, upgrades: *venomous*), Venomous Spittle (blinding attack II: 20 ft. ray; Will DC 15 or become *blinded* for 2d6 rounds)

Treasure: 1A, 2L

NIGHTMARE

These gaunt or skeletal horses are wreathed in flame and reek of brimstone. They often serve corrupt beastmasters and vile paladins, with whom they wreak great havoc. Some say nightmares are descended from the mount of Death itself, for their footfalls echo with the faint screams of the tormented and every step sets fire to the land of the living.

Tactics: Nightmares are quite intelligent, though they choose not to speak with lesser beings (read: everything that still lives). They're also cunning, turning *incorporeal* and bursting through walls to blindside and Trample Medium and smaller characters. When they're feeling their oats, they stick around and use their flaming hooves to kick the tar out of bothersome enemies.

Nightmare (Large Beast Spirit Flier/Walker — 112 XP): Str 14, Dex 12, Con 14, Int 10, Wis 12, Cha 10; SZ L (1×2, Reach 1); Spd 100 ft. flight, 40 ft. (Run 200 ft.); Init VIII; Atk VII; Def VIII; Res IX; Health V; Comp II; Skills: Intimidate V, Notice VI, Sneak V, Survival VI; Qualities: *Damage reduction 3, darkvision II, improved stability, superior runner I, stench*

Attacks/Weapons: Bite I (dmg 1d10+2 lethal; threat 18–20), Flaming Hooves (Kick II: dmg 1d8+2 fire; threat 19–20), Trample II (dmg 1d10+2 fire; threat 19–20; notes: Medium and smaller only, Fort (DC equal to damage) or become *sprawled*)

Treasure: None

OGRE

Ogres are handled with a rogue template *(see page 249)*. Species feats can be applied for additional archetypes, such as oni and merrow.

OOZES

Oozes are semi-sapient, invertebrate blobs commonly found in dark, dank dungeons and caves. They all share core characteristics but each variety is uniquely adapted to its particular hunting and feeding methods.

Gelatinous cubes are massive, mindless blocks of transparent goo that slowly creep through hallways and tunnels, absorbing everything in their path. They're nearly invisible in the dim subterranean tunnels they call home.

Oozes

Jellies are skulking amoeba that move equally well across horizontal and vertical surfaces. Their cilia excrete a mild acid that converts organic matter into a paste they can absorb.

Puddings are malevolent colonies of aggressive single-celled organisms with rudimentary hive intelligence. Their pitch-black color is a warning of the danger they present — many an adventurer has hacked away at one, only to watch in horror as it splits into two or more of the acidic monsters.

Tactics: While diverse in their makeup, oozes all attack in the same way, smothering or engulfing enemies with their gloopy bodies. Gelatinous cubes have no true predatory instinct, preferring to wait for their prey to come to them, while jellies and puddings are attracted to anything that looks edible.

Puddings are the most dangerous of the three, thanks to their acidic *natural defense.* Weapons used to hit them, natural and man-made, are often slagged in the process.

Gelatinous Cube (Huge Animal Ooze Walker — 76 XP): Str 10, Dex 2, Con 18, Int 1, Wis 2, Cha 2; SZ H (4×4, Reach 2); Spd 15 ft. ground; Init I; Atk IV; Def I; Res I; Health IV; Comp —; Skills: Athletics III; Qualities: *Blindsight, chameleon II (caverns/ mountains, indoors/settled), critical hesitation, damage immunity (electrical), shambling, tough III*

Attacks/Weapons: Slam I (dmg 1d10 acid; threat 20), Engulf (Swallow II: dmg 2d8 acid; notes: Grapple benefit — Medium and smaller only), Paralyzing Pseudopods (paralyzing attack III: Fort DC 20 or become *paralyzed* for 3d6 rounds, upgrades: *supernatural attack (slam)*)

Treasure: 2A

Jelly (Large Animal Ooze Walker — 44 XP): Str 12, Dex 2, Con 16, Int 2, Wis 2, Cha 2; SZ L (2×2, Reach 1); Spd 10 ft. ground; Init I; Atk III; Def I; Res I; Health V; Comp —; Skills: Athletics III; Qualities: *Achilles heel (fire), blindsight, critical hesitation, damage splitter, shambling, superior climber II, tough I*

Attacks/Weapons: Slam II (dmg 1d8+1 acid; threat 19–20; upgrades: *grab*), Squeeze II (dmg 1d12+1 acid; notes: Grapple benefit)

Treasure: None

Pudding (Huge Ooze Walker — 64 XP): Str 14, Dex 2, Con 16, Int 4, Wis 2, Cha 2; SZ H (4×4, Reach 2); Spd 20 ft. ground; Init I; Atk V; Def I; Res I; Health VI; Comp I; Skills: Athletics IV; Qualities: *Blindsight, critical hesitation, damage splitter, natural defense (acid), superior climber II, tough I*

Attacks/Weapons: Slam III (dmg 2d10+2 acid; threat 19–20; upgrades: *grab*), Squeeze III (dmg 4d8+2 acid; notes: Grapple benefit)

Treasure: None

ORC

Orcs are handled with a rogue template *(see page 249).* Species feats can be applied for additional archetypes.

PECH

Pech are handled with a rogue template *(see page 249).* Species feats can be applied for additional archetypes, such as hairfoots and gnomes.

PEGASUS

The blood of the gods is said to flow through the veins of these noble, winged horses. Sometimes, when the mightiest heroes prove their worth, one of these steeds may agree to become his mount.

Tactics: Pegasi aren't as bashful about combat as their wingless cousins. They still prefer escape when greatly outnumbered but otherwise they're perfectly willing to wade into the thick of melee, using their size and the blasting wind beneath their wings to disorient and subdue foes.

Pegasus (Large Animal Flyer/Walker — 62 XP): Str 12, Dex 14, Con 12, Int 5, Wis 10, Cha 10; SZ L (1×2, Reach 1); Spd 100 ft. winged flight, 50 ft. ground (Run 250 ft.); Init IV; Atk II; Def IV; Res V; Health IV; Comp —; Skills: Acrobatics V, Notice IV; Qualities: *Feat (Agile Flyer), improved sense (scent), natural spell (Gust of Wind), superior runner I, superior traveler II*

Attacks/Weapons: Kick II (dmg 1d8+1 lethal; threat 19–20), Trample I (dmg 1d10+1 lethal; threat 20; notes: Small and smaller only, Fort (DC equal to damage) or become *sprawled*)

Treasure: 1L, 2T

RAKSHASA

Rakshasa are malicious, spellcasting demons that wear many faces — sometimes of men but more commonly of monkeys or tigers. They're spiteful, haughty creatures thriving on fear and mortal suffering, be it magical torment, physical anguish, or (best of all) profound emotional pain. They hide in the guises of noblemen and aristocrats, casting Invisibility as needed to escape detection. Only when their true faces will cause the most psychological damage do they drop their complex ruse.

Tactics: Despite their animalistic appearance, rakshasa dislike melee combat, preferring instead to dominate foes with powerful combat and illusionary spells. They're tremendously resistant to magic but have a peculiar weakness against crossbow bolts and arrows, particularly those blessed by holy men. They attack archers before all others, casting Haste and Mage Armor to close in safety. Failing this, they fall back to cover and use Magic Missile to attack the archers from a distance. Rakshasa quickly withdraw when their vitality or spell points run dry.

Rakshasa (Medium Outsider Walker — 113 XP): Str 10, Dex 12, Con 12, Int 10, Wis 12, Cha 14; SZ M (1×1, Reach 1); Spd 40 ft. ground; Init V; Atk III; Def II; Res III; Health II; Comp V; Skills: Bluff VII, Resolve VII, Spellcasting V; Spells: Haste, Illusionary Images I, Invisibility, Mage Armor, Magic Missile; Qualities: *Damage reduction 8/bows, darkvision II, shapeshifter I, spell defense IV, telepathic, treacherous, veteran I*

Attacks/Weapons: Bite III (dmg 2d8 lethal; threat 17–20; upgrades: *keen 4*), Claw II × 2 (dmg 1d6 lethal; threat 19–20)

Gear: Mage's pouch, 2 × mana potion, vitality potion

Treasure: 1L, 2M

RAPTOR

These large flightless birds are skittish and violent in the wild but take to saddle training surprisingly well. They're not as effective for hauling loads as horses or other pack animals but their natural predatory instincts make them quite effective in melee. *Choco!*

Tactics: Raptors flee opponents their own size but fight smaller targets and respond in kind when cornered by an aggressive opponent. They attack with vigor and ferocity, favoring Cheap Shots at the legs (to reduce Speed).

Riding Raptor/Wild Raptor (Large Animal Walker — 51 XP): Str 12, Dex 14, Con 10, Int 3, Wis 12, Cha 8; SZ L (1×2, Reach 1); Spd 50 ft. ground (Run 250 ft.); Init II; Atk IV; Def IV; Res IV; Health III; Comp —; Skills: Acrobatics IV, Athletics IV, Notice II; Qualities: *Feat (Pathfinder Basics (plains)), superior runner I, superior traveler I, tricky (Cheap Shot)*

Attacks/Weapons: Bite II (dmg 1d10+1 lethal; threat 17–20; upgrades: *bleed*), Claw I (dmg 1d8+1 lethal; threat 20)

Treasure: 1T

War Raptor (Large Animal Walker — 65 XP): Str 12, Dex 12, Con 12, Int 4, Wis 12, Cha 8; SZ L (2×2, Reach 1); Spd 50 ft. ground (Run 250 ft.); Init II; Atk V; Def IV; Res IV; Health IV; Comp —; Skills: Acrobatics IV, Athletics IV, Notice V; Qualities: *Fearless I, feat (Pathfinder Basics (plains)), superior runner I, tough I, tricky (Cheap Shot, Fully Engaged)*

Attacks/Weapons: Bite III (dmg 2d10+1 lethal; threat 17–20; upgrades: *bleed*), Claws I (dmg 1d8+1 lethal; threat 20)

Treasure: 2T

RHINO

Rhinos are thick-bodied mammals generally found in warm climes. They may appear docile but aggressively protect their herds.

Tactics: Rhinos circle and attempt to run off all who approach too close. Those who linger get to see them back up, aiming a charge and lining up their thick horns…

Rhino (Large Animal Walker — 65 XP): Str 16, Dex 10, Con 10, Int 2, Wis 10, Cha 6; SZ L (2×2, Reach 1); Spd 30 ft. ground; Init V; Atk IV; Def II; Res VI; Health VI; Comp —; Skills: Athletics V, Intimidate III, Notice III; Qualities: *Damage reduction 4, fearless I, feat (Charging Basics)*

Attacks/Weapons: Gore III (dmg 2d8+3 lethal; threat 18–20), Trample I (dmg 1d10+3 lethal; threat 20; notes: Small and smaller only, Fort (DC equal to damage) or become *sprawled*)

Treasure: 1T

ROOTWALKER

Rootwalkers are handled with a rogue template *(see page 249)*. Species feats can be applied for additional archetypes.

RUST MONSTER

Rust monsters look like the offspring of a bizarre beetle/armadillo pairing, with small mandibles, long antennae, a propeller-like tail, and thick-plated hides the color of oxidized metal or sulfur. They're feared not for their incredible fighting prowess or deadly magical abilities, but their diet. Rust monsters subsist on ferrous metals such as iron and steel, savoring refined alloys like fine delicacies. A single brush of their long antennae can corrode a pricy suit of armor or powerful weapon, breaking them down to a fine dust they consume with glee. Such is their appetite that they shadow adventuring parties for days, even weeks, hoping to snack on their most expensive (and tasty) equipment.

Tactics: Rust monsters are simple creatures with dog-like intelligence, driven by their cravings. They care little for combat except to acquire food. When they identify a new source using their *improved sense,* they discreetly approach, avoiding contact with anything that's moving. They flee if attacked but soon return unless the source of metal has been exhausted.

Rust Monster (Medium Animal Horror Walker — 65 XP): Str 10, Dex 14, Con 10, Int 2, Wis 12, Cha 8; SZ M (1×1, Reach 1); Spd 40 ft. ground; Init V; Atk V; Def VI; Res VII; Health IV; Comp —; Skills: Notice III, Survival IV; Qualities: *Damage reduction 1, darkvision I, improved sense (scent), improved stability*

Attacks/Weapons: Bite I (dmg 1d8 lethal; threat 18–20), Rusting Touch (rusting attack V: dmg 1d12 lethal per 2 TL (metal objects only); threat 20)

Treasure: None

SALAMANDER

Salamanders are mysterious beings born in their fiery bosom of the earth, riding lava flows up through volcanoes to explore the world of men. They look vaguely like humans with great serpent tails and thick, stony skin that glows like magma. Salamanders have near-complete control of fire and use it to forge weapons and gear of such craftsmanship that even the dwarves look on with envy. They sometimes trade these items with "toplanders," asking for beautiful art and other treasures in return. Merchants are wary, however, as all have heard the stories of caravans burned to the last, their cargo stolen, with nothing but melted trails left as evidence of the crime.

Tactics: Intensely passionate, salamanders pour everything they have into everything they do. This feeds their creative spark but it also makes them fiercely unpredictable and quick to anger. Still, they never lose their heads, not even in the heat of battle. They fight with calculated fury, casting Wall of Fire to cut opponents off from one another and then rushing in to skewer them with Polearm Basics. Salamanders are sometimes seen in the company of other fiery creatures, such as elementals and hell hounds, and command them in battle with vicious precision.

Salamander (Medium Outsider Walker — 87 XP): Str 12, Dex 10, Con 12, Int 12, Wis 12, Cha 10; SZ M (1×1, Reach 1); Spd 20 ft. ground; Init III; Atk VIII; Def III; Res IX; Health V; Comp IV; Skills: Crafting VI, Search VI; Qualities: *Achilles heel (cold), damage immunity (fire, heat), damage reduction 2, feat (Crafting Basics, Polearm Basics), grueling combatant, natural spell (Wall of Fire)*

Attacks/Weapons: Superior glaive (dmg 1d8+2 lethal; threat 19–20; qualities: *keen 4, reach +1*), Squeeze III (dmg 2d10+1 fire; notes: Grapple benefit), Tail Slap III (dmg 2d8+1 heat; threat 19–20; upgrades: *reach +1*)

Gear: Blacksmith's tools

Treasure: 1G, 2L

SAURIAN

Saurians are handled with a rogue template *(see page 249).* Species feats can be applied for additional archetypes, such as frog-men and chameleons.

SCAVENGER WORM

Every ecosystem has bottom feeders, living on the scraps left by others: cities have vermin, forests have various insects, and dungeons have worms — *big* worms — eight-foot long, segmented worms lined with sticky sucker-feet, bearing lamprey-like mouths ringed in short stinging tentacles. These subterranean vacuum cleaners are mindless eating machines, indiscriminately consuming all carrion in their paths.

Tactics: Scavenger worms aren't natural predators, generally only attacking creatures already close to death. The danger in confronting a scavenger worm isn't the damage it inflicts but rather its Combat Instincts, which let it use its Paralyzing Tentacles out of turn.

Scavenger Worm (Large Animal Horror Walker — 69 XP): Str 12, Dex 14, Con 10, Int 1, Wis 12, Cha 6; SZ L (1×2, Reach 1); Spd 30 ft. ground; Init IV; Atk I; Def IV; Res IV; Health V; Comp —; Skills: Athletics VII, Search III, Survival III; Qualities: *Damage reduction 2, darkvision II, feat (Combat Instincts), improved sense (scent), superior climber II*

Attacks/Weapons: Bite I (dmg 1d10+1 lethal; threat 18–20), Paralyzing Tentacles (paralyzing attack II: Will DC 15 or become *paralyzed* for 2d6 rounds)

Treasure: 1A

SEA DEVIL

Sea devils are disgusting, fish-like humanoids with saggy, bloated bodies, slick eely hides, and buggy eyes. They live in theocratic cities deep beneath the waves but periodically surface to crusade against seaside towns and merchant kingdoms. They're intensely xenophobic, eradicating or enslaving all who don't share their beliefs, even other sea devils with slightly different interpretations of their religious hymns or practices. Such is the will of their draconian rulers, an intolerant priesthood that's forged their labyrinthine laws for millennia.

Having spent most of their lives underwater, sea devils express themselves through changes in pigmentation. This is useful when silent communication is needed but it's often difficult for other species to parse their rainbow phrases.

Tactics: These savage zealots are utterly ruthless in combat, fearing little more than the wrath of their own leaders. They open most combats with volleys of harpoons, then charge in with machetes and shields at the ready. Sea devils are difficult to pin down on the battlefield thanks to high Defense scores and virtual immunity to Grapples due to their slick hides.

Sea Devil (Medium Folk Walker — 67 XP): Str 10, Dex 10, Con 10, Int 10, Wis 12, Cha 8; SZ M (1×1, Reach 1); Spd 20 ft. ground; Init II; Atk IV; Def V; Res IV; Health III; Comp II; Skills: Crafting III, Notice V, Resolve III; Qualities: *Aquatic II, banned action (Bluff), condition immunity (entangled, held), contagion immunity, damage defiance (electrical), damage reduction 2, darkvision II, improved sense (sight), light-sensitive, superior swimmer VIII*

Attacks/Weapons: Machete (dmg 1d8 lethal; threat 20; qualities: *AP 2*), hooked hide shield (dmg 1d3 subdual; threat 20; qualities: *guard +2, hook*), harpoon (dmg 1d8 lethal; threat 18–20; range 20 ft. × 3; qualities: *bleed, cord*)

Treasure: 2C

SHADOW BEAST

Shadow beasts are darkness given shape, black as midnight with cruel eyes that sparkle like dying stars. Their forms are blurry and always shifting but those who've seen them in the light swear they're great hunting cats with tentacles of dark energy coiling out of their backs. Shadow beasts prowl the wild on moonless nights, searching for game and lonely homesteads they can raid for food. Victims are snuffed out, their life absorbed into the creature, giving it the strength to kill again.

Tactics: Battling a shadow beast is arduous as blows seem to pass harmlessly through its vaporous form (a characteristic represented by its lethal and subdual *damage defiance*). Shadow beasts hunt in pairs and go straight for the jugular, lashing out with their lithe tentacles at anyone who gets too close (Combat Instincts). The best way to take them out is with magical or elemental attacks, which they use Evasive to escape.

Shadow Beast (Large Beast Outsider Walker — 86 XP): Str 14, Dex 12, Con 12, Int 5, Wis 10, Cha 8; SZ L (1×2, Reach 2); Spd 40 ft. ground; Init IV; Atk VIII; Def X; Res X; Health VI; Comp II; Skills: Blend VI, Sneak V; Qualities: *Damage defiance (lethal, subdual), damage reduction 2, darkvision I, feat (Combat Instincts, Evasive)*

Attacks/Weapons: Bite I (dmg 1d10+2 lethal; threat 18–20), Tentacle Slap I × 2 (dmg 1d10+2 lethal; threat 19–20; upgrades: *bleed, reach +1, trip*)

Treasure: None

SKELETON

"Skeletal" is a monster template, which may be applied to any monster or rogue *(see page 294).*

SLIME

Slimes are massive colonies of toxic mold growing on dungeon ceilings. They're sensitive to vibration and changes in air pressure, which trigger their defense mechanism: dripping portions of the colony onto those below. A passing party can find itself covered in the mold, which quickly burrows into flesh, feeding and propagating at an alarming rate. Before long the victims' bodies become fresh colonies, lying in wait for others.

Tactics: Slimes are mindless, attacking only the closest target each round. Fortunately, they're vulnerable to fire (and other forms of energy), so a party with torches can best them quickly (if not safely).

Slime (Huge Immobile Plant — 41 XP): Str 10, Dex 1, Con 10, Int 1, Wis 1, Cha 1; SZ H (4×4, Reach 2); Spd —; Init I; Atk I; Def I; Res I; Health V; Comp —; Skills: None; Qualities: *Achilles heel (fire), blindsight, chameleon I (indoors/settled), critical hesitation, damage immunity (lethal, subdual), infectious conversion, killing conversion, tough I*

Attacks/Weapons: Drip (acid damage attack II: dmg 1d6 acid per 2 TL, threat 20)

Treasure: 1A

SPIDERS, GIANT

These giant arachnids are much like their tiny cousins: solitary predators, hunting by spinning elaborate webs to trap prey. At their size, however, "prey" is defined quite differently.

Brown stalkers are about the size of a large dog and willing to chase potential dinner over a considerable distance. Fortunately for them, their poisonous bites soften muscles, bringing any pursuit to a rapid conclusion.

Great Lashers approach the size of a horse with gleaming red carapaces. Sticky filaments at the tips of their forelegs act like whips, ensnaring smaller creatures.

Tactics: Spiders prefer ambush and spend most of their time sitting motionless in their webs, in shadows, in shallow holes, or beneath forest litter. Their main attack is their venomous bite, which in the brown stalker's case requires an immediate save due to Venom Master.

Brown Stalker (Small Animal Walker — 47 XP): Str 14, Dex 14, Con 10, Int 3, Wis 10, Cha 8; SZ S (1×1, Reach 1); Spd 30 ft. ground; Init VI; Atk III; Def III; Res II; Health III; Comp —; Skills: Acrobatics IV, Notice IV, Sneak IV; Qualities: *Superior climber III, superior jumper III, tricky (Venom Master)*

Attacks/Weapons: Bite I (dmg 1d6+2 lethal + slowing poison; threat 18–20; upgrades: *venomous*)

Treasure: 1A, 1T

Great Lasher (Large Animal Walker — 60 XP): Str 12, Dex 12, Con 10, Int 1, Wis 10, Cha 6; SZ L (3×3, Reach 1); Spd 30 ft. ground (Run 150 ft.); Init IV; Atk IV; Def III; Res III; Health V; Comp —; Skills: Athletics III, Notice III, Tactics V; Qualities: *Darkvision II, damage reduction 2, fearsome, grappler, superior climber III, superior jumper II, superior runner I*

Attacks/Weapons: Bite I (dmg 1d10+1 lethal + necrotic poison; threat 18–20; upgrades: *venomous*), Web (entangling attack I: 20 ft. ray; Fort DC 10 or become *entangled* for 1d6 rounds)

Treasure: 1A, 2T

SPORLING

Sporlings are sentient fungi taking many forms, most commonly toadstools, shelf fungus, and puffballs. They live in tribal circles deep under the earth and in damp tropical forests and rarely show interest in anything other than other sporlings. They've been known to walk past non-threatening folk without a glance. Other subterranean creatures hunt sporlings for sport and food, which is why they've evolved a coating of toxic slime that wreaks havoc with digestion. Their bodies also expel spores that cause hallucinations, though this trait has backfired, with other species harvesting the spores to make poisons and ceremonial drugs.

Tactics: Sporlings are inherently non-confrontational and lack aggressive instinct. They can communicate via pheromone-laced spores but rarely bother, preferring to ignore anything that doesn't try to attack them. A threatened sporling's first impulse is to run, relying on *chameleon* to get out of sight and *natural defense* to deter determined pursuit. When cornered or struck, it releases a Spore Cloud to disorient the threat and flees. The only way to potentially rouse a sporling to violence is to directly threaten its tribal circle but even then their attacks are half-hearted and disorganized.

Sporling (Small Plant Walker — 39 XP): Str 10, Dex 10, Con 12, Int 8, Wis 10, Cha 8; SZ S (1×1, Reach 1); Spd 20 ft. ground; Init II; Atk II; Def II; Res II; Health II; Comp I; Skills: Blend III; Qualities: *Chameleon I (forest/jungle), darkvision I, light-sensitive, meek, natural defense (acid), telepathic*

Attacks/Weapons: Slam I (dmg 1d4 acid; threat 20), Spore Cloud (slowing attack I: 20 ft. aura; Will DC 10 or become *slowed* for 1d6 rounds)

Treasure: None

STIRGE

Stirges are loathsome parasites with the look of giant feathered mosquitoes. They're common pests in warm climes and tropical jungles, where vast schools of them hang from trees and inside shady caves, swarming out to feed at dusk.

Tactics: A stirge *swarm* sweeps past enemies, individuals latching onto victims with hooked feet and plunging 6-in. proboscises through the skin to feed on their blood (Blood Drain). A couple of these attacks is merely annoying but a swarm can consist of dozens or even hundreds of stirges, each potentially bringing a victim one step closer to death.

Stirge (Tiny Animal Flyer/Walker — 48 XP): Str 9, Dex 14, Con 10, Int 1, Wis 10, Cha 6; SZ T (1×1, Reach 1); Spd 40 ft. winged flight, 10 ft. ground; Init VI; Atk IV; Def I; Res V; Health II; Comp —; Skills: Notice IV, Sneak X; Qualities: *Darkvision II, swarm*

Attacks/Weapons: Blood Drain (attribute draining attack I: Fort DC 10 or suffer 1 temporary Con impairment)

Treasure: None

TARASQUE

The tarasque is Armageddon made flesh, a force of indiscriminate, perhaps inevitable destruction. Towering over the landscape at over 50 ft. tall, this immense creature has a hide of nearly impenetrable scales, a giant shell thick as a castle wall, six squat legs, horns that could skewer an elephant, and a gaping maw lined with three-foot teeth. No one knows if the tarasque is intelligent, though the swath of destruction in its wake certainly shows its temper. Fortunately, it sleeps for decades or centuries at a time. Its coming is an epoch-defining event heralding the end of a civilization — and one day, perhaps, the world.

Tactics: This apocalyptic beast has no rival and knows it. It stalks the land with the angry confidence of a vengeful god, interested in nothing short of utter devastation. It shows no mercy, callously crushing everything in its path. Its Trample inflicts explosive damage due to its incredible weight and power, and its Terrifying Roar can shatter armies, sending them fleeing into enemy forces or even over cliffs if needed.

The tarasque tends to be the center of any fight, taking full actions to lash out with all six of its natural attacks in each round. It starts to *frenzy* when reduced to half its vitality, causing as much death and collateral damage as possible. This "tantrum" is, perhaps, the most telling of its behaviors, showcasing the monster's astoundingly underdeveloped personality. It's not unlike a wrathful child with the power to destroy *anything* that displeases it.

With *tough VIII, monstrous defense III,* and *damage reduction 10,* the tarasque is nigh-invulnerable. Magic has little effect on it, as spell defense 35 lets it ignore virtually all spells up to Level 7 and *spell reflection* redirects even the most powerful arcane volleys. Worst of all, *regeneration 40* and the Explorer's *lifeline* class ability ensure that even if a party manages to injure the tarasque (reduce its vitality below 0) it refreshes and recovers 40 points at the end of the round. As a final insult, the tarasque is *everlasting,* destined to return even when killed (though probably not in most of the characters' lifetimes).

The tarasque's most significant weakness is its solitary nature — a concerted effort by a large and particularly skillful (and lucky) party might be able to punch through its defenses and get ahead of its healing curve. It's still got numerous advantages, however, from *dramatic entrance* shifting the rules in its favor to *veteran* improving its already impressive statistics.

Tarasque (Colossal Beast Walker — 438 XP): Str 28, Dex 12, Con 22, Int 3, Wis 12, Cha 12; SZ C (12×18, Reach 4); Spd 40 ft. ground; Init X; Atk X; Def VII; Res X; Health X; Comp I; Skills: Notice III, Survival II; Qualities: *Cagey III, charge attack, class ability (Explorer: lifeline), critical surge, damage reduction 10, dramatic entrance, everlasting, frenzy II, grappler, menacing threat, monstrous attack I, monstrous defense III, regeneration 40, spell defense V, spell reflection, tough VIII, treacherous, veteran V*

Attacks/Weapons: Bite V (dmg 6d8+9 lethal; threat 16–20), Claw II × 2 (dmg 1d12+9 lethal; threat 19–20), Gore II × 2 (dmg 1d12+9 lethal; threat 18–20; upgrades: *bleed*), Swallow III (dmg 4d10+9 acid; notes: Grapple benefit — Huge and smaller only), Tail Slap II (dmg 2d8+9 lethal; threat 19–20; upgrades: *reach +1*), Trample IV (dmg 4d8+9 explosive; threat 18–20; notes: Huge and smaller only, Fort (DC equal to damage) or become *sprawled*), Terrifying Roar (frightening attack IV: 50 ft. aura; Will DC 25 or become *frightened* for 4d6 rounds)

Treasure: 10A

TIGERS

These great hunting cats inspire awe and terror in those who encounter them… and survive. They rule the jungle not so much as 'kings' but assassins, striking from stealth with incredible power and precision.

Tigers are sleek, efficient jungle-dwellers that can pull down animals many times their own size. Their striking orange-and-black coloration blends into the dappled shade of their native habitat with uncanny efficiency.

Saber-tooth tigers are adapted to frigid conditions. They're stocky, with bulky fur to keep them warm in harsh weather. Their massive fangs have likewise evolved, able to penetrate similarly thick hides.

Tactics: Tigers are overtly territorial, launching most attacks from ambush. Against opponents of similar or larger size, they often sink their teeth into the target and ravage it with both sets of claws.

Tiger (Large Animal Walker — 63 XP): Str 14, Dex 16, Con 10, Int 4, Wis 12, Cha 8; SZ L (1×2, Reach 1); Spd 40 ft.

ground; Init VI; Atk V; Def III; Res III; Health V; Comp —; Skills: Athletics V, Notice IV, Sneak IV; Qualities: *Chameleon I (forest/jungle), grappler, rend*

Attacks/Weapons: Bite III (dmg 2d10+2 lethal; threat 17–20), Claw II (dmg 1d8+2 lethal; threat 19–20)

Treasure: 2T

Saber-Tooth Tiger (Large Animal Walker — 70 XP): Str 18, Dex 14, Con 10, Int 4, Wis 12, Cha 8; SZ L (1×2, Reach 1); Spd 30 ft. ground; Init V; Atk VI; Def III; Res V; Health V; Comp —; Skills: Athletics III, Notice V, Sneak III; Qualities: *Damage defiance (cold), rend*

Attacks/Weapons: Bite V (dmg 3d10+4 lethal; threat 16–20; upgrades: *grab*), Claw II (dmg 1d8+4 lethal; threat 19–20)

Treasure: 3T

TROGLODYTE

Troglodytes are cave-dwelling reptilian humanoids and distant cousins to saurians. They're distinguished by a stiff "comb" frill that runs along the top of their heads and down their backs; their slick glossy hide, which shifts slightly to match the surroundings; and long slender bodies with stubby legs like those of a simple lizard. Their most memorable feature, however, is their "musk," an acrid odor like that of a week-old carcass rotting in the sun, shoveled up and tossed in an open latrine.

Fiercely inbred, "trogs" are disproportionately hostile toward everything and everyone they don't immediately recognize. When not fighting other species or between themselves, they spend their time rutting with siblings, scrounging for bits of metal to adorn their homes, and lounging in deep, damp caves swilling mushroom spirits deadly to most surface dwellers.

Tactics: Troglodytes are light in the head but know how to lay a decent ambush. Most encounters with them start with some sort of "surprise attack," typically from concealment using slings or javelins (range is pretty much the only thing that conceals their *stench*). Once their position is revealed troglodytes quickly close to melee, where the smell weakens foes and blunts an effective counterattack. Trogs are born survivors and flee when a quarter or more of them fall in battle.

Troglodyte (Medium Folk Walker — 38 XP): Str 10, Dex 10, Con 12, Int 8, Wis 10, Cha 10; SZ M (1×1, Reach 1); Spd 30 ft. ground; Init I; Atk III; Def VII; Res II; Health IV; Comp II; Skills: Survival III, Tactics III; Qualities: *Chameleon I (caverns/mountains), cold-blooded, damage reduction 2, darkvision II, light-sensitive, stench*

Attacks/Weapons: War club (dmg 1d8 lethal; threat 19–20; qualities: *bleed*), sling (dmg 1d4 subdual; threat 20; range 60 ft. × 6; qualities: *load 1*) or javelin × 3 (dmg 1d8 lethal; threat 19–20; range 30 ft. × 3), Bite I (dmg 1d8 lethal; threat 18–20)

Treasure: 1C

TROLL

Trolls are lumbering giants, ten feet tall and nearly as broad. Their skin is leathery and elephantine, and their faces are flat, ugly, and perpetually twisted in bafflement or rage. Trolls have amazingly recuperative powers: their wounds close in a matter of seconds and they can even regrow severed limbs in weeks. Couple this with the fact that they're too stupid to fear anything and you have a significant threat indeed.

Storytellers say that trolls were once stones, given life and pressed into service for the armies of an ancient god. Perhaps there's a bit of truth to those tales… or perhaps they're simply folklore sparked by the brutes' incredible toughness and thick-headedness. Regardless, trolls are deadly foes found nearly everywhere: swinging battering rams in orc armies; performing manual labor for kings; harassing travelers who cross remote bridges; and more.

Tactics: Trolls express fun, affection, and anger in pretty much the same way — with hammering blows about the head and body. They're blasé attitude extends to everything that's smaller, which includes most opponents and all but a few siege weapons. They take the shortest path available to any combat, pausing only for the most shocking displays of wonton violence (and then usually in admiration rather than alarm).

Troll (Large Folk Walker — 91 XP): Str 16, Dex 12, Con 18, Int 6, Wis 9, Cha 6; SZ L (2×2, Reach 2); Spd 25 ft. ground; Init IV; Atk IV; Def III; Res V; Health VIII; Comp II; Skills: Athletics III, Notice III, Survival V; Qualities: *Class ability (Explorer: lifeline), damage reduction 2, darkvision I, fearless I, improved sense (scent), regeneration 5, rend*

Attacks/Weapons: Large mace (dmg 1d10+3 lethal; threat 20; qualities: *AP 4*), Claw II (dmg 1d8+3 lethal; threat 19–20)

Treasure: 2G

TURTLE, GIANT

If hippocampi are the horses of the sea, giant turtles are the mules, widely employed as draft animals for ships and beasts of burden for travelers on (and under) the high seas. Though sluggish of mind and body, they take instruction well and their sharp beaks can shear a man's arm clean from his body with a single bite.

Tactics: Giant turtles have no love of fighting but they're often too slow to escape when combat springs up around them. They make for water and submerge if possible, snapping at foes that insist on bothering them.

Giant Turtle (Large Animal Walker — 65 XP): Str 16, Dex 6, Con 14, Int 1, Wis 10, Cha 9; SZ L (2×2, Reach 1); Spd 15 ft. ground; Init I; Atk II; Def III; Res VII; Health VI; Comp —; Skills: Athletics III, Survival III; Qualities: *Aquatic I, damage reduction 4, improved stability, lumbering, meek, monstrous defense I, superior swimmer VIII, superior traveler II*

Attacks/Weapons: Bite III (dmg 2d10+3 lethal; threat 17–20)

Treasure: 2T

UNBORN

Unborn are handled with a rogue template *(see page 249).* Species feats can be applied to adjust construction and composition.

UNICORN

Common symbols of purity, unicorns are also a favorite companion of paladins and other righteous heroes. Like many fey, unicorns favor forest glades and other natural environments, guarding the natural balance and continued survival of their inhabitants.

Tactics: Unicorns are honest, well-meaning creatures of unrelenting charity, but they're not above impaling the unworthy upon their pearlescent spiraled horns.

Unicorn (Large Beast Fey Walker — 81 XP): Str 12, Dex 14, Con 10, Int 8, Wis 12, Cha 12; SZ L (1×2, Reach 1); Spd 50 ft. ground (Run 250 ft.); Init VII; Atk IV; Def IV; Res V; Health V; Comp III; Skills: Athletics V, Sense Motive V; Qualities: *Attractive II, contagion immunity, improved sense (hearing), improved stability, natural spell (Cure Wounds III, Neutralize Poison), superior runner I, tough I*

Attacks/Weapons: Gore III (dmg 2d8+1 divine; threat 18–20; upgrades: *bleed*), Kick I (dmg 1d8+1 lethal; threat 20)

Treasure: 1L, 1T, 1M

VAMPIRE

"Vampiric" is a monster template, which may be applied to any monster or rogue *(see page 294).*

WATCHER IN THE DARK

Few things invoke universal dread like watchers in the dark. Their reputation is legendary in adventuring circles yet few can describe them. Some claim they're bits of living shadow; others, great floating orbs or masses of lashing tentacles and eyestalks; still others, creatures out of time and space, predating the eldest fey. One characteristic remains constant, however — unblinking eyes, staring out from the darkness, that can wrench a man's soul from his body, cause him to bleed from every orifice, flood him with mind-shattering fear, and even render him unto ash. No one knows what the watchers want, or why they're here, but one thing is clear: they hate all life, slaughtering all with impunity.

Tactics: Watchers are horrifying, unfathomable foes whose many Beam and Gaze attacks can decimate a party in just a few rounds. They're clever and spiteful, pressing every advantage to dominate the enemy, which is the only thing that keeps them from using *frenzy* to apply *every* Judgement *every round.* In a toe-to-toe fight, watchers use Petrifying and Searing Judgments to suppress closing groups, Fearful and Sluggish ones to turn back specialized melee fighters, and Weakening and Wounding ones to pick off ranged and hurting combatants. Their Bite is a weapon of last resort, though they might charge with it when absolutely necessary.

Watcher in the Dark (Large Beast Horror Flyer — 163 XP): Str 10, Dex 12, Con 14, Int 14, Wis 12, Cha 12; SZ L (2×2, Reach 1); Spd 20 ft. flight; Init X; Atk III; Def VII; Res V; Health IV; Comp IV; Skills: Search VIII, Sneak V; Qualities: *Condition immunity (flanked), damage reduction 4, darkvision II, feat (Charging Basics, Charging Mastery, Iron Will), frenzy III, improved sense (sight), veteran II*

Attacks/Weapons: Bite I (dmg 1d10 lethal; threat 18–20), Fearful Judgment (frightening attack II: 120 ft. gaze; Will save DC 15 or become *frightened* for 2d6 rounds), Petrifying Judgment (petrifying attack II: 20 ft. beam; Fort DC 15 or be turned to stone), Searing Judgment (divine damage attack III: 40 ft. beam; dmg 1d8 divine per 2 TL, Ref DC 20 for 1/2 damage), Sluggish Judgment (slowing attack II: 120 ft. gaze; Will save DC 15 or become *slowed* for 2d6 rounds), Weakening Judgment (fatiguing attack II: 120 ft. gaze; Fort DC 15 or become *fatigued*), Wounding Judgment (lethal damage attack II: 120 ft. gaze; dmg 1d6 lethal per 2 TL, Ref DC 15 for 1/2 damage; upgrades: *bleed*)

Treasure: 2A, 1M, 1T

WATER SERPENT

Water serpents are distant aquatic cousins of drakes, with lithe bodies much like those of massive snakes and frilled heads filled with venomous fangs. They're sometimes used as war-steeds or battering rams by evil residents of the sea, who relish their brutal efficiency in battle.

Tactics: Obedient and savage, water serpents show no quarter, snapping at their masters' targets until the waves run red with their blood. They coil around any survivors and squeeze until their organs come out both ends.

Water Serpent (Large Animal Swimmer — 62 XP): Str 12, Dex 14, Con 10, Int 8, Wis 10, Cha 4; SZ L (1×3, Reach 1); Spd 80 ft. swim; Init II; Atk IV; Def V; Res IV; Health V; Comp —; Skills: Athletics IV, Intimidate III; Qualities: *Aquatic II, damage reduction II, fast healing, grappler, grueling combatant*

Attacks/Weapons: Bite II (dmg 1d10+1 lethal; threat 17–20 + numbing poison, upgrades: *venomous*), Squeeze II (dmg 1d12+1 lethal; notes: Grapple only)

Treasure: 1T

WIGHT

Wights are age-old victims of pagan sacrifices, animated by the bitter spirits still trapped in their flesh. Their flesh is stretched taut by peat and time, and they return imbued with the chill of death itself. Their mere touch fills a man with bone-chilling dead, enough to bring a stout warrior to his knees or kill a lesser man outright. Victims of this grisly assault become the wight's eternal companions, driven by the same dark impulses.

Tactics: Wights predominately hunt at night near burial grounds, sacrificial sites, and lonely swamps. They rarely speak except in rage, though they sometimes interrogate lordly and scholarly characters for information about their murderers. Unless a wight is very young, however, these characters are likely long dead, and this realization drives the creature even deeper into wrathful despair.

Wight (Medium Undead Walker — 70 XP): Str 10, Dex 10, Con 10, Int 10, Wis 12, Cha 12; SZ M (1×1, Reach 1); Spd 30 ft. ground; Init III; Atk III; Def II; Res IV; Health VI; Comp II; Skills: Search V, Sneak X; Qualities: *Damage reduction 2, feat (Night Fighting), killing conversion*

Attack/Weapons: Claw II (dmg 1d6 cold; threat 19–20), Chill of the Grave (soul draining attack II: Fort DC 15 or die (standard character), lose 1 action die and 10 max. vitality (special character); upgrades: *supernatural attack (claw)*)

Treasure: 1G, 1L, 1T

WILL O' WISP

Will o' wisps are found in lonely forests and fields, flitting playfully about and silently enticing travelers to join their merry dance. Woe be to those who fall for this ruse, however, for will o' wisps are in fact mischievous spirits that feast on the anxiety of others. They lure the unwary into precarious situations — over a dangerous cliff on a moonless night, for example, or into a pair of grizzly bears at mating season, or the camp of an orc warband — and then feed on the characters' panic and fear.

Tactics: Will o' wisps are ridiculously difficult to dispatch. They're small and fast, with high Defense and Resilience scores, and they can become *incorporeal* and *invisible* at will. Without the means or interest in direct confrontation, however, they instead rely on traps and tricks, especially those that end in other creatures finishing off their prey. As mentioned, their favorite tactic is to draw characters into dangerous situations (using the *beguiling* quality and starting with those who appear dimmest). They save their Shocking Touch for moments when escape appears impossible any other way.

Will o' Wisp (Small Spirit Flyer — 87 XP): Str 1, Dex 20, Con 10, Int 12, Wis 12, Cha 10; SZ S (1×1, Reach 1); Spd 60 ft. flight; Init X; Atk V; Def VIII; Res X; Health IV; Comp III; Skills: Bluff VI, Notice VIII; Qualities: *Beguiling, critical surge, invisibility*

Attacks/Weapons: Shocking Touch (electrical damage attack I: dmg 1d4 electrical per 2 TL, threat 20)

Treasure: None

WOLVES

These canine predators are feared and hated by farmers and peasants the world over for making away with livestock in the dead of night.

Pack wolves are the common type encountered in the wild, foot-soldiers determined to guard pack leaders even at the cost of their own lives.

Pack leaders are larger specimens that have clawed their way up the pack's social ladder.

Riding wolves are pack leaders that have been captured, domesticated, and trained as battle steeds by the smaller folk races. A few are bred in captivity but this is rare.

Vargr are savage beasts that may or may not be related to common pack wolves. Brutes with keen intelligence, they often understand a handful of folk languages, though they use them sparingly.

Tactics: Wolves are pre-eminent pack hunters, found in groups of a dozen or more and employing a wide array of complex group tactics. They fight in pairs and make extensive use of their Wolf Pack feats to improve attack and damage bonuses. Though ferocious and determined, packs are more interested in their continued survival than the kill and retreat to lick their wounds when they lose half or more of their numbers.

Pack Wolf (Small Animal Walker — 41 XP): Str 10, Dex 12, Con 10, Int 3, Wis 12, Cha 6; SZ S (1×1, Reach 1); Spd 30 ft. ground (Run 180 ft.); Init II; Atk III; Def IV; Res III; Health III; Comp —; Skills: Acrobatics I, Search III, Survival V, Tactics III; Qualities: *Feat (Wolf Pack Basics, Wolf Pack Mastery), improved sense (scent), superior runner II, superior traveler I*

Attacks/Weapons: Bite I (dmg 1d6 lethal; threat 18–20; upgrades: *trip*)

Treasure: 1T

Pack Leader/Riding Wolf (Medium Animal Walker — 57 XP): Str 12, Dex 10, Con 12, Int 5, Wis 10, Cha 10; SZ M (1×1, Reach 1); Spd 30 ft. ground (Run 150 ft.); Init II; Atk IV; Def IV; Res III; Health IV; Comp —; Skills: Acrobatics II, Search IV; Sneak II; Survival IV, Tactics IV; Qualities: *Feat (Wolf Pack Basics, Wolf Pack Mastery), improved sense (scent), superior runner I, superior traveler I, tough I, trick (Called Shot)*

Attacks/Weapons: Bite II (dmg 1d8+1 lethal; threat 17–20; upgrades: *trip*)

Treasure: 2T

Vargr (Large Beast Walker — 58 XP): Str 16, Dex 10, Con 10, Int 9, Wis 10, Cha 10; SZ L (1×2, Reach 1); Spd 30 ft. ground (Run 150 ft.); Init II; Atk V; Def IV; Res III; Health V; Comp I; Skills: Acrobatics II, Sneak IV, Survival IV, Tactics IV; Qualities: *Improved sense (scent), superior runner I, tough I, treacherous*

Attacks/Weapons: Bite II (dmg 1d10+1 lethal; threat 17–20; upgrades: *trip*)

Treasure: 1L, 1T

WYVERN

Ill-tempered, dim-witted cousins of the dragon, these birdlike creatures have broad wings, leathery hides, and long tails tipped with poisonous barbed stingers.

Tactics: Unlike their sophisticated relatives, wyverns are straightforward predators that employ few true tactics. Their main strategy is to attack from above, using Charging Basics to weaken the target with flyby attacks. They close when a victim looks close to death, stinging with their Tail Slap. Wyverns only retreat when severely outnumbered or facing a vastly superior foe.

Wyvern (Large Beast Flyer/Walker — 85 XP): Str 14, Dex 10, Con 12, Int 6, Wis 10, Cha 9; SZ L (2×3, Reach 1); Spd 60 ft. winged flight, 20 ft. ground; Init III; Atk VI; Def III; Res VI; Health VII; Comp I; Skills: Search VI, Sneak V; Qualities: *Condition immunity (paralyzed), damage reduction 4, feat (Charging Basics), improved sense (scent), light sleeper*

Attacks/Weapons: Bite III (dmg 2d10+2 lethal; threat 17–20), Tail Slap II (dmg 1d10+2 lethal + paralyzing poison; threat 20; upgrades: *reach +1, venomous*), Wing Slam × 2 (Slam I: dmg 1d8+2 lethal; threat 20)

Treasure: 1A, 1T

ZOMBIE

"Risen" is a monster template, which may be applied to any monster or rogue *(see page 293).*

MONSTER TEMPLATES

The Rogues Gallery and Bestiary contain many examples of "standard" NPCs and monsters but individuals can and should frequently differ. The following templates offer quick, easy-to-apply 'upgrade' packages to keep the game interesting and the party on its toes. Simply add the listed XP and make the listed changes (plus any other modifications you like), and you've got a whole new threat!

Special Note: A monster's XP value does *not* decrease when a template reduces attribute scores, even if the scores start higher than 10. Similarly, templates may add XP without effect when a template raises a statistic above its maximum or adds a quality the NPC already has. Rule-breaking combinations may also arise, like Competence scores rising above Signature Skills. In these and other cases where templates interact strangely with base NPCs, the GM should make the call that best fits his setting and story.

ALPHA (+20 XP)

Alpha monsters are chieftains and champions of their race, the strongest and best their kind can muster. They're often found leading their fellows into battle.

Benefit: The NPC's Initiative, Attack, Defense, Health, and Competence rise by I each and his Strength and Dexterity rise by 2 each. He also gains *class ability (Captain: battle planning I), treacherous,* and *veteran II.*

EXAMPLE: ALPHA HOBGOBLIN

This thick-bodied creature is a lord in his clan, guiding younger, weaker warriors into battle by bloody example.

Alpha Hobgoblin (Medium Folk Walker — 53 XP): Str 12, Dex 12, Con 12, Int 10, Wis 9, Cha 8; SZ M (1×1, Reach 1); Spd 25 ft. ground; Init IV; Atk V; Def IV; Res III; Health IV; Comp II; Skills: Intimidate III, Tactics III; Qualities: *Class ability (Captain: battle planning I), darkvision I, fearless I, feat (Shield Basics), treacherous, tricky (Fully Engaged), veteran II*

Attacks/Weapons: Halberd (dmg 1d10+1 lethal; threat 19–20; qualities: *AP 4, reach +1*), short sword (dmg 1d8+1 lethal; threat 19–20; qualities: *keen 4*), metal shield (dmg 1d4+1 subdual; threat 20; qualities: *guard +2*)

Gear: Partial scalemail with light fittings (DR 4; Resist Edged 2; DP –2; ACP –2; Spd –5 ft.; Disguise –12)

Treasure: 2C, 1G

EXAMPLE: ALPHA SABER-TOOTH TIGER

An exceptionally dangerous specimen, this wizened hunter is always found at the front of his pack, inspiring the rest to greater skill and deadliness.

Alpha Saber-Tooth Tiger (Large Animal Walker — 90 XP): Str 20, Dex 16, Con 10, Int 4, Wis 12, Cha 8; SZ L (1×2, Reach 1); Spd 30 ft. ground; Init VI; Atk VII; Def IV; Res V; Health VI; Comp —; Skills: Athletics III, Notice V, Sneak III; Qualities: *Class ability (Captain: battle planning I), damage defiance (cold), rend, treacherous, veteran II*

Attacks/Weapons: Bite V (dmg 3d10+5 lethal; threat 16–20; upgrades: *grab*), Claw II (dmg 1d8+5 lethal; threat 19–20)

Treasure: 3T

ANCIENT (+20 XP)

Experience is a valuable asset — and one that few monsters gain with "adventurer" becoming such a popular career path. Ancient NPCs are methuselahs of their kind, slightly diminished in body but greatly strengthened in mind. They're commonly surrounded by younger, stronger specimens and frequently become masterminds of their people, hatching complex and nefarious plots to turn the tables against those troublesome "heroes."

Benefit: The NPC's Strength, Dexterity, and Constitution drop by 2 each but his Intelligence and Wisdom rise by 4 each. His Competence rises by 3 and he also gains *burden of ages, cagey II, class ability (Courtier: master plan I, never outdone; Keeper: bright idea II),* and *fatal falls.*

EXAMPLE: ANCIENT GHOUL

An ancient ghoul is a corpulent, withered king, bloated by great feasts on the dead and many years of relative comfort. Though somewhat less adept in combat than his "subjects," this vile creature's surprisingly sharp mind more than makes up the difference.

Ancient Ghoul (Medium Undead Walker — 78 XP): Str 8, Dex 10, Con 8, Int 14, Wis 16, Cha 10; SZ M (1×1, Reach 1); Spd 30 ft. ground; Init IV; Atk III; Def III; Res V; Health VI; Comp IV; Skills: Sneak V; Qualities: *Burden of ages, cagey II, class ability (Courtier: master plan I, never outdone; Keeper: bright idea II), fatal falls, feral, improved sense (scent), stench, swarm*

Attacks/Weapons: Bite I (dmg 1d8–1 lethal; threat 18–20), Ghoul Fever (sickening attack II: Will DC 15 or become *sickened* for 2d6 rounds; upgrades: *supernatural attack (bite)*), Claw I (dmg 1d6–1 lethal; threat 20), Paralyzing Claw (paralyzing attack I: Will DC 10 or become *paralyzed* 1d6 rounds; upgrades: *supernatural attack (claw)*)

Treasure: 1L, 1G, 1T

EXAMPLE: ANCIENT NAGA

A self-appointed avatar of Sssyt, god of snakes, this wrinkled, bitter creature's malicious streak has only grown over the long ages. She eschews common barbarism, preferring trickery, riddles, and other deception.

Ancient Naga (Large Beast Fey Walker — 100 XP): Str 14, Dex 10, Con 14, Int 16, Wis 18, Cha 14; SZ L (1×3, Reach 2); Spd 40 ft. ground; Init IV; Atk II; Def II; Res V; Health V; Comp VIII; Skills: Resolve IX, Sense Motive IX, Spellcasting IX; Spells: Command II, Divine Favor, Fireball I, Mirror Images, Ray of Enfeeblement, Righteous Aura; Qualities: *Burden of ages, cagey II, class ability (Courtier: master plan I, never outdone; Keeper: bright idea II), damage reduction 4, darkvision I, fatal falls, feat (Iron Will, Lightning Reflexes), menacing threat, tricky (Venom Master)*

Attacks/Weapons: Bite II (dmg 1d10+2 lethal; threat 17–20 + necrotizing poison, upgrades: *venomous*), Venomous Spittle (blinding attack II: 20 ft. ray; Will DC 15 or become *blinded* for 2d6 rounds)

Treasure: 1A, 2L

CLOCKWORK (+20 XP)

Clockwork creatures are the product of mad scientists and craftsmen seeking to replicate life in mechanical form. Each is a wonder of science — made of steel and iron, moved by pistons and cogs, and powered by magic, steam, coal, or other mysterious technologies. Most clockwork creatures serve as ageless sentinels or testaments to their master's craft but some escape into the wild, or are released to further the experiment.

Requirements: Non-Construct

Benefit: The NPC gains the Construct Type, *damage reduction 3,* and *Slam III.*

EXAMPLE: CLOCKWORK SPRITE

These wind-up faerie were created by a lonely artificer, to entertain and carry out small tasks. With their master gone, these little angels have become tiny terrors, attacking all who enter his quiet laboratory...

Clockwork Sprite (Diminutive Construct Fey Flyer/ Walker — 92 XP): Str 10, Dex 18, Con 10, Int 10, Wis 10, Cha 14; SZ D (1×1, Reach 1); Spd 40 ft. winged flight, 10 ft. ground; Init VI; Atk I; Def IX; Res IV; Health I; Comp II; Skills: Acrobatics VII, Bluff III, Impress III; Qualities: *Chameleon II (forest/jungle), class ability (Burglar: he did it!), damage reduction 3, feat (Agile Flyer), shapeshifter I*

Attacks/Weapons: Diminutive short bow + 30 standard arrows (dmg 1d4 lethal; threat 19–20; range 20 ft. × 6; qualities: *AP 2, cavalry, poisonous*), Slam III (dmg 2d3 lethal; threat 19–20)

Gear: Fast-acting baffling poison (3 uses)

Treasure: None

EXAMPLE: CLOCKWORK WATCHMAN

Common in the lairs of arcane tinkers, these lanky iron men move with stiff mechanical precision and speak in tinny artificial voices. They defend their masters' lair to the (un)dying end.

Clockwork Watchman (Medium Construct Folk Walker — 57 XP): Str 10, Dex 10, Con 10, Int 10, Wis 10, Cha 10; SZ M (1×1, Reach 1); Spd 30 ft. ground; Init V; Atk II; Def II; Res III; Health III; Comp II; Skills: Investigate V, Notice V, Search V; Qualities: *Damage reduction 3, feat (Basic Skill Mastery (Investigator), Combat Instincts), improved sense (hearing)*

Attacks/Weapons: Club (dmg 1d8 subdual; threat 20), mancatcher (dmg 1d6 subdual; threat —; qualities: *reach +1, trip*), Slam III (dmg 2d6 lethal; threat 19–20)

Gear: Partial hardened leather armor (DR 3; Resist Fire 3; DP –1; ACP –1; Spd –5 ft.; Disguise –2), hooded lantern, manacles, whistle

Treasure: None

DIRE (+20 XP)

Dire creatures are massive examples of their kind, worshipped by some primitive cultures as messengers of the gods. While no more intelligent or skilled than their smaller kin, they're magnitudes more dangerous, possessing incredible strength, boosted resilience, and the ability to inspire raw, animal terror in all who face them.

Requirements: Animal, Beast, Ooze, or Plant

Benefit: The NPC's Size increases by 2 categories (adjust his footprint accordingly). His Strength and Constitution rise by 4 each and he gains *tough II* and *unnerving*.

EXAMPLE: DIRE BEAR

Also known as cave bears, these ferocious creatures are nearly 25 ft. of famously bad attitude.

Dire Bear (Huge Animal Walker — 89 XP): Str 20, Dex 8, Con 16, Int 3, Wis 12, Cha 10; SZ H (2×5, Reach 2); Spd 30 ft. ground (Run 150 ft.); Init III; Atk V; Def III; Res V; Health VI; Comp —; Skills: Athletics IV, Intimidate V, Notice IV; Qualities: *Grappler, menacing threat, superior runner I, tough III, unnerving*

Attacks/Weapons: Bite II (dmg 1d12+5 lethal; threat 17–20), Claw II (dmg 1d10+5 lethal; threat 19–20), Squeeze II (dmg 2d8+5 subdual; notes: Grapple benefit)

Treasure: 1T

EXAMPLE: DIRE GELATINOUS CUBE

This translucent terror slowly roams the halls of titanic dungeons, filling entire rooms with its immense bulk. It's been known to swallow entire parties in the process.

Dire Gelatinous Cube (Colossal Animal Ooze Walker — 96 XP): Str 14, Dex 2, Con 22, Int 1, Wis 2, Cha 2; SZ C (20×20, Reach 2); Spd 15 ft. ground; Init I; Atk IV; Def I; Res I; Health IV; Comp —; Skills: Athletics III; Qualities: *Blindsight, chameleon II (caverns/mountains, indoors/settled), critical hesitation, damage immunity (electrical), shambling, tough VI, unnerving*

Attacks/Weapons: Slam I (dmg 2d8 acid; threat 20), Engulf (Swallow II: dmg 2d10 acid; notes: Grapple benefit — Medium and smaller only), Paralyzing Pseudopods (paralyzing attack III: Fort DC 20 or become *paralyzed* for 3d6 rounds, upgrades: *supernatural attack (slam)*)

Treasure: 2A

GHOSTLY (+40 XP)

Some who die linger, unable or willing to embrace their afterlife. They remain fettered to the physical realm as terrifying apparitions, manifesting to destroy the spirits from unsuspecting adventurers...

Requirements: Animal, Beast, Fey, Folk, Horror, Ooze, Plant, or Undead

Benefit: The NPC gains the Spirit and Undead Types and *everlasting.* He also gains the Ghostly Wail (shaking attack III: 40 ft. aura, Will DC 20 or become *shaken*) and Shadow of Death (soul draining attack III: Fort DC 20 or die (standard character), lose 1 action die and 10 max. vitality (special character)) extraordinary attacks. Depending on the creature, you might want to remove some or all of its other attacks.

EXAMPLE: GHOSTLY HELL HOUND

This fearsome apparition has haunted generations of a cursed family, forcing each member of the damned clan to atone for their forebears' misdeeds... or driving them irrevocably insane.

Ghostly Hell Hound

Ghostly Hell Hound (Medium Animal Outsider Spirit Undead Walker — 114 XP): Str 10, Dex 10, Con 10, Int 6, Wis 10, Cha 6; SZ M (1×1, Reach 1); Spd 40 ft. ground; Init VII; Atk VIII; Def IV; Res VIII; Health V; Comp —; Skills: Acrobatics III, Notice IV, Sneak IX, Survival IV; Qualities: *Achilles heel (cold), damage immunity (fire), darkvision II, everlasting, feat (Wolf Pack Basics), improved sense (scent), nocturnal*

Attacks/Weapons: Fiery Bite (Bite III: dmg 2d8 fire; threat 17–20), Flame Breath (fire damage attack II: 10 ft. cone; dmg 1d6 fire per 2 TL, Ref DC 15 for 1/2 damage), Ghostly Wail (shaking attack III: 40 ft. aura, Will DC 20 or become *shaken*), Shadow of Death (soul draining attack III: Fort DC 20 or die (standard character), lose 1 action die and 10 max. vitality (special character))

Treasure: None

EXAMPLE: GHOSTLY GOBLIN STRUMPET

A lonesome victim of a horrible hate crime, this angry ghost jerks through the air like a deranged mutant rag doll. Drunkards wandering home from a late night at the pub might think her a hallucination, or some bizarre street performer's lost plaything — but her days as a plaything are over, as she's happy to illustrate to the unwitting and the unfortunate.

Ghostly Goblin Strumpet (Small Folk Spirit Undead Walker — 69 XP): Str 10, Dex 10, Con 10, Int 10, Wis 10, Cha 10; SZ S; Spd 30 ft. ground; Init II; Atk III; Def I; Res II; Health III; Comp I; Skills: Bluff IV, Haggle IV, Impress II, Prestidigitation II; Qualities: *Beguiling, class ability (Courtier: slanderous), darkvision I, everlasting, feat (Ambush Basics), light-sensitive*

Attacks/Weapons: Ghostly Wail (shaking attack III: 40 ft. aura, Will DC 20 or become *shaken*), Shadow of Death (soul draining attack III: Fort DC 20 or die (standard character), lose 1 action die and 10 max. vitality (special character))

Treasure: None

HEAVENLY (+10 XP)

Heavenly creatures — what many call "avatars" — embody justice, hope, and truth. They're dispatched to assist to the peoples of the world, some with messages of peace, others helping mortals to evolve, or even ascend. All are what their species considers 'ideal': an extraordinarily beautiful and graceful human, an exceptionally strong and fair horse, a gold-scaled dragon glowing with inner radiance, and the like.

Requirements: *Interests (Alignment)* quality

Benefit: The NPC gains the Outsider Type, his Wisdom and Charisma rise by 2 each, and he gains *devoted (Good II)* and *natural spell (Bless, Divine Favor).*

EXAMPLE: HEAVENLY GRIFFON

This magnificent creature patrols the skies of righteous kingdoms, striking with deadly precision those who would undermine the rule of the just.

Griffon (Large Animal Outsider Flyer/Walker — 76 XP): Str 14, Dex 14, Con 12, Int 5, Wis 12, Cha 8; SZ L (1×2, Reach

1); Spd 80 ft. flight, 30 ft. ground; Init III; Atk VI; Def III; Res IV; Health V; Comp —; Skills: Acrobatics III, Notice III; Qualities: *Devoted (Good II), feat (Charging Basics), improved sense (sight), interests (Alignment), natural spell (Bless, Divine Favor), rend, tough I*

Attacks/Weapons: Bite I (dmg 1d10+2 lethal; threat 18–20; upgrades: *bleed, keen 4*), Talon II (dmg 1d8+2 lethal; threat 19–20)

Treasure: 2T

EXAMPLE: HEAVENLY KNIGHT

Once a knight errant questing for sanctified artifacts, this warrior supped from a sacred vessel and was infused with divine grace.

Knight (Medium Folk Outsider Walker — 78 XP): Str 15, Dex 10, Con 10, Int 10, Wis 12, Cha 12; SZ M (1×1, Reach 1); Spd 30 ft. ground; Init IV; Atk VI; Def IV; Res V; Health V; Comp II; Skills: Athletics V, Impress III, Resolve V, Ride V, Tactics III; Qualities: *Class ability (Lancer: master rider I), devoted (Good II), fearless II, feat (Armor Basics, Charging Basics), honorable, interests (Alignment), natural spell (Bless, Divine Favor)*

Attacks/Weapons: Lance (dmg 1d8+2 lethal; threat 19–20; qualities: *AP 4, cavalry, massive, reach +1*), long sword (dmg 1d12+2 lethal; threat 20), metal shield (dmg 1d4+2 subdual; threat 20; qualities: *guard +2*)

Mounts and Vehicles: War horse (Spd 50 ft. ground (Run 250 ft.); Travel 5; SZ/Def L/IV)

Gear: Full plate (moderate platemail with heavy fittings: DR 7; Resist Blunt 2; DP –4; ACP –4; Spd –10 ft.; Disguise obvious)

Treasure: 1L, 1M

INFERNAL (+10 XP)

Infernal monsters draw strength from the netherworld and serve unholy masters, spreading corruption, plague, and strife in exchange for power, wealth, and glory. Their evil manifests in many ways — wicked horns, sickly skin, nasty personality traits, and more — but the foul stain on their spirits is universal.

Requirements: *Interests quality (Alignment)*

Benefit: The NPC gains the Outsider Type and his Strength and Intelligence rise by 2 each. He also gains *devoted (Evil II)* and *natural spell (Command I, Disguise Self)*.

EXAMPLE: INFERNAL HAG

Twisted and hideous, this witch consorts with dark powers to gain even greater power over men's minds.

Infernal Hag (Medium Outsider Flier/Walker — 141 XP): Str 18, Dex 10, Con 14, Int 18, Wis 12, Cha 10; SZ M (1×1, Reach 1); Spd 60 ft. flight, 30 ft. ground; Init III; Atk VI; Def V; Res VII; Health VI; Comp IV; Skills: Bluff VIII, Crafting V, Sense Motive VIII, Spellcasting VIII; Spells: Bestow Curse, Control Weather I, Disguise Self, Geas, Hold Person, Scare I, Scrye III, Tiny Shelter; Qualities: *Achilles heel (divine), beguiling, bright I, class ability (Assassin: black vial; Mage: spell secret III (Bestow Curse, Disguise Self, Scrye III)), darkvision II, devoted (Evil II), everlasting, feat (Black Cat, Iron Will, Jinx, Tough Luck), interests (Alignment), natural spell (Command I, Disguise Self), repulsive I, spell defense II, spell reflection, tough I, treacherous, veteran II*

Attacks/Weapons: Dagger (dmg 1d6+4 lethal; threat 19–20; qualities: *bleed, hurl*), Evil Eye (stress damage attack II: 60 ft. gaze; dmg 1d6 stress per 2 TL, Ref DC 15 for 1/2 damage)

Gear: Chemist's kit, invisibility potion, love potion, mage's pouch

Treasure: 1A, 3M

EXAMPLE: INFERNAL TROLL

Spawn of an unholy union between demon and troll, these terrifying monsters are stronger and more dangerous than either.

Infernal Troll (Large Folk Walker — 101 XP): Str 18, Dex 12, Con 18, Int 8, Wis 9, Cha 6; SZ L (2×2, Reach 2); Spd 25 ft. ground; Init IV; Atk IV; Def III; Res V; Health VIII; Comp II; Skills: Athletics III, Notice III, Survival V; Qualities: *Class ability (Explorer: lifeline), damage reduction 2, darkvision I, devoted (Evil II), fearless I, improved sense (scent), interests (Alignment), natural spell (Command I, Disguise Self), regeneration 5, rend*

Attacks/Weapons: Large mace (dmg 1d10+4 lethal; threat 20; qualities: *AP 4*), Claw II (dmg 1d8+4 lethal; threat 19–20)

Treasure: 1G, 1M, 1T

IMMATURE (-20 XP)

Young and baby monsters can still challenge many parties.

Benefit: The NPC's Size decreases by 2 categories (adjust his footprint accordingly) and his Reach decreases by 2 (minimum 1). His Attack, Defense, Resilience, Health, and Competence drop by 2 each, as do the grades of his natural and extraordinary attacks (minimum I).

EXAMPLE: IMMATURE BULETTE

These creatures are sometimes found hunting with their mothers. It's a rare chance to find two or more members of the species together.

Immature Bulette (Medium Animal Burrower/Walker — 91 XP): Str 18, Dex 12, Con 14, Int 2, Wis 10, Cha 6; SZ M; Spd 10 ft. burrow, 50 ft. ground; Init IV; Atk V; Def III; Res VI; Health IV; Comp —; Skills: Acrobatics VI, Athletics III, Notice III; Qualities: *Blindsight, damage reduction 4, darkvision II, fearless I, improved sense (scent), superior jumper III, tough I*

Attacks/Weapons: Bite I (dmg 1d8+4 lethal; threat 18–20), Claw I × 2 (dmg 1d6+4 lethal; threat 20; upgrades: *AP 2*), Swallow I (dmg 1d10+4 acid; notes: Grapple benefit — Tiny and smaller only)

Treasure: 1A, 1T

EXAMPLE: IMMATURE FIRE DRAGON

Small but packing a serious punch, dragon spawn are still extremely fierce opponents.

Immature Fire Dragon (Medium Beast Flyer/Walker — 223 XP): Str 22, Dex 10, Con 18, Int 14, Wis 16, Cha 14; SZ M; Spd 140 ft. winged flight; 40 ft. ground; Init III; Atk IV; Def I; Res IV; Health IV; Comp II; Skills: Athletics X, Haggle V, Intimidate X, Notice V, Resolve V; Qualities: *Achilles heel (cold), damage immunity (fire, heat), damage reduction 7, darkvision I, dramatic entrance, fearsome, ferocity, improved sense (sight), light sleeper, menacing threat, monstrous defense II, never outnumbered, tough II, treacherous, veteran II*

Attacks/Weapons: Fiery Breath (fire damage attack II: 50 ft. cone; dmg 1d6 fire per 2 TL, Ref Save DC 15 for 1/2 damage), Bite II (dmg 1d8+6 lethal; threat 17–20; upgrades: *reach +1*), Talon I × 2 (dmg 1d6+6 lethal; threat 20), Tail Slap I (dmg 1d8+6 lethal; threat 20; upgrades: *reach +1, trip*), Trample I (dmg 1d8+6 lethal; threat 20; notes: Tiny and smaller only, Fort (DC equal to damage) or become *sprawled*), Wing Slam × 2 (Slam I: dmg 1d6+6 lethal; threat 20)

Treasure: 1A, 2C

KAIJU (+125 XP)

Kaiju are titanic beings of unimaginable power, forces of nature so immense they can crush buildings underfoot. Mercifully, they're quite rare, created and woken by powerful magic, cosmic accident, or the gods themselves. Kaiju are a diverse lot with little in common except for their sky-blotting size and limitless appetite for destruction.

Benefit: The NPC's Size increases to Enormous (adjust his footprint accordingly), his Reach increases by 4, and his Strength and Constitution rise by 5 each. He also gains *clumsy, condition immunity (frightened), contagion immunity, damage immunity (stress, subdual), damage reduction 5, fearsome, frenzy II, knockback, lumbering, menacing threat, monstrous defense III, never outnumbered, tough V, unnerving, veteran V,* and *Trample V* (dmg 6d8 lethal; threat 18–20; upgrades: *AP 10;* notes: Gargantuan and smaller only, Fort (DC equal to damage) or become *sprawled*).

EXAMPLE: KAIJU ELDER WATER ELEMENTAL

This terrifying force is a tsunami brought to life, rising from the sea to sweep entire cities into a watery grave.

Kaiju Elder Water Elemental (Enormous Elemental Walker — 280 XP): Str 25, Dex 10, Con 25, Int 6, Wis 10, Cha 10; SZ E (30×30, Reach 6); Spd 70 ft. ground; Init V; Atk V; Def V; Res IV; Health VI; Comp IV; Skills: Athletics VII, Search IV; Qualities: *Achilles heel (cold, heat), blindsight, class ability (Burglar: evasion II), clumsy, condition immunity (frightened), contagion immunity, damage immunity (bows, edged, stress, subdual), damage reduction 5, everlasting, fearsome, feat (Ferocity Basics, Ferocity Mastery, Ferocity Supremacy), frenzy II, grappler, improved stability, knockback, lumbering, menacing threat, monstrous defense III, natural spell (Mass Water Walk, Move Water), never outnumbered, superior swimmer X, tough VII, unnerving, veteran VII*

Attacks/Weapons: Slam IV (dmg 2d12+7 subdual; threat 18–20; upgrades: *grab, reach 1*), Drown (Swallow III: dmg 4d10+7 lethal; notes: Grapple benefit — Small and smaller only), Riptide (stunning attack III: 30 ft. beam; Will DC 20 or become *stunned* for 3d6 rounds), Trample V (dmg 6d8+7 lethal; threat 18–20; upgrades: *AP 10*; notes: Colossal and smaller only, Fort (DC equal to damage) or become *sprawled*)

Treasure: 6A

EXAMPLE: KAIJU TYRANNOSAURUS REX

This king of all monsters stalks a warm jungle island in the south, waiting for the siren call summoning him to save all mankind... or destroy it.

Kaiju Tyrannosaurus Rex (Enormous Animal Walker — 231 XP): Str 26, Dex 10, Con 22, Int 4, Wis 10, Cha 10; SZ E (20×40, Reach 5); Spd 40 ft. ground (Run 200 ft.); Init IV; Atk VII; Def III; Res V; Health VIII; Comp —; Skills: Athletics II, Search VI, Survival VI; Qualities: *Class ability (Scout: trail signs), clumsy, condition immunity (frightened), contagion immunity, damage immunity (stress, subdual), damage reduction 8, fearsome, frenzy II, grappler, impaired sense (scent), knockback, lumbering, menacing threat, monstrous defense III, never outnumbered, superior runner I, tough VII, treacherous, unnerving, veteran V*

Attack/Weapons: Bite IV (dmg 4d8+8 lethal; threat 16–20; upgrades: *AP 2, grab*), Swallow III (dmg 4d10+8 lethal; notes: Grapple benefit — Medium and smaller only), Trample V (dmg 6d8+8 lethal; threat 18–20; upgrades: *AP 10;* notes: Gargantuan and smaller only, Fort (DC equal to damage) or become *sprawled*)

Treasure: 2A, 3T

LICH (+70 XP)

Liches are the immortal remains of sorcerers or magical creatures that have traded their souls for eternal "life," and like most unholy bargainers they've paid a terrible price. Their bodies are shriveled and their skin is taut and pallid. Their eyes are sunken pits of balefire and they give off an aura of unearthly menace, withering all who approach. They're a bitter mockery of life, desperately clutching tenuous threads that should have snapped long ago.

Lich

Requirements: Spellcasting Signature Skill

Benefit: The NPC gains the Undead Type and his Intelligence, Wisdom, Charisma rise by 2 each. His Health rises by 2 and he gains *condition immunity (enraged, fatigued, frightened, shaken), damage immunity (cold, electrical), damage reduction 5, dread, everlasting* and *turn immunity*. He also gains Lich Touch (paralyzing attack III: Will DC 20 or become *paralyzed* for 3d6 rounds)

Special: Most liches keep a phylactery, a special container that stores their soul and protects them from harm. Finding a lich's phylactery makes a great adventure objective and should it be destroyed (Hard 4) the lich loses this template.

EXAMPLE: LICH NECROMANCER

Necromancers turn to lichdom all too often, usually to avoid losing the control they enjoy in life.

Lich Necromancer (Medium Folk Undead Walker — 123 XP): Str 10, Dex 10, Con 10, Int 12, Wis 12, Cha 12; SZ M (1×1, Reach 1); Spd 30 ft. ground; Init II; Atk II; Def III; Res V; Health VII; Comp III; Skills: Intimidate VIII, Medicine V, Resolve V, Spellcasting V; Spells: Animate Dead II, Deathknell, Deathwatch, Dominate Undead I, Speak with Dead; Qualities: *Condition immunity (enraged, fatigued, frightened, shaken), damage immunity (cold, electrical), damage reduction 5, dread, everlasting, feat (Ghost Basics, Glint of Madness), stench, turn immunity*

Attacks/Weapons: Shod staff (dmg 1d8 lethal; threat 19–20; qualities: *double, trip*), Lich Touch (paralyzing attack III: Will DC 20 or become *paralyzed* for 3d6 rounds)

Gear: Moderate padded armor (DR 1, Resist Cold 5; DP –0; ACP –0; Spd —; Disguise +0), mage's pouch, mana potion

Treasure: 2L, 2M, 2T

EXAMPLE: LICH ROYAL DRAGON

As if dragons weren't greedy enough, some focus their natural magic ability toward living forever.

Lich Royal Dragon (Huge Beast Undead Flyer/Walker — 326 XP): Str 16, Dex 10, Con 16, Int 20, Wis 18, Cha 18; SZ H (3×6, Reach 1); Spd 200 ft. winged flight, 60 ft. ground; Init III; Atk VII; Def III; Res X; Health IX; Comp V; Skills: Disguise VI, Impress IX, Investigate VI, Resolve VI, Spellcasting VI; Spells: Bless, Command II, Geas, Mark of Justice, True Seeing, Zone of Truth; Qualities: *Bright II, cagey II, class ability (Captain: virtues of command I), condition immunity (enraged, fatigued, frightened, shaken), contagion immunity, damage immunity (cold, divine, electrical), damage reduction 9, dramatic entrance, dread, everlasting, light sleeper, monstrous defense I, never outnumbered, shapeshifter II, spell defense IV, spell reflection, superior swimmer IV, tough II, turn immunity, unlimited spell points, veteran IV*

Attacks/Weapons: Radiant Breath (divine damage attack III: 80 ft. beam; dmg 1d8 divine per 2 TL, Ref DC 20 for 1/2 damage),

Bite III (dmg 2d12+3 lethal; threat 17–20; upgrades: *reach +1*), Claw II × 2 (dmg 1d10+3 lethal; threat 19–20), Tail Slap III (dmg 2d12+3 lethal; threat 19–20; upgrades: *reach +1*), Trample II (dmg 1d12+5 lethal; threat 19–20; notes: Medium and smaller only, Fort (DC equal to damage) or become *sprawled*), Lich Touch (paralyzing attack III: Will DC 20 or become *paralyzed* for 3d6 rounds)

Treasure: 3A, 3M

PREDATORY (+15 XP)

Predatory NPCs have honed their tactics to a razor's edge. They fight with clever tactics and innovative ploys, besting opponents as often with their heads as their hands.

Benefit: The NPC gains the Tactics V Signature Skill, *feat (Coordinated Attack, Misdirection Basics, Wolf Pack Basics, Wolf Pack Mastery),* and *swarm.*

EXAMPLE: PREDATORY GNOLL

These bloodthirsty creatures are charged with eliminating intruders and acquiring man-flesh for gnoll families and elders.

Predatory Gnoll (Medium Folk Walker — 38 XP): Str 12, Dex 10, Con 10, Int 8, Wis 10, Cha 8; SZ M (1×1, Reach 1); Spd 30 ft. ground; Init II; Atk IV; Def II; Res I; Health IV; Comp I; Skills: Notice II, Survival II, Tactics V; Qualities: *Darkvision I, feat (Coordinated Attack, Misdirection Basics, Wolf Pack Basics, Wolf Pack Mastery), improved sense (scent), nocturnal, swarm, tricky (Relentless Attack)*

Attacks/Weapons: Axe (dmg 1d10+1 lethal; threat 20; qualities: *AP 4*), hide shield (dmg 1d3+1 subdual; threat 20; qualities: *guard +2*), bola × 3 (dmg 1d6+1 subdual; threat 19–20; range 20 ft. × 3; qualities: *cavalry, trip*)

Gear: Partial studded leather (DR 2; Resist —; DP –1; ACP –0; Spd +0 ft.; Disguise +0)

Treasure: 1C, 1G, 1L, 1T

EXAMPLE: PREDATORY MYRMIDON

A few myrmidon soldiers possess an uncharacteristic "spark" beyond the hive mind. They make leaps their comrades don't, like finding ways to turn opponents around and trap them in their tunnels. These exceptional myrmidon are the unsung, oft-misunderstood heroes of their species.

Predatory Myrmidon (Medium Folk Walker — 107 XP): Str 12, Dex 14, Con 12, Int 10, Wis 10, Cha 8; SZ M (1×1, Reach 1); Spd 40 ft. ground; Init V; Atk VII; Def IV; Res IX; Health IV; Comp IV; Skills: Athletics VI, Crafting V, Tactics X; Qualities: *Banned action (Bluff, Impress, Intimidate), contagion immunity, damage reduction 2, fearless I, feat (Coordinated Attack, Misdirection Basics, Wolf Pack Basics, Wolf Pack Mastery), hive mind, honorable, improved stability, superior jumper II, swarm*

Attacks/Weapons: Bite I (dmg 1d8+1 lethal; threat 18–20), Claw I (dmg 1d6+1 lethal; threat 20), Gore II (dmg 1d6+1 lethal + weakening poison; threat 18¬–20; upgrades: *bleed, venomous*), Chakram × 3 (dmg 1d6+1 lethal; threat 20; range 20 ft. × 3; qualities: *keen 4*)

Treasure: 2G

RISEN (+5 XP)

Foul necromancy is often used to animate the husks of the recently dead, pressing them into service as zombified soldiers and brain-dead guardians. These shambling corpses become inured to pain and fear, but they also develop an unearthly appetite for the flesh of the living — perhaps attempting to recapture the spark of life.

Requirements: Animal, Beast, Folk, or Horror

Benefit: The NPC gains the Undead Type, his Resilience grade increases by 2, and his Initiative and Competence grades decrease by 2 each. He also gains *devour, monstrous defense I* and *shambling.*

EXAMPLE: RISEN PEASANT

The walking dead are a common sight in lands infested with necromancers and dread lords, usually as the unfortunate victims of a biological or magical plague.

Risen Peasant (Medium Folk Undead Walker — 25 XP): Str 10, Dex 10, Con 10, Int 10, Wis 10, Cha 10; SZ M (1×1, Reach 1); Spd 30 ft. ground; Init I; Atk II; Def III; Res VI; Health II; Comp I; Skills: Athletics III, Bluff III, Survival III; Qualities: *Devour, meek, monstrous defense I, shambling*

Attacks/Weapons: Bite I (dmg 1d8 lethal; threat 18–20)

Treasure: None

EXAMPLE: RISEN WATCHER IN THE DARK

Evil overlords must sometimes hunt Watchers when conquering dungeons. The savvy ones reanimate them, gaining access to their mighty abilities without the pesky independence.

Risen Watcher in the Dark (Large Beast Horror Undead Flyer — 168 XP): Str 10, Dex 12, Con 14, Int 14, Wis 12, Cha 12; SZ L (2×2, Reach 1); Spd 20 ft. flight; Init VIII; Atk III; Def VII; Res VII; Health IV; Comp II; Skills: Search VIII, Sneak V; Qualities: *Condition immunity (flanked), damage reduction 4, darkvision II, devour, feat (Charging Basics, Charging Mastery, Iron Will), frenzy III, improved sense (sight), monstrous defense I, shambling, veteran II*

Attacks/Weapons: Bite I (dmg 1d10 lethal; threat 18–20), Fearful Judgment (frightening attack II: 120 ft. gaze; Will save DC 15 or become *frightened* for 2d6 rounds), Petrifying Judgment (petrifying attack II: 20 ft. beam; Fort DC 15 or be turned to stone), Searing Judgment (divine damage attack III: 40 ft. beam; dmg 1d8 divine per 2 TL, Ref DC 20 for 1/2 damage), Sluggish

Judgment (slowing attack II: 120 ft. gaze; Will save DC 15 or become *slowed* for 2d6 rounds), Weakening Judgment (fatiguing attack II: 120 ft. gaze; Fort DC 15 or become *fatigued*), Wounding Judgment (lethal damage attack II: 120 ft. gaze; dmg 1d6 lethal per 2 TL, Ref DC 15 for 1/2 damage; upgrades: *bleed*)

Treasure: None

SKELETAL (+15 XP)

Magically animated skeletons are comprised solely of bone with no connecting tissue. Even their brains have boiled away, leaving them mindless. They feel nothing, fear nothing, and can't be reasoned with. All they do is kill.

Requirements: Animal, Beast, Folk, or Horror

Benefit: The NPC gains the Undead Type, as well as *damage defiance (edged), damage immunity (bows),* and *ferocity.*

EXAMPLE: SKELETAL MAN-AT-ARMS

At a distance these soldiers might easily be mistaken for living military troops. Up close, however, the unnatural sound of clacking bones in hollow armor gives them away.

Skeletal Man-at-Arms (Medium Folk Undead Walker — 51 XP): Str 10, Dex 10, Con 10, Int 10, Wis 10, Cha 10; SZ M (1×1, Reach 1); Spd 30 ft. ground; Init IV; Atk IV; Def III; Res II; Health IV; Comp I; Skills: Athletics III, Intimidate III, Notice III, Tactics III; Qualities: *Class ability (Soldier: rugged weapons), damage defiance (edged), damage immunity (bows), feat (All-Out Attack, Combat Instincts), ferocity*

Attacks/Weapons: Glaive (dmg 1d8 lethal; threat 19–20; qualities: *keen 4, reach +1*), metal shield (dmg 1d4+2 subdual; threat 20; qualities: *guard +2*), short sword (dmg 1d8 lethal; threat 19–20; qualities: *keen 4*)

Gear: Partial chainmail with light fittings (DR 3, Resist Edged 2; DP –1; ACP –1; Spd –5 ft.; Disguise –8)

Treasure: 1C

EXAMPLE: SKELETAL TRICERATOPS

Skeletal dinosaurs make remarkable siege engines, offering all the versatility and reaction time of a trained mount with none of the fickle behavior or problematic morale issues.

Skeletal Triceratops (Huge Animal Undead Walker — 103 XP): Str 22, Dex 8, Con 18, Int 1, Wis 10, Cha 8; SZ H (3×4, Reach 2); Spd 30 ft. ground; Init I; Atk VII; Def IV; Res V; Health IX; Comp —; Skills: Notice IV; Qualities: *Charge attack, damage defiance (edged), damage immunity (bows), damage reduction 5, ferocity, improved sense (scent), tough I*

Attacks/Weapons: Gore III (dmg 2d10+6 lethal; threat 18–20; upgrades: *bleed*), Trample IV (dmg 2d12+6 lethal; threat 18–20; notes: Medium and smaller only, Fort (DC equal to damage) or become *sprawled*)

Treasure: 2T

Skeletal

VAMPIRIC (+45 XP)

Vampiric monsters are abominations against nature, damned to forever feed on the life force of others, even their own kind.

Requirements: Beast, Fey, Folk, Horror, Outsider, or Plant

Benefit: The NPC gains the Undead Type, his Defense and Health increase by 2 each, and his Strength, Wisdom, and Charisma rise by 2 each. He also gains *Achilles heel (divine, fire, flash), beguiling, damage defiance (cold), damage reduction 3, darkvision II, fast healing, killing conversion, light-sensitive, nocturnal, shapeshifter I* and *superior climber II,* as well as Bite I and Drain Blood (life draining attack II: Fort DC 15 or suffer 1 lethal damage per TL, the NPC healing the same amount; upgrades: *supernatural attack (bite)*).

EXAMPLE: VAMPIRIC ELF NOBLEMAN

Centuries ago, this nobleman blasphemed against the gods. They damned him to a life of animalistic bloodlust, which he sates on the front lines of wars he arranges.

Vampiric Elf Nobleman (Medium Fey Undead Walker — 93 XP): Str 12, Dex 10, Con 10, Int 10, Wis 14, Cha 12; SZ M (1×1, Reach 1); Spd 40 ft. ground; Init III; Atk III; Def IV; Res V; Health IV; Comp III; Skills: Impress V, Intimidate IV, Ride IV, Sense Motive IV; Qualities: *Achilles heel (divine, fire, flash), attractive II, beguiling, burden of ages, class ability (Courtier: only the finest, with a word), damage defiance (cold), damage reduction 3, darkvision II, fast healing, feat (Repartee Basics, Repartee Mastery), improved sense (hearing, sight), killing conversion, light-sensitive, light sleeper, nocturnal, shapeshifter I, superior climber II, tricky (Parry)*

Attacks/Weapons: Dagger (dmg 1d6+1 lethal; threat 19–20; qualities: *bleed, hurl*), rapier (dmg 1d8 lethal; threat 19–20; qualities: *bleed, finesse*), Bite I (dmg 1d8+1 lethal; threat 18–20), Drain Blood (life draining attack II: Fort DC 15 or suffer 1 damage per TL, the NPC healing the same amount; upgrades: *supernatural attack (bite)*)

Mounts and Vehicles: Riding horse (Spd 50 ft. ground (Run 250 ft.); Travel 7; SZ/Def L/IV) or none

Gear: Ceremonial partial leather armor (DR 0; Resist Fire 3; DP –1; ACP –0; Spd —; Disguise +0)

Treasure: 2C, 2L

EXAMPLE: VAMPIRIC CHAOS BEAST

A roiling mass of eyeballs, fangs, and slathering tongues, this elder horror is found in the deepest and most corrupt places of the world, waiting to feed on the flesh of the living.

Vampiric Chaos Beast (Medium Ooze Outsider Undead Walker — 165 XP): Str 14, Dex 10, Con 10, Int 10, Wis 12, Cha 12; SZ M (1×1, Reach 1); Spd 20 ft. ground; Init IX; Atk VII; Def V; Res VII; Health V; Comp IV; Skills: Acrobatics VII, Athletics VI, Sneak V; Qualities: *Achilles heel (divine, fire, flash), beguiling, condition immunity (paralyzed, stunned), damage defiance (cold), damage immunity (sneak attack), damage reduction 5, darkvision II, fast healing, feat (Elusive, Mobility Basics), killing conversion, light-sensitive, monstrous defense III, nocturnal, shapeshifter I, spell defense II, superior climber II, tough I, unnerving*

Attacks/Weapons: Claw I (1d6+2 lethal; threat 20), Chaos Touch (enraging attack II: Will save DC 15 or become enraged for 2d6 rounds, upgrades: *supernatural attack (claw)*), Devolving Touch (slowing attack II: Will save DC 15 or become slowed for 2d6 rounds, upgrades: *supernatural attack (claw)*), Bite I (dmg 1d8+2 lethal; threat 18–20), Drain Blood (life draining attack II: Fort DC 15 or suffer 1 lethal damage per TL, the NPC healing the same amount; upgrades: *supernatural attack (bite)*).

Treasure: 3A

OGL CONVERSIONS

There are dozens of monster books and thousands of creatures available under the Open Gaming License — enough to satisfy nearly every GM's taste and needs, and far more than we can include in this book. The Rogues Gallery and Bestiary include many popular fantasy favorites but when you want to add an old standby rather than build something new, you can turn to this handy conversion system.

These rules work with nearly all NPCs and monsters from SRD, 3.0, and 3.5 roleplaying products, generating a balanced *Fantasy Craft* stat block. As with original NPCs the result can be used at any Threat Level and easily modified on the fly. Necessarily though, the initial process is a bit more complex than an original build, so you should set aside a little time for that.

CONVERSION BASICS

The following steps walk through the entries in a standard OGL monster description (except Organization, which isn't part of *Fantasy Craft* NPC construction). Detailed instructions are provided for each step beginning on the pages listed in parentheses. Keep in mind that your judgment is just as important as any rule. These steps can't handle every situation and there's no such thing as a "perfect" conversion, only one that works best at your table. Feel free to tweak and adjust as desired to keep things interesting and fun.

Step 1: Size and Type *(see page 296)*: Type determines an NPC's Competence grade and assigns starting qualities.

Step 2: Hit Dice *(see page 297)*: Hit Dice set the NPC's Health grade and related stats.

Step 3: Abilities and Natural Attacks *(see page 297)*: Natural attacks convert cleanly to *Fantasy Craft* counterparts.

Step 4: Other Attacks and Qualities *(see page 300)*: Here you'll port over many unique OGL abilities.

Step 5: Skills *(see page 301)*: OGL skills translate directly in most cases.

Step 6: Feats *(see page 302)*: OGL feats can translate to *Fantasy Craft* feats, NPC qualities, or stat grades.

Step 7: Gear and Treasure *(see page 302)*: OGL treasure rating converts to *Fantasy Craft* Treasure Rolls.

Step 8: Remaining Entries *(see page 302)*: Here you'll convert everything else.

Step 9: Final Tweaks *(see page 303)*: In this optional step, you can tweak to taste.

Step 10: XP Value *(see page 303)*: Total the XP value of the converted stat block and you're ready to go!

CONVERSION THREAT LEVEL

OGL characters and monsters are designed as proper threats in only a narrow level range while Fantasy Craft NPCs scale to any level. Fortunately, it's easy to convert most non-scaling OGL stats into grades. Start by finding the NPC's Conversion Threat Level, which is equal to the OGL Challenge Rating (maximum 20), or Hit Dice (if there's no CR). You'll use this value when converting many stats.

Example: A remorhaz's Challenge Rating is 7, so its Conversion Threat Level is also 7.

STAT LIMITS

No stat may exceed the minimum or maximum listed in the standard NPC creation rules. Conversion rules are often provided for surplus but in all other cases excess is ignored.

STEP 1: SIZE AND TYPE

The NPC's Size remains unchanged and defines the NPC's maximum footprint *(see page 217)*. *Fantasy Craft* characters aren't always perfectly square, so you may want to adjust the footprint — listed as an OGL creature's "Space" — to a more logical shape. Footprint also translates directly from feet into squares.

Table 6.10: Type Conversion

OGL Type/Subtype	Competence Grade *	Fantasy Craft Type/NPC Qualities/Other Option
Type		
Aberration	II	Horror
Animal	—	Animal
Construct	I	Construct or Elemental
Dragon	III	Beast
Elemental	II	Elemental
Fey	III	Fey
Giant	II	Folk
Humanoid	III	Folk
Magical Beast	I	Animal or Beast
Monstrous Humanoid	II	Folk or Beast
Ooze	None or I	Ooze
Outsider	III	Outsider
Plant	None or I	Plant
Undead	None or I	Undead or Spirit
Vermin	None or I	Animal or Beast
Subtype		
Air	—	*Damage immunity (sonic)*
Angel	—	*Damage defiance (electrical, fire), telepathic*
Aquatic	—	*Aquatic II*
Archon	—	*Damage immunity (electrical), fearsome, telepathic*
Augmented	—	—
Chaotic	—	*Interests (Alignment)*
Cold	—	*Achilles heel (fire, heat), damage immunity (cold)*
Earth	—	Burrow Speed *(see Step 8)*
Evil	—	*Interests (Alignment)*
Extraplanar	—	—
Fire	—	*Achilles heel (cold), damage immunity (fire, heat)*
Goblinoid	—	—
Good	—	*Interests (Alignment)*
Incorporeal	—	*Spirit*
Lawful	—	*Interests (Alignment)*
Native	—	—
Reptilian	—	*Cold-blooded*
Shapeshifter	—	*Shapeshifter*
Swarm	—	*Swarm*
Water	—	*Aquatic II*

* The NPC's Competence grade is equal to this or his OGL Intelligence bonus, whichever is higher (maximum X). A "mindless" creature gains no Competence score.

Table 6.11: Hit Dice Conversion

OGL Hit Dice/Challenge	Fantasy Craft Health Grade (min. I, max. X)
d6	II
d8	III
d10	IV
d12	V
Challenge Rating vs. Number of Hit Dice	
Challenge Rating Greater	–1 Health per 3 difference (max. –5)
Equal or fractional difference (**or** *no CR*)	—
Hit Dice Greater	+1 Health or *tough I* per 3 difference (max. +5 in each)
Size	
Smaller than Medium	–1 Health per category
Medium	—
Larger than Medium	+1 Health **or** *tough I* per category

Example: A remorhaz is a Huge creature and stays the same in *Fantasy Craft.* Its Space is 15 ft. × 15 ft., which the GM translates to a footprint of 3 wide × 4 long (an arbitrary but plausible choice).

OGL type and subtype(s) set the NPC's Competence grade and may add one or more qualities, as shown on Table 6.10: Type Conversion *(see page 296).* When a character has 2 or more OGL types, apply the highest Competence generated by any of them. A character without an OGL type becomes Folk or an Animal, as appropriate. You can apply additional qualities at this point if you like to bring the NPC in line with a "common" non-human species *(see page 230),* though it isn't necessary.

Example: The remorhaz is a "Magical Beast" with an Int score of 5 (–3 bonus). This translates to the Animal or Beast Type in Fantasy Craft. Given the creature's Intelligence and SRD description, Animal (and Competence —) seems a better fit.

STEP 2: HIT DICE

The NPC's OGL Hit Dice, Challenge Rating, and Size determine its *Fantasy Craft* Health grade and possibly grant the *tough* quality, as shown on Table 6.11: Hit Dice Conversion *(see above).*

Example: A remorhaz has 7d10+35 Hit Dice, a CR of 7, and a Size of Huge. The die type sets the Health grade to IV and the other stats convert to 2 combined grades of Health and *tough I.* The GM decides to apply 1 grade to each, so the remorhaz winds up with Health V and *tough I.*

STEP 3: ABILITIES AND NATURAL ATTACKS

Add each of the NPC's OGL ability modifiers to 10 to obtain the corresponding *Fantasy Craft* attribute score. Unless the NPC is an Animal, reduce odd attribute scores by 1. Ability scores below 10 translate directly.

Example: A remorhaz has the following OGL ability scores: Str 26, Dex 13, Con 21, Int 5, Wis 12, Cha 10. These translate to Str 18, Dex 10, Con 15, Int 5, Wis 10, Cha 10 in Fantasy Craft.

If the NPC has any OGL natural attacks, compare the maximum damage of each, sans Strength modifier, with the same attack's maximum damage in *Fantasy Craft* at Grades I, III, and V (again, without Strength). Apply the grade that's closest without going over. If the maximum OGL damage is 50% or more of the way toward the next *Fantasy Craft* grade, raise the grade by 1 more (increasing the attack's threat range by 1).

Example: Without its Strength modifier, the remorhaz has an OGL Bite inflicting 2d8+4 damage (a max. of 20). At the creature's Size (Huge), the closest Fantasy Craft Bite that doesn't exceed this is Grade I (dmg 1d12; threat 18–20). The maximum OGL damage is more than 50% of the way toward the maximum Bite II damage, though, so the remorhaz gains Bite II (dmg 1d12; threat range 17–20).

Apply the NPC's Strength modifier to the resulting *Fantasy Craft* damage.

Example: The remorhaz's *Fantasy Craft* Strength modifier is +4, so its Bite damage becomes 1d12+4.

Finally, apply any natural attack qualities needed to simulate OGL effects.

Table 6.12: Other Attack and Quality Conversions

OGL Effect	Fantasy Craft Option
Ability score damage or drain	Attribute draining extraordinary attack
Acid	Extraordinary or natural attack inflicting acid damage
Alternate form	*Shapeshifter* quality
All-around vision	*Condition immunity (flanked)* quality
Amphibious	*Aquatic II* quality
Augmented critical	*Treacherous* and/or *monstrous attack II* quality
Aura, damaging	Extraordinary attack with Aura Area
Aura, spell-like	*Natural spell* quality
Aversion to daylight	*Light-sensitive* and/or *nocturnal* quality
Barbed defense	*Natural defense* quality inflicting lethal damage
Berserk	*Feral* quality
Blindsense	*Blindsight* quality
Blindsight	*Blindsight* quality
Blood drain	Attribute (Con) draining extraordinary attack
Breath weapon	Extraordinary attack with Beam or Cone Area
Burn	Extraordinary or natural attack inflicting fire damage
Burrow	Burrow Speed *(see Step 8)*
Camouflage	*Chameleon* quality
Carapace	*Spell reflection* quality
Change shape	*Shapeshifter* quality
Climb	Athletics Signature Skill *(see Step 5)* and/or *superior climber* quality
Cold	Extraordinary or natural attack inflicting cold damage
Crush	Trample natural attack *(see Step 3)*
Constrict	Squeeze natural attack *(see Step 3)*
Create spawn	*Killing conversion* quality
Darkvision	*Darkvision* quality
Damage reduction	*Damage reduction* quality (reduce to 1/2 OGL amount, rounded down)
Daylight powerlessness	*Light-sensitive* and/or *nocturnal* quality
Death attack/ray	*Natural spell (Finger of Death)* quality
Death throes	*Death throes* quality
Despair	*Fearsome* quality
Disease	Extraordinary damage or natural attack with the *diseased* quality
Drag	Athletics Signature Skill *(see Step 5)* and/or extraordinary or natural attack with *grab* quality
Earth glide	Burrow Speed *(see Step 8)*
Energy drain	Soul draining extraordinary attack
Engulf	Swallow natural attack *(see Step 3)*
Etherealness	Spirit Type *(see Step 1)*
Evasion	*Class ability (Burglar: evasion)* quality
Fast healing	*Fast healing* and/or *Regeneration* quality
Fear	*Fearsome* quality and/or extraordinary or natural attack inflicting stress damage
Fear aura	*Fearsome* quality and/or extraordinary or natural attack inflicting stress damage
Feed	*Devour* quality
Ferocity	*Ferocity* quality
Flight	Flight Speed *(see Step 8)*
Freeze	*Chameleon II* quality
Frightful presence	*Fearsome* quality
Gaze attack	Extraordinary attack with Gaze Area
Heat	*Grueling combatant* quality and *natural defense* quality inflicting subdual damage
Hive mind	*Hive mind* quality
Hold breath	*Aquatic I* quality
Immunity to condition	*Condition immunity* quality
Immunity to damage	*Damage immunity* quality
Immunity to magic	*Spell defense* quality
Immunity to poison	*Contagion immunity* quality
Impale	Athletics Signature Skill *(see Step 5)* and/or Talon natural attack
Improved critical	*Treacherous* and/or *monstrous attack II* quality

Improved grab	Natural attack with *grab* quality
Incorporeal	Spirit Type *(see Step 1)*
Keen senses	*Improved sense* and/or *darkvision* quality
Leap	Acrobatics Signature Skill *(see Step 5)* and/or *charge attack* quality
Light blindness	*Light-sensitive* quality
Low-light vision	*Darkvision* quality
Maneuverability	Acrobatics Signature Skill *(see Step 5)*, or lack of it if the creature is clumsy
Melt weapon	Extraordinary attack inflicting fire damage
Natural weapon	Natural attack
Paralysis	Paralyzing extraordinary attack
Petrification	Petrifying extraordinary attack
Pincer	Claw natural attack
Poison	Extraordinary damage or natural attack with the *venomous* quality
Pounce	Acrobatics Signature Skill *(see Step 5)* and/or *charge attack* quality
Powerful charge	Extraordinary or natural attack
Psionics	*Natural spell* and/or *telepathic* qualities
Quickness	*Swift attack* quality
Rage	*Feat (Rage Basics)* and/or *feral* qualities
Rake	Bite or Claw natural attack
Ray	Extraordinary attack with Ray Area and/or *natural spell* quality
Regeneration	*Regeneration* quality
Rend	*Rend* quality
Resistance to energy	*Damage defiance* quality
Roar	*Fearsome* quality
Rust	Rusting extraordinary attack
Scent	*Improved sense (scent)* quality
See in darkness	*Darkvision* quality
Single actions only	*Shambling* quality
Sneak attack	*Class ability (Scout: sneak attack)* and/or *feat (Ambush Basics)* quality
Sonic attack	Extraordinary attack inflicting sonic damage
Spell immunity	*Spell defense* quality
Spell resistance	*Spell defense* quality
Spell-like ability	*Natural spell* quality
Spells	Spellcasting Signature Skill *(see Step 5)*
Split	*Splitter* quality
Stability	*Improved stability* quality
Stench	*Stench* quality
Stun	Stunning supernatural attack
Summon	*Natural spell* quality
Supernatural ability	*Natural spell* and/or other qualities
Swallow whole	Swallow natural attack
Swim	Athletics Signature Skill *(see Step 5)* and/or *aquatic* quality
Tail slap	Tail Slap natural attack
Telepathy	*Telepathic* quality
Tongues	*Telepathic* quality
Trample	Trample natural attack
Transparent	*Chameleon* quality
Tremorsense	*Blindsight* quality
Trip	Extraordinary or natural attack with the *trip* quality
True seeing	*Natural spell (True Seeing)* quality
Turn resistance	*Feat (Iron Will)* and/or *turn immunity* qualities
Uncanny dodge	*Class ability (Burglar: uncanny dodge)* quality
Vulnerable to damage	*Achilles heel* quality
Vulnerable to energy	*Achilles heel* quality
Water breathing	*Aquatic* quality
Weakness	Attribute draining extraordinary attack
Web	Entangling extraordinary attack
Wing	Slam natural attack
Wounding	Wounding extraordinary attack, or extraordinary or natural attack with the *bleed* quality

Example: The remorhaz's Bite is linked to its OGL improved grab special attack, which is easily handled in *Fantasy Craft* with the *grab* quality. The final natural attack in *Fantasy Craft* is Bite II (dmg 1d12+4; threat 17–20; upgrades: *grab*).

Don't worry if you miss something. The next step converts the rest of the NPC's attacks and you can make any necessary changes or additions there.

STEP 4: OTHER ATTACKS AND QUALITIES

This step is the trickiest, especially when converting complex characters and monsters. OGL "Special Attacks" and "Special Qualities" are flavorful in part because each one is a little different (in name and function), which makes it hard to sync every one of them up with an identical *Fantasy Craft* parallel. Most options are available but they have different names and may operate a little differently, so it's extremely helpful for you to be as familiar as possible with the regular NPC construction rules.

Start by carefully identifying what all the original options do. Include remaining non-weapon attacks as well, as the process of converting them is similar. Focus on *effects* rather than flavor, as most *Fantasy Craft* options can easily be "re-skinned" to achieve the same mechanical result through different means (an identical Wisdom drain, for example, might appear as a breath weapon on one monster and a fear aura on another).

Once you have a firm grasp of the OGL options, consult Table 6.12: Other Attack and Quality Conversions *(see page 298)*. If this doesn't provide the necessary conversions, flip through Chapters 1–3 to see if an available class ability, feat ability, or spell effect works (in which case you should grant the NPC the *class ability*, *feat*, or *natural spell* qualities). Note that some class abilities aren't available to NPCs *(see page 232)*, primarily because they interact strangely with the base NPC rules.

If you still haven't found a parallel, you may have to improvise. Fortunately, *Fantasy Craft* has a robust game system simulating a wide variety of effects with skill checks, combat actions, class and feat abilities, events, action die uses, and many other tools. One of them is likely to give you the rule you need and from there it's just a matter of adapting it to your needs.

Don't feel obliged to convert every attack and quality. It's generally only a good idea to add what you expect to use in each adventure; everything else needlessly complicates the NPC and bloats its XP. Stat blocks can and should vary a bit between adventures anyway, so leaving room for future expansion can only help.

Example: The remorhaz also has heat, which translates to the *grueling combatant* and *natural defense* (heat) qualities. It also has swallow whole, which translates to a Swallow natural attack. The OGL attack inflicts a maximum of 28 points of fire damage when the victim is consumed and an additional 48 points per round. The GM averages this damage to 38 for conversion's sake and uses Step 3 to produce a *Fantasy Craft* natural attack: Swallow III (which at Huge Size produces a maximum damage of 32 points). The remorhaz gains Swallow III (dmg 4d8+4 fire; notes: Grapple benefit — Medium and smaller only).

Table 6.13: Skill Conversion

OGL Skill	Fantasy Craft Option
Alchemy	Crafting (Chemistry)
Animal Empathy	Survival
Appraise	Haggle
Balance	Acrobatics
Bluff	Bluff
Climb	Athletics
Concentration	Resolve
Craft	Crafting
Decipher Script	Investigate
Diplomacy	Impress
Disable Device	Prestidigitation
Disguise	Disguise
Escape Artist	Athletics
Forgery	Crafting
Gather Information	Investigate
Handle Animal	Survival
Heal	Medicine
Hide	Blend or Sneak
Innuendo	Bluff
Intimidate	Intimidate
Intuit Direction	Survival
Jump	Acrobatics
Knowledge	*Interests* quality *(see page 234)*
Listen	Notice or Search
Move Silently	Sneak
Open Lock	Prestidigitation
Perform	Impress
Pick Pocket	Prestidigitation
Profession (chosen area)	None
Read Lips	Search or Sense Motive
Ride	Ride
Scry	Spellcasting
Search	Search
Sense Motive	Sense Motive
Sleight of Hand	Prestidigitation
Speak Language	*Interests* quality *(see page 234)*
Spellcraft	Investigate
Spot	Notice
Survival	Survival
Swim	Athletics
Tumble	Acrobatics
Use Magic Device	None
Use Rope	Athletics
Wilderness Lore	Survival

STEP 5: SKILLS

Fantasy Craft groups skill checks differently than most OGL games, ensuring that all characters are broadly capable, and that a point invested in one skill is just as useful as a point invested in another. Analogs are provided on Table 6.13: Skill Conversion *(see page 300)*. Competence provides a bonus for all skills except Spellcasting, so you only need to convert that (if needed) plus 1–3 of its most critical OGL skills. If the NPC has 4 or more OGL skills, convert up to 3 and increase its Competence grade by 1 per 2 skills not converted.

For each converted skill, the NPC gains the lowest possible Signature Skill grade that includes the OGL skill bonus in the Conversion Threat Level column of Table 6.1 *(see page 229)*. If no Grade includes the bonus, the NPC gains Grade X and the *bright* quality (grade equal to 1/3 the surplus bonus, rounded down).

Remember that a Signature Skill grade must exceed the NPC's Competence. When a converted grade is lower, the NPC probably doesn't need that Signature Skill.

Example: Per its OGL description, a remorhaz has Listen and Spot at +8 each. Notice and Search cover these skills in *Fantasy Craft* and at a Conversion Threat Level of 7 the +8 bonus translates to Grade II.

Table 6.14: Feat Conversion

OGL Feat	Fantasy Craft Option
Ability Focus	Extraordinary or natural attack grade
Alertness	Notice or Search Signature Skill
Awesome Blow	Knockback quality
Blind-Fight	Feat (Night Fighting) quality
Cleave	Feat (Cleave Basics) quality
Combat Casting	Resolve Signature Skill
Combat Expertise	Feat (Elusive) quality
Combat Reflexes	Feat (Combat Instincts) quality
Die-Hard	Ferocity quality
Dodge	Defense grade
Empower Spell	Feat (Spell Conversion: Effect) quality
Extra Turning	Class ability (Priest: rebuke) quality
Far Shot	Feat (Bow Mastery) quality
Flyby Attack	Feat (Charging Basics) quality
Great Cleave	Feat (Cleave Mastery) quality
Great Fortitude	Feat (Great Fortitude) quality
Improved Bull Rush	Athletics Signature Skill
Improved Critical	Monstrous attack and/or treacherous qualities
Improved Disarm	Feat (Expert Disarm) quality
Improved Initiative	Initiative grade and/or Feat (Lightning Reflexes) quality
Improved Natural Armor	Damage reduction quality, damage defiance quality, and/or damage immunity qualities
Improved Natural Attack	Extraordinary or natural attack grade
Iron Will	Feat (Iron Will) quality
Leadership	Feat (Followers) quality
Lightning Reflexes	Feat (Lightning Reflexes) quality
Multi-Attack	Feat (Darting Weapon) and/or Feat (Two-Hit Combo) qualities
Multi-Weapon Fighting	Feat (Two-Weapon Fighting) quality
Power Attack	Feat (All-Out Attack) quality
Quick Draw	Feat (Quick Draw) quality
Quicken Spell	Feat (Spell Conversion: Casting Time) quality
Run	Superior runner quality
Snatch	Extraordinary or natural attack with the grab quality
Spring Attack	Feat (Charging Basics) quality
Toughness	Feat (Combat Vigor) and/or tough qualities
Track	Survival Signature Skill
Weapon Focus	Attack grade

STEP 6: FEATS

Feats are probably the second most challenging part of conversion, with nearly as much variation as Other Attacks and Qualities. Fortunately, the number of OGL feats that find regular use is fairly narrow. *Fantasy Craft* features ready parallels for most as shown on Table 6.14: Feat Conversion *(see page 301)*. For those not listed, consult Step 4 and see if you can match the feat's effect with an NPC quality or other option.

As in the previous step, focus only on the most vital feats and ignore the rest. More than a few feats can make an NPC difficult to play anyway, requiring lots of memorization or book reference.

Example: The SRD remorhaz has 3 feats: Awesome Blow, Improved Bull Rush, and Power Attack. These translate to *knockback,* the Athletics Signature Skill, and *Feat (All-Out Attack),* respectively. The GM assigns both qualities and arbitrarily adds Athletics IV to the NPC's stat block.

STEP 7: GEAR AND TREASURE

Gear translates directly; just flip through Chapter 4 to find the appropriate item(s).

Treasure is a little less obvious. Where SRD creatures possess multiples of "standard" treasure, *Fantasy Craft* NPCs have letter-coded Treasure Rolls that can lead to a vast number of potential rewards for their defeat *(see page 344)*. Converting between these isn't difficult but requires a few choices. Start by consulting Table 6.15: Treasure Conversion *(see below)*, which shows the number of Treasure Rolls the NPC should have. The specific treasure codes (categories) should be assigned based on the NPC's personality, his background, and his role in the story. To get you started, we offer some common guidelines on Table 6.16: Treasure Roll Suggestions *(see page 303)*.

Example: A remorhaz's OGL treasure code is "None," which translates to 0 or 1 *Fantasy Craft* Treasure Rolls. The GM decides that the specific monster in his game has recently eaten a traveling royal, so he assigns a code of 1C.

Table 6.15: Treasure Conversion

OGL Treasure	Fantasy Craft Treasure Rolls
None	None or 1
1/10th Standard	1
1/2 Standard	2
Standard	3
Double Standard	4
Triple Standard	5
Quadruple Standard	6

STEP 8: REMAINING ENTRIES

With the most complicated parts of the conversion done you can run through the remainder of the OGL stats. This section covers them in the order of standard monster presentation. Any entries not listed here are ignored.

RACE AND CLASS

Fantasy Craft NPCs don't gain full race and class options but abbreviated species templates are provided on page 248 and some class abilities can be applied with a quality *(see page 235)*. As seen in the other conversion steps, you should use these options sparingly, applying only the ones that are most vital or iconic to making the NPC memorable in your game.

INITIATIVE

The NPC's Initiative grade is equal to its OGL initiative bonus + 2. If the result is 0 or lower, the NPC gains Initiative I and *critical hesitation.* If the result is 11 or higher, he gains Initiative X and *critical surge.*

Example: The remorhaz's initiative bonus is +1, so its Initiative grade becomes III.

SPEED/MOBILITY

Determine whether the NPC is a Walker, Burrower, Flier, or Swimmer as shown on page 227. Its Speeds remain unchanged, though OGL maneuverability is ignored. Apply the *banned action* quality if the NPC can't climb, jump, or swim.

Example: The remorhaz can burrow and walk so it becomes a Burrower/Walker with its OGL Speeds (20 ft. and 30 ft., respectively).

ARMOR CLASS

Add 1/2 the OGL natural armor bonus (rounded up) + Armor Class bonuses from sources other than attributes, Size, and gear. The NPC gains the lowest possible Defense grade that includes the result in the Conversion Threat Level column of Table 6.1 (minimum I). If no grade includes the result, he gains Defense X and *monstrous defense* (grade equal to 1/3 the surplus result, rounded down). If the OGL natural armor bonus is +1 or higher, he also gains *damage reduction* (1/4 the natural armor bonus, rounded up, maximum 10).

Example: The remorhaz's AC is 20 (–2 size, +1 Dex, +11 natural). Scanning down the TL 7 column, +6 translates to Defense IV. Given the natural armor bonus of +11, our fiery friend also gains *damage reduction 3.*

Table 6.16: Treasure Roll Suggestions

Type	Common Treasure Rolls	Uncommon Treasure Rolls	Rare Treasure Rolls
Animal	(C)oin, (T)rophies	(A)ny, (G)ear	(L)oot, (M)agic
Beast	(G)ear, (T)rophies	(C)oin, (L)oot	(A)ny, (M)agic
Construct	(L)oot, (M)agic	(C)oin, (G)ear	(A)ny, (T)rophies
Elemental	(A)ny, (M)agic	(C)oin, (G)ear	(L)oot, (T)rophies
Fey	(C)oin, (T)rophies	(A)ny, (M)agic	(G)ear, (L)oot
Folk	(C)oin, (G)ear	(L)oot, (M)agic	(A)ny, (T)rophies
Horror	(G)ear, (L)oot	(C)oin, (M)agic	(A)ny, (T)rophies
Ooze	(A)ny, (G)ear	(M)agic, (T)rophies	(C)oin, (L)oot
Outsider	(L)oot, (M)agic	(A)ny, (C)oin	(G)ear, (T)rophies
Plant	(A)ny, (T)rophies	(C)oin, (G)ear	(L)oot, (M)agic
Spirit	(G)ear, (M)agic	(A)ny, (C)oin	(L)oot, (T)rophies
Undead	(A)ny, (C)oin	(G)ear, (M)agic	(L)oot, (T)rophies

BASE ATTACK

The NPC gains the lowest possible Attack grade that includes his OGL base attack bonus in the Conversion Threat Level column of Table 6.1. If no grade includes the bonus, he gains Attack X and *monstrous attack* (grade equal to 1/3 the surplus bonus, rounded down).

Example: The remorhaz's base attack bonus is +7, which translates to Attack V.

REACH

Reach translates from feet into squares (1 square per 5 ft.). If any of the NPC's OGL attacks have additional reach, add the *reach* quality to the corresponding *Fantasy Craft* attacks.

Example: The remorhaz has a Reach of 10 ft., which becomes Reach 2.

SAVES

The NPC gains the lowest possible Resilience grade that includes his *second-highest* OGL save bonus in the Conversion Threat Level column of Table 6.1. If no grade includes the bonus, he gains Resilience X and *cagey* (grade equal to 1/3 the surplus bonus, rounded down).

Example: The remorhaz's second-highest save is +6, which translates to Resilience VI.

ALIGNMENT

If the NPC's Alignment is available in the current campaign, he gains the *interests* quality.

Example: The remorhaz is "usually neutral." In the unlikely event this Alignment is available in a Fantasy Craft game, the remorhaz gains *interests (Neutral Alignment).*

STEP 9: FINAL TWEAKS (OPTIONAL)

By now you should have a working *Fantasy Craft* NPC but you might still want to tinker with it a bit. If so, feel free to boost or lower his stats, add qualities, adjust gear, and make other changes as desired.

STEP 10: XP VALUE

As with a standard build, just sum the XP values from all the *Fantasy Craft* options you've applied and you're good to go! If you've created new qualities for the NPC, simply add 1 to 5 XP for each, based on how useful you think it'll be in the game.

Here's our completed example creature! XP values follow each item with a cost in brackets.

Remorhaz (Huge Animal Burrower/Walker — 85 XP): Str 18 [+8], Dex 10, Con 15 [+5], Int 5, Wis 10, Cha 10; SZ H (3×4, Reach 2 [+1]); Spd 20 ft. burrow, 30 ft. ground [+3]; Init III [+3]; Atk V [+5]; Def IV [+4]; Res VI [+6]; Health V [+5]; Comp — [+0]; Skills: Athletics IV [+4], Notice II [+2], Search II [+2]; Qualities: *Damage reduction 3* [+9], *feat (All-Out Attack)* [+2], *grueling combatant* [+2], *knockback* [+2], *natural defense (heat)* [+7], *tough I* [+5]

Attacks/Weapons: Bite I [+2] (dmg 1d12+4; threat 17–20; upgrades: *grab* [+2]), Swallow III [+6] (dmg 4d8+4 fire; notes: Grapple benefit — Medium and smaller only)

Treasure: 1C

CHAPTER 7: WORLDS

As a *Fantasy Craft* GM, you're not just a master of the game but also of your domain, which consists of two distinct worlds: the setting in which the characters live and the physical or metaphorical table where you and your friends turn ideas into adventure. You create the setting and the challenges facing the party in your communal fantasy world, and you manage rules and interpret player desire here in the real world. This may sound like a lot to handle but it's also one of the most rewarding parts of the roleplaying experience.

Let's start at the beginning, with the stars and the skies and the mountains and the seas, in those places the characters will soon call home, where their legend will soon be forged...

WORLD BUILDING

A new setting starts with a general concept and improves with every specific decision. You don't have to decide everything before you play — just the bits that are critical to the story you'd like to tell and the backgrounds of the characters the players are building. Often, you can begin with just a paragraph or two and expand as you go, discovering the world as you present it to the players. This works best for groups that have previously enjoyed fantasy RPGs together, especially if they've developed expectations about the worlds their characters inhabit.

For other groups, and those unsure where to start, this section offers a comprehensive approach, starting with general decisions and moving toward narrow ones. To get started, ask yourself a question.

WHAT'S THE SPIRIT OF YOUR GAME?

This can be a tricky question to answer but it's also one of the most important. It's difficult because it's deceptively complex, touching on many facets of play, but that's also why it's important. Defining spirit sets many expectations right up front, giving you a point of reference when making other decisions about your game. It eases the rest of the world building process.

Consider what you're after when playing a fantasy RPG. Are you mostly interested in bold and bloody action? Intense character drama? Light-hearted comedy? Complex courtly intrigue? The thrill of exploration and discovery? As you can see, the "spirit" of your game is all about how you feel when you're playing. That's the core of the question: what do you want your game's emotional impact to be?

If you're unsure, you might want to think about your favorite fantasy movies, books, and video games. What do you get out of them? Ask the same of the players and look for common ground. Imitation being one of the sincerest forms of flattery, it's perfectly acceptable to borrow flavor and even concepts. It can also makes the game more accessible, which generally translates to more fun — and fun is never bad or wrong.

WHAT'S YOUR GAME'S GENRE?

Another way to narrow your options and help your world take shape is to define your fantasy genre. This basic list is by no means complete but it covers the most common options.

Traditional Fantasy: Sometimes called "high fantasy," this genre focuses on the struggle between good and evil in a world of magic and monsters. *Examples:* Lord of the Rings; The Hobbit; The Lion, the Witch, and the Wardrobe; Dungeons & Dragons

Sword and Sorcery: This genre features brave heroes, visceral action, romance, and corrupting magic. Though the heroes may change the world, it's often by accident. *Examples:* Conan; Fafhrd and the Grey Mouser; Elric of Melnibone

Dark Fantasy: This offshoot genre infuses sword and sorcery with horror. The bad guys have won, evil is absolute, and the "good guys" are merely the least selfish of the bunch. *Examples:* Mistborn; The Black Company; Midnight; Ravenloft

Epic Fantasy: Like the champions of Greek and Norse myth, this genre's heroes are godlings, legendary generals and warriors slaying unique monsters, crushing nations, and determining the fate of the entire world. *Examples:* God of War; Beowolf; King Arthur and the Knights of the Round Table

Gonzo Fantasy: Typified by Japanese pop culture and wuxia films, this relatively new genre shamelessly embraces the most extreme elements of the spectrum, reveling in over-the-top humor, melodrama, and action. *Examples:* Crouching Tiger, Hidden Dragon; Final Fantasy; Avatar: The Last Airbender; Naruto; World of Warcraft

Political Fantasy: This genre is fraught with intrigue and danger, the heroes navigating a complex landscape of clashing kings and warring states. *Examples:* A Song of Ice and Fire; Birthright

WHAT'S YOUR GAME'S ERA?

Fantasy RPGs can span many time periods and technologies, making cultural touchstones a valuable tool in establishing your world's baseline. Medieval Europe is the most common inspiration but your game could just as easily present the exploits of prehistoric barbarians, Renaissance swashbucklers, mystical Victorians, or a thousand other characters throughout history.

For simplicity, Mastercraft divides time into "eras," each grouping a set of roughly concurrent social, cultural, and technological advancements. The *Fantasy Craft* "baseline" covers four eras: **primitive, ancient, feudal,** and **reason**. A fifth era, **industrial**, is presented to allow for slightly "futuristic" games.

Your choice of era determines the gear available in your game (as shown on the tables throughout Chapter 4).

PRIMITIVE

The earliest era covers the dawn of civilization, before the foundations of the world's first great societies. In many ways, it's analogous to the real world's Stone Age and Neolithic period.

The most common social unit of the primitive era is the tribe — a collection of individual family groups sharing resources and skills to survive. Most tribes survive as hunter-gatherers, living off the land and following migrating herds of animals as they move with the seasons.

The peoples of a primitive world are culturally unsophisticated. They rarely possess a written language, though pictographs may be common. Most live in relative isolation and languages are often confined to single tribes or close clusters of tribes.

Leaders are named in many ways. Some are divinely inspired and others gain rank through age and wisdom. Still others benefit from lineage, heroic deeds, or conquest. Warfare is generally limited to minor skirmishes and raids sparked by old feuds and desire for resources. Wandering warriors and tribal champions often become heroes in primitive settings as professional soldiers and standing armies are virtually unheard of.

Primitive technologies are based on items that are easily cultivated or modified. Metalworking is either non-existent or extremely rare, so most tools are simple and crafted from natural materials such as stone, bone, shell, obsidian, and wood. Clothing and armor are made from leather, hides, fur, and soft plant materials like cedar, grass or reeds. Transportation centers on beasts of burden and early domesticated animals like horses, mastodons, and other riding animals.

Medicine and magic are rarely distinguishable in the primitive era, with herbs, naturally-occurring drugs, and animal materials being the most common components of both tonics and spellcasting. Primitive magic often focuses on channeling natural forces and beings, while religions draw power from animistic spirits of nature, their ancestors, or great abstracted gods.

ANCIENT

The ancient era is more sophisticated and structured than its predecessor, pioneering the first steps toward science, literature, and lasting cultural advancement. Ancient societies span the Bronze Age through the classical antiquity of our world, with examples including Egypt, Greece, Rome, Sumer, India, Mexico, and China.

The basic social unit of an ancient campaign is the city-state, a small independent nation built around a particular ideal, culture, religion, or ruling dynasty that outlasts any one family or individual. Unlike primitive tribes, city-states are permanent and have set social, political, and economic structures based on birthright, species, military status, or other qualities. This complexity lets a few ancient societies grow into kingdoms, empires, or even dynasties lasting centuries and encompassing huge swaths of land.

Ancient cultures feature spoken and written languages, commonly shared across great distances thanks to expansion and conquest. Education is available but the new disciplines of literacy and philosophy are primarily confined to the wealthy and clergy. Trade and interaction with other city-states is common, and economic and political concerns are a key part of everyday life. Members of ancient societies no longer struggle to subsist, letting them specialize in trades and professions, or pursue education or the arts.

Leaders rise through many different means: social status, heredity, military conquest, popular support, and economic dominance are all common. A more diverse range of governments are seen here than in any other era, including autocracies, democracies, theocracies, and oligarchies. Warfare expands beyond simple skirmishes to bloody clashes over resources, trade, and territory, and standing armies press mercenaries, slaves, and citizens into service in roughly equal numbers.

Technology approaches but still falls a bit short of the "fantasy standard." Weapons and tools are metal (typically copper, bronze, or iron). Armor and shields are made of leather or linen, often with metal scales or rings. Huge strides in engineering allow for magnificent buildings, aqueducts, efficient farming and transport tools, and devastating weapons of war. Domesticated animals are common and medicine comes into its own, surgeons and alchemists providing reliable cures for injury and disease.

Magic and faith are highly structured, featuring pantheons of deities with distinct personalities and benefactions. Mages are philosophers and mystics with solutions to problems that society's nascent sciences can't yet solve, though magic and technology remain close enough that mages are still learned and respected advisors, philosophers, and mystics. This changes quickly in the feudal era.

FEUDAL

The "classic" fantasy era is a time of kings, knights, wars, and princesses, resembling the Dark Ages to the Late Medieval period in our world. Society becomes even more structured, with massive political, military, and social systems dwarfing all but the most heroic individuals. This is the time of Charlemagne, Byzantium, Vikings, Samurai, the Moors, the Crusades, and the Hundred Years' War.

The kingdom is the most basic feudal social unit, a fully-developed, well-armed culture with a defined social and political hierarchy. Small kingdoms rival ancient city-states, relying on trade and alliances to thrive while larger kingdoms can be entirely self-sufficient with regularly expanding borders.

Feudal societies perfect several ancient advancements, particularly those protecting the sovereignty of their leaders. Education is still uncommon but is also far more widespread, with books preserving knowledge for future generations. Languages encompass entire continents thanks to military conquest and expanding travel, though most people remain uneducated and agrarian. Strict social hierarchies limit social interaction and opportunities by class: nobility, clergy, military, and peasants.

Leaders typically gain authority by divine or heredity birthright (often, they are considered one and the same), though some earn it through conquest as well. Warfare is a premier art form, with national armies perpetually battling for king and country. Professional soldiers, such as knights and men-at-arms, may even form a warrior class, giving low-born citizens a chance to serve as a means of social advancement.

Like ancient culture, the era's technology refines what's come before. Iron and steel are widely used to manufacture weapons and armor, and complex blacksmithing techniques are making gear ever stronger and more deadly. Engineering provides feudal kingdoms with unassailable castles, magnificent places of worship, and massive siege engines to batter them down. Medicine advances but is still only available to the nobility.

Magic is as strictly segregated as social classes: divine casters are often missionaries of massive, structured faiths while arcanists lose traction in accepted circles. Increasing knowledge, the rising availability of machines, and the exhortation of the clergy make arcane casters less needed and less trusted, often driving them to form secret guilds and other elusive groups.

REASON

This is an era of incredible growth and discovery, of far-reaching exploration and conquest. New technologies and modes of travel bring wildly disparate cultures together for the first time, making it a turbulent and wondrous time to be alive. Reason encompasses our Renaissance period through our Age of Enlightenment.

The primary political and social units of the era are nations — autonomous, clearly defined countries with a distinct cultures and national identities. Not all nations are physically large but all maintain seasoned militaries and strong sets of values.

Culture is defined by curiosity and humanism, which is a far cry from the stricture and willful ignorance of the feudal era. Education, literacy, and knowledge are widely available to the masses for the first time, thanks to printing, philosophers, and national leaders. The inexorable advance of science and technology paves the way for amazing discoveries, freeing the common man to engage in professional and intellectual pursuits. Star-charting, refined mapping, and other navigation advances help explorers travel beyond and between continents, and languages spread through extensive trade, learning, and military networks.

Hereditary and military leadership are still most common but individuals also rise to power by accumulating wealth, gaining popular support, and simple, underhanded scheming. Nations may be led by a wider array of characters, including merchant princes and great philosophers. Warfare remains a vital facet of international relations and it's bloodier than ever, though diplomatic and economic alliances are on the rise. 'Warrior' is a profession rather than a social caste.

Science impacts nearly every aspect of life. Gunpowder changes warfare forever, prompting armorers to shift away from heavy plate to light and flexible suits that encourage mobility (read: dodging). As an added benefit, these suits can also be worn socially, which helps to integrate warriors more fundamentally into other circles. Machinery is available and often mastered by common folk. Transport includes grand wagons and great ships (some even floating on air), and medicine becomes available to the masses through chemists and professional healers.

The advancement of science also has a great impact on religion and magic. As people gain new options for their ills, they start to rely less on their faiths, at least for healing. Technology continues to displace magic, forcing mages to specialize and cloister, though some embrace and change with the times. These few, and their divine counterparts, use their power in new and exciting ways, experimenting as much as the great thinkers of the time.

INDUSTRIAL

Steam, steel, and strife define this era, which is a time of empires, revolution, and the triumph of science. In these and many other ways, the industrial era is like our own 19th century.

The industrial era's basic social unit is the empire, which acts like a nation but spans continents or even entire worlds. Empires are sometimes leagues of independent nations though they can also be massive colonizing powers ruled by a powerful individual or governing body. Relations between empires are formal and complex, and when war becomes the sentiment of the day it's comparatively brief and decisive.

Refinement and pursuit of perfection are hallmarks of the industrial era. Colonizing powers seek to conquer their subjects militarily and culturally, stamping out "savage" peoples and converting those who submit. As a result, languages and faiths tend to spread worldwide, as do books and education. Long-distance communication methods develop toward the end of this era, permitting rapid communication between empires, and travel is likewise improved via steam-, coal-, and arcane-powered engines.

A new leader arrives in the form of the revolutionary, who employs radical ideas like socialism and democracy to fuel his cause. The revolutionary threatens the sovereignty of industrial empires, sparking as many internal wars as colonists ignite abroad. The status of the army is also in flux during this period, as common firearms cheapen life and let empires field less-trained warriors. The bloody meat-grinder of modern warfare is just a few steps away.

Industrial technology focuses primarily on speed and volume, drawing society away from artisanship to mass production of easily replaced items. Gunpowder weapons approach the apex of their development, making melee weapons and armor obsolete without specialized training. Complex devices like clockwork and steam-powered gadgets are increasingly common and locomotives, steamships, zeppelins, and other mechanical transports dominate the roads, rails, and skies of the world. Medicine is still crude by modern standards but is nonetheless an exacting science, with doctors and surgeons applying widely-accepted techniques.

Magic often combines with science in the industrial era, resulting in magical technologies beyond imagination. "Steampunk" sorcerers create lightning bolt guns, time-travel sleds, clockwork animals, and other wild gadgetry that baffles even modern minds. A few mages continue to reject science, however, retreating from society to become witches and cultists.

WHAT DO PEOPLE BELEIVE?

Belief systems are an integral part of fantasy, ranging from worship of specific, strongly characterized deities (as in the Norse, Greek, and Egyptian pantheons) to axiomatic moral codes (like Good, Evil, Order, and Chaos) to abstracted philosophies and cosmological viewpoints (like Far Eastern elemental affinities). Beliefs form a common ground for characters of diverse ethnicities, geographies, and occupations, and often drive devotees to rise above their roots, to get involved and potentially change the world.

In *Fantasy Craft,* beliefs are represented by **Alignment**. Each character may only have one Alignment at a time, though each Alignment may feature multiple beliefs.

Example: A simple dark fantasy game may feature only two Alignments: Good and Evil. Characters without an Alignment are neutral, which means their beliefs either don't fall in line with the world's established faiths or are too mild to warrant a full Alignment.

Alternately, in a traditional fantasy game, each Alignment may consist of a single choice from each of two different pairs: Good or Evil, Order or Chaos. Characters can be Good and Order, Good and Chaos, Evil and Order, or Evil and Chaos. Again, neutrality means a character falls outside the accepted norms or is without powerful beliefs.

Ask yourself four primary questions when defining your world's beliefs.

- What Alignments are available?
- How do Alignments impact society?
- Are miracles real?
- If miracles are real, how do they impact society?

Don't worry if you're not ready. These questions are important for every world but you may not have a firm enough handle on your idea to answer them yet. If that's the case, skip forward to magic *(see page 314)* and come back to this section later.

WHAT ALIGNMENTS ARE AVAILABLE?

First and foremost, Alignments are *optional.* Not every world's beliefs are strong or structured enough to require them, and unless miracles are real Alignments boil down to glorified Interests *(see page 61).* They can still be useful to support religious factions and as ways to expand character backgrounds, however.

If you want to include Alignments, consider the hallmarks of belief in your world. Concentrate on the things that attract the most loyal and/or numerous followers. Alignments can focus on anything: gods, moral codes, ethical ideals, rules of etiquette, viewpoints, elements, constellations, animals, bloodlines, nations, colors, symbols... The sky's the limit. Your world can even feature Alignments of multiple types (bloodlines and stars, for example), though the options can get complex fast so it's probably best to start small: pick one set and jot down all the options you'd like characters to have (e.g. for elements, you might jot down "Air, Earth, Fire, and Water").

Likewise, Alignments can be organized however you want. Characters may choose one item from a list (one element: Air, Earth, Fire, or Water), or choose one item each from multiple lists (e.g. Good or Evil and Order or Chaos). A character's Alignment consists of all choices made. Remember, *each character may only possess one Alignment at a time.*

HOW DO ALIGNMENTS IMPACT SOCIETY?

Alignment can be an integral and perhaps mandatory part of daily life (e.g. in a culture that reveres constellations and divides their calendar into seasons accordingly, everyone might be born under a specific group of stars), or it can be a decision made by worshippers (e.g. each character choosing whether to adhere to one of a common set of ideals or not). It can be based on irrefutable truth (e.g. gods who walk among men) or driven entirely by faith (e.g. cults formed around differing religious interpretations of ancient script, despite evidence that the script is nothing more than a mundane primitive language).

These are just two of the most profound ways Alignment can shape your world. There are, of course, countless more. Are established orders devoted to some or all Alignments, or are each character's beliefs purely personal? If orders exist, how do they interact with each other and the rest of society? Are

Table 7.1: Example Alignments

Alignment	Alignment Skills	Paths	Ritual Weapon	Avatar *	Opposed Alignments
Elements					
Air	Acrobatics, Blend, Investigate, Prestidigitation	Air, Travel	Boomerang	Air Elemental V	Earth
Earth	Athletics, Crafting, Ride, Survival	Earth, Metal	Maul	Earth Elemental V	Air
Fire	Acrobatics, Athletics, Bluff, Ride	Fire, War	Jagged sword	Fire Elemental V	Water
Water	Disguise, Search, Sneak, Tactics	Life, Water	Bullwhip	Water Elemental V	Fire
Traditional Fantasy Alignments					
Chaos	Acrobatics, Disguise, Prestidigitation, Survival	Chaos, Destruction	Hand claw	Chaos Beast	Order
Evil	Blend, Bluff, Ride, Sneak	Evil, Darkness	Scourge	Anarchy Demon	Good
Good	Athletics, Haggle, Ride, Tactics	Good, Light	Bastard sword	Guardian Angel	Evil
Order	Crafting, Investigate, Search, Tactics	Order, Protection	Long staff	Stone Golem	Chaos

* These elementals can be found in the Grimoire *(see page 125)*. The traditional fantasy avatars are in the Bestiary *(see page 253)*.

they endorsed by, sponsored by, or perhaps a part of the world's governments (or vice-versa)? Do they have allies and enemies?

A character's Alignment might demand little of him (e.g. mild dietary requirements or short, unobtrusive rituals) or represent a major commitment (e.g. daily regimen and/or hefty tithes). The same is true — perhaps more true — of orders focusing on Alignments, which often develop extensive expectations of members, along with detailed selection processes to dissuade casual observers.

If divine powers exist, they may be keenly interested in the lives of mortals (like the Greek gods) or they might be cold and indifferent (like the gods of Hyboria). They may exist in harmony or oppose each other (with obvious ramifications for believers should the powers make themselves known).

Again, skip ahead if you're unsure how to address some or all of these possibilities. The gaps may be filled by other decisions in the world building process. If not, and you're still unsure when you have what you consider enough to get playing, you can always follow up when you need to know.

ARE MIRACLES REAL?

In fantasy RPGs, belief can be a palpable force, gifting the devout with supernatural assistance and/or various controllable abilities and spells. This power can be granted by a god, tap latent reserves of mystic or magical clout, align a character with various sources of external energy, or come from somewhere else. You may define the source and nature of any miraculous power however you like but for the purposes of game play you only need to start with one question: Do miracles ever happen in any form? If not, you can skip forward to magic *(see page 314)*.

If miracles do happen, start by applying the *miracles* campaign quality *(see page 324)*. Then ask yourself two questions. The answer to one or both should be yes.

- Do characters benefit from unexpected miracles? If so, then you may (and periodically should) use Narrative Control to produce these effects *(see page 366)*.
- Can characters invoke miracles? If so, then they need to gain access to Paths *(see page 310)*. The most common way this occurs is through classes like the Priest and the Paladin *(see pages 44 and 56)*, though the Blessed feat grants a single Step *(see page 105)*. If you'd rather not feature divine caster classes, you can work Paths into another part the system, such as feats (1 Step per "New Step" feat) or Career Levels (1 Step every 2 or 4 Levels, starting at Level 1), though the latter isn't balanced, increasing PC power at no actual "cost."

When the *miracles* quality is applied, each Alignment also gains several game features defined by its concept and description (which can include its patronage(s), common followers, and any other details you deem relevant).

Paths: Choose 2–5 Paths that flavorfully represent the Alignment *(see page 310)*.

Alignment Skills: Choose 4 skills, excluding any that are already class skills for one or more divine caster classes in your game (i.e. in the default *Fantasy Craft* game, which features the Priest and the Paladin, you should exclude Impress, Intimidate, Medicine, Notice, Resolve, or Sense Motive). The chosen skills become class skills for divine caster classes in your game.

Ritual Weapon: Choose a specific weapon wielded by devout followers of the Alignment (e.g. a sickle for a nature deity or a broad axe for the god of executioners). Make sure this weapon is available in your game's era.

Avatar: Choose or build a specific NPC or creature, up to 120 XP, as the Alignment's incarnate representative in the physical world (e.g. a Guardian Angel of Good or a Dire Mammoth for a Thunder Alignment).

Opposed Alignments (Optional): Some Alignments clash so fiercely that their followers automatically become adversaries. In these cases the Alignments become "opposed," triggering or altering many class abilities and spells.

Here's an example. You can also find the traditional fantasy Alignments (Good and Evil, Order and Chaos) and an elemental set on Table 7.1: Example Alignments *(see page 308)*.

DEGMOS STONE-FATHER

Degmos is the Dwarven patron of blacksmiths, warriors, and fathers. He's a cold and stern god, and his clergy are grim and wizened, prone to espousing his manly wisdom on craft and home life to all who'll listen (and some who'd rather not). Degmos' devotees routinely wage holy crusades against the goblins threatening the god's temples and protected territories.

Paths: Earth, Metal, Strength

Alignment Skills: Athletics, Crafting, Search, Survival

Ritual Weapon: Mallet

Avatar: Earth elemental V *(see page 125)*

Opposed Alignments: Razgeth Bloodblade, Demon Lord of Goblins

LOSING YOUR RELIGION

Like characters, beliefs change over time: a god may abandon a character; an Alignment may become unavailable; or a significant event may leave a character questioning his values or even the order of the universe. Any situation in which the character loses his Alignment, voluntarily or not, prompts a Crisis of Faith Subplot *(see page 381)*. In a game with the *miracles* quality, this Subplot gains several special rules.

- The character loses his Alignment but does not lose the Interest "slot" *(see page 61)*. Instead, it becomes frozen until the Subplot ends, at which point he may fill the slot with his new Alignment.

- For the duration of the Subplot, the character loses access to his Alignment Paths, skills, avatar, class abilities, feat abilities, and other character options requiring or supporting an Alignment. He gains access to his new Alignment's options and may re-allocate his Steps when the Subplot ends.
- The character retains his ritual weapon but loses access to any special abilities or options related to or supported by it for the duration of the Subplot. Thereafter, he receives his new Alignment's ritual weapon.

If Subplots are not part of your game, the character instead permanently loses access to the Interest slot, as well as his current Paths, skills, avatar, class abilities, feat abilities, and other character options requiring or supporting an Alignment. He must devote a new Interest slot to an Alignment to gain access to its options. He may re-allocate Steps at that time as well, along Paths associated with his new Alignment.

HOW DO MIRACLES IMPACT SOCIETY?

When belief has a palpable impact on the world, the world tends to sit up and take notice. Supernatural manifestations, especially those clearly prompted by a higher power, have a profound influence on society. They bring people together (in religious groups, governments, or civilizations) and tear them apart (particularly when miracles come from opposed Alignments). They beget champions to spread the word and smite infidels, and forge resentful enemies even when there's no clear benefit in opposing the faith. Sadly, they also spark bloody, bitter wars beyond imagination.

All these things can and do happen without true miracles, which is all the more reason to seriously consider the reactions of a society faced with genuine power beyond their control — and perhaps beyond their understanding. What do worshippers hope to gain from their Alignments and how do they use them in everyday life? How do religious factions leverage their followers' power and how do governments and other groups respond?

If your game features Priests and Paladins, are they trained by and/or answer to one or more religious factions? Whether they do or not, what's their role in society? Are they soldiers, activists, saviors, or all three? Are their services available to the masses or restricted to the elite? What special allowances and indulgences do they enjoy? How heavily do others rely on them to survive and/or thrive?

Widely accepted miracles can prompt all these questions and many more. Rare, if not unknown, is the world that witnesses such power without fundamental change.

THE FLAVOR OF MIRACLES AND MAGIC

When miracles and magic are real, your choices don't end with their impact on society. You can also decide how these incredible powers look, sound, and feel, both to observers and those invoking them. Is every miracle accompanied by a sense of euphoria? Does every arcane spell make the hairs on the back of your neck stand up? You can go without this extra description, of course, but where's the fun in that?

Adding flavor is simple: think in terms of the five senses and choose key visual, auditory, tactile, olfactory, and gustatory cues as desired. One or two for each (miracles and magic) is plenty unless you're really inspired. Cues can also be set for individual abilities and spells, or groups, but to avoid information overload you should probably reserve that option for effects important to the plot. This option's handy when you want to spark a player realization with narration (e.g. "The room floods with the smell of sulfur.").

PATHS

Alignments are often complex and multidimensional, with many facets expressing their personality or influence, or that of the power behind them. For example, the indifferent Cimmerian god Crom is patron of strength, martial prowess, and craftsmanship, while the culture's evil god Set grants his followers magical skill, great and mysterious secrets, and hypnotic attractiveness. In *Fantasy Craft*, these facets are represented by "Paths," spheres of influence that may be tapped by an Alignment's followers when the *miracles* quality is applied.

There are five **Steps** along each Path, each granting one or more miraculous abilities and/or spells. A single Alignment can feature two to five Paths and each time a character with that Alignment is permitted to take a Step, he may take it along any one his Alignment's Paths.

Example: Fallow, a Priest, is Aligned to the dwarf god Degmos *(see page 309)*, which grants him access to the Earth, Metal, and Strength Paths. At Level 1, Fallow's *acolyte* ability lets him take a Step along one of his Paths. He chooses Metal I, which grants him the Crafting (Metalworking) focus and a +5 bonus with Crafting (Metalworking) checks. Two class levels later, *path of the devoted* lets Fallow take another Step. He chooses Strength I, which grants him a +5 bonus with Athletics checks. After another two class levels, Fallow may gain Earth I, Metal II, or Strength II (but only one of those three).

CASTING PATH SPELLS

When a character casts a spell granted by a Path, he's considered a divine caster *(see page 110)*.

PATH OF AIR

Air I: You gain Bang and Electrical Resistance equal to 3 times your Air Step.

Air II: You may convert damage inflicted by your melee and unarmed attacks to electrical damage. You may also cast Gust of Wind once per scene.

Air III: You may cast Air Walk and Wall of Wind once per scene.

Air IV: You may cast Call Lightning II and Control Weather III once per scene.

Air V: You may cast Deadly Draft II and Control Weather IV once per scene.

PATH OF BEASTS

Beasts I: You gain the Animal Partner feat.

Beasts II: You may cast Hold Animal and Nature's Ally I once per scene.

Beasts III: You may Turn animals a number of times per combat equal to your Beasts Step.

Beasts IV: All your Animal Partners' Threat Levels are equal to your Career Level.

Beasts V: You may cast Nature's Ally IV and Wild Side III once per scene.

PATH OF BEAUTY

Beauty I: You gain the Comely feat.

Beauty II: You may cast Charm Person I once per scene. You also gain *beguiling (see page 231)*.

Beauty III: You gain the Elegant feat.

Beauty IV: You may roll twice when making an Impress check, keeping the result you prefer.

Beauty V: You may cast Charm Person IV once per scene. You also gain the Enchanting feat.

PATH OF CHAOS

Chaos I: When you roll an action die to boost an Alignment skill check and the number shown is odd, double it and add it to your result; when the number shown is even, subtract it from your result instead.

Chaos II: One of your attributes, determined at random, rises by 1. Also, you may cast Entropic Shield once per scene.

Chaos III: You may cast Confounding Images and Devotion Hammer once per scene.

Chaos IV: Once per scene, you may increase your threat and error ranges by 4 each.

Chaos V: One of your attributes, determined at random, rises by 2. Also, you may cast Scintillating Pattern once per scene.

PATH OF CURSES

Curses I: You gain the Black Cat feat.

Curses II: You may cast Blindness/Deafness and Ray of Enfeeblement once per scene.

Curses III: You may cast Bestow Curse and Geas once per scene.

Curses IV: You gain the Jinx feat.

Curses V: You may cast Insanity III and Maze once per scene.

PATH OF DARKNESS

Darkness I: You gain *darkvision I (see page 233)* and a +5 bonus with Sneak checks as long as you're not in direct sunlight.

Darkness II: You may cast Blur and Darkness I once per scene.

Darkness III: You may cast Darkness II and Phantasmal Killer once per scene.

Darkness IV: You may cast Mass Cause Wounds III and Shadow Walk once per scene.

Darkness V: Once per scene, you may become *incorporeal* for a number of rounds equal to your starting action dice.

PATH OF DEATH

Death I: Each of your attacks against a living character inflicts 2 additional damage. You may also cast Deathwatch at will.

Death II: You may cast Death Knell and Dominate Undead I once per scene.

Death III: You may cast Animate Dead II and Speak with the Dead once per scene.

Death IV: You may inflict critical hits on undead characters. You may also cast Animate Dead III once per scene.

Death V: You may cast Dominate Undead II and Finger of Death once per scene.

PATH OF DECEIT

Deceit I: You gain the Repartee Basics feat.

Deceit II: You may cast Disguise Self and Mirror Images once per scene.

Deceit III: You may cast Flawless Fib and Invisibility once per scene.

Deceit IV: Your Charisma score rises by 1 and you may cast Project Presence once per scene.

Deceit V: You gain the *bald-faced lie* class ability *(see page 31)*.

PATH OF DESTRUCTION

Destruction I: Each of your melee and unarmed attacks gains the *armor-piercing* quality equal to your Destruction Step.

Destruction II: You may convert damage inflicted by your melee and unarmed attacks to acid damage. Also, you may cast Shatter once per scene.

Destruction III: You may cast Counter Magic I and Rusting Grasp once per scene.

Destruction IV: You may cast Harm and Quake Touch once per scene.

Destruction V: Each of your attacks inflicts 4 additional damage. Also, you may cast Disintegrate once per scene.

PATH OF EARTH

Earth I: You gain the Pathfinder Basics (caverns/mountains) feat.

Earth II: You may Turn constructs once per combat and cast Magic Stone once per scene.

Earth III: You can burrow at 1/2 your Ground Speed and cast Shape Stone once per scene.

Earth IV: You may cast Move Earth and Wall of Stone once per scene.

Earth V: Your Constitution score rises by 2 and you may cast Earthquake once per scene.

PATH OF EVIL

Evil I: You inflict additional damage against *helpless* and *sprawled* characters equal to your Evil Step.

Evil II: You may cast Consecrate and Scare II once per scene.

Evil III: You may cast Castigate I and Cause Wounds III once per scene.

Evil IV: You gain the Horror Type and *unnerving (see pages 227 and 235).*

Evil V: You may cast Purge and Sacred Aura once per scene.

PATH OF FIRE

Fire I: You gain Fire and Heat Resistance equal to 3 times your Fire Step.

Fire II: You may convert damage inflicted by your melee and unarmed attacks to fire damage. You may also cast Scorching Ray once per scene.

Fire III: You may cast Conjure Elemental II (fire elementals only) and Fireball I once per scene.

Fire IV: You may cast Elemental Shield (fire) and Wall of Fire once per scene.

Fire V: You may cast Fire Storm and Fireball II once per scene.

PATH OF FORTUNE

Fortune I: You gain the Fortunate feat.

Fortune II: You may activate a threat as a critical hit or success without spending an action die a number of times per session equal to your Fortune Step.

Fortune III: You gain a magic bonus with action die results equal to your Fortune Step.

Fortune IV: You may use your Fortune II and Fortune III abilities on allies you can see and hear.

Fortune V: You gain the *proven worth* class ability *(see page 48).*

PATH OF GOOD

Good I: You gain a bonus when contributing to cooperative checks equal to your Good Step.

Good II: You may cast Calm Emotions and Consecrate once per scene.

Good III: You may cast Castigate I and Prayer once per scene.

Good IV: You gain the Angelic Heritage feat.

Good V: You may cast Purge and Sacred Aura once per scene.

PATH OF HEROISM

Heroism I: You gain two bonus action dice at the start of each Dramatic scene. You may immediately give one of these dice to a hero who can see or hear you.

Heroism II: You may cast Command I and Heroism I once per scene.

Heroism III: You gain the *battle planning I* class ability *(see page 34).*

Heroism IV: You may cast Heroes' Feast and Heroism II once per scene.

Heroism V: You gain DR 4/special characters.

PATH OF KNOWLEDGE

Knowledge I: You gain a +5 bonus with Knowledge checks.

Knowledge II: You may cast Detect Emotions and Insight once per scene.

Knowledge III: Choose one Alignment skill. Your maximum rank in that skill increases to your Career Level + 8.

Knowledge IV: You may cast True Seeing and Tongues II once per scene.

Knowledge V: Your Intelligence score rises by 2 and you may cast Hindsight once per scene.

PATH OF LIFE

Life I: You gain the Bandage feat.

Life II: You may cast Cure Wounds II and Restoration I once per scene.

Life III: You may cast Cure Wounds IV and Neutralize Poison once per scene.

Life IV: You may cast Heal and Mass Cure Wounds II once per scene.

Life V: You may cast Regenerate and Resurrection I once per adventure.

PATH OF LIGHT

Light I: You're immune to flash damage. You may also cast Flare and Glow I at will.

Light II: You gain a trick:

Blinding Blow (Ritual Weapon or Unarmed Attack Trick): Your target must also make a Fort save (DC equal to damage inflicted) or be *blinded* for 1 round. You may use this trick a number of times per combat equal to your Light Step.

Light III: You may cast Glow II and Searing Ray once per scene.

Light IV: You may cast Light's Grace and Sunlight I once per scene.

Light V: You may cast Scintillating Pattern and Sunlight II once per scene.

PATH OF MAGIC

Magic I: You may Read Magic at will and gain a +2 magic bonus with saves vs. spells.

Magic II: You may cast Detect Magic and Identify I once per scene.

Magic III: You may cast Counter Magic I once per scene. Also, your bonus with saves vs. spells increases by 2 (total 4).

Magic IV: You may cast Anti-Magic Field and Identify II once per scene.

Magic V: You may cast Counter Magic II once per scene. Also, your bonus with saves vs. spells increases by 2 (total 6).

PATH OF METAL

Metal I: You gain the Crafting (Metalworking) focus and a +5 bonus with Crafting (Metalworking) checks.

Metal II: Each metal weapon you own gains a gear bonus to damage equal to your Metal Step. You may also cast Tinker II once per scene.

Metal III: You gain a 20% discount when purchasing metal armor/weapons. You may also cast Keen Edge once per scene.

Metal IV: You gain Metal Weapon Resistance 4.

Metal V: Your metal gear can never be broken or destroyed. You may also cast Iron Body once per scene.

PATH OF NATURE

Nature I: You gain a +5 bonus with Survival checks.

Nature II: You may cast Entangle and Pass without Trace once per scene.

Nature III: You may cast Tree Walk and Verdure once per scene.

Nature IV: You may cast Natural Attunement and Nature's Ally III once per scene.

Nature V: You may cast Conjure Elemental IV and Control Weather IV once per scene.

PATH OF ORDER

Order I: When you roll an action die to boost an Alignment skill check and the number shown is less than your Wisdom modifier, it becomes equal to your Wisdom modifier (minimum +1). This may not cause the action die to explode.

Order II: Your lowest attribute rises by 1 and you may cast Zone of Truth once per scene.

Order III: You may cast Devotion Hammer and Mantle of the Mundane once per scene.

Order IV: You may cast Mark of Justice and Permanency once per scene.

Order V: Your lowest attribute rises by 2 and you may cast Purge once per scene.

PATH OF PROTECTION

Protection I: You gain a +5 bonus with Notice checks.

Protection II: You gain an insight bonus to Defense equal to your Protection Step. You may also cast Shield Other once per scene.

Protection III: You may cast Glyph of Protection I and Resilient Sphere I once per scene.

Protection IV: When you or a teammate makes a saving throw, the roll is made twice, keeping the result you prefer. You may also cast Wall of Counter Magic once per scene.

Protection V: You may cast Protection from Spells and Lift Curse III once per scene.

PATH OF SECRETS

Secrets I: You gain a +5 bonus with Bluff checks.

Secrets II: You may cast Obscure Object and Pass without Trace once per scene.

Secrets III: You gain the *cold read* class ability *(see page 30).*

Secrets IV: You gain the Repartee Supremacy feat.

Secrets V: You may cast Mind Blank and Mass Invisibility once per scene.

PATH OF SPIRITS

Spirits I: You gain Spirit Resistance equal to your Spirits Step. You may also cast Dancing Lights and Whispers at will.

Spirits II: Your Wisdom score rises by 1 and you may cast Scrye I once per scene.

Spirits III: You may cast Dimension Door and See Invisible once per scene.

Spirits IV: Your Wisdom score rises by 1 and you may cast Living Library II once per scene.

Spirits V: You gain the *virtues of command I* class ability *(see page 35).*

PATH OF STRENGTH

Strength I: You gain a +5 bonus with Athletics checks.

Strength II: You may cast Brawn I (Strength or Constitution) twice per scene.

Strength III: Your Size increases by 1 category (max. Large).

Strength IV: You gain Unarmed and Natural Attack Resistance 4.

Strength V: Your Strength score rises by 4.

PATH OF TRAVEL

Travel I: Your Speed increases by 5 ft. and you may cast Orient Self at will.

Travel II: You may cast Knock and Jump once per scene.

Travel III: Your Speed increases by an additional 5 ft. and you may cast Freedom of Movement once per scene.

Travel IV: Your Speed increases by an additional 5 ft. and you may cast Find the Path once per scene.

Travel V: Your Speed increases by an additional 5 ft. and you may cast Phase Door once per scene.

PATH OF WAR

War I: You inflict additional damage with your ritual weapon equal to your War Step.

War II: You may cast Mage Armor and True Strike I once per combat.

War III: You gain the Contempt feat.

War IV: You gain a trick:

War God's Blessing (Ritual Weapon or Unarmed Attack Trick): If your target is a standard NPC with DR 4 or less, he automatically fails a Damage save (no damage roll required). You may use this trick once per round.

War V: Your Strength score rises by 2 and you may cast War Cry once per scene.

PATH OF WATER

Water I: You gain a bonus with Reflex saves equal to your Water Step. You may also cast Create Water and Water Walk at will.

Water II: You gain *aquatic II* and *superior swimmer IV*.

Water III: You may cast Move Water and Wall of Ice once per scene.

Water IV: You may cast Cone of Cold and Winter's Domain II once per scene.

Water V: You gain the *take heart* class ability *(see page 48)*.

PATH OF WILDERNESS

Wilderness I: You gain the Pathfinder Basics feat and may cast Endure Elements at will.

Wilderness II: You may cast Goodberry and Concealing Countryside I once per scene.

Wilderness III: You gain the Pathfinder Mastery feat.

Wilderness IV: You gain the Pathfinder Supremacy feat.

Wilderness V: You gain the *master tracker 1/session* class ability *(see page 50)*.

CAN PEOPLE CAST SPELLS?

Common and powerful spells are often synonymous with fantasy, though they don't have to be. In the Arthurian legends and the Lord of the Rings trilogy spells are cast only by a select few (any of whom may be NPCs, depending on how the material is adapted). Other possible inspirations, like the Gormenghast and Kushiel novels, feature no spellcasting at all.

If spellcasting is possible, apply the *sorcery* campaign quality *(see page 325)*. Then ask yourself two questions. The answer to one or both should be yes.

- Can characters cast spells? If so, then you should allow one or more arcane caster classes (in this book, the Mage and perhaps the Alchemist and/or Rune Knight).
- Can NPCs cast spells? If so, then apply the Spellcasting Signature Skill as desired *(see page 228)*.

If only one may cast spells, develop a reason why. Maybe spellcasting is restricted to an elite class (all of whom are player or other special characters). On the flip side, spellcasting might be the exclusive province of diabolists (NPCs) who are encroaching upon a civilized, non-magic society (the PCs' home).

You can also limit spellcasting in your world by excluding any spells you think will be problematic. Note that this has a ripple effect across the system, eliminating certain gear (especially scrolls and elixirs), and potentially certain character options as well (including certain Path Steps).

If people can cast in your setting, you should also define how spells are acquired. It can be as simple as new formulae "dawning" on casters as they grow in power, it can involve complex and specific quests, or the process may be unique to your world.

HOW DOES SPELLCASTING IMPACT SOCIETY?

The ability to bend reality to one's will is monumental, touching every corner of civilization, from civic life and health to business and war. Imagine a world where magical healing rendered medicine, and perhaps even natural healing, obsolete... Where effective long-range scrying dominated espionage without risking a single life... Where a thriving golem industry eliminated the need for common labor? None of these worlds would, or could, progress as we expect. All of them would revolve in some way around magic.

The effects of spellcasting don't have to be this widespread but to make this happen you need to think about the nature and limitations of magic. Is it an omnipresent power understood by everyone or an elusive secret protected by a guarded cabal? Is it easily mastered or an exacting specialty trained by a select few? Is it safe and painless or fraught with peril and woe? The second answer to each of these questions can help curb the sweeping impact of spellcasting and simultaneously give magic some character in your world.

These questions may naturally lead you to define the origins of magic, which can also help structure additional limitations. Spells won't change the world quite as much if every casting destroys valuable components, or drains the life forces of those in the vicinity (perhaps even the caster), or weakens the veil between your world and... another (presumably more dangerous) place.

With the origin, nature, and limitations of spellcasting in hand, you can start to ask the tough questions. Who casts spells and why? Are spells tools of war, commerce, healing, transport, theft, all of these things, or something else entirely? Who employs casters and toward what end? Do groups or governments support, protect, capture, or eradicate spellcasters? When, how, and why are they trained? How are they viewed by the general populace in each region? Try to imagine what living in your world must be like given your vision of magic, and expand from there.

WHAT SPECIES EXIST IN YOUR GAME?

With all the metaphysical questions answered for your world, it's time to sprinkle mortals across the land! There are two things to consider here: heroic species and monsters.

WHAT ARE YOUR HEROIC SPECIES?

By default, *Fantasy Craft* features twelve heroic (playable) species: drakes, dwarves, elves, giants, goblins, humans, ogres, orcs, pech, rootwalkers, saurians, and unborn. This assumes an extremely diverse high fantasy setting, which may not be to your liking. Feel free to prohibit any of these, making them monsters *(see next)* or excluding them altogether.

Next, take a moment to personalize each of your heroic species. In your world, do their appearances vary from the Origin descriptions? Do they have an unusual history? How commonly are they seen? Do they have population centers (cities, towns, or villages) or live in the wild? Do they have common characteristics, personality traits, or quirks? Do they speak a unique language? Do they specialize in anything or have any cultural weaknesses? Do they favor or eschew certain weapons, gear, or tactics?

After you've run *Fantasy Craft* a couple times and you're comfortable with the rules, you might also want to consider which splinter races are available in your world and how they interact with the root species and each other. The easiest way to do this is to look through the Species feats *(see page 99)*, identifying which you want to disallow and/or make monsters, and answering important questions for those available to the players.

WHICH MONSTERS EXIST?

The Bestiary in Chapter 6 includes over 70 unique monster types and many more individual monsters and template combinations. This dizzying menagerie can easily populate hundreds of unique fantasy worlds or overrun a single high fantasy setting. It isn't necessary to decide whether each and every one is part of your game right off the bat — and in fact, it's counterproductive.

Instead, ask whether any are iconic adversaries. It's generally a good idea to start with at least three to five monsters the characters can immediately identify as "the enemy." Remember that heroic species can also be monsters, whether they're disallowed to player characters or not.

You don't need to answer nearly as many questions about monsters, nor do you have to go into as much detail. Unless you'd like to change something, you can keep it as simple as a list of iconics and maybe another for those you're sure will never appear.

CHANGING THE RULES

Fantasy Craft's heroic species and monsters are based on commonly accepted concepts (with a few interesting twists to keep things interesting and "kick it up a notch"). However, you're in no way obliged to include them as is, and making a few changes is a great way to add a bit of extra personality to your setting. Perhaps in your world only elves have the gift of magic. Maybe dwarves can't ride mounts. Brain fiends might be mute and drakes might be wingless (flying magically, mechanically, or not at all).

Many adjustments to heroic species are simple: swapping out attribute modifiers and bonus feats, for example. You can also restrict base and expert classes, Specialties, and even feats to or from a species, and apply the *banned action* quality to keep certain skills or combat activities out of a species' hands. There's a careful balance in play throughout the system but a few minor tweaks here and there aren't going to break anything. If you're really worried, visit the Crafty Games forum (**www.crafty-games.com**), where new rules are constantly being devised, reviewed, and tested.

Monster adjustments are even easier and perfectly balanced at all times — simply add, remove, or swap the abilities you want and modify the XP value accordingly!

STIRRING THE MELTING POT

Finally, take a look at your heroic species and monsters and think about how they interact. Is the world basically civilized with pockets of monsters or overrun by creatures surrounding a few beleaguered points of light? Which species and/or monsters trade with each other and how (e.g. across established naval channels, with informal merchant caravans, or maybe through a thriving black market)? Are any species allied or at war with others? Is interspecies sex and/or marriage common or taboo? Is there racial or ethnic prejudice and if so, is it merely chilly (like the old grudges between dwarves and elves in The Lord of the Rings) or violent (akin to the savage wars between dwarves and goblins in the mines of Moria)?

Are any species dominant, controlling the majority of the land, law, or currency? This is especially telling: a world overrun by orc hordes is probably a gruesome, warlike place where only the strong survive, while one shared in roughly equal number by exotic species may see relatively little racial tension, as well as vastly diverse nations and cultures.

If your world has a bit of history and you'd like to shake things up, consider how insular each species is and whether it's picked up traits from other cultures. The classic perception, for instance, is that elves live in forest glades and universally rise above or ignore the eccentricities of other species, retaining an unswerving focus on nature, beauty, and order despite thousands of years of inter-species relations. Likewise, dwarves are often portrayed with a single face — that of surly mountain-, cave-, and gem-loving hermits unfazed by visitors and neighbors. How much more interesting would it be if centuries of negotiations between these two cultures had rubbed off on individuals and groups, merging elements of their cultural and ethnic identities — if they'd started to share religions, language, art, gear and technologies, crafting techniques, naming trends, proverbs, and a thousand other things?

This "realistic" approach isn't easy, as isolated tweaks can seem out of place in an otherwise undisturbed world, especially if they lack plausible ramifications. Following just a few fundamental influences through to their natural conclusion can bring a world to life, however, creating rich opportunities for roleplay.

No matter how you stir the melting pot, be sure to include ways for player characters of all the allowed heroic species to adventure together. Most mature players can get past a bit of mild species bias, and to a few it's a roleplaying gold mine, but nothing good can come of outright, universal rancor between characters. It's a license for the childish and impudent to act out, and a recipe for disaster in a gaming group.

NATIONS AND ORGANIZATIONS

In traditional fantasy gaming, the heroes are usually a little like cowboys, wandering swordsmen and shiftless do-gooders who stumble from one adventure to the next in a quest for personal glory and/or fabulous wealth, bound only by loyalty to one another. Conversely, heroes of legend, mythology, and literary fiction often serve the greater good (or evil), becoming champions of a desperate kingdom, errant knights sent to recover a precious relic stolen from their masters, or a fellowship sent by free people to destroy an artifact of ultimate evil.

Even if the heroes (and players) in your game defy authority, refusing "missions" without something in return, nations and organizations can be powerful storytelling forces and in your game. They can establish laws, put on festivals and other events, employ NPCs, and drive the plot forward as supporters or adversaries. One of the most common fantasy organizations, the guild, is a bottomless well of play potential, sometimes rivaling or exceeding the local city government in power and scope. Guildmasters are often portrayed as the crime kingpins of the fantasy world but they can just as easily become benevolent campaigners for just causes.

In many ways, nations and organizations fill the same game role as deities. Their actions shift the setting, establishing background and creating situations against which the party's adventures unfold. Though the characters might sometimes get involved directly, such moments should be rare and meaningful. The day the party is arrested for a crime, whether they committed it or not, is an excellent opportunity to showcase the local government, and a corrupt guild might make a great ultimate threat for an ongoing political campaign.

When building the nations and organizations in your world, focus initially on the few that matter most in the game you want to play. Size and scope aren't as important as their role in your game. It isn't helpful to develop all the nations on the planet if your characters will never get out of a single valley, for instance, but if the local merchant caravans all pay a chunk of their profits to a connected mogul who commands a small army, that's relevant — and a great source of story.

All the choices you've made thus far should help here. You aren't likely to see a globe-spanning empire in an ancient setting, for example, because the infrastructure needed to communicate with and transport to remote regions is missing. Conversely, a world of lost gods and powerful magic might naturally suggest underground cults of religious zealots or clans of despotic mage-kings (perhaps both, leading to a war for divine truth). If unborn are the dominant species, any government you build is likely to be sterile and mechanical, which may lead you to install one or two upstart organizations for the "lesser" organic species.

IN HIS MAJESTY'S SERVICE

In *Fantasy Craft*, a character's social standing is represented by his Reputation, or more accurately his Renown. This statistic grants a character the ability to keep Prizes and request Favors *(see page 187)*, but it also awards him titles by which he's known in your world. These titles are one of the strongest ways to personalize your setting, immediately establishing a vernacular for the commonly accepted pecking order. If you wanted, you could even create honorifics unique to one or more nations or organizations.

You can also customize Renown by restricting benefits to characters belonging to certain nations and organizations. For example, it follows that a knight of the king's court with a high Military Renown should be able to spend Reputation for holdings (fiefdoms awarded by his lord for brave service) and Favors (conferred by his title). He might not be able to keep magic items, however, bound by a pledge to return them to the royal museum or local armory.

Another example might find a master thief loved by the people due to a high Heroic Renown, which grants him the option to keep magic items and purchase Contacts (though his guild), but denying him holdings (which are deemed too risky by his guildmaster).

A high-ranking cardinal in the royal church, flush with Noble Renown, might enjoy all the Renown benefits thanks to the church's far-reaching hand, immense wealth, and bountiful political influence. This might compensate for other difficulties he faces in your world, such as fewer class options (or even a mandated class progression).

WAY OF LIFE

It's easy to gloss over the lives of everyday people in an RPG ("they wear poor clothes, eat broth, and look downtrodden"), but this squanders a great opportunity to give your world that extra spark of personality and just as importantly, to establish a framework for the questions to follow.

Again, your previous decisions offer many initial hooks: era defines trade and available technologies; Alignment informs common moral codes and beliefs, and possibly how fearful and/or pious the people are; the commonality of magic might suggest the populace's reliance on supernatural assistance and/or popular opinion about spellcasters; every species contributes to the lifestyles of the others and the melting pot — or lack thereof — can tell you how xenophobic or tolerant people are; and the states and groups you've developed may hint at how citizens relate to authority. Naturally this is just the tip of the proverbial iceberg but it's a great base and offers you plenty of starting detail.

CLASS AND CASTE

Most societies feature class systems, where people are born and grow up in one class but have the opportunity, however slim, to improve (or worsen) their lives. A few have caste systems, establishing social standing at birth, with no chance of enrichment. As a rule, caste systems are more common in early eras and class systems become more pronounced in later ones. Many primitive fantasy settings determine standing by age while feudal settings tend to divide by social or economic role (nobles at the top, followed by knights, merchants, and peasants at the bottom). Any, all, or none of this may be true in your world, however.

Start with the basic question (class or caste system?) and expand from there. Is standing dictated by birth, sex, wealth, race, religious orientation, ownership, merit, or other factors? How important is one's class to *other* parts of society? How do members of different social strata relate? Is everyone treated equally under the law or does hierarchy override justice? Do heroes rise from all strata or only certain segments of society? In a class system, what's required to promote oneself or take a tumble down the social ladder?

Mechanically, ask whether the social system in your world limits a character's Reputation. In a feudal fantasy game, for example, only nobles and knights might earn full Reputation from adventures; merchants might only earn half and peasants none at all. Characters might only be able to earn so much Reputation (e.g. peasants "capping out" at 0 and merchants capping out at 100), or they might have limited access to Favors (e.g. none costing more than 20 Reputation for merchants). As in the previous section, a character's class or caste might restrict him from certain Reputation purchases altogether, and it certainly has an impact on the titles he can hold.

EVERYDAY LIVING

For all these large-scale social questions, fortunately, there are also simple ones. Consider the daily lives of the classes or castes the characters likely hail from and those they'll likely interact with (adventures often draw parties into the lowest social tiers, though it depends on the story). In these circles, what do people eat, drink, and wear? Are they generally literate and/or educated? Are they mostly upbeat or gloomy? What do they do for fun? Are they social or do they keep to themselves? What jobs do they take (and realistically desire)? What's their daily routine? These details may seem trivial but they can have tremendous impact when describing and roleplaying scenes. As usual, you don't want to overload the players with detail but ignoring the little flourishes can sabotage even the most intriguing world concept.

TRADE AND CURRENCY

All civilized societies engage in trade, exchanging valuable commodities, goods, and services. In *Fantasy Craft*, all trade, no matter what's being exchanged, is measured with a "silver standard." Currency can take the form of actual coin (made of silver and/or other materials) or anything else that fits your world: valuable ingots, spices, raw materials, beads, future services…

You're fine even if you don't use actual silver pieces — just measure each unit of your world's currency against the silver values in Chapter 4. It's easiest if you have an analog for a single silver piece (e.g. 1 bead-stone equals 1s), but you'll be fine as long as the silver conversion is simple (e.g. 1 iron ingot equals 15s).

When deciding on your currency, consider what's scarce, valuable, or prized in your world. A primitive society that has no use for shiny rocks might cherish fine pelts for clothing or spices to preserve food for the winter. Likewise, the coins of different nations might have different values across the land, based on perceived strength, stockpiles of precious items, and outright bias (indeed, some nations may refuse their enemies' currencies).

Though far from necessary, you might also want to consider the breadth of trade across your world. Is it strictly local or does it span continents? Does it cross seas? What trade goods are highly sought? Is any nation or region the exclusive source of a treasured resource? Answering these questions prepares you to present your world's markets with confidence and style.

GEAR

Chapter 4 offers a huge selection of gear, available by era and based on real world technological growth to prevent anything from going dramatically "wrong" with an out-of-the-box campaign. As the GM, you have the right and responsibility to tailor this selection to fit your world, based on the specific advancements made, the edicts of leaders, your group's preferences, and as always, the needs of your story.

RESTRICTING GEAR

By default, all gear in Chapter 4 is available on the open market, but you have two options for restricting items, individually or in groups.

- Make the gear so rare it never appears on the market. This option preserves your right to introduce the restricted item as an adventure reward *(see page 344)*.
- Make the gear non-existent in your world. This option's best reserved for items you know will disrupt or derail the flow of play.

One of the most common gear issues involves black powder weapons. You might decide that there's no place in your world for longarms, for example, but retain sidearms as a specialty item crafted by a select few smiths. This keeps troublesome weapons out of the characters' hands and also gives them a reason to invest in the Crafting skill themselves (assuming they don't want to make friends with a smith or perhaps acquire one as a Contact).

Scrolls and elixirs can also be problematic, though they're automatically limited if you exclude any spells from your world *(see page 314)*. You can also specifically remove them, though in the case of scrolls it's probably best to remove all scrolls or none (as they're all made in much the same fashion). With elixirs you have a little more room for discretion, as you can explain their absence with unavailable components (making them rare or non-existent in your world, just like any undesired gear).

Magic items are a huge sticking point for some. The big question is whether characters can buy them with Reputation *(see page 194)*. This should only be allowed in high magic games where items are so readily available that an economy can plausibly develop around them. For ways to control the frequency and power of magic items, consider the *flexible magic items, greater magic items, monty haul, plentiful magic items*, and/or *rare magic items* campaign qualities *(see page 322)*.

Also keep in mind that removing any gear — magic or otherwise — may require re-rolls on the treasure tables and/or cause complications for certain classes (like the Alchemist if all elixirs are removed).

Always inform the players of what's not available, though you can withhold whether an item is permanently out of play or just held in reserve (there's no need to ruin the surprise when and if the party finds one, and keeping this decision to yourself also lets you change your mind if you later need to introduce a "non-existent" item).

MIXING ERAS

Fantasy is, well, fantastic — which can account for many deviations from true history. There's no reason your world can't include anachronistic gear, so long as it's plausible enough to *your group*. Advanced technology can be made available worldwide (e.g. rapiers across a feudal setting or metal swords throughout a primitive one), or you can limit them to certain cultures (e.g. primitive tribal orcs alongside feudal elves and industrial dwarves) or regions (an ancient culture on one continent and primitive ones everywhere else).

When fiddling with technology, avoid making too much work for yourself. If you change more than about 3 categories of gear, you might want to consider advancing the era instead. The last thing you want to do is create a baseline your group can't easily grasp in play.

RESTRICTING CRAFTING

The final decision you may need to make about gear is what characters can craft versus what "professional" crafters can make. This is important because Crafting can become an easy way to circumvent gear restrictions. Allowing characters to make black powder weapons that have been restricted to adventure rewards, for example, defeats the purpose; likewise letting them make scrolls if none exist in the world. Be sure to inform players of the restriction or absence of certain crafting options so they can make character-building choices with confidence.

WORKSHOPS

Most heroes don't have ready access to their own workshops *(see page 159)* but may be able to find them in town or build them into their holdings *(see page 193)*. Given the benefits of Crafting in a workshop, it's likely they'll become vital in a game where any of the characters use the skill. Thus it's important for you to establish the minimum size population center that has a workshop and the average cost of using it (in silver pieces by the day). If you'd like to make things simple, this cost can be deducted from the Crafting check result.

Certain types of workshops may not appear in certain parts of the world (where vital raw materials are missing, for example, or where the resulting items are in low demand). Some may be restricted to certain species, classes or castes, or organizations. Some may have a premium price (perhaps even costing Reputation instead of silver).

LANGUAGES AND STUDIES

Characters may or may not spend one Interest to take an Alignment but the rest go to languages spoken and fields studied, which are another great opportunity to flesh out your world.

Languages can develop within nearly any significant group. They're most common among cultures but species, nations, organizations, and even Alignments can have their own tongues (e.g. the black and twisted words spoken between followers of a dark god). Niche languages are prevalent among groups that trade, militaries using signals to convey orders, and secretive factions speaking in code (e.g. thieves' guilds). Keep languages simple and relevant: a list of up to 10 languages across your entire setting is plenty unless you're running a complex multinational, multi-species epic. Also, avoid defining languages too narrowly — it may seem flavorful to give infernal bugbears their own tongue but unless they're routinely encountered the chance of a player investing an Interest in it is pretty slim.

Studies, on the other hand, can literally be anything — a character could follow regional gambling or the tales of a particular mythology, cook in a certain style or debate a particular philosophical outlook. Rather than defining what studies are possible, it's better to come up with a list of the most common and useful studies that heroes might take. This is one of the most-open ended ways to establish world flavor (i.e. "Worship of Hashur, Lord of the West" rather than "religion" or "Sips of the Fang Rock Strangle Plums" rather than "wines"). This can ground your players a bit and provide a ready list of interesting story and plot hooks.

THE CALENDAR

Measuring time is often overlooked in setting design but it's yet another powerful tool in your world-building toolbox. For instance, on a world close to the sun, "winter" may just be slightly cooler than summer, having little if nothing to do with snow. A world with multiple moons may mark the change of seasons with regular eclipses or lunar convergences. Another world might measure years in 10-day weeks and 5-week months.

One of the most flavorful elements of building your calendar isn't in its justification but in the names people have for years, months, weeks, and days (or whatever increments you wind up using). A swamp world once ruled by fierce flightless dragons might use a general term for years ("molts," after the amount of time a dragon is believed to have kept his skin), but name months after the most ancient dragons (who might also be gods in the setting) and weeks after saurian heroes throughout time. Days might be named for the scale tones of the four major saurian splinter races in the world, and a cornerstone of their ongoing political stability (each splinter race retaining a favorable negotiating position on its day).

You might also want to think about significant social, political, or magical events throughout your year — what they mean to the people, how they're observed, and what they're called. For example, the greatest feast of the year may be held on the solstice, bringing society to a halt for the revelry. Ley lines that fuel sorcerous magic might only flare at the new year, reserving the most powerful spells for that day alone.

CRIMES AND PUNISHMENT

Laws in fantasy worlds can be fluid, even progressive policies maintained by small collectives, but more often they're staid edicts laid down by gods, philosopher-kings, or leaders of old. They can be brazenly prejudiced, favoring certain species, social classes, and religions over others, or surprisingly egalitarian, exhibiting fairness in court that's rarely seen elsewhere. In a well-conceived system they can also incorporate willful supernatural acts, like spells and reliable miracles, establishing whether it's lawful to raise the dead against their will, or secretly scrye on others, study or practice certain magical Schools and Disciplines, or pursue certain Alignments.

Something else to consider is the government's involvement in keeping the peace. Are enforcers numerous and omnipresent or few and far between? Are they dogged and unwavering or passive and forgiving? Do they forgive certain crimes but not others? Do any of them take the law into their own hands, dispensing justice on their terms? Is this, in fact, expected (perhaps because courts don't exist in the land, or are only used when a criminal requests a trial)? When trials happen, what's the process? Where do they occur and who passes judgment on the accused? Are the courts receptive to bribes? When someone is found guilty, where are they punished? Is their punishment a private affair or a public spectacle?

LAYING DOWN THE LAW

Parties run afoul of the law, even when they're trying not to — it's a frequent byproduct of RPG adventuring — so it's helpful to identify crimes in your world and the punishment(s) typically inflicted for each. Common crimes and punishments are found on Table 7.2: Trials *(see below)*. Some or all of these may not apply and you can and should introduce more as appropriate. For example, assault and murder may not be crimes in a hardened sword and sorcery world, while possession of certain sacred fruits by anyone but a shaman might be grounds for flogging.

If trials occur, you should also establish the crime's severity in the eyes of the court (minor or major).

TRIALS

In a particularly enlightened world, every character accused of a crime may stand trial, though in most fantasy settings a trial must be requested, if the option is available at all. Mechanically, a trial is a Complex Task using information from Table 7.2 *(see below)*.

Crime: The worst crime for which the defendant is on trial determines the number of successful skill checks the defendant must make to win the Task and escape punishment.

Crime's Severity: The crime's severity determines the DC of each check during the Task. When a minor crime is heinous in nature, you may arbitrarily upgrade it to major.

Table 7.2: Trials

Crime	*Successes Required*
Adultery	2
Arson	3
Assault	3
Bearing false witness	3
Blasphemy	2
Desecration of a sacred place	3
Fraud	2
Heresy	4
Indecency	3
Kidnapping	3
Murder	5
Prostitution	2
Rape	3
Theft	3
Treason	5
Trespassing	2
Using forbidden magic	4
Vandalism	2

Severity/DC	*Sample Punishments*
Minor (DC 15)	Imprisonment (1d6 weeks); flogging (2d6 wound damage); 1d6×100s fine; banishment
Major (DC 20)	Imprisonment (2d6 months); branding (–1 Appearance modifier); maiming (–1 to physical attribute); execution

Court	*Additional Tries*
Kangaroo	–1 (at least one critical success is needed to escape punishment!)
Hostile	+0
Antagonistic	+1
Neutral	+2
Amiable	+3
Friendly	+4

Bribing the Court: This dangerous option can easily backfire if the court isn't receptive. When a character offers incentives for preferential treatment and the GM hasn't already determined whether the court is receptive to bribes, the GM should roll 1d6: a result of 1–2 means the court resents the attempt, reducing the character's additional tries by 1, while a result of 5–6 means the court is receptive, increasing his additional tries by 1. A result of 3–4 indicates a principled or unfazed court, with no modifier to additional tries.

Court's Demeanor: The court's demeanor determines the number of Challenges available to the defendant in relation to the number of necessary successes.

Example: Brungil is caught raiding an ancient king's tomb. In his world theft is typically a minor crime but as the king was especially well loved the GM upgrades the severity to major, setting a DC of 20 for all Challenges. Not having a pre-established court in place, the GM decides on the fly that it consists of antagonistic nobles who don't take kindly to "commoners" defiling their grave sites. This means poor Brungil has to succeed with 3 (for theft) out of 4 Challenges (for the antagonistic court), each with a DC of 20, to escape punishment.

A character may attempt each Challenge with one of the following skills: Bluff (lie to the court), Haggle (plead or trade information for leniency), Impress (play on the court's sympathies), Intimidate (harass a witness or bully the court), or Investigate (offer evidence). He may use each skill no more than twice during the Task and never twice in a row. A character using a legal advocate gains a morale bonus with each check *(see page 169)*.

If the character wins the Task he avoids punishment; otherwise, he suffers the punishment commonly inflicted for the crime in your world. If no punishment is established, you choose one based on the crime's severity, as shown on Table 7.2.

Example: Brungil's trial begins. For the first Challenge, he decides to throw himself on the mercy of the court, using his Impress skill and scoring a success. He can't use that tactic in the second Challenge, so he tries to Bluff the court instead. He isn't a terribly good liar, though, and fails. Brungil falls back on his Impress skill for the third Challenge and succeeds again. The fourth Challenge is do or die, so Brungil takes a risk and argues for a lack of evidence using his Investigate skill....

Unfortunately, he fails this last Challenge as well, so he's found guilty. Normally, the punishment for theft on Brungil's world is a 1d6 × 100s fine but as the GM decided this particular theft was a major crime he also has to choose a punishment. He sends Brungil to prison for 2d6 months. Looks like he'll have some Downtime on his hands until someone breaks him out...

As with any Complex Task, a trial can benefit from roleplay, especially when the verdict marks a turning point in the game. You could run every minute but it's far easier to highlight the important bits. Before rolling for each Challenge, let the defendant present one part of his argument — preferably the part most relevant to the skill being used — and apply a discretionary modifier based on the argument's strength and his delivery in the eyes of the court. To include everyone, let the other players take the roles of spectators, awarding action dice to those who make the experience more thrilling and fun for everyone. If the spectator commentary is plausible for the world you can even use it to help determine your discretionary modifiers for each Challenge.

HISTORY

Just as our world's events are an outgrowth of its people, cultures, and way of life, so can your fantasy world's history come from all the decisions you've made about thus far. Determining some critical turning point events can help develop a spine for other the details of your world, as well as the story of your game. As an example, turning points in *The Lord of the Rings* include the arrival of the Men of the West, the forging of the rings of power, and the ends of the Ages (not to mention the wars fought along the way). These events shaped the world that Frodo and his companions found themselves in, as well as their adventures through the books.

Turning points should be significant, if not world-changing. Major wars, cataclysmic environmental changes, widespread plagues, the arrival of new species, and the rise and fall of empires are all good examples, though in a narrowly focused fantasy world even the death of a parent, the loss of a family relic, or the start of a feud might qualify. When outlining turning points, focus on the big picture — what happened, who was involved or affected, how the event resolved, and who benefited from it (if anyone). If a turning point is recent, you might also ask if any instigator(s) still live and if the event is still happening (and if so, who can use it to their advantage).

GEOGRAPHY AND CLIMATE

These factors can be as instrumental in defining flavor, inhabitants, cultures, and story as any event or god. A world covered almost entirely by water naturally develops primarily amphibious and aquatic species, a strong sea trade, and navies over armies. Conversely, a desert world may consider water more precious than gold (perhaps even using it as currency), build with sand and brick instead of wood and plant matter, and keep a nocturnal schedule to avoid the blazing heat. A continent crisscrossed with treacherous mountain ranges might host cultures that have never seen or heard of each other, each with its own unique era of technological and cultural development.

When physically building a world, your first instinct might be to start with terrain and weather, laying cultures and history over it, but the opposite approach works just as well. To include a few nations, cultures, and species that share languages and defend one another's borders, make them neighbors and adapt the terrain to justify their growth in those locations. If you'd like two groups to constantly be at odds, place them both close to a valuable natural resource (such as a deep water port) and develop reasons neither of them can permanently capture it (such as powerful storms which ravage the port and smash occupying navies). Build impassable geographic barriers to funnel the party through dangerous areas during an important adventure, introduce periodic volcanoes and/or earthquakes to upset potentially stagnant areas, and use intermittent but disastrous weather to isolate regions or force the party to rely on fewer resources.

THE WORLD MAP

A visual map is a valuable tool for sharing your vision and making sure everyone understands where they are and what's around them — but there are many potential pitfalls. First, be sure to keep your map's scale practical. While it's commendable to map four full continents and thousands of square miles of land, it's pointless unless the players are going to travel all the way around the world. Start with what's immediately relevant to your story and let the map develop organically as need and inspiration demand.

Likewise, you can keep the geography beyond the party's starting surroundings vague, at least at first. Highlight important features — continents, oceans, mountain ranges, deserts, rough climates, and well-known landmarks — and add detail as the adventure moves into new regions. Undiscovered countries are wonderful sources of inspiration when a game gets stale, and they're just as exciting for the party to discover.

Note any important geopolitical borders, particularly as they relate to the story you intend to tell, and show locations important to the party: national capitals, major cities and towns, ports of call, the headquarters of any groups they know, the homes of their Contacts, and the last known positions of enemies. The occasional flourish usually won't hurt — "Here There Be Monsters" — but be careful not to make them too interesting or the party may ignore the plot to investigate.

CAMPAIGN QUALITIES

No two fantasy worlds are the same — some are dominated by evil powers, others feature wild and terrible magic, and still others feature god-forsaken populations living and dying in brutal strife. The default *Fantasy Craft* rules are perfect for most fantasy gaming "out of the box" but when you're looking for something a little different, or if your world diverges from traditional fantasy gaming, consider adding campaign qualities. These optional rules alter the system in small or dramatic ways to fit your world and vision. Everything from character creation to combat to magic and Alignment can be tweaked, granting absolute control over your game.

Campaign qualities can be used in two ways — as permanent effects or as temporary conditions. Permanent campaign qualities are active for the duration of your game but you can add temporary campaign qualities to an adventure at any time by spending one or more action dice *(see page 365)*. Temporary campaign qualities last until the end of the current scene, making them a great way to represent fleeting effects, dramatic episodes, and other exciting moments.

Example: Kevin is running a *Fantasy Craft* game and reaches the final climactic encounter. Wanting it to be a little more dangerous, he spends 3 action dice to add the *deadly combat* quality. The threat ranges of attacks increase by 2 for the rest of the scene. The party won't soon forget this encounter!

Some campaign qualities, like *miracles* and *sorcery*, are labeled "Permanent" and may not be activated using action dice. These qualities have fundamental or lasting impacts on the game and make no sense over just a scene. Both *miracles* and *sorcery* may be tailored in various ways, some of which may be triggered like temporary campaign qualities.

Example: Kevin starts another game in a world of his own creation. Spellcasting is possible, so he adds the permanent *sorcery* quality, but he also wants it to periodically become uncontrollable. Fortunately, this is easily handled with strategic, temporary application of the *wild magic* quality. Alternately, he could add *wild magic* as a permanent quality, keeping arcane casters on their toes at all times.

Initially, you should probably add no more than 3 permanent qualities to each game and 1 temporary quality to each scene. More than that and it might get hard for players to keep track of the optional rules. As you gain more experience, you could go as high as 5–7 permanent qualities per game and 2–3 temporary qualities per scene, though his is pretty ambitious and requires a great memory and strong understanding of the core rules. As with any mechanical changes, less is often more.

ADVENTURE INSURANCE (PERMANENT)

People respect the stout of heart, even when fate doesn't. If a hero loses a Prize while being heroic or through no fault of his own (e.g. drops a magic sword into a chasm to catch a falling teammate, suffers the accidental death of a Contact, etc.), he immediately regains 1/2 the Prize's Reputation value (rounded down). This "rebate" is granted at the GM's sole discretion and should *not* apply when a hero deliberately gives up a Prize without a heroic reason, or when he loses a Prize for callous or greedy reasons (e.g. knowingly puts a Contact at risk, trades a magic item for personal gain, etc.).

BEEFY HEROES (1 ACTION DIE)

A ripped physique is all the armor a real hero needs! Special characters gain Lethal and Subdual Resistance equal to their Strength modifier (min. 0).

BLEAK HEROES (3 ACTION DICE)

These are dark times and the odds are stacked high against heroes. Each hero's starting action dice decrease by 2 and none of his action dice explode. Abilities based on the number of starting action dice are unaffected (i.e. they're calculated using the hero's normal number of starting action dice).

BOLD HEROES (1 ACTION DIE)

Heroes are larger than life and rely on luck as much as skill. Each hero's starting action dice increase by 2 and his action dice explode with a 1 *and* the natural highest result (e.g. a "6" on a d6). Abilities based on the number of starting action dice are unaffected (i.e. they're calculated using the hero's normal number of starting action dice).

CODE OF HONOR (2 ACTION DICE)

The world observes one or more strict social codes or taboos of the GM's creation (e.g. "never strike an unarmed foe," "don't enter the sacred faerie glades," etc.). Each time a hero willingly violates one of these codes, he loses 2 Reputation. If this drops his Reputation below 0, the remainder becomes a debt against future awards.

COMPLEX HEROES (PERMANENT)

Heroes are forged not only in fierce battles to save the world but also in intimate struggles of a most personal nature. The XP rewards from Subplot objectives are doubled.

DEAD MEANS DEAD (3 ACTION DICE)

Life is fleeting and once you check out, you don't come back. Characters may not Cheat Death or benefit from the *everlasting* quality. Also, the Preparation Cost of Resurrection and other spells that return a character to life are doubled.

DEADLY COMBAT (3 ACTION DICE)

Combat is a life-or-death affair, with death being a very real possibility. The threat ranges of attacks increase by 2.

DOMINANT HEROES (2 ACTION DICE)

Carnage abounds as true heroes carve their way through lesser foes. Whenever a hero or special NPC scores a threat with an attack check, it automatically becomes a critical hit unless the attacker spends 1 action die.

DOOMED HEROES (4 ACTION DICE)

Threats against heroes automatically become critical hits.

DRAMATIC PACING (PERMANENT)

Time bends to meet the needs of the story. Durations and time restrictions lasting more than 1 hour instead last until the end of the scene (e.g. a balm that typically lasts 8 hours instead lasts the rest of the scene and a potion that may typically be used once per day may instead be used once per scene).

FAST ATTRIBUTES (PERMANENT)

Each player character gains 1 bonus attribute point at Career Level 3 and every 3 levels thereafter. This replaces the bonus attribute points on Table 1.4: Career Level *(see page 27)*.

FAST FEATS (PERMANENT)

Each player character gains 1 extra feat at Career Level 2 and every 2 levels thereafter. This replaces the extra feats on Table 1.4: Career Level *(see page 27)*.

FAST INTERESTS (PERMANENT)

Each player character gains 1 bonus Interest at Career Level 2 and every 2 levels thereafter. This replaces the extra bonus Interests on Table 1.4: Career Level *(see page 27)*.

FAST LEVELS (PERMANENT)

The XP required to gain each level decreases to 1/2 normal (rounded up), and player characters may gain up to 2 levels between adventures.

FAST PROFICIENCIES (PERMANENT)

Each player character gains 1 bonus proficiency at Career Level 1 and at every Career Level thereafter. This replaces the bonus proficiencies on Table 1.4: Career Level *(see page 27)*.

FEAT EXCHANGE (PERMANENT)

Whenever a hero gains a specific feat, or a feat from a specific tree, he may instead gain a feat from a specific tree chosen by the GM. For example, when feat exchange (Species) is applied, a character who gains a bonus feat from any other tree may choose a Species feat instead. So can a character who earns any specific feat (e.g. Combat Instincts or Polearm Basics).

FLEXIBLE MAGIC ITEMS (PERMANENT)

Magic items are diverse and may have Charms and Essences in any combination (i.e. 2 Essences, 2 Charms, or 1 Essence and 1 Charm).

FRAGILE HEROES (PERMANENT)

Heroes can fall as easily as lesser men. Their class vitality bonus decreases to 1/2 normal (rounded down). For example, a hero who typically has a vitality bonus of 9 instead gains only 4 vitality per level.

GREATER MAGIC ITEMS (PERMANENT)

Magic items are especially powerful and may have up to 2 Charms and 2 Essences. Also, when randomly generating a magic item, roll twice on table 4.31 and apply *both* results *(see page 194)*.

HEARTY HEROES (1 ACTION DIE)

Heroes are exceptionally resilient and bounce back quickly from injury. They benefit from natural healing even while they're not resting, and their natural healing rate is doubled while they do rest.

HEWN LIMBS (2 ACTION DICE)

The world is a brutal place where no injury is trivial. Characters must save to avoid a critical injury when they suffer 16–25 points of damage in a single attack; with a failed save, the character rolls 2d20 and adds the result to his damage to determine the critical injury suffered. Also, characters must save against Massive Damage when they suffer 26 or more points of damage in a single attack *(see page 208)*.

IRON HEROES (1 ACTION DIE)

Heroes scoff at the threat of permanent injury. Heroes must save to avoid a critical injury when they suffer 36–60 points of damage in a single attack; with a failed save, the character rolls 1d10 and adds the result to his damage to determine the critical injury suffered. Also, heroes must save against Massive Damage when they suffer 61 or more points of damage in a single attack *(see page 208)*.

JACKS OF ALL TRADES (1 ACTION DIE)

Heroes are masters of improvisation. They never suffer untrained skill check penalties, even when they have 0 ranks or lack a required kit.

LARGER-THAN-LIFE HEROES (PERMANENT)

Heroes stand head and shoulders above their peers. At character creation, player characters start with 40 points to buy attribute scores and may purchase scores above 18 at 5 points per score beyond 18 (i.e. a starting score of 20 costs 32 points).

LESSER HEROES (PERMANENT)

Heroes are everyday men and women with more courage than raw ability. At character creation, player characters start with 32 points to buy attribute scores and may not start with scores above 18 (even after applying Origin benefits).

LUCK ABOUNDS (1 ACTION DIE)

Luck plays a significant role in the world. Action dice increase by 1 die type (i.e. d4s become d6s, d6s become d8s, and so on), to a maximum of d12. Also, a character may spend any number of action dice when boosting an attack check, skill check, or save.

MIRACLES (PERMANENT)

Alignments grant fantastic powers — perhaps controlled, perhaps not *(see page 309)*. You may tailor miracles with these additional qualities.

Beneficent Universe (Permanent): The universe rewards the pious. When a character gains his first Alignment, he immediately takes the first Step along one of its Paths.

Fickle Universe (2 Action Dice): The universe is temperamental, shaping the daily lives of the devoted. At the beginning of each session, roll 1d6 and consult Table 7.3: Fickle Forces *(see page 325)*.

Generous Universe (1 Action Die): The universe rewards success. Each time a character performs a service supporting his Alignment (e.g. slays a special character with an opposing Alignment or recovering an artifact of his religion), he gains two action dice.

Indifferent Universe (1 Action Die): The universe ignores the faithful. Divine assistance may not be used as a justification for Narrative Control *(see page 366)*.

Strict Universe (Permanent): Characters are aligned by birth or cosmic arrangement. Every character gains an Alignment at the start of the game and may never change or lose it.

Warring Universe (2 Action Dice): The universe is in turmoil and this conflict extends to the mortal realm. Every Aligned character gains an insight bonus with attack checks and opposed rolls targeting characters with an opposing Alignment equal to their Charisma modifier (min. +0).

Wrathful Universe (2 Action Dice): The universe does not abide defiance. Every Aligned character is subject to a permanent Mark of Justice spell (triggered by violating his Alignment's codes).

MONTY HAUL (PERMANENT)

Real heroes *never* leave valuable treasure behind. Player characters suffer no penalties from a heavy load and may keep twice the normal number of Prizes and any number of artifacts.

NON-SCALING NPCS (PERMANENT)

The world has a set pecking order and if the heroes survive long enough, they'll eventually reach the top. Every NPC and monster's Threat Level is set when it's introduced and never changes. For example, the GM decides at the start of a game that all kobolds are TL 2 and all dragons are TL 14. This remains the case regardless of the PCs' Career Levels, the adventure's Menace, and other rules.

PARANOIA (2 ACTION DICE)

NPCs are exceptionally cautious, perhaps even suspicious. Disposition modifiers from skill checks and abilities decrease by 5 (min. 0) and the Persuasion DCs of Contacts increase by 10.

PLENTIFUL MAGIC ITEMS (PERMANENT)

Magic items are especially common and impressive. The party gains a +10 bonus with Treasure Rolls on Table 7.15: Magic and may choose not to roll if directed to Table 7.11: Any, instead claiming a result of "1M."

RAMPANT CORRUPTION (1 ACTION DIE)

Everyone has their price. Bonuses granted by incentives are doubled *(see Table 2.12, page 75)*. Also, incentives offered to a receptive court earn the defendant 1 additional try during a trial *(see page 320)*.

RARE MAGIC ITEMS (PERMANENT)

Magic items are especially uncommon (though no less desired). The party suffers a –10 penalty with Treasure Rolls on Table 7.15: Magic *(see page 350)*. If this reduces the result below 0, roll on Table 7.11: Any, re-rolling Magic results *(see page 345)*.

REPUTABLE HEROES (1 ACTION DIE)

Heroes are paragons in the eyes of the people and always given the benefit of the doubt. Reputation rewards are doubled.

REVILED HEROES (2 ACTION DICE)

Heroes are scorned by the people as trouble-makers, outlaws, or worse. Reputation rewards decrease to 1/2 normal (rounded up).

SAVAGE WILDS (2 ACTION DICE)

Vile creatures stalk the wilds, always on the lookout for a fresh meal. The action die cost of travel encounters decreases to 1/2 normal (rounded down, min. 1). If travel encounters are determined randomly *(see page 373)*, the result range triggering an encounter doubles (e.g. a range of 1–3 becomes 1–6).

SORCERY (PERMANENT)

Magic is real and may be harnessed and controlled in the form of spells. NPCs gain this ability with the Spellcasting Signature Skill *(see page 228)*, while player characters may take levels in one or more arcane caster classes *(see page 110)*. You may tailor magic with these additional qualities.

Corrupting Magic (3 Action Dice): Magic is a vile force that twists the caster's body and mind. Each time a character casts a spell, he must also make a Will save (DC 10 + the number of spell points spent to make the check). With failure, he gains 1 grade of the following condition.

Tainted (I–IV plus special): The character suffers a –2 penalty with Will saves and Charisma-based skill checks per grade suffered. If a character with *tainted IV* is *tainted* again, he instead becomes an NPC under the GM's control. A character loses 1 *tainted* grade at the end of each scene.

Cyclical Magic (2 Action Dice): Magic ebbs and flows like the tides (e.g. according to lunar cycles or calendar periods, or as a finite source is depleted). At the start of the scene, roll 1d6: with a 1–2, all characters' spell points decrease to 1/2 (rounded down); with a 4–5, they remain the same; and with a 5–6 they increase by 50% (rounded up). This effect lasts the entire scene.

Table 7.3: Fickle Forces

Result	Effect
1	*Capricious:* Each Aligned character gains a +2 bonus with unopposed Alignment skill checks and a –2 penalty with opposed Alignment skill checks.
2	*Gracious:* The starting action dice of each Aligned character rise by 2.
3	*Meddling:* Once per scene, each Aligned character must re-roll one successful skill check, attack check, or saving throw of the GM's choice. The second result stands, even if it's also successful.
4	*Mercurial:* The threat and error ranges of each Aligned character's skill checks increase by 2 each.
5	*Mirthful:* Once per scene, each Aligned character may re-roll one failed skill check, attack check, or saving throw. The second result stands, even if it's also a failure.
6	*Spiteful:* Each Aligned character's starting action dice decrease by 2.

Difficult Magic (3 Action Dice): Magic is a rare and exotic art, exceedingly difficult and time-consuming to perform. The DCs of Spellcasting checks increase by 5 and the Casting Times of spells double.

Easy Magic (1 Action Die): Magic is easily mastered and may be performed with a literal flick of the wrist. The DCs of Spellcasting checks decrease by 5 and the Casting Times of spells decrease to 1/2 (min. 1 free action).

Lost Magic (Permanent): One or more Schools or Disciplines have been lost, though a fledging black market exists for the knowledge. Choose any number of Schools and/or Disciplines. To gain a spell from one of them, a character must also spend Reputation equal to 5 × the spell's level (min. 5).

Potent Magic (2 Action Dice): Magic is particularly powerful and difficult to resist. The Save DCs of spells increase by 5 and the numerical results of spells, if any, increase by 50% (rounded up).

Random Magic (Permanent): Magic is an unpredictable talent. When a character learns one or more spells, he selects the spell's level and randomly generates the spell learned on Table 3.2: Spells *(see page 114)*. The character may re-roll the result if he already knows this random spell.

Ubiquitous Magic (Permanent): Magic is a common or innate talent available to virtually everyone. Every character automatically knows a number of Level 0 spells equal to his Wisdom modifier (min. 0) and may cast these spells automatically once per session with a Casting Level of 1.

Wild Magic (2 Action Dice): Magic is unpredictable or difficult to control, leading to... *exciting* critical successes and failures. The threat and error ranges of Spellcasting checks increase by 2 and when a character scores critical success or failure, roll 1d6 and consult Table 7.4: Wild Magic *(see below)*.

TENSE (2 ACTION DICE)

Fear and tension grip the world. Stress damage is doubled and no character may take 10 with skill checks.

THRIFTY HEROES (PERMANENT)

Heroes manage their coin well. Money saved/earned through Prudence increases by 15% (e.g. a hero with a Prudence of 0 has a starting Money Saved/Earned of 30%).

TRIUMPHANT HEROES (PERMANENT)

Tales of heroes' outrageous exploits spread quickly. Whenever a hero scores a critical hit or success, he immediately gains Reputation equal to the number of action dice spent to activate the success minus 1.

Table 7.4: Wild Magic

Result	Effect
Critical Success	
1	*Attunement:* The spell point costs of spells you cast in this scene decrease by 1. This benefit is cumulative but may not decrease a spell's cost to below 0 spell points.
2	*Devastating Spell:* The spell's Area and/or number of targets doubles. If the spell has no Area or targets, its Duration doubles instead.
3	*Empowered Spell:* The spell's save DC increases by 5 and all its numerical results increase by 50% (rounded up).
4	*Forked Spell:* Choose a second target within the spell's range. That target is also affected by the spell. If the spell has no target, its Duration doubles instead.
5	*Penetrating Spell:* Saves against the spell automatically fail, the spell cannot be countered, and it ignores Spell Resistance and reflection.
6	*Power Surge:* Your spell points immediately refresh at maximum.
Critical Failure	
1	*Memory Loss:* You may not use this spell again during this adventure.
2	*Miscast:* A spell goes off but not the one you intended. Roll for a random spell of the same level on Table 3.2: Spells *(see page 114)*.
3	*Backfire:* The spell goes off but affects a new target chosen by the GM (the new target may be anyone or anything, even you or another party member).
4	*Backlash:* You suffer 1d6 lethal damage per spell point used to cast the spell. This cannot reduce your wounds to below 1.
5	*Overload:* You immediately fall unconscious.
6	*Power Drain:* Your spell points immediately drop to 0.

VERSATILE HEROES (PERMANENT)

Heroes are world-wise veterans with diverse skill sets. A hero may gain ranks in any non-class or non-Origin skill at a cost of 2 skill points per rank.

WIRE FU (1 ACTION DIE)

The world sees high-flying action… literally. Special characters may move in any direction and across any surface — even up walls, over water, and through the air. If at the end of a character's movement he isn't on a solid surface, he falls (or submerges). Also, falling damage decreases to 1/2 normal (rounded up).

ADVENTURE BUILDING

An adventure is a loose script for one episode in the party's saga — it may stand alone as a uniquely enjoyable and fulfilling experience or become one part of a **campaign**, a series of adventures that may or may not share plot, adversaries, locations, and other elements *(see page 356)*. Here we introduce the basics for every adventure.

Most adventures consist of three to five **scenes**, each focusing on a sequence of events or series of problems. A scene is similar to an act in a television episode or stage play, though the action isn't confined to a single location (if desired, it can span an entire region, or beyond).

A scene is further divided into one or more **encounters**, each consisting of a single challenge facing the party, such as a combat, puzzle, investigation, series of linked skill uses (like a Complex Task), or a pivotal and important roleplaying exchange (like a negotiation or interrogation).

The duration and scope of each scene are left up to you, as they depend on the adventure's story, though natural breaks should become apparent as you develop your adventure. Conversely, an encounter's duration and scope are largely fixed and set by the specific challenge at hand.

STORY SEEDS

All adventures start with one or more story seeds, or big hooks to spark the action. Decide the basic thrust of your story up to the point when the characters become involved. Don't worry about how they might respond, or even how they'll get involved, but make sure the idea offers plenty of room for them to have an impact on the outcome.

If you're stumped for ideas, choose or randomly roll one on Table 7.5: Story Seeds *(see page 328)*, or read through the examples for inspiration. Most of these seeds are deliberately incomplete so you can adapt them to your world and ongoing campaign (if you're running one).

YOUR FIRST ADVENTURE: KEEP IT SIMPLE

When building an adventure it's easy to bite off more than you can chew: complex story seeds can confuse or frustrate the players; elusive or difficult goals or clues can lead the party astray; too many NPCs can make it hard to keep track of the cast; and too many adversaries, or too many types of adversaries, can bog the game down.

It's best to start small, easing into greater detail as you get comfortable being a *Fantasy Craft* GM. In your first adventure, it's probably best to limit yourself to one story seed, a single clear motivation (preferably for the whole party), and no more than two to three types of adversaries (with standard adversaries outnumbering the party by no more than two to one). You'll find this a boon in those inevitable moments when the adventure goes somewhere unexpected, forcing you to improvise.

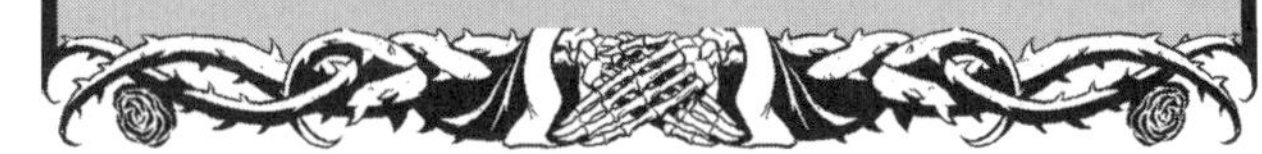

PC MOTIVATIONS

Equally important are the characters' reasons for getting involved, which can include curiosity, moral or ethical outrage, greed, lust, fear, anger, remorse, resentment, loyalty, a yen for excitement or discovery, a burning desire for revenge, the desperate need to survive, the simple need to win, or anything else that ignites the party's passion.

It's important that the characters' motivations justify the risk (to them), which can be tricky given that most adventures involve at least some chance of serious injury or death. You might take away that every adventure should whip the party into a frenzy but this is problematic for two reasons: first, extreme emotions are taxing and wear on player stamina, especially over time; and second, some players may see this as justification to act out or even cross the line, pushing the game into dark, amoral territory.

The best motivations are tailored specifically to the characters, hitting them where they live and driving them to decisive, personal action. Any part of a character's background may work for this but Subplots are especially useful; threatened Dependents, the object of a Search, or the appearance of a Nemesis or Rival are just a few of the many highly effective options *(see page 379)*. Of course, Subplots don't always apply to the entire party, so it's a good idea to come up with something for the other characters as well.

Table 7.5: Story Seeds

Roll	Story
1	The party learns that a savage orc war-tribe intends to attack a local trading post in three days' time.
2	A friend of the party is (presumably) framed for murder.
3	Farms are being ravaged by giant insects.
4	The greatest diplomats of the civilized world are gathering to discuss a potentially explosive border dispute.
5	Children are being abducted, reportedly by a gypsy clan.
6	A strange melody haunts a local monastery, which has closed its doors and is refusing visitors.
7	Graves are being robbed — or are they? Arcane symbols are scorched into the gravesites, sparking rumors of a dark cult.
8	A mysterious smoking sinkhole appears along a major trade route.
9	The party learns of treasure in a dangerous area (e.g. a forbidden swamp, an ancient tomb, or an inhospitable desert).
10	A town's water supply is tainted by something upstream.
11	A character receives an apocalyptic vision from a higher power.
12	Coastal villages are being raided for slaves (and worse).
13	A traveling vendor sneaks a strange little creature into the party's saddlebags.
14	Weapons and objects bought at market are animating and stealing their owners' belongings.
15	A noble calls on the party to help settle a squabble between neighboring fiefdoms without bloodshed.
16	Rumors spread that a powerful and corrupt archmage has died, leaving the contents of his impregnable fortress up for grabs.
17	A famous swordsman challenges a character to a duel, claiming the character committed and affront no one remembers.
18	Monstrous vermin are destroying the foundations of a character's home.
19	Dark storm clouds and fierce lightning besiege a lone tower in town, yet neighboring buildings are untouched.
20	The party learns that a great hero is riding into a trap.

Most parties can be enticed to adventure with the simple promise of… more. Fantasy characters are notoriously hungry for coin, treasure, and power — all of which are available as a matter of course in nearly every *Fantasy Craft* adventure. These old standbys are useful but like extreme conditions can grow tiresome if overused. Vary the motivations from adventure to adventure and watch for opportunities to introduce new reasons for the characters to adventure.

ADVERSARIES AND OTHER NPCS

Chapter 6 covers adversaries and other NPCs in great detail, whether they're monsters or corrupt player species. It offers near-limitless control over every aspect of an NPC, from its statistics to its abilities to its demeanor and more. It also makes building NPCs a snap, even on the fly, which can be helpful when your adventure skews in an unexpected direction. To keep this to a minimum, however, you should dedicate some effort to making NPCs that serve your adventure's story and appropriately challenge the party.

Don't waste your time building every NPC the characters might meet and every adversary they might fight, and don't slather every character with piles of background the players will never hear or mind. Start with the characters most vital to your adventure and ask yourself what makes them interesting and fun (both to you and to the players). The Beyond the Stats section in Chapter 6 can get you started with several random tables for names, quirks, and motivations *(see pages 249–252)* but again, you should try to tailor each character to your adventure whenever possible.

Think about what each character wants and needs, and how he fills his days. Not every villain must be vile, nor must every town champion be righteous. Creating three-dimensional characters with personal likes and dislikes, biases and creeds, will go a long way toward making your world believable and captivating, and can only draw the players deeper into the action as they start to wonder about what's going on inside the heads of friends, enemies, and others. It will also give you plenty of grist for getting into character, making the experience unique to each NPC the party meets and fights.

With opponents you should take the process a step further, exploring their strategies and battlefield behavior. Intelligent combatants with something special to bring to the fight are far more interesting enemies for everyone — you'll find them more fun to play and the heroes will appreciate that they're matching clashing steel with worthy foes. Even animals and other low-Intelligence enemies, driven by base needs like hunger, anger, fear, curiosity, and protecting their young, leave you plenty of options: an unusual attack style or clever maneuver can work wonders, making the opponent memorable and (potentially) more dangerous.

Always consider the types of adversaries the players want to fight. Do they prefer to fight mobs of standard NPCs or solitary, powerful opponents? Are they more excited by straightforward bash 'em ups, guerilla combats with periodic lulls between short-

YOUR FIRST ADVENTURE: GETTING THE PARTY TOGETHER

It's easy to start with the party already together, especially if the players know each other and have a rhythm. In this case they might devise the party's history when creating their characters or develop it over time as interesting ideas come up in play. These are excellent chances for you to award them action dice.

If you're playing with strangers, or want to give the players the chance to roleplay their party coming together, you can start with their first meeting. Characters can join forces by accident (wrong place, right time), through mutual acquaintances or organizations (like guilds), or out of necessity (say, to escape from a kobold warren where they're all held). The story of the party's origin could easily become a full adventure but in your first outing it's best to keep it to a brief scene with a single encounter, perhaps two if you include a small combat.

You can run the scene as a flashback if you'd like it to precede your first adventure by a while *(see page 334)*, but even if you do be sure to include rewards as normal *(see page 342)*. It's part of the party's saga, after all, even if the risk is somewhat lower (and it should be — heroes shouldn't die before the opening credits).

but-fierce skirmishes, explosive matches against creatures with lots of flashy abilities, complex tests of wit and will that demand their full attention, or something else entirely? Most groups prefer a combination of these options, which places the onus on you to shake the NPCs up in each adventure.

Adversaries, especially humanoids and their servants, often have hierarchies that you can exploit to great effect. Their organization and relations between enemy ranks can define them just as much as their abilities and tactics.

- A troll answering to a hobgoblin tribe is instantly intriguing. How did this relationship come about and what keeps it in place? If the troll is enslaved or resents his servitude, perhaps the characters can use that to their advantage. This would be an excellent new objective in the adventure.
- The leaders of a massing enemy army might not agree on how best to use it. Not only could one or more of them become allies, their differences of opinion could be showcased with radically divergent approaches to dealing with the PCs.

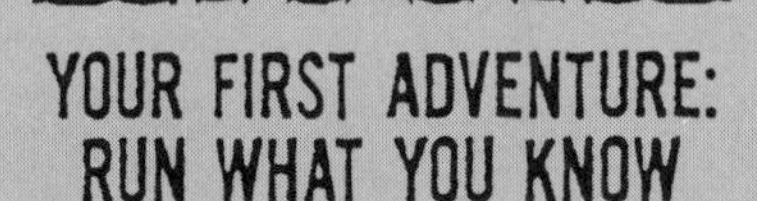

YOUR FIRST ADVENTURE: RUN WHAT YOU KNOW

Not sure where to begin? No problem. You can base NPCs on people you know in the real world, historical figures, or even characters from movies or books. You can do the same with locations, scene concepts, puzzles, and even plot points. This is especially helpful when you're short on time.

It's best to use ideas you're reasonably sure the players haven't encountered, but you can "re-skin" the ones they might recognize. For example, you might base a sage on the wizard Akiro from the *Conan the Barbarian* movies, replacing his signature furs with heavy robes or swapping out his voice for a booming baritone.

LOCATIONS

There are many things to consider when deciding where adventures take the party, but the most important is fun. Adventures can take place anywhere: in sprawling cities or quaint towns; in deep, dank dungeons or the cold, sterile halls of an abandoned castle; in any wilderness you can imagine; and beyond. Every location has its own flavor and you can use this to deepen and drive the adventure.

Consider the history of the place. Who lived there and why? Does anyone (or anything) remain? What was their culture and how much, if any of it remains? What momentous events occurred there? Was it the site of famous battles, desperate treaties, religious trials, or unexplained phenomena? What happens at the site today? Is it important to any nations, organizations, or individuals? How frequently is it visited and why? What do visitors see, hear, smell, taste, and feel?

Ecology is a critical question for any location that's home to living creatures: What do they eat and where do they sleep? What's their daily routine? Where and how do they breed? How do they interact with other inhabitants? Do they hunt other creatures or are they hunted themselves?

The answers to these questions can be as fantastic and wild as you like but no matter how incredible the location it has to be plausible within the setting — to you and to the players — or it threatens the integrity of your game. A traditional high fantasy campaign can withstand the improbable a great deal more easily than, say, a political or dark one. Also keep in mind that the more remarkable a location is, the greater the chance the party will fixate on it — potentially instead of the adventure's plot. Too much detail can have the opposite effect, turning the players off or worse, overshadowing the greater experience.

The best locations offer plenty of choices and things for the characters to do without giving the characters so much freedom that they can accidentally skip the scene(s) you've prepared for the area. In a military scenario, for example, a wide canyon might offer a waterfall to hide behind, evading enemies, tall trees that can be used to launch ambushes against unwitting soldiers passing below, soft earth allowing for pit traps and gear caches, unstable cliff faces that can be collapsed to block pursuers or create advantageous terrain, and more. At the same time the canyon is a self-contained location, preventing the characters from wandering too far from the action.

Locations can also offer plenty of challenge. In an epic fantasy setting, a contested crossroads might be a confluence of sheer rock outcroppings spiking up out of what's believed to be a bottomless chasm separating the civilized lands of men and the untamed wilds beyond. The characters might track a group of brigands there, seeking to regain the holy relic they stole, setting the stage for a perilous battle against a thrilling backdrop. The GM could take this a step further by having the brigands weaken the bridges or plant traps on them, or maybe enlist the help of a boulder-chucking troll who pummels the bridges with tons of ferrous rock.

A few more things to keep in mind when developing locations: First, don't fret about details that won't come into play. Foraging options are well and good but only if you intend to ask the party for Survival checks in the area. Second, try to view locations through the party's eyes. Unless rushed by the plot, characters almost always look for ways to get more information before proceeding. What can they hear through a door, or see and hear from each part of the area? What's likely to be most interesting or enticing to them (and is it where you want them to go most)? Finally, never underestimate a party's greed or its potential to derail an adventure. Yes, fixtures made of gold are impressive but they're also likely to slow the party's progress as they try to pry them from the walls.

MAPS

Depending on your play style and the needs of your adventure, you may have to draw maps for some locations. You can do this by hand (it's easier and more accurate with graph paper), or use one of many online or software options developed for fantasy RPGs. *Fantasy Craft* uses the standard grid scale (1 square = 5 ft.), which works great with the most commonly used miniatures and dry and wet erase play mats on the market.

As you place halls, rooms, doors, traps, obstacles, secret areas, fixed treasure, and other features, it's helpful to keep some things in mind, including party and character size and speeds, line of sight, potential terrain modifiers, spell and ability ranges, and scrying and other far-viewing options. You might also want to note locked doors and portals, as well as any NPCs, adversaries, and magic effects in each area.

If any events in your adventure change the location itself, you might want to draw before and after maps as well.

YOUR FIRST ADVENTURE: RUN WHAT YOU'VE GOT

Just as you can draw from your experience when building an adventure, you can steal to fill in the gaps. Don't have time to draw a map for your next adventure? Rummage through your adventure collection and lift one from an old classic (perhaps making a few revisions to disguise your thievery). Recycle NPC stats with a few strategic changes or borrow those from adventures or the Crafty Games forums. Collect art from your favorite websites and products and build a gallery you can draw from when you need to give the players visual reference for an NPC, monster, or location. You can even factor your collections into your adventure building process, choosing the visuals and creating statistics or other missing components to support them in play.

SCENES AND ENCOUNTERS

Commonly, adventures span three to five scenes organized like a three-act stage play or multi-act TV episode.

Opening Scene (Setup): This introduces the initial problem or challenge facing the characters, as well as initial adversaries and important NPCs, and compels the party to act. It kicks off with a bang, frequently *in media res* (the action already in progress), stirring the players and immediately drawing them into the adventure, and often ends with a minor plot twist or turning point in the story.

Middle Scenes (Pursuits and Confrontations): These scenes feature rising action and tension, periodically pausing for the party to regroup and take stock. Challenges and adversaries grow more powerful and dangerous, and the story urges the characters ever onward, leading to revelations and commonly a major turning point in the story (and possibly one or more significant plot twists as well).

Closing Scene (Resolution): The characters learn any remaining secrets and face the greatest adversaries the adventure has to throw at them. In the best closing scenes, the party's actions in previous scenes determine the conditions of the final confrontation, including pivotal perks or disadvantages. Regardless, the locations and action are the most epic and extraordinary here, providing the perfect backdrop for a meaningful victory or defeat. Some adventures fade with a fitting denouement and offer hooks for more in subsequent game sessions.

Your adventure may vary, of course, having any number of scenes and reordering or revising as you like.

SCENE CONSIDERATIONS

As a rule, each scene should focus on a single sequence of (related) events or problems. The action can take place in one or more locations, though in most cases multiple areas should be close together or some kind of swift travel should be available. Any prolonged pause in the action, due to travel or other factors, is probably grounds for a separate scene. There are exceptions, of course, like a single scene that covers all the events in a week-long political caucus or one that covers random events over a month of guard duty at the edge of an army encampment.

Given the incredible versatility and wide number of options available when building scenes, there aren't many rules for doing them well — what works for one group may fail for another and there's always room for improvement. Experience is your best guide but here are a few pieces of accumulated wisdom, some specific to *Fantasy Craft,* some universal to all systems.

General Scene Guidance

- Don't assume the characters will pursue any particular path, choose any particular option, or respond in any particular way (even if you think they're "obvious" or "right" (or even when they're established at the outset as "heroic" or "appropriate" things to do). Include multiple, interesting ways to accomplish each objective and whenever possible prepare for the party to ignore or change objectives as well.
- Don't employ *deus ex machina* (the sudden introduction of a plot device to save the day) or sideline the party. Players rarely have fun when they're denied the spotlight and/or control of the action.
- Don't shy away from exciting ideas, no matter how weird they are (this is fantasy, after all), but do ensure that everything in your scenes is plausible in your world.
- Avoid truly random events and situations (that come out of nowhere, independent or contrary to previous events and situations). The best events and situations believably arise from previous ones.
- Build scenes that keep the energy level high but be sure to also give the players chances to breathe (excitement is fun but non-stop excitement can burn everyone out, including you).
- Experiment with scene construction. Try different ways to introduce and support story. At the very least, make sure each scene in a single adventure presents its own unique flavor and challenge.

Promoting Story

- Offer regular opportunities for the players to get into and stay in character, including ample chances for in-character dialog and plenty of engaging questions and ideas to address. Put the characters in positions where they have to define or defend their personal beliefs.
- Develop NPCs that challenge the characters intellectually and emotionally as well as physically and magically. A duel of wits and will can be just as exciting as the most desperate combat — and sometimes more.
- Confront the characters with tough emotional, strategic, or heroic decisions, sometimes with no clear path to victory. Empower them to forge their legends in the face of adversity and they'll only ever win (even when they lose). A word of caution: don't dangle mechanical rewards to influence the party's decisions, or openly deny them rewards for choosing the "wrong" course. This can lead to resentment and damage the players' respect for you as a Game Master.
- Use the characters' decisions, however small, to change the world and course of the adventure. Plan for these watershed events when building adventures but watch for them during play as well — some of the most defining moments in your game will be unplanned.
- Create reasons for the party to embrace the story. Make them not want to skip it to get to the next die roll. Do this by making the story directly relevant and exciting to the *players*. Hook them and the character will follow.

Challenging the Party

- Don't pre-empt or negate the characters' abilities. They've worked hard to gain them.
- Develop encounters that play to, and test, the characters' strengths. Players appreciate being good at things. They appreciate winning through excellence even more, especially if it's by the skin of their teeth.
- Create objectives the party can accomplish as a team. Likewise, don't leave any of them with nothing to do.
- Test the party with unconventional situations that demand unconventional solutions. Require the players think about what *else* their characters can do.
- Don't let NPCs steal the spotlight. Likewise, make sure NPCs aren't in a position to, even if the players ask for their help.

Developing Encounters

- Vary the types and pacing of encounters from scene to scene, and within each scene (combat, skill use, problem solving, roleplaying, investigation). Try to make each encounter distinct and special.
- Especially at first, follow the guidance on page 243 regarding how many adversaries to throw at the party. Be careful not to make fights too easy or difficult, and when in doubt skew low. You can always add reinforcements with action dice *(see page 368).*
- Incorporate reasons for characters to vary their tactics and use sub-optimal abilities, perhaps offering bonus action dice or Instant Rewards for doing so *(see page 344).*

- Don't hinge success on a single die roll or choice, even one of those tough choices mentioned two sections back. Not only does this dramatically increase the chance of failure, it's horribly anti-climactic.
- Give the enemy a reason not to kill player characters outright. No one wants to lose a character because they fail a saving throw and it's always more interesting when the players have a chance to chat with the opposition face-to-face.

SCENE TRANSITIONS

Characters can move from one scene to another by performing or completing tasks, acting on information, moving from one location to another, or even without knowing (e.g. if the scene shift occurs at a certain time or due to an event the party doesn't know is happening). You may keep the players abreast of the scenes they're in or wait for it to come up (usually when the players ask if they can use an ability or option that's limited by scene).

Moving between scenes can be one of the trickiest aspects of running *Fantasy Craft*, especially when the party's options aren't obvious or, for one reason or another, the story hasn't progressed to a point where the action can fluidly shift. One of your most important jobs as Game Master is keeping the pace of play brisk and engaging at all times, which means that while the players are busy staying in character, chasing down enemies, and completing objectives you're performing a delicate balancing act to keep them occupied.

Ideally, while one scene is playing out, you should be thinking about the next and considering contingencies if the party strays from the expected path (and they will). Redundancy is your greatest tool here. In a perfect world, each scene transition should feature at least two unconnected avenues, one of which you can prompt without action from the characters (such as information plausibly acquired by allies or clues you can reveal in the party's current location, no matter where they are). Each additional way to get from one scene to another is that much less chance the adventure falters if the characters overlook or misinterpret critical pointers.

THE ADVENTURE FLOWCHART

One of the easiest ways to organize your scenes is with an adventure flowchart. Start with a box containing the title of your first scene and draw a line from it to a box containing the title of each scene into which it might transition (scenes often lead into two or more others, especially when the action is driven by character choice, as during an investigation). Repeat this for each avenue you've built into the adventure, labeling each line. If you like, you can add the necessary clue(s) or other triggers alongside these labels.

This gives you a visual guide you can reference during play and can also highlight any potential issues with your scene structure, like too few avenues into a critical scene or optional side scenes that don't push the characters back to the main plot.

THE ADVENTURE TIMELINE

Another helpful tool you can incorporate into your adventure is a timeline of fixed events, as well as those triggered by player actions. Fixed and triggered events are a great way to keep the action going, especially when you leave yourself the option to put them into play early if the adventure slows down. They can also help the players feel like they're part of a living, breathing world where things happen even without their direct involvement, and also put pressure on them to keep moving forward (lest opportunities slip through their fingers).

PLANNING YOUR REVEALS

One of the easiest ways an adventure can go astray is lack of information. Characters missing a vital clue can unknowingly focus on unimportant details or worse, become convinced that a red herring is the intended plot. Part of building a successful adventure is making sure the party finds the all-important details that explain the story and lead them in the right direction(s).

On the flip side, it's often critical to withhold information. For instance, revealing a villain can be a dicey proposition as players are notoriously single-minded — and short-sighted — when it comes to the enemy. They'll rush headlong into a fight with anything short of a god if they think he's behind their current woes (and might still charge in unless there's hard evidence that the god can kill them — because after all, why would you put anything in their line of sight they can't knock over?).

Fortunately, it's pretty easy to determine the order in which characters should learn details, even if you can't control how the players will react to them. Build a checklist in the desired order of revelation and you can also use it as a record of facts gained during play. Again, make sure that every important detail can be found in multiple ways, at least a few of which should seem obvious to the *players* (every play group is different, so this will take some second-guessing). Flag reveals you think the players will act on immediately, possibly with an asterisk, and when you're running the adventure you'll know to take an extra moment to consider whether they might jeopardize a scene or encounter.

Keep in mind that many player characters have access to spells and abilities they can use to learn information early, so you might want to pad your revelation list with some interesting but less pivotal facts, or even questions that get the players thinking along the right lines without providing the full truth. Flag these separately, perhaps with a triangle or another symbol of choice.

CLUES AND HINTS

Every piece of information built into your adventure and every detail on your revelation list is by default a clue *(see page 335)*, which means that characters can learn them through various abilities and skill uses, among other means. You can also offer them as hints *(see page 366)*, which is another way to ensure the essentials are revealed to the party. Again, you can simply tick off items as they're discovered.

LEAVING ROOM TO IMPROVISE

No matter how much preparation you put into an adventure, the players are bound to take it in directions you never dreamed possible. This is the beauty and the curse of a roleplaying game — the characters can at least *attempt* to do anything, no matter how irrational or outlandish. What this means is that there's a very real limit to the amount of work you can put into an adventure before it starts working against you. The more you set in stone, the less room you leave yourself to react to the players' actions.

What's the practical limit? It's different for every GM and adventure but the best advice we can give is to stop building just as soon as the adventure makes sense. After that you're just embellishing, which is something that's often best handled during the game anyway.

TESTING YOUR ADVENTURE

The last step before running your adventure is *test*-running it. If possible, take a couple days after completing your initial build. This will clear the details from your head and help you spot any issues that might otherwise seem fine. If you've got them handy, glance over the player characters, paying close attention to what they can do and the gear they have. Read through your adventure top to bottom, scene by scene, and try to anticipate the party's actions and reactions. Note any changes but don't make them until you're done with your pass.

Make any changes and if you have time (and unless you're confident the adventure's good to go), repeat the process. It's amazing how just a couple dry runs in the right mindset can improve the experience for everyone.

YOUR FIRST ADVENTURE: WHAT TO INCLUDE

From the outset, you'll find yourself drawn to build and record adventures in your own way. You might prefer comprehensive, meticulously organized files or loose lists of notes, each condensing a complete thought into a word or phrase. You might prepare full scripts to read as the characters arrive at each location and face each event, or you might improvise them from memory. Use whatever method works best for you and organize your materials however will help you find things fastest in play. The process can be refined over time but the most important thing is to develop a reliable system. This will keep you from shuffling for things you need at the table.

CINEMATIC SCENE STYLES

Movies and television can teach us a lot about RPG storytelling. Not only are the story structures similar but many of the same tools can be exploited to great effect — like these alternate scene styles.

CUT SCENES

A cut-scene shifts the *players'* perspective to simultaneous events at another location, leaving the characters oblivious ("Meanwhile..."). You can use a cut-scene to reveal details without the characters reacting but there's a significant pitfall: some players respond poorly to losing control of the story. Their reaction may worsen if the cut-scene is long or dull.

There are a couple workarounds. First, always keep cut-scenes short and concise, and give the players plenty of chances to ask questions. Alternately, you might prepare a cut-scene as a playable encounter or scene, letting the group assume alternate roles. For example, the players could become minions acting in service to a villain. Not only do they get to play the bad guys for a bit but their superiors could reveal important information about the enemy's plans that for storytelling reasons you want the players to know.

DREAM SEQUENCES

Another excellent way to safely convey information is the dream sequence, which poses two dangers. First, unless there's an explanation for more than one character sharing a dream — e.g. magic or supernatural abilities — only one player may be involved. Second, unless you state upfront that the characters are having a dream you run the risk of betraying their trust or destroying their suspension of disbelief.

Once you work out the reasons for a shared dream, however, you can use this method to remind players about important clues, foreshadow upcoming events, or raise new questions, perhaps in surreal or frightening ways. Dreams being what they are, you can get away with a lot when building them, taking the characters to places and confronting them with creatures and situations they'd never encounter in the waking world.

FLASHBACKS

A flashback focuses on past events, with the players taking other roles or playing younger versions of their characters. This is a popular way to reveal how the party came together, or let the players take an active role in a big setting or story reveal. The issue, of course, is that the past can't change, not in any way that's established as canon, which is why it's critical that you spend extra time looking for potential paradox and developing ways to explain any that might arise.

As an example, when playing through a flashback revealing the secret history of a powerful mage in the modern setting, the party might inadvertently cause his death. You could let him escape death *(see page 385)*, or you might work his death into the story *as a new reveal.* Make it the moment the characters realize that the modern mage is an imposter, perhaps with a nefarious agenda.

FLASH-FORWARDS AND MONTAGES

With a flash-forward *(see page 367)*, you can advance to a more interesting period of play. It's helpful when the action heads into tedious or unscripted (and unimportant) directions. As with any cinematic scene style, there's a chance that using a flash-forward will irk some players, so it's a good idea to politely suggest it rather than spring it on the group without warning. Some players may prefer to redirect their actions without interruption and if that can happen quickly you should probably oblige.

You can sometimes turn a shaky flash-forward into an asset by revealing fun bits about the "missing" period over time, starting at the point when play resumes. Cut to a new location, add several bizarre details ("You ride up to the inn at dusk the next evening, covered in tar and acorns. You dismiss questions with an irritated wave of your sticky arms, mutter something about demented pixies, and stomp up to your rooms."), and let the players wonder. You can go back to the gag whenever you like, even introducing NPCs that the characters met, fought, loved, and lost, but be careful — this is a tactic best used sparingly, with great respect and not a little wit.

Another variant on the flash-forward is the montage, which lets you summarize lengthy and mundane periods of play with a brief, often pithy description. Players can get involved as well and if you're up for it you could even turn the scene into a round-robin or free-for-all storytelling exercise. Montages are a wonderful way to handle Downtime *(see page 371).*

PARALLEL SCENES

When interesting things happen in two places at once (e.g. the party splits up or some of them are captured), you can run a parallel scene, in which you shift the focus back and forth, highlighting important activities in each area. This keeps everyone involved but it runs the risk of players getting bored when your focus is elsewhere.

Thus it's best to run parallel scenes at a brisk pace — there's no room for combat, Complex Tasks, or other lengthy endeavors without some kind of streamlined play or group shorthand. Flash-forwards may be required if the scenes bog down anyway.

MENACE

With your story, adversaries, and other elements in hand, it's time to apply the rules. Though you can do this in any order, it usually starts with the adventure's "Menace," or difficulty. Menace levels range from I to V (1 to 5) and adjusts Threat Level *(see page 335)*, the number of Dramatic scenes *(see page 335)*, and encounter threat *(see pages 243–244)*, as well as the GM's starting action dice *(see page 365)* Adventure rewards are automatically adjusted as well *(see page 342).*

Your choice of Menace is arbitrary, based entirely on how dangerous you want the adventure to be.

I (TRIFLING)

The adventure poses little true threat.

Threat Level: –2

Dramatic Scenes: None

Encounters: Minor

II (ROUTINE)

The adventure is dangerous but nothing your average group of heroes can't handle.

Threat Level: +0

Dramatic Scenes: 1

Encounters: Minor to Significant

III (CHALLENGING)

The adventure gives true heroes pause — but only for a second. Then it's time to wade in and hope everyone comes back alive.

Threat Level: +1

Dramatic Scenes: 1–2

Encounters: Average to Serious

IV (DANGEROUS)

Chances are someone's not coming home with their skin intact.

Threat Level: +2

Dramatic Scenes: 2–3

Encounters: Significant to Extreme

V (DEATH-DEFYING)

After this, your party will want to buy new loincloths and invest in some dye to get back to their original hair color.

Threat Level: +4

Dramatic Scenes: All

Encounters: Serious to Extreme

THREAT LEVEL

An adventure's "Threat Level" (TL) gauges its danger specific to the party. Like Career Level, it ranges from 1 to 20 but instead of representing aptitude it's used to calculate NPC statistics *(see page 240)* and to calculate XP rewards *(see page 342)*.

An adventure's Threat Level is calculated at its start and generally remains the same throughout. To find Threat Level, simply average the characters' Career Levels, rounding down (sum them and divide by the number of characters). If the adventure's Menace is other than II (Routine), apply that modifier as well.

Example: The TL for a team of 5 characters Levels 4, 7, 9, 10, and 18, is 9 (48 divided by 5, rounded down). If the adventure's Menace is IV (Dangerous), the adventure's TL is 11.

Specific NPCs can be calculated with modified Threat Levels. When this happens the NPC retains this TL for all purposes until the end of the adventure.

SCENES

You need to ask yourself four primary rules questions about every scene...

- Is it Standard or Dramatic?
- What are the Clues?
- What are the Objectives?
- Who are the Adversaries?

Let's start at the top with...

IS IT STANDARD OR DRAMATIC?

Every scene is either "Standard" or "Dramatic," indicating its general importance to the plot and/or the trouble characters will face therein.

During a **Standard scene**, the playing field is generally level and the chance of overall success is high. All standard *Fantasy Craft* rules apply.

During a **Dramatic scene**, the odds are stacked against the PCs and success is far from assured. Many rules change...

- The GM may spend any number of action dice on NPC die rolls and when healing NPCs *(see page 365)*.
- Standard adversaries may activate critical successes and hits.
- Player characters may not Cheat Death *(see page 384)*.

An adventure's Menace determines the number of Dramatic scenes it has. You may distribute these any way you wish, though it's generally a good idea to assign them to moments of high crisis in the story.

WHAT ARE THE CLUES?

As discussed in Scene Considerations *(see page 331)*, it's crucial to include several ways for the party to get from scene to scene. Clues are details worked into the plot that point the party in the right direction. They can be gained through class abilities like *notebook* and *master tracker (see pages 39 and 50)*, or learned with the Investigate skill *(see page 76)*. Clues can be standalone or strung into chains, one leading to the next.

When taking a final look at your scenes, search for potential clues to add. You never know when the characters will need a little help. Three or four for each avenue into or out of a scene is plenty. Clues that don't rely on specific knowledge are especially helpful, as they can double as hints *(see page 366)*.

WHAT ARE THE OBJECTIVES?

When building your adventure's story you came up with plenty of things for the party to accomplish *(see page 336)*. In the *Fantasy Craft* rules, each of these that doesn't involve traps or evading, defeating, or otherwise "besting" adversaries becomes an "objective," generating experience points for success *(see page 337)*. Objectives include traditional quests and all the Complex Tasks, puzzles, and other obstacles the party must overcome along the way, as well as tasks the party undertakes to further Subplots *(see page 379)*.

Start by compiling a list of things your party can do to enhance the story or further the plot. It may help to walk through each scene as you expect it to unfold (or to follow the adventure flowchart), noting each of the party's steps along the way.

Depending on your play style, objectives can be loose and fluid or carefully defined. If you're at all worried about confusion or debate at the table, we recommend you make sure each objective meets these four criteria.

1. One Accomplishment per Objective

Limit each objective to just one achievement. It's easy to lump objectives together but this can also lead to confusion. For example, "sneak into the castle" might involve nothing more than evading guards, which is fine. However, if the scene also calls for the party to access deeper parts of the castle that are more heavily defended, then you might want to break it down into individual tasks or steps.

2. Be Specific

An objective should be something the party can definitively finish, without potential misunderstanding. "Avoid harm," "safely enter a location," "humiliate an NPC," and similarly subjective

phrases only work when you're prepared to determine whether the party completes the objective on the fly, and reasonably certain the players will accept your ruling.

Instead, keep objectives simple and clear, without room for confusion (e.g. "Complete the scene without losing any wounds," "enter the location undetected," or "plant the (already introduced) incriminating evidence in the NPC's quarters").

Be careful also not to specifically limit an objective to an *activity*. "Search for keys" isn't a strong objective because it's not an accomplishment, though it *does* lead to one; instead, go with "obtain the keys," which also covers stealing them, duplicating them, and other possible solutions.

A common mistake when building objectives is to add "perform a cool cinematic maneuver," which should be rewarded but not as part of the adventure. Instead, watch for these as part of regular play, offering Instant Rewards when they come up *(see page 344)*.

3. Turn Negatives into Positives

It's bad form to inflict XP penalties, reducing the party's XP reward (or worse, their existing XP total). This rules out objectives that penalize but fortunately it's easy to turn those around. "Don't get caught" can become "evade the guards," for example, and "don't let the king die" can become "prevent the king's death" or "save the king."

4. Always Leverage Risk

Every objective should involve some degree of risk and consequences for failure; otherwise it's just free XP, which is hardly heroic. "Accept the quest" is a horrible objective, for example, as it requires nothing of the party and serves no purpose in the game other than to determine what the characters face next. Planning and entering locations are similarly problematic (unless the characters must convince someone to accept their plan, for example, or the location somehow threatens intruders).

For each objective, ask yourself whether the characters are in danger. If not, the task probably isn't an objective.

OBJECTIVE CHAINS

Next, consider whether any objectives can be accomplished in escalating or subsequent steps. For example, a party interrogating a miscreant named Fortunado might earn a base amount of XP for gleaning 1 clue and progressively more for each additional one. The clues lead to a brigand hideout and more XP based on the number of characters who sneak or bluff their way in. Finally, the party earns additional XP for each covert step they take to bring the gang down.

In all these cases, a single objective becomes a "chain" and is structured accordingly. Here are some examples.

A. 1 clue gleaned
B. 2 clues gleaned
C. 3 clues gleaned
D. 4 or more clues gleaned

A. 1–2 characters inserted into the hideout
B. All characters inserted into the hideout

A. Sabotage brigands' weapons without notice
B. Shoo away brigands' horses without notice
C. Set traps at 1–2 hideout exits without notice
D. Set traps at 3–4 hideout exits without notice
E. Set traps at all the hideout exits without notice

The party only receives one XP reward in each chain. In the last example, if they set up traps at 3 exits, they earn XP for the "D" stage of that chain, not A, B, C, or E. Alternately, that could be structured as two or even three chains, allowing separate XP rewards.

A. Sabotage brigands' weapons without notice

A. Shoo away brigands' horses without notice

A Set traps at 1–2 hideout exits without notice
B. Set traps at 3–4 hideout exits without notice
C. Set traps at all the hideout exits without notice

OBJECTIVE REWARDS

Finally, assign each objective an XP value based on its difficulty and/or importance. For simplicity you can value objectives in increments of 25 XP, and for a rough gauge you can compare them to the adversaries featured in the same adventure. Very difficult objectives and those critical to the plot, the party, or the party's employers should generally be valued significantly higher than the rest. The actual XP values are entirely up to you, though you should shoot for a total of 750 to 1,000 XP in combined objectives and adversaries if you want your campaign to progress at the default rate *(see page 342)*.

Each step in an objective chain gets its own escalating XP reward. Here are some examples.

A. 1 clue gleaned: 25 XP
B. 2 clues gleaned: 50 XP
C. 3 clues gleaned: 75 XP
D. 4 or more clues gleaned: 100 XP

A. 1–2 characters inserted into the hideout (critical): 50 XP
B. All characters inserted into the hideout: 100 XP

A. Sabotage brigands' weapons without notice: 50 XP
B. Shoo away brigands' horses without notice: 75 XP
C. Set traps at 1–2 hideout exits without notice: 100 XP
D. Set traps at 3–4 hideout exits without notice: 200 XP
E. Set traps at all the hideout exits without notice: 300 XP

WHO ARE THE ADVERSARIES?

The rules for developing adversaries of all kinds, including monsters, are found in Chapter 6. Selecting statistics, qualities, attacks, and other options generates an adversary's XP value, which is earned each time the party defeats the adversary, in or out of combat (sneaking past guards, for example, or dosing sleeping enemies before they can attack). XP is *not* earned for merely encountering an NPC (even an adversary); as with objectives, an element of risk must be involved.

Adversary XP values are applied differently for standard and special NPCs.

Standard Adversaries: These appear in "mobs" equal in number to the player characters. The party earns the XP value for each mob defeated, with fewer yielding proportionately less *(see page 240)*.

Special Adversaries: These appear singly. The party earns the XP value for each individual defeated. Special Adversaries may also be designated "villains," which gives them the option to ignore Disposition and Morale effects *(see pages 373 and 379)* and Cheat Death *(see page 384)*, among other benefits.

When building an adventure, you should have a stat block ready for each adversary the party may face and each of these should be designated standard or special (and if special, potentially a villain). The story will generally inform your decision (e.g. packs of gnolls should probably be standard, perhaps with a special leader), but if you're unsure it's best to ask whether each adversary deserves to be special; if not, then make them standard. Don't worry, you can upgrade any single standard NPC to special by spending 2 action dice in play *(see page 365)*.

You can even vary NPC designations between adventures!

Example: In a murder mystery, the characters find themselves hunting the killer of a beloved prince. The trail leads to a local merchant, who until now has been a standard NPC the players occasionally interact with when selling the spoils of their labors. This time around he's a witness, the last person to see the prince alive, and potentially a prime suspect once the characters learn he recently sold the prince's royal jewelry. The GM could still keep him a standard NPC but decides to upgrade him to a special adversary so he's a bit more capable when the characters set their sights on him. After the truth comes to light (that the merchant sold the prince's jewelry to help fund his fake death and escape from his corrupt father), the merchant might go back to being a pleasant bit player, probably with a shift back to standard as well.

NPCs share the same basic statistics whether they're standard or special and whether they're adversaries or not, which makes it a simple process to change things up whenever you want.

TRAPS

This section covers location traps like lava pits, collapsing ceilings, and giant crushing balls rolling through corridors *(see Table 7.6: Traps, page 339)*. Portable traps can be found in Chapter 4 *(see page 160)*.

Unlike portable traps, these generate XP *(see page 342)*, though only when the party overcomes them. A party that never encounters a trap earns no XP for it.

Every location trap starts with a good concept. What does it look like? How big is it? How does it work? How is it triggered? What excruciating fate does it offer its unfortunate victims? Most of these questions are answered by defining five trap traits. This also determines the trap's XP value (simply add the trait values together).

Mechanism: This defines the trap's physical appearance and/or trigger, as well as a second skill that may be used to bypass the device *(see page 339)*. A bypassed trap is not triggered and may be set off later.

Difficulty: This sets the Complexity and number of Challenges needed to Bypass or Disable the trap (as a Complex Task). Failure with even one Challenge attempt triggers the trap, as does failing the Task.

Concealment: This is the trap's Stash bonus, which opposes Notice and Search checks to spot it (when the installer is known, his Stash bonus is used instead). A party that doesn't spot a trap before stumbling into it automatically triggers it.

Target: This determines which characters are affected when the trap is triggered and offers a few sample trap actions. You can and should add new trap actions.

Effect: This is what happens to the trap's target (damage, suffocation, loss of action dice, etc.).

SAMPLE LOCATION TRAPS

Bubbling Oil Pit (65 XP): Mechanism: Pit; Difficulty: Simple; Concealment: None; Target: Entire Party; Effect: Draining

Crushing Boulder (35 XP): Mechanism: Tripwire; Difficulty: Average; Concealment: Average; Target: Random Party Member; Effect: Lethal damage

Giant Cage (80 XP): Mechanism: Pressure plate; Difficulty: Intricate; Concealment: Superior; Target: Entire Party; Effect: Captured

Guardian Idol (35 XP): Mechanism: Trial; Difficulty: Sophisticated; Concealment: None; Target: Triggering character; Effect: Curse

Horrific Exhibit (45 XP): Mechanism: Grotesque display; Difficulty: Simple; Concealment: Average; Target: Entire party; Effect: Condition (*frightened*)

Poison Darts (20 XP): Mechanism: Light beam trigger; Difficulty: Simple; Concealment: Poor; Target: Triggering character; Effect: Poison (necrotizing poison)

COMPLEX TASKS

As discussed in Chapter 2 *(see page 67)*, Complex Tasks can turn what might be a single, anticlimactic roll into a tense, multi-check event. However, unless you and your group are quick on your feet and possess strong improv skills, you should probably put a little thought into a Task before including it. Otherwise you run the risk of turning the event into just another series of dull, sterile rolls.

PROGRESS VS. PRECISION TASKS

The basic rules on page 67 describe Progress Tasks, in which the characters advance a step in the process with each successful Challenge. The Task may be timed (with the party racing to complete the last step before the clock runs down), or not (in which case the Task determines how long the whole process takes).

When desired, there's another option. In a Precision Task, the action advances a step whether the characters succeed or fail and each Challenge becomes an independent step or stage in the process. Precision Tasks are always timed and the party wins if by the end they score more successes than failures. Ties may be defined as success or failure, as you prefer.

To determine the type of Task that best suits your adventure, take a look at the action. Can the characters attack the problem in more than one way or complete steps out of order? If not, then you're definitely looking at a Progress Task. Is the Task more about getting things *done* or doing things *right*? Can the characters fail and keep going? Is there a time limit? The solution should quickly become clear.

SCRIPTING PERIL

Critical for many groups is the "Task script," which defines the skill(s) used and adds flavor, obstacles, and/or danger to the process. Ideally, a script develops unique identity for each Challenge (or in a timed Task, each Challenge *attempt*). It doesn't have to be long or complex — one distinct detail per Challenge is plenty, and you can even leave some brief or simple Challenges open to be described as you go. A well-conceived script lends to this, giving the players plenty of ideas for filling in the gaps.

To get started just pick a skill and check DC for each Challenge, then add one or two of the following events. Feel free to skip events for Challenges you feel the characters will easily overcome.

Table 7.6: Traps

Mechanism	*Bypass Skill*	*XP Value*
Clockwork/mechanical device	Crafting	—
Grotesque display	Resolve	—
Illusion	Sense Motive	—
Light beam trigger	Sneak	—
Logic/word puzzle	Investigate	—
Password	Sense Motive	—
Pit	Acrobatics (Balance) or Athletics (Climb)	—
Pressure plate	Acrobatics (Jump)	—
Riddle	Bluff	—
Trial (of character, spirit, etc.)	Resolve	—
Tripwire	Notice	—
Visual puzzle	Search	—

Difficulty	*Complexity and Challenges*	*XP Value*
Simple	10 + 1/2 Threat Level — 2 Challenges	+5
Average	15 + 1/2 Threat Level — 3 Challenges	+10
Sophisticated	15 + Threat Level — 3 Challenges	+15
Intricate	20 + Threat Level — 4 Challenges	+20

Concealment	*Stash Bonus*	*XP Value*
None	—	+0
Poor	+5	+5
Average	+10	+10
Superior	+20	+20

Target	*Sample Trap Actions*	*XP Value*
Triggering character	Needle; puff of dust; ray of light; shackle	+0
Random party member	Spray of darts; small gas cloud; swinging log; falling rocks	+5
Entire party	Collapsing ceiling; cloud of gas; avalanche; gaping pit; giant barred gates	+10

Effect	*Damage or Other Effect*	*XP Value*
Acid damage	1d6 acid damage per 2 TL, Ref DC 15 for 1/2 damage	+20
Alarm	Adversaries in vicinity become aware the trap has been triggered	+10
Attribute impairment	1d6 temporary impairment with 1 attribute, Will DC 20 to negate	+30
Cave-in	Pinned beneath rubble (1d20 × 1,000 lbs.)	+20
Captured	Held in place, Prestidigitation DC 30 to escape	+30
Crushing	1d6 lethal damage per round until trap is Disabled	+30
Condition	1 condition for 3d6 rounds, Fort DC 20 to negate	+20
Curse	–2 action dice	+20
Divine damage	1d6 divine damage per 2 TL, Ref DC 15 for 1/2 damage	+20
Draining	Fort DC 15 each round or lose 1/2 current vitality and wounds (rounded up)	+50
Drowning	Suffocation *(see page 217)*	+30
Electrical damage	1d6 electrical damage per 2 TL, Ref DC 15 for 1/2 damage	+10
Explosive damage	1d6 explosive damage per 2 TL, 5 ft. blast increment	+20
Falling damage	1d6 falling damage per 2 TL, Ref DC 15 for 1/2 damage	+20
Fire damage	1d6 fire damage per 2 TL, Ref DC 15 for 1/2 damage	+20
Lethal damage	1d6 lethal damage per 2 TL, Ref DC 15 for 1/2 damage	+10
Knocked out	Unconscious, Fort DC 20 to negate	+30
Pain	–2 penalty with all checks for rest of the scene, Will DC 20 to negate	+10
Poison	Ranged attack (+10 attack bonus); with a hit, target is exposed to 1 poison	+10
Stress damage	1d6 stress damage per 2 TL, Ref DC 15 for 1/2 damage	+10
Subdual damage	1d6 subdual damage per 2 TL, Ref DC 15 for 1/2 damage	+10

- *Combat:* Perhaps for succeeding or failing at a Challenge, perhaps when the characters reach a Challenge or at a specific time, adversaries arrive to make their lives difficult.
- *Damage for Failure:* The characters suffer a certain amount of damage if they fail the Challenge attempt.
- *Extra Check:* One or more characters unexpectedly have to make a check in addition to the Challenge. Unless the check is a free action, the characters making it may not be able to help with the current Challenge.
- *Extra/Less Time:* Generally with a successful or failed Challenge attempt, the characters gain a bit more or less time to complete the Task.
- *Gear Bonus/Penalty:* A particular piece of gear is especially helpful or hurtful when attempting the Challenge, applying a bonus or penalty.
- *Reward:* For taking a particular action, the characters gain a reward (e.g. 1–2 Reputation, a Treasure Roll, etc.).
- *Skill Bonus/Penalty:* Conditions present during the attempt apply a bonus or penalty with the Challenge or another skill.
- *Trap:* With failure, the characters trigger a trap *(see page 338)*.

Over time you'll develop your own events, giving you even more options. Complex Tasks are a great place to experiment with the *Fantasy Craft* system, as you can test mechanics for just one Challenge attempt without worry that a bad call will have lasting negative impacts on your game.

Vary the skills and events, playing to the party's strengths *and* weaknesses, and don't stack the odds too heavily for or against them. Look for ways to expand and evolve the Task's story with each new Challenge or attempt, compounding and raising the stakes. Think of a Complex Task like a riveting sequence in your favorite high adventure movie, when the music swells and the heroes sweat. The best of these sequences periodically introduce new problems to ratchet the tension and keep the audience nervous, but they also throw the heroes a bone every so often to relieve the audience's pressure. It's exactly this kind of roller-coaster action that should guide every Complex Task.

Finally, it's crucial to plan for any characters who wind up uninvolved in the Task. Concurrent combats are good for this, especially when the Task unfolds round-by-round. Another option is to create a second Task for the rest of the characters to complete. Perhaps they can support the characters attempting the Task with activities on the side (finding gear or information to help them, or preparing a location before the Task moves into it). Maybe the players have something to discuss — a recent plot development or an upcoming plan — while their characters root for the others? They could even make a team check once per attempt to turn their rooting into a morale bonus! The sky's the limit but the important thing is that everyone have something to do throughout.

Here are some examples of scripts in action, expanding the ideas in the base Complex Task rules.

TASK SCRIPT: THE CLOCKWORK MONSTER

In this Progress Task, a massive clockwork automaton is marching toward the heroes' home village, sent to enact revenge for the party's efforts against its creator. The party must complete 5 Challenges in 8 rounds, after which the automaton reaches the village and starts destroying buildings. The Task continues even then, until the characters disable the monster, but the village loses a random building for every 3 additional rounds they take.

Challenge 1 (Acrobatics or Climb DC 20): With success, an character clambers up and enters the automaton (a grappling hook is especially helpful here, granting a +2 bonus with either check). Each character must attempt this check on his own but all of them may benefit from the same grappling hook. Up to three characters may enter the automaton at once but the rest of the party is still involved; each round they may help clear the village before the automaton arrives (a second Task script could be prepared for this group).

Challenge 2 (Search DC 18): With success, this cooperative check lets characters within the automaton find its clockwork heart, a mind-boggling array of tubes, gears, and pistons. This Challenge features no events.

Challenge 3 (Prestidigitation DC 15): With success, this cooperative check disables a gear that blocks access to the pistons running the automaton's legs (the gear is inconsequential otherwise, at least for the purposes of this script). Unfortunately, with failure, the characters attempting the Challenge get caught in the gears instead, suffering 1d8 lethal and 1d6 stress damage each.

Challenge 4 (Prestidigitation DC 20): Now that the characters are at the leg pistons, success wreaks havoc with the automaton's movement. It's not enough to stop it cold but the metal beast slows, its motion erratic. As a surprise bonus, the characters get 2 additional rounds to complete the Task! Unfortunately, any of them without at least 4 ranks in Acrobatics suffer a –2 penalty due to the automaton's jerky movement.

Failure is worse; sections of the automaton's innards break free, "waking up" to defend it from within. One additional mob of these standard adversaries awakes with each failure (these mobs are equal in number to the characters inside the automaton, not the whole party). The first time they sprout from the surrounding gears they gain a surprise round against the party. They share sentience with the larger monster and go dormant when the Task is won. They have the following statistics.

Automaton Defenders (Small Construct Walker — 32 XP): Str 10, Dex 16, Con 12, Int 10, Wis 6, Cha 6; SZ S (Reach 1); Spd 20 ft. ground; Init III; Atk II; Def II; Res IV; Health II; Comp I; Skills: Acrobatics IV, Athletics III; Qualities: *Achilles heel (electrical), always ready, damage reduction 1, natural defense*

Attack/Weapons: Gear Grind (Slam II: dmg 1d4 lethal; threat 20)

Treasure: None

Challenge 5 (Prestidigitation DC 25): The combat continues through this Challenge. With success, the characters finally disable the monstrous automaton and its defenders, but its momentum continues to carry it forward even as its leg gears have locked in place. The automaton tips and collapses, finishing the job. If this is the last round before it reaches the village, it takes out the most outlying building in the process. The fire burning in its crystal eyes dims and the immediate threat is over.

But what of the heroes within? The last event finds each of them making an Acrobatics check to grab hold of something or dive free as the automaton comes down. With success, a character emerges unscathed but if he fails he suffers 3d6 lethal damage from falling and battering debris.

TASK SCRIPT: THE TRAPPED TOMB

In this timed Precision Task, the party is trapped inside a tomb that will fill up with poison gas in 10 rounds. The tomb contains the life's writings of the paranoid architect, who buried clues to escaping throughout his journals. Three successful Investigate checks are required to find and decipher the clues; thereafter, the characters are exposed to concentrated lethal poison once per round until they escape or die.

The first Challenge is DC 10, the second is DC 15, and the third is DC 20. As an added complication, the Challenges are a linked puzzle and all three must be deciphered correctly in a row; failure with even one leads the characters to the wrong conclusion, resets the process, and opens a random wall panel as shown on Table 7.7: The Trapped Tomb *(see below).*

DISEASES

Except for the very mildest bugs, diseases should only be introduced to serve the plot of a prepared adventure. Many are lethal or inflict permanent disabilities, which can easily derail or even end a game without the proper forethought. Always consider whether an antidote is available and if so, who controls it. Compare a disease's stats against the Fortitude save bonuses of not only the party but important NPCs. Be prepared for the disease to become a primary focus of the players' attention, and likely that of the local population as well.

Diseases tend to look and act the same no matter the time period or genre (though in fantasy games their perceived origins are often little more than ludicrous hysteria). Table 7.8 includes a selection of common modern diseases with potential fantasy analogs *(see below).* Feel free to use these or consider them a

Table 7.7: The Trapped Tomb

d6 Result	Contents of Panel
1	More gas! The room floods with gas 1 round sooner.
2	Missile trap! Each character is immediately hit by a Magic Missile *(see page 136).*
3	Snakes! A pile slithers out and disappears under the rising blanket of gas. Each round, one random character is attacked (Attack III, Bite II (dmg 1d4 lethal + baffling poison; threat 18–20; *qualities*: venomous). The characters can't see the snakes to attack them in return and even if they could there isn't enough time to kill all of them
4	Pit trap! A pit opens beneath one random character. With a failed Reflex save (DC 15), the character falls in, suffering 2d6 falling damage (Ref DC 15 for 1/2 damage).
5	Fire trap! Each character is immediately attacked by a Fireball (Spellcasting II; Casting Level 6)
6	Treasure! Roll 1d20+5 and consult Table 7.11: Any *(see page 345).*

Table 7.8: Diseases

Name	Effect	Incubation	Possible Fantasy Name and Perceived Origin
Anthrax	–4 Str, –4 Con	1d6 days	Herdsman's curse (spread by animals)
Bubonic plague	–6 Str, –6 Con	1d6 days	The Black Death (spread by monsters)
Dementia	–4 Int, –4 Cha	1d6 years	The Mumbles (not thought to be a disease but a weakness)
Ebola	–8 Str, –8 Con	1d6 days	The Purple Death (the wrath of the gods)
E coli	*Sickened* for 1 Incubation Period	1d6 days	Glutton's pain (punishment for eating too much)
Encephalitis	–2 Con, –2 Wis	1d6 days	Brain bugs (tiny insects crawling in the ears and nose)
Flesh-eating virus	–4 Con	1d6 days	Mummy rot *(see page 276)*
Influenza (flu)	–2 Con	1d6 days	Traveler's cough (spread by visitors)
Leprosy	–2 Dex, –2 Cha	1d6 years	The Slough (comes from consorting with the dead)
Lupus	–2 Str, –2 Con, –2 Cha	1d6 years	The Wilding (gained in dark forests and secluded locales)
Smallpox	–2 Con, –2 Cha	1d6 days	Pockles (contracted by romancing out of status)
Typhoid fever	–2 Str, –2 Con	1d6 days	Thieves' plague (punishment for stealing)
Yellow fever	–2 Dex, –2 Con	1d6 days	Blood sweats (a sign that the victim has killed before)

guide for your own contagions. You can and should modify save DCs, Incubation Periods, effects, and other details to satisfy the needs of your story. *For more information about diseases, see page 216.*

EXPERIENCE

Experience Points, or "XP," represent a character's personal growth — what he takes away from his adventures translated as raw learning. When a character earns enough XP his Career Level rises, many of his statistics improve, and he may apply the level to a class *(see page 27)*. This process is often called "leveling" (e.g. a Level 3 character "levels" when his total XP reaches 5,000). No matter how much XP a character gains, he may only level once per adventure.

Characters don't generally earn XP individually but rather gain it as their party completes adventures. This keeps the bookkeeping simple (one XP total for everyone), but it also keeps Career Levels equal, ensuring the characters all have the abilities and raw numbers to stay effective against the same challenges. On occasion, one or more characters may break away from their party, completing objectives and/or defeating adversaries on their own. These characters earn additional XP and if this happens enough they may level ahead of their teammates. In these cases you might want to consider giving the rest of the party a chance to catch up, perhaps with by running additional encounters or even a special adventure just for them.

XP REWARDS AND CAREER PACING

It's your job as the GM to determine XP rewards, near the end of building each adventure. XP is awarded for completing objectives *(see page 335)*, encountering traps *(see page 338)*, and defeating adversaries *(see page 337)*. As a rule, the sum of these awards should fall between 750 and 1,000 XP for a single adventure, though you can go as high as 1,500 XP for a truly landmark outing.

Assuming you stick to these numbers, your party should level approximately once per adventure through Level 5. After that the rate should drop off to about once per two adventures until Level 11, then remain steady at once per three adventures until the late game (Level 17). Four adventures per level common from then until Level 20. Over the course of a character's entire career, this translates to somewhere between forty and fifty adventures total. For a group that finishes an adventure every two weeks or so, this should result in about two years of play from Level 1 to the pinnacle of heroism.

Each group is a little different, of course, and these expectations can vary dramatically based on the amount of XP you hand out. More than a couple landmark adventures and your group will pull ahead; more than a few low-yield outings and your group will take longer to cap out. If you're looking for another way to speed up leveling, consider the *fast levels* campaign quality *(see page 323)*.

APPLYING XP

XP can be awarded at the end of each scene or at the end of each adventure, as your group prefers. Awarding XP by scene gives the characters the chance to level during an adventure but it may also slow the game down as players make choices for their new levels. Especially if this is your first time roleplaying, we recommend awarding XP by adventure so everyone can take the time they need.

Whenever you apply XP, it must first be multiplied by the adventure's Threat Level, including any adjustments from Menace *(see page 334)*. The result is added to each character's total.

Example: A party of five characters Levels 4, 7, 9, 10, and 18 (TL 9) completes an adventure with a total base reward of 800 XP. The adventure's Menace is IV (Dangerous), which increases the TL by 2 (to 11). Each character gains 8,800 XP.

If any characters have fallen 2 or more levels behind the others, consider giving them a bonus of 10–25% of their adventure XP (to help them catch up). You should only do this if the player is present for the whole adventure and contributes frequently and positively.

PLAYING WITHOUT EXPERIENCE

If you find tracking XP tedious, consider playing without it. Just decide when you want the characters to level: per the story (after important or defining adventures, for example); after a set number of adventures; or when the group decides they want a little more variety.

This approach is tricky, as you need to plan ahead (past the next adventure), develop a formula that works for your group, or stay on top of it with your players, asking every adventure or two if they're still having fun at their current level. Regardless of the method you choose, you should always keep characters at the same level when playing without experience.

REPUTATION

Reputation basics are covered in Chapter 4 *(see page 186)*. Characters earn Reputation in two ways.

- Each character earns Reputation when his party completes an adventure, as shown on Table 7.9: Adventure Reputation *(see page 343)*. His Legend is added to this total *(see page 29)*. This reward is fixed and requires no special preparation.

- The party or an individual character may earn Reputation as an Instant Reward *(see page 344)*.

In both cases this Reputation signifies word spreading about the character and/or party's exploits. You can portray this in play by having shop keeps, tavern masters, squires, town criers, and others bring it up, even if they don't recognize the characters *(see page 187)*. The greater the Menace, the more spectacular the stories should be. Remember also that gossip tends to warp the facts over time — you can and should see the characters' saga shift as it passes from one NPC to the next.

Table 7.9: Adventure Reputation

Menace	Reputation Reward *
I	2 + Legend
II	5 + Legend
III	10 + Legend
IV	15 + Legend
V	20 + Legend

* This reward increases by 1 per critical objective completed.

REPUTATION PENALTIES

Characters can also *hurt* their Reputation by betraying their public allies and values. Word tends to spread even more quickly when a nominally heroic party sacrifices or lets innocents come to harm, even in order to win the day. No one trusts heroes that lie, steal, or cheat, and no one hires characters — even mercenary or villainous ones — who ignore job instructions.

When building an adventure, consider also how the characters might injure their Reputation: actions they might take to disappoint friends, employers, and others who rely on them. Just a few representing the most egregious offenses is plenty. Avoid minor slights, as they're not worthy of Reputation loss.

Assign each offence a penalty of –1 to –3 Reputation. The combined total from all offences in each adventure should be no higher than –10 Reputation. These penalties are applied simultaneously with Adventure Reputation and *may* reduce a character's Reputation to less than he had before. If they drop his Reputation to less than 0, his Reputation resets to 0 and his Renown in the most appropriate track drops by 1. This may have additional impacts, such as forcing the character to give up a Prize.

Example: Lord Bloodpyre, leader of the bloodthirsty orc tribes of the Vile Wash, honors a debt he's owed for years by letting a caravan pass through the tribe lands without paying tribute. Despite the fact that he treated the caravan with fairness (and potentially earned Reputation for doing so), he betrayed his tribe, triggering one of the game's longstanding Reputation penalties.

Indeed, Lord Bloodpyre has shown kindness several times recently and his Reputation is flagging as a result. This latest offence drops his Reputation to –2, so he loses 1 Noble Renown (the GM decides that his peoples' doubt is most fiercely leveled at his ability to lead). Lord Bloodpyre is at his Prize Limit, so he must also lose one of those. He chooses Bwarg the Goblin King, a contact and leader of an allied humanoid tribe. He's had a shaky relationship with Bwarg for some months now; after this, he shouldn't expect any support from the tiny quivering ones.

You may inform the players of potential Reputation penalties ahead of play or let them discover them as they commit their corresponding offences. The *offences* should be clear from the outset, however, preferably explained as part of the story or through NPC dialog (e.g. "Lord Bloodpyre, your continued mercy tries our patience.").

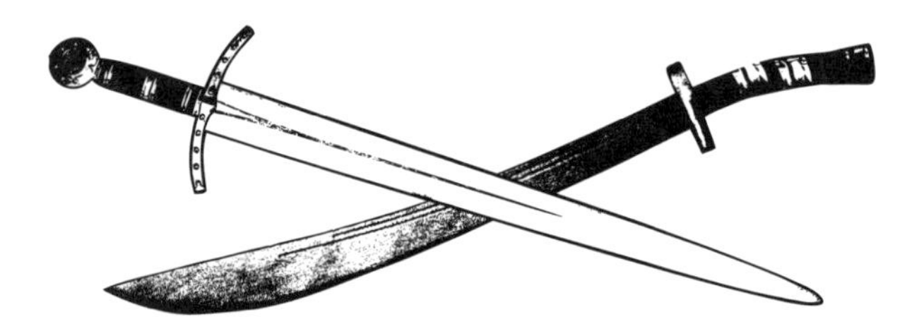

INSTANT REWARDS

Some actions are immediately memorable and some stories change a character's life forever. A hero is remembered for a daring and spectacular stunt, an ally is won with a single momentous decision, a debt of honor is offered for particular kindness, an unexpected inheritance leaves a character with an impressive family homestead, or a title is bestowed for an act so courageous that nothing short of a new name will do. All these are examples of "Instant Rewards," or awards of Reputation or Prizes earned immediately for pre-scripted actions and decisions in play.

Instant Rewards are built into adventures. They're a bit like objectives but pay off immediately in the form of 1–3 Reputation (for exciting, cinematic, and innovative actions) or a single Prize (when appropriate to the story). It's helpful to prepare one or two of these in each adventure, especially if any "pop out" at you as you build the story and apply the rules. You can also award them on the fly (with no preparation), and in both cases they work the same.

- The reward is immediately applied to the character's sheet.
- If the reward is a Prize and it takes the character over his Prize Limit, he must refuse it or sacrifice one of his other Prizes at the end of the adventure.

Instant Reputation Rewards are fairly trivial but Instant Prizes can sometimes rankle the other players. You should keep track of which characters receive them and make sure to compensate the other characters as soon as you can, perhaps with their own Instant Prizes, boosted Renown, more story focused on their characters, bonus action dice, fortuitous Favors, or useful gear. In groups where this is likely to become an issue, it's probably also a good idea to avoid individual Instant Prizes whenever possible, instead awarding them to the whole party (e.g. a grateful patron leaves them his estate when he dies, for example, or they're all knighted at once).

TREASURE

Treasure basics are explained as part of NPC construction *(see page 239)*. After defeating any number of NPCs with treasure, the party makes the listed number of **Treasure Rolls** for each group of identical NPCs in the encounter, no matter how many individual characters were defeated.

Example: Brungil's party sneaks into a hobgoblin camp and, over the course of several hours, defeats 20 of them. The hobgoblins all share the same statistics, which include a treasure entry of "1C, 1G." The party makes 1 Coin roll and 1 Gear roll for the entire camp.

Example: A hobgoblin chieftain with separate statistics and his pet warg are also located at the camp. Defeating them generates separate rolls even if they share the same treasure entry because they have different statistics. In this case the GM has assigned the same treasure code to the chieftain but only 1T to the warg. Assuming the party defeats everything in the camp they make 2 Coin rolls and 2 Gear rolls (for the hobgoblins and the chieftan), and 1 Trophy roll (for the warg).

For each Treasure Roll, the party rolls 1d20, adding the NPC's Threat Level and any relevant modifiers from Table 7.10: Treasure Roll Modifiers *(see page 345)*. Find the result on the appropriate treasure table (7.11–7.16) to learn what the characters recover.

Example: Following the first of the two previous examples, Brungil's party consists of 5 characters (including him) and the Threat Level is 8. For each Treasure Roll, the party totals 1d20 + 8 (the TL) + 5 (because the hobgoblins are in their lair) + 15 (because the NPCs outnumber the party by 4-to-1 (20 vs. 5). Thus, each Treasure Roll is 1d20 + 28.

Example: Following the second of the two previous examples, each Treasure Roll remains 1d20 + 28 unless the TL changes, as the NPCs are still located in their lair and they outnumber Brungil's party by the same ratio. If there were 4 wargs instead of 1, the ratio would rise to 5-to-1, making each roll 1d20 + 33.

PRESET TREASURE

Of course, the GM can feature specific treasure in an adventure anytime he likes. This allows him to carefully control the rate at which the party acquires wealth and has the added benefit of tailoring treasure precisely to each encounter. When the GM assigns treasure, he should reduce the adversaries' treasure codes accordingly.

Artifacts, in particular, make good candidates for preset treasure. Though it's (remotely) possible to randomly roll one on the treasure tables, the Game Master is strongly advised to build them into adventures, preferably one at a time, making each a capstone reward for monumental success (e.g. defeating the Big Bad in a campaign, preventing the destruction of a region, etc.).

Table 7.10: Treasure Roll Modifiers

Circumstance	Modifier
Encounter is in or leads to NPC's lair, nest, or camp	+5
Total NPCs outnumber the party by 2-to-1	+5
Total NPCs outnumber the party by 3-to-1	+10
Total NPCs outnumber the party by 4-to-1	+15
Total NPCs outnumber the party by 5-to-1 or more	+20

Table 7.11: Any

Result	Treasure
2–5	1T
6–10	1G
11–15	1C
16–20	1L
21–25	1M
26–29	2 categories of GM's choice (additional –5 modifier for each)
30–33	2 categories of party's choice (additional –5 modifier for each)
34–36	1T (additional +5 modifier)
37–39	1G (additional +5 modifier)
40–42	1C (additional +5 modifier)
43–45	1L (additional +5 modifier)
46–48	1M (additional +5 modifier)
49	2 categories of GM's choice (no additional modifiers)
50	2 categories of party's choice (no additional modifiers)

Table 7.12: Coin

Result	Silver Pieces (or equal value in any coin(s) of the realm)
2–5	1/4 × NPC's XP value (rounded down)
6–10	1/2 × NPC's XP value (rounded down)
11–13	1 × NPC's XP value (rounded down)
14–16	2 × NPC's XP value (rounded down)
17–19	3 × NPC's XP value (rounded down)
20–22	4 × NPC's XP value (rounded down)
23–25	5 × NPC's XP value (rounded down)
26–28	6 × NPC's XP value (rounded down)
29–31	7 × NPC's XP value (rounded down)
32–34	8 × NPC's XP value (rounded down)
35–37	9 × NPC's XP value (rounded down)
38–39	10 × NPC's XP value (rounded down)
40–41	20 × NPC's XP value (rounded down)
42–43	30 × NPC's XP value (rounded down)
44–45	40 × NPC's XP value (rounded down)
46–47	50 × NPC's XP value (rounded down)
48	75 × NPC's XP value (rounded down)
49	100 × NPC's XP value (rounded down)
50	Choose any 1 lower result + roll 1 additional result (applying TL but no other modifiers)

Table 7.13: Gear

Result	Treasure			Page Reference
2–4	Cheap goods (roll 1d20)			158
	1–2: Garrote	9: Brand	16: Pick or shovel	
	3: Lanyard	10–11: Canteen or waterskin	17: Pipe	
	4: Whistle	12: Fishing pole or net	18: Saw	
	5–6: Hand axe	13–14: Tool hammer	19: Umbrella	
	7–8: Blanket or bedroll	15: Average map	20: Grappling hook	
5–6	Spoiled food & drink (roll in next entry, gaining 2d6 servings with no effect or value)			165
7–9	Food & drink (roll 1d20 and gain 2d6 servings of result)			165
	1–2: Common meals	9–10: Comfort food	17–18: Spirits	
	3–4: Animal feed	11–12: Filling food	19: Fresh food	
	5–6: Rations	13–14: Hearty food	20: Spices	
	7–8: Coffee or tea	15–16: Booze		
10–11	Spoiled or destroyed consumables (roll in next entry, gain 1d4 items with no effect or value)			162
12–14	Consumables (roll 1d20 and gain 1d4 of result)			162
	1–2: Candles	11: Bandages	16: Tonics	
	3–4: Pints of oil	12: Jars of body paint	17: Jars of leeches	
	5–6: Pieces of chalk	13: Sheaves of paper	18: Salves	
	7–8: Jars of common ink	14: Smelling salts	19: Balms	
	9–10: Torches	15: Jars of invisible ink	20: Ointments	
15–17	Valued goods (roll 1d20)			158
	1: Hemp rope (50 ft.)	9: Chain (10 ft.)	15: Glasses or goggles	
	2–3: Firesteel or tinderbox	10: Game (GM's choice)	16: Bandolier	
	4: Grooming case	11: Magnet	17: Manacles	
	5–6: Candle lantern	12: Snowshoes	18: Silk rope (50 ft.)	
	7: Skis	13: Tent	19–20: Hooded lantern	
	8: Block and tackle	14: Hourglass or sundial		
18–19	Destroyed container (roll in next entry, gaining an empty container with no effect or value)			158
20–22	Container (roll 1d20 + roll 1 additional result as noted for contents, applying TL but no other modifiers *)			158
	1–2: Jar/jug (Any)	9–10: Saddlebags (Any)	15–16: Large sack (Any)	
	3–5: Pouch (Coin)	11–12: Backpack (Any)	17–18: Small chest (Any)	
	6–8: Purse (Coin)	13–14: Small sack (Any)	19–20: Large chest (Any)	
23–24	Destroyed weapon (roll 1d20 and gain 1 weapon of party's choice in resulting category with no effect or value)			176
	1–5: Blunt	11–15: Hurled	19–20: Black powder (re-roll if unavailable)	
	6–10: Edged	16–18: Bows		
25–26	Broken weapon (roll 1d20 and gain 1 weapon of party's choice in resulting category that may be repaired)			176
	1–5: Blunt	11–15: Hurled	19–20: Black powder (re-roll if unavailable)	
	6–10: Edged	16–18: Bows		
27–30	Weapon (roll 1d20 and gain 1 weapon of party's choice in resulting category)			176
	1–5: Blunt	11–15: Hurled	19–20: Black powder (re-roll if unavailable)	
	6–10: Edged	16–18: Bows		
31	Upgraded weapon (roll 1d20 and apply result to a weapon in the previous entry **)			185
	1–2: Craftsmanship (roll on Table 7.17 — no rules unless playable species)			353
	3: Crude materials	9: Bayonet	15: Bleed	
	4: Lure	10: Massive	16: Guard	
	5: Cord	11: Hurl	17: Injector †	
	6: Grip	12: Trip	18: Armor-piercing	
	7: Hook	13: Bludgeon	19: Superior materials	
	8: Cavalry	14: Keen	20: Finesse	

Result	Treasure			Page Reference
32–34	Precious goods (roll 1d20)			158
	1–2: Mirror	8–9: Flag or standard	16: Music box	
	3–4: Bullseye lantern	10–11: Seal or signet ring	17: Spyglass	
	5: Poison ring †	12: Magnifying glass	18: Pocket watch	
	6: Detailed map	13–14: Musical instrument	19: Holy symbol (GM's choice)	
	7: Hand scale	15: Astrolabe	20: Holy book (GM's choice)	
35–36	Upgraded precious good (roll 1d20 and apply result to a good in the previous entry)			159
	1–12: Durable	13–16: Hollow	17–20: Masterwork	
37–38	Spoiled poison (roll in next entry, gaining 1d4 uses with no effect or value)			166
39–41	Poison (roll 1d20 and gain 1d4 uses of result)			166
	1: Putrid	8: Intoxicating	15: Paranoia	
	2: Deafening	9: Maddening	16: Lethal	
	3: Sickening	10: Stupefying	17: Knockout	
	4: Numbing	11: Weakening	18: Baffling	
	5: Agonizing	12: Debilitating	19: Blinding	
	6: Necrotic	13: Disorienting	20: Paralyzing	
	7: Slowing	14: Enraging		
42	Upgraded poison (roll 1d20 and apply result to a poison in the previous entry)			166
	1–3: Concentrated	10–12: Potent	17–18: Virulent	
	4–6: Persistent	13–14: Fast-acting	19–20: Cocktail (2 random poisons)	
	7–9: Exotic	15–16: Gas		
43	Destroyed armor (roll in entry after next, gaining armor with no effect or value)			174
44	Broken armor (roll in next entry, gaining armor that may be repaired to regain full effect and value)			174
45–47	Armor (roll 1d20)			174
	1–2: Padded (partial)	10: Heavy fittings	16: Hardened leather (moderate)	
	3–4: Leather (partial)	11: Chainmail (partial)	17: Platemail (partial)	
	5–6: Padded (moderate)	12: Hardened leather (partial)	18: Scalemail (moderate)	
	7: Light fittings	13: Studded leather (full)	19: Platemail (moderate)	
	8: Studded leather (partial)	14: Scalemail (partial)	20: Articulated plate (moderate)	
	9: Leather (moderate)	15: Chainmail (moderate)		
48	Upgraded armor (roll 1d20 and apply result to an armor in the previous entry — re-roll fittings)			175
	1–3: Craftsmanship (roll on Table 7.17 — no rules unless barding and playable species)			353
	4–5: Fitted	11: Fireproofed	18: Discreet	
	6–7: Crude materials	12: Ceremonial	19: Cushioned	
	8: Vented	13: Blessed	20: Reinforced	
	9: Warm	14–15: Superior materials		
	10: Insulated	16–17: Lightweight		
49	Plot item (roll on Table 7.18, applying the result to the GM's choice of any 1 item on this table)			354
50	Choose any 1 lower result (rolling for specifics) + roll 1 additional result (applying TL but no other modifiers)			—

* If the resulting item is too large to fit in the container, the container is instead empty.

** Upgrade restrictions still apply.

† This item comes with 1d4–1 uses of 1 random poison.

Optional Detail

Species: Though this table only generates species results for armor and weapons, you can roll on Table 7.17 to suggest flavor for any item *(see page 353)*. Goblin food is bound to be quite different in your setting than human food, for instance, just as brain fiend medicines and poisons are bound to vary from those crafted by driders.

Table 7.14: Loot

Result	Treasure			Value
2–3	1 set of raw materials (by Crafting focus — roll 1d20, weight equal to silver value in lbs.)			1d20s
	1: Carving	9–10: Metalworking	18: Scrolls	
	2–3: Carpentry	11: Pharmacy	19: Elixirs	
	4: Chemistry	12–13: Pottery	20: Magic items	
	5–6: Cooking	14–15: Stonecutting		
	7–8: Inscription	16–17: Tailoring		
4–5	1 set of trade goods (roll 1d20)			1d20 × 2s
	1: Bone/ivory (10 lbs.)	8: Furniture/décor (50 lbs.)	15: Oil (10 lbs.)	
	2: Chemicals (2 lbs.)	9: Grains (25 lbs.)	16: Paint/dye (5 lbs.)	
	3: Cosmetics/perfume (2 lbs.)	10: Herbs/spices (10 lbs.)	17: Paper/parchment (10 lbs.)	
	4: Drugs (5 lbs.)	11: Incense (2 lbs.)	18: Stone (100 lbs.)	
	5: Fabric (50 lbs.)	12: Livestock (750 lbs.)	19: Tobacco (10 lbs.)	
	6: Fruit/vegetables (25 lbs.)	13: Metal (100 lbs.)	20: Wood (25 lbs.)	
	7: Fur/hide (25 lbs.)	14: Nuts (25 lbs.)		
6–7	1 piece of art (roll 1d20)			1d20 × 5s
	1: Architecture (1,000 lbs. *)	8: Ornate jewelry (roll on Table 7.16)	15: Sculpture (10 lbs.)	
	2: Book/scroll/text (5 lbs.)	9: Ornate clothing (roll on Table 7.16)	16: Sheet music (1/10 lb.)	
	3: Crystalware (5 lbs.)	10: Ornate gear (roll on Table 7.13)	17: Statuary (500 lbs.)	
	4: Embroidery (5 lbs.)	11: Magic art (1d20 lbs.)	18: Stuffed critter (roll on Table 7.17)	
	5: Glassware (5 lbs.)	12: Mosaic/relief/carving (1,000 lbs. *)	19: Tableware (5 lbs.)	
	6: Illusion (0 lbs., no value)	13: Painting/drawing/etching (2 lbs.)	20: Woodblock print (2 lbs.)	
	7: Invention (1d20 lbs.)	14: Pottery (5 lbs.)		
8–9	1 gem (roll 2d20, weighs 1/25 lb.)			1d20 × 10s
	2: Agate	15: Emerald	28: Opal/fire opal	
	3: Alexandrite	16: Garnet	29: Pearl	
	4: Amber	17: Hematite	30: Peridot	
	5: Amethyst	18: Iolite	31: Quartz	
	6: Aquamarine	19: Jacinth	32: Rhodochrosite	
	7: Azurite	20: Jade	33: Ruby	
	8: Beryl	21: Jasper	34: Sapphire	
	9: Bloodstone	22: Jet	35: Sard	
	10: Carnelian	23: Lapis lazuli	36: Spinel	
	11: Citrine	24: Malachite	37: Topaz	
	12: Coral	25: Moonstone	38: Tourmaline	
	13: Corundum	26: Obsidian	39: Turquoise	
	14: Diamond	27: Onyx	40: Zircon	
10–11	1 set of raw materials			1d20 × 2s
12–13	1 set of trade goods			1d20 × 5s
14–15	1 piece of art			1d20 × 10s
16–17	1 gem			1d20 × 25s
18–19	1 set of raw materials			1d20 × 5s
20–21	1 set of trade goods			1d20 × 10s
22–23	1 piece of art			1d20 × 25s
24–25	1 gem			1d20 × 50s
26–27	1 set of raw materials			1d20 × 10s
28–29	1 set of trade goods			1d20 × 25s
30–31	1 piece of art			1d20 × 50s
32–33	1 gem			1d20 × 100s
34–35	1 set of raw materials			1d20 × 25s
36–37	1 set of trade goods			1d20 × 50s

Result	Treasure	Value
38–39	1 piece of art	1d20 × 100s
40	1 gem	1d20 × 250s
41	1 set of raw materials	1d20 × 50s
42	1 set of trade goods	1d20 × 100s
43	1 piece of art	1d20 × 250s
44	1 gem	1d20 × 500s
45	1 set of raw materials	1d20 × 100s
46	1 set of trade goods	1d20 × 250s
47	1 piece of art	1d20 × 500s
48	1 gem	1d20 × 1,000s
49	Plot item (roll on Table 7.18, applying the result to the GM's choice of any 1 item on this table)	—
50	Choose any 1 lower result (rolling for specifics) + roll 1 additional result (applying TL but no other modifiers)	—

* This item is immobile and fixed in the environment. It may be separated at the same rate as clearing rubble *(see page 154)*.

Special Note on Loot Value

The values of loot rise at higher results but the types, weights, and quantities generally don't. This is because loot spans a broad range of quality — not all diamonds shine with the same luster, nor do all crops or works of art demand the same price. As with many treasure results, specific flavor is left to the GM and the group to allow for varied and setting-specific details. A more valuable diamond might be slightly larger, for example, or it might be uncut. Crops with a higher silver value might have been grown in particularly rich soil and greater art might have been created by an accomplished or aspiring master.

Optional Detail

Other Loot as Raw Materials: The raw materials entries represent various resources that are especially well suited to crafting, often because they've already been prepped in some fashion (treated wood, polished stone, etc.). With the GM's permission, however, a character might be able to use some other loot as raw materials (e.g. wood trade goods in carpentry). In such cases, the materials are worth 1/2 their normal loot value as raw materials, rounded down (e.g. 120s in wood trade goods is worth 60s as carpentry raw materials).

Supply and Demand: The value of loot can shift significantly depending on area, season, how much is being brought in and sold, and many other factors. Listed values are the highest the party will see but the GM can vary them by rating **demand** and **supply** each on a scale of 1–10, subtracting supply from demand, and multiplying the result by 10. This becomes a percentage applied to the listed value.

Example: The GM determines that hides are in high demand (because people are stocking up for winter) but that few are coming in (due to dwindling animal populations in the area). He rates demand as 8 and supply as 2, for a result of 6 (+60% of listed value). Thus a stack of hides listed at 300s would actually be worth 480s on the open market.

This rule could actually be applied to any treasure, or indeed any gear, but it's most appropriate for loot.

Table 7.15: Magic

Result	Treasure
2	1 Level 0 scroll (roll on Table 3.2: Spells)
3	1 Level 1 scroll (roll on Table 3.2: Spells)
4	1d4 purifying oils or sustaining potions (party's choice)
5	1d4 weak acid vials
6	1d4 vitality potions
7	1 Level 2 scroll (roll on Table 3.2: Spells)
8	1d4 repairing oils
9	1d4 magic weapon oils
10	1d4 blessing oils
11	1d4 weather vials
12	1d4 striking potions
13	1d4 shattering vials
14	1d4 healing potions
15	1d4 mana potions
16	1 Level 3 scroll (roll on Table 3.2: Spells)
17	1d4 obscuring oils
18	1d4 resisting oils (roll 1d6 for each) 1: Acid, 2: Cold, 3: Electrical, 4: Fire, 5: Heat, 6: Sonic
19	1d4 consecrating oils
20	1d4 darkvision potions
21	1d4 blurring oils
22	1d4 mage armor oils
23	1d4 wilding oils
24	1d4 confidence or refreshing potions (party's choice)
25	1d4 strong acid vials
26	1d4 hold person vials
27	1d4 restoration oils
28	1 Level 4 scroll (roll on Table 3.2: Spells)
29	1d4 tongues potions
30	1d4 love potions
31	1d4 sanctifying oils
32	1d4 animating vials
33	1d4 invisibility potions
34	1 Level 5 scroll (roll on Table 3.2: Spells)
35	1d4 anointed vials
36	1 Level 6 scroll (roll on Table 3.2: Spells)
37	1d4 boost attribute potions
38	1 Level 7 scroll (roll on Table 3.2: Spells)
39	1 oil cocktail (roll 1d20 twice, ignoring duplicate results) 1–2: Blessing, 3: Blurring, 4: Consecrating, 5–6: Mage armor, 7–8: Magic weapon, 9–10: Obscuring, 11–12: Purifying, 13–14: Repairing, 15–16: Resistance, 17: Restoration, 18: Sanctifying, 19–20: Wilding

Result	Treasure			
40	1 potion cocktail (roll 1d20 twice, ignoring duplicate results)			
	1: Boost attribute	5–6: Healing	10–11: Mana	15–16: Sustaining
	2: Confidence	7: Invisibility	12: Refreshing	17–18: Tongues
	3–4: Darkvision	8–9: Love	13–14: Striking	19–20: Vitality)
41	1 vial cocktail (roll 1d20 twice, ignoring duplicate results)			
	1–4: Animating	9–12: Hold person	17–20: Weather	
	5–8: Anointed	13–16: Shattering		
42	1 magic item (party chooses object, 1 Lesser Essence or 1 Lesser Charm — party's choice)			
43	1 magic item (party chooses object, 1 Greater Essence or 1 Greater Charm — party's choice)			
44	1 magic item (party chooses object, 1 Lesser Essence & 1 Lesser Charm)			
45	1 magic item (party chooses object, 1 Greater Essence & 1 Lesser Charm)			
46	1 magic item (party chooses object, 1 Lesser Essence & 1 Greater Charm)			
47	1 magic item (party chooses object, 1 Greater Essence & 1 Greater Charm)			
48	1 artifact (party chooses object and GM secretly rolls 1d20 for Essences and 1d20 for Charms)			
	1–4: 2 Lesser	9–11: 3 Lesser	15–16: 4 Lesser	19: 5 Lesser
	5–8: 2 Greater	12–14: 3 Greater	17–18: 4 Greater	20: 5 Greater
49	Plot item (roll on Table 7.18, applying the result to the GM's choice of any 1 item on this table)			
50	Choose any 1 lower result (rolling for specifics) + roll 1 additional result (applying TL but no other modifiers)			

Optional Detail

Elixirs: Roll 1d20: With a result of 17–18 the elixirs are distilled and with a result of 19–20 they're gaseous.

Scrolls: Roll 1d20: With a result of 17–18 the scroll's material is heavy and with a result of 19–20 it's solid.

Table 7.16: Trophies

Result	Treasure			Value
2–5	1 body part (roll 1d20 *, gaining body part with no value)			—
	1: Brain/control mechanism	8: Heart/engine/rib cage	15: Skull/jaw/horn	
	2: Ear/lobe/sensor	9: Knuckle bone/joint gear	16: Spine/fin/barb	
	3: Entrails/blood/slime/ooze	10: Limb/tail/wing	17: Teeth/mandible/pincer/stinger	
	4: Eye/antenna/sensor	11: Loins/breast	18: Tongue/tentacle/vine	
	5: Finger/toe/claw/talon	12: Nose/snout/beak/gills	19: Venom sack/gas gland/fire lung/silk spinner	
	6: Hair/fur/feather/leaf	13: Scalp/mane/face	20: Pristine body (perfect for stuffing!)	
	7: Hand/foot/hoof/paw/root	14: Skin/hide/bark/scale/shell		
6–7	1 flawless body part (roll in previous entry, gaining valuable body part)			1d20 × 2s
8	1 ruined piece of clothing (roll 1d20 in next entry, gaining an item with no value)			—
9–11	1 piece of clothing (roll 1d20)			1d20s
	1: Belt	8: Gloves	15: Shirt	
	2: Boots	9: Handkerchief	16: Shoes/sandals	
	3: Coat	10: Hat/headband	17: Tunic	
	4: Cloak/cape	11: Loincloth/stockings	18: Veil	
	5: Dress	12: Pants	19: Vest	
	6: Eyepatch	13: Robe	20: Vestments	
	7: Glasses/monocle	14: Sash		
12–13	1 flawless piece of clothing (roll in previous entry)			1d20 × 2s
14	1 ruined piece of jewelry or personal effect (roll 1d20 in next entry, gaining an item with no value)			—
15–17	1 piece of jewelry or personal effect (roll 1d20)			1d20 × 25s
	1: Amulet	8: Collar/choker	15: Pendant	
	2: Anklet/bracelet	9: Crown/tiara	16: Ring	
	3: Armband/bracer	10: Earring/piercing	17: Scepter	
	4: Brooch/medal	11: Fastener (comb, pin, etc.)	18: Talisman	
	5: Cane/walking stick	12: Locket	19: Tattoo (with skin)	
	6: Charm/trinket (per GM)	13: Mask	20: Torc	
	7: Circlet	14: Necklace		
18–19	1 flawless piece of jewelry or personal effect (roll in previous entry)			1d20 × 50s
20–22	1 body part			—
23–24	1 flawless body part			1d20 × 5s
25	1 ruined piece of clothing			—
26–28	1 piece of clothing			1d20 × 5s
29–30	1 flawless piece of clothing			1d20 × 10s
31	1 ruined piece of jewelry or personal effect			—
32–34	1 piece of jewelry or personal effect			1d20 × 100s
35–36	1 flawless piece of jewelry or personal effect			1d20 × 250s
37–39	1 body part			—
40	1 flawless body part			1d20 × 10s
41	1 ruined piece of clothing			—
42–43	1 piece of clothing			1d20 × 25s
44	1 flawless piece of clothing			1d20 × 50s
45	1 ruined piece of jewelry or personal effect			—
46–47	1 piece of jewelry or personal effect			1d20 × 500s
48	1 flawless piece of jewelry or personal effect			1d20 × 1,000s
49	Plot item (roll on Table 7.18, applying the result to the GM's choice of any 1 item on this table)			—
50	Choose any 1 lower result (rolling for specifics) + roll 1 additional result (applying TL but no other modifiers)			—

* If none of the defeated creatures have the body part, the player can re-roll or the GM can choose from parts the creature does have.

Body Parts as Raw Materials: Raw materials are various resources that are especially well suited to crafting, often because they've already been prepped in some fashion (e.g. polished bone). With the GM's permission, however, a character might be able to use certain body parts as raw materials (e.g. bones in carving). In such cases, the materials are worth 1/2 their normal trophy value as raw materials, rounded down (e.g. 20s in bone trophies is worth 10s as carving raw materials).

Table 7.17: All Things Great and Small

Result	Species			
1–2	Tool-using species I (roll 1d20)			
	1: Angel	6: Doppelganger	10: Faerie	16: Gorgon
	2: Brain fiend	7: Dragon	11–12: Ghoul	17: Hag
	3–4: Bugbear	8: Drider	13–14: Gnoll	18: Harpy
	5: Demon	9: Elemental	15: Golem	19–20: Hobgoblin
3–4	Tool-using species II (roll 1d20)			
	1: Homunculus	6: Manticore	11–12: Myrmidon	17–18: Troglodyte
	2: Imp	7–8: Merfolk	13: Naga	19: Troll
	3–4: Kobold	9: Minotaur	14: Rakshasa	20: Wight
	5: Lamia	10: Mummy	15–16: Sea Devil	
5–10	Heroic species (roll 1d20)			
	1: Drake	6: Giant	12–13: Ogre	18: Rootwalker
	2–3: Dwarf	7–8: Goblin	14–15: Orc	19: Saurian
	4–5: Elf	9–11: Human	16–17: Pech	20: Unborn
11–12	Common mount (roll 1d20)			
	1–3: Camel	7–10: Donkey/mule	13–17: Horse/pony	
	4–6: Dog	11–12: Elephant	18–20: Wolf	
13–14	Animal (roll 1d20)			
	1: Ape	6: Dinosaur	11: Livestock/game animal	16: Spider, giant
	2: Basilisk	7: Eagle	12: Monstrous insect	17: Stirge
	3: Bear	8: Griffon	13: Pegasus	18: Tiger
	4: Bulette	9: Hippocampus	14: Raptor	19: Turtle, giant
	5: Darkmantle	10: Kraken	15: Rhino	20: Water serpent
15–17	Other creature I (roll 1d20)			
	1–3: Barghest	8–10: Chimera	14: Jelly	18–19: Nightmare
	4–5: Burrowing behemoth	11: Gelatinous cube	15–16: Mimic	20: Pudding
	6–7: Chaos beast	12–13: Hell hound	17: Monstrous plant	
18–20	Other creature II (roll 1d20)			
	1–2: Rust monster	8–9: Shadow beast	13–14: Unicorn	18–20: Wyvern
	3–4: Salamander	10–11: Sporling	15: Watcher in the dark	
	5–7: Scavenger worm	12: Tarasque	16–17: Will o' wisp	

Using This Table: All playable species and most creatures in the Bestiary appear here, which is helpful in some cases (identifying a stuffed critter or a second-hand trophy), but can produce weird results in others (determining the race that made and/or uses a weapon or piece of armor). For this reason, tool-using species, heroic species, mounts, and animals are broken out into their own results so you can easily roll one when needed. To determine a random armor- or weapon-wielding species, roll 1d10 (or 1d12 if you want a chance of mount barding).

Table 7.18: There's Always More to the Story

Result	Plot
1	The item was created with a purpose. *Example:* It was a symbol of peace between rival cultures — until thieves stole it for a war-mongering military leader fearing an end to his illustrious career. The thieves were instructed to destroy the item but instead sold it, leaving a chance,however slim, that its purpose may yet be fulfilled. *Example:* It was made for the Patron Saint of Adventure, who is long gone but watches over those bold few exploring the fringes of society. Followers claim that the Saint's gear conveys a potent blessing but is also a sign of impending desperate need. *Example:* It was fixed in the earth where the last of the elder titans, progenitors of mortal man, perished. So long as it remained there the titans would slumber, leaving their descendants to their fate. Perhaps that explains the tremors of late…
2	The item hails from a previous age. *Example:* When it was constructed to aid a party of adventurers in vanquishing a vicious beast. The creature's blood stains the item but it's visible only under moonlight, when a Resurrection III spell can be cast on the item to bring the beast back. *Example:* When its presence comforted a dying queen in the twilight of her empire. It can do the same for party members, healing 1d6 stress damage each night it remains within a few feet of a slumbering character. Anyone healed in this fashion wakes from dreams of pleasant conversations about the world that was, and the dark forces that undermined it — forces that loom again. *Example:* Or rather, *its* previous age. The item travels backward through time, coincidentally taking its owners along for the ride.
3	The item… isn't an item. *Example:* It's a wounded mimic that's lost the ability to shapeshift. The characters could kill it or sell it to an apothecary — or they could nurse it back to health, gaining a free Animal Partner *(see page 108)*. *Example:* It was given physical shape by the fever-dreams of an ailing sorcerer, and it's just one (rather benign) invention; unless the sorcerer is cured, and quickly, his nightmares might soon follow. *Example:* It's a concealed construct sent out into the world by an aging inventor looking for worthy heirs to his collection of oddities. If the party proves it can treat gear with respect, perhaps the construct will lead them back to its creator.
4	The item features sockets or other crevasses. *Example:* The sockets are custom-made for a series of magically charged gems, each held by a predatory collector or monster. *Example:* The sockets are mouths that feed on fear, regret, and other negative emotions. This can be helpful, as it renders the party immune to stress damage. Of course, they aren't alone — everyone near the item is immune, including enemies. *Example:* The item is a key, fitting perfectly into the belly of an iron maiden. Learning the item's true purpose is hollow consolation however, when the torture device takes on the form of an actual maiden, a battle-maiden cursed centuries ago for war crimes. She plucks the name of the party's greatest foe from their minds and sets out on a crusade to destroy the enemy, leaving a gory trail of massacred innocents in her wake.
5	The item is… odd. *Example:* No matter how much damage it takes, it's always in perfect shape in the morning. If only the same could be said for whatever it sits on overnight. Everything beneath it crumbles to dust and the earth below turns black. Days later, perhaps long after the party has moved on, the charred earth cracks open and spews forth imps and other outsiders elated to finally be free. *Example:* If the party were to crack the item open they'd find flesh and bone… Where did it all come from? *Example:* The item's an illusion projected from its actual location — in the heart of an enemy camp.
6	The item is part of a set. *Example:* The full set awakens a powerful force or unlocks a secret location *Example:* The full set grants membership in an organization and special training (apply the Mentor/Patron Subplot) *Example:* The full set animates and serves its owner(s) as simple, non-combatant custodians. They cook, clean, and amuse.
7	The item is made from an unusual material. *Example:* It's composed of an element (air, earth, fire, or water) and can be used once per day to cast any spell of that element up to Level 2. Unfortunately, its use is taxing and inflicts 1d6 subdual damage. It must also be recharged once per year at a remote elemental temple guarded by a fungoid demon queen. *Example:* It's made with the harvested bits of a particular species (roll on Table 7.17). Its kin want the remains back, plus one or two of the new owners to make some items of their own. *Example:* It's made of solid sound and emits a constant, low hum. It works just as it's supposed to until a louder sound drowns it out, at which point it disappears until the louder sound is gone.
8	The item bears a unique crest or other identifying mark. *Example:* The mark is a unique piece of art commissioned to celebrate the love between a high-ranking noble and his beautiful bride. Should the party return the item to the couple, the noble promises them a free Favor (up to Noble Renown 7). *Example:* Though it may not be immediately obvious, the mark depicts a location — from another location. At the second location is a burial site where the artist's body lies, along with his greatest masterpiece. *Example:* The mark belongs to the item's long-dead maker. He was widely regarded as one of the foremost in his craft and if the party can find his hidden workshop and decipher his personal code, they just might learn from him (i.e. gain +5 ranks in Crafting).
9	The item is central to a prophecy (apply the Chosen Subplot). *Example:* "The fallen shall rise and the risen shall fall. So the cycle has been and so the cycle must be." *Example:* "To his earth place the Wood of N'gai, wither may come He Who is Not to be Named." *Example:* "And a band of heroes shall discover the vessel and bear witness to the last gasp of their world."

Result	Plot
10	The item is haunted by one or more ghosts or other spirits (apply the Haunted Subplot). *Example:* The spirits are victims of the previous owner and seek to scour all trace of him from the world — including the item. *Example:* The item is haunted by a single spirit, a former storyteller who never penned a great adventure epic. With the help of a friendly witchdoctor, the storyteller bound his spirit to the item, hoping it would fall into the hands of a band of heroes. Now… it has, and the spirit harangues the party with questions about their plans, histories, and escapades. *Example:* The spirit was killed by its shrewish spouse (who now lives in their luxurious home with a new lover). If the party helps to resolve the situation so the spirit can pass on, it leads them to the home's hidden deed (so they can claim it as a free Holding).
11	The item is hollow (apply the *hollow* upgrade). *Example:* It was made to smuggle items past port officials and city guards — items like the small vial of clear fluid the party finds inside. Maybe the liquid's part of a vile alchemical concoction or maybe, just maybe, it's the only cure for a terrible malady. *Example:* Anything put in the item disappears, replaced with something entirely different. *Example:* The item contains a vermin nest and the critters aren't happy about losing their home. They follow the party, seeking to steal the item back. Should combat ensue, the vermin share statistics with any random critter (roll on Table 7.17).
12	The item is stolen. *Example:* Or so it would seem. The item's actually a copy of the original, which is in the possession of the counterfeiter. *Example:* It was stolen from a widespread and pervasive cult with its eyes on the throne. It's one of many items that can be activated with a unique code phrase to communicate with, or observe, other spies and saboteurs working for the cult. *Example:* It was stolen from a prestigious religious museum. If returned, the party gains 5 Heroic Renown.
13	The item was involved in recent events. *Example:* The item is pivotal in a war or political crisis (apply the Military/Political Entanglement Subplot) *Example:* The item has been demanded as ransom by a shadowy group that kidnapped a wealthy family's firstborn son. *Example:* The item was used in a murder and can be used to identify the killer. The owner gains the Hunted Subplot as the killer tries to eliminate the lead. If a witness or a local constable sees the owner with the item, he also gains the Wanted Subplot.
14	The item contains or bears a map or clues leading to a location. *Example:* The item was stolen from the location, a crypt containing the spoils of a long-dead adventuring party. They hunted and killed the thief, then returned to the location to guard the spoils of their long career together. *Example:* A captive is held at the location. If freed, he becomes a new Contact for the party at no cost. *Example:* At the location, the item can become anything the party wants it to be, but only for the next 24 hours, and only so long as it stays in their possession. After that, the item vanishes.
15	The item is famous. *Example:* It's also ostentatious, immediately identifying the party wherever they go, and automatically shifting initial Dispositions by 1d20 for or against them. *Example:* As a vessel of ultimate destruction. Though it may be harmless now, people still avoid its presence and speak of it in hushed tones. *Example:* As part of a carnival act or stage play that brought great joy for generations. Everywhere the party goes they hear new stories.
16	The item was forged by the divine (randomly determine the item's Alignment from those available in the setting). *Example:* It also opposes the arcane, any spell use within 30 ft. of it triggering an Anti-Magic Field I spell centered on its location. *Example:* It "records" events and can be tapped to learn about the surrounding area's past. The events unfold like memories and become part of the viewer's recollections, which can be confusing to the uninitiated. *Example:* The item is a magnet for situations best solved by acting in accordance with its Alignment. If the party uses these tactics 3 or more times they gain the item's Alignment or (if they have an incompatible Alignment) suffer a Crisis of Faith Subplot.
17	The item changes shape and function once a day at a random time (roll on the "Any" treasure table for daily forms). *Example:* It takes the form of an object within 1 mile held by a person in profound emotional turmoil. *Example:* The item is a construct familiar cursed by its spiteful former master. It tries to communicate with the party (e.g. forming words on its surface, making repetitive or suggestive sounds, etc.) and begs for their help in killing its master and lifting the curse. *Example:* It's part of a grand bet staged by a trickster demigod and his orderly father. Each new form is crucial to solving a problem that crops up in the area. If the party figures it out and solves enough of the problems the father wins the bet and the trickster withdraws for 20 years; otherwise his father does. Either way the item vanishes.
18	The item is cursed (apply the Cursed Subplot). *Example:* It periodically invokes fear in those the party meets (possibly by warping their appearance in the minds of observers). *Example:* The item teleports the party to a random location once per day. *Example:* It saps the party's life force, increasing incoming damage by 1 point per injury.
19	The item is intelligent (Int and Wis 1d8+10 each + *telepathic* quality) *Example:* It wants to be returned to its previous owner and does everything it can to leave a trail for him to follow. *Example:* It's been around long enough to become jaded and delights in ribbing the party every chance it gets. It would be easy to just chuck it into a pit or sell it for scrap — if it weren't so damned helpful the rest of the time. *Example:* It animates when the party sleeps and/or leaves, destroying pieces of other gear out of jealousy.
20	Game Master Fiat

RAW MATERIALS

Certain Loot and Trophy results include raw materials, which can be used in Crafting *(see page 72)*. After an encounter, a party may also want to scavenge the area for more (e.g. prying metal and stone from fixtures, rendering animals for bones and hide, ripping apart location traps, tearing down structures, etc.). This is especially true if the game is entering Downtime.

No skill check is required. A character simply spends the required time and gains the listed silver piece value in raw materials, as shown on Table 7.19: Scavenging Raw Materials *(see below)*.

An item or patch of scenery may be scavenged by no more than 1/4 the characters who can stand on, in, or adjacent to it, rounded up (they need the extra room to work). Each time the number of characters scavenging an item or patch of scenery doubles, the time required drops by 1/2 (rounded up).

Example: Though nine characters may stand adjacent to a Medium marble statue, only three may scavenge it. When three characters work together, the time to scavenge the statue decreases to 1 hour (from 2 hours).

Scavenged materials may only be applied to certain Crafting projects (by Crafting focus), as defined by the GM when they're acquired. Raw materials weigh 1/10 their silver value in pounds (rounded up).

Only ruined items and scenery (including location traps) may be scavenged, and can only be scavenged once. Working and broken gear may be Dismantled with similar results *(see page 73)*.

CAMPAIGNS

In a campaign, adventures are run in succession, each a new episode in a continuing story. The same rules for developing an adventure story can apply to a campaign, producing an opening adventure, closing adventure, and many installments in-between, though if a campaign goes on long enough you may want to consider breaking your campaign into **seasons**, each with its own premiere and finale (just like a U.S. TV season or British series).

Campaigns usually feature recurring themes and concepts, which can be supported mechanically with campaign qualities *(see page 322)*. They sometimes also invoke a particular flavor, like horror, swashbuckling, wuxia, or one of the genres described on page 305, for which qualities are also a good fit.

Thanks to the Menace and scaling rules, you can start a campaign at any Career Level without modifying your adventures. Just set each character's XP to the minimum required for the desired level and dive into the action!

CAMPAIGN LENGTH

It's almost always a good idea to plan for the end of your campaign before it begins. This supports the overall structure of a campaign, helping you plan for the closing adventure as you move through the opening and middle ones. It allows proper foreshadowing and helps you set an appropriate pace every step of the way.

Unless you're lucky enough to have a play group without many commitments, it's best to plan for a window of opportunity (e.g. a summer vacation, a school year, or the duration of the "slow months" at work). Once you know how many sessions you can play, build adventures to span half of them. Assume the rest will be consumed by schedule conflicts, illness, unexpected work nights, and other life issues. Plus, if you actually manage to play through them all, you get a bonus campaign!

ADVENTURE PLAY VS. UNBROKEN PLAY

Campaigns can unfold in two ways — as a series of discreet episodes (each an adventure) or as an ongoing game with no perceptible breaks (this is common when the party controls the direction of the campaign, deciding what parts of the world to explore and what rumors and events to pursue). The former option changes nothing about the game but the latter raises an important question.

Table 7.19: Scavenging Raw Materials

Ruined Item/Scenery Size	Time Required	Raw Materials Scavenged
Diminutive *	15 minutes	1s × average Crafting bonus
Tiny	30 minutes	2s × average Crafting
Small	1 hour	5s × average Crafting bonus
Medium	2 hours	10s × average Crafting bonus
Large	6 hours	25s × average Crafting bonus
Huge	1 day	100s × average Crafting bonus
Gargantuan	1 week	200s × average Crafting bonus
Colossal	1 month	500s × average Crafting bonus
Enormous	2 months	1,000s × average Crafting bonus
Vast	6 months	2,500s × average Crafting bonus

* Smaller items and scenery cannot be scavenged.

WHEN DO ABILITIES AND TIMERS REFRESH?

Per adventure abilities and timers refresh after an arbitrary number of sessions you define (we recommend three). Per scene and per session abilities and timers are unchanged (you should still play with scenes and encounters, even if you abandon the full adventure format).

PAYING THE BILLS

Fortunately, this isn't an issue. Each character's upkeep — including the rental of inn rooms and other general travel costs — is folded into Prudence *(see page 153)*.

CONTINUITY

One of the most important decisions you can make when building a campaign is the frequency and magnitude of recurring locations, NPCs, adversaries, and stories. There's no right answer — old faces and places can appear in every installment or become major events. If your campaign revolves an arch-villain and his legions, then your course is probably set, at least toward the end of the campaign, but otherwise you can link as often as feels right.

The one, all-important watchword of campaign continuity — and indeed, adventure continuity as well — is *consistency*. No matter how often you include locations, characters, and stories, never contradict what's come before without an extremely well-considered reason. Permanent physical injuries, intense prejudices, family ties, and irrefutable truths witnessed by large crowds are all campaign truths and shouldn't be sacrificed for anything short of a game-changing revelation.

PLAYER PACKS AND CAMPAIGN LOGS

When prepping a campaign, you might find it helpful to develop a player pack, which presents the campaign concept and many world details such as important locations and NPCs, religions and myths, rumors, and general character knowledge. A player pack can also list possible character roles, available character options (if less than the full offering), anticipated goals, and expected behavior. This document can be a great asset, establishing an accepted baseline out the gate, and can help to keep everyone on the same page throughout the campaign.

Another helpful document is your campaign log, which is simply a list of important notes that grows as you develop new information for the game. It can be used to remember character and location names you come up with on the fly, house rules, ideas for upcoming sessions that come to you during play, and more. Over time you'll develop your own organization for this but to start we recommend Characters, Places, Miscellaneous, Rules, and Ideas.

RUNNING FANTASY CRAFT

Building worlds and adventures is only half your job — the rest is the business of promoting fun, making rules calls, and keeping the party and story moving forward. It's not easy. Running an RPG requires you to be equal parts team manager and stage director. You have to make decisions quickly and confidently, present ideas clearly and concisely, and be ready to improvise when the unexpected happens (and the unexpected will happen — it *always* happens).

Fortunately, the rewards are substantial: as a creator you see your vision realized more directly and intimately than any script writer or novelist; as an entertainer you enjoy a more immediate and interactive response from the "audience" than any actor on stage or screen; and as a judge you have complete control over an entire universe of places, characters, and events. It's your show — though you still have to make sure the players are happy in it. Let's start there, with your role at the table.

THE IMPARTIAL CHAMPION

The first thing to remember as Game Master is that you're the voice of success *and* failure. In order to remain equal and impartial in all things, you must remain positive and avoid bias at all times. You can't give in to anger, resentment, or spite, or let any players' negative emotions undermine your confidence and positive outlook, lest the whole game be dragged down with you.

When you remain level-headed and fair, and ensure your world and NPCs never strain credibility or take advantage of the party, there's no limit to your potential.

FUN FIRST

People play games for a reason: because they're *fun*. In this game, you're the conductor of fun. You write the chords and look for harmony with your players. If one of them falls out of tune, it's your responsibility to guide him back, hopefully without losing the others.

You have many tools at your disposal: a deep understanding of your story (and hopefully the game rules), insights about what your players enjoy, improvisational skill, and a sense of humor. Make the most of these and keep an eye out for disengaged or distracted players. They're the ones who need your attention the most.

LEAD BY EXAMPLE

Players also expect you to set the tone. If your NPCs are ruthless and adversarial, then they'll return the favor. If the challenges are relentless or exceedingly difficult, they'll start playing against *you* rather than their foes. Keep your game grave but not grim, challenging but not cruel, honor the characters in success *and* defeat, and the players will rise to every occasion

DEVELOPING YOUR STYLE

Over time, you'll develop your own personal GMing style. You might become a dedicated roleplayer, indulging in heavy drama and serious stakes, or you might run a "beer and pretzels" game that lets everyone goof off and laugh as much as they want, no matter what's going on in the story. You might be committed to using the rules "properly," or prefer a fast-and-loose method where anything that isn't essential to the core game is ignored or decided on the fly. All these options are equally valid ways to play the game but the only style that really matters is yours.

So what sort of GM are you? If you've never run before, you might not know. Taking a cue from Alignments *(see page 308)*, a Good GM might enable the players and story, cutting the heroes slack so long as the adventure advances and everyone has a good time, while an Evil GM might delight in foiling the players' best-laid plans, cooking up conniving plots and dastardly monsters to use against them. An Orderly GM might stick to the rules closely, keeping the game fair and "by the book" at all times, while a Chaotic GM might pitch the rules out the window the first time they interfere with his next move.

Most GMs are a blend of these. They champion and discard the rules as needed to keep the game fair and entertaining, and balance their adversarial and supportive roles to make sure the players usually win, though not always easily.

ROLE-PLAYING VS. ROLL-PLAYING

Roleplaying games are improvised theatre presented as a tactical exercise, play-acting governed by percentages, averages, and bell-curves. Like players, most GMs lean either towards roleplaying (focusing on story, character development, and plot) or "roll-playing" (focusing more on tactical elements, rules, and combat). Both options have advantages and pitfalls. Immersing the players too heavily in roleplay can leave character statistics unused (wasting the time spent choosing them), but rolling the dice for every action eliminates the human element, denying the PCs one of the greatest weapons in their arsenal — the players' instinct and problem solving ability.

Your approach should depend partially on the nature of your group but striving for a balance is helpful in most cases. Injecting opportunities for emotional and character investment between exciting fights (or vice-versa) should keep everyone interested and engaged.

HISTORY VS. FANTASY

Many fantasy games are set in the real world, or a world very close to ours: Ancient Greece and China, feudal Europe and Japan, the age of the Vikings and even the dawn of man are all popular choices. A real-world analog can provide a valuable touchstone for culture, technology, NPC details, and more, but it can also lead to problems if one or more players (including you) disagree about how rigidly to adhere to the record. If you embrace history at all, be sure to discuss your plans with the group and come to a consensus before you start the game. Ask history and fantasy enthusiasts their opinion directly, as they're the most likely to take issue with any conflicts they see, which can stall the game and cause unwanted friction.

REALISM VS. PLAUSIBILITY

Another balance to consider is that of what's possible in the real world vs. what's possible in your game. This being a fantasy RPG, magic and miracles can explain virtually anything, no matter how unrealistic or even implausible it is. Again, however, it's important to get all the players on the same page. As with history vs. fantasy, your GMing style needs to support the group's common preference.

BE FLEXIBLE

No matter how much your group discusses the game beforehand, and no matter how hard you work to develop a matching GM style, surprises will abound. You might find that the historical precedents the group's so fiercely committed to including produce too staid a setting, or that you have to make things up when you're all stumped about details, only to find you rather enjoy the result. You might initially want to keep the rules in the background, only to find everyone picking up the dice at every available opportunity. These aren't failures to implement a plan but rather signs that the plan might not actually be what you're after.

Remember, there are no right ways to play an RPG and every group must find its own happy medium (even if it's not really a medium at all!). In the end you should do what feels right and run for your group, being open to new options and styles as they present themselves.

WORKING WITH THE PLAYERS

One of your most important duties is managing the *player dynamic*, which boils down to entertaining the group, keeping their trust, and treating them with respect. Don't speak down to them, or make them feel dense for not "getting" the world or the adventure. Never make them feel like your job is more important than theirs — in fact, do exactly the *opposite* by keeping them at the center of the action except when you have to pass along vital details.

This isn't as difficult or selfless as it sounds. Every RPG revolves around the players and it's simple to apply this mindset to everything you do. Though your actions frequently "oppose" the player characters, every adventure you design, every monster you build, every decision you make, and every unexpected twist you conceive — it's all there to entertain the players, your friends.

Experienced GMs know to let the players take charge every so often, especially with things that aren't pivotal to the plot. Not only does it draw the players deeper into the campaign, it makes your job easier as well.

CHALLENGING THE HEROES

No party appreciates what it doesn't earn. Part of being a fair and impartial GM is making sure the party works hard for its successes — at least as hard as you work to provide the evening's adventure. Trial breeds triumph, and triumph breeds commitment to the setting, the storyline, and its creator. Make them sweat and at the end of the day their reward will taste twice as sweet.

Challenges are many and varied, and not all must involve combat. Tough moral and ethical choices, cerebral trials like puzzles and tactical exercises, and even intense debates — especially in character — can be just as stimulating, and offer their own unique rewards to boot.

MAKING RULES CALLS

No RPG can account for every possible situation, which is one of the reasons for a GM. You're the final arbiter when the rules fall short of exactly handling the action. Your call is the last word and so you need to ensure your rulings are both fair and best for the situation at hand. Consider the effects of every ruling: What other rules and character options might be affected? Will the ruling change anything about the world and adventure? Perhaps most importantly, how will the players react?

With the right answer in hand — a ruling that's fair and promotes fun — present it evenly and dispassionately. A cavalier, argumentative, or dictatorial ruling can cause resentment and may also provoke the players to argue. Your goal when making a ruling is to avoid debate or, failing that, to keep them as brief and concise as possible. Letting the game grind to a halt over a single rule helps no one. When in doubt, make the best call you can and let everyone know you'd like to discuss it after the session.

Remain as consistent as possible when revising and applying rules — the players rely on them to make important decisions, during and between games. If you change your mind about a previous ruling, give the players ample warning so they can raise any questions as needed.

LISTEN TO THE PLAYERS

One of the best things you can do for your game is listen to the players. *Constantly.* Never assume the game is working for them — not even if it was a month ago. Even if you talk to your players all the time, periodically start or end your session with a quick request for feedback, and preferably a few pointed questions. Have they particularly enjoyed or disliked anything about the game lately? Have they seen any movies or read any books they'd recommend as inspiration? Is there something they want out of the game that they're not getting?

You can also use this opportunity to get to know the *characters*. What's the heroes' take on recent events in the game? What do they want and how do they intend to get it? Who do they see as their biggest allies and threats? Are there plot threads the heroes want to resolve?

The answers should provide valuable insight and may spark ideas to keep the group interested. You don't have to give up your goals for the story, so long as you're incorporating the players' desires as well. Let them have a say and they'll keep coming back week after week, with dice in hand and smiles on their faces.

INVEST IN THE CHARACTERS

Players like to see their characters grow, on and off their record sheets, and elevating a hero beyond the stats — expanding on his background, aspirations, foibles, and triumphs — can dramatically increase a player's stock in the game. He'll be ecstatic to see his contacts blossom into recurring NPCs the party can rely on in perilous adventures, and won't even mind when old foes return, looking for revenge. He'll thank you for periodically adding new details about his improving lifestyle, embellishing on shiny new possessions and holdings, and coming up with inventive honorifics for NPCs to bestow upon him when they meet.

Of course, character development is a joint effort. You can certainly get the ball rolling — by incorporating character background into the next adventure, for example, or setting a scene in one of the characters' homes — but after that you should encourage the players to be just as involved. The very best campaigns are forged when creative people work together to make them a reality.

REWARD FAILURE

One of the most direct ways to get the players involved is to reward their *efforts* (not necessarily their successes — those are usually reward enough). Here's an example: a burglar suffers an error when scaling a castle wall. You *could* spend action dice to

trigger a critical failure, having the hero fall noisily and alert the royal guards, but that would penalize the player for doing what he's built to do. Instead, you could ignore the roll and let the character try again (or better yet, not call for the roll in the first place). After all, the burglar is doing something he's trained for… Why not just let the player describe how he does it, especially if the roll isn't crucial to the adventure's success?

If you're a stickler for random happenstance, use unlucky results to introduce moments of tension. Using the previous example, the burglar might barely catch himself, three fingers on a window ledge, as guards pass below. The window opens and a curious woman arches her eyebrow at the burglar, clearly amused. This puts the burglar in a more desperate position that doesn't rely on the same skill(s) as before. It raises the stakes and forces him to think on his feet. It also gives him new things to do rather than merely asking him for another identical roll. Who knows? Perhaps the burglar will discover his inner lothario and not only turn the situation around but come out ahead.

THE FIRM HAND

There are two very important exceptions to the "kid gloves" approach. First, any player who repeatedly and intentionally acts to the detriment of the group, ruining everyone's fun, demands a swift and strong response. If the problem involves his character's in-game actions (e.g. he's abusing allies or being unnecessarily violent), NPC reactions might be enough to bring him in line. Failing that, calm observations may be required and if the problem still persists, you might have to make an appointment to speak with the troublemaker away from the group. Never lose your composure in situations like this. Remain focused on the problem and resolved that the player needs to adjust his behavior. Explain that if he doesn't improve he'll be politely asked to leave the game.

The second instance is an adventure's climax, when everything hangs in the balance. Most of the time, this will happen in a Dramatic scene, when special rules raise the stakes and you have greater control over the game *(see page 335)*. However, this is only half the equation — even a Dramatic scene falls flat without a powerful dilemma and a compelling reason to tackle it. Emphasize the stakes with your very best dialog and descriptions. Drive the scene home with as much energy as you can muster. Stand. Few things get the players' attention as quickly as the GM getting out of his chair.

CHARACTER DEATH

The line between challenging the PCs and overwhelming them is fine indeed and recognizing it before it's crossed requires years of experience. It isn't just a matter of rules and probability — it's reading the players, anticipating their actions (especially the suicidal ones), and when needed, rescuing them from themselves.

When you're planning a deadly adventure, try to give the players a bit of warning, if not directly then certainly through the tone and escalating situations facing them in the game. Ideally, no adventure will require the death of a player character but in the event that one does it's even more vital the players see it coming. Prophesies are helpful for this, as are visions and other supernatural phenomena.

Of course, characters die accidentally: the party might underestimate a monster's threat, or you might not realize how deadly it is when building it; a failed saving throw can pitch a character into a lake of boiling acid; or a mook can score a lucky shot in a Dramatic scene. In any of these cases, and particularly when a hero's death would be anti-climactic or hurt the story, you can fall back on the rules for Cheating Death *(see page 384)*.

No matter when or how death occurs, give the player a final bit of glory, a chance to go out in style — with a closing phrase, action, or just a moment of reverence. All PCs are heroes when they die; it's the nature of things. The players will appreciate you making an effort to portray this at the table.

INTRODUCING NEW CHARACTERS

When a PC dies, it usually falls to you to introduce his replacement. This is a lot like bringing the party together for the first time *(see page 329)* and motivating the party in each adventure *(see page 327)*. Linking the new character's arrival to the previous character's death is by far your strongest option — perhaps he's a mutual enemy of the hero's killer, or a close friend or relative interested in justice (or vengeance) — though you could just as easily bring him in as a mercenary hired to help with the next quest, or assigned by the party's patron.

New characters can enter the campaign at the party's average Career Level, or perhaps one level lower if you'd like them to "earn their stripes" (this can discourage players from "recycling" characters when they discover a better set of options, and also forces them to work a bit harder to establish themselves in a veteran party). When characters are introduced at a lower Career Level, be sure to let them earn a little bonus XP until they catch up *(see page 342)*.

KEEPING THINGS ON TRACK

If there's one universal rule for GMs, it's this — none of your plans will survive contact with the players. They'll invariably take adventures into uncharted territory, interpret your plots in ways you couldn't imagine, and do things that defy your best efforts and planning. This isn't malicious — it's merely players assuming their natural role as "chaos" in the make-believe universe. Fortunately, you have some options for guiding the party back to the beaten path.

NUDGE THE PARTY

It's usually best for a party to return to the plot on its own terms, without your direct intervention. Players understandably like to be captains of their own destinies and that's part of what makes a tabletop RPG so much fun. Of course, affording them that latitude and still keeping them on target is can be tricky. The keys are subtlety and plausibility. Whenever possible, try to fold pointers back to the plot into the situation at hand.

For instance, when the party sails to a remote island to face a lich lord, you might not have the time or desire to map out miles of sea in every direction. Instead you can establish, early on or as the characters investigate the surrounding terrain, that the seas are infested with serpents and the neighboring islands are home to dangerous cannibals. Hopefully the players will think twice before diverting their charted course.

Take care not to overuse this option. If every scene involves the characters moving strictly from point A to point B, the PCs will start to feel powerless, not so much captains of destiny as stowaways in your story.

FOLLOW THEIR LEAD

Sometimes the players will suggest something that, despite falling outside the adventure, is too much fun to pass up. Indulge them! You've got all the tools you need at your fingertips: dozens of ready-made monsters and rogues in Chapter 6, plenty of random treasure and other rewards for victory *(see page 344)*, and Complications to keep things interesting *(see page 366)*. All that's needed is a little ingenuity and the time and willingness to go along for the ride.

Consider the previous example. Perhaps one of the players deduces that the lich lord hasn't conquered the cannibal islands because they have some power over him. This isn't something you've planned for but it sounds like an opportunity to enrich the adventure, so you run with it. After a brief course change (and a scuffle with a sea dragon run directly out of Chapter 6), the party encounters a tribe of cannibals and their necromancer king, learning that he keeps the lich lord at bay with a scepter topped with a golden monkey skull (a minor artifact you whip up on the fly using the rules at the back of Chapter 4). If the party can steal it, they'll have a new edge against the adventure's villain but even if they don't the players will still see the value of their input. They'll know they can command the story as decisively as you, which is more important than any planned scene or encounter.

LET THEM WIN

Statistically, 5% of all rolls fail (with a natural 1), which makes sense in isolated situations — especially dire, desperate ones. It breaks down a bit in relatively harmless situations, however, when the characters should be largely immune to misfortune. Fortunately, there's a simple answer: don't make them roll unless failure will mean something. For example, if the characters have lots of time and can simply retry a skill check, there's no reason to roll (they'll just try again, probably without penalty).

The watchwords here are "risk" and "consequence" — rolling without either is a pointless waste of time. What constitutes "risk" and "consequence" is entirely up to you. A character might not have to Impress a current lover to receive help, but a spurned former lover is another thing altogether (there's a risk of being turned away). If that lover's *also* sleeping with the sheriff, there's consequence too.

Keep your eyes peeled for "dice fatigue." Excessive die rolling can bog the game down, particularly when most of the characters are highly skilled and most of the checks are unopposed (a recipe for constant success, and lots of meaningless rolls). In these cases, you might want to let any character whose total bonus exceeds a DC succeed without rolling. As an example, let's say the party is scrambling across a narrow beam over a pit (Acrobatics DC 15). If the characters' Acrobatics bonuses are +18, +15, and +5, you might only make the third character roll as he's the only one with a *reasonable* chance to fail. Table 7.21: Chance of Success is your best friend when making these kinds of calls on the fly *(see page 370)*.

FAILURE IS AN OPTION

In any world where risk is constant, failure isn't far behind. Characters sometimes lose but it's important to remember that *players* don't. Every player, including you, wins just for showing up and having a good time. Some players take failure personally — whether it's losing a fight, letting a valuable piece of treasure slip through their fingers, or falling short of an objective — but you can turn it around for them. As in the earlier burglar example *(see page 359)*, the trick is turning the failure into new chances for adventure.

Let's say, for example, that the party fails to stop a doppelganger from kidnapping and replacing an influential lord in the king's court. This is a sad outcome and may have lasting impacts on the larger setting, but there's no reason for the adventure to end there. What if, in the process of hunting the creature, the party also discovered a far-reaching conspiracy against the throne? Suddenly the opportunities for redemption abound! There's less time for the players to grouse about their setback when they're mounting a resistance against the new regime.

SO IS LYING

When running a game, the adventure is your Bible and the rules are your Commandments, yet one of the most effective ways to keep things on track is to ignore them. Don't hesitate to seize opportunities to improve the game, even if they contradict the story you've laid out or the DCs and stats you've built. Have the players suggested a way out of a trap that's more interesting than what you've built into the adventure? Let them escape and applaud their ingenuity. Will a roll that's just a bit too low derail the adventure? Lower the DC and describe the narrow victory.

This is harder when you make everything known to the players, of course, which is why a little mystery can make all the difference. Limiting descriptions to just what the characters immediately sense is a good start. Some GMs also play with a screen to hide their rolls (so they can cheat for both sides), and others make critical rolls behind cupped hands.

HANDLING ACTION

Daring sword fights, nail-biting chases, and explosive magic duels are hallmarks of high adventure fantasy, regardless of world or adventure, so it's extremely helpful to develop a style for running action sequences. Ask yourself how important action is to the game you're running: How often does it appear, and how intense does it get? What flavor of action do you enjoy most: Flashy or restrained? Outlandish or grounded? Chaotic or tactical? Escalating or decisive? Should your action style change from adventure to adventure? Most importantly, how would the *players* answer these questions?

Action is often easiest to define with references to movies, comics, or video games you'd like to emulate. This can quickly translate what often amounts to a feeling, putting the whole group on the same page and providing them with handy cues to fall back on during the game. Common references can also quickly illustrate any differences between your tastes, and might suggest ways to blend them together as something new.

ACTION ADVENTURE PHYSICS

One of the first things to decide is the point at which action goes too far. If your world is "low fantasy" or very grounded, then "realistic" physics and human capabilities are the goal and a lot of movie action is right out. Over-the-top gonzo action is much easier, as there really aren't any true limits. In-between are most established fantasy worlds, like Middle Earth, Narnia, Westros *(The Song of Ice and Fire)*, and the Domination *(The Black Company)*.

Unmodified, *Fantasy Craft* is somewhere in the middle, its action similar to that seen in most high fantasy film and roleplaying. The heroes regularly push themselves beyond the limits of normal men, stand toe-to-toe with brutal monsters, weather savage magic, and survive against all realistic odds. Real world physics apply, though magic and other forces can break them, and many rules bend them to keep the action fast and fun (the hero on page 6 is a great example — there's really no way he could topple an idol that large on his own, but it's fun so it's allowed).

There are lots of ways to adjust this baseline. Campaign qualities are one of the most direct *(see page 322)*, and you could also disallow or adjust certain skill DCs and feats, though much of what defines action adventure physics in your world won't necessarily be supported (directly) by rules. Rather, they lie in what's impossible. With a high enough Acrobatics rank, can a character perform a standing back flip? How far can a character fall before he's well and truly dead? Can the party really survive being catapulted 300 ft. over a wall of fire, landing in a somersault over burning coals without injury? Any or all of these options are fine, so long as everyone knows what to expect.

ACTION CUES

Players sometimes find the uncertainty of adventure maddening, especially when it comes to drawing their weapons. They know brandishing steel too early can derail the narrative but doing so too late can cost them valuable tactical advantages. Establishing a few non-verbal cues that it's time for violence can smooth this shift and generally improve the flow of play. You can speed up or alter the tone of your voice, roll a special initiative die, or (if you're not using the tactic to keep energy high), just stand up. All that's important is keeping the cue(s) consistent.

DESCRIBING ACTION

A frequently overlooked way to generate excitement is "choreographing" attacks, describing with more flair than "you hit" or "you inflict 12 points of damage." It helps to have a strong mental picture of the "set;" keep track of the characters' locations at all times and their surroundings will suggest quite a few ways to spice up your action descriptions. For example, in a bar fight a critical miss with a bow might send the arrow over the target's shoulder, tipping over a cask of highly flammable alcohol. Later, a hit with a Bull Rush in the same area might send another target careening across the spill, which might lead to him going up like a Roman candle if he's later attacked with fire (or caught in the blast of a fireball).

Other useful details when describing action are the difference between the attack result and the target's Defense (or the difference between a save result and the DC), and amount of damage suffered. These are hard numerical gauges of severity you can use to fuel narrative outcomes. Despite the fact that a hit with a result of 16 against a Defense of 14 likely has the same mechanical effect as a hit with a result of 22 against a Defense of 12, the two should *feel* entirely different. For instance, you might describe the first as "a glancing blow that draws a thin line of blood across the enemy's arm," and the second as "burying the blade deep in his chest, leaving him gasping for air." Narrative details not only give everyone a better picture of the action but draw them further into it, and may also make up for a lackluster roll.

IMPROVISING DAMAGE

In the heat of a fight, an enthusiastic hero might grab a mundane object to use as a weapon (like a large rock or severed body part), or he might come up with an unusual variation on a weapon (e.g. coating his spear in oil and setting it alight). Though the damage of each weapon is set, you can always change or add to it. One-handed improvised weapons tend to inflict 1d6 damage, two-handed ones 1d8, and really large ones 1d10. You can also swap out damage types — in the case of the flaming spear, for example, from lethal to fire — but make sure each weapon inflicts only one damage type.

Another way to adjust damage is with stress *(see page 211)*. If you feel the target is measurably unnerved by an attack, inflict stress damage as described (equal to half or all the damage inflicted). Going back to the flaming spear example, a light-sensitive goblin might suffer half stress damage while a creature with the *Achilles heel (fire)* quality might suffer an equal amount.

TRACKING INITIATIVE

Fantasy fights can get pretty involved, especially with many combatants. Grouping Initiative for each side can speed things up *(see page 203)*, though this works best for mobs and other standard NPCs (special characters should get the chance to set up their own tactics in their own time). Adopting a system for tracking initiative is also a great help, preventing the action from stalling as you work out the next fighter. The simplest option is to jot down the names and Counts of each character, then scan the list after each action, though you could also put some of the onus on the players. Assign one of them "initiative keeper" so you can stay focused on resolving and describing action, or hand out numbered cards to each player — in the order they're set to act — and have them flip them over as they complete their turns.

BALANCING ENCOUNTERS

In combat, it's easy to think of yourself as the party's enemy (they often think so), but remember that you're there in part to make sure they have a good time. They want a challenge — but they also want to win, and even more importantly, they don't want their teeth kicked in. Injury and death are universal constants in a violent RPG world and the players know that, but they also invest a lot of time and energy into their characters and don't like starting over. Don't make them without a good reason (and a fitting send-off).

There are lots of lessons here: Don't circumvent or shut down the party's only way to beat an enemy. Don't ruthlessly pummel the party. Look for reasons not to kill characters. Spread the enemies and their attacks around. Remember that every combat has a "temperature." You want to raise the heat by degrees, but not to a boil. When the players are hurting, feel free to turn up the flame, but when they're *dying*, find reasons not to. Introduce reinforcements to distract the enemy, or flare tensions in the enemy's ranks, having them fight each other for a round or two. Intelligent enemies might prefer to take prisoners, or taunt their opponents. Unexpected events like cave-ins and stampeding wildlife can separate combatants, and are especially fitting when they're supported by previous events in the story or the combat. Never hesitate to expand a combat's narrative to save the party's bacon.

NPCs have many special advantages that make them interesting for you to run and exciting for the players to fight. A monster with three or more natural attacks can flurry to attack once with *each* of them. Qualities like *charge attack* and *frenzy* add even more offensive capability, while *rend* and *swift attack* grant free attacks that can even be used on the move. Extraordinary attacks are particularly powerful but may only be used once per round (except during a frenzy), and most still require an attack check. The options are balanced in a vacuum but given the open-ended nature of NPC design it's easy to go overboard, making adversaries unstoppably powerful. Take special care not to overbuild NPCs and even if you do, remember that you don't have to throw everything an adversary has at the party, especially not every round.

Finally, keep the enemy's psychology in mind. The Bestiary describes how creatures tend to behave in combat, but you can and should adjust by circumstance and to taste. Not only can this justify non-lethal actions, it can make fights unique. Going toe-to-toe with a territorial pack hunter should be a very different experience than exchanging precision blows with an honorable swordsman. A combat could even change mid-way through (say,

YOUR FIRST ADVENTURE: COMBAT

Fantasy Craft combat is loaded with options — enough to be overwhelming the first time out, especially if you or your players haven't played d20 or OGL games. Make it easy on yourself — stick to the basics and introduce new rules as your confidence grows.

Before running your first combat, read pages 203–207 to get a handle on the core rules — initiative, movement, attacks, defense, and injury. Master those before getting fancy. Design an encounter using a mob of standard NPCs with relatively few rules, like the Goon or Mercenary rogues _(see page 246)_. Fill out an NPC tracking sheet _(see page 400)_ so you don't have to pick up the book midstream, and use simple initiative, rolling once for each side. If you have miniatures and a battle mat, you may want to use those too; they make determining range and movement much easier. If you're _really_ new to game mastery, you can also stick to basic combat actions like Standard Attacks and Standard Moves until you're ready for more sophisticated maneuvers.

And don't worry if you don't fully grasp the rules the very first time out. It takes practice and comes easier with experience. The game is modular, so you can add rules in pieces as you prefer. Start with things that intrigue you most — perhaps a few NPC qualities, damage types, conditions, and tricks. You may never end up incorporating the whole of Chapter 5, and that's OK — the rules will always be there if you need them!

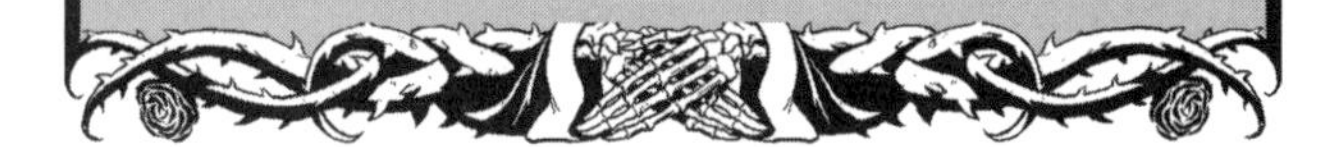

when the sorcerer magically dominating a troll is slain, shifting the behemoth from a sluggish weapon of brute force into a raging force of nature, looking to take its anger out on anything that moves).

Predators and small humanoids often rely on ambushes and concentrate their attacks on weak and slow targets. Scavengers and parasites attack by opportunity, fleeing when they face resistance or eat their fill. Peaceful and herd creatures fight only if cornered and to drive away threats to their young (and rarely pursue those who flee). Nearly every creature has a breaking point, which you can decide arbitrarily before the combat (e.g. a special adversary losing half its vitality or a standard adversary suffering 15 or more damage), or you can apply Morale *(see page 379)*.

CHANGING THE RULES

One of your greatest powers is the authority to tailor the rules for your game and group, but it's important to do so with your eyes wide open. Every *Fantasy Craft* rule was designed for a specific purpose and it's not always obvious how changing a rule might impact the rest of the system. Before you make changes of your own, take a look through campaign qualities *(see page 322)*, which are all built to plug fluidly into the greater game. If you're still not happy with a rule, ask yourself some questions: Why am I changing the rule? Am I clear about how it really works? Why do I think the rule exists? Do I know what *other* rules might change if I adjust this one? Will changing the rule imbalance the game or give certain character types, classes, or species an unfair advantage or deficit? Will the change make more players happy than not?

Ask the players for input. Discuss rules changes before implementing them. Players tend to engage with the rules very differently than GMs, and their perspective can be invaluable. When you're comfortable with a change, test it out for a few sessions and see how it fares. Don't be afraid to take it back if it doesn't work out but when you find a house rule you really like, visit the Crafty Games forums and share!

IGNORING THE RULES

Easier than changing the rules is ignoring them. Again, it's important to consider the ramifications. Take, for example, the movement rule that you must stop whenever adjacent to an opponent. This may seem like a small and inconsequential mechanic, but ignoring it also disables one of the most useful Acrobatics checks (Tumble), and more importantly reduces a party's ability to shield its weaker combatants with tougher ones.

AVOIDING BURNOUT

Eventually, your campaign may start to wind down, or you may eventually get tired of running and want to *play* the game instead. Consider stepping aside and letting someone new take over your duties. There are a number of possible solutions.

INTERLUDES

Sometimes a brief respite is all the break you need. Let one of the other players take over as GM for just one or two adventures — maybe in the same continuity, maybe with all-new characters. If you'd like to preserve your story and still enjoy an interlude, carve out a separate region for the new GM and let him do what he likes, so long as he doesn't impact anything you've already introduced (you can give him a short list of other things to avoid as well, unless you're worried they'll spoil upcoming play).

Interludes are excellent chances to try out different styles of play, perhaps with different campaign qualities and trial rules. They're also great for following up with interesting plots previously left by the wayside (such as rescuing a village that was taken over by an oppressive warlord, or following up on leads about treasure in a distant jungle). Regardless of the details, interludes should always be self-contained — unless, of course, they turn into troupe play.

TROUPE PLAY

Some groups, particularly those with multiple experienced GMs in their ranks, may consider a round-robin approach in which two or more GMs trade off, running adventures in the same or splinter storylines. This is a great approach for groups with irregular attendance but can produce uneven results without careful management. At the very least, all troupe GMs should agree on basic boundaries and rules to avoid contradicting each other or damaging the campaign's continuity.

PASSING THE TORCH

When and if it's time for you to retire as the group's GM, the group needs to consider whether your successor will follow your setting and storyline or start something new. While everyone's involved, the greatest voice must be yours, as you'll be the one deciding whether to resolve any outstanding plotlines (if you haven't already).

If the new GM takes over in the same world, be sure to pass along any notes or materials he may need, and wash your hands of it. Separation anxiety is very real but it's vital that you support and respect the new GM's work if the game is to keep going strong.

SHARING THE WORK

When you're starting to feel overwhelmed by the work of running, consider assigning some of it to the players. Think of yourself like a U.S. President with the players as your cabinet — you can have a Secretary of Defense (who manages initiative), an Attorney General (who stays abreast of mechanical disputes and advises you before rules calls), a Secretary of the Interior (who sets up the play area before games), and even a Secretary of Agriculture (who gets munchies)! Just a few duties off your plate can make your job worlds easier, and get everyone more involved to boot!

EMBRACING YOUR LIMITATIONS

Yours is a big job and you're just one person. Be careful not to bite off more than you can chew when you start, and increase the scope of your game slowly over time. Watch for things you do well and things you don't, and look for ways to redistribute the latter. The players are there to have a good time and they won't mind helping out. Focus your game on the things you and the players do best and you'll all have a much better time.

GM ACTION DICE

Action dice can be one of your greatest tools to keep the heroes on their toes and your game on track. Like PCs, you can boost rolls, activate threats and errors, and heal NPCs, but you can also introduce campaign qualities and Dramatic scenes, rescue and promote NPCs, and more! All this power comes with a great responsibility, of course: You shouldn't look at your dice as a way to make the characters' lives difficult but rather as a way to make sure the *players* have fun. Never use your dice to pick on a player, or to spoil a player's moment of glory — it ruins everyone's fun. Instead, use your dice to raise the stakes and encourage the characters to step up, improving the game for everyone.

You receive a number of action dice at the start of each game session equal to the number of player characters present + twice the adventure's Menace.

Example: Five PCs are present for a Menace IV adventure. You begin the session with 13 action dice.

You gain more action dice for awarding PC action dice *(see right)* and offering hints *(see page 366)*. All action dice not spent at the end of each session are lost.

Your action dice may be spent in the following ways. When one of these options asks you to roll a die on behalf of an NPC, roll 1d6 (if the NPC is standard) or 1 die type higher than the highest action die rolled by the PCs (if the NPC is special).

Example: The most experienced PC at the table is Level 11. He has no feats or other options that improve his action die type, so he rolls d8s. When rolling on behalf of a special NPC, you roll d10s.

1. BOOST AN NPC DIE ROLL

You may spend 1 action die to boost an NPC die roll as if he were a player character *(see page 62)*.

2. BOOST AN NPC'S DEFENSE

You may spend 1 action die to boost an NPC's Defense as if he were a player character *(see page 63)*.

3. ACTIVATE AN NPC'S THREAT

When a special NPC or a character with the *treacherous* quality scores a threat, you may spend 1 or more action dice to activate the threat *(see page 235)*.

4. ACTIVATE A PC OR NPC'S ERROR

When an opponent within an NPC's line of sight suffers an error with an attack or skill check, you may spend 1 or more action dice to activate it as a critical miss or failure *(see page 208 and 65, respectively)*.

5. HEAL AN NPC

You may spend any number of action dice to heal an NPC *(see page 212)*.

6. PROMOTE A STANDARD NPC

You may spend 2 action dice at any time to promote a standard character to special character for the duration of the current adventure *(see page 337)*.

7. HAVE A VILLAIN CHEAT DEATH

You may spend 4 action dice to let a villain Cheat Death *(see page 384)*. The players don't vote or otherwise influence the story of his escape; instead, you develop the reasons — potentially when building a later adventure — and reveal them as a natural part of the story. The villain does suffer a random Impact, however: roll 1d4+1 (or a higher die type, if you want a less controlled result), and consult Table 7.28: Cheating Death *(see page 386)*.

XP is awarded as if the villain was defeated. He may not return in this adventure.

8. ADD A TEMPORARY CAMPAIGN QUALITY

You may spend action dice at any time to add a campaign quality for the rest of the scene. You may only add a campaign quality with an action die cost *(see page 322)*.

9. PROMPT A DRAMATIC SCENE

You may spend 4 action dice to upgrade the current scene to Dramatic *(see page 335)*.

AWARDING PC ACTION DICE

Action dice are a valuable commodity at the game table, giving everyone the power to tweak the odds and change the rules when needed to keep the game fun and challenging. Everyone starts with a small pool of them but it's your job to keep them flowing. Any time you're impressed with a player or PC's behavior or performance at the table, you can award the player a bonus action die and gain one for yourself.

You can award action dice for many things and you'll quickly develop your own criteria but as a general rule you can hand one out...

- Anytime a player attempts something heroic or selfless, whether he's successful or not
- Anytime a player roleplays well or makes decisions supporting his character concept
- Anytime a player acts in service of his Alignment
- Anytime a player exhibits strong leadership or problem-solving ability
- Anytime a player helps to move the story along
- Anytime a player promotes fun and enjoyment at the table

It's especially important to reward acts that meet these criteria despite any game penalties they might inflict, as it reinforces daring actions and keeps the players taking chances. Likewise, you should spend your action dice to support those chances, and do everything in your power to ensure PCs don't needlessly suffer for their effort — because without that effort, they'd never win.

On average you should hand out at least 1 action die every 20–30 minutes. Action dice are the grease that keeps the *Fantasy Craft* game engine running, and a healthy stream of them not only makes the players comfortable spending the ones they've got but keeps your stack high as well. Try to spread rewards between all the players — if someone's shy, nervous, or just not having a great day it's all that much more important to highlight his noteworthy moments.

HINTS

Sometimes the players get stuck. They find themselves stumped by a puzzle, at a loss in an investigation, unsure how to beat a foe, or just asking "What are we missing?" At times like this you can offer them a hint.

Unlike clues, hints don't necessarily point the way to upcoming scenes but rather focus on what's happening to the party right now. They might give the party additional insight about enemies, describe things from a different perspective, remind players about something they've forgotten, point to clues they've missed, or just give them something new to think about. Hints can be as pointed or vague as the situation demands but they should always be immediately useful. The best hints get the players halfway there and let them figure it out from there.

Hints are best presented when you have a firm grasp of your party's problem solving abilities, so you'll get better at offering them over time. At first it's best to err on the side of caution, giving more information rather than less. The worst you can do is push the game along a little faster than expected.

For each hint you offer, you gain 1 action die. Some players may have abilities that prompt you to give hints, in which case they usually gain an action die if you refuse; otherwise, PCs neither gain nor lose action dice for hints.

NARRATIVE CONTROL

Action dice not only change the odds, they can change the world! Using these optional rules, anyone can spend one to four action dice to subtly shift details in their favor. The more action dice spent, the bigger the shift. In many ways this is like activating critical hits/successes and misses/failures *(see pages 207 and 65)*. It's a way to mildly nudge the story to help or hinder the party, or make life interesting for everyone.

Shifts enacted by players are called **Perks**. When a Perk directly affects more than one character, those involved may pool action dice to request it (e.g. two characters spending 2 dice each for a four-die Perk, one character spending 2 dice and two others spending 1 each, etc.). Perks can help get players out of a bind but they shouldn't eliminate challenge or undermine encounters. Here are some examples.

1 Action Die: Fortuitous terrain (stairs or a table offering "higher ground," a chandelier allowing a character to swing around an enemy, etc.) offers a +1 bonus with 1 character's attacks for 1 round; nearby cover (1/4); a guard straying a bit from his post (–2 with Notice and Search checks); a hero fallen into a pit discovers rough handholds on the pit wall (Climb DC 25 to escape); favorable travel conditions (conventient bridges, a friendly caravan, etc.) let the party move 1 MPH faster for 1 Downtime period; room available at a booked or busy inn (common lodging)

2 Action Dice: Fortuitous terrain offers +1 bonus to 2 characters for 1 round; nearby cover (1/2); a guard preoccupied with other tasks (–4 with Notice and Search checks); a hero fallen into a pit discovers a vine dangling within reach (Climb DC 20 to escape); auspicious travel conditions let the party move 2 MPH faster for 1 Downtime period; room available at a booked or busy inn (up to fancy lodging)

3 Action Dice: Fortuitous terrain offers +1 bonus to 3 characters for 1 round; nearby cover (3/4); a guard who's fast asleep; a hero fallen into a pit discovers a rusty but working pulley that lasts long enough to get him out (Climb DC 15 to escape); remarkable travel conditions let the party move 3 MPH faster for 1 Downtime period; room available at a booked or busy inn (up to luxurious lodging)

4 Action Dice: Fortuitous terrain offers +1 bonus to whole party for 1 round; nearby cover (total); an alarm summons all but essential guards to another location; a hero fallen into a pit discovers a secret tunnel leading out (and perhaps leading to greater adventure!); miraculous travel conditions let the party move 4 MPH faster for 1 Downtime period; room available at a booked or busy inn (up to extravagant lodging)

Shifts you enact are called **Complications**. Manipulating fluid details is part of your normal job, of course, but Complications provide a fair framework for various common mechanical events and obstacles. Whenever possible you should apply action die costs to shifts you apply on the fly (above and beyond any prepared adventure). It helps to promote the action die economy, illustrates your commitment to fair play, and gives the players an exciting peek "behind the screen." Here are some examples.

1 Action Die: Collapsed pillar, tree, or other large debris fills 1 square; surface changes across area (giant boiling pot tipped over, loose debris scattered everywhere, magic ice covers area, etc.), reducing Speed by 5 ft.; cover damaged or destroyed (drops by 1/4); item malfunctions (1 half action to fix); up to Tiny scenery destroyed by collateral damage (falling pillar or boulder, ballista shot, etc.); a dropped item disappears under furniture or into a tight crevice (1 extra half action to retrieve); troublesome travel conditions (brigands handled off screen, a nosy portmaster, etc.) slow the party by 1 MPH for 1 Downtime period (minimum 0); the only room at an inn is poor lodging

2 Action Dice: Large debris fills 2 squares; surface changes across area, reducing Speed by 10 ft.; cover damaged or destroyed (drops by 1/2); item malfunctions (1 full action and Crafting DC 10 to fix); Medium scenery destroyed; a dropped item disappears through a grate or under a locked door; ill-fated travel conditions slow the party by 2 MPH for 1 Downtime period (minimum 0); no rooms at the inn

3 Action Dice: Large debris fills 3 squares; surface changes across area, reducing Speed by 15 ft.; cover damaged or destroyed (drops by 3/4); item malfunctions (1 full action and Crafting DC 15 to fix); Huge scenery destroyed; a dropped item lands at an enemy's feet; wretched travel conditions slow the party by 3 MPH for 1 Downtime period (minimum 0); someone at the inn remembers the characters… bitterly

4 Action Dice: Large debris fills 4 squares; surface changes across area, reducing Speed by 20 ft.; cover destroyed (entirely); item malfunctions (1 full action and Crafting DC 20 to fix); Colossal scenery destroyed; a dropped item is lost or destroyed (e.g. is swallowed by a passing wyvern, falls into a vat of acid, etc.); disastrous travel conditions slow the party by 4 MPH for 1 Downtime period (minimum 0); the party resembles a group on a poster at the inn (a wanted poster)

You determine the cost of Narrative Control based on the desired impact. As shown in the previous examples, minor, extremely likely changes cost only 1 die while larger, less plausible changes cost up to 4.

Narrative Control is *not* absolute control — certain rules and limitations apply.

- When Narrative Control is allowed, it's available to everyone (you and all players).
- No one may change established reality. If something's already happened or been proven, it's permanent.
- You must approve every Perk and Complication before it enters play.
- Action dice may not be spent to counter or cancel Narrative Control, no matter who enacts it. Once a Perk or Complication is approved, it becomes a permanent change to the world. If you and the party both spend action dice on the same thing (e.g. on travel conditions), your dice are applied and the party regains their dice.

Narrative Control is an excellent way to handle divine assistance. It lets everyone introduce potentially miraculous events with as much (or as little) heavenly flavor as you like. Other Complications appear throughout *Fantasy Craft*, including critical miss effects *(see page 208)* and travel encounters *(see page 372)*.

Perks and Complications are best introduced when conditions suggest them. A Stolen Item Complication is best introduced when the party visits a seedy part of town, and a Sympathetic Adversary Perk is most likely when the enemy's leader is hateful and draconian. Among other factors, plausibility should guide whether you allow a Perk or introduce a Complication.

The following are just a few of the many things you can do with Narrative Control. Tweak them to taste and work with the players to develop more.

PLAYER PERKS

Unless otherwise specified, the party may only use each of these scripted Perks once per adventure. Perks you (the GM) decline don't count toward this limit, and non-scripted Perks may show up as often as you allow.

FLASH-FORWARD

Sometimes an encounter isn't working. No one's into it or the solution to the problem is eluding everyone. In these cases the party can spend 4 action dice to suggest the action "flash forward" to the next encounter (past the current fight or death trap, out of an ugly social situation that no one's excited about, etc.). If you agree, you may concoct whatever story or circumstances you like to explain the intervening time — indeed, the party is giving you this right by enacting this Perk — though you may ask for ideas if you're at a loss and/or would like to include the players in the narrative. All rewards from the encounter are forfeit, including XP and treasure.

I HAVE ONE OF THOSE!

The party may spend one or more action dice to "remember" they brought a non-magical item with them (retroactively adding the item to their inventory), to find one in the area, or to find something that makes a good improvised version *(see page 73)*. Improvised versions have a few drawbacks but may be the only option when there's little or no chance of finding the real item in the area. The item's Complexity may not exceed 5 per action die spent (maximum 20).

NEVER TELL US THE ODDS

As Initiative is rolled, the party may opt to worsen the odds, spending 2 or 4 action dice. If you agree, the number of adversaries increases by 1 special NPC or 1 mob of standard NPCs per 2 action dice spent. This is a Perk because the party benefits from extra XP and potentially better treasure as a result *(see pages 342 and 344).*

SYMPATHETIC ADVERSARY

The party may spend one or more action dice to sway a standard adversary to their side for the rest of the scene. The NPC's XP value may not exceed 20 per action die spent (maximum 80). The NPC is Neutral with the party and won't risk his life. Unless detained, he leaves at the end of the scene, though he could potentially make subsequent appearances if it supports the story.

UNEXPECTED HELP

The party may spend one or more action dice to introduce a single NPC from the Rogues Gallery *(see page 244)*, who helps them for the rest of the scene. This Perk otherwise operates like Sympathetic Adversary, except that the NPC is Friendly with the party.

GM COMPLICATIONS

As illustrated here, Complications don't include tools you need to manage scenes and move the story along (such as guards, suspicious NPCs, endangered bystanders, and surprise combats). Instead, they present various impediments and difficulties that may befall the party, some of which might leave a bad taste in the players' mouths without a concrete cost. The GM can (and periodically should) enact Perks as well, especially when the party is having a hard time.

ADVENTURERS IN TOWN!

You may spend up to four action dice to have local merchants realize adventurers have arrived and raise their prices (by 25% per action die spent).

LOST OR STOLEN ITEM

You can spend up to three action dice to have the party misplace an item (Search DC 10 + 5 per die spent to find it). Alternately, you can spend four action dice to have an item go missing (dropped, left behind, or stolen). Take care not to eliminate cherished items, as this can cause resen-tment.

NATURE'S FURY

You may spend one or more action dice to introduce a natural disaster or taxing weather in the party's area, as shown on Table 7.20: Nature's Fury *(see page 369).*

REINFORCEMENTS

You may spend one or more action dice to introduce new adversaries to an ongoing fight (1 action die per 20 XP). You may introduce no more than 1 mob of standard adversaries or 1 special adversary per round.

SHODDY ITEM

You may spend up to four action dice to increase the error ranges of all attacks and skill checks made with a single item by twice the same amount (i.e. +2 error range for 1 die, +4 error range for 2 dice, etc.). This lasts until the end of the combat or scene, whichever comes first.

MANAGING SKILL DIFFICULTY

The DCs in Chapter 2 are fixed, meaning that each result has a set difficulty that never changes. As the characters gain levels and their skill ranks improve, these results become easier and new results become available. By the highest levels your characters can master several skills and become extremely capable with most if not all of the rest (some classes offer more skill points and better skill bonuses and benefits than others, so results will vary).

Using this system of **static DCs**, a higher level character specializing in a skill should best a lower level one specializing in the same skill the vast majority of the time, especially as the level gap widens. Static DCs are excellent when you want the characters' to become experts over time, growing from highly competent heroes at Level 1 to world-class badasses at Level 20.

An optional alternative, **sliding DCs**, uses a simple formula to calculate each DC, incorporating Threat Level *(see page 335)*. This keeps the difficulty of each skill attempt at roughly the same as the characters rise in level, making the play experience roughly the same throughout. New levels grant more options but not necessarily more power. Sliding DCs are superior when you want to set the scope of your game at Level 1 (the characters becoming acknowledged champions in their fields, for example) and have that remain the case mechanically until Level 20.

Note that attack ability naturally follows a sliding scale, as do opposed skill checks, as the "DCs" of both (Defense in the case of attacks) commonly rise with the opponent's level. This choice of static vs. sliding DCs only matters with unopposed skill checks.

USING STATIC DCS

The DCs in Chapter 2 should cover most needs. When the characters want to do something unopposed that isn't covered there, simply apply a DC of 10 (easy), 15 (average), 20 (tricky), 25 (hard), or 30 (desperate). Recognize that even a Level 1 character can quickly render easy results trivial if they specialize (with a +2 attribute bonus and maximum skill ranks, a Level 1 character

Table 7.20: Nature's Fury

Action Dice	Intensity or Duration	Effect
Cold/Heat Wave		
1	1d6 hours	Subdual damage *(see page 210)*
2	2d6 hours	Subdual damage *(see page 210)*
3	3d6 hours	Subdual damage *(see page 210)*
4	4d6 hours	Subdual damage *(see page 210)*
Dust/Fog/Rain/Snow		
1	1d6 hours	–20 ft. to visual range increments
2	2d6 hours	–40 ft. to visual range increments
3	3d6 hours	–60 ft. to visual range increments
4	4d6 hours	–80 ft. to visual range increments
Earthquake		
1	1d6 rounds	–2 penalty with attack and Dex-based skill checks
2	2d6 rounds	–4 penalty with attack and Dex-based skill checks; Ref DC 15 each round or become *sprawled*
3	3d6 rounds	–6 penalty with attack and Dex-based skill checks; Ref DC 20 each round or suffer 1d6 lethal damage and become *sprawled*
4	4d6 rounds	–8 penalty with attack and Dex-based skill checks; Ref DC 25 each round or suffer 2d6 lethal damage and become *sprawled*
Fire		
1	1 square	1d6 fire damage
2	2 × 2 squares	2d6 fire damage
3	3 × 3 squares	3d6 fire damage
4	4 × 4 squares	4d6 fire damage
Flood/Landslide		
1	Flash flood/mudslide	3d6 subdual damage, Ref DC 15 for 1/2 damage
2	Minor landslide	6d6 lethal damage, Ref DC 15 for 1/2 damage
3	Major landslide	9d6 lethal damage, Ref DC 15 for 1/2 damage; failed save = buried (1d20 × 1,000 lbs.)
4	Avalanche	12d6 lethal damage, Ref DC 15 for 1/2 damage; failed save = buried (1d20 × 1,000 lbs.)
Lightning		
1	Distant strike	1d6 stress damage, Will DC 15 for 1/2 damage
2	Local strike	2d6 stress damage, Will DC 15 for 1/2 damage
3	Near strike	3d6 stress damage, Will DC 15 for 1/2 damage; 1d6 flash damage; Ref DC 15 for 1/2 damage
4	Direct strike	12d6 electrical damage + *sprawled*, Ref DC 15 for 1/2 damage
Wind		
1	1d6 rounds	–2 with hurled attack checks; –5 ft. Speed against wind
2	2d6 rounds	–4 with hurled attack checks; –10 ft. Speed against wind
3	3d6 rounds	–6 with hurled attack checks; –20 ft. Speed against wind
4	Tornado	Hurled attacks and movement impossible; Fort DC 20 or be sucked in (12d6 lethal damage + *sprawled* 1d6 miles away, Ref DC 15 for 1/2 damage)

can beat a DC of 10 with a roll of 4), and that this discrepancy grows as the characters gain levels.

For a specific percentage chance of success, subtract the character's total skill bonus from the DC and consult Table 7.21: Chance of Success *(see below)*. Be careful not to assign impossible DCs unless you want to eliminate that particular option for the character.

USING SLIDING DCs

Sliding DCs are assigned using the same rough difficulty scale — easy, average, tricky, hard, and desperate — but the actual numbers are based on an individual character's Career Level (if he's working alone) or the party's Threat Level (when they're working together). With these details in hand, simply consult Table 7.22: Sliding DCs *(see below)*.

You can also use this table to convert static DCs found in Chapter 2. Round the static DC to the nearest multiple of 5 and use the column that most closely matches: easy for 10, average for 15, tricky for 20, hard for 25, and desperate for 30 and above.

This table assumes progressively higher rolls and attribute bonuses with each degree of difficulty, but keeps the skill rank investment fairly level, and subdued, throughout the character's career. Thus a character who specializes has an edge, even against a sliding DC.

Table 7.21: Chance of Success

DC Minus Skill Bonus	Chance of Success
1 or less	100%
2	95%
3	90%
4	85%
5	80%
6	75%
7	70%
8	65%
9	60%
10	55%
11	50%
12	45%
13	40%
14	35%
15	30%
16	25%
17	20%
18	15%
19	10%
20	5%
21 or more	Impossible

Table 7.22: Sliding DCs

Career/Threat Level	Easy	Average	Tricky	Hard	Desperate
1–2	10	13	16	19	22
3–4	11	14	17	20	23
5–6	12	15	18	21	24
7–8	13	16	19	22	25
9–10	14	17	20	23	26
11–12	15	18	21	24	27
13–14	16	19	22	25	28
15–16	17	20	23	26	29
17–18	18	21	24	27	30
19–20	20	23	26	29	32

MANAGING DOWNTIME

Downtime is a powerful time management tool, giving you the opportunity to "gloss over" parts of the game that offer little or no challenge or roleplay potential. It also lets the players pursue interesting but lengthy projects like building and repairing things, conducting research, and treating complex illnesses without interrupting the game for everyone else.

Most Downtime activities should resolve cleanly per the rules and any choices you need to make — such as the focus to apply during a Build or Repair check — should be obvious. Your chief concern is when to start and stop each Downtime period. Frequently, opportunities will present themselves in play — as the characters embark on a long journey, as they settle into town for a couple weeks' relaxation, as they begin Downtime skill checks, etc. — but you can also plan for them as part of adventures. This is especially helpful when filling gaps in your story.

Downtime can happen as often or as rarely as you like, though you should avoid using it as a crutch to prop up underdeveloped adventures or to quash party initiative. Likewise, you should make sure the players don't come to rely on it as a way to circumvent tough or undesirable encounters. Generally, Downtime is best used to fill "empty" game time and quickly resolve long and dull skill checks (many of which are already flagged in Chapter 2).

The length of a Downtime period is also up to you, though it should never be less than a full day, and shouldn't extend beyond the first character returning to regular play (while Downtime is going on, all characters should be involved). It's much easier to run one long Downtime period than many short ones, and constantly alternating between Downtime and standard play can get tedious, so it's a good idea to "group" brief Downtime periods whenever possible, shifting standard encounters to happen before or after.

You can also be a bit duplicitous with Downtime, initially declaring a longer period and cutting it short. This is helpful when you need to conceal an upcoming (unexpected) event or plot twist, but it can go awry if used too often. No more than once every two or three adventures and you're probably fine.

TRAVEL

One of the most common Downtime activities is travel. Vehicles have set Travel Speeds *(see page 171)*, while mounts and characters have Travel Speeds in miles per hour equal to 1/10 their Speed (rounded up).

Example: A hippocampus has a Swim Speed of 60 ft. Its Travel Speed is 6 MPH.

Travel Speeds are modified by terrain and weather, as shown on Table 7.23: Travel Speed by Terrain *(see below)*. Once per Downtime period of travel, you may optionally make a team Survival check in secret against the DC listed on Table 7.23.

Table 7.23: Travel Speed by Terrain

Conditions	Travel Speed	Survival Check DC
Terrain		
Aquatic	—	12
Arctic	—	12
Caverns/mountains	–1	16
Desert	—	12
Forest/jungle	–1	20
Indoors/settled	—	8
Plains	—	12
Swamp	–1	20
Weather		
Dust/fog/rain/snow (1 die)	—	+2
Dust/fog/rain/snow (2 dice)	—	+4
Dust/fog/rain/snow (3 dice)	—	+6
Dust/fog/rain/snow (4 dice)	—	+8
Wind (1 die)	–1 / +1 *	—
Wind (2 dice)	–2 / +2 *	—
Wind (3 dice)	–3 / +3 *	—
Wind (4 dice)	–4 / +4 *	—

* In the air and at sea, the modifier to the left of the slash applies when moving against the wind while the modifier to the right applies when moving with it. On the ground these modifiers decrease to 1/2 (rounded down).

With failure, the party becomes lost, wasting a number of hours equal to the difference. Their side trek should only be detailed if you have something interesting prepared or want to apply a travel encounter.

TRAVEL ENCOUNTERS

Travel may also be interrupted by planned encounters built into the adventure or impromptu encounters introduced as Complications *(see page 366)*. This lets you decide on a case-by-case basis whether you want to spring something on a traveling party, rather than making it a matter of a random roll. If you'd prefer genuinely random encounters, see page 373.

Once per Downtime period of travel, you may spend one or more action dice to interrupt the journey with an encounter. You can choose the adversaries involved or randomly roll them on Table 7.24: Travel Encounters *(see page 374)*. Paying the base action die cost introduces 1 special adversary or 1 mob of standard adversaries, and you may increase the number encountered by spending additional dice. You can also create mixed encounter groups in the same fashion. You can set the conditions of the encounter or roll them on Table 7.25: Encounter Conditions *(see page 377)*.

Though many encounters can be presented as surprise attacks, it's a good idea to periodically work one into the ongoing story. Characters hunting a villain, for example, might gut a defeated scavenger worm, finding the remains of the villain's manservant in its belly. Perhaps the manservant was carrying an item important to the villain, in which case they might be able to use it to lure him out of hiding. These kinds of links make seemingly "random" encounters feel like natural, organic extensions of the larger plot (like interludes in many great movies and novels).

Alternately, you can use a travel encounter to launch new story. In a desert, for example, the party might find a camel wearing royal vestments they've never seen before. They could appropriate the animal, leaving the vestments to rot in the dust, or they could follow it back to its owners in a thieves' hideout modeled after the caliphates of old. Exotic adversaries and monsters appearing in unusual terrain are especially evocative of new story. Angels and demons are almost always portents of impending turbulence. A water serpent found in the jungle might indicate a strange migration up a tributary, but why? A young rakshasa found in the arctic might be on a pilgrimage seeking enlightenment, or he could be seeking superior prey to display as a badge of his adulthood.

Encounters can also feature location traps *(see page 338)*, though these aren't listed on Table 7.24 because they should be introduced sparingly and only with intent. Location traps should always be introduced as part of the story or setting, even if it's as simple as them being left over from previous battles or civilizations.

Planned and Complication encounters won't always add to the party's XP reward. Merchants, for example, aren't adversaries in the traditional sense but rather a chance to restock and perhaps find a few interesting baubles from far-off lands. The same holds for true adversaries that are merely avoided, rather than defeated *(see page 337)*.

Lastly, it's bad form to introduce travel encounters when the party has hired safe passage *(see page 190)*. They've spent hard-earned silver to ensure a safe trip and you should avoid squandering their purchase without a solid story reason. If you must interrupt their journey, be sure to give them a little help from the Rogues Gallery (e.g. bowmen supporting them from afar or guides, hunters, mercenaries, outriders, or watchmen engaging alongside, generally equal in number to the action dice spent to trigger the Complication).

RANDOM TRAVEL ENCOUNTERS

If you'd prefer truly random encounters, simply roll 1d20 once during each Downtime period of travel. If the result falls within the range listed below, an encounter occurs.

Aquatic	1–2
Arctic	1
Caverns/Mountains	1–4
Desert	1
Forest/Jungle	1–3
Plains	1–2
Swamp	1–3

This range narrows by 1 if the party secured hired passage *(see pages 168 and 190)*. For example, there's a 1 in 20 chance of a random encounter in aquatic terrain when using hired passage, or a 1–2 in 20 chance in a swamp, etc.

You should still decide on the number and types of adversaries, as well as traps and story, in order to tailor them to the party's ability and the needs of the plot.

DISPOSITION

All sentient beings are guided by their emotions; indeed, they're often slaves to them. They trust and doubt, love, hate, and ignore. Every relationship is different and informs actions and reactions. *Fantasy Craft* handles all this with Disposition.

Every character has a Disposition toward every other character — a modifier ranging from +25 to –25. Most Dispositions start at +0 (Neutral). Higher values indicate affection and trust while lower values translate to dislike and doubt. A character's Disposition modifier is applied to any check targeting him that relies on his emotional investment in the acting character, such as Bluff, Haggle, Impress, or Investigate/Canvass. It is *not* applied to Intimidate and Sense Motive checks, which don't rely on the target's opinion.

Disposition has another effect, as shown on Table 7.26: Disposition *(see page 378)*. First, when you want to randomly determine whether an NPC helps someone without being prompted, you can roll 1d20. If the result is equal to or less than the number in the Assistance column, the NPC offers aid; otherwise, he doesn't. This number can also be used when you want an NPC to randomly choose sides — equal to or lower and the NPC helps a character (or the character's side); higher and the NPC goes the other way. As with successful Persuade and Coerce checks, PCs and villains may ignore an Assistance result by spending 1 action die.

A character's Disposition modifier can change in a variety of ways, most notably successful Influence and Browbeat checks *(see pages 74 and 75)*. Player characters and villains are somewhat resistant to suggestion and changes to their Disposition may be only half as effective if they desire (rounding in their favor).

Example: Lord Bloodpyre negotiates with Bwarg the Goblin King to reestablish the alliance between his tribe and the tiny quivering ones. Both are special characters. Bloodpyre begins with a successful Browbeat check, mentioning the awful losses the goblins have suffered since the alliance was broken. His result would normally improve Bwarg's Disposition (toward Bloodpyre's tribe) by 5 but since the Goblin King is a special character his Disposition only rises by 2.

Bwarg later attempts to smooth-talk Bloodpyre, Impressing him with what the goblin hopes are favorable terms. He doesn't realize Bloodpyre secretly needs the talks to go well to retain his tribe standing (Bloodpyre made a strong display of not wanting anything to do with the goblins to potentially improve his bidding position), so when his Impress result changes Bloodpyre's by a whopping 8, Bloodpyre accepts the full adjustment.

ATTITUDE

When a character's Disposition shifts into a new range on Table 7.26, his Attitude is adjusted. This is important because Attitudes are lasting where Dispositions fade given time for reflection. At the end of each scene, a character's Disposition sets to the number within his current range closest to Neutral.

Example: At the end of the first summit, Bloodpyre's Disposition (toward the goblins) is +18 and Bwarg's Disposition (toward Bloodpyre's tribe) is +7. As the scene ends, Bloodpyre's Attitude settles to Supportive and Bwarg's Attitude settles to Intrigued. The negotiations will continue. Soon, there will be attempts to Persuade and Coerce tribute between the tribes, which is potentially where it'll get messy. Pray for folk in the region.

Unless otherwise specified, a character's Attitude may not adjust more than 1 grade in either direction during each scene.

WHAT DO THE ATTITUDES MEAN?

Attitudes affect various rules throughout *Fantasy Craft*, most notably Bluff, Haggle, Impress, and Investigate checks. Here are some pointers for roleplaying them. Player characters are subject to Disposition as well and you should award action dice to those who take this responsibility seriously.

Devoted: The character reveres or worships the subject, or is madly in love with them.

Supportive: The character cherishes the subject as a dear friend and misses them when they're apart for any length of time. In a romantic liaison, the character is fascinated, bordering on what might be called "love."

Friendly: The character is close with the subject, or wants to be. He looks for chances for them to meet and misses the subject when they're not together for longer than a couple weeks. In a romantic liaison, the character is attracted and wants to learn more.

Table 7.24: Travel Encounters

d20 Result	Action Die Cost	Adversary/Encounter
Aquatic Terrain		
1–5	—	Common encounter (roll below)
6–7	1	Hippocampus (46 XP)
8–9	1	Merfolk (47 XP)
10–11	2	Water serpent (62 XP)
12–13	2	Turtle, giant (65 XP)
14–15	2	Sea devil (67 XP)
16	4	Kraken (182 XP)
17	4	Dragon, sea (184 XP)
18	—	Monster from different terrain (GM's choice of table)
19	—	Exotic encounter (roll below)
20	—	Template (roll again, re-rolling 20, and roll on a template table below)
Arctic Terrain		
1–6	—	Common encounter (roll below)
7–11	2	Saber-tooth tiger (73 XP)
12–16	2	Mammoth (82 XP)
17	4	Dragon, frost (197 XP)
18	—	Monster from different terrain (GM's choice of table)
19	—	Exotic encounter (roll below)
20	—	Template (roll again, re-rolling 20, and roll on a template table below)
Caverns		
1–3	—	Common encounter (roll below)
4	1	Troglodyte (38 XP)
5	1	Sporling (39 XP)
6	1	Slime (41 XP)
7	1	Jelly (44 XP)
8	2	Pudding (64 XP)
9	2	Darkmantle (65 XP)
10	2	Rust monster (65 XP)
11	2	Scavenger worm (69 XP)
12	2	Gelatinous cube (73 XP)
13	2	Drider (82 XP)
14	3	Burrowing behemoth (97 XP)
15	3	Bulette (113 XP)
16	4	Watcher in the dark (163 XP)
17	4	Dragon, fire (243 XP)
18	—	Monster from different terrain (GM's choice of table)
19	—	Exotic encounter (roll below)
20	—	Template (roll again, re-rolling 20, and roll on a template table below)
Desert		
1–10	—	Common encounter (roll below)
11–12	1	Camel (40 XP)
13	1	Donkey (43 XP)
14	2	Mummy (74 XP))
15	2	Basilisk (76 XP)
16	2	Lamia (89 XP)
17	3	Bulette (113 XP)
18	—	Monster from different terrain (GM's choice of table)
19	—	Exotic encounter (roll below)
20	—	Template (roll again, re-rolling 20, and roll on a template table below)

d20 Result	Action Die Cost	Adversary/Encounter
Forest/Jungle		
1	—	Common encounter (roll below)
2	1	Fire beetle (34 XP)
3	1	Slasher vine (38 XP)
4	1	Spiders, giant (47–60 XP)
5	1	Elk (48 XP)
6	1	Stirge (48 XP)
7	1	Fanged vase (55 XP)
8	2	Pegasus (62 XP)
9	2	Spriggan (63 XP)
10	2	Tiger (63 XP)
11	2	Bear (68–85 XP)
12	2	Sprite (72 XP)
13	2	Sidhe (77 XP)
14	2	Ape (78–89 XP)
15	2	Unicorn (81 XP)
16	2	Velociraptor (71 XP)
17	4	Dragon, forest (222 XP)
18	—	Monster from different terrain (GM's choice of table)
19	—	Exotic encounter (roll below)
20	—	Template (roll again, re-rolling 20, and roll on a template table below)
Mountains		
1–8	—	Common encounter (roll below)
9	1	Goat/sheep (15 XP)
10	1	Llama (38 XP)
11	1	Donkey (43 XP)
12	1	Eagle, giant (57 XP)
13	2	Hippogriffon (65 XP)
14	2	Griffon (66 XP)
15	2	Wyvern (85 XP)
16	3	Troll (91 XP)
17	3	Chimera (101 XP)
18	—	Monster from different terrain (GM's choice of table)
19	—	Exotic encounter (roll below)
20	—	Template (roll again, re-rolling 20, and roll on a template table below)
Plains		
1–4	—	Common encounter (roll below)
5	1	Cattle/oxen (24 XP)
6	1	Wolf (42–56 XP)
7	1	Horse/pony (41–55 XP)
8	1	Dog (46–52 XP)
9	1	Raptor (51–65 XP)
10	1	Horse, race (53 XP)
11	1	Bison (54 XP)
12	2	Rhino (65 XP)
13	2	Elephant (74 XP)
14	2	Will o' wisp (87 XP)
15	2	Triceratops (88 XP)
16	3	Tyrannosaurus Rex (104 XP)
17	4	Dragon, royal (256 XP)
18	—	Monster from different terrain (GM's choice of table)
19	—	Exotic encounter (roll below)
20	—	Template (roll again, re-rolling 20, and roll on a template table below)

Table 7.24: Travel Encounters (Continued)

d20 Result	Action Die Cost	Adversary/Encounter
Swamp		
1–8	—	Common encounter (roll below)
9	1	Bleeding murk (32 XP)
10	1	Bugbear (49 XP)
11	1	Harpy (55 XP)
12	2	Naga (75 XP)
13	2	Manticore (87 XP)
14	3	Chimera (101 XP)
15	3	Rakshasa (113 XP)
16	3	Hag (131 XP)
17	4	Hydra (160 XP)
18	—	Monster from different terrain (GM's choice of table)
19	—	Exotic encounter (roll below)
20	—	Template (roll again, re-rolling 20, and roll on a template table below)
Common Encounters		
1	1	Gnoll (23 XP)
2	1	Kobold (27 XP)
3	1	Hobgoblin (33 XP)
4	1	Merchant (33 XP))
5	1	Damsel (37 + roll another encounter for her harasser)
6	1	Outrider (37 XP)
7	1	Brigand (38 XP)
8	1	Con man (40 XP)
9	1	Cutpurse (41 XP)
10	1	Mercenary (43 XP)
11	1	Fortune teller (44 XP)
12	1	Nobleman (45 XP)
13	1	Bugbear (49 XP)
14	1	Necromancer (53 XP)
15	1	Ghoul (56 XP)
16	1	Treasure Hunter (56 XP)
17	2	Knight (68 XP)
18	2	Wight (70 XP)
19	2	Warlord (71 XP)
20	—	Template (roll again, re-rolling 20, and roll on a template table below)
Exotic Encounters		
1	1	Homunculus (54 XP)
2	2	Imp (62 XP)
3	2	Minotaur (65 XP)
4	2	Gorgon (71 XP)
5	2	Hell hound (74 XP))
6	2	Mimic (82 XP)
7	2	Shadow beast (86 XP)
8	2	Salamander (87 XP)
9	3	Myrmidon (92 XP)
10	3	Barghest (93 XP)
11	3	Doppelganger (95 XP)
12	3	Nightmare (112 XP)
13	3	Golem (58–115 XP)

d20 Result	Action Die Cost	Adversary/Encounter
Exotic Encounters (Continued)		
14	3	Chaos beast (120 XP)
15	4	Brain fiend (145 XP)
16	4	Elemental, elder (150 XP)
17	4	Demon (100–164 XP)
18	4	Angel (79–177 XP)
19	4	Dragon, storm (225 XP)
20	—	Template (roll again, re-rolling 20, and roll on a template table below)
Rogue Templates		
1	+1	Drake (+14 XP)
2–3	+1	Dwarf (+11 XP)
4–5	+1	Elf (+2 XP)
6–7	+1	Giant (+7 XP)
8–9	+1	Goblin (+2 XP)
10–11	+1	Ogre (+7 XP)
12–13	+1	Orc (+4 XP))
14–15	+1	Pech (+2 XP)
16–17	+1	Rootwalker (+11 XP)
18–19	+1	Saurian (+6 XP)
20	+1	Unborn (+4 XP)
Monster Templates		
1–3	+1	Alpha (+20 XP)
4	+1	Ancient (+20 XP)
5	+1	Clockwork (+20 XP)
6–8	+1	Dire (+20 XP)
9	+2	Ghostly (+40 XP)
10	+1	Heavenly (+10 XP)
11	+1	Infernal (+10 XP)
12	–1	Immature (–20 XP)
13	+4	Kaiju (+125 XP)
14	+3	Lich (+70 XP)
15–17	+1	Predatory (+15 XP)
18	+1	Risen (+5 XP)
19	+1	Skeletal (+15 XP)
20	+2	Vampiric (+45 XP)

Table 7.25: Encounter Conditions

d20 Result	Conditions
1	Adversaries caught in a trap *(see page 338)*
2	Adversaries wounded (1/2 vitality or –2 with Damage saves)
3	Sleeping adversaries in their lair, nest, camp, or communal area (–1 action die to introduce more as they return from the wild)
4	Sleeping adversaries in the wild
5–7	Waking adversaries in their lair, nest, camp, or communal area (–1 action die to introduce more as they return from the wild)
8–11	Waking adversaries in the wild
12–14	Ready patrol (adversaries gain +2 morale bonus with Notice and Search checks)
15–17	Hungry, greedy, or mated adversaries (adversaries immune to Morale penalties)
18–20	Set ambush prepared by the adversaries *(see page 83)*

Intrigued: The character is fond of the subject and enjoys spending time with them. He doesn't seek the subject out, however — their relationship is limited to casual meetings unless the subject feels more strongly. If the liaison is romantic, the character's interest in the subject is budding but uncertain.

Neutral: The character is ambivalent toward the subject of his Disposition. His opinions and judgments are based on his personal beliefs as he's developed no personal feelings toward the subject. He only gets involved in the subject's affairs when his Alignment or other factors compel him to do so.

Cold: The character is aloof and distant around the subject. His Attitude might be the result of mistrust or dislike but it's not strong enough for the character act against the subject without cause. Mostly he just ignores the subject and hopes the favor is returned.

Unfriendly: The character actively dislikes the subject and doesn't pass up an opportunity to act against them but he probably doesn't hate them, especially if it's against his Alignment to do so.

Hostile: The character hates the subject and goes out of his way to make trouble for them. He usually stops just short of physical violence and breaking laws, though — unless it's a sure bet he won't be caught.

Adversarial: The character does everything in his power to hurt the subject, up to and including murder.

ROUSING THE MASSES

Actions don't happen in a vacuum — they impact everyone who witnesses them, subtly swaying their opinions. Most of the time there's no need to track these Disposition changes as they're both too small to affect Attitudes and immaterial to the overall story. Occasionally, however, someone will do something so kind (or so divisive) that everyone watching (and potentially everyone hearing about it after) may instantly shift their stance. In these cases, you can automatically adjust the Attitude of each standard character who witnesses the act (in the appropriate direction). PCs and villains are also adjusted unless they make a successful Will save (DC 12). They may not spend action dice to avoid this effect.

Example: Toward the end of their summit, Bwarg takes a chance and reminds Bloodpyre of his weaknesses *(see page 373)*. The words are caustic and heard by the assembled tribes, which Bloodpyre can't abide. With one fell swing of his mighty great axe (and a lucky critical hit), Bloodpyre severs Bwarg's offending head and raises it so all the goblins can view their king's final, stunned expression. This could really go either way, the GM automatically shifting the goblins' Attitudes by 1 in either direction, but with the orc tribe present he decides to adjust it favorably (from Intrigued to Friendly). Bloodpyre has new followers! They quiver too much for his liking but they're also small enough to make exceptional spies. Pray for *everyone* in the region.

ALLIES AND ENEMIES

The transition from ally to enemy is gradual — at least two scenes (the time required to go from Intrigued to Cold and vice-versa), which offers plenty of time to roleplay such changes. When an ally or Neutral character becomes an enemy, you should probably also total his XP (just in case).

CONTACTS

Contacts are long-term allies whose Disposition toward the character must remain at least Supportive at all times *(see page 191)*. Should a Contact's Disposition drop below this threshold — perhaps because the character abused their trust or needlessly endangered them — the character must give the Contact up, regaining the Prize slot. Reputation invested in the Contact is *not* regained, however.

Table 7.26: Disposition

Disposition	Attitude	Assistance *
+21 to +25	Devoted	18
+16 to +20	Supportive	16
+11 to +15	Friendly	14
+6 to +10	Intrigued	12
+5 to –5	Neutral	10
–6 to –10	Cold	8
–11 to –15	Unfriendly	6
–16 to –20	Hostile	4
–21 to –25	Adversarial	2

* If the endeavor involves serious risk (e.g. combat), this number drops to 1/2 (rounded down).

MORALE

Fantasy adventure is fraught with peril — terrifying dragons, hordes of savage humanoids, and devastating magic can rattle even the stoutest heroes to their core. Morale is an optional rule for groups wanting a more "realistic" way to model stress and fear. When used, it affects *all* characters, even the PCs.

Several Morale Triggers are shown on Table 7.27: Morale *(see below)*. Immediately when one or more of these occurs, and each time a new one happens thereafter in each scene, each affected special character and mob of standard NPCs must make a Resolve check against the highest listed DC that applies. With success, the character(s) may continue to act as normal, and with a critical success the character(s) become immune to Morale penalties for the rest of the scene.

With failure, the character(s) suffer a penalty with their next actions, based on the amount by which they failed the check *(see next)*. With a critical failure, the character(s) immediately surrender.

MORALE PENALTIES

Hesitation (failed by 5 or less): The character(s) may not move toward or take an action against opponents this round. A hero or villain may spend 1 action die to ignore this result.

Withdrawal (failed by 6–10): The character(s) must take at least 1 Move action away from his opponents this round. A hero or villain may spend 1 action die to ignore this result.

Retreat (failed by 11–15): The character(s) must continue to move away from opponents until they escape or gain 1/2 cover from all opponents. A hero or villain may spend 2 action dice to ignore this result.

Rout (failed by 16–20): The character(s) abandon any notion of conflict and Run as directly away from opponents as possible, not stopping until they escape or get out of range of the opponents' attacks. A hero or villain may spend 2 action dice to ignore this result.

Surrender (failed by 20 or more): The character(s) drop their weapons and beg mercy from their opponents. They may not act against their opponents again during this scene. A hero or villain may spend 3 action dice to ignore this result.

SUBPLOTS

The lives of *Fantasy Craft* characters are often peppered with private concerns and lingering business. Much of this "personal baggage" is handled with Subplots, which let one or more players identify elements of the ongoing story and/or incidental play as important or interesting to them. This alerts you to include more of those elements, giving the characters a chance to expand and advance their individual stories without interrupting the regular flow of play. Even better, these experiences create new objectives, offering the whole party another way to earn XP.

NOMINATING POTENTIAL SUBPLOTS

This optional system lets anyone introduce secondary objectives based on things they think are cool in the game. Anyone can nominate anything as a Potential Subplot, even you (the GM). You can even introduce Subplot ideas in advance, just to see how the players react to them *(this is essentially tentative foreshadowing, which is more fully discussed on page 332)*.

Potential Subplots can come up anytime — even during character creation — though at first it's probably best that everyone simply be aware of them and how they work. Most of the time, opportunities will become apparent in play. The party will take a liking to an NPC or a story point ("This guy's a jerk. I like him."), they'll notice something about their character(s) that isn't explained or might lead to interesting adventures ("Anyone else wonder why the constable in every city seems to hate us?"), or they'll get themselves into a situation that's best resolved alongside the main plot ("Really? That was a *loan*?"). Subplot suggestions can be clinical ("That treasure hunter seems like a good Rival."), sarcastic ("No really, that guy's a *jerk*."), or roleplayed ("You, sir, are an interesting fellow. Would you care for some traveling companions?").

However a nomination comes up, every player automatically gets the chance to suggest ideas you might incorporate into the Subplot story: "Maybe the constables are on the take!", "You think these loan sharks have duped other parties like this?", "I hope this guy doesn't turn out to be another brigand in disguise!",

Table 7.27: Morale

Morale Trigger	Resolve DC
Outnumbered less than 2-to-1	10
25% or more of group unconscious or slain / outnumbered 2-to-1	15
50% or more of group unconscious or slain / outnumbered 3-to-1	20
75% or more of group unconscious or slain / outnumbered 4-to-1 or more	25

and so on. Every player who makes a suggestion that piques your interest earns a bonus action die. This step is entirely optional and you shouldn't pressure the players to offer ideas. Provide the opportunity and if anything sparks, all the better. Ideas can also come later, as play continues, but each player can only earn one action die per Potential Subplot no matter how many ideas he contributes.

Your group can nominate as many Potential Subplots as they like but you shouldn't let it interrupt the regular flow of play. The process should always be organic and last only as long as everyone is having fun suggesting ideas. Jot those down and get back to the adventure in progress as soon as you can.

SUBPLOT OBJECTIVES

Nominating a Subplot doesn't make it real — only you, the GM, can do that. When you sit down to build an upcoming adventure, take a look at your Potential Subplot notes and ask yourself which, if any, might work as part of the plot. Strong candidates should suggest one or more objectives, which in turn generate XP for success *(see page 337)*. Sometimes, a Subplot will naturally become the backbone of an entire adventure, or even a series of adventures. This is fine, so long as everyone is having fun. If one or more players seem put out, you might want to focus on their characters' Subplots soon, or let the Subplots take a back seat in your game.

No matter what ideas were suggested, Subplot stories are ultimately up to you. This lets you merge them fluidly with the rest of the ongoing story and also gives you the chance to shock and surprise the players with plot twists. So long as you stay true to the Subplot's inspiration (e.g. avoid radically changing an NPC the players like or twisting a plot the players see as heroic into a moral or ethical quagmire), you can develop Subplots in very much the same way as any other adventure seed.

Subplot objectives should always involve the entire party, even when the supporting story focuses on a single character. For example, a Chosen character might be charged by divine forces to defend the kingdom from a dark counterpart, but that doesn't mean his story can't expand to include his allies. The dark champion might amass an army, prompting the king to enlist the rest of the party as generals in a brutal war. Alternately, it might become clear that the character's destiny lies in vanquishing the dark champion, who resides at the heart of a deadly dungeon. In both these cases the character needs the entire party's help to succeed, and everyone has a chance to shine and gain experience in the process.

You can integrate as many Subplots as you like into each adventure, though at first you should stick to just one (if you use Subplots at all). Unless you're used to running epic character dramas with lots of diverging storylines, it's probably not a great idea to include more than three or four.

ENDING SUBPLOTS

Like any story, a Subplot must eventually end. The length of a Subplot is entirely up to you, and should depend entirely on the amount of fun the group is having with it. One Subplot might last for months or even years of game time and wind up something you and your friends discuss about long after the campaign is over. Another might fizzle at the nomination stage, never making it into actual play. Most will be featured in an adventure or two and then close out, maybe with fanfare and a true climax, maybe not.

Initially you're the gauge of which Subplots to include and how integral to make them to the game's story (though you're acting on nominations shared by the entire group, which should give you a few ideas about what they might like to see). You might see a lot of potential in a Subplot, brainstorming several adventures ahead, or you might only see it as a one-off. Follow your instinct but try to make sure that when a Subplot doesn't end in the next adventure the characters at least have some satisfactory closure.

Following the objectives example in the last section, you might set up the next adventure against the dark champion to resolve with a pivotal battle at the edge of the kingdom, (presumably) with the party successfully routing the enemy's troops. The dark champion still lives and the Chosen character's destiny is not yet fulfilled but the heroes win the day and you can let the plot settle into the background for a while.

In these ideal cases, after each adventure in which one or more Subplots are featured with a degree of closure, ask the party whether they want to see that plot continue. If they do, keep your notes and watch for more chances to work Subplot objectives into future adventures. If not, then focus on other things and let that story fade away. Take a vote if the party can't reach consensus on their own, with the Subplot character breaking a tie.

Ending a Subplot is still an option even when closure isn't achieved but it may demand that you resolve the story off screen. For example, if the party failed to fight back the dark champion's forces and no one wanted to see that Subplot again, you might explain during Downtime or in the next session's introduction that the king's allies rallied and won the day later. Alternately, the dark champion's forces could fall back without explanation, perhaps re-igniting interest in the Subplot.

Again, what's important is that every Subplot runs only as long as it's welcome, and that it gets the sendoff the group wants for it. Anything else and the Subplot becomes a burden rather than a way for players to personalize the campaign's storyline.

SUBPLOT CONSIDERATIONS

First and foremost, Subplots are optional. Only players interested in enriching their characters' stories should introduce them, and you should only pursue them if you're interested in adding more player-driven content to adventures.

Second, Subplots are collaborative. Even though you get to choose whether each Potential Subplot makes it into future adventures (and how), the players get to choose whether an unresolved Subplot should continue. Everyone has the chance to contribute ideas. All the players and all their characters are involved, even when the story focuses on just one or two of them. Without this shared responsibility and care, Subplots can easily become distracting or even annoying. In these cases it's critical that you consult those who aren't engaging with a Subplot and discern the source of their disinterest. Many times you can adjust the Subplot to get everyone's juices flowing but when you can't it might be best to retire the story and move on.

Third, Subplots are unobtrusive. These rules only demand attention at very specific times (when someone notices something intriguing or takes note of someone else's interest, as you build an adventure, and after an adventure when Subplots appear). Just as important, everyone's involved when they come up in play. Potential Subplot nominations take advantage of table chatter that happens anyway, and Subplot objectives are (or should be) tailored to challenge the whole party instead of just one or two characters.

Finally, Subplots are yours to modify and mutate as you like. The following list is merely a set of suggestions to get you started. Your list might splice or merge Subplots, add or remove rules, introduce new and exciting objectives… The sky's the limit!

CHOSEN

One or more characters have a calling. It might be handed down by a god, a church, the people, voices no one else can hear, or just a feeling, but the character(s) are charged with a duty they can't ignore (though they might try). Chosen characters are often guided by or caught up in prophesy.

Potential objectives can include anything Chosen characters must do on the path to fulfilling their destiny: saving innocents, defending locations, converting the faithless, and maybe even discovering the nature of the obligation in the first place. Adversaries are almost always enemies of the group or force guiding the characters, such as disciples of a rival deity or religion, the people of an opposing region, or adventurers compelled by equally enigmatic and mutually exclusive power.

CRISIS OF FAITH

The faith of one or more characters is shaken, perhaps because they question their religion's values or maybe because they experience something that contradicts them. Now they search for a fresh direction and watch for meaning in everything they see and everyone they meet.

Potential objectives can include learning about newly encountered faiths and making tough ethical and moral choices with lasting impact on the world. Adversaries exclusive to this Subplot are rare though members of the characters' former faith might take it upon themselves to antagonize or undermine the party. Conversely, followers of opposing religions might court the characters with false promises of spiritual bounty, more interested in corrupting their souls than saving them.

In any campaign, a character caught in a Crisis of Faith is considered a traitor to his beliefs and the Dispositions of characters with his former Alignment decrease by 10 when they realize his state of mind. In a campaign with the *miracles* quality, several special rules apply *(see page 309)*.

CURSED

One or more characters are victims of a curse inflicted by a spellcaster, a monster, blind fate, or cosmic coincidence. The curse might have specific consequences (e.g. dooming the characters to loveless lives or turning friends to enemies), it might inflict a permanent injury (–1 wound), or it might doom them to constant misfortune (+1 error range with checks or 1 fewer starting action dice).

Potential objectives usually include learning the source of the curse and taking the steps required to lift it. These steps often involve the character(s) righting their wrongs or satisfying karmic requirements. When a spellcaster, monster or other NPC places the curse, the characters may be able to locate and confront them, and with luck and a little groveling they might even be able to convince them to lift it. Maybe killing them will lift the curse (or maybe it will make it permanent).

DEBT

One or more characters owe money to dangerous groups or individuals. At a minimum, the Debt should involve more coin than the entire party can raise in a day. Unless owed to charitable sorts, debts often compound unless paid quickly (e.g. doubling each month).

Potential objectives can involve anything the party has to do to raise the required cash. Alternately, the party can look for ways to satisfy the debt without repaying it (e.g. undertaking jobs for the loaners, or in a less than heroic game eliminating or framing them). As for adversaries, NPCs who loan sizable sums commonly employ hired muscle to "remind" characters of their debt, and make examples of them when time runs out.

DEPENDENTS

One or more characters are responsible for one or more largely helpless NPCs (e.g. family members, friends, wards, people they've rescued who have nowhere to go and no one else to protect them, etc.). Dependents are often recklessly fond of the party, unwittingly following them into spectacularly bad situations, and foolishly curious, getting into remarkable trouble when left alone.

Potential objectives include all the tasks involved in keeping the dependents safe, whether the threats come from their backgrounds or the party's adventures. Adversaries can range from hungry monsters the dependents "find" to angry drunks they "console" to con men they trust with the party's gear and more.

HAUNTED

One or more characters are plagued by ghosts, visions, or memories that distract and disturb them. Whenever the source of their anguish comes up, the characters suffer a –2 penalty with attack and skill checks.

Potential objectives include anything that helps put the source of the haunting to rest (e.g. helping a ghost resolve his worldly ills, fulfilling a vision, or righting a wrong the characters can't forget). Except for spirits, adversaries are uncommon with this Subplot.

HUNTED/WANTED

One or more characters are on the run from powerful adversaries who want to capture or kill them. The hunters might be individuals acting for their own reasons (Hunted) or emissaries of the law (Wanted). The characters may be guilty of whatever their hunters claim, they might have been framed, or they could just be victims of unfortunate circumstance.

Potential objectives include evading or eliminating the hunters, but they can also include overcoming obstacles the hunters use to slow them down and challenges that arise in the hunt (e.g. rescuing innocent bystanders, learning new information about the hunters, gaining new allies against them, and clearing their names). The primary adversaries are, of course, the hunters and their allies.

MENTOR/PATRON

One or more characters answer to a trainer (Mentor) or benefactor (Patron). Their service might be religious (acolytes), martial (squires), or involve an art or craft (apprentices). In any case, their sponsor takes a direct interest in their lives, encouraging or demanding pursuits related to their service.

Potential objectives can include virtually any task that develops the characters' skills or supports their backer. Squires might be charged with demonstrating a precise sword technique, or a patron might send his servants to fetch ingredients for his latest culinary concoction — pollywogs found in the deepest, dankest swamp in the land. Adversaries can include anyone or anything opposing their various errands, including Rivals and other beneficiaries of the backer's gifts. For an interesting twist, give the mentor or patron a Rival or Nemesis of his own — one who competes or threatens him through the characters.

MILITARY/POLITICAL ENTANGLEMENT

One or more characters are embroiled in large-scale turmoil. They could be in positions of power, in positions of influence near those in power, or just swept up in the chaos. This Subplot can cover war, choosing a successor to the throne, or any other regional or natural issue that places demands on the party.

Potential objectives include forging and splintering alliances, claiming new or lost territory, winning over supporters, and breaking enemy forces, among many other similar activities. Adversaries can be drawn from the ranks of opposing soldiers or court figures, as appropriate.

MISTAKEN IDENTITY

One or more characters are mistaken for someone else (e.g. different adventurers, criminals, experts with knowledge the characters lack, etc.). Mistaken identities rarely outlast a single adventure and often promote comic or slapstick situations. They also require a good deal of forethought to handle correctly, as situations must constantly arise to prevent the characters or others in the know from correcting the error.

Potential objectives can include overcoming challenges facing the persons for whom the characters are mistaken (e.g. saving their loved ones and defeating their enemies), successfully acting like the real persons (when desired or needed), and correcting the error (which is never as simple as merely blurting it out, and is often interrupted by a steady stream of more pressing concerns). Adversaries include the real persons' enemies and anyone who suspects a ruse and gets in the party's way.

NEMESIS/RIVAL

An adversary takes a special interest in one or more characters, wishing to defeat them in any way he can (Nemesis), or best them in some specific fashion, possibly winning the heart of a mutually desired love or proving himself better than the characters in a shared profession (Rival).

Potential objectives include fighting off a Nemesis' schemes, winning competitions against a Rival, and ending the hostility. The nemesis or rival is the primary adversary, though he may have many allies and minions.

RESCUE

One or more characters seek to liberate someone held against their will, possibly a friend, relative, love interest, or party member (which can be useful when a player leaves the game, takes a break, or retires a character to start a new one).

Potential objectives include locating the captive, penetrating defenses, and escaping with the captive in tow. Adversaries include those guarding the captive and those who took him or her prisoner in the first place.

QUEST

One or more characters have accepted a crucial but dangerous task (e.g. clearing an area of monsters, bringing fugitives to justice, or reuniting a shattered people). An NPC may have bestowed the task or the characters might have taken it upon themselves. Either way, the Subplot ends when the task is accomplished. Quests sometimes compensate characters, especially when bestowed, but are just as often their own reward.

Possible objectives include all the demands of the task as well as solving problems that arise while performing it (e.g. destroying a gate through which the monsters are arriving, tracking and apprehending those who helped the fugitives escape, or locating survivors of the shattered civilization and extracting them from their current circumstances). Adversaries are many and varied, depending on the nature of the quest.

SEARCH

One or more characters are looking for something. It could be an item, lost knowledge, or even a lost love. Clues are fleeting and often wrong, but always lead to new adventure.

Potential objectives include solving all the problems the clues lead to, a few of which may actually yield important details about what's been lost. Adversaries might include rival searchers and those who wish the past to remain buried.

SECRET IDENTITY

One or more characters hide their true identities, possibly because they're on the run (Hunted/Wanted), or maybe to avoid problems in their real lives.

Potential objectives always risk revealing the characters' real identities (e.g. requiring skills not in keeping with their aliases, interacting with characters who know their real names, etc.). Adversaries can include anyone searching for the characters (for reasons left behind in their real lives) and opponents of their aliases.

TROUBLED ROMANCE

One or more characters are entangled in messy romance, perhaps even with the same love interest. They may crave the interest's affection or hope to protect them from heartbreak. Troubled romances are often tragic, involving hard choices between love and duty.

Potential objectives can include scripting and delivering passionate messages, composing and performing heartfelt musical pieces, making a fool (but not acting the fool), sacrificing for love, and similarly grand gestures (they can also include pech cocktails and getting caught in the rain). Adversaries can include rival suitors, protective or objecting family and friends, and meddling enemies who may or may not understand that the characters just want a moment's peace with the person of their dreams (oh, and kooky romantic ballad singers — them, too).

CHEATING DEATH

There's nothing more humiliating for a hero than an ignoble death — fumbling while climbing a cliff, failing a critical save against an acid pit trap, getting backstabbed by a common (standard) goblin during a Dramatic scene… These aren't the ways a hero should go out. Fortunately, *Fantasy Craft* offers a loophole: heroes can often Cheat Death, beating the odds to adventure another day. Like all miracles, though, Cheating Death has a price.

A character may only Cheat Death once per adventure, and only with your approval. The option shouldn't be extended to characters whose deaths were reckless, foolhardy, or a result of violating the basic principles of the game (e.g. acting ruthlessly in a heroic game, betraying the party, supporting the enemy, or being disruptive).

With your approval, the player proposes a plausible reason for his character's survival, as well as a lasting impact the experience has on his character's background or the campaign world.

Example: At the conclusion of a daring rescue operation, Brungil holds Lord Bloodpyre's men off long enough for his companions to escape. He lands a critical hit on the orc but overextends himself, giving Bloodpyre the chance to sink a dagger deep between Brungil's ribs. Brungil stumbles back and gets hammered with arrows from Bloodpyre's men, tumbling over the side of a cliff. He disappears in a forest canopy nearly 100 ft. below.

By the rules, Brungil is good and dead, having suffered enough damage to bring his wounds to –28. This is even enough to pulp his body when it hits the forest floor, but Brungil's player has another thought. Rootwalkers have yet to make an appearance in this game, so he proposes that the trees he falls through are in fact slumbering NPCs who break his fall and nurse him back to health.

The GM's current story deals with Bloodpyre's tribe expanding its territory, an effort that's pillaged much of the natural environment and threatens the local fey population. Brungil wagers that the Rootwalkers aren't happy with the tribe's actions, and that they might be open to negotiating an alliance with the region's folk — through Brungil.

Everyone else at the table, including you, jointly rates these proposals on a scale of 1 (horrible) to 5 (brilliant). These are averaged — added together and divided by the number of people rating the proposals, rounding up — and the result is recorded. It'll be important in a second.

Example: Brungil's player is one of four at the table, plus the GM (a total of five). The other three players love the suggested story, rating it 5, 4, and 4, respectively. The GM likes it but is a bit concerned about it being so self-serving, so he rates it a 3. The average rating is 4 (5 + 4 + 4 + 3 = 16, divided by 4).

The player rolls 1d20 and consults Table 7.28: Cheating Death *(see page 386)*. His character seemingly dies but actually suffers the fate corresponding to the averaged rating (1 being Catastrophic, 2 being Ruinous, 3 being Tragic, 4 being Damaging, and 5 being Petty). His character earns no XP or other rewards for this adventure.

Example: Brungil's player rolls a 7. The average rating of 4 translates to a Damaging fate, which with a result of 7 on Table 7.28 yields "He [Brungil] is regularly visited by spirits of fallen enemies and suffers a –2 penalty with Morale checks." The GM jots this down and starts planning.

The character may return in the next adventure, suffering the listed penalty (if any). **This penalty is permanent** (though the character can sometimes recoup over time, as is the case with lost Renown).

Example: Early into the following adventure, which the GM shifts to several days later to allow Brungil time to heal, the dwarf returns with his Rootwalker saviors. Talks of alliance begin and the party rejoices that their friend survived. A week later, as the alliance is prepping its first retaliatory strikes against Bloodpyre's tribe, the party is sent to spy on the orcs' main camp. This is a Dramatic scene and when the party accidentally alerts an orc patrol the GM indulges in a bit of deceptive description, portraying more orcs to Brungil than there were in the patrol. His attacks pass harmlessly through the newcomers, confirming they're spirits, or visions, or... something, and he recognizes a couple from previous battles. He soon realizes he's being haunted and if the patrol manages to alert the camp, outnumbering the party many times over with reinforcements, he'll also suffer the penalty. Both will remain with him for the rest of his career, so he'll never forget that fateful fall into the arms of the leafy, slumbering giants...

For heightened drama, the proposal ratings can be recorded secretly and handed to you without the player learning the results. If *you* also roll on Table 7.28 the player will be completely in the dark about his character's fate until it's revealed in play.

Example: The previous example is a great illustration of this tactic's potential. It would be so much more powerful if Brungil had returned without the player knowing his fate — if he'd put it together himself on that battlefield, as orcs seemingly appeared from nowhere... Even the fact that he's haunted wouldn't necessarily reveal the penalty. With five possible fates, the player would be left guessing until a Morale trigger came up.

With your approval, a character may Cheat Death more than once. All fate effects are cumulative.

NPCS CHEATING DEATH

Villains and certain other NPCs can also Cheat Death, generally at the cost of 4 GM action dice. When an NPC Cheats Death, the players don't vote; rather, you roll 1d20 for the general result and 1d4+1 for the NPC's specific fate. Again, it's often best to keep these results secret — the GM doesn't even need to announce he's spending the dice — so the villain's survival can be revealed as a surprise down the line.

Example: Turning the tables for a second, what if Bloodpyre had been sent plunging off that cliff instead? The GM could spend 4 action dice and roll a d20 and a d4 to find that he survived the fall an amnesiac (Rootwalker magic at work?), or without Contacts (and thus expelled from the tribe, perhaps to be come an unlikely ally against the orcs' new leader), or with a reduced Constitution score (a weakness the party can exploit in an upcoming adventure). The possibilities are limitless.

Table 7.28: Cheating Death

Result	Fate
1	The character returns with a story to tell. 1. *Catastrophic:* The story is an embarrassment. The character loses all accumulated Renown. 2. *Ruinous:* The story is needlessly self-aggrandizing. The character's error ranges with Cha-based skill checks increase by 2. 3. *Tragic:* The story is less than flattering. The character's highest Renown rank drops by 1. 4. *Damaging:* The story is greeted with good-natured skepticism. The character's error ranges with Impress checks increase by 1. 5. *Petty:* The story is impressive and widely recanted in taverns and dens of iniquity across the land.
2	The character returns without some of his memories. 1. *Catastrophic:* His addled mind impacts everything he does. He gains *baffled I*. 2. *Ruinous:* He loses core knowledge (1/2 his ranks in an Origin skill of the GM's choice). 3. *Tragic:* He loses knowledge he uses every day (1 skill focus or 2 spells of the GM's choice). 4. *Damaging:* He loses bits of obscure knowledge (1 Interest or proficiency of the GM's choice). 5. *Petty:* He "forgets" portions of his background, gaining the chance to reinvent himself. He can even take a new name!
3	The character returns with physical scars. 1. *Catastrophic:* The scars are monstrous (e.g. extensive burns, mangled face, etc.), inflicting *restricted action (Influence, Persuade)*. 2. *Ruinous:* The scars are frightening (e.g. seared skin, missing nose, etc.), decreasing his Charisma score by 2. 3. *Tragic:* The scars are unnerving (e.g. frozen eyelid, missing ear, etc.), decreasing his Appearance modifier by 1. 4. *Damaging:* The scars are unsettling (e.g. cloven lip, missing fingernails, etc.), inflicting a –2 penalty with Cha-based skill checks. 5. *Petty:* The scars increase the character's mystique and make for interesting conversation pieces
4	The character returns with emotional scars. 1. *Catastrophic:* He becomes paranoid and anxious, gaining the *shaken I* condition. 2. *Ruinous:* He becomes dangerously unstable. Once per scene, the GM may spend 2 action dice to cause him to become *enraged*. 3. *Tragic:* He develops a phobia. Once per scene, the GM may spend 1 action die to cause him to become *frightened*. 4. *Damaging:* He's more easily overwhelmed. Once per scene, the GM may spend 1 action die to cause him to become *slowed* for 1d6 rounds. 5. *Petty:* He's moody, perhaps brooding, which actually earns him points with some (like emotionally immature sexual partners).
5	The character returns with spiritual scars. 1. *Catastrophic:* He becomes despondent and lethargic, gaining the *fatigued I* condition. 2. *Ruinous:* His sadness is crushing, decreasing his Wisdom score by 2. 3. *Tragic:* His melancholy impacts his ability to bounce back after a fight. His natural healing rate decreases to 1/2 normal (rounded up). 4. *Damaging:* His determination wanes. His base Will save bonus decreases by 2. 5. *Petty:* He's depressed and sullen, perhaps prone to alcoholism or drug abuse.
6	The character returns to find his next of kin have started liquidating his assets. 1. *Catastrophic:* Too late! All his worldly possessions are gone, including all coin, gear, and physical Prizes (he retains his Contacts). 2. *Ruinous:* All but my…! All his coin, his full Stake, all his gear, and half his Prizes excluding Contacts (GM's choice) are lost. 3. *Tragic:* Those greedy gits! All his coin, his full Stake, and all his gear have been claimed, donated, or sold. His retains his Prizes. 4. *Damaging:* Could have been worse! All his coin and half his Stake have been donated to a local church. He retains his gear and Prizes. 5. *Petty:* Just in time! He retains his coin, gear, and Prizes but gains no Income next adventure.
7	The character actually *returns from the dead…* and he's not alone. 1. *Catastrophic:* He's a subconscious conduit for violent spirits craving death and destruction. When he sleeps, the GM can spend 1 action die to have them slip through his dreams and into the waking world, lingering just long enough to kill a standard NPC the character's encountered in the last 24 hours. Alternately, the GM can spend 2 action dice to kill a special NPC the character's encountered in the same period. The murders are brutal and all evidence points to the character as the culprit (this is, of course, because they look like the character, possess the same weapons, and use the same tactics). It gets worse if the character dies — his body explodes in a nimbus of hellfire, inflicting 1d6 divine damage per Career Level with a blast increment of 1 square. This also releases a small army of the spirits (1 per Career Level), each a standard Ghostly NPC (max. 75 XP), freeing them to murder at will — starting with the rest of the party. 2. *Ruinous:* He's hunted by servants of a malevolent god he escaped in the afterlife. Once per adventure the GM may spend 2 action dice to attack the character with a single special Ghostly NPC or a mob of standard Ghostly NPCs (max. 100 XP). He may spend additional action dice for Reinforcements *(see page 368)*. The GM is encouraged to build one or more of these NPCs in advance to have them ready and maintain continuity. If the NPCs kill the character, they drag his soul to their master, forever preventing the possibility of another return (even via resurrection). 3. *Tragic:* He's harassed by a malicious spirit in moments of mortal danger. He suffers a –2 penalty with attack and skill checks during Dramatic scenes. 4. *Damaging:* He's regularly visited by spirits of fallen enemies and suffers a –2 penalty with Morale checks. 5. *Petty:* He periodically sees the spirits of dead friends and relatives, who offer cryptic and sometimes infuriating "advice."

Result	Fate
8	The character returns without apparent incident — but Fate isn't done with him. 1. *Catastrophic:* His spark of heroism flickers like a candle on the coast. His starting action dice decrease by 2 (min. 0). 2. *Ruinous:* He and his party will be chasing that rainbow for a long, long time. His party suffers a –10 penalty with Treasure Rolls. 3. *Tragic:* His margin for error is particularly slim. His action dice never explode. 4. *Damaging:* Even when he sets his mind to something, it can still go wrong. He suffers a –1 penalty with action die rolls. 5. *Petty:* He's plagued by minor mishaps: dice and cards never favor him, people spill drinks on him, and so on.
9	The character returns with a significant physical injury. 1. *Catastrophic:* He loses a hand or arm. He can no longer use 2-handed gear and suffers a –4 penalty with Dex-based skill checks (among other obvious effects). 2. *Ruinous:* He loses a foot or leg. His Speed decreases by 10 ft. he can no longer Run. 3. *Tragic:* He loses an eye, suffering a –4 penalty with ranged attacks and visual Notice and Search checks. 4. *Damaging:* He's partially deaf, suffering a –4 penalty with auditory Notice and Search checks. 5. *Petty:* He loses his sense of smell.
10	The character returns to a… *complicated* personal life. 1. *Catastrophic:* He becomes a social leper, unable to acquire new Contacts. 2. *Ruinous:* His social network has collapsed into spiteful infighting. The character loses all his Contacts. 3. *Tragic:* He's blamed for *everything* — even things he couldn't possibly have done. The Dispositions of all characters drop by 10 when they learn who he is. 4. *Damaging:* One of his close friends is nowhere to be found. The character loses 1 Contact (GM's choice) 5. *Petty:* Everyone's moved on, resulting in cascading repercussions. Allies and family speak candidly — perhaps *too* candidly — about their fallen friend. Lover(s) find comfort in new arms. When the character returns, chaos and hilarity ensue.
11	The character returns to find his social standing tarnished. 1. *Catastrophic:* Any prestige he once enjoyed is gone. He loses all Reputation and Renown. (among other obvious effects). 2. *Ruinous:* Now he fights for every kindness. His Reputation costs increase by 50% (rounded up). 3. *Tragic:* The slander makes rebuilding his good name an uphill battle. His Legend decreases by 2. 4. *Damaging:* He recoups, but not without social injury. He loses 50 Reputation (or, if he has less, he loses 1 Renown). 5. *Petty:* His enemies seize the opportunity to spread lies about him, resulting in countless unfortunate assumptions and misconceptions.
12	The character returns a celebrity — and it only gets worse from there. 1. *Catastrophic:* Even when disguised, he tends to attract passionate neophytes hoping to "learn from the master." Once per adventure the GM may spend 2 action dice to introduce an overprotective, overzealous standard NPC seeking to become the character's new apprentice (max. 50 XP, built by the GM or chosen by him from the Rogues Gallery). This NPC "helps" the party in every way possible (whether they ask or not), up to and including attacking the party's enemies, attempting critical skill checks, and wandering ahead to "scout the area." Unfortunately, the party earns no XP for anything the NPC accomplishes for them, and should he die or be sent away, the party earns no Reputation for the adventure. 2. *Ruinous:* Even when disguised, he's routinely swarmed by oblivious sycophants. Once per adventure the GM may spend 1 or more action dice to introduce the same number of doting admirer mobs (max. 40 XP, built by the GM or chosen by him from the Rogues Gallery). These admirers follow the party around, vying for the character's attention and generally getting in the way (they also prevent the party from adopting disguises of any kind). Should any of the admirers die or be sent away, the character earns no Reputation for the adventure. 3. *Tragic:* Even when disguised, he's regularly attacked by rivals wanting to claim his celebrity as their own. Once per adventure the GM may spend 1 action die to attack the character with a single special NPC or a mob of standard NPCs (max. 100 XP). He may spend additional action dice for Reinforcements *(see page 368)*. The GM is encouraged to build one or more of these NPCs in advance to have them ready and maintain continuity. 4. *Damaging:* Unless Disguised, he's automatically recognized *(see page 73)*. Also, his Holdings are constantly full of doting admirers, taking up half the maximum guest capacity (rounded up). 5. *Petty:* Unless Disguised, he's regularly pestered by inquisitive scribes, fawning fans, needy nobles, and other annoyances.
13	The character returns with an allergy to a common species or substance (GM's choice). 1. *Catastrophic:* When he's within 30 ft. of his allergy trigger for more than a round, he must make a Will save (DC 18) each round or begin suffocating *(see page 217)*. Once the character fails a save, he can only breathe again when he moves more than 30 ft. away. 2. *Ruinous:* When he's within 30 ft. of his allergy trigger for more than a round, he must make a Will save (DC 16) each round or suffer 1 temporary Con impairment. 3. *Tragic:* When he's within 30 ft. of his allergy trigger for more than a minute, he must make a Will save (DC 14) each round or suffer 1d6 lethal damage. 4. *Damaging:* When he's within 30 ft. of his allergy trigger for more than a minute, he must make a Will save (DC 12) each round or become *sickened* for 1 round. 5. *Petty:* His eyes water and his nose runs when he's near his allergy trigger for more than a few minutes.

Table 7.28: Cheating Death (Continued)

Result	Fate
14	The character returns with a weakness. 1. *Catastrophic:* His massive damage threshold against 1 type or from 1 source (GM's choice) decreases to 25 points *(see page 208)*. 2. *Ruinous:* He suffers double damage of 1 type or from 1 source (GM's choice). 3. *Tragic:* He suffers a –2 penalty with saves against stress or subdual damage (GM's choice). 4. *Damaging:* He suffers a –2 penalty with saves against spells and other magic effects. 5. *Petty:* He suffers excruciating pain — but no penalties — from hits inflicting 1 damage type or from 1 source (GM's choice).
15	The character isn't quite as brawny when he returns. 1. *Catastrophic:* His error ranges with unarmed and melee attacks increase by 2. 2. *Ruinous:* His Strength score drops by 2. 3. *Tragic:* Damage reduction is twice as effective against the character's attacks. 4. *Damaging:* His suffers a –2 penalty with unarmed and melee damage. 5. *Petty:* He's noticeably scrawny, lacking much of his former bulk.
16	The character isn't quite as quick on his feet when he returns. 1. *Catastrophic:* He gains the *flat-footed* condition. 2. *Ruinous:* His Dexterity score drops by 2. 3. *Tragic:* His base Initiative bonus decreases by 4. 4. *Damaging:* His base Reflex save bonus decreases by 2 5. *Petty:* He's noticeably less agile and prone to minor physical foibles.
17	The character is a bit more fragile when he returns. 1. *Catastrophic:* His maximum vitality decreases to 1/2 standard (rounded down). 2. *Ruinous:* His Constitution score drops by 2. 3. *Tragic:* Poisons and diseases affect him twice as fast (1/2 Incubation Period) and twice as severely (doubled effect). 4. *Damaging:* His base Fortitude save bonus decreases by 2. 5. *Petty:* He's pallid and gaunt, his features sunken.
18	The character's mind isn't quite as sharp when he returns. 1. *Catastrophic:* Skill ranks cost twice as many skill points for him. 2. *Ruinous:* His Intelligence score drops by 2. 3. *Tragic:* He's often exploited at market. His silver prices increase by 25% (rounded up). 4. *Damaging:* He suffers a –2 penalty with Int-based skill checks. 5. *Petty:* He's sometimes slow on the uptake, taking an extra moment to gather his wits.
19	The character looks the same but something's just not right. 1. *Catastrophic:* He's like a whole new person. The GM and player take turns selecting class levels to replace the character's previous choices. The GM chooses first. 2. *Ruinous:* His talents aren't the same. The GM and player take turns selecting feats to replace the character's previous choices. The GM chooses first. 3. *Tragic:* He specializes in different activities. The GM and player take turns investing his skill ranks to replace the character's previous choices. The GM chooses first. 4. *Damaging:* He pursues new things. The GM and player take turns selecting new Interests to replace the character's previous choices, including Alignment. The GM chooses first. 5. *Petty:* His mannerisms are different (e.g. he speaks with a new accent, makes uncharacteristic gestures, etc.).
20	The character returns a changed… person? 1. *Catastrophic:* The character comes back as the party remembers him but over time he… changes. Once per adventure, during a period of Downtime or when the character sleeps, the GM may introduce any 1 NPC type or quality by spending a number of action dice equal to the XP cost. This process continues as long as the GM wishes 2. *Ruinous:* He periodically shapeshifts, losing control of his transformed body. He doesn't remember what he does while shifted, though he may suffer the consequences. Once per adventure the GM may spend 2 action dice to trigger the transformation and take control of the character for up to 12 hours. Ideally, this should happen during Downtime or between adventures so the player isn't left out of the game. The GM determines what happens in the intervening time. If needed, he can build the character's alternate shape using the NPC construction rules (max. 100 XP). 3. *Tragic:* He gains the Beast Type *(see page 226)* and a natural attack of the GM's choice in place of his hands. 4. *Damaging:* Non-adversary animals fear him and flee whenever possible. He can't ride an animal, even if it's trained. 5. *Petty:* He gains a disturbing but harmless characteristic that's "alien" to his species (e.g. tentacles in place of fingers).

OPEN GAME LICENSE

OPEN GAME CONTENT

INDEX

Primary references are in bold.

CHARACTER NAME | SPECIES/TALENT | SPECIALITY

FIRST CLASS/LEVEL | SECOND CLASS/LEVEL | THIRD CLASS/LEVEL

PLAYER NAME | CURRENT XP | NEXT LEVEL

GENDER | AGE | HEIGHT | WEIGHT | EYES | HAIR

FantasyCraft™

ACTION DICE

STARTING DICE | DIE TYPE

PHYSICAL ATTRIBUTES

ATTRIBUTE NAME	SCORE	MODIFIER	IMPAIRED SCORE	IMPAIRED MODIFIER
STR STRENGTH				
DEX DEXTERITY				
CON CONSTITUTION				

MENTAL ATTRIBUTES

ATTRIBUTE NAME	SCORE	MODIFIER	IMPARED SCORE	IMPAIRED MODIFIER
INT INTELLIGENCE				
WIS WISDOM				
CHA CHARISMA				

SKILLS

MAX RANKS

ORIGIN SKILL	SKILL NAME	SUGGESTED ATTRIBUTES	SKILL BONUS		RANKS		ATTRIBUTE MOD.		MISC. MOD.	THREAT RANGE
☐	ACROBATICS	DEX		=		+		+		
☐	ATHLETICS	STR		=		+		+		
☐	BLEND	CHA		=		+		+		
☐	BLUFF	CHA		=		+		+		
☐	CRAFTING *	INT		=		+		+		
☐	DISGUISE	CHA		=		+		+		
☐	HAGGLE	WIS		=		+		+		
☐	IMPRESS	CHA		=		+		+		
☐	INTIMIDATE	WIS		=		+		+		
☐	INVESTIGATE	WIS		=		+		+		
☐	MEDICINE	INT		=		+		+		
☐	NOTICE	WIS		=		+		+		
☐	PRESTIDIGITATION	DEX		=		+		+		
☐	RESOLVE	CON		=		+		+		
☐	RIDE *	DEX		=		+		+		
☐	SEARCH	INT		=		+		+		
☐	SENSE MOTIVE	WIS		=		+		+		
☐	SNEAK	DEX		=		+		+		
☐	SURVIVAL	WIS		=		+		+		
☐	TACTICS	INT		=		+		+		

FOCUSES

CRAFTING | RIDE

INTERESTS

TOTAL STUDIES

SUBPLOTS

☐ COMPLETED ☐ COMPLETED ☐ COMPLETED

☐ COMPLETED ☐ COMPLETED ☐ COMPLETED

COIN

COIN IN HAND

STAKE

LIFESTYLE

TOTAL LIFESTYLE

PANACHE | PRUDENCE

APPEARANCE BONUS | MONEY SAVED/EARNED %

INCOME

NON-COMBAT ABILITIES: CLASS ABILITIES, FEATS, AND OTHER OPTIONS

NAME	NOTES	NAME	NOTES

DEFENSE

_____ = 10 + _____ + _____ + _____ + _____ – _____
TOTAL | CLASS BONUS | DEX MOD. | SIZE MOD. | MISC. MOD. | ARMOR MOD.

INITIATIVE

_____ = _____ + _____ + _____
TOTAL | CLASS BONUS | DEX MOD. | MISC. MOD.

VITALITY

TOTAL | CURRENT

WOUNDS

TOTAL | CURRENT

CRITICAL INJURIES

SUBDUAL

CURRENT | ☐☐☐☐ FATIGUED

STRESS

CURRENT | ☐☐☐☐ SHAKEN

CONDITIONS

SIZE

SIZE	FOOTPRINT	REACH

GROUND SPEED	OTHER SPEED	TRAVEL SPEED
BASE	BASE	MPH

PROFICIENCIES

PROFICIENT	FORTE		PROFICIENT	FORTE	
☐	☐	UNARMED	☐	☐	BOWS
☐	☐	BLUNT	☐	☐	BLACK POWDER
☐	☐	EDGED	☐	☐	SIEGE WEAPONS
☐	☐	HURLED			

BASE ATTACKS

ATTACK TYPE	TOTAL		BASE ATTACK		ATTRIBUTE MOD.		MISC. MOD.
UNARMED	_____	=	_____	+	_____	+	_____
MELEE	_____	=	_____	+	_____	+	_____
RANGED	_____	=	_____	+	_____	+	_____

SAVING THROWS

SAVE TYPE	TOTAL		BASE SAVE		ATTRIBUTE MOD.		MISC. MOD.
FORTITUDE	_____	=	_____	+	_____	+	_____
REFLEX	_____	=	_____	+	_____	+	_____
WILL	_____	=	_____	+	_____	+	_____

WEAPONS

WEAPON 1
TYPE | ATK | DMG | THREAT | SZ/HAND | WGT
RNG | SHOTS | QUALITIES/UPGRADES

WEAPON 2
TYPE | ATK | DMG | THREAT | SZ/HAND | WGT
RNG | SHOTS | QUALITIES/UPGRADES

WEAPON 3
TYPE | ATK | DMG | THREAT | SZ/HAND | WGT
RNG | SHOTS | QUALITIES/UPGRADES

WEAPON 4
TYPE | ATK | DMG | THREAT | SZ/HAND | WGT
RNG | SHOTS | QUALITIES/UPGRADES

ARMOR

ARMOR
TYPE | DR | DP | ACP | SPEED | WGT
DISGUISE | RESISTANCES | UPGRADES

COMBAT ACTIONS

ACTION	BONUS/MOVE	TIME	EFFECT
Attack Actions			
Standard Attack	_____	half	1 attack against 1 target
Bull Rush *	_____	full	Move up to Speed toward 1 opponent; opposed Athletics check to push target 1 square + 1 additional square per 4 over opponent result; target becomes *sprawled*
Coup de Grace	_____	full	(*Helpless* adjacent target only) hit = unconscious or automatic critical hit + save vs. death (Fort DC 10 + Damage)
Disarm *	_____	half	Standard Attack vs. Standard Attack to disarm 1 target in Close Quarters
Feint	_____	half	Prestidigitation vs. Notice to render adjacent opponent *flat-footed*
Grapple *	_____	full	Athletics vs. Athletics to render target *held*; both characters become *vulnerable* and may make additional Athletics (Str) checks to gain Grapple benefits
Pummel	_____	full	Unarmed attack: hit = triple subdual damage
Taunt	_____	half	Sense Motive vs. Sense Motive to force opponent in Close Quarters to attack you with next action
Threaten	_____	half	Intimidate vs. Resolve to inflict 1d6 stress damage to opponent in Close Quarters
Tire	_____	half	Resolve vs. Resolve to inflict 1d6 subdual damage to adjacent opponent
Trip *	_____	half	Acrobatics vs. Acrobatics to render target *sprawled*
Initiative Actions			
Aim		half	(Unmoving target only) +1 with Standard Attack
Anticipate		half	Sense Motive (DC 10 + target base attack bonus); success = dodge bonus to Defense equal to Wis mod (min. +1) for 1 full round
Delay		free	–1 Initiative for this round; max (10 + Init bonus) times
Distract		half	Bluff (Dex) vs. Sense Motive to reduce opponent's Initiative by 2d6 for this round only
Ready		full	1 half action taken later during this round
Refresh		1 round	If not attacked, regain 1 action die's result in vitality and 2 wounds
Movement Actions			
Standard Move	_____ ft.	half	Move up to Speed in any direction
Handle item	0 ft.	half	Draw, sheath, pick up, or manipulate 1 object
Mount/Dismount	0 ft.	full	Prepare to ride 1 trained animal or vehicle
Reposition	0 ft.	half	Stand or drop *prone*, become *flat-footed*
Run	_____ ft.	full	Move 4 × Speed in straight line (3 × Speed in full armor); become *flat-footed*
Total Defense	_____ ft.	full	1 Standard Move; +4 dodge bonus to Def for 1 full round

** The larger opponent gains a +2 bonus per category of Size difference (except in the initiation of a Grapple, when the smaller opponent gains this benefit).*

COMBAT ABILITIES: CLASS ABILITIES, FEATS, TRICKS, AND OTHER OPTIONS

NAME	NOTES	NAME	NOTES

CARRYING CAPACITY

LIGHT LOAD ____________ HEAVY LOAD (–2 DEF/PHYSICAL, 1/2 SPEED) ____________

OVERLOADED (–5 DEF/PHYSICAL, CAN'T MOVE) ____________

LIFT (2 × HEAVY LOAD, NO MOVEMENT) ____________

PUSH/DRAG (2 × HEAVY LOAD, 1/4 SPEED) ____________

REPUTATION AND RENOWN

LEGEND ____________ REPUTATION ____________ RENOWN ____________

HEROIC RENOWN ____________ TITLE ____________

MILITARY RENOWN ____________ TITLE ____________

NOBLE RENOWN ____________ TITLE ____________

GEAR

NAME	EFFECT	SZ/HAND	CONST	WEIGHT	NAME	EFFECT	SZ/HAND	CONST	WEIGHT

MOUNT

NAME ____________ SIZE (FOOTPRINT)/REACH ______ (__________) /________ SPEED ____________ TRAVEL ____________

ATTRIBUTES ____________ INIT ________ ATK ________ DEF ________ RES ________ HEALTH ________ COMP ________

SKILLS ____________

QUALITIES ____________

ATTACKS ____________

VEHICLE

NAME ____________ SPEED ____________ TRAVEL ____________ SIZE/DEF ____________ OCC/LOAD ____________ CONST ____________

QUALITIES ____________

CONTACT 1

NAME ____________ TRUST ______ SIZE/REACH ______ SPEED ______

ATTRIBUTES ____________ REP COST ______

INIT ______ ATK ______ DEF ______ RES ______ HEALTH ______ COMP ______

SKILLS ____________

QUALITIES ____________

ATTACKS ____________

GEAR ____________

CONTACT 2

NAME ____________ TRUST ______ SIZE/REACH ______ SPEED ______

ATTRIBUTES ____________ REP COST ______

INIT ______ ATK ______ DEF ______ RES ______ HEALTH ______ COMP ______

SKILLS ____________

QUALITIES ____________

ATTACKS ____________

GEAR ____________

HOLDING 1

NAME ____________ SCALE ______ GUESTS ______/ MAX ______

UPGRADES ____________

____________ REP. COST ______

HOLDING 2

NAME ____________ SCALE ______ GUESTS ______/ MAX ______

UPGRADES ____________

____________ REP. COST ______

MAGIC ITEMS

NAME	ITEM LVL	ESSENCES	CHARMS	REP COST

CASTING LEVEL ______ **SPELL POINTS** ______

SPELLCASTING BONUS ______ TOTAL = ______ RANKS + ______ INT MOD. + ______ MISC. MOD.

SPELLS KNOWN ______ TOTAL = ______ RANKS + ______ WISDOM SCORE + ______ MISC. MOD.

SAVE DC ______ TOTAL = 10 + ______ CHA MOD. + ______ FEATS

SPELL LIST

NAME/SCHOOL	LEVEL	CASTING TIME	DISTANCE	AREA	DURATION	SAVING THROW	PREP COST	EFFECT

SPELLCASTING ABILITIES: CLASS ABILITIES, FEATS, PATHS, AND OTHER OPTIONS

NAME	NOTES	NAME	NOTES

NON-PLAYER CHARACTER

NAME ______ (SIZE: ______ TYPE: ______ MOBILITY: ______ — ______ XP):

STR ______ /+______, DEX ______ /+______, CON ______ /+______, INT ______ /+______, WIS ______ /+______, CHA ______ /+______;

SIZE ______ (FOOTPRINT: ______ × ______, REACH ______); SPEED ______ FT. GROUND, ______ FT. BURROW, ______ FT. (WINGED) FLIGHT, ______ FT. SWIM;

INIT ______ /+______; ATK ______ /+______; DEF ______ /+______; RES ______ /+______; HEALTH ______ /+______; COMP ______ /+______;

SKILLS ______

SPELLS ______

QUALITIES ______

ATTACKS/WEAPONS

NAME ______ × ______ (ATTACK/WEAPON: ______: DMG ______, AREA ______, THREAT ______, RANGE ______; SAVE ______;

QUALITIES/UPGRADES/NOTES ______

NAME ______ × ______ (ATTACK/WEAPON: ______: DMG ______, AREA ______, THREAT ______, RANGE ______; SAVE ______;

QUALITIES/UPGRADES/NOTES ______

NAME ______ × ______ (ATTACK/WEAPON: ______: DMG ______, AREA ______, THREAT ______, RANGE ______; SAVE ______;

QUALITIES/UPGRADES/NOTES ______

NAME ______ × ______ (ATTACK/WEAPON: ______: DMG ______, AREA ______, THREAT ______, RANGE ______; SAVE ______;

QUALITIES/UPGRADES/NOTES ______

GEAR/MOUNT/VEHICLE/TREASURE

GEAR ______

MOUNT/VEHICLE ______

TREASURE ______

NON-PLAYER CHARACTER

NAME ______ (SIZE: ______ TYPE: ______ MOBILITY: ______ — ______ XP):

STR ______ /+______, DEX ______ /+______, CON ______ /+______, INT ______ /+______, WIS ______ /+______, CHA ______ /+______;

SIZE ______ (FOOTPRINT: ______ × ______, REACH ______); SPEED ______ FT. GROUND, ______ FT. BURROW, ______ FT. (WINGED) FLIGHT, ______ FT. SWIM;

INIT ______ /+______; ATK ______ /+______; DEF ______ /+______; RES ______ /+______; HEALTH ______ /+______; COMP ______ /+______;

SKILLS ______

SPELLS ______

QUALITIES ______

ATTACKS/WEAPONS

NAME ______ × ______ (ATTACK/WEAPON: ______: DMG ______, AREA ______, THREAT ______, RANGE ______; SAVE ______;

QUALITIES/UPGRADES/NOTES ______

NAME ______ × ______ (ATTACK/WEAPON: ______: DMG ______, AREA ______, THREAT ______, RANGE ______; SAVE ______;

QUALITIES/UPGRADES/NOTES ______

NAME ______ × ______ (ATTACK/WEAPON: ______: DMG ______, AREA ______, THREAT ______, RANGE ______; SAVE ______;

QUALITIES/UPGRADES/NOTES ______

NAME ______ × ______ (ATTACK/WEAPON: ______: DMG ______, AREA ______, THREAT ______, RANGE ______; SAVE ______;

QUALITIES/UPGRADES/NOTES ______

GEAR/MOUNT/VEHICLE/TREASURE

GEAR ______

MOUNT/VEHICLE ______

TREASURE ______